Born of Yorkshire parents in Eccles in 1897, Lettice Cooper lived from a very early age in Leeds. After reading classics at Oxford she returned to Leeds and spent some time working in the family business. It was during this period that her first novel, *The Lighted Room* (1925) was published, and was followed by, among others, *We Have Come to a Country* (1935) and *The New House* (1936). It was Leeds which inspired some of her greatest work, notably *National Provincial* (1938).

In the 1930s Lettice Cooper moved to London and joined the staff of the influential literary journal, *Time and Tide*, of which she was Associate Editor from 1939-40.

During the war Miss Cooper worked in the public relations division of the Ministry of Food and could spare no time for writing. But in 1947 *Black Bethlehem* appeared and also her biography of Robert Louis Stevenson. This was followed by *Fenny* (1953), *Three Lives* (1957), *A Certain Compass* (1960) and *The Double Heart* (1962). Her most recent book, *Unusual Behaviour*, appeared in 1986. Altogether, Lettice Cooper has published twenty novels, fifteen children's books (which she started to write in 1961) and one biography. She was the *Yorkshire Post*'s book reviewer for ten years, also contributing reviews to national papers.

Lettice Cooper was the President of the English Centre of International P.E.N. from 1977 to 1979 and is a founder member, with Maureen Duffy, Brigid Brophy, Francis King and Sir Michael Levey, of the Writers' Action Group. She was awarded the O.B.E. in 1978 and has lived for many years in Hampstead, London.

GW00584874

NATIONAL PROVINCIAL

NATIONAL PROVINCIAL

by

LETTICE COOPER

LONDON
VICTOR GOLLANCZ LTD
1987

First published in Great Britain 1938
by Victor Gollancz Ltd
14 Henrietta Street, London WC2E 8QJ

Reissued 1968

First published in Gollancz Paperbacks 1987

British Library Cataloguing in Publication Data
Cooper, Lettice
    National provincial.
    I. Title
    823'.912 [F]   PR6005.04977

    ISBN 0-575-04173-0

Printed and bound in Great Britain
by Richard Clay Ltd, Bungay, Suffolk

To Valentine and Bonamy Dobrée

PREFACE TO THE 1987 EDITION

National Provincial, a novel in which all the action is set in Leeds, was first published by Gollancz in June 1938. I had been writing it all through 1937, a year when the war in Spain was still going on, when Hitler was steadily growing in power and aggression. Half England recognized that a war was coming, half refused to believe it.

I had been South for school and college, had lived most of my life in my parents' home in Yorkshire, where I had written several novels. My family were staunchly Conservative, as they had been for generations. I had lately joined the Labour Party. I had moved that way at Oxford and was confirmed in it during the slump when I worked in a centre for unemployed men. I came in contact with many different kinds of people in the town, and felt a growing desire to write a book which would give as just a picture as possible of the "many streams" that were meeting in this one salt sea. I believed that this small world was a microcosm of the world in general, and that actions and causes could be more clearly seen in miniature.

I chose for my viewpoint of this scene a young woman; a young woman who had been working for a few years in London but had come back to her home in Leeds where she was needed to help look after a semi-invalid mother. Through the eyes of this girl, much interested in looking again at a scene which she had known from childhood, I watched the development of two themes.

One was a strike in a big ready-made clothing factory where the Union had put up a demand for a rise in wages. One of my chief characters, John Allworthy, an elderly, experienced Union member, aimed to secure only a part of what had been asked for. He had a young friend, Tom Sutton, who had been something like a son to him and who worked in the same factory. Tom resented what seemed to him the slow movement of the Union, their readiness, in his view, to compromise. Hostility broke out between the two men and increased as Tom saw his own aims being defeated by his old friend.

Then, in the local election which followed, Tom Sutton stood for the seat on the City Council which John Allworthy had held for many years and which the Conservatives had never contested. Because the Labour vote was divided the Conservatives no longer refrained from putting up a candidate and the election was bitterly fought.

There are many other strands in this piece of Yorkshire tapestry, loves and friendships, hatreds and jealousies, which readers will find for themselves. But perhaps the theme which stands out most clearly now is the clash between the moderates in the Labour party who followed and trusted the unions, and the activists who wanted quicker and more decisive action, even, if necessary, against the unions. When I wrote the book fifty years ago, I believed and wrote that Tom and his kind, although defeated in everything then, would be the winners in the end because they were the future, and John Allworthy and his kind, however admirable, were the past. I was at that time glad of this. I believe the same now: that the militant left, I hope the more rational part of it, will not be so easily defeated but may be the future. Am I glad of it? I think only in proportion as they are motivated by love of their fellow men, more than by hatred of what they see as the enemy. I would wish for what all the politicians so glibly talk about—but which is so difficult to achieve—an undivided nation.

Lettice Cooper
London, June 1987

NATIONAL PROVINCIAL

PART I

"As many ways meet in one Town
As many fresh streams meet in one salt sea."

SHAKESPEARE, *Henry V.*

Until the train ran into Sheffield station at four o'clock, Mary did not rouse herself to look out of the window. The placid and uneventful Midlands, heavy with the green of July, slid by her unnoticed. At Sheffield the family who were sharing her carriage got out. As the door slammed behind them, she shut her book, lit a cigarette, and settled down in her corner to the luxury of solitary travelling.

The rhythm of the train carrying her from one life to the next released her thoughts but dulled her feelings, so that she was able to see clearly but with a certain detachment this retreat which was almost a disaster. Almost but not quite, because it was not her fault. That comfort sustained her as the thought of early, hard-won victories might sustain an army turned back by a flood or by an earthquake, or by any other act of God. It was consoling now to remember that in that first difficult year in London she had neither written for money nor gone home. Brought up in a household that made a luxury of resigning itself to the worst, she had, ever since she was a stubborn little girl, attached great importance to not being beaten.

She looked out of the window at the sliding panorama of streets, warehouses, chimneys, slag-heaps, railway sidings and colliery shafts. She was too familiar with such scenes to be struck by their ugliness, but she saw with a fresh eye their beauties, the subdued harmonies of grey and brown, the taut perfection of springing line in crane and chimney, all softened to-day in a sunlight thickened by smoke to a haze of gold. The industrial North, one of the battlefields of that sporadic war of which so many people were still unaware, seeing each battle separately and with surprise in terms of their own emotional or social colouring. But you could not look at anything separately nowadays, and there was not much surprise left to anyone who had been on a newspaper.

Mary was twenty-seven and had been on the *Daily Tribune* for three years, during which she shared a studio in Hampstead with a friend who designed modern furniture. In her spare time, if any was left over from friends and conversation, she tried to write short stories which were often not finished, and if finished, were usually rejected. She did not yet know what she wanted to write, but knew that she could not bear the impact of life unless she tried to do something with it, there was too much of it and it was too exciting. Even now, in spite of her disappointment, she was also secretly and ecstatically happy. It was impossible for her to go on a railway journey without feeling that at the other end of it there was likely to be something interesting.

It's so long, she thought, since I've been home for more than a week-end. It's difficult to tell things from letters, from their letters, anyhow. I wonder what Doris's Frank is really like? I don't know Arthur a bit, he'd grown up so much at Christmas, and boys at school are the most difficult people to know. What will it be like at home without Doris? With some dismay she saw herself alone in the house with her elderly mother and young brother, without the mixture of solid affection, mental disparity, occasional quarrels and friendly companionship that had made up her relationship with her sister. Odd to think of Doris a bride, married to her county cricketer, and living in another house! Odd to look forward to being the one at home while Doris came back for visits! It would be like returning to the time when Doris, always her mother's favourite, had been a pretty and good little girl and she a naughty and plain one of whom only Aunt Grace hoped great things. That time had been obscured by the years of Mary's success at school, her prizes, her friends, her scholarship to Oxford, her adventures and independence in London. And during those years Doris had stayed at home and looked after the family and worked as a typist in a solicitor's office. Certainly it was her turn!

Mary stood up, balancing herself against the rhythm of the train. She powdered her face and touched up her lips, looking at her reflection in the oblong square of glass above the seats. It was a brown face without much colour, with good bones, space between the eyes, and a wide mouth. Doris's pink, white and blue had been her childish idea of beauty, she had accepted for a long time the fact that she was plain, and it had been fun when she first discovered that she could look nice and that people thought so.

Sitting down again in her corner, she looked out of the window at the familiar landscape of the West Riding of Yorkshire, the villages that were half towns, the green hills humped up to the sky above valleys filled with smoking chimneys, the fields divided by unmortared stone walls, old, square, solid houses, mills and mill yards, surprising patches of wood and meadow. They were approaching the outskirts of the city. A ring road swept away from the railway line on either side, tiny cars and buses moving on it like toys on a nursery floor. The remains of stone cottages, standing alone or partly demolished, divided the uncooked rawness of new housing estates, some of which had sprung up since Mary's last visit, proof, no doubt, to Uncle John that the world was moving forward, though their ugliness among the bare patches of ground and temporary rubbish heaps was depressing, and made you wonder if it was moving in the right direction.

The train slid through the outskirts, and ran into the heart of the old city. Mary looked down upon the tops of trams, swaying down narrow streets, across the roofs of warehouses and factories, broken here and there by the whitish dome of a new cinema, or the darkened spire of a church or chapel. The streets parted to show a glimpse of a river, green and sluggish as a canal. Mary saw wharves, a slow-moving barge, the square black tower of a church rising above them, then a wider street, imposing shops, trams, cars, buses, pavements thick with people.

She stood up, collecting her book, coat and bag. The dark arch of the station enclosed them. The porters and passengers hurrying along the platform had a familiar and, to her, a welcoming look, lively, ugly, interested; the voices all round her sound pleasantly broad and full after the sharp Cockney twang. By the barrier at the end of the platform, she saw two expectant faces, Doris fair, smiling, lovely under the brim of a dark blue hat, Aunt Grace with her dark eyes alive as coals, her nose and chin thrusting forward, so that she looked like the figurehead of a ship that had come through stormy weather. They were waving, and Mary, whose hands were too full to wave back, smiled and hurried towards them.

The three of them, carrying Mary's luggage between them, walked out of the station and crossed the square to the tram stop.

"Frank would have come to meet you with his car," Doris said. "They've got two days off this week. They don't have to go to Gloucester till to-morrow night, but he has to give the prizes this evening at some sports for a Working Men's Club out near Baildon, and he found he wouldn't be able to get there in time."

Doris's tone was innocently proud and consequential. Evidently Frank was a person of importance, as befitted his rising reputation. His place in the Yorkshire team had been secure for three years, and he was talked of for Australia.

"Didn't he want you to go with him, Doris?"

"I didn't want to go your first night at home."

"I was going to meet you for her," Aunt Grace amplified, "but she was set on coming."

Mary, who knew that Doris had, like her mother, a gentle obstinacy of self-sacrifice, hoped that Frank had not minded.

"They're playing here the week after next, so we shall all be able to go and watch him."

"That's right!" Aunt Grace agreed heartily. "We'll take our lunch and have a real day out!"

Mary smiled at her. Ever since she was a little girl she had heard those words in that tone, and never without a quick stir of response in her own heart. She had known when she heard them that they would all go for the day trip to Scarborough or the afternoon in the Park, that her mother would be fretful, Doris tired, that Uncle John would sit down somewhere with a pipe and withdraw amiably but silently into his own thoughts, but that Aunt Grace would share her own ardent intensity of enjoyment, wanting to see and do everything, wanting the day not a minute shorter. It was always Aunt Grace who would come with her on the rocks or to the

12

end of the pier when the others wanted to sit down, who said, "Take your shoes and stockings off, love!" when her mother was debating whether it was too cold to paddle, who made friends with the other people in the railway carriage on the way home. It was from Aunt Grace that she had first learned that the world was a place of wider possibilities than it was allowed to be in her own home, Aunt Grace who had always been on the side of the positive. "Stuff and nonsense, Emily! What's going to hurt the child! What does it matter what the neighbours think?" It had been odd to go up to Oxford from her High School, a shy, priggish, self-conscious eighteen-year-old aware of a humble background and afraid of doing the wrong thing, and to find that in the very absence of that fear Aunt Grace had been her best preparation for the company of people used to a wider world. Mary looked at the taut, eager face under the red straw hat—how Aunt Grace always loved red hats—and smiled with warm affection.

On a seat of the tram that would only hold two, with Doris a row or two behind them, they were private enough for Grace to say,

"I'm sorry about this, Mary! It's hard on you. I wish you hadn't had to come home. Your Uncle John and I have been really grieved for you!"

"It can't be helped. After all, it's my turn. Doris has done her share—more than her share, I've often thought."

"Oh, Doris is a good girl. But you were always my girl, Mary."

Mary touched the ungloved hand lying on her aunt's knee. It was a hand which even when slack and at rest looked full of energy, the fingers ready to make and do.

"It will be nice being near you again!"

"You must come round to-morrow and see Uncle John, and we'll have a good talk. We thought we'd leave you to your mother to-night. When do you start on the paper?"

"I'm going down to the office to-morrow to find out. I'm sorry the paper's on the other side, Aunt Grace! Will you and Uncle John feel ashamed of me?"

"You've got your living to earn!" Grace's tone was almost fierce, as though defending her darling.

13

"I shan't be touching politics anyhow, only parties and weddings and race meetings, worse luck!"

Someone got up from the seat opposite to them, and Doris moved into it. Too far off to talk in the clanging tram, she was near enough to smile at Mary. She sat still, her face composed and happy, her blue eyes thoughtful.

"Doris looks happy! Is her Frank nice?"

"Yes, he's a nice enough fellow. He means to have his own way, but that's no harm."

"Doris looks prettier than I've ever seen her, and she's lost that fretting look."

"She does fret sometimes still. She's like your mother, she wouldn't be easy unless she could, but she's very fond of him and he's fond of her. He's a grand cricketer and a very sensible, level-headed fellow; keeps very cool with it all."

"You don't like him much, Aunt Grace!"

"He's not my sort, that's all, Mary. A bit too canny! I like a man to risk something, and think a bit of something besides his own affairs. Well, you know what I like! But Frank's right enough for Doris, if they don't get stubborn with one another. I'm glad she's happy, only I wish it didn't bring you back home. I was thwarted enough when I was a lass! I've set me heart on it you shouldn't be!"

"Perhaps it's a good thing to go back to your roots sometimes."

Grace shook her head emphatically.

"I don't care what they say, it's never good for anyone to be thwarted doing anything they want to do and can do, without it's something wrong! That's all I've ever cared about, really, and all I've worked for and struggled over. It isn't that I want our people to have a lot more money. You can have a good life without a lot of money. I want them to have a chance to use everything that's in them! Now there was my mother, your Grannie that you can't remember. She had a lovely voice, a great big voice that would have filled the Town Hall or a theatre, and her ear was as true as true, but there was no money for singing lessons and no chance to learn, and she never sang except to us children sometimes when she wasn't too tired. Well, that's what I can't bear for our

14

people, to think of all the things they could do and haven't had a chance, all there is wasted."

"Not so much now, surely?"

"Oh no, it's a lot better than it was, but there's room for it to be better still."

With the look that Mary as a little girl had called her "fighting face," Aunt Grace stared straight before her, one hand beating on her knee as though impatient to set about the universe.

The tram was climbing a hill between rows of old-fashioned, solid houses with narrow gardens sloping to the street. Behind them, row upon row of smaller houses with no garden but a shrub or two at the door covered the shoulder of the hill. Doris leaned forward.

"Here we are. Will you come in to tea, Aunt Grace?"

"No, love, thank you. I've got to get back and give my old man his tea at home. But I'll help you take Mary's things up the road."

They had moved into No. 4, Birchgrove Terrace when Mary was eleven years old, and from the first she had felt and resented the atmosphere of the house as a place into which they had crept to hide themselves after defeat and disgrace, a place in which it was permissible to work, sleep, eat, do one's duty and keep up appearances, but not to have fun. Emily Welburn, cooking, sewing and cleaning all day for her two little girls and her baby boy, diffused a spirit of expiation, made in the house a continual Lent. The children were checked if they laughed or played noisily. If they asked for a small treat, even a treat that cost nothing, such as sitting up half an hour later, or dressing up, Emily conveyed to them that there had been something indecent in the request. The climax came when Mary wanted to ask three little girls to tea on her twelfth birthday. She had always had a party, often with trifle and crackers and presents. She knew that they were too poor this year for the crackers and presents, but she was a sociable child and she thought that Betty and

Kathleen and Jean might come to tea. She suggested it at breakfast and saw her mother's mouth droop and tighten. When her mother said, "No dear. I'm afraid not. We can't have parties now," she was shrewd enough to detect a certain satisfaction in the refusal.

"Not a party," she persisted. "Just Betty and Kathleen and Jean? And not any crackers or presents. Just having them to tea. Can't I?"

" No, Mary."

"Why not? Why shouldn't I?" Her quick flare of temper was not so much at the loss of her treat as something primmed, righteous and disapproving in her mother's face.

Emily, getting up to clear the table, replied with bitterness, "You'd better ask your father."

Mary could not do that, since he no longer lived with them. It was the first time her mother had mentioned him since they came to No. 4, and she had been told that he had gone away and would not be coming back. Shyness and a sense of unknown issues involved kept her from probing further, but that evening, on the way back from school, she went to see her Aunt Grace. Aunt Grace was baking. Arms deep in a bowl of flour, she looked at the child who came in, tossed her satchel and school hat on a chair and stood silent and uneasy by the table, rubbing one shoe against another. She said, "What is it, love?"

"I wanted to have Jean and Kathleen and Betty to tea on my birthday, and Mother says I can't."

"Perhaps you could have them another day?"

"No, she said not at all. I said, 'Why?' and she said, 'Ask your father.' "

For a minute, while she made up her mind, Grace did not speak. Her hands worked, kneading the soft mass of dough. Then briskly and unemotionally she told Mary about her father. Suppressing her own personal resentment against the weak, spoiled young man who had fallen in love with her sister like a child crying for the moon, married her in a fit of perversity, and led her a harassed life for fourteen years, she told Mary that he had grown tired of married life, had run away from her mother with someone else, a girl in the office

16

of the firm for which he travelled, and that he was now living with her. Mary stopped rubbing her shoe with the toe of her foot. She said, "It's not Mother's fault!"

If it were in any way, the shades were too fine for a child.

"No, not at all," Grace said at once.

"Then need we—must we——?"

It was her inarticulate protest against the shadow of disgrace and penance in which they lived, against her mother's underlining of distaste. She could not express her revolt against the dramatized situation, nor explain her distaste for the enforced sorrow, but she came near to it for her years when she said desperately,

"Can't we ever be ordinary again?"

Aunt Grace wiped the flour off her arms, came round and took Mary on her knee and promised to ask Jean and Betty and Kathleen to tea at her house, and to make a birthday cake. Much comforted, Mary ran home and danced into No. 4, flinging her books on the table.

"Aunt Grace is going to have a tea-party for me on my birthday."

Her mother said,

"Aunt Grace can please herself in her own house, of course."

Resentment that it should be so was clear in her tone, Mary thought, and was not far wrong in thinking, "She doesn't want us to have fun." It was not until years later that she understood how their misfortunes had provided a sanction for her mother's natural Puritanism and made a righteous abnegation of her desire to keep herself to herself. At the time she only stood there in a turmoil of feeling, sorry for her mother and annoyed with her, angry with her father and wanting him back, impatient at the shadow on her own life. She said crossly and woundingly, "I wish I didn't live here! I wish I lived with Aunt Grace." Then, shocked at her own feelings and miserable because she had hurt her mother, she burst into tears. Her mother wept too. Mary was forgiven and talked to and sent to bed with an uncomfortable consciousness of sin, and a determination, of which she was less fully aware, to get away from home.

And here I am back again, she thought, as she put her suitcase down inside the front door and was enclosed in the indefinable atmosphere of home, deeply familiar, alien, and yet part of her. The table at one side of the passage, on to which she had always thrown her books and gloves, the hat-rack above, with the peg where her school hat had hung from its elastic, were a reminder of innumerable home-comings, of reluctant home-comings from the busy, absorbing life of school, triumphant home-comings with a prize or a small success, of tired and hungry home-comings on days when work had been difficult and the scholarship had looked remote and tea had seemed the one bright prospect. Arthur's school cap hung now on the hat-stand and an old felt hat which Doris wore in rainy weather. Some books, probably Arthur's were stacked untidily on the table. The door into the sitting-room was open, and her mother's voice called, "Is that Mary?" as it had often called when she came running in from school out of the cold air, banging the front door behind her.

Arthur came out into the passage to meet her, moving diffidently, with self-conscious jerks of his shoulders. He had grown much taller, and looked all wrists and ankles. He said, "Here you are!" and after a moment's hesitation kissed her incompetently on the edge of her hair. "Mother's downstairs," he said, and wriggled as though displeased with himself for the obvious statement. Mary went past him into the room.

Her mother was sitting in a chair by the fire with a shawl round her shoulders. She had once been like Doris, pretty and fair, with a white skin and large blue eyes. Her eyes, though faded in colour, were still beautiful, well shaped and well set, but dissatisfaction, worry and pain had so dragged and changed her face that it was only by looking closely at the structure of the bone that it was possible to see the likeness to her daughter. She had suffered for six years with rheumatoid arthritis, was crippled in hands and arms and only able to walk on good days with a stick. On her bad days she could not walk at all. She had always had a grievance against life, and life had taken her at her word and supplied her with definite grievances, an unsatisfactory, unfaithful husband, three children to bring up on a tiny income, and a painful, crippling illness.

Seeing her face more fragile and lined than it had been six months ago, Mary felt a warm rush of tenderness and compassion. She ran across the room and put her arms round her.

"Mother, darling! How are you?"

Her mother turned her cheek to be kissed, but as though she were performing a duty. Emily had never been able to respond to demonstrations of affection. From her childhood they had made her uneasy and self-conscious, and the facile caresses and words of affection with which her husband had varied his long bouts of neglect had confirmed her in her distaste. She was devoted to her children, had worked herself to the bone for them, and was never able to help holding them off from her by a manner faintly grudging and tinged with disapproval.

"Well, Mary," she said, "your train must have been late. I suppose your Aunt Grace met you? I dare say you'd be glad to see her?"

She was bitterly jealous of the affection between Mary and her aunt. It seemed unfair when she had given up her life to her children and done everything for them, and Grace, always busy with her Labour Movement and her committees and her public work, had seen them perhaps once a week, given them an occasional treat or present, Mary should be so fond of her that her face changed when her aunt came into the room. Emily suffered a double pang that Mary should love Grace, and that Grace, her sister who should have put her first, should centre her heart on Mary. Her own response had been to make much of Doris so far as she could make much of anyone. She turned to her now.

"There's a piece about Frank in the evening paper, saying that he's giving the prizes to-night, and about how he used to stay at Baildon with his Grannie. Where is the paper, Arthur?"

"It's in the kitchen. I'll get it." Arthur slipped out of the room as though glad to go.

"You really ought to have gone with Frank, Doris," her

19

mother said. "If Grace had told us she was going to meet Mary, you could have gone."

"I wanted to meet her too," Doris protested sturdily, but there was a faint frown on her forehead, her lips drooped at the corners. Inside the house, her serenity and certainty were less secure, she looked childish, uneasy, troubled, like the little girl Doris who had suffered agonies whenever she had to make up her own mind, although she would never be moved from her decision afterwards.

"Well, Mary," her mother said, "what have you been doing?"

A daunting question, which at the end of a crowded Oxford term or of a busy six months in London had always made her feel that she had been doing nothing. One life fell away at the inrush of another. The flat in London, Jill, Taddy, the *Daily Tribune* office, her friends, parties, had become the airy fabric of a dream in this too warm, familiar room in which the small tendrils of family life stretched out and curled round her.

"Oh, I haven't been doing much," she said. "I've written two short stories, but I don't know if anybody will have them."

"There's a lot to do for Doris," her mother said more briskly. "All her things to see to, except what she's been making these last few weeks. And there's the house. Frank has seen one or two he wants to go and look at. He thought of a flat so that they could shut it up easily if she went round with him in the summer, but Doris doesn't seem to fancy a flat."

"I've always been used to a house," Doris agreed, faintly complacent. "It's what you've been used to, isn't it?"

"It might be more fun to try what you haven't been used to."

"I don't think I should like it," Doris shook her fair head. "Let's take your bags upstairs, Mary."

In the bedroom which they had always shared, Doris put Mary's suitcase down by the end of the bed, and threw her arms round her.

"Oh, Mary! I'm ever so glad you've come! I'm glad we

shall be in here together again for a bit. I do want you to see Frank! I know you'll like him. Look, that's his new photograph. Just fancy! The photographers take him for nothing so that it can be used in the papers. And they took one of me, too, with him, and gave us two free copies. That's one on the mantelpiece. Don't you think he's nice-looking?"

Mary looked at a determined young face.

"Yes, he is, and so are you. You've got prettier and prettier."

"I'm ever so happy!" They hugged one another until Doris broke away, laughing.

"I'm frightened of his mother! I'm sure she thinks I'm not good enough for him! They live in a little house they built out at Fairfield. They all came to tea here one Sunday about a fortnight ago with Aunt Grace and Uncle John. I was afraid they might get arguing about politics. Frank's father is a Conservative, you see."

"Is Frank?"

"He doesn't bother his head about it. I think he gets tired of Aunt Grace talking sometimes. Well, you know, Mary, she does go on! He likes her very much, of course," Doris added perfunctorily.

It was no use saying, "I should hope so," since he obviously didn't. Mary pushed her fingers through her flattened hair.

"What is Arthur like now, Doris? I haven't seen him since Christmas, you know, and then I only had two days, and we seemed to be cooking and eating all the time. He's grown inches."

"He's been growing too fast, I think. He's a funny boy, very quiet. He's doing quite well at school. I'm afraid he's not much good at games! Frank took him up to the County Ground and let him have a practice at the nets, but he said he couldn't make much of him. He thinks he wants rousing up a bit and taking out of himself."

I hope, Mary thought, that I'm not going to dislike Frank! It was odd to find Doris looking at her family through outside eyes. It would have to happen, of course. Soon Doris would be in another house, a visitor and a stranger, coming back, as Mary herself had done in the last few years, to see her own home as other people saw it. Now she would be part of it

21

again. She felt caught in a trap, her own bright, free casual world slipping away from her.

"It was lucky," Doris said serenely, "that you could get this job on the *Guardian* just now. And it's such a good paper. Frank knows one or two of the people on it. He says their cricket notes are some of the best. He was ever so pleased when he heard about you."

Mary had an impulse, which she despised, to say, "Oh, was he! Well I don't want the job. I've given up a better one with more chances, I hated leaving London, I didn't want to come home." But it would be asking for pity, breaking into Doris's soft cocoon of happiness and complacency. It was no use making a fuss. It was no use thinking of Jill and the studio, of London at dusk in October, of spring mornings in Regent Street and the walk over the Heath towards the white spires of Highgate, of people coming in and out ready to argue about anybody and anything, careless, easy-going, happy-go-lucky people to whom any point of view was interesting. It was never any use regretting.

"I'll just run down and make the tea," Doris said. "I left everything all ready."

When she had gone Mary stood by the window, looking out. Birchgrove Terrace stood on the last of one of the spires of hill that radiated from the heart of the city. Ridge upon ridge the roof-tops, feathered with smoke, fell away below the high window to the jumble of flat roofs, towers and spires and domes that clustered thickly round the Town Hall. The evening was so clear and still that in spite of the haze of smoke Mary could see across the city to the suburbs and new housing estates on the far hillsides, even to a curve of unspoilt grassy hill, to the church spire of a distant village rising above a clump of trees, and to chimneys, small and fine as pencils against the summer sky. Between those far-off chimneys and her own window, sprawling in the once green valley that it had defaced, lay a whole world, ugly, dirty, teeming, noisy, alive, rich in humanity, in passion and hope, sorrow and joy, suffering and humour.

Mary thought to herself. It's mine. Mine to take and make something of it, and I don't want anything of it except to

22

make something of it. So I'm free. As having nothing and yet possessing all things. It doesn't matter where I am, really. If I can't make something out of all this, I shall never be a writer.

She remembered what Vivian had said to her at her farewell party, leaning against the studio wall, his head tilted a little sideways,

"I shan't be sorry for you, Mary! I'm sorry for us losing you, but I won't be sorry for you. I think you're lucky and I'd like a year down there. We know more about Abyssinia here than we do about the provinces. To us they're either Beauty Spots or Distressed Areas. If something startling happens, we turn the limelight on them for a moment, but we never see their average life. There's always been a gap between us and them, and the gap's widening. I noticed it last month when I had a week-end in Liverpool. I expect you'll find it stiffer and slower there, you'll probably run up against a lot more settled prejudices than you do with our lot here, but don't be a fool and waste time down there wishing you were back. You soak it in. I don't believe you can do anything much in England unless you've got the feeling of the provinces. They're the main body and we're the advance-guard. An advance-guard that gets out of touch with the main body isn't any more use. Besides, if you want to write, you couldn't have a better chance of seeing life all round than a reporter's job on a provincial paper."

That was unusually serious for Vivian, who had perhaps been a little drunk, but often talked sense in his cups. There below her window lay the world at which he had been guessing, her own world in which she had been brought up, and to which she had come back a stranger.

"I've made the tea, Mary!" Doris called up the stairs. Mary left the window and went down to the family meal.

On the smooth turf in front of Greenoak Hall, the Civic Players were performing *A Midsummer Night's Dream* to an audience who had dined well, if early, and who were now comfortably settled on garden chairs. A clouded afternoon, which had given the organizers of the performance some qualms, had cleared into an exquisite evening. Rooks were flying home to the tall trees behind the square stone house, the light had a quality in which every flower stood out with its full colour and value. The stage sloped up a little towards the herbaceous border at the foot of the terrace. Two great holly trees at either side marked its boundary and served as wings from which lovers, fairies and yokels emerged on to the grass. The audience sat with their backs to the long avenue, and to the sunk fence which divided the garden from a hay-field, but the players on the stage could see the tops of cars and buses passing on the road, and the sprawling huddle of the city beginning on the rising ground beyond it. From the audience, Greenoak might have been a country house, the manor house of a remote village. From the stage, and from the terrace and windows behind, chimneys and house-tops and the smoke of the town were visible. The house confronted squarely the scene of the labour by which it was built, the yards and workshops whose profits had piled its stones, smoothed its turf and planted its great border of roses.

The house belonged to William Marsden, who stood behind the rows of chairs with his brother-in-law, Lionel Harding, looking across the heads of the audience at the stage. He was not listening to the play, but his dry, thin face wore an expression of contentment and approval. It pleased him to lend his garden for so good an object as the new wing of the Infirmary, and for anything so undeniably right as Shakespeare. Not naturally sociable, he was always glad to see his friends at his house, feeling it due to the house, to himself and to them that he should entertain them as handsomely as possible at suitable intervals. His sense of duty was as powerful and unflagging as his sense of what was due to him, and his life ran between those two lines. He excited both admiration and amusement in his brother-in-law, who lounged beside him smoking a pipe. They were of the same age to within eight months, and William had gone to Cambridge in the same week that Lionel went to Oxford. Now the casual observer might have guessed ten years between them. Lionel, half a head shorter, had kept his fresh colour and a good deal of brown in his hair. He stood more loosely, moved more restlessly, had a livelier eye, looking for particular friends in the audience rather than surveying a gathering of people.

"Like a chair, Lionel? There are one or two more in the summer-house."

"No, thanks. I'd rather stroll about. I never can sit still and listen to anything out of doors."

Lionel was looking at six chairs in the second row. His wife, Alice, sat erect, her grey head rising above the collar of her fur coat. She was never too warm, even in the summer. Clare, his daughter, was all but hidden from him by the man behind her. A bit of cheek and a curve of dark hair alone were visible. Next to her, his elder son, Robert, lounged in a deck-chair, a cloud of smoke rising above his dark head. Almost certainly bored, his father thought, smiling, just as Stephen, his junior, was probably enjoying himself. The light glinted on the high golden head of Stephen's wife, Joy, whom Lionel admired with a touch of rueful alarm. A lovely, but an intolerant, and in some ways a stupid, young woman. Not his pigeon, and he could have sworn not Stephen's, but heavens, how crazy the boy had been about her! Stephen always took things harder than Robert. For Robert's wife, Beryl, Lionel had a more comfortable affection. She was good-tempered, sweet, and no fool, in spite of her high, childish voice and little round face.

"Before you go," William said, "you must have a look at my new delphinium."

In speaking of his flowers, his voice took on warmth and depth. He could think of people in the mass, but flowers were individuals to him, needing individual consideration and rewarding it with their unblemished beauty.

"Very pretty the whole place looks this evening!" What will have become of it, Lionel wondered, in twenty years' time? It will be a housing estate or a convalescent home, I suppose. Even if Humphrey and Will had lived they probably couldn't have kept it on. But perhaps it would have been a different world if the best of our young men weren't out of it. Wrinkling his face behind his pipe, he felt again the stab of that wound nearly twenty years old which he shared with William. He should have borne it the more stoically of the two, he had often thought, should have been the one to comfort and console, for both the Marsden boys had been killed, while he had only lost one of three sons. But what a son! It was not only he who had discerned in Neville some rare quality, something vivid, a sensitive integrity, an ardent idealism which seemed to have been the peculiar grace of that generation of young men. Neither Robert nor Stephen had the same quality, though in Stephen there was a look of Neville, a flash of his spirit, but they had grown up during the war years and after and had never, even at eighteen, had that bloom on the mind, that hopeful expectancy. Perhaps they were better without it in the post-war world. Did William now think often of his two young sons who had so often raced across this lawn to play cricket in the field below the sunk fence? He had never given way nor broken down, had worked all through the war years, growing thinner, drier, greyer. A braver man than I am, Lionel thought humbly. He was sometimes remorseful because he could not help being amused at his brother-in-law. The amusement had never detracted from friendly respect, and both were in an old tradition.

The friendly antagonism between the two families went back to their parallel rise to prosperity in the early days of Victoria. The Hardings, country stock from the Westmorland fells, were Tories and Churchmen, admirers of Pusey and Keble. At the time of the Kensitite agitations, three tall Harding sons took their seats every Sunday in St. Jude's Church in the pew nearest to the door, and waited hopefully for the threatened arrival of Kensit and his followers. They sang lustily and tunefully, one eye on the door, but Mr. Kensit never came, the Vicar continued to light candles on the altar undisturbed, and after a few weeks, the Harding boys, disappointed, lapsed from such exacting standards of church-going and took the dogs out again on Sunday morning.

But their allegiance to the Church never wavered, and in their mature years they led their children into the family pew, acted as churchwardens, and opened bazaars with genial aplomb.

John Marsden, the first in the firm, had been a Wesleyan, bringing with him from a new chapel in a Manchester street a consciousness of sin which did not impede his worldly progress. In later life he was a rigid, pious old man, strict about Sunday observance in his household, prolonging family prayers while the eggs and bacon cooled, and fond of reading sermons aloud. His eldest son married into a Unitarian family, and became a Unitarian in which two of his brothers followed him. The Marsdens were Liberals, inclining to intellect and the regeneration of humanity, while the Hardings turned their attention to hunting, shooting and intermittently to racing. The Hardings made contacts with the County and the Church, produced a General of inconsiderable fame and a Colonial Bishop. The Marsdens' outside connections were in the educational and literary world, they boasted the editor of a Liberal paper, a headmistress of a pioneer girls' school and a brace of dons. They travelled observant but aloof in most European countries, whereas the Hardings were apt to stay at home and take domestic holidays with babies, buckets and spades. Both families were devoted to their city and gave generously of energy and money to its needs. Both measured importance in terms of that city and were therefore innately aware that it was something to be a Harding or a Marsden. During the slump of the 1930s, both families had suffered, the Hardings more heavily. The Marsdens, who were in textiles, had bigger reserves and were able to hold on until things turned the corner. They were, on the whole, better men of business, with a strong strain of prudence and foresight. The Hardings, of gayer, easier blood, picked up new ideas more readily, but were liable to impulsive decisions and suffered from a fatal tendency to spend as fast as they earned. Each family cherished a certain tolerant contempt for the other. "Always were prigs, the Marsdens," "Not exactly progressive, the Hardings"—but the contempt was far outweighed by a respect and esteem that saw in the other family

27

what Yorkshire sees in Lancashire, something unlike themselves, but much more like them than the rest of the world. Everyone on both sides had been delighted forty years before at the marriage of Lionel Harding to Alice Christine Marsden, everybody, that is, except Cicely Dawson, who thought her too dull for Lionel, and an old aunt of the Marsdens who was displeased that the wedding was in church and not in the Unitarian chapel. But Alice had gone to church with her husband and brought up her children to go to it, just as she and her brother now voted for a Conservative Government. In 1935 the Marsden and Harding traditions were merging.

Stephen lay back in his chair, his eyes on the strip of green grass between the two holly trees. Helena, after declaring her speech with self-conscious emphasis, had vanished behind the bush with a flutter of yellow and blue draperies. Helena was pretty but no good, had perhaps been given the part for one of those reasons which in Amateur Dramatic Societies thrust the merely lucky between talent and its opportunity. Now Bottom was calling the roll of his company, who squatted on the turf in their browns and greens, looking very much at home there, suitable visitors for the orderly and exquisite garden. Yorkshiremen made good natural comedians, and the broad voices suited the rustic parts. They played with gusto, enjoying themselves.

The scene, the words, the feeling of things, individual, sturdy and gay, touched Stephen to a sense of nostalgia. With all the nonsense talked about Merrie England, he was conscious of something vividly present in this fourth-rate performance, and not present in everyday life, not, certainly, in everyday life at Alfred Ward's. His eye wandered down the row of chairs to the end where Mrs. Ward and Marjorie were sitting. Shakespeare was nothing to them, but no doubt they were pleased to be here. There had been no difficulty about bringing them to-night, since anyone could buy tickets to help the Infirmary. It was the favours and social privileges that could not be bought that were difficult. He would not have been able to persuade his uncle to ask them to a private party, and he had not been able, so far, to get Ward made a member of the Country Club. He did what he could, prompted by gratitude, genuine liking, and an uneasy feeling that he was not performing the intangible and unmentioned duties for which he had perhaps been given his job. He had wanted the job so badly seven years ago when their own firm went down, and Joy and his three months' distant wedding depended on finding work at once.

Shifting himself in his deck-chair, he clasped his hands round his knees and tilted his head back, looking up at Joy, who sat erect, her eyes on the players. She would not be thinking about them at all. What would she be thinking about? The boys, the week's holiday at her own old home next month, her brother, her tennis match on Saturday? Something actual and concrete, whatever it was. The ways of her body were familiar and dear, the ways of her mind were still strange to him. It was an orderly, definite mind that saw no distances and half lights, recognized problems, felt no hesitations. Its certainty had seemed to him like strength, and was only now beginning to seem like a stone wall from which his perplexed fumblings and uneasy inquiries recoiled as impotently as the shallow waves of a neap tide.

Looking along the rows, he thought how difficult it would be to talk about those perplexities to his friends. He had known most of these people all his life. He had gone to tea with them and shared dancing classes and drill classes, had played cricket and tennis with his contemporaries, danced with their sisters, worn his top-hat at their weddings, fetched his little boys home from tea with their children. Yet they now seemed remote from him, entrenched in a security which he had once shared, but from which he now felt himself cast out. It was a security that the slump had not really shaken. Businesses had crashed, cars had been put down, entertaining had been curtailed, there was some real hardship and much talk of it, but their order had been undisturbed by any thought of radical change. They had borne something, and had borne it cheerfully, greatly sustained by the fact that they were all in the same boat. It had seemed to them

29

that they were bearing a great deal, and that no more could be demanded of them. The return of prosperity had been a justification of their confidence. Even Mussolini's threatened impertinences in Abyssinia, though they roused some indignation, did not affect them closely as anything to do with themselves. They lived still in the old world of separate compartments.

And a good world it had been, a damned good world! He had only to reach back into his childhood to evoke the flavour of it, a flavour of ease and leisure and hope as definite as the smell of hot grass on a cricket field. There had been no incongruity to a child in the life lived so prosperously in the big stone houses with their lawns and rose gardens, side by side with the life lived in the streets round the works, where barefooted children and shawled women with lined faces clustered in the doorways of dingy houses. All that was just there. You went down to the works, were given blue pencils in the office and allowed to see the crane move in the shop, unconsciously absorbing deference. Sometimes at home, if tiresome over rice pudding, you were told that poor little boys would be glad of it, but you did not believe that, it was what was now called salesmanship, a grown-up wile to get the filthy stuff off on you. In your distaste for the pudding and for adult insincerity, you never really thought about the poor little boys. You were in one compartment and they in another. The mere fact that they were alleged to like and want the rice pudding robbed them of reality.

He looked again at Joy, at the firm curve of her neck rising from the Chinese coat that Hilary had sent her. How she loved that coat! He had never been able to give her any present so successful! Hilary had had a leave in Pekin during his five years' station in India; Stephen could see now Joy's face as she unwrapped the parcel, and picked up the note from the shining, folded silk, could hear her say, "Oh, Hilary!" and see the softening of lips and eyes. It was absurd to be jealous of her brother! Absurd to think, as he sometimes did, that she liked Lin better than Jack, the lithe fair sprig of her own family better than the square, dark Harding. She was devoted to both of them. She was an incomparable mother for small

30

boys, anyhow for small boys growing up in the accepted tradition of their kind. There it was again, the question that would thrust its way up. Were they being brought up in a dying tradition that ought by now to be dead? He felt tired of speculation and tried to devote his whole attention to the play. Titania was speaking:

> "*The Spring, the Summer,*
> *The chilling Autumn, angry Winter, change*
> *Their wonted liveries, and the mazed world,*
> *By their increase, now knows not which is which.*"

He felt rather like that about the world himself. Impatient this evening of his sense of flux and change, he tried to jerk himself out of it by looking at the faces of those near him who were not aware of it; Robert amiable, sturdy and bored, Beryl amiable, interested and pleased, Joy like a carved figure looking before her at the green stage, beyond her the rows of their friends, some obviously bored like Robert, some mildly interested, but all to outward appearances serene, prosperous, undisturbed, having their private troubles, no doubt, but living against a permanent background. What none of them saw was perhaps not there. Stephen slumped down into his chair again and let the play steal his uneasy spirit from the everyday world.

Mary sat in the back row of chairs next to Freda Lewis, a young Jewess who was reporting for the *Yorkshire Echo*, the rival paper to the *Guardian*. It could hardly be called a rival nowadays since the *Guardian* so firmly held the field, but it professed Liberal views, reported Labour meetings at some length, and courted Nonconformity as opposed to Church interests. In its early days it had been considered startlingly progressive. It had specialized in profound if obscure articles by leading Unitarians, had run Liberal candidates for Parliament, and had been partly financed by the Marsden family. Its hey-day had been during Mr. Gladstone's third ministry, when a Harding and a Marsden had contested the

31

northern borough of the city in a by-election. The *Echo* had trumpeted freedom and progress against the *Guardian's* cry of order, loyalty and tradition. It had upheld the unselfish nobility of William Marsden, and denounced the reactionary selfishness of Harry Harding. One of its leading articles was reprinted on the Liberal electioneering pamphlets and caused Marsden in private life to offer a stately apology, received with a shrug, a twinkle and a "Not your fault! Always was a sour rag!" from Harry Harding.

The rise of the Labour Party had been the downfall of the *Echo*, which turned its back on them from the first, and thus found itself in a few years no longer the radical and progressive organ, but a second fiddle on the side of stability and reaction. In this field it had no chance against the *Guardian*, which was the property of great Conservative families, and had in the eyes of the chief citizens of Aire something of the settled dignity and authority of the Church of England. All that the *Echo* could do was to grumble and to keep on striking the note of intellect by wooing contributions from head masters and notable preachers. Soon there was a small Labour weekly in the city, kept going by the blood and tears and sacrifice of the young Labour Party. The *Echo*, troubled by falling circulation, fell a prey to the insidious temptations of the new journalism. While the *Guardian*, secure in the support of all right-minded people, rejected sensational articles, avoided stunts and scoops, and devoted a bare line to the more feverish elements of modern life, the *Echo* began to coquette with the private lives and personal affairs of notorieties, to publish revealing articles by actresses and criminals, and to interview the notables of the town on their reactions to the modern novel, the modern girl, spiritualism and jazz. At the time of the 1931 crisis it supported the National Government, but after the election it sometimes gave a qualified support to the Opposition. Its readers were mostly among the chapel-going clerks and shop-keepers, but William Marsden continued to take it in. It had appeared on his father's breakfast-table every morning and must appear on his, since like many Liberals he was more Conservative than any Tory. Every morning his light eyes under their prominent, grizzled eyebrows, slid distastefully over its flaunting personalities and artless self-revelations. He still had a few shares in the property, and out of deference to so respectable a supporter, the Editor printed long and full accounts of his speeches and parties.

Freda Lewis, licking the point of her pencil, made a perfunctory note or two on her pad and said to Mary:

"A dud evening. I can get home early."

"I was rather enjoying it," Mary protested.

"There's more for you to do, of course. These people all read the *Guardian*. A lot of them don't read anything else. They'll look in the morning to see if you've got their names in. They don't read the *Echo*, hardly know it's there. All I need is half a column because the Editor thinks old Marsden likes it, and a good notice of the play so that they'll send us an advertisement of their next performance."

Mary looked at the block of smooth and curled heads in front of her.

"I shall have a job to find out who all these people are."

"Not once they know who you are. They'll come and tell you. Some of them, that is. The old lot wouldn't think it dignified. But you belong up here, don't you? Don't you know them all?"

"I've been away most of the time since I left school, and anyhow I wasn't brought up in these circles. My uncle is in Alfred Ward's, in the works. He's a shop steward."

"What's his name?"

"John Allworthy."

"Of course I know him. Leader of the Labour Party on the Council and an old stalwart of the movement. We interview him sometimes. That's Mrs. Ward in the front row in the stamped velvet coat, and that's the daughter."

"Marjorie Ward? She was at the High School for a bit when I was. She was a junior, of course, but we once acted in a play together." Mary leaned forward and looked between the heads. "She's grown up nice-looking."

"She's all right. She doesn't know what to do with herself. They can't quite get in with the people Mrs. Ward wants them to get in with, and she tries to keep clear of the others for fear of queering her chances. It's one of the funny things about this town, seeing it's an industrial town and built up on money making, money doesn't get you in anywhere—not new money. You've got to have had it for a couple of generations. Marjorie Ward hasn't had sense enough yet to make friends for herself, and the Marsdens and Hardings and so on won't have anything to do with the parents if they can help it. Old Ward's very unpopular."

"Why?"

"I think because he always makes it clear that he wanted to get on in the world. People think he's ostentatious. And he's not genial or easy to get on with, doesn't seem to like anyone. Something about him puts them off."

"Perhaps he's shy."

The little Jewess shrugged her shoulders.

"That's old William Marsden going behind the holly tree now to speak to the actors. He'll feel it's his duty, like royalty. That's Lionel Harding with him."

"Oh, I remember him! I once went to a bazaar when he opened it. Are the young ones all married?"

"Both the sons. Not the daughter. Stephen married a beauty, county family from the dales. There, in front, in the Chinese coat, with yellow hair. He's in Ward's you know. Sort of staff manager and right-hand man, one of Ward's fancies. I shouldn't think he's worth his screw, and he probably doesn't like it much, but your uncle will tell you about that. Robert's a solicitor—went in with Lawson and Marsh and became a partner last year. He's got a nice little wife, rather overshadowed by the family so far. He was engaged to the Johnson girl for two years and then she jilted him."

Mary looked round at the lengthening shadows on the smooth turf, the bright flowers, the heavy trees.

"This place is lovely! And not a bit spoilt! It's still like a country house. They haven't built near it!"

The little Jewess snorted.

"Trust them to see to that! The Marsdens still pull their weight on the Council. Ask your uncle!"

"Who are those four young ones together, the red-headed

34

young man who looks so cross and the other young man and the two girls?"

"They're some of the University staff, the junior lecturers and their wives. They don't matter."

"They look interesting."

"I mean they aren't news. That's the Vice-Chancellor over there, Sir George Callardine, I don't think Lady Callardine is here, he's with Professor Ellison and his wife. You'd better mention her, she'll expect it."

"What is he like?"

"Sir George? He's only been here a year. He's a very good public figure. Fine manners, good speaker, looks well on the platform. They say in the office that he never says anything. He's your paper's money but not mine. He's a bit stuffy with us about interviews. Refused to answer a questionnaire last month about Breakfast or No Breakfast for Brain Workers. We had to get Mrs. Allison in the end to represent the University. She'll always give an interview and go round to all her friends afterwards saying, 'Have you seen that nonsense in the *Echo*? Really, the Press is disgusting!'"

"Isn't that Canon Halliday leaning forward to speak to her? He's got much stouter."

"Yes, he's the comfortable kind of clergyman. He's got a new High Church curate who made a stir in the town a few months ago by preaching a sermon about housing. He went for the Town Council and the Property Owners' Association and the employers of labour and everybody else he could think of. We interviewed him the next morning and got him to write an article for us called 'The Eye of a Needle,' but the Editor had to cut it and alter it a bit, and the young man went off the deep end about that, so we haven't had any more from him. Forrester, his name is, Mark Forrester."

"He sounds interesting."

"A bit cracked, if you ask me. Doesn't know when to stop."

"Is he here to-night?"

"Oh no, he doesn't come to this sort of thing much. He wouldn't be too welcome if he did."

"They'd really mind, would they?"

The little Jewess, closing her pad with a snap, looked sideways at Mary under her long, dark lashes.

"Of course they would. They're frightened, though they don't know it!" She slipped off her chair and nodded. "I've got all I shall need. See you again soon, I expect. So long." She tiptoed away across the grass.

Night was falling, and in the border below the terrace a change of front took place like the counter-marching of an army, the red, blue and violet flowers retreating into the shadows, the white advancing, till they stood out, globes and stars and bells of something that seemed more light than substance, poised on invisible stems, half hidden by invisible leaves. Lights were turned on to the theatre, making green turf and solid trees look as improbable as stage scenery. In the oval of light, Puck swept, the twigs of his broom rasping on the dry grass. Oberon and Titania came in from behind the holly tree, the stage was filled with glimmering figures. For a minute or two at the end the enchantment of the play held all the audience. Even those who had been bored realized that their penance would soon be over, and that they would not have to sit there much longer, a resentful prey to midges.

As soon as the players had taken their calls, the audience began to move. The two young lecturers from the University with their wives drifted towards the front of the house. Someone had said that there were to be refreshments, but they were not quite clear whether these were only for invited guests. To Angus and Grizel Grant, the question was important. They had taken a chance on it, and had had no supper before coming out. They did their own cooking and it was sometimes worth while missing a meal and taking a party on trust. They could always eat bread and cheese when they got home. Each of them secretly felt willing to go home now and eat bread and cheese, for they were not entirely happy in the company of Claud and Naomi Unwin. Angus felt sure that Claud was going to start a serious conversation with him about the play. He disliked serious conversations about English literature except with his most intimate friends, and with Claud he could not adopt his usual protective covering of light mockery, for you could not speak lightly to Claud at all, and he took all mockery in deadly earnest.

Claud opened his mouth, and Angus, much alarmed, interrupted hastily.

"I haven't been here before. It's a lovely place, isn't it? You'd never know it was a town garden."

He had no sooner spoken than he realized his mistake. Of course! He had held a match to a dry bonfire! Such a house and such a garden, especially when built with profits earned in the mean and dirty streets of the town, were an outrage to all Claud's principles. Claud began to say something about "an epitome of bourgeois, selfish comfort." Now he's off, Angus thought despairingly. He tried to hang back, hoping that Grizel would come to his rescue, but she and Naomi had dropped behind.

And of course, thought Angus, what he was saying was perfectly true. True, but arid, and to him not interesting. It was very wrong that some people should have large, comfortable houses and other people too small, uncomfortable houses, but he could not pretend to himself that he really cared about either..He had none of Claud's sense of responsibility for the Universe, and he was irritated by what seemed to him to be a flood of clichés. They were true and Claud meant them, but they were dragged into every subject on every occasion, and that very fact made clichés of them, since truth and sincerity were not enough without the intelligence that made them appropriate. In a way Claud, probably, almost certainly, a very good economist, was a stupid fellow. But unhappy, thought Angus, looking at him sideways, at the sharp profile, and the jerky movement of his red head. Some private deprivation of his own, whether real or fantasy, rasped in his voice and pointed his denunciations. Karl Marx was the stalking-horse for his private griefs, which did not alter the fact that Karl Marx might be right and necessary, even if unpalatable.

Grizel knew from the set of Angus's shoulders that he was depressed, and tried to move Naomi on more quickly, hoping

37

to join them, but Naomi loitered, intent on what she was saying.

"Of course you know, this Abyssinian business is only the beginning. There's going to be civil war in Spain. We had a friend of ours staying for a couple of nights last week, a Spanish girl, an artist, a most intelligent person and she said . . ."

All the Unwins' guests were foreigners and artists and most intelligent people! Grizel knew very well that Naomi only tolerated her domestic activities, her Scotch ordinariness because Angus was one of the very small number of his colleagues with whom Claud had not yet quarrelled. As though anyone, even Claud, would be likely to quarrel with Angus!

"And Germany are certain to make trouble on the Rhine next year. We had a letter from a friend, an exile now living in Czechoslovakia . . ."

Yes, that was the other thing they were besides artists— exiles, and still and always very intelligent, and generally living in Czechoslovakia. A sudden desire to laugh rose in Grizel, but she suppressed it, ashamed. Naomi was really clever, so very much cleverer than she was. And on the whole patient with her. As though to answer this thought, Naomi stopped talking about her intelligent friends, and inquired politely for Alistair and Elspeth.

"They're very well, thank you. I had them both out in the pram this afternoon."

Would the Unwins ever have a child? It was difficult to imagine one fitting into their energetic life. Not easy to see Naomi as a mother, but still harder to see Claud as a father. All the ordinary relationships seemed to fit awkwardly on Claud. He would be a most uncomfortable person to go to bed with. Grizel began to tell an anecdote about Bunny and Biddy, probably very boring to Naomi, but she could think of nothing else to say. She was really thinking that she must make Angus get his hair cut again, and missed Naomi's sigh at the end of her story, knowing nothing of the pang of envy in her heart.

The two young men waited for them in the doorway.

Grizel sent a glance and a smile at Angus, who smiled back suddenly warmed and reassured, aware that Claud was funny. Shyness descended on the Grants and on Claud as they entered the hall of the strange house. In Grizel and Angus it was the shyness of children at a party, in Claud the defensive armour of an enemy entering a hostile world. Only Naomi was unabashed, looking round her at the house and at her fellow guests, her eager mind absorbing material which she would grind up in its mills and add to the store of her penetrating and dogmatic convictions about life.

"You can tell," she said to Angus, "that the minds of the people in this house are dated 1890."

But how, thought Angus, could you tell anything with so much certainty? You advanced with so small a candle into such a large dark room. Your guesses were insults laid upon the darkness. He felt sure that Naomi was going to have a serious conversation with him. His worst forebodings were justified, for she said,

"Do you ever see an amateur dramatic society up here do any play that has any bearing on contemporary life?"

Was it possible to say what had any bearing on contemporary life! Anyhow, he would have liked to suggest to Naomi that Shakespeare would outlast it, but he could not manage to say such a thing to her, she might start discussing Shakespeare with him!

"I don't often seem them do any plays," he said. Why they said he was brilliant, God only knew! He was an escapist, childish, bourgeois to the bone! Of course *A Midsummer Night's Dream* was exactly right for him! Naomi gave him up. She and Claud often gave up the Grants and were unaware that they liked being with them, did not realize that it was they who suggested the next meeting which Grizel and Angus were too kind and polite, too unready in social guile to avoid.

The four of them came in a bunch to the door of the dining-room where refreshments were spread on the long tables, and maids waited, stiff in frilled caps and aprons, behind coffee-pots and jugs of pale lemonade. Grizel turned round, smiled at Angus and whispered, "Strawberries and cream!"

Lionel Harding walked into the house with Mrs. Ward, Stephen following with Marjorie. How often, Stephen reflected, his father had made things easier for him, in small ways, in his difficult relationship with the Ward family! He would have been polite to them, anyhow, out of gratitude and decency, but it was galling to have to be polite to them to keep his job. Not that anything had ever been put into words, and perhaps he exaggerated a self-conscious sense of obligation, but old Ward, though he could be generous, liked his money's worth. If he and Joy could have laughed over the thing and done it together cheerfully! But it sickened her, she loathed the Wards and hated his position with them. He felt remorsefully that he was sometimes obliged to force upon her company which she could not bear, and uneasily suspected that the necessity lowered him in her eyes.

Yet really Marjorie was not a bad girl, and would probably have been a very nice one if she had had anything to do but spend too much money, and share in her mother's social activities and disillusionments. Left to herself she might have achieved a good deal of what her mother wanted, for she was good-looking, played tennis and bridge well, and her generation were easier. She was not left to herself enough, because Mrs. Ward, who was inclined to despise the friends she could have had, had no one else to go about with, and clung to her daughter.

"I've always thought I'd like to act," Marjorie said, "I did one or two parts in plays at school and I loved it, but there doesn't seem to be much chance afterwards."

"Couldn't you join this company?"

"I did once think of it, but there are a lot of people in it that we don't know."

"You'd soon get to know them, wouldn't you?"

"Well, then, you see, Mother thinks it might be awkward. They're rather queer sort of people."

"What rot it all is!" Stephen exclaimed.

Marjorie looked at him, startled.

"What is?"

If he had answered truthfully, he would have said, the whole thing, Joy thinking it beneath her to know you, you

40

and your mother thinking it beneath you to mix with the Civic Players. Human beings deliberately shutting themselves off from one another, from experience, novelty, enrichment, and what for? To preserve some fancied superiority, to avoid some imaginary contamination! For fear, perhaps, of being seen with the wrong people by some others who were presumably the right people, but who were the same sort of stiff, frightened and negative creatures as they were! It was not that fear with Joy, she was too sure of herself. It was simple distaste. Marjorie and her mother climbing up the social scale were more timorous, more careful of taking a step back.

"I meant," Stephen said, "it seems a pity not to join the Players if you'd enjoy it, whoever belongs to it. After all, it's amusing to meet different kinds of people."

He touched some chord in Marjorie's urgent and unsatisfied youth. She said, "Yes I think it is. I like having a lot of friends, but you know how Mother and Dad feel about things."

Stephen did not conceive it to be part of his duty to suggest to his employer's daughter that she should tell Mother and Dad not to be silly. They had reached the refreshments, and he supplied her with sandwiches and coffee, and looked round the room for someone of her own age to introduce to her. His eye fell upon the young Grants standing side by side with plates of strawberries and cream in their hands. They looked, he thought, like Hansel and Gretel, Angus with his slim body and untidy brown hair, Grizel with her freckled face, and wide grey eyes, the most nearly silver eyes he had ever seen. He had met them casually at University parties. Nice people! He was going to bring them to Marjorie, but saw Mrs. Allison swoop down upon them to give them the few kind words which she thought due to them as junior members of the University staff. They drew together, smiling politely at her over their strawberry plates. A pleasant, quiet, shy young couple, she thought, being naturally unaware that Angus called Biddy's stuffed monkey "Mrs. Allison," and caused it to stalk about the dinner table, making gracious bows, while he imitated her party conversation.

Looking round, Stephen saw Joy with his mother at the far side of the room. It was generally easy to see her at a party. Not only was she an inch or two taller than most of the women there, but she carried her head like a swan. It had been extraordinary to him that anyone so beautiful should love him, should leave her own world for him. She had always hated towns, had cried, they told him, as a little girl when she first encountered the noise and dirt and ugliness. It was true that they did not actually live in the town, since they had built their house at Barton, seven miles out of it, before Lin was born, but their life centred on the town, their friends were urban, young people who had moved outside when they got married and who carried on the rhythm of urban life. Joy was different, as different as the life lived in the square stone house that smelled of flowers in summer and wood smoke in winter, the house where "going to the village" was so often the central activity of the long leisurely day. Remembering the smell of that house, here in his uncle's lit and crowded dining-room, he was carried back to the rapture and agony of those early visits before he was sure of Joy, when after ringing the bell, he had stood on the doorstep suffocated by the beating of his heart.

"There are a lot of people here that I don't know!" Marjorie said. There was a complaining note in her voice, and her full lip dropped sulkily. She was not enjoying herself. Stephen felt remorseful. Seeing his sister-in-law, Beryl, alone for a minute, he moved across to her.

"Come and talk to Marjorie Ward for a bit!"

Beryl came at once, ready to be nice to anyone. She said cordially, "Oh, I've met her. I like her." It struck Stephen how few people she disliked. She was an easy, friendly creature, always, so far as he had seen, willing to go anywhere and do anything. He wondered if Robert's family took her too much for granted, and remembered that lately he had thought her more serious and silent. But then they all talked a good deal too much, Joy said, and Beryl usually listened as though she enjoyed it, her blue eyes moving from one to the other. "A nice little thing," was what everyone called her, and all that he himself knew of her. She and Joy got on well

42

enough, but he thought that Joy was not interested in her, perhaps even a trifle contemptuous of her, and that had prevented him from getting to know her. Joy did not like very many people. She loved with an ardent intensity the boys, himself, Hilary, her father and mother, and drew round that small group an invisible line, shutting off the rest of the world.

He saw when he took Beryl up to Marjorie that she had found a friend, a girl not in evening dress, but in a dark frock and a small hat. Marjorie was talking with some animation, and turned a smiling face to him.

"May I introduce Mr. Harding—Miss Welburn—Mrs. Robert Harding——" Her ceremonious introductions and careful, formal tone were an exact copy of her mother's, but she added in a cheerful schoolgirl voice, "I haven't seen Mary for ages! We used to be at school together. Fancy! She's a reporter on the *Guardian*. She's reporting this party." She giggled. "She'll have to put it all in the paper!"

"I don't think we are important enough." Then, afraid that he might have hurt Marjorie's infernal social sensitiveness, he added quickly, "We're not old enough. We only get in at our time of life when we get engaged or married. Otherwise it's for our elders and betters when they open bazaars and make speeches. Isn't that right, Miss Welburn?"

"I don't really know," Mary confessed. "I haven't done quite this kind of thing before. This is my first evening on the job. I ought to know all about everybody, but I don't. It's so long since I was up here, except for week-ends."

"You do belong up here, do you?"

"I told you she went to school with me," Marjorie broke in.

"I expect you know my uncle," Mary said to Stephen. "He is in Alfred Ward's. John Allworthy."

"Oh, of course I know him!" He smiled. "You couldn't be in Ward's and not know him. He keeps us all in order."

He glanced at Mary with a sudden interest, thinking that he would not have expected old John to have this kind of niece who looked very much more at home at his uncle's party than his employer's daughter. Perhaps the flick of surprise showed in his eyes. Mary's tone was defensive, and

43

she said quickly, "Uncle John's a wonderful man. I'm very fond of him."

"Oh, of course. He's a grand fellow."

To her ears he sounded careless, kind, patronizing. She felt an unaccountable desire to shake his easy superiority. She remembered Freda Lewis's suggestion that he was a luxury in the firm and did not earn his screw, and wanted to tell him that he would have to work hard to be worth as much as her uncle. Before she could speak, Marjorie broke in.

"But surely—Isn't John Allworthy the *Labour* man who made the strike a few years ago?"

Her face was so full of ingenuous horror and surprise that both Mary and Stephen laughed. Stephen said comfortably, "That's all past history. It was before I came into the firm."

"I remember it," Mary said, "I was at school. I remember my uncle coming round in the evening while I was doing my homework and telling us that the men were coming out next day. It lasted three weeks."

"Did they get what they wanted?"

"Some of it, of course. Not all."

"I should hope not!" Marjorie exclaimed indignantly. "Those sort of people are always wanting something, and the more you give them, the more they want! They're never satisfied!"

The words were so obviously a quotation, the tone was so full of childish and virtuous disapproval, that both her hearers laughed again.

"Perhaps they really haven't enough?" Stephen suggested lightly.

"Father would always give them everything they ought to have! You know he would, Mr. Harding!"

Before her indignant challenge, Stephen grew grave and answered,

"He's a lot more generous to his work-people than a good many employers."

Mary saw that he had not answered, but Marjorie was satisfied.

"You ought to come and see the Works," she told Mary

44

"They've got a splendid new rest room with Vitaglass and a swimming-bath and a library, and all sort of things. It's like an hotel. And they have the most lovely lunch, very cheap. Mother and I and Leslie went and had it in the new canteen the day it was opened, and we saw it all cooked first."

"Leslie is your brother, isn't he? I remember him in the kindergarten at the High School. Is he going into the business?"

Marjorie looked doubtful.

"Well, I don't know. He doesn't want to. But I expect he will in the end. He's going to the University first. He doesn't know what he wants to do."

"Perhaps he'll find out while he's at the University."

Marjorie looked startled at the suggestion.

"Father would be very disappointed if he didn't go into the business."

It was evident that the Ward family were not expected to make up their own minds. Mary was not sure whether she saw or fancied a slight, impatient jerk of Stephen's head.

At that moment his wife came up to him, nodded to Marjorie, and said to Stephen,

"Let's go, are you ready? I've said good-bye to your mother." She added, in a voice that she might have used to one of her children, "Have you had some strawberries?"

"No, I don't mind about them."

"I'll wait if you like. I've had some."

There were faint shadows like bruises on the fair skin under her blue eyes. She said to Marjorie, "I was playing in a tennis match this afternoon. You get awfully tired standing about at this sort of party."

"She doesn't enjoy any party unless it's out of doors," Stephen's voice was affectionate, the tone of a husband proud of his wife's idiosyncrasies. He said "Good-bye, Miss Welburn. Good-bye, Marjorie, see you again soon, I expect," and moved off after his tall and lovely wife.

"I don't like her!" Marjorie said discontentedly. "She's stuck-up and snobbish."

"She's beautiful, isn't she?"

"Yes, I suppose she is. But he's much nicer than she is.

45

Dad thinks it's ruined him, marrying her. Her family are county, you see, and all in the Army, and he thinks that makes Stephen look down on business and prevents him from putting his back into it. That's why Leslie isn't going to Oxford or Cambridge, he's going to the University here so that he shan't get to think himself too superior to work. Oh, I forgot. You went to Oxford, didn't you?"

"Yes. But I'm not too superior to work. Anyhow, I've got to."

Marjorie said, with round eyes open, "But writing for newspapers must be so interesting. It isn't like ordinary work."

"Sometimes it is—very like it!"

Marjorie laughed, obviously incredulous. She was too young, self absorbed and discontented to be capable of grasping any existence but her own. She liked Mary, and said eagerly, "I do hope we shall meet again. Won't you come to tea or dinner? Is Sunday a good day for you? Or Saturday? I'll look in my book when I get home and send a postcard. I think I ought to go and find Mother now."

It was a long time, Mary reflected, since she had been at a party where people felt that they ought to find their mother now. Standing for a moment alone by the refreshment table, she watched the groups shifting under the electric lights in the long dining-room, moving now and then to disclose the dark oil-paintings on the walls in their heavy gold frames. The babel of talk was deafening, but had a steadier note than the parties to which she had lately been accustomed. At those parties in studios or in the sitting-rooms of clubs or modern flats, people moved about more quickly, with freer, looser movements, shouted more loudly, though perhaps it was because there would certainly have been cocktails and sherry instead of the tea and coffee and lemonade which the two neat elderly maids were serving at the long tables, often with a smile or nod in response to a friendly greeting or recognition from one of the guests. These people were not casual acquaintances, they all knew each other, they even knew one another's servants. They gave an impression of stolidity and stability and what a lot of grey heads in the room! You felt that most

46

of the guests had not come as units, but in families, father, mother and grown-up children had come together and would probably leave together, most of them going off, per-haps, to a square, solid house like this, where maids who had been with them for years left the light turned on in the hall, and whisky on the drawing-room table, and shining brass cans of hot water in the bedrooms.

Mary, who was very hungry and would have to go back to the office before going home, turned and helped herself to sandwiches and took a cup of coffee from the maid behind the urn. A hand jerking out quickly towards a plate caught the edge of her saucer, the cup rocked and heeled over, pouring coffee on to her wrist and sleeve and skirt, and on to the polished wood of the table.

"I'm so sorry! I'm most awfully sorry! How stupid of me!"

The red-haired young man who was stammering an em-barrassed apology, sounded annoyed as well as remorseful, he looked at Mary as though he thought she ought not to have put her coffee cup there to cause him this moment of humiliation.

"Let's rub it quickly." That was a girl standing at his side, a girl with short, light-brown hair, silvery-grey eyes, and a faint Scotch inflection in her voice.

"Give me your hanky, Angus," she commanded. Another young man obediently handed over a large handkerchief. He had thick, ruffled, mouse-coloured hair, and a serious pale face, which brightened into a surprisingly charming smile.

"I'll get you some more coffee," he suggested.

"It doesn't matter a bit," Mary protested. "Don't bother!"

The girl with the silvery eyes was still rubbing her skirt. Mary had noticed her a few minutes ago looking shy and lost like a little girl alone at a party. Now she was as kind and competent as a young mother dealing with a child.

"I don't think it will mark it much." Her tone was meant to reassure, not only Mary, but the red-haired young man who had upset the cup, and who still stood awkwardly before her, looking unhappy and cross as though the small mis-adventure had disconcerted him out of all proportion. He seemed to think that he ought to make some amends, picked up a plate and thrust it towards her, saying, "Have a sandwich." At that moment a thin, dark girl with eager eyes came up and caught him by the arm.

"Come over here, Claud. I've just met a most interesting man! One of the players, the one who was doing Quince. He's a workman and so intelligent! I think he'd like to join the Literary Society. Do come and talk to him!"

She towed him off, awkward and unwilling but obedient. Angus murmured, "Poor fellow!" without specifying whether his compassion was for Claud or the workman, bit into an asparagus sandwich and then paused in alarm with his mouth full as Mrs. Allison bore down upon them. I thought we'd had our turn, he said to himself, but eyed her with a limpid innocence over the half-eaten sandwich.

"Sir John Ormerod is here," she informed him. "I've just been having a long talk with him. Such a charming man! I think he may come on the Committee of the Children's Home!"

Having relieved her excitement, she smiled graciously upon them, and swept off with a rustle of skirts. And, oh, thought Angus, we're a funny lot!

"Queer things, parties!" he said to Mary with his shy, delightful smile. Then, having gone rather nearer to seriousness than was his habit with a stranger, he added, "Will you eat some more with us and then we can eat some more with you and we shan't feel so greedy? You see, we didn't have dinner before we came here, and obviously all these respectable people did. So it makes us a bit diffident about concentrating on the refreshments. Try one of these, they're very good."

The last of the party to leave, the Hardings, stood on the doorstep, saying good-bye to William and Isobel Marsden. The group wore the relaxed air of those who realize that the strangers have now gone, and the family is alone. In the light from the open hall door the likenesses among them would have been clearly visible to anyone enough interested

48

to look for them. Alice and Isobel were plainly sisters, and in Clare and Robert, dark, high-coloured Hardings though they were, were looks and movements that linked them with William, and even if they had known it, with the portrait of William's grandfather who confronted them across the hall from a forest of side-whiskers. Only Beryl, having no share in their blood, stood a little apart, until Clare turned with a friendly word and drew her into the group. She looks a bit forlorn, Clare felt rather than thought. Her own consciousness that it was something to belong to their family, made her careful of those outside it. Beryl was free from the continual itch of expecting to be noticed, and her mood was sober for other reasons.

William was saying in his precise voice,

"It was very good of you all to come."

"Oh, no, William, we've enjoyed it. I hope they've done well out of it for the Infirmary."

"Oh, I think we've done pretty well. Quite a lot of people were kind enough to come and take tickets."

Even with his sister and brother-in-law William was never informal. Had there never been a time, Beryl wondered, when he was a small boy and other children called him Bill and rolled him down the banks in the garden? Such a lovely garden for children, too. An involuntary sigh escaped her. She held out her hand.

"It was lovely, Uncle William, thank you. I did enjoy the play."

"Has Stephen gone?"

"Yes, he went early. Joy was tired."

Alice said with some asperity,

"She's never tired if it's tennis or a walk."

There was a note of apology in Lionel's reply.

"Well, she'd been playing in a tennis match all the afternoon."

Clare said, "She lives for them."

Invisibly the group on the doorstep drew together, closing their ranks against Stephen's wife, the intruder in the family, who had slighted their party and their company by being tired and going home early. It was as the voice of the group, praising and including Beryl by contrast, that Aunt Isobel said kindly,

"You don't look tired my dear! What a pretty frock that is! I hope you were warm enough."

"I wanted a word with Stephen," Robert grumbled.

"We'll ask them to supper on Sunday, darling."

"I believe he said they'd got to go to those infernal Wards."

There was a faint groan of universal sympathy for Stephen and dislike for the infernal Wards. Only Lionel Harding cocked an eyebrow, disagreeing. They were not so bad, really! It was pathetic to have made all that money and not to know what to do with it, to buy a big, ugly, handsome house, and live an uneasy life in it, like people carefully and painfully speaking a foreign language learned at school.

"I saw Stephen labouring with the girl this evening."

Lionel said quickly,

"Ward was good to Stephen, gave him a job when he badly wanted one. I don't think it will hurt him, or anybody for that matter, to show a little kindness and civility to Ward's daughter."

"What I think one dislikes," William said, "is the feeling that it's expected of him."

Alice nodded.

"I hate the poor boy to have to go and hand round tea at their horrid parties for fear of losing his job! And it's trying for Joy to be patronized by that woman!"

There was a murmur of agreement. The feeling of the group swung towards Joy, part of their family set upon by strangers.

But Lionel thought, I don't know, it's half patronage, but half kindness. The Wards see things in terms of money, and they're rich and Stephen and Joy comparatively poor, so they give them theatre tickets and expensive presents for the children. After all, what have we all been helping the Infirmary for to-night, half patronage and half kindness. It seemed to him that if half a thing was good, it was perhaps as much as anyone had a right to expect, but he knew himself easy, without what people called proper pride, and on the whole too much interested in his fellow creatures, too curious about

50

them to be kept apart from them by unnecessary barriers. And Alice's proper pride had kept him from too many of what his friends and relations might have called eccentricities. But I wonder what would have happened, he mused, if I'd married Cicely. Somewhere beneath the stout, elderly Cicely Dawson, whom he had met and shaken hands with that evening, was buried his first love, Cicely de Saumerez, the reckless, spirited, vivid girl who had led him such a dance for two years, and stirred in him an intensity of feeling never reached again, except, but so differently, when Neville was killed.

"Come along," he said to his family. "You must be tired, Isobel, and want to get rid of us. Let's go home."

When they had gone, Clare driving her father and mother in the old Austin, and Robert and Beryl tucked into their Morris, William Marsden turned back into the hall.

"Don't wait, Isobel," he said. "I'll lock up." He added with stiff courtesy. "Thank you for all your trouble. I thought it was a very successful evening."

"I'm glad you were pleased, William. Good night." As Isobel went upstairs to her room, she thought how odd it was that as a little girl she should have adored William, have said, "When I'm grown up I'll marry William and live with him," and now after the years of his life with Esmée and the boys, after her years in the settlement in East London, when she was Aunt Isobel coming to stay with him at Christmas and in the summer, here she was back in the old house where she had made that childish resolution, living with William and keeping house for him. She was not a woman of general observations, and it never occurred to her how often people get what they most want in unrecognizable ways. She only said to herself above a deep content that she was glad he had been satisfied with his party, she must tell Agnes again to have the hot water ready at the beginning for the urns. Upstairs, taking off her heavy gleaming rings, and placing them one by one on the branches of the porcelain tree which had been a twenty-first birthday present from an old governess, she thought about Alice and Lionel and the boys and Clare, who had been her one little niece, her favourite, and

Stephen's two sons, who were such fine sturdy boys, full of life and spirit. There was a warmth and security in the feeling that the family were all round her, her contemporaries growing old with her, the younger ones springing up like trees to outlast her. As she lifted the old-fashioned silver-backed brush and brushed out her fine hair where the light-brown still showed among the grey, she thought that perhaps some day Stephen might have this house. His two sons might play cricket in the field and come running up the slopes to tea with flannel shirts open at the neck and flapping round their wrists as once William's two dead boys, Humphrey and Bill, had run in, crying out, "Are there sandwiches?" In that way, as the years went on, the lasting hurt in the house might be healed.

Downstairs William fastened the dining-room windows and drew the curtains across them with stiff, methodical movements. Before shutting the front door, he went out for a moment on to the steps, and looked across the garden to the lights of the town. They climbed the opposite hillside as though they climbed into the dark sky, the regularly spread lights of street lamps, the scattered lights of houses. It would be a good thing, William's doctor had told him, if he could retire and finish his life in the South away from the harsh east winds, the smoke and the long cold springs of the West Riding. William's only answer had been a grunt, a flick of his dry, wrinkled eyelids. To say to the doctor that a plant dies cut off from its roots would have been a flight of words beyond him, a translation not of a thought but of a feeling. To Isobel he said, "The young man's a fool, Isobel. I know what's good for me. I ought to, at my time of life." Standing on the step with his sleeping house behind him, and the invisible flowers of his garden at his foot, he followed with his eyes the curve of hill that was now a warren of new streets and houses, but had been a green field when he was a child, even when his boys were children playing on the terrace. An innate dislike of any change was always at odds with the conscientious belief in progress that he had learnt from his father, and in the day-time he could not avoid the feeling that the new red houses were an affront so painfully spoiling

52

the view from his own terrace, but night was kind to him and to them, and gave him back the country of his youth. He went inside, put on the chain and slid the heavy bolts across the door as if he were securing the gates of a fortress.

When Joy and Stephen had first thought of building Lane End, a house in the country, their great desire, or Joy's great desire, had been to make it as far as possible like her old home. A nostalgia for her old life, dormant during the first five years of marriage, had stirred into an active feeling as soon as she began to carry her second child. She fretted for her father and mother as she had never done when Jack was on the way, insisted on going home for Christmas and stayed on into the New Year, returning with her heart set on a house which should be at least a shadowy reproduction of Stackhouses.

The architect, the builder, their finances, and, more than anything else, the three hundred odd years through which Stackhouses had confronted wind and weather were against them. Lane End, when finished, was very much like any other neat, compact and convenient modern villa. It stood a hundred yards back from the main road at the end of a narrow strip of shadeless garden, but there was a clump of trees at the side of the house, and a thicket of bramble bushes behind divided it from green fields, and made Joy promise herself September blackberry parties for the children when they should be old enough. She planted fruit trees in front of the house, shoulder high, so that in spring you walked out of the front door into a wave of the sea, and in autumn you picked your fruit with the minimum of exertion. Stephen begged plants from his Uncle William when he divided his herbaceous border, and annoyed him by the impertinence of producing better specimens in the cleaner air and unused soil. Lane End was only eight miles from the centre of the city, a bus ran past it, and they had plenty of near neighbours, for other young married couples had dotted the green slopes on both sides of the road with houses of red brick or pale stone, and new, successful gardens.

In fact, thought Stephen, looking out of the bathroom window as he shaved, Lane End should have satisfied all their demands. It was what house agents called an ideal situation. It was perhaps cantankerous of him to feel that it was a mushroom house among other mushroom houses, part of a rootless, gutless civilization. Not that it would have mattered if it was what Joy wanted, but it wasn't. It was no more a country house than the Eiffel Tower. It was a house put down in the country. It had not grown there for any reason. It was a building imposed upon a field. A charming, convenient building with the undeniable advantages of air and space, but an empty shell without spiritual roots, without those deep, invisible connections that bound Stackhouses to the church and the rectory, to the Women's Institute and the pub, to the cottages and farms around, even to the local poachers and the village idiot. That was real, and his own father's house was real, built within an hour's walk of the works that had paid for it, linked to the city by a hundred ties of obligation, affection and irritation. Living out here, Stephen thought, there's nothing to annoy us except ourselves and one another. He thought of his father-in-law angry over the misdeeds of the Parish Council, grumbling about his colleagues on the bench, struggling with the preparations for the local Show. He thought of his mother-in-law narrating the ups and downs of the Women's Institute, of his own father coming back from stormy Town Council meetings, of his mother flushed with triumph from her committees or warm with indignation. At Lane End they were right out of all that sort of thing. Both he and Joy had grown up in the middle of it, with the affairs of town and parish and village and countryside in the air. He wondered if she felt as he did, that they now lived in a cardboard house in a group of other cardboard houses.

Yet it seemed ungrateful to be dissatisfied when he came downstairs and into the one long living-room which ran across the front of the house. In winter they curtained off one end and used it for a dining-room, but in summer the narrow oak table, which had once come from a refectory, was pushed up to the sliding window doors that opened on to the verandah. The doors were wide-open this morning. His two sons sat with their backs to the garden because their attempts to see the cars and buses passing on the road always distracted them from the business of eating. They looked up as he came in, Jack with a piece of toast half way to his mouth, Lin with his mug in his hand, and a white moustache of creamy milk above his short upper lip. They were both deeply sunburnt, Jack to his own ruddy colouring, Lin with the same golden brown as Joy's fair skin. Joy, in a white shirt and green linen skirt, sat at the end of the table reading a letter. The smell of coffee penetrated the garden smell of grass and flowers. There was a blue plate on the table piled with raspberries picked by Joy before breakfast, and a great bee, blundering in through the window, hovered over the bowl of small, dark-red carnations. Wife and children and home and a summer morning—what more could anyone want?

"You're a bit late, Daddy." Joy spoke absently, one hand on the coffee-pot, the other turning the sheet of notepaper.

"I know. I dawdled. I shall have to be quick."

"Did you see Grandpapa at the party?" Jack inquired. He had from the very first adored his grandfather Harding, of whom he was a small copy, and not only in looks. He was a sociable, curious, humorous, friendly child, without shyness. In games and races, in spite of his twenty months' superiority, he often allowed himself to be beaten by the taut determination of his junior.

Joy laid down the letter.

"Oh, Stephen! Hilary got home last Friday, and he wants to come to us next week-end. Mother says he hasn't changed a bit!" She looked at the letter again. "He's coming by road. He'll be here for dinner on Friday!"

"Oh, good!" Stephen exclaimed heartily, too heartily, if Joy had had a sensitive ear for finer shades, or had been thinking about him. She had all her younger son's power of concentration on one object at a time.

"I wonder if he'll stay till Wednesday. We were going to the Ambers' to dinner on Tuesday."

"We'll ask if we can bring him."

"I think he'd probably rather stay here in peace. You go, and I'll stay with him."

"If you like."

"And on Monday we might have a whole day at the County Match. Could you get off, Stephen?"

"I don't think I'd better ask for a day just now. I'd rather not. We had that long week-end in June."

"What a pity!" Was it his imagination that her regret was perfunctory? "Oh, and Sunday, Stephen, you'd better let the Wards know we can't come."

"I'll ask if we can bring him too. They won't mind."

"I'm not going to inflict that on him!"

"Oh, come, it's not quite as bad as all that! I don't want to cry off again. We did that last week about their tennis."

"I'm not going to play tennis there. That wretched boy loses his temper and I can't stand the other people you have to play with. They're all outsiders, and they haven't even any manners! They argue about the score!"

Jack began to giggle. "Miss Law said we hadn't none of us any manners yesterday when the blackboard fell off the stand and we all laughed."

"Get along out, you two, if you've finished."

Joy waited until her sons had rolled and tumbled down the grassy slope below the verandah like a pair of puppies off the lead.

"I'm sorry, Stephen. I know you've got to go there, it's beastly for you and I hate you having to do it. I'll go to their terrible pompous dinner parties and their tea fights sometimes, and I'll have them here when you think we ought, but I won't play tennis there again, and I just won't drag Hilary into it."

To his own surprise, Stephen said crossly,

"They're good enough for me but not for him, are they?"

"Don't be silly! He hasn't got to bother about them. You have—worse luck! It's degrading to have to truckle to people because they've got the whip-hand of you! I loathe it for you!"

Stephen said slowly, "You know—I partly loathe it, but

I'm sorry for them, especially for those two young ones! There they are with all that money having hardly any fun out of it because they simply don't know how. It's too late for the parents, but I think it's a pity someone doesn't get hold of Marjorie and Leslie and give them a shake and show them how. I thought school might do it for them, but it hasn't. Marjorie went to a silly snob place where she didn't meet the sort of girls whose parents would ask her to stay, and Leslie's so shy and moody he probably just had a rotten time at Harrow and didn't make any friends at all. Yet they're not really a bad couple. Marjorie's got any amount of energy and quite a lot of undeveloped sense, and Leslie's intelligent. I never go to one of those dreary dinners without feeling sorry for them."

"I should have thought at Harrow they might have taught Leslie not to swear and throw his racquet across the court when he lost a game."

Stephen had the feeling that most of what he had said to her had passed over her head. Leslie, the human being with unsatisfied needs and undeveloped possibilities, was to her, simply the underbred boy who threw his racquet across the court at the end of the game. With the same finality, the same clear view of one question, she concluded,

"You go if you like, Stephen, if you think you ought, I mean, but I shan't come on Sunday and I won't take Hil there at all, ever. If you've finished, I'll clear the table now. It's Ivy's day out."

Leaving the car for Joy, who was playing tennis that afternoon, Stephen caught the bus into town. He took the *Yorkshire Guardian* with him. Joy had it at breakfast, glanced at the births, marriages and deaths, ran a casual eye over the picture page, read the cricket, and having thus disposed of the outside world, passed the paper to Stephen.

Stephen's habit had been to glance at the chief news headlines, look at anything that seemed interesting, turn to the book reviews and musical criticisms, and finally to read the cricket. Lately he had found himself spending more time on the middle pages of the paper. This business of Mussolini was disquieting. Stephen read the first leading article, a sober comment on the negotiations then taking place between Eden and Laval, a sober forecast of the League Council meeting to be held in two days' time. The gist of the article seemed to be that the situation was grave, but that a war made by one member of the League on another, a war of aggression begun by a European power, was a thing that nowadays did not happen. The *Guardian*, always anxious to be fair, admitted provocation, hinted at the possibility of concessions to Italy's needs, but warned Mussolini that going to war about it was not done. Only, thought Stephen, suddenly sceptical, the people who don't care whether a thing is done or not have such an enormous pull over the people who do. There rose dimly on the edge of his mind, like a black cloud, a vision of a world in which nobody kept the rules, and an unformed suspicion that people like himself, born with the rules in their blood, would find themselves hopelessly at sea in it. Sometimes it seemed to be coming nearer, and then again he thought that he must have got nerves. He had never supposed himself to have them, but there must be something to account for this curious state that was growing on him in which his senses were alert for any mention of the day's news, his spirit often heavy with a presage of disaster. Were other people the same, he wondered. He looked round the bus at the blank, placid faces of people apparently serene and absorbed in their own affairs. He ached for company at this moment and would have liked to talk to somebody who felt as he did, or perhaps to somebody who knew that such feelings were absurd, that these undisturbed faces in the bus were the reality, and his intangible forebodings were only nightmares. Feeling unable to broach the subject to any of the strangers who sat near him, he turned the pages of the newspaper, and read a review of a book of modern poetry. It appeared to his sharpened wits that the same conflict arose here. The poet, somewhat obscurely, was writing in terms of a new world, the reviewer was trying in a worried way to measure his writing by the standards of

58

an old one. Stephen was conscious that he felt with the reviewer, but was beginning reluctantly to see with the poet. He did not like what he saw. He turned another page and read the cricket with resolution.

The office and works of Alfred Ward stood in an unimposing street a little way behind the Town Hall Square. By degrees they had extended all along one side of the street, and swallowed up several blocks of houses behind them. The buildings made a square with an open space in the middle, which had been laid out as a garden and included two hard tennis-courts and a covered swimming-bath for the use of the employees. The employees used the swimming-bath a good deal during the lunch hour but seldom made use of the tennis-courts, and the question of whether it was worth keeping them up was to be raised at the next Board meeting. The real sports-ground of the firm, with its cricket and football field, grass tennis-courts and pavilion, was about three miles away on the edge of the town.

Stephen turned in at the main door, nodded to the porter in his box on the left, and paused for a moment in the wide entrance hall. After the heat and dust outside, the coolness of the regulated temperature was welcome, but the place depressed him, and he realized this morning for the first time that his spirits always sank a little on entering. It was not that he disliked work, his job was not arduous, and was sometimes interesting. It was the richness, efficiency and completeness of his surroundings that felt like a stone on his heart. So much satin-smooth wood, such thick carpet, so much shining chromium and Vitaglass, so many rest-rooms, buffets, first-aid stations, shower-baths, and ventilators gave him a sensation of being over-fed. It isn't, he thought, a sensible feeling. All this care and comfort for work-people, this fussing over conditions is a darned good thing, one of the best things that ever happened. He thought of the excellent meals served in the bright, airy restaurant, of the medical examinations, the clean, luxurious cloakrooms, and reminded himself of the days when men and women worked intolerable hours in dark, fetid buildings, and eight-year-old children were ducked to keep them awake for another hour's work. One ought to thank Heaven for the chromium and the ventilators and the escape from those cruel days! To his astonishment he found himself thinking, at least then both sides had their gloves off! There were moments at Alfred Ward's when he felt that the chromium and polished wood, the well cooked lunches and the swimming-bath were only part of soft, well lined gloves.

His own room was on the first floor and had two windows overlooking the central square. A private washing cabinet opened off it, with a built-in wardrobe where he kept an old mackintosh and a few odds and ends. At the opposite side of his room, a door opened into his secretary's office. He had two comfortable leather-backed chairs as well as the modern furniture which Ward favoured for the whole building. If he did not want to have lunch or tea in the staff dining-room, he could telephone for what he wanted, and have it brought to him.

All the office staff and the fabric and furniture of the place were under his control, and as a natural consequence, he received almost more brisk attention and service than Ward himself.

His father, accustomed all his life to cramped and old-fashioned offices between the canal and the railway station, spoke of "Stephen's luxury liner," and Robert, frankly envious, called him a fatted calf.

So I am, he thought, sitting down at his table. How lucky, oh, how lucky he had been to get this job! He had been engaged to Joy for six months when the family firm went down, and he still remembered like a nightmare those desperate weeks, seeing his marriage receding into the distance, finding himself unemployed, trying to jerk himself out of his own selfish misery to sympathize with his father's feeling at closing down a business that had been in the family for three generations and at turning off clerks in the office and men in the works whom he had known all his life. Into the midst of that nightmare Ward had stalked like a queer, grey, dry fairy godmother, offering a job with ungracious abruptness, and giving no hint of his reason, unless in the remark which he seemed to make unwillingly, "Your father and me have always agreed well enough." Lionel Harding's uncalculating kindness and his easy geniality that made no distinctions had been bread upon the waters for his children more often than he or they knew.

Stephen read the pile of letters and memoranda on the table before him, made a note or two, rang for his secretary and began the morning's work of dictating, interviewing, telephoning. His most immediate business was the arrangements for the annual outing of all the employees of the firm. This took place in the second week of August. Everyone, works, office staff, travellers, agents, and Ward himself, went by special train to some seaside place, lunched copiously with speeches, disported themselves as they pleased in boats, swimming-pool or amusement park, and dined even more copiously on the train coming home. Stephen would have enjoyed the day if he had not been responsible for it, did contrive to enjoy a good deal of it. He wondered if Joy would come with him again this year. If not, perhaps he might be able to take Jack. He would like his son to grow up used to all sorts and conditions of men. He himself as a little boy had always been to the annual picnics and cricket match of his father's firm, and remembered as one of his great treats the drive home in a char-à-banc late at night, drowsy with fresh air and excitement.

Yet there had been a difference between that outing and this. It was not only that his father's firm had belonged to simpler days and had been content with simpler ways, tea and pork pies and tea cakes in the dining-room of the country pub whose cricket field they hired for the afternoon. There was about this far superior and more highly organized treat of Alfred Ward's an unacknowledged element of compulsion. Ward said that he liked to have all his people there, and the heads of the general office and foremen in the works, taking their cue from him, made their subordinates feel that to miss the Annual Outing was, if not a crime, at least a breach of taste likely to make them lose favour. Somehow that element of compulsion got into all Ward's kindnesses. At the dinner parties which Joy found so dreary you felt that the guests had been dragged there by pertinacious hosts, and would rather have been at home.

Stephen checked the list of those who were coming and looked through the menu for dinner on the train, thinking, well, anyhow it's my job to make a success of the day, I don't have to bother about what it's really worth to them or to Ward. Suddenly he thought that perhaps that was the canker in his happy life, he never did have to think whether anything was right or not. He was a glorified, well paid private secretary. He was necessary to Ward because of these Annual Outings and Sports Grounds and Rest Rooms, because of all the complicated fabric that enclosed the business of making ready-made clothes for money. He was a luxury living on other luxuries. It was his business to accept the major premises, to assume that the system was all right and attend to the detail, and lately he had wondered whether the system was all wrong. Sometimes he thought that this great, shining elaborate place was the monstrous temple of a dead faith. Then again his traditional and everyday self laughed at the fancy and drove it back. Such unwelcome ideas were still only a small part of him.

Picking up the memorandum about the tennis-courts, he reflected that it would be as well to mention it to John Allworthy before suggesting to the Board that they should be grassed over. He did not believe that the men and girls out of the works ever used them, an occasional dilatory single between two clerks out of the office was all that he had ever seen, but if the courts were done away with, it might become a grievance. He would probably then discover that the workrooms were full of people who had just been going to play on them, and who considered that they had been deprived of their rights. It was always a good thing before making any minor change to have a word with old John. Ward from policy, Stephen from courtesy and good will, took counsel regularly with the Senior Shop Steward and Branch Secretary of the Union. Besides, John was a character, not only in the firm, but in the city. He and Alfred Ward,

62

leaving school together at eleven years old, had started in the same week as fitters' boys, but while Ward had pushed on to make his fortune, Allworthy had thrown his energies into politics. He had been one of the earliest supporters of the Labour Movement, had fought its battles on the Town Council, in the Press and in his firm, had suffered and lost and struggled for his cause, and had now reached the stage at which he was the acknowledged local leader to the older men in the movement, a check upon the young hotheads, and an object of kindly regard, almost of vicarious pride, to the Conservatives of the town, who called him Long John, ragged him at Council Meetings, and felt for him that affection which Englishmen often feel for an opponent of long standing.

There was a gentle knock at the door. John Allworthy came into Stephen's room, nodded and smiled in reply to his greeting, made a cheerful remark about the weather, and sat down in the chair that his secretary had just left. It was difficult to believe that this man had been a firebrand, made history, and taken every man and woman in the place out on strike ten years ago. He seemed, no, he *was*, a mild-mannered, kindly, elderly Yorkshireman, who looked like a foreman in his Sunday clothes. He was small, with a high forehead, from which the hair, once sandy but now grey, had receded, except for one long wisp that came forward in moments of agitation. It was his habit when speaking to smooth it down every few minutes, and anyone in the audience who was interested might notice then that his hands were shapely, fine and flexible. His eyes were small, greenish-grey, his smile diffident and sweet, his ears very large, his nose shaped like Punch's. High forehead and ears and nose gave him an oddly disarming appearance, which was useful for cartoons in the local Press, and remained in the mind of the casual observer who often did not notice the strength and determination in the well-shaped mouth and chin. Stephen had known John Allworthy as an opponent of his father's at Municipal Elections and on the Council before he ever came

63

to Alfred Ward's. In the firm, he had found him easy enough to get on with, and often congratulated himself on the improved relations between employers and employees. There was not likely to be any real difficulty so long as he and Ward and Allworthy could have lunch together and talk it over like sensible people. Stephen's attitude to the Union Branch Secretary was that of a man who keeps a tiger as a domestic pet and is disposed to pet it the more because it obliges him by staying domestic. Like the Conservatives on the City Council he experienced a peculiar pleasure, a pleasure decidedly tinged with condescension, in his cordial relationships with the other side.

It would have surprised him very much to know that there was a good deal of condescension in John Allworthy's attitude to him. Stephen Harding, John thought, was a nice lad with very good manners, a nice, pleasant lad very young and ignorant and inexperienced, knowing nothing at all about life. Life for John, as for a good many people, meant his own life. It meant sleeping three in a bed, and going to school barefoot and hungry. It meant leaving school at eleven and working as a fitters' boy in the old workshop of Ernest Miller's, down by the yard of the steelworks. It meant skimping and saving to buy books, growing up to the dawn of the Labour Movement, becoming a political orator at nineteen, marrying at twenty-three, organizing a strike at twenty-five, and being knocked down in a street fight by a policeman. It meant years and years of elections and conferences, of the business of the Union and of the Movement, of reading newspapers and making speeches and handing out leaflets, of meeting strange speakers in deserted stations on Sunday afternoons or of travelling himself by slow Sunday trains to mount the platform in hot or draughty halls where rows of unknown faces looked up expectant and hopeful through the thick cloud of cheap tobacco smoke like birds waiting to be fed. It meant an ardour that had changed with the slow growth of time into an untiring patience. It meant poverty and hard work and exhaustion and triumph and satisfaction and disillusionment, and one belief and purpose running through the whole like a spinal cord. John Allworthy looked

64

kindly at Stephen, the young and untried, who had never been short of a meal, never fought or suffered for a cause. Stephen, in the unconscious security of having been born into the favoured section of humanity, with an inbred sense of superiority of which he was unaware and which he would instantly have denied, looked kindly at John Allworthy, thinking him a very decent old fellow.

"It's about those tennis-courts, John." The whole firm called Allworthy John. "I never see anyone playing on them, and it seems to me they might as well be grassed over. It would make a bit more room for people to sit about, and look nicer, and the surface of the far court really wants redoing. Mr. Ward noticed it the other day. It's not worth having it done if nobody plays on it."

"I don't think they seem to use them at all, Mr. Harding. I don't know why, I'm sure. I said to one of the girls the other day, why don't you bring your racquet and have a game of tennis at dinner-time instead of sitting indoors and giggling? But they don't want to, and I reckon they might as well be grassed over. They'd make a very good lawn, perhaps, with a couple of nice flower-beds cut out here and there? I'm sure those antirrhinums round the far side of the swimming-bath have been a picture. You ought to have brought your uncle to see them, Mr. William Marsden. I know he's a great gardener. He once showed me all round his garden. It will be a sight just now, I dare say."

"Yes, it's lovely. I was there last night." A recollection flashed across Stephen's mind. "Oh, I met your niece—isn't it your niece? She said she'd just got a job on the *Guardian*."

"Yes, that's Mary, my sister's eldest. She's a clever lass. She got a scholarship to Oxford and she was in London doing well, but she had to come home because her mother's an invalid. Doris, the younger one, is getting married. She's marrying Frank Varley."

"The cricketer? Really? What's he like?"

"He seems a nice young fellow."

"He's a very good bat. I saw him play last year. Do you follow cricket much?"

"I don't go to the matches often nowadays, but I keep an

65

eye on the score and I like to have an afternoon there when I can."

"You'll certainly have to if Varley's going to marry into your family. I see he got eighty-nine yesterday against Gloucester."

Allworthy's eye was on the folded newspaper under Stephen's hand. He was thinking, I suppose that's all that really interests him, the cricket. It's the only news I've ever heard him talk about. As though the thought had passed to him across the table, Stephen said,

"What do you think of this Abyssinian business?"

Allworthy answered gravely, "It's bad, sir, I don't like it."

But he thought, I can't tell that lad why I don't like it. He could not begin to explain to Stephen as he would cheerfully have explained to an audience his private conviction that his Government and France were going to betray Abyssinia to Italy, if they had not already done so. The League Council were to meet in two days and the League Assembly in September, but he was an old Town Councillor and knew just how much business was arranged on committees and in private conversations, and how much of the actual Council Meeting was shop-window dressing for a few reporters and the outside world. He always kept off politics with the heads of the firm, confining himself to Trade Union business, and polite conversation. He genuinely did not want to offend Stephen, but at the mere thought of Mussolini and Abyssinia his mouth shut and tightened and his eyes shone, and for a moment a gulf yawned. Stephen was an enemy on the other side, even if he did not know it. Stephen felt the division and thought, of course he hates Mussolini and feels all sentimental about the poor Abyssinians, lot of lousy rascals, these Labour people judge everything by sentiment, that's why they make such a mess of handling things. He had stepped back from the gulf on to his own side, and said in the cheerful and polite tone his father would have used to a gardener,

"Well, all right, John. I'll see about the tennis-courts." His voice meant, you can go, but as John Allworthy was

66

turning away, there was a perfunctory knock. The door opened at once and Alfred Ward came in.

There were times when Stephen tried by stretching his imagination to evoke that legendary small boy, Alf Ward, who had started work at eleven years old with the small boy, John Allworthy, in the tailor's shop behind the old steel-works. The small John was easy. You could see him with eager eyes and large ears protruding under a man's discarded cap too big for him, with a firm but childish chin above a blue neckcloth. He would have looked like dozens of bright, plain, undersized children starting work to-day, except that his clothes would probably be shabbier than the clothes of the working-class boy nowadays, and he would be a good three years younger in age, although he must even then have had the maturity of a settled purpose, for he had always meant, he once told Stephen, to save up and buy books and learn things and "do summat about it all." Stephen felt that he could reconstruct a probable and convincing young John, but he had never been able to make any mental picture of young Alfred. "A boy" was all he could arrive at. The boy had no connection with the Alfred Ward who was sixty-nine, lived in the pseudo-Gothic splendour of Grey Manor, and was a captain of big business. It was impossible to reclothe the strong bones of that dry, grey, wrinkled face with the rounded flesh of childhood, impossible to imagine the eyes bright and ingenuous, the lips full and soft, the whole personality open and unwary. The only thing one could say for certain was that at the age of eleven, or at any other age, Alfred Ward must have been a remarkable child.

You always know, Stephen thought, when he comes into a room. Yet the feeling that he brought with him was oddly impersonal. You did not feel an onrush of warmth or gaiety or friendliness as you did with some people. You did not even feel the chill of hostility or bad temper. It was more as though a big machine had been started up, and you could feel in the air the vibrations of its impersonal vitality. It was a machine enclosed in a strong fence. But against what, Stephen wondered, was he fenced? He was a bold man afraid of something, a man rigorously positive in affairs and action, but negative in personal relationships. Of his ability there could be no doubt. His feelings, loves and hates and longings were guess-work. Of his private life beyond its circumstances Stephen knew only two things, that he did not have friends and he did not have fun.

"Morning, Harding. Oh, you here, John," Ward said, and nodded. Allworthy said briskly, "Good morning, Mr. Ward."

The relationship between the two who had been Alf and John setting out to work together at eleven years old, had always intrigued Stephen, sure of one thing only, that either would have minded separation. Sometimes he thought that to Ward, the presence of John Allworthy, a shop steward in the works, a poor man living in a little house, was the measure of his own success. In his dry way he spoke almost affectionately of old John. John's attitude to him was that of a cat in front of her kittens facing a large dog. At any moment the large dog, the employer, might pounce upon the workpeople, might dock some right or privilege, try to get some little bit of extra work done for nothing. The cat crouched, bright eyes and vigilant, the hair on her back bristling if the dog moved a paw, yet she would have got on quite well with the dog if the kittens had not been there, and did over anything in which they were not concerned.

Really, Stephen thought, the two men managed a very successful relationship by each feeling superior. Ward, the man who had got on, could afford to be tolerant of the man who had not. John, the man who had spent his life, as it seemed to him, for the things that mattered, could afford to be tolerant of the man who had worked for himself alone. In fact, you can get on all right with other people, even people who disagree with you, so long as you have your own platform, self-respect or vanity, whichever you like to call it, it's your most precious possession. Take that away from a man and he's dangerous,—or from a country, as we all did from Germany? He wondered, what's my platform? With a

68

sense of shock he discovered that in his relationship with anyone at Alfred Ward's, it was probably the accident of better birth, breeding and education. So I'm a snob after all! A horrid discovery! Especially, he thought, with a wry inward smile, as my platform with Joy's people has always been not being a snob. How virtuous and disapproving he had sometimes felt when they were talking in their casual, well-bred voices about "the sort of people one doesn't know," "our sort of people." The deuce of a lot of their lives human beings managed to spend, when you came to think of it, in feeling superior!

"I'll go along now, Mr. Harding," Allworthy said.

"All right, John, I'll be seeing you later. We might have a look at the tennis-courts together."

As the door closed behind him, Ward drew a chair up to the table.

"I wanted a word with you about those Americans coming next week. They'll have lunch here in the Staff Room, of course, but you'd better take them round the place yourself. Reingart is a big man. You'll see about rooms for them if they stay the night?"

"You don't want to put them up at Grey Manor, sir?"

"No, I don't think that would be convenient for Mrs. Ward."

Ward had, as Stephen knew, an inveterate distaste for visitors staying in the house, probably because he was too shy to be left alone with them in those hours at the end of the evening or after breakfast when the host must bear the brunt of his male guests. That was one of the things wrong, Stephen thought, with Marjorie and Leslie. The house ought to have been full of their young friends, exasperating their parents by dropping cigarette ash all over the place, and being late for meals. But Leslie had never had a friend to stay, and a schoolgirl who once came back with Marjorie, a fair, plump child, cheerful on arrival, had wilted and gone home a day before her time. Sometimes, as now, Stephen thought of the young Wards and tried to break into the formal isolation of the household, but he was seldom successful.

"You'd better bring them up to dinner," Ward said uneasily. "But take rooms for them at the Midland."

69

"We could have put Reingart up if he'd been coming alone, but we haven't room for his secretary too. Oh, I forgot, we couldn't anyhow, my wife's brother will be here with us. By the way, sir, I'm afraid Joy won't be able to come up to supper with me on Sunday. He'll be there, and she won't like to leave him."

"I hope you will bring your brother-in-law, too."

"Thank you very much, but I think they will want a little time to themselves. She hasn't seen him for five years. He's been in India with his regiment and only just come home." He felt that it sounded lame, and that Joy had refused a good many invitations to Grey Manor lately, and added in a voice that sounded too hearty, "I'm looking forward very much to coming." He wondered for one wild moment whether he could induce Beryl and Robert to come with him, but although Beryl probably wouldn't mind, Robert, whom he had once taken to make up the numbers at a dinner party, had afterwards stated firmly and frankly that he wasn't going to be butchered again to make a Ward holiday, and would probably stick to it. For purposes of intercourse with the Wards, Stephen thought it would really be more convenient if he'd married Beryl and Robert had married Joy. Partly to suppress this thought, and partly to prevent Ward from issuing a wholesale invitation for a later date when Joy and Hilary might be supposed to have got over the reunion, Stephen said hastily, "What do you think of the news this morning?"

Ward replied, "I think Mussolini means business, and isn't going to let the League stop him. Why should he? It's an idea, that's all. It's got no force, only a backing of sentimental idealism. You can't stop a man who knows what he wants and means to get it by asking him to be nice about it." He added, and the words had a ring of personal pride, "It's very hard to stop any man who knows exactly what he wants and means to get it. No, he'll go for Abyssinia. All I hope is we don't get dragged into a quarrel with Italy by sentimentalists like Stanley Baldwin and Eden trying to stop him when they can't."

"I think we ought to try and stop him."

Ward shrugged. "We should only make fools of ourselves. He won't be stopped."

Stephen found himself saying irritably, "He jolly well ought to be. I don't hold with dictators."

"It isn't a question of what you hold with, but of what's there," Ward added dryly. "There are worse things than dictators."

Some personal feeling flickered between them, as Stephen answered, "I don't think so."

"Of course there are—Communism, anarchy, revolution. A country can be perfectly prosperous and well governed under a dictator and no country is prosperous and well governed in a state of anarchy, or during a revolution. You've got too many ideas in your mind, Harding. You've got to clear your mind of ideas nowadays and stick to facts." For an instant Stephen, silent and mutinous, had a glimpse of the young poet's new, hard world, saw himself like the reviewer, trying to measure it by the standards of the old one. Then Ward took a paper out of his pocket-book and said, "But I didn't come in here to talk politics. I want you to look at this estimate."

At twelve o'clock, Stephen went down into the South Work-room, looking about him for Allworthy. Accustomed as he was to the scene, he never saw the orderly rows of men and women at work without an uneasy qualm for the whole of civilization. That anyone should spend so many hours of their day on a mechanical repetition of one job, or rather of a tiny part of a job, seemed to him an outrage against all that men and women were meant for. A good deal of this feeling, he supposed, was sentimental. Hours of mechanical repetition of the same action would have been intolerable to him, but he knew that many of them not only did not find it intolerable, but even liked it. Girls who got married and left pined for the work-room and often came back again. Men returning from their holidays said, with obvious sincerity, that a bit of a change was all right, but they were glad to be back. Evidently to many of them it seemed a good life.

But even if it does, he thought, there's something wrong with them or something wrong with the world that can't offer them anything better. He stood at the end of one of the long tables watching a girl who was working a machine that fastened buttons on the waistcoats. The waistcoats slid towards her out of a wooden funnel that disgorged them flat on to the table, the side awaiting the buttons marked with chalk crosses, and turned towards the machine. One sure movement of her hands flicked the waistcoat into place, a second dropped the buttons into a small tray at the side of the machine, which immediately absorbed them. As she pressed a treadle with her foot, the machine released the buttons each into its place on the chalk crosses. Needles shot down and stitched the buttons on to the cloth with firm, strong stitches. Another pressure of her foot raised the needles and released the cloth, a quick twist of her hand pulled the waistcoat past the machine into another flat wooden funnel that conveyed it to the next table, where another girl was waiting to operate on it with a machine for making button-holes. This button machine was new and one of the show pieces of the work-room. Stephen had brought his mother to see it, but she had observed placidly, "They'll all come off at once, dear. I've never worn anything ready made without sewing on the buttons first." Those five movements of hand and feet, endlessly and exactly repeated, distressed her as they distressed Stephen, and she asked, "Don't you get very tired of doing it?" but the girl, who was pretty, with carefully curled hair, delicately plucked eyebrows, and a bright painted mouth, smiled and said that she liked it. How can she, Stephen thought, as he stood now watching her warm young flesh and blood moving with the precision of a machine.

"That's Tom Sutton's girl," Allworthy's voice said at his elbow. "He brought her round to our house a month or two ago. Olive Walters, her name is."

"Tom Sutton? Oh, the foreman cutter in the next room? The fellow that came on that deputation about having the windows open? I remember."

72

Allworthy walked at Stephen's side between the long tables and the rows of backs bent over the machines.

"Ah, I was a bit vexed about that business. By rights they ought to have come to me first."

"It was when you were away with bronchitis, wasn't it?"

"Aye, but I was only off ten days. They could have waited while I came back. But Tom's always in a hurry. Always the same ever since he was a little lad and used to come to our house, with his father and mother. Always as soon as he came in at the door, 'When do we get our teas, Aunt Grace?' 'What can I play with, Uncle John?'" Allworthy chuckled. "He always called us Aunt and Uncle, you see, his mother being such a friend of Mrs. Allworthy. Ah, he's a grand lad, is Tom. But he'll have to learn patience."

Allworthy had forgotten for the moment that he was talking to Stephen Harding. Tom'll have to learn patience, he was thinking, if he's to do any real good in the Movement. He won't help things on by ranting and raving the way he did that last night he came, talking nonsense about men that's been in the Movement before he was born or thought of, men that have done work in the Unions for forty years. It isn't all such an easy matter as the young men think it is. When you get on a bit, you know that nothing's ever plain sailing. All that talk about traitors and snobs, the Unions being in the hands of a caucus, it makes bad blood and doesn't help anyone. It's a pity Tom goes about with that Communist friend of his! It does him no good. Allworthy had a distaste for Communists compared with which the feeling of the average Conservative towards them might be described as a mild liking. He frowned, remembering certain wild words that Tom had spoken on his last visit. His brow cleared as they approached the table where the young man was working, his brown face with the crisp dark hair growing back from its wide forehead bent above the shining scissors that snipped their way with such delicate assurance through the thin cloth. Tom was a good cutter, one of the best he'd ever known. A good workman and a good lad, the son of his old friends. He smiled and nodded as he passed.

Tom Sutton's answering nod was a trifle sulky. He paused for an instant with the scissors suspended above the cloth, and looked after the retreating backs of John and Stephen. There was Celtic blood somewhere in his family, and his face with its high cheek-bones, brown skin and dark-blue eyes, looked more alive, more like a face and less like a pudding than a lot of those around him. He saw Stephen and John pause in the doorway, turn to one another and laugh, saw John stand back to let Stephen pass him, saw Stephen put a hand on his shoulder urging him through. Tom bent to his cloth again, a snake of suspicion stirring in his heart. He suspected both of them, but whereas his suspicion of Mr. Harding, the gentleman, the class enemy, the master, was automatic and almost perfunctory, his suspicion of John Allworthy, the workman, the Trade Union man, the stalwart of the Divisional Labour Party, was a vivid and uncomfortable emotion.

He owed a lot to his so-called Uncle John, his start at Alfred Ward's, his early training in Socialism, as well as a great deal of personal kindness, John Allworthy had been his friend and mentor and also his hero. Had he not known and talked with Edward Carpenter, and Hyndman and William Morris? Had he not started and led the great gas workers' strike of 1890 which had so changed the position of Municipal workers? Had he not organized the strike at Alfred Ward's ten years ago? It was only lately that it had occurred to Tom that his hero, instead of raising fresh standards of revolt, was trying to pull down those already raised. He began to think that Allworthy was always opposing direct action, that he temporized and hung back and talked too much about patience and steadiness. "Rome was not built in a day," Allworthy had said at the last Divisional Labour Meeting, and a young, dark-eyed girl, a student at the University had flashed back at him, "No, but Soviet Russia was, pretty nearly!" Tom had joined in the burst of applause, which followed her sally, and had seen Allworthy's mouth fold and tighten, heard him say gently and decidedly, "Aye, but this isn't Russia." There had been another burst of applause, from a different quarter of the room, from the grey-headed

74

men and broad-bottomed elderly women on the front benches. The sense of divided aims, of being held back, kept in check, had irritated Tom, and made him wonder why he did not join the Communist Party straight away like his friend, Harold Pearson. He often thought of it but could never bring himself, to the point. He had grown up in the tradition of the Labour Movement, his friends were in it. He recognized the weight and value of so large a body, and respected its history. Although he agreed on the whole with Communist aims, he did not like the idea of instructions from the Komintern. His spirit, strongly individualist, rebelled against the disciplined and dedicated life which Harold Pearson led in the Communist Party. Also, he had a feeling, of which he was not aware, that it was more interesting to be an extremist in the Labour Movement than one among a small knot of extremists. He had remained in the Labour Party so far, but began imperceptibly to distrust John Allworthy and to go less often to his house. The Allworthys would have thought more of this and he himself would have been more awake to the difference if he had not lately been courting Olive Walters.

There was another of his troubles! He had met Olive at a whist drive got up by his work-room to raise money for the Infirmary. He very seldom went to such things, but he had been fool enough to buy a ticket and go. During the evening he had done something more foolish still. He who never troubled himself much about girls had stuck at one table for three hands with a girl, and had found himself at the end of that time dry in the throat, hollow in the stomach and weak in the knees for fear he should never see her again. He had discovered her name and her place in the South Work-room, and of course he had seen her again. He often thought that it would be much better if he hadn't. In his saner moments he knew that she would never be a suitable wife for him. She cared passionately for her clothes and her hands and her hair, for good times and for what she called "having things nice." She was alarmed by his politics so far as she understood them, she hated arguments, and was not at all interested in his ideas. She loathed the kind of holidays and treats he liked best, long walks in the country, evenings spent talking to friends. Nothing would induce her to stay at a Youth Hostel or go to a political meeting. Her relations were all the sort of people Tom couldn't get on with. Her parents were all right, decent working folk without any ideas, but without any pretensions and kindly. Tom liked them, but he couldn't do with her married brother, Herbert, who lived in one of the new housing estates with his wife and little girl. They were petty-bourgeois in every bone, always thinking about how things would look to the neighbours, and aping the standards of the real bourgeoisie. He couldn't do with the unmarried brother, Fred, either, he was another of the same kind. Fred's girl, Rosie, wasn't so bad. The rest of the family, or anyhow Herbert and Mabel, looked down on her a bit because she was in domestic service and her people were colliers. Tom himself was scornful of anyone who submitted to what he thought a servile occupation, but he couldn't help liking Rosie, who was sturdy, human flesh and blood beside the thin gentility of her future in-laws. She would have been a better wife for him than Olive. But it was Olive who made his heart beat and produced unfamiliar sensations in his body, whose face haunted and yet eluded him at work and at meetings.

As soon as the hooter sounded at half-past twelve, he went out into the uncovered square to wait for her. They met every day for a minute or two before she went off to the women's rest-room and lunch-rooms, and he plunged into the swimming-bath. He could not persuade her to try and swim in the bath, though she liked bathing at the sea, and was knitting an elaborate bathing dress for her holiday. She had it with her now, a bundle of striped green and white wool tucked under her arm and speared by long green needles. She came up to Tom, smiling. Her long morning at the button machine did not seem to have tired her. She was delicately pink and white. Her dress of some white cotton stuff sprigged with little yellow buttercups had short puffed sleeves, and a belt of plaited yellow ribbon round her narrow waist. Her slim brown legs were bare and she wore green and white plaited sandals tied round her ankles. Without her working

76

overall, which she had left on her chair, she looked ready for a picnic. Tom's heart turned over with love and longing.

"It's hot, isn't it?" Olive said, smiling at him.

"Why don't you come and have a try in the pool, Olive? I'll teach you to swim."

"Oh, I wouldn't like to start learning with all these people watching!"

"They wouldn't watch. People who can't swim go in every day of the week. They splash about and nobody looks at them. They're all too busy themselves."

Olive shook her head decidedly.

"I don't want to get my hair all messed up. I don't want to go and have it set again while Monday."

Tom checked a sigh of exasperation. Olive's hair was one of his minor troubles. She was always washing it or having it waved or having it set at Haley's, the big, new multiple store at the corner of Highgate. So far as he could see, it was lovely anyhow and did not need these constant attentions. It was tiresome that when he did coax Olive out for a walk or for a day on the moors, she was always fiddling with her bunch of curls, pushing little pins in, and adjusting a net over them to keep them from being disarranged by wind or weather. Once on a Saturday outing he had persuaded her to lie down with him in the grass. Low down between the springing stems and small flowers, with a bee humming close to them, he drew her to him and coaxed her to relax into his arms, her cheek against his shoulder. The sweetness and warmth of those moments had been such as he had never known, a vivid and tender surprise, but when they scrambled up again as though they were awaking from a dream, Olive had exclaimed, "Oh, Tom! My hair!" She had grabbed her handbag from the grass and taken out the little mirror, and sat there peering into it, patting and pulling her curls, and had finally exclaimed, "I look ever such a mess! We mustn't do that again, Tom. It's common." He had felt as though she had smacked him in the face, and the day had ended in a gloomy and expensive tea in a café, and a silent bus ride home. He remembered this now, but pushed the thought away from him.

"I reckon," he said, "you wouldn't like to come to the meeting with me on Sunday night?"

"What meeting?"

"It's a big meeting in support of the Jews that have been turned out of Germany."

"I don't like Jews. They're ugly and dirty. I won't sit next to one in a tram if I can help it."

"Don't say that, Olive!" Tom cried vehemently.

"Why ever not?"

"Oh, because——" He stopped. What was the use of saying to her that it was against human decency and kindness, that it meant allying herself with the oppressors against the oppressed, joining in with the wrong side? She did not even know that there were any sides. She would have a vote at the next election, but probably would not use it. If she did, it would be at the chance direction of something she had heard or seen in the paper. And there were thousands like her!

"Besides," Olive added, "I'm going over to my Aunty's on Sunday."

She too was exasperated. Why did he always want to take her to meetings instead of to the Regal or the Tivoli or somewhere to have a bit of fun? Why couldn't he be more like other boys, joking and laughing and wanting good times? She had been carried off her feet at his first approaches by his eagerness, his good looks and his vitality. Now she was fond of him, proud of him, bored by him, and a little afraid of him. A dim instinct warned her that he might marry her and sweep her into a life of strenuous ardours and activities in which her personal life of small vanities, pleasures and refinements would be swamped. Obeying this instinct, she held him off. She was prim when he tried to talk about a house and a wedding. She would not always go out with him when he asked her, but invented excuses. She was proud of having such an interesting young man, a foreman cutter admired by a lot of the girls in the work-room, but she was not really as happy in his company as she was walking up and down Highgate with a girl-friend, or at home, altering a dress or manicuring her nails with loving care.

78

"Shan't I be seeing you Sunday, then?" Tom asked. For the moment he was neither the pragmatical politician nor the capable workman, but a young man in love, pleading humbly. It was a mistake, if he had known it, to be humble with Olive. She felt that she had scored a point in a game in which she was generally beaten. She said, "Well, I've to help Mother get the dinner in the morning, and then we've to catch the bus as soon as we've cleared up. My Aunty lives at Cleckheaton and we shan't be back while bed-time."

"Well, Saturday? Let's take a bus ourselves Saturday and go out on the moors."

Olive loathed the moors. It was such hard work walking through the heather, you had to lift your feet up so high every time, the heather stems scratched your ankles, the dust from the heather blew up in your face, and the wind blew your hair about. Not only that, but it was almost frightening to Olive to be in the middle of so much space, with nothing but miles and miles of heather around her and miles and miles of sky above her. She felt little and lost and as though she had no clothes on. And Tom would talk and talk, telling her things about politics that did not interest her, often getting angry with people she had never heard of, and thumping the palm of his hand with his clenched fist, so that she wondered what people would think if they saw him. No, she was not going on the moors. She said, "Let's go up to the Park, Tom, and have our teas at the café and listen to the Pierrots. Maybe Herbert and Mabel would come along too and bring Doreen. It would be a treat for the kiddy."

Tom would have liked to say bitterly that he didn't want to go with a trip. For twopence he would have told her what he thought of her smug brother and sister-in-law and their spoilt brat. He saw himself trailing drearily round the Park, listening to Herbert's conversation, and having tea in a hot café, sickened by the fatuous admiration which Herbert and Mabel and even Olive accorded to Doreen's pert remarks. Somehow he did not say any of it. He looked at the clear curve of Olive's cheek and throat, at the wide grey eyes under the firm arches of her plucked eyebrows—such silly little lines on the white skin that he had an absurd desire to stroke them with his finger. He muttered, "All right, if you like."

"I must go and get my dinner," Olive nodded, smiled brightly, and turned away, not without a faint feeling of relief as though the day's ordeal were past. Tom looked after her, sulky, yearning, unsatisfied, disturbed to the very depths of his being. Then he shrugged his shoulders and slouched off to join Harold Pearson, who was waving to him from the terrace round the swimming-bath.

Stephen was driving his family along the Ring Road that skirted the northern suburbs of the town. They were on their way to Sunday afternoon tea in his old home. By his side, Jack, whose turn it was for the front seat, shouted out the make of each approaching car, occasionally disputing one with Lin, who was sandwiched in the back seat between his mother and his Uncle Hilary. Joy and Hilary were talking about some relation, a cousin perhaps, who had just come home from India and had taken a farmhouse in Devonshire where there would be a bit of rough shooting and ponies for the boys. They had so many relations, Stephen thought, and so many of them came home from India and had farms or boys with ponies, or bits of rough shooting that it was impossible for him to keep up with them, and he was not going to try. All decent people disliked their relations outside their immediate families. Joy and Hilary seemed to take a morbid interest in the houses and families and fortunes of their most distant cousins. Stephen, who had been left out of the conversation all through lunch and had savagely eaten too much of the roast beef and Yorkshire pudding that Joy never failed to order in any weather, felt hot, sleepy and cross.

"What are you going to do about riding for the boys, Joy?" Hilary enquired.

"Well, I don't know. When we go home for holidays, they get a bit on the Grangers' pony, but I haven't done anything here, yet. There is a place, but it's rather expensive and I don't think the man teaches well. And there are ponies at one of those awful, twopenny-halfpenny riding schools, but the poor brutes are all skin and bone. Still, I must do something. It's time they began seriously."

"Why?" Stephen threw over his shoulder.

"Well," Hilary's slow, pleasant voice sounded surprised, "Jack's six, isn't he?"

"I'm getting on for thirty-six, and I never ride."

"But you learnt. You can."

"Yes, I can, but a lot of use it is to me. Jack and Lin are growing up into a mechanized world, and will probably live in towns and go into business. I don't know that it will be much use to them."

Stephen, who had discussed riding lessons for the children quite favourably several times, was being perverse, and Hilary was puzzled. The Army was of course to be mechanized so that what Stephen said about the world might be true, but still if one didn't learn to ride at six years old, what did one learn? He said tentatively, "Perhaps they won't go into business."

"They shan't if I can help it!" Joy cried, hugging Lin to her.

Hilary felt embarrassed, just as he had sometimes felt at children's parties when Joy came out with a blunt comment. He hoped that husband of hers didn't mind. He didn't know yet what to make of Joy's husband. He couldn't get used to her having a husband at all. If ever he had dimly envisaged her as married, he had thought of her living in a house in the country, rather like Stackhouses, with a husband who was only a blur in his imagination, but who would probably be some friend of theirs, someone who as a small boy had ridden his pony with theirs at the local show, and driven into the nearest market town for the same dancing class. Instead of that vague extension of themselves, here was the reality, this square, dark young man with brisk movements, who sometimes laughed when there was no joke, and made remarks whose point escaped Hilary, but which were, he thought, sarcastic. This young man had been brought up in a town, did not often ride, had done very little shooting, had never hunted in his life. Of course it was not his fault, but it was an established if unexpressed fact in Hilary's mind that people brought up in and belonging to a town were never as good as people brought up in and belonging to the country. It seemed odd that Joy should have married one, but she had, and here he was. It was queer how things turned out, Joy and himself scrambling on the moors together, and paddling in the streams and riding and learning to fish and coming towards them in the future out of a town this square, dark Stephen, this alien who did not belong.

"I'm not going into business," Jack announced. "I'm going to drive a racing car."

Lin murmured, "I'm going to be a soldier. I want to learn to ride."

Stephen called out over his shoulder, "I expect they'd better learn," and added, feeling ashamed of his bad temper, "I've had too much lunch."

"So have I," agreed Hilary, who hadn't, but was anxious to meet his brother-in-law half way.

The house in which Neville, Stephen, Clare and Robert had grown up stood on a slope of rising ground at the northern end of the town. It had originally been called the Mill House, because its stable wall abutted on the buildings of a mill, now disused and falling into ruins. A more pretentious Harding in the 'eighties had changed the name of the house to Mill Hall. Like so many other houses in the neighbourhood, it was built of grey stone. It was square, solid, unbeautiful, dignified in its plainness, and distinguished chiefly by three magnificent copper beeches, one at the side of the house sheltering the path to the old stables, two opposite the front door on the other side of the lawn. Clare had once christened these two Mr. and Mrs. Harding. Beyond Mr. and Mrs. Harding, a low beech hedge divided the garden from a field. The stream that wavered across the field had been for the young Hardings and their Marsden cousins every river in romance and history. They had crouched on its banks listening for the sound of Indian canoes, had waded it to throw bloodhounds off their trail, had forded it with crusaders, Jacobites, smugglers and explorers. Now, as the car turned in at the gates, and the gravel of the short drive crunched

82

under their wheels, Jack began to bounce up and down in his seat, shouting out, "Can we go and play in the stream after tea?" Joy replied, "You must ask Grannie, but I expect you can. You left your rubber boots here last time, didn't you?" Lin pleaded, "Will you come and play, Uncle Hilary?" Stephen saw his father scuffling the soil between his roses on the far side of the lawn, and Clare in a blue dress got up from her deck chair and came towards them, smiling. He no longer felt as he had felt at lunch, an outsider in a strange family, he was at home once again with his own people.

His mother came out to meet them, and the whole party crowded into the hall. Some of the furniture in the house was old and beautiful, a good deal was Victorian and ugly, but the general effect was easy and much lived with; although only Clare and her parents were now left in it, the house still kept the feeling of a large, casual family. The drawing-room was a place where people came in and out, smoked and talked and read and sewed. It had none of that suggestion of being preserved in lavender which clung to the drawing-room at Greenoaks. As at Greenoaks, heavy oil-paintings and gold frames hung on the dining-room wall, but they failed to make intimidating a room that suggested Christmas dinners, family lunches and children's tea-parties rather than the elderly men drinking their port whose ghosts seemed permanently established in the high-backed chairs of the Greenoaks dining room. At Greenoaks where the young men had died before they were twenty it was as though at that moment someone had stopped the clocks, and life in the house had become static. At Mill Hall, Robert, Stephen and Clare bringing in their friends and assailing their parents with their ideas had kept time moving.

Our children teach us more than we teach them, Lionel Harding reflected humbly as he took his seat at the end of the long table, and looked across its dark wood and bright flowers to his wife handling the cups behind the big Queen Anne tea-pot. When you are young, you aren't willing to learn, you think you know. When you come to my time of life the one thing you do know is how small your knowledge is. He had scouted the idea of learning anything at all from his father's experience. His mind was open to receive and consider the experience of Robert and Stephen. There was so much of life and so little time to learn in, he had long ago abandoned the conceit and assurance that were the greatest stumbling-block to learning. Perhaps if there was a definite time, he had abandoned them in the last year of Neville's life. It had honestly seemed to him that the boy was so much better, a so much more rare and valuable person than he himself had ever been or would ever be. Looking round the table now at his sons and their wives, at his little grandchildren, he felt the pang of Neville's loss of life and love and maturity, of these years when he too should have learnt from his children. He said to himself, there must be no more wars! Catching fragments of a conversation between Hilary and Robert about Abyssinia, he felt that his one desire in the matter was that England should keep out of it.

Hilary and Robert were discussing possible military operations in Abyssinia with careful politeness. Hilary, who did not consider the territorial Robert a soldier, was kind enough to want to conceal it. Robert detected the patronage and thought to himself, the good old Regular Army! They disagreed about the probabilities. Hilary was quite certain that Mussolini did not mean to fight, and would never get to Addis Ababa if he did. Robert thought that Mussolini did mean to fight, and opined, more from perversity than from any real knowledge or conviction, that a bunch of untrained blacks would never hold him up. Both of them grew, if not hot, a trifle stiff, and Clare joined in the conversation to ease matters. Round the Sunday tea-table in the West Riding industrial town the names "Abyssinia," "Addis Ababa" ran through the conversation like motifs in an opera. A year ago, thought Lionel Harding, most of us would have had to look at a map to see where they were, and Addis Ababa sounded as remote and irrelevant as Babylon or Manoa. Who can tell what is coming into my children's lives?

Stephen sat by Beryl, who was quiet, listening, with bright eyes. Beryl was nice to be with, she made no demands on you, but responded quickly to your mood. While the others were arguing about Mussolini and the League, she said to him suddenly,

"Do you know a girl in your works called Olive Walters? And a man called Tom Sutton?"

"I know Tom. He's a foreman cutter, a very good workman. I believe he's something in his Trade Union, a delegate or something like that. I just know Olive Walters by sight. As a matter of fact, she was pointed out to me this week. She works a machine for putting on buttons. But why did you ask? Do you know them?"

"I know all about them. Rosie—you know Rosie, our little maid?—her boy is called Fred Walters and Olive is his sister. Fred works in a chemist's shop. It's rather a condescension for him to walk out with Rosie, and for Olive to know her because she's in service."

"Good Lord!"

"Yes! But it's very important. That's why people don't want to be maids. Rosie doesn't care much, she's very cheery and sensible. She knows Tom Sutton, you see, because of Olive. Sometimes they all do things together. Tom Sutton's a Communist, I think. Rosie says he's a daft lad, but she's seen worse. She doesn't like Olive very much. She said darkly that she was too much of a lady."

"I didn't know we had these links with the works in private life. Tell me some more about them."

"I don't know very much more. There's a married Walters brother living in one of the new housing estates. They've got one little girl called Doreen, who comes to tea in the kitchen sometimes. Rosie's got a whole large family of her own living in a colliery village near. They're always going out on strike and having weddings and babies and operations and funerals."

"And I suppose Rosie wants days out for them all?"

"Well, yes, she does. But I don't mind, really, as long as it's not too often. I like her, she's such good company, and it doesn't matter, when——" Beryl paused. She had been going to say, when there's only me at home, and I haven't much to do. If ever I have my baby, she thought, it will be different. But she was not going to let herself think about that in the middle of tea. "It must be interesting," she said to Stephen, "being in big works like that with so many different kinds of people. I've been realizing I've led a very shut-up life—shut up, I mean, with our kind of people. I've never heard so much about colliers and poor people, and people like the girl in your works before. It's only since I've had Rosie and she's always talking about them. It makes you think, doesn't it?"

"It does indeed. What have you been thinking?"

Beryl looked round the long room, out of the wide windows at the sunlit garden and the waving trees, back to the cheerful company assembled round the table.

"That I've never done a single thing to earn all the things I've had. I've never done any work, and I've never had to do without anything, or had anything but good times. It isn't fair, altogether—is it, Stephen?"

"No, it isn't. I feel the same."

"You work. It's different for you."

"I don't produce anything, or make anything or do anything worth doing. I just oil wheels that would probably run quite smoothly without me."

"Oh, I don't think they would, or surely Mr. Ward wouldn't have you?"

At the word of sense kindly spoken, Stephen laughed. His mother heard the laugh and looked down the table with approval. Stephen had not been looking very cheerful lately. What was the matter, was he hard up, or not getting on with Joy, or was Mr. Ward worrying him? Anyhow at the moment he seemed happier. She smiled at Beryl. A kind little wife Robert had, easier to live with, perhaps, than Joy. Remembering her duty to Joy's brother, now silent on her right, she asked him how his mother was and said how glad she must have been to see him home again. One found oneself saying things like that to Hilary rather often. Very nice-looking, Alice thought, and very nice manners, but she preferred her own noisier, livelier, more obstreperous brood. Firmly pursuing her duty, she asked him how his father was, and if he was going to Scotland this year.

Robert said to Joy, "When are you bringing Hilary round to see us?" Hilary was a bore, he had decided, but they must help Stephen out with him. They could play bridge after dinner.

"Come back to supper with us to-night?" Beryl looked at Joy.

"We can't, Beryl. Thanks awfully. Nannie is out, I've got to put the rabbits to bed."

"You come, Stephen, and bring Hilary?"

"I can't, thanks, Robert. I'm going to the Wards'."

"Ah well," Robert said cheerfully, "you'll get a much better supper. I don't suppose they put a bit of parsley on the beef and drag it back again."

"Robert, be quiet! Your wife feeds you very much better than you deserve! Poor Stephen, must you go dear? What a bother for you!"

"There's just one thing to be thankful for," Robert observed. "You don't have to wear Ward's suits. I wonder he doesn't insist on it."

Hilary laughed at a joke which he could understand. He had an unexpectedly high and feminine laugh which did not match his voice. The sound irritated Stephen, who had not thought Robert's remark funny, had been flicked by it in some sore and secret place. He got up, "Do you mind if I take the boys down to the stream, Mother? Come on you two, if Grannie says you may get down."

A minute or two later, Lionel Harding saw them pass the window. Jack and Lin raced ahead, shouting and pushing one another, released from the constraint of good behaviour. Stephen followed slowly, lighting his pipe. He lifted his hand and jerked the match away into the flower-bed with a quick movement eloquent of exasperation. That gibe of Robert's, Lionel thought, was a bit near the nerve. He does almost have to wear Ward's livery. He knew that he was behind the times, but it seemed to him a pity that so few of the young men nowadays were running their own businesses or would ever have a chance of running their own. He felt oppressed by the size of the machines into which they were all absorbed. He had seen the gradual destruction of small concerns by large ones, the sporadic death of private enterprise. His own firm, the firm started by his great-grandfather, had been a casualty in that silent war. No doubt there was greater economy and efficiency. No doubt he was, as that red-headed young don from the University had told him the other day, flogging the dead horse of individualism. He had laughed at the crude young man, but not without a certain envy of his power of accepting an unpleasant future world—even perhaps of conforming his manners to it. he thought with a wry smile. A different world was coming. If it were possible to preserve in it the things that mattered, humanity, toleration, liberty, integrity, kindness, perhaps it could only be by rendering oneself free from regrets for the old one, by working out these vital necessities in terms of the new one. But that was for the younger men, for Robert and Stephen. He was rooted in the departing world, too old for the job. He said to Hilary,

"How does England strike you, coming back to it again after five years? Where do you most feel the difference?"

Hilary blinked at the impact of a question that might make him think. He considered, turning his fair head courteously towards his host.

"Well, sir, I don't know that there is much difference. It was one of the first things I thought when I'd been home a day. Thank Heaven it was just the same!"

"At your own home, yes, I dare say. But you've been in London on the way, and been at your club, talked to people. Does it strike you that things have changed at all?"

"I don't think so, sir. I never could stand London at any time. Too noisy for me, and too much of a rush."

"Business is a lot better than it was when you left," Robert informed him. "Unemployment's gone down. Food's gone up. We've climbed up out of the slump."

"Ah," Hilary said wisely, "I suppose that's the National Government."

"It's a relief to have things a bit better again," Alice said briskly. "It was dreadful when you woke up every morning to find that someone else's firm had shut up. It was like an epidemic. You didn't know which of your friends would go down next. And everybody tried to be cheerful, but looked so anxious. And the unemployment was terrible. It was awful to see decent men hanging about deteriorating every day

88

through no fault of their own, and their wives went so short of everything."

Lionel was silent. Yes, it had been a bad time. He himself had been badly hit, in pride, in pocket, and, deeper still, in the severance from his life's work and from the men who had worked with him, in the loss of their livelihood, in the blow to Stephen's prospects. All the same, he thought, in some ways it was a better time than this. We were more aware of things, more aware of one another, as we were in the War. Now I think we're harder, more self-enclosed again. Well, I suppose there's bound to be another slump. He looked at Hilary's fair, clear-cut face, undisturbed and placid behind his pipe, and wondered if there would be changes that even he could see if he came back to England in another ten years.

Stephen really preferred going to the Wards' alone. When Joy went with him, he was always sensitively aware that they were irritating her, and that she was appearing stuck-up and stand-offish to them. Sorry to have to inflict on her company that she disliked so much, he still wished that she could take them more easily.

He was obliged to admit that Grey Gables was a nasty house, a tasteless erection of bad brick tormented with unnecessary turrets, and set in a garden whose successful bedding out made you feel that even flowers could be ugly. As he turned in at the gates between the two thickets of ornamental shrubs, he saw Leslie strolling from the tennis-courts towards the front door. They reached it at the same time. The boy came up to open the door of the car, smiling uneasily. Everything about Leslie was uneasy, his nervous movements, the twitching muscles round his eyes, his wavering, uncertain smile, his shy, hurried speech. He should have been nice-looking. He had good features, a fair skin, and good grey eyes, but what should have been a clear picture was blurred by the inner dislocation. His own discomfort made other people uncomfortable, and put them off him, which was unfortunate for him, since he yearned for sympathy, comfort and friendship. As a little boy he had been his mother's darling, but when he went to school she lost touch with him, and made Marjorie the centre of her life. Marjorie's clothes and doings were more intelligible to her than the needs of an awkward, sulky schoolboy.

"Hulloa!" Leslie said. "Here you are! Glad to see you." His assumption of a grown-up ease of manner emphasized his insecure youth, but he liked Stephen and his smile was genuine.

"Well, how are you? Glad to have finished with school?" Stephen thought to himself: My God, what silly questions one does ask the young!

"Darned glad." Leslie kicked a loose stone on the drive. "It isn't quite time for supper," he said. "Come round here and have a look at the roses."

Surprised that Leslie should know which the roses were, Stephen nodded and sauntered by his side round the corner of the house. Leslie produced his cigarette case, and lit cigarettes for them both with an exaggerated grown-up casualness, but it was in a child's voice of frightened defiance that he blurted out,

"I've asked someone to supper."

"Oh. Who?"

"A clergyman. Mr. Forrester. Mark Forrester. Do you know him?"

"The new curate at St. Jude's, who——" Stephen had been going to say, "who preached the sermon that upset everybody," but stopped. "I've met him once, just to shake hands with, you know. My father knows him."

"He's a wonderful fellow!" Leslie said defiantly.

"Is he? Tell me about him."

"Well, I met him last holidays. It was at an awful civic lunch I had to go to, and he was there and I sat next to him. It was a lunch of a Society in Aid of Something, and we talked. He was awfully easy to talk to. You felt it didn't matter what you said to him. And he had different ideas from anyone I've ever spoken to before. He thought different things mattered. He wasn't just interested in eating and

90

sleeping and making a lot of money and getting on in the world, or in playing games and behaving like other people." Leslie broke off short and said angrily and defensively, "I expect you think I'm an ass, talking like this."

"No, I don't, Leslie. Far from it. Go on."

"Well, I went to his church and heard him preach, and afterwards he was at the bottom of the church talking to people, and I stopped and spoke to him. He asked me to go and see him one evening and I went. We made tea and sandwiches ourselves in his room, and talked." Leslie drew a deep breath. "And I went to his church again and he wrote to me twice in the term and I wrote to him. And as soon as I got back I went to see him, but he was out, and he's been busy all the week, he rang me up to say so, so I asked him to supper, and he's coming to-night after church." There was a sudden drop from excitement to panic, as he added nervously, "I don't suppose Father will like him."

"I shouldn't worry too much about that. You and Marjorie are sure to have a lot of friends coming here now you're both grown-up and at home, one's parents just put up with it." Stephen knew that what applied to his own tolerant and liberal-minded mother and father did not necesssarily apply to the Wards, but there would be some hope for Marjorie and Leslie if they could be persuaded to assume that it did.

"That's part of the trouble. Marjorie's asked a girl to supper to-night, too."

"You're both coming on!"

"Mother and Father are furious about it! You see, this girl's uncle is a shop steward in the works. Oh, of course you'll know him, John Allworthy."

"I've met the niece, she's nice."

"There's been an awful row about it. Mother said she wouldn't have the work people's relations coming to this house as guests. And Marjorie got very angry and said that this girl was as much of a lady as she was." Good for Marjorie, thought Stephen. "And she said anyhow she'd asked her, and she couldn't possibly put her off. So—as a matter of fact I haven't said anything yet about having asked Mr. Forrester

—Mark—I just slipped in and told them to lay an extra place—
and I thought perhaps I'd sort of leave it and it might sort
of seem as though he'd just come in of his own accord."

"But won't that be very awkward for him?"

"Do you think it would? If I thought that, I wouldn't do
it," Leslie said heroically.

"Let's go round to the front now in case he turns up, and
you can just say casually before he comes that you've asked
a friend in to supper."

"Yes, perhaps I ought."

They turned and walked back along the side of the house.
Leslie was so visibly nervous that the hope of his being able
to say anything casually seemed small. Stephen, brought up
in a sociable, free and easy household, where the parents'
authority was lightly used, felt very sorry for him, and rather
sorry for his unwary guest. Ward must know what all the
city knew about the housing sermon and was not likely to
have much sympathy with young iconoclasts.

In the long drawing-room, where everything looked stiffened and unused, Ward stood by the window with his hands
in his pockets, staring out at the garden. His wife sat in her
chair by the fireplace, where a group of hothouse flowers in
pots masked the empty grate. Marjorie lounged ungracefully
on a sofa as though she had flounced there. She had an
illustrated paper open on her knee, but was not reading it.
The air of the room was heavy with feeling. Almost anyone
could have told that it had lately been the scene of a family
row. Ward turned, nodded to Stephen, and turned back again.
Mrs. Ward, who liked him, greeted him much less agreeably
than usual. She was a tall woman with carefully waved
iron-grey hair, a skin which had been clear and pale but was
now a little sallow, and much powdered. She had been a
teacher of music of the kind who painfully acquire an L.R.A.M.,
and proclaim it on a little plate on the door of a neat house
whose windows are screened by ornamental curtains. She had
married Ward when she was thirty-five, unable to believe her
good fortune. In those days he was a partner in his old firm
but had not yet started his own huge business. He had been
about half-way up his climb to prosperity, already dry and

grey in his 'forties. Gwendolen was his second wife. Somewhere in his incredible past there had been a girl whom he had married after a brief courtship, and with whom he had lived for a year in a three-roomed house near the railway goods station, until she and her baby died. None of his present acquaintances had known her, no picture or record of her remained, and Stephen had never heard Ward mention her, but he sometimes wondered what difference it would have made if she had lived, and whether any trace of the dead girl and her dead baby lingered in Ward's heart. The second Mrs. Ward was a devoted wife and mother, an inexpert social climber, and had a passion for clothes and household goods of the conventional and fashionable kind.

Stephen sat down by Marjorie and tried to talk to her, but received sulky, indifferent answers. Joy was right, he reflected, about the young Wards' manners. It was not their fault, perhaps, but they both wanted smacking sometimes. Leslie drifted to a small table near the fireplace, and began to fidget with the things on it, opening and shutting a silver box, playing with the tassel of an elaborate box of matches covered with velvet and gold braid. It certainly seemed an unpropitious moment in which to burst even the smallest bomb on his family. Stephen felt and sympathized with his aphasia. Yet what nonsense it was that so small a thing as an invitation to Sunday supper should be causing such agitation! After all, there would be enough to eat!

The door opened, and a maid announced,

"Miss Welburn."

A girl in a black frock with some kind of white frill at the neck was coming down the long room. Marjorie jerked herself off the sofa, trying to look pleasant, and succeeding about as well as inexperienced people usually do when they have to make the transition too suddenly. Leslie, who had opened the match-box, dropped it on the floor, spraying the hearthrug with coloured matches. Marjorie muttered introductions with a note of defiance. Her parents' greeting could not be said to be cordial, and Leslie's was perfunctory. Between his shyness, his desire to pick up the matches, and his utter

93

inability to make his announcement, he hardly knew what he was doing.

The girl was smiling, a little shy in the strangers' house, but bearing up very well, Stephen thought, against a reception whose chill she must have felt. She looked at Leslie with a face ready to be friendly, remarked: "Shall I help?" and stooped over the hearthrug, the fur of some animal in which Leslie was feverishly rooting. Her brown waved hair, brushed close to her head, finished with a knot on her neck.

"You are an ass, Leslie!" Marjorie said. "Don't bother, Mary! I'll help him."

The front-door bell rang and Stephen, sorry for Leslie, was conscious all the same of a desire to laugh. Leslie, scarlet both from stooping and from embarrassment, dropped the box of matches again and scrambled to his feet, exclaiming in a voice which was meant to be off-hand, but sounded merely desperate,

"Oh, I say. I've asked a fellow to supper."

Stephen saw Mrs. Ward turn and look at her son with surprise just as the door opened, a maid announced "Mr. Forrester," and a plump, pink-faced young clergyman came briskly into the room.

It was a good thing, Stephen thought, that Joy hadn't come. The cocktails and sherry handed round by a parlourmaid always roused her ire. She said that if you wanted to read a paper in the Ward house, you would be expected to ring for a maid to turn over the pages. Certainly it was always difficult for a small group in that large drawing-room to become convivial, even while drinking Ward's excellent sherry. This evening they did not begin to achieve conviviality. Nor were things any better when, in response to the booming of a gong that might have summoned a regiment, they all streamed into the dining-room, and took their seats at the long table. Leslie was still silent from alarm, Marjorie from the remains of temper. Ward was always quiet at home, and the young clergyman appeared to have no small talk, and to feel no obligation to make any. Perhaps he was absorbing his young friend's family and surroundings, possibly disapproving of them, thought Stephen, remembering the sermon. Certainly the place reeked of misapplied wealth, which bore heavily on the spirit because nobody seemed to be enjoying it. They worked through the lavish food with no more appetite than is usual with people at the end of a well-fed Sunday. Only the young clergyman seemed hungry.

Stephen began to ask him if he belonged to the North, if he liked it, if he had known it before he came to St. Jude's. An odd business, this approaching a stranger with questions, trying to pick up the end of a thread here, to give it a little pull and find your way into the warp and woof of another life. Mark Forrester replied that he came from Newcastle and had only been through Aire once before coming there to the parish.

"My people live in your parish," Stephen said. "My father, Lionel Harding, often goes to your church. I expect you know him."

"Oh, yes, he asked me to supper, but I wasn't able to go. He's a friend of the Vicar's."

Something in his tone was faintly dismissing, as though to be a friend of the Vicar's meant a very different thing from being a friend of Mark Forrester.

"You've got a big new housing estate dumped down on you!"

"Yes," the young man replied shortly, "and nothing being done about it, and no hope of doing anything."

"I suppose you really can't cope with it, just the two of you?"

Something seemed to be unlocked in Mark Forrester. "It's not that. We—I—get round it pretty well as far as visits are concerned—at least we shall in time. But they've dumped down twelve hundred living souls in a dead parish! The whole thing's run by a group of people whose ideas are at least a hundred years old. They finance the church and the parish and keep it as their private preserve. They've no more living religion than this chair I'm sitting on. The church smells of dust and decay."

95

"Surely," Mrs. Ward said coldly, "that could be seen to?"
Mark Forrester swept on unheeding.

"They won't allow any change. They don't want to let anyone else in. The church is an exclusive club, a club for old ladies and old gentlemen. They subscribe handsomely to its funds and go there on Sundays in their Sunday clothes and meet their friends and criticize the sermon. I didn't know there was anything left like it in what's called this year of grace! And there are twelve hundred people denied the living word of God simply because the place is such a snob hole that they daren't put their noses inside it!"

In the painful silence which followed an allusion to God at the supper-table, Marjorie half stifled a nervous giggle. The eyes of Mary Welburn danced discreetly and Stephen observed,

"They can't all be quite as bad as that! I don't think you could call my father either dead or a snob."

"I didn't mean anything personal," the young clergyman replied with obvious sincerity. Stephen saw that Leslie was gazing at his friend with admiration. He himself felt that there was force in the young man, and a serious honesty, unimpaired by tact.

"Of course," Mark Forrester went on, "it's the same with everything. Look at this nation! Look at the world! A few dogs in the manger, crammed with ideas a hundred years behind the times, sitting on everything and keeping it to themselves while the majority are shut out, and go short." He brought his fist suddenly down on the table, making the knives and forks rattle. "I can't understand," he cried, "how anyone can sit still and let it go on happening!"

"Don't you think," Mary said in the silence that followed, "that a great many people still don't realize that it is happening?"

"Then it's our business to make them!"

"Yes, of course. I agree. But I think we can't expect to do it all in a minute. I have an uncle and aunt—he is in Mr. Ward's business—who have spent their whole lives trying to make people realize it. I think they would tell you that it's a slow job. Of course now, the pace has got to be faster."

Mark Forrester nodded.

"There isn't time for slow jobs nowadays."

"That's the worst of it. When things have to be done quickly, they're so often done badly."

"But one can't shelter behind that and do nothing at all."

"Like the Parliamentary Labour Party!"

Marjorie, who had not understood, said scornfully, "Oh, well, of course, no decent people belong to the Labour Party!"

But Stephen thought, Good God, these two are like that poet! They've accepted a different world. In the girl and in the curate he was aware of a strange maturity. Their eyes were open to harsh necessities that he dimly perceived. He climbed hastily on to a platform of superiority. They were younger than he was, of course, and in the 'twenties one expected to change the world. They did not know what they were talking about.

Ward spoke suddenly from the head of the table,

"Mr. Forrester, how many of the people in your housing estate want to come to your church, and would know how to behave themselves if they got inside?"

Forrester answered steadily,

"A small proportion at present."

"Isn't it the same with the nation and the world? Those people who want to get on in the world and have the ability to do it, can. Most people don't want it, at least not with any real strength of purpose, and have not the ability to manage things if they got to the top. The average man is lazy and has only an average intelligence. I'm prepared to swear that if there was a man in your housing estate who was deeply religious and who had a strong desire to take part in the life of the parish, he would come to your church and probably in a short time be on your parish council."

The young clergyman, whose mind was obviously direct and vigorous rather than quick, considered a moment. It was Mary who answered.

"But, Mr. Ward, things couldn't be left like that, do you think? It isn't a question of what happens to exceptional people. They're always all right. Isn't it a question always of a fair chance for the average man?"

Ward shook his head.

"Not in a real world. There's no such thing as what you call a fair chance for the average man. He should have what's necessary provided for him, opportunity to earn, food, a house, clothes, leisure and reasonable entertainment. But you can't make him more than he is. Mr. Harding here will tell you that there's nobody in my works goes short of anything he ought to have. But if a man's born to take orders you can't make him a foreman, and if he's not up to the job you can't make him a traveller, and as for my job"—the words were so matter-of-fact that they did not sound like a boast—"there's nobody in the works or the office who could do it at all. Isn't that so, Stephen?"

"Yes," said Stephen, who thought it was. He saw Mary give him a quick glance and took it for scorn. He thought suddenly and furiously. That's what she thinks I am, a yes man, paid to agree with the boss's statements and bolster up his pride.

Forrester leaned forward across the table and said earnestly,

"In the eyes of God, Mr. Ward, you are no more important than the average man."

Ward replied dryly,

"Don't make too sure that the eyes of God are your eyes, Mr. Forrester."

Marjorie, whose idea of social ease and grace was still to thrust herself into any conversation from which she was for the moment excluded, broke in,

"I don't understand what you want, Mr. Forrester?"

He answered her readily enough,

"I want to convert England!"

Marjorie had thought that England was converted. She looked puzzled and said doubtfully,

"To the Church?"

"To a living Christianity. To a people that will seek peace and ensue it and have all things in common."

"In fact," said Leslie in a sudden husky croak, "to Communism."

He would have caused very much less consternation in his own family if he had said, "To Mohammedanism." Marjorie exclaimed, "Oh, Leslie!" and looked at him with

98

round eyes. Leslie was not much disturbed by her, but he felt in every bone the look his father gave him. Mrs. Ward rose up in her place with the expression of a woman who had stood all she could and more. She gave both her younger guests an indignant glance as she said,

"I think we'd better go and have our coffee in the drawing-room."

"I wish you'd go out, Stephen," Mrs. Ward said, "and tell them all to come in. It's getting too dark for them to be wandering round the garden. Tell them we're going to have some tea." As Stephen went obediently through the French windows, he heard her say plaintively to Ward, "I do hope Marjorie and Leslie will soon make some *nice* friends." Ward muttered, "It's a great mistake to try and combine religion with politics. That young man will find it out." "And the girl," his wife said tartly, "giving her opinion about all sorts of things she couldn't possibly understand." There was something about "That man's niece. We can't possibly have it," but Stephen heard no more, as he stepped thankfully from the stiff, brilliant room into the blue dusk of the garden.

He saw a light dress against the trees on the far side of the lawn, but did not hurry, being by no means anxious to spoil what was probably the most satisfactory evening Marjorie and Leslie had ever spent in their own home. Marjorie and Mary Welburn were sitting together on a garden seat. Leslie and Mark Forrester were strolling together along a path by a wall covered with fruit trees. The white muslin covers protecting the gardener's show fruit made ghostly patches in the dusk. Stephen gave his message first to the girls and then to the young men, sorry when he noticed Leslie's guilty start. As the whole group moved towards the house, he found himself dropping behind with the boy, who seized his arm and shook it, stammering in his excitement as he asked,

"Stephen! Don't you think he—Mark—is a wonderful fellow? Don't you think he's one of the most interesting people you've ever known?"

"I should think he's very honest and brave."

"Yes! You see, he doesn't mind what he says to anyone!"

They walked on for a moment in silence. There was a lamentable drop in Leslie's voice when he next spoke.

"Is—is my father annoyed about Mark? About what he said at supper."

"Leslie, I'm afraid you'll find that your father won't always like your friends. You're different from him, you see. You'll be bound to like different sorts of people. If I were you I'd stick to the ones you do like and try not to worry too much. I once brought a friend home for the week-end and my father said he was the most fat-headed ass he'd ever seen."

"Did he? Did he really?" Leslie, in the relief from tension, laughed more heartily than the comment deserved, but he added shrewdly a moment later, "It's different, though. Your father's different, you know, Stephen. Mine doesn't think much of me. You see, I'm not much good at things. And of course he's so able and so capable, it's disappointing for him. And I never can tell him how much I admire him."

"Have a try," Stephen suggested. He could not quite imagine what reception Ward would give to so personal an approach, but most people warmed and thawed to admiration.

They arrived in the drawing-room to find Mary Welburn saying good-bye.

"I have to get back early, my sister is away for the week-end, and I have to help my mother to bed. She can't manage alone."

"Well, we mustn't keep you," Mrs. Ward said. Her manner was that of one addressing an inferior, and perhaps because of it, Stephen exclaimed, "I can run you home. I mustn't be late, because I want to have a pipe with my brother-in-law before he goes to bed."

He fancied that his offer had not pleased the Wards, but he did not much care. They said good-bye to Mary without cordiality, but Marjorie came with them to the door, said boldly, "You must come again," and bumped her cheek against her visitor's in an open, impulsive, school-girlish gesture which the other girl seemed to like, for she responded warmly and said, "You must come and do something with

100

me. If you like we'll go round the paper." She and Stephen climbed into the car.

As the door slammed on them and the car started, Stephen gave an involuntary sigh of relief. The girl at his side laughed, and said,

"You know, it's very odd to me coming back here to live in my own town with my own people to find how much everything is family life. I've been living mostly in a group of people who were on their own, working. Some of them were married, of course, but most of those were fairly young and perhaps had one small child. Even then the parents were often working at separate jobs. They didn't, on the whole, do things because the family did them and think things because the family thought them. But up here it's terrific!"

"It was terrific to-night, certainly!"

"I know. That poor boy! I'm sure he's going to be told not to ask his queer friend again! I rather think Marjorie's being told now not to ask me."

"Are you a queer friend, too?"

"Of course I am! My uncle's in Mr. Ward's works, and a great Labour man, and a person that Mrs. Ward wouldn't know socially!"

"But he and Ward started life together."

"That makes it worse!"

Stephen was silent. Her voice went on at his side, interested, with an undercurrent of amusement as though it were on the edge of laughter.

"And it's the same thing in my own family! I've got a sister engaged and just going to get married. You'd think that where they lived and what they did was mostly their business, but it isn't anything nearly so simple as that. It's involved with what both families think they ought to do, and with what each family thinks about the other family's ideas of what they ought to do. I've often thought since I came back how little my friends in London really knew about ordinary people—though of course they did know things that most ordinary people here don't seem to know."

"What sort of things?"

"Well, the things we were talking about at supper."

"Oh," said Stephen. "Politics!"

"Yes, but you can't say 'politics' in that sort of voice nowadays, can you?"

"What sort of voice did I say it in?"

"As though it was something separate, like keeping bees, or playing chess."

"And you don't think it is something separate?"

"Well, do you, really? It seems to me it's everything—how we live and behave to each other, how we bring up children, what sort of world we want to make it." She added, "Of course, I've heard it going on all round me in my uncle's house since I was small. He's fought all his life for Socialism. Being in his house was always like being with a regiment on active service."

"I was brought up in the opposite camp."

"Yes, of course, you would be."

An obscure ease stole over Stephen, a feeling of being able to speak freely. He said,

"I'm not at all sure that I'm in it now."

"No, I don't expect you are. I don't think any generous or intelligent person will be able to stay in it much longer."

"Of course, my father—nobody could say he's not generous and intelligent. He's a stout Tory.

"That generation decently could be."

"And our generation decently can't?"

"I think not."

They were both silent for a moment. Then in a lighter tone, Mary said,

"If you go over into the other camp, you won't get asked to Sunday supper at the Wards' either."

She had spoken gaily, without thinking, but suddenly she realized the implications of her remarks. She had for the moment forgotten his position with Ward. She saw that much more than Sunday supper might be at stake. She had blundered into something which was perhaps the crux of the whole business for him. Her cheeks grew hot in the darkness at her own stupidity. She felt that he knew of her discomfort. He answered lightly, "Well, you must ask me to Sunday supper with you instead." He was rather surprised at himself after he had said it. It was a long time since he had felt rising in him, as he felt now, a sudden sense of gaiety and freedom. He said more seriously,

"I should like to have a talk with your uncle about things."

"Why don't you? He'd be very glad. Go to see him at home some evening. Then you'd see Aunt Grace, too."

"I've met her once or twice when the firm has had outings and parties."

"She's a wonderful woman. I owe her a lot. She was the first person who made me feel that the world was a big place and living was an adventure. I think I did feel it without knowing what the feeling was. But you know what the first person means to you who gives you vigorous support from outside for the things stirring in you? My own family were poor and unhappy. My father ran away from us when I was ten, and my mother felt that nothing could ever go right with us. When I wanted to try for a prize at school or for a scholarship she always said, 'I'm afraid you'll be disappointed.' But Aunt Grace said 'Try!' Aunt Grace and Uncle John had a difficult time, you know. In the days when they began to be Labour, it was damaging. It could mean losing your job, and they were very poor. They had to keep Aunt Grace's mother and invalid brother for years, and they had one baby boy and lost him. They've had hard times. But Aunt Grace has always kept her bonnet cocked, and always had time to spare to help other people, and always carried about with her the feeling that life was worth living. Those are the people who are worth a lot, aren't they? The people who make more life by giving you that feeling."

"Yes, I suppose they are. I should like to know her."

An easy silence fell upon them, broken only when Stephen said, "Up here? Is this the turn?" And she said, "Yes, second on the right."

"I can't ask you in, I'm afraid," she said at the door. "My mother hasn't been well all day and only got up just before I came out. I ought to get her straight to bed."

He had an impression of her standing on the doorstep of her house, extraordinarily brave, young and sincere, and with a power of facing life which he envied. He said good night and drove off, feeling as though something in him had been liberated by the brief conversation.

There may have been, it is thought, a village at Aire before the Romans came, leaving traces of their occupation in the open fields north of the city. A Saxon cross in the chancel of the parish church bears witness to a Christian settlement, and the Manor of Aire appears in Doomsday as a large and prosperous agricultural estate. It became a borough a year after the signing of the Great Charter, but was not rich enough to meet its responsibilities and declined into a small market town. Its position at the end of a long valley with a great stretch of moorland and hills behind it made it a good market for wool, and a natural centre for cloth making. The town grew slowly and steadily, very much alive but little heard of, until King Charles I gave it its charter, and it sent its first representative to a Parliament soon to be involved in war against its King. In the eighteenth century, Aire was a busy and increasing town, its houses built plainly of the local stone, its more prosperous citizens raising stately mansions for themselves on its outskirts.

The Industrial Revolution swept over it, building, adding, enriching, destroying old land-marks. The town became a city, sprawling across the valley and up the sides of the surrounding hills. It swallowed up the grass with its streets and darkened the sky with its chimneys. It bears to this day the mark of the vigorous and wealthy generation of citizens who were begotten of the Industrial Revolution. They put up its public buildings, some of them ugly, some tolerable, all with a durable solidity and built for permanence. They started its musical and literary societies, laid the foundation-stones of its schools, gave and endowed its public parks, built its churches and chapels, began to raise a fund for its university. Its culture in the nineteen-thirties still bears their stamp, and its streets, in spite of modern shops and new buildings, are signed with their seal. A stranger's first impression of the City of Aire is of grime and solidity, of a brisk and lively air from the hills not altogether dulled by smoke, of a city built to last in the days when men sometimes built without taste but never without confidence.

The city which they left fell roughly into three divisions. South of a double dividing line made by river and railway were the works and warehouses and the working-class districts of Albeck and South Albeck, Worbeck and South Worbeck and Onslet. North of the river a belt of the principal shops and offices and public municipal buildings. North again of these were the more prosperous residential districts, terraces and streets of solid houses merging into the fringe of the city, already half country, where big stone houses stood alone in beautiful and carefully tended gardens.

The centre of the city was not much changed, but the slow and unconscious revolution of the twentieth century had caused any number of permutations in the outlying circle. There were bare, empty spaces in South Worbeck and South Albeck where condemned houses had been pulled down. New housing estates were springing up in districts that had never expected to see with their own eyes how working people lived. Half the big houses were empty, some were now Corporation property, institutions, or blocks of flats. A little further out in the country the sons and daughters of the men who owned them had built for themselves new villas of more manageable size. Gradually, contrasts were being reduced, barriers between one section of society and another were falling. The new-comer whose first impression of Aire was of permanence and solidity, would, if he stayed long enough, discover a city and a society in a state of flux, preoccupied with any number of small adjustments, but unaware, for the most part, of the general principle in obedience to which it flowed.

The offices of the *Yorkshire Guardian* were in the middle of the city, a block wedged between a café and a photographer's. They were small for their purpose. The paper's prestige was out of all proportion to its circulation and a good deal of its office equipment was old-fashioned. There hung about the awkward corridors, narrow stairs and small, untidy rooms the atmosphere of a family business. There was no chromium or vitaglass, none of the uniformity of Alfred Ward's. In the reporters' room, at the long tables, were two or three solid office chairs, a couple of wooden kitchen chairs, and a beautiful Chippendale armchair, in whose worn and faded seat the faint colours of the old tapestry, maroon, greyish green and soft blues, still showed. On the walls hung portraits of the earlier directors and previous editors of the paper. It had recently celebrated its centenary, and a framed copy of the *Yorkshire Guardian* of 1833 hung over the fireplace in the upstairs room. About the whole place was an air of tradition, of a certain dignity and integrity, independent of great wealth or of waves of popular feeling.

To Mary, accustomed to the impersonal bustle of a big London newspaper office, there was a curious charm about the *Guardian's* more personal flavour. The *Daily Tribune* had been written for the public. The *Yorkshire Guardian* was written for the Yorkshire public, and for a definite section of them. First of all, its detractors said, for country gentlemen in large houses and rectors in country villages. Secondly, for the industrial squiredom in the towns, for the educated business and professional men, the doctors, architects, heads of firms, the Hardings and Marsdens and their friends. The paper had a solid country and county flavour, followed Mr. Baldwin in the letter and spirit of its politics, and gave all possible prominence to local news. One of the first things impressed upon Mary was that a piece of news mattered to the paper because it was connected with Yorkshire, a politician, scientist or novelist born in Yorkshire or speaking about Yorkshire was given a little more space than an equally important politician, scientist or novelist from another part of England speaking about anything else. World affairs were not allowed to obliterate local interest. There must be a full report of the speech made at Sheffield or Bradford or Leeds by the Prime Minister or Winston Churchill, but there must also be a paragraph reporting the remarks of the local member who proposed a vote of thanks. Mussolini and Hitler, however outrageous their doings, must not be allowed to crowd out the Agricultural show at Otley or the account of the performance by the Bradford Civic Players or the Halifax Thespians. When Hitler, Mussolini or Soviet Russia were in its eyes particularly outrageous, the *Guardian* was grieved, firm and indignant, always implied as a last reproach that what they were doing was not done, but never allowed itself to be agitated. Behind the measured phrases of its leaders, the sober summary of its photographers one caught a half smile and a resigned "These Foreigners!" A trifle old-fashioned, stodgy and some said snobbish, the paper was never cheap and refused to panic. English, provincial, middle-class in every line of printer's ink, it confronted a shattering world with a steady but incurious faith in an unexamined liberty and democracy, an instinctive belief in human decency and a healthy interest in local affairs.

"In fact," young Guy Runnacre raged to Mary, "it simply doesn't know there's anything happening in the world! It'll have nice soothing leaders about the good feeling and moderation of the English people up to the morning of the revolution, and it will go on yammering about liberty and democracy under the Fascist government afterwards. That is if it isn't still saying that war is an out-of-date way of settling things till a bomb bursts in the office."

He sat on the edge of the upstairs table, swinging his long legs, and scribbling on a pad on his knee, a chewed end of pencil between his brown-stained fingers. He was an impatient, elegant, nervous youngster, a year down from Oxford. He liked Mary, but thought her old-fashioned in her outlook.

"You know," Mary said, "it's all true. Liberty and democracy are the things that matter. The English people are full of moderation and patience. And there is a widespread feeling that war is an out-of-date way of settling things."

"Unfortunately," the young man returned, "it isn't spread quite wide enough! The trouble with you, Mary, is that you've got a bourgeois mentality. You don't share this paper's views—I don't want to say there's absolutely *no* hope for you—but you share its feelings. You do put your faith in all this moderation and good feeling of the English people. Let me tell you there isn't going to be much use for moderation and good feeling in the next ten years, and if there is, there oughtn't to be. And no amount of moderation or good feeling is going to be any kind of use as a gas mask."

Mary finished transcribing a paragraph of her shorthand, flipped over a page, and observed,

"The funny thing is, Guy, that I think you're enjoying yourself. You're just a little bit like Tommy Traddles drawing skeletons."

"Tommy?"

"Traddles. David Copperfield. Dickens. Haven't you read it?"

"Don't think so."

"Well, you should. It would be a change for you."

Guy Runnacre snapped the elastic over his notebook, slipped it into his pocket, and lit a cigarette. He said,

"You're wrong if you think I enjoy myself raising horrors. I think I keep on raising them because I've a kind of feeling that if I do, they won't give me such a shock when they come. But I know they will, all the same. Or else it's like when you're going to the dentist and you can't keep your mind off thinking how he'll hurt you."

Mary looked up at the young man and saw the muscles twitching under his smooth brown cheek, and the restless movements of his hands. She thought, Poor boy, he oughtn't to be like this, and had a spontaneous and momentary desire to pull his dark head down on to her knee and stroke his hair.

Hudson, one of the senior reporters, came into the room. He was an older man of the solid, sturdy Yorkshire type, educated at a local Grammar School, and trained by a long apprenticeship on various small papers. He had a house in the suburbs, a comfortable wife, two children at school, and a garden on which he lavished his spare time and affection. He said "Good evening" to Mary, nodded to Runnacre, and sat down in the chippendale chair, squaring his elbows firmly to the table. He remarked,

"I see the Reverend Forrester's been going off the deep end again."

"Oh, has he? I met him out at supper last Sunday night. What's he been doing?"

"Speaking at a Peace Meeting. Said the sort of thing people do say at peace meetings, that we ought to go to war with Italy at once on behalf of Abyssinia, and that it was our peculiar obligation because it was our fault. We had set Mussolini the bad example by annexing half the globe, and ought to pay for it in blood and tears. Suggested a national penance week and an ultimatum to Italy."

"The last half," Runnacre observed, "is a good idea."

Hudson, who had been special correspondent for two years in France and Gallipoli, replied soberly,

"There aren't many things worth a war."

"The trouble with people of your generation," Runnacre responded, "is that you still see things separately. You think that a war in Abyssinia and a strike in Glasgow are two entirely unconnected things. You don't see there's one great crack stretching across the world and jerking everybody on to one side or the other."

"If by one side or the other, you mean Fascists or Bolsheviks," Hudson retorted sturdily, "I'm not going to be jerked on to one side or the other. I've no use for either of them. Besides, they aren't one side or the other. They're the same dogs with different collars. If there is this crack you talk about, and I don't know that there is, it's between the sane people and the insane."

Guy Runnacre stubbed the end of his cigarette viciously on the ashtray.

"You just don't know what you're talking about! Your crack's a fancy one, mine's real. It's economic. Talking about Communists and Fascists being the same thing is just like sticking an old-fashioned poultice on a broken leg and saying it's set. There's all the difference in the world between people trying out a new economic system and people hanging on like grim death to an old one."

"So far as I can see, there's very little difference in behaviour."

"Oh!" Runnacre shrugged. "Behaviour!"

At the deep, dismissing contempt of his tone, Mary and Hudson both laughed.

"Rather important, don't you think?" Mary suggested.

"Just now I think hardly at all, any more than manners when you're running away from an earthquake." He slid off the table, straightened his long easy length and remarked with finality as he strolled to the door,

"Judging ideologies nowadays from the point of view of behaviour is expecting to measure the world by the standards of the lower middle class."

As the door slammed behind him, Hudson said unresentfully, "And I hope it keeps fine for him! Had any supper, Miss Welburn?"

"No. I've finished when I've turned this in. I thought I'd go home—at least to my uncle's. What will happen about Mark Forrester? Will he have to go?"

"I've no doubt his vicar would like him to, but it's not so easy to get rid of a curate in the Church of England."

Hudson, who had sung in the parish church choir as a boy, was a pillar of his own Church and well up in ecclesiastical detail. "No, unless he leaves of his own accord, I expect he'll just go on here thinking he's John the Baptist until he learns sense." He added, "I'm not in favour of ultimatums to Italy dictated by the Reverend Forrester, but I sometimes think a national penance week wouldn't do the young men of this country any harm. With all the men who should have been in their forties now wiped out, they're like little boys that haven't had bigger boys to smack their heads. They've been pampered in their teens with Youth Movements and rubbish about the views of youth till they think any idea of theirs is good enough to settle the universe. Well, I suppose they'll learn in time—and they do get to hear of things nowadays! It's wonderful what my two hear of at school with the wireless and everything!" He added with a cheerful pride that belied his strictures on youth, "My boy and girl will soon be able to teach their father."

Two other reporters whom Mary hardly knew came in, from a race-meeting, and began to discuss horses and probable tips with Hudson. Mary finished off her report, handed it in, and left the office.

As her tram swung up the steep hill out of the Jewish quarter, she reflected rather sadly about Guy Runnacre and Hudson. The terribly clear-sighted, unstable young, the sturdy, balanced middle-aged with their eyes closed. Each in his way so sure of his own world and unable to see the other's. Yet at present, and because of that very assurance, able to meet on friendly terms. Here in England the crack had not widened enough to jerk everybody on to one side or the other. There were rumblings below the surface, but the upper soil still held, and men like Hudson walked on it contentedly, hating all extremes, wishing no one any ill, calmly pursuing their private lives. If and when the soil cracked under their feet, which way would they go? Would they throw their solid decency and kindness and sense of fair play on one side or the other, or would they tumble into the crack, leaving the world to those who preferred ideologies to behaviour? Or would the crack never quite come here with the same violence? It would depend perhaps how quickly they saw and which way they moved, these men like Hudson and Stephen Harding.

Mary began to think about Stephen Harding. What sort of a life did he have at Ward's, devilling for that grim buttoned-up old man whose children were so much afraid of him? He was beginning to be aware of the rumblings. An uncomfortable state of mind, probably, for one brought up in the Harding family. Probably being brought up in the best of the old tradition made it harder to accept the new. Easier for Marjorie and Leslie to revolt against Grey Gables and Ward's great factory and Ward himself than for Stephen to turn against the liberal, gracious tradition of his home, and against a united and friendly family! But of course it was all much less difficult nowadays for anybody of twenty than for anybody of thirty-five, nurtured in the old world and unfit for the new. Besides, Stephen was married. The image of Joy's white neck and golden head floated across Mary's mind, bringing with it a faint irritation and sense of loss of which she was hardly aware. She got off the tram a little disheartened, feeling tired, and thinking that it was a difficult world.

Grace Allworthy came to the door of the house to meet her, hugged her warmly and exclaimed, "That's right, Mary! I'm ever so glad you've come! We've got quite a party. Would you like to leave your hat upstairs? Well, go straight in then. We've got Doris here and her Frank. And Tom Sutton's just come in and brought his girl, and her brother's here and his girl, Rosie Jenkins, her name is. She seems a nice lass. You go on in and talk to them. I had some sandwiches ready but I'm just going to cut a few more and make some coffee. We'll have a real jolly evening!"

Mary returned her hug.

"Oh, Aunt Grace! It's always nice to see you! I don't see enough of you!"

"Well, you're so busy and you've a lot to do at home with Doris's wedding and all. But you know you're always welcome here, Mary."

The warmth that had never failed her in that house stole round Mary's heart.

"Let me come and help you with the sandwiches."

"No, love. You know I like messing about on my own. You can come and help me carry them in if you will. I'll call you. But go in and see them all first."

Mary went in, kissed her Uncle John and was introduced to those of the company whom she did not know. Tom Sutton's girl, a pretty little thing in a thin two piece suit and small hat with an eye veil, said, "How do you do?" in a languid voice, and gave Mary a limp shake of a daintily manicured hand. A lanky youth with the same grey eyes, apparently her brother, shook hands and muttered, "Pleased to meet you." His Rosie was a broad-faced, healthy-looking child whose cheeks matched her name. She greeted Mary with a good imitation of Beryl Harding's manner to her guests, but her green eyes danced, looking hopefully at a new comer for friendliness or fun. Mary slipped into a chair by Frank, and the whole party sat sown again.

Aunt Grace had been unduly optimistic, Mary thought, in prophesying a jolly evening. Uncle John, in his chair by the fireplace, puffed serenely at his pipe and smiled hospitably on his guests. Rosie Jenkins, in spite of her company manners, was quite obviously ready to be jolly if anyone would be jolly with her, but the expressions of the rest of the company were unpromising. Fred looked shy. Tom, humped on a chair near the door, looked as black as thunder. He had promised to come here this evening and Olive had not wanted to. When he insisted, since they had refused half a dozen invitations, she had, out of pure perversity, he thought, tacked her brother Fred and his girl, Rosie, on to the party. This was the more annoying because, as a rule, when he suggested going out with them, she refused on the ground that Rosie was common. She preferred the company of her married brother, Herbert, and his wife Mabel, who had gone up in the world, and had a cocktail set with little cocks on the glasses, and two bedroom suites with enamel trimmings. She was a snob, a little bourgeois snob, thought Tom, watching the sulky movements of her pretty head and aching to take her out of this room full of tiresome people and hold her in his arms, out in the dark under the stars at any street corner the way she said only low-class people did.

Frank was smoking a cigarette placidly and looked slightly bored, but not unamiable. He was a bronzed, blue-eyed, fair-haired young man, with a compact and limber body whose movements were a pleasure to the eye. Mary liked him much better than she had expected, perhaps because he unmistakably liked her. His world, like hers, was wider than the world of either of their families. They both had ambitions, knew something of the business of carving a career out of life, had encountered disappointments, and appreciated the incidental experiences and pleasures. Mary saw that Frank was honestly in love with Doris, and put up with the rather uncongenial company of her relations for her sake. That he did not intend to put up with them too much was also clear, but she did not really see why he should. He was sensible, probably selfish but not disagreeable. He set a good value on himself but not a fantastic one, and if he appreciated his successes, he was good-tempered about his failures. Altogether he seemed likely to be a very successful husband for Doris, and quite a nice brother-in-law.

Doris, Mary saw, was looking miserable and much less

pretty than usual. Her fair good looks varied with her spirits, and at present her face was harassed, her mouth turned down at the corners, and her body was stiff with some constraint. She was suffering acutely the self-consciousness of someone obliged to mix two worlds. She felt and exaggerated Frank's boredom. She dreaded any political conversation between her uncle and Tom Sutton. She thought that Fred, Rosie and Olive were most unsuitable people for Frank to meet, people whom he could not possibly like, but at the same time she thought that Frank had glanced approvingly one or twice at Olive, and wished that she herself had put on her two-piece suit, and not come round in her office frock. She was as glad to see Mary as a child at a party to see its mother. She pulled her into the chair near Frank, and thought with relief that she would be able to talk to him.

"Come from the paper?" Frank asked. He respected newspapers, and thought Mary's job interesting and rather creditable. It smacked of that wider world into which he was vigorously pushing his way. Newspapers reported his achievements, and took photographs of him and occasionally asked him what he thought about physical training or slimming diets, or Why Young Men Do Not Go to Church. For one paper he had even written an article.

Mary began to talk about a garden fête which she had been reporting that afternoon. There had been some pompous speeches and something almost like a quarrel between two organizers on the platform. Doris and Frank listened and laughed, John Allworthy smoked peacefully, Fred smiled nervously and politely, Tom continued to glower, Olive listened eagerly to the account of a party in high life. Rosie, sitting upright on the edge of her chair, thought despairingly, aren't we *ever* going to have any fun? Wouldn't they put on some variety on the wireless or make some real jokes and everybody shriek with laughter, and all start shouting and laughing and rolling about on the cushions and getting hot? Why, you might as well be in Church or at one of Her parties.

Why we 'ad to come here I don't know, thought Rosie, instead of going to the pictures and having a right good time.

It's that Olive! Reckon she can't care much for Tom any road, or she'd want to be off alone with him same as I do with Fred. And Fred's such a great soft lad, 'e's too gormless to tell her to go to Pudsey! I'll play Hamlet with 'im if he lets her spoil my evening out next week!

John Allworthy, knocking out his pipe against the side of the fireplace, said,

"Well, Tom? Found a house yet?"

"No," Tom replied shortly.

"We've looked at a lot," Olive put in with nervous haste, "but we can't find one we seem to fancy like."

"Can't find one you seem to fancy," Tom amended.

"Well, it's the woman that has to live in it," John reminded him. "It's right she should choose. What do you say, Miss Jenkins?"

Rosie, feeling unequal to comment among strangers, grinned at him broadly and wondered if they were going to have a cup of tea. It seemed at the moment about the only hope in ·life. She saw that the lady who had come in, the one who called the old man Uncle John, was smiling at her, and smiled back. Then she looked at Tom Sutton and felt sorry for him. That Olive wasn't in no hurry to find a house and give up going out to work and spending her money on her own back. Rosie would be surprised if she put by every week. She was the sort that expected the boy to do it all.

"It's a job finding what you want," Frank said amiably to Tom.

"Most people can't get it anyhow," Tom replied, not at all amiably.

Frank, who could not help knowing of a good many young men who would be quite pleased if he spoke to them, resolved not to bother himself any more about that sulky fellow in the corner. Doris began to talk nervously and hurriedly about houses and furnishing. Mary, who was tired, tilted her head back against the chair and clasped her knees.

What talk she had listened to in this room! How often as a little girl she had sat on a hassock between her aunt and the fireplace, half asleep in that warm corner, half listening to her elders. Sometimes it had been friends who dropped in. Sometimes it had been a speaker resting before a meeting or having a cup of tea and one of Aunt Grace's cheese-cakes afterwards. Sooner or later the talk had always been about the same thing—the Movement. As she grew into her teens, Mary had a picture of the Movement in her mind. She saw it as an advancing mass of people, walking steadily forward into a forest, cutting down a tree here, making a road there, clearing a swamp, digging a well, blazing a trail for others to follow. This image was so deeply embedded in her young mind that it was at first very strange to her to go to school and to Oxford and meet so many people who had never heard of that marching army with its strategy, its victories and defeats, except vaguely as "Socialists" or "people that vote Labour." In this very town where she now lived were men and women who had grown up beside her, people like Stephen Harding who had been grown up when she was at school, to whom that advancing army was only a vague menace, an enemy not dangerous enough to hate. And now? If the issues were forced and the enemy became visible and dangerous, would they hate? Would that alien plant of hatred take root at last in English soil? Surely a man like Stephen Harding would not hate if he understood. His eyes and his smile were kind.

In the meantime, this was a very sticky party. Mary opened her eyes and said desperately, "Isn't there anything on the wireless, Uncle John?" Rosie looked hopeful for a minute, but her hopes were speedily dashed as the second movement of a Tchaikowski symphony flooded the room, making a cover under which they all relaxed a little, feeling less acutely the strain of that obligation to present social faces to one another which they were so incompetently fulfilling.

Mary stepped out of the room and into the kitchen. There was a good smell of coffee, and the sandwiches and cakes were ready on a tray. Aunt Grace, adventurous even in food, made sandwiches of cream cheese and anchovies and chopped nuts while her friends would have bought pots of paste, or, for occasions, slices of ham and tongue. She was buttering the last of them, the sleeves of her spotted red blouse rolled up to her elbows, her dark hair, hardly yet grey except on the temples, straying over her forehead. She had cut it short in the shingling fashion and refused to grow it, being charmed with the unencumbered feeling. On the table beside the plates, a sleek, striped, six-inch tiger of a tom kitten sat erect on his haunches, ardent eyes on the food. He put out a paw, disproportionately large for his slender body, and made a dab at Aunt Grace's hand. She picked up the last of anchovies between her fingers, and held it to the greedy little pink tongue. The kitten, turning his head sideways with an exquisite movement, pulled the anchovy out of her fingers, and settled down on all four paws to eat it.

"Specially lovely they are when they're being greedy," Mary stroked the tiger coat. "Not a bit like us! Have you found him a home yet?"

"Not yet. Mrs. Hodgson would have had him, but she want's to have him doctored, so I won't let him go there. He's such a proper little tom, it seems a shame."

Mary smiled. It was so like Aunt Grace, who could not bear to thwart life or cramp anyone's style, though it often made the placing of her tom kittens a problem.

"I've just done. Are they enjoying themselves in there?"

"No, I don't think they are much. They're all shy and rather quiet."

"And my old man smoking away like a chimney, I suppose, and thinking everybody else is as happy as he is."

Mary picked up a sandwich and bit it.

"I oughtn't to, but I'm hungry. I didn't have supper."

"Cut yourself a good slice of bread and butter, love. There's nothing in these little things. See, there's plenty of cream cheese left. I'll spread some for you."

"What's the matter with Tom Sutton, Aunt Grace? He used to be such a bright, eager, friendly boy. I can hardly get a smile out of him."

"I don't know what's come to him. He's not been nigh us for months. That girl's no good to him."

"She's pretty, isn't she, but she looks a bit bloodless. I'd rather have the other one, Rosie Jenkins, is it? She looks a good, stout, cheerful child. If she could once get over her company manners, I think she might enliven the party."

Aunt Grace picked up the tray.

"Tom's got with a lot of Communists and such like that have done him no good. Your uncle's very much distressed with the way he behaves sometimes at the Branch Meetings, finding fault with people that have given their lives to working for the Union and that were in the Movement before he was born."

"You know, Aunt Grace, the young ones do feel that things are moving a bit too slowly."

"The young ones always do. I've been to Russia, Mary, as you know, and there's no one admires a lot of what's been done there more than I do. But this country's different and that's what these young ones don't see. England's pace is a slow pace. You can't rush the British people. I took a long time to learn that myself and it was your Uncle John taught me. Many's the time I've walked up and down this kitchen wringing my hands and biting my lip till it bled because I thought we should never get people to see and never get anything done! But your uncle was always patient, always said 'slow and steady does it' and we've seen a lot done in our life time." She added, "But I mustn't get talking now. I've always been fond of Tom, and it grieves me when he vexes your uncle. But he'll learn sense. Bring the coffee, will you, Mary."

The company thawed a little over coffee and sandwiches, helped by Aunt Grace's genial presence. Doris seemed to feel safer with her aunt in the room. Mary thought that Frank did not altogether like being rallied quite so heartily about his house and wedding, but Olive was apparently ready to be interested in any house and wedding except her own, and Rosie and Fred, losing shyness, became companionable. Mary sat down by Tom and said, "It's years since I've seen you, Tom. Do you remember that evening when they were all talking here, and Aunt Grace gave you and me a shilling each to go to the Feast on Whiteroad Moor? And we meant to buy her a present, but we spent all our money and only had a gingerbread pig left at the end, and we said we'd keep that for her; but do you remember, we got so hungry, we broke it in two and ate half of it on the way home, and gave her half a pig?"

Tom laughed, the sulky mask of his face breaking up into sudden charm.

"Aye, I remember that well. We saw the boy selling rabbits, and I'd have bought one only I hadn't enough money. I should have had a job to get it home!"

Olive heard his laugh and glanced across at them, faintly resentful. Do her good, Mary thought, smiling inwardly. She began to tell Tom about her work and exchange ideas with him. The conversation prospered. He was intelligent and eager, he read a good deal and talked vividly about books with a shrewdness drawn from life. This was the grown up Tom Mary would have hoped to find. They were both absorbed when Olive's voice said sharply,

"Tom! Did you hear Miss Welburn's sister was asking about the firm's outing?"

Doris, whose question had been put to Olive, smiled across at Mary meaning, I didn't want to interrupt you. Mary smiled back at her, thinking, No, certainly not the right girl for Tom! What a pity! Only I suppose that's what peoples' friends always think about their girls. But she is rather a little bitch, or would be if there was enough to her. She caught a fragment of conversation from near the fireplace. Uncle John's getting on to old times. Doris won't like that, Frank will be bored and she'll worry. If she could only feel secure, just know that he does get bored with her family sometimes, but it doesn't matter because he loves her!

Doris had no grasp of that security. Uncle John was going to talk and talk about the time when he was young, when he was desperately poor and making all sorts of strikes and trouble. It would be so much better to forget all that! A man like Frank, who was getting on in the world and went everywhere and stayed in the very best hotels and knew all sorts of people, well, naturally he didn't want to hear about his fiancée's uncle being knocked down by a policeman, or about how he and Aunt Grace both went to work for years after they were married because they had to help their families. Aunt Grace and Uncle John had been wonderful, but it was a sort of wonderful that didn't belong to Frank's world. To be easy in mixed worlds requires an inner poise and harmony which Doris painfully lacked. As Uncle John's voice dominated the other voices in the room and he became a speaker with an audience, she shrank and suffered, feeling as though she, or rather Frank, were naked under a cold shower-bath.

Frank did not suffer nearly as much as she suffered for him. He had been playing cricket all day, he was sleepy with fresh air and full of bodily well-being. Old Allworthy was a bore and a crank, but then old men did run on about what they had done when they were young. His own father was always drawing up from the well of his past tales of antediluvian cricket matches with which to regale Frank and his friend. Frank smoked and thought about the bowling he would have to face at Sheffield on Saturday. He knew his own weak spot. He did not like the first ball from a slow bowler after an over of fast bowling. He was born to play fast bowling. He had trained himself to play slow. His danger point was in that first minute of adjustment from the born to the trained bat. But if this weather held they would not put Carter on first, they would begin with Armstrong and Medway and with luck he would be settled before he had to deal with that slow, accurate, dangerous ball, curling in past his toes. Frank's own world, a green field with white figures performing on it the exquisite minutiae of their art, enclosed him comfortably and shut off that world of struggle and hardship and faith which John Allworthy was unrolling like a film in the room. Mary and her Aunt Grace knew the film, Olive and Fred were puzzled and bored by it. Rosie listened with a degree of interest. What it was all about she did not know, but ardour and adventure touched her young vitality to an uncomprehending sympathy and she said to herself that old Mr. Allworthy had seen some goings on!

But it was not to any of them John Allworthy spoke. He was looking at the corner of the room where Tom Sutton sat clasping his knees, and staring at the floor. Outside dusk was falling. The light in the room was growing dim, but

120

nobody troubled to move. Tom's face was a pale blur in the shadows, except once when he lit a cigarette, and in that brief illumination his cheek-bones, his deep-set eyes and the broad forehead below the crisp hair stood out with more than natural clearness like a painting of a face accentuating its qualities.

"You'll mind my telling you, Tom, what a night that was! There hadn't been a gas lamp lit in the city for four days, not since the beginning of the strike. We knew they were bringing out the soldiers against us, and we didn't know which way the ordinary folk might turn. We, the six of us that had done it all, sat in the little room above a warehouse where we always met, and waited for the dark. We knew they'd got their gang of blacklegs ready in the Town Hall to take them along to the Gas Works as soon as it was dark and we knew we'd got to stop them, or let them break the strike and break us and put the clock back fifty years. I mind once we sat there with it getting darker and darker, and because of what we'd done ourselves we couldn't light the gas, and Larry McGee that was a great red-headed Irishman was whistling all the time between his teeth. It made me feel that I could kill him. I wanted to tell him to stop, but I thought, if we have words among ourselves to-night over anything big or small, we're done for. It was our only hope, sticking together like brothers."

He broke off and added in a different tone, "It's our only hope now, eh, Tom?"

Tom did not answer. For a second the film was broken in two, the present returned to the room. Fred coughed, Rosie settled herself more squarely on her chair and sighed. Doris tried to see Frank's face in the dusk. In the theatre of Frank's mind the bowler behind the opposite wicket was arrested with his hand in the air. Frank shifted his shoulders, thought, Lord, I was nearly asleep! Grace Allworthy, rocking herself gently in her chair, looked towards Tom and thought, Drat the lad, what's come to him? He might give my old man a kind word.

"As soon as it was dark, we went down to the old bridge where we meant to hold them up. A lad came running up to us as we took our places and said the soldiers were coming. They didn't come, not till later on, but we all thought we could hear them. I heard horse's hooves a dozen times while we were waiting, and I know I wasn't the only one. I could feel the sweat running down me inside my shirt, and yet I was cold right through me though it was a warm night.

"When you plan a thing beforehand, you think everything will happen one after another like a play at a theatre, one thing waiting to begin till the other's finished. But it isn't like that when things really happen; everything comes at once, all of a muddle and you're in the middle of it before you know it's started. I don't rightly know what we heard first, whether it was the blackleg workmen coming with the police marching in front and beside them, or the people shouting. I heard afterwards they'd been held up almost before they got to the bridge. There was half the working folk of the town out to help us, and not only the men. I know later on, when I was lying on the ground after the policeman had knocked me out, I saw a woman chasing one of the blacklegs along the pavement with a rolling-pin. I don't ever want to see men and women fighting again in the streets of this city, but what we did that night was worth it! Eh, Tom? They fetched the soldiers in the end, but they never risked the blacklegs in the Gas Works. There was too much feeling, and they'd brought in all sorts of men in a hurry that didn't know the work, and people took fright and were afraid the town would be blown up. They came to terms with the strikers and gave them their shorter hours, and Larry and George Booth started the first union for municipal workers in this country." He ended with an old man's regretful sigh, "Ah, those were great days."

Tom Sutton, speaking for the first time, said, "It seems they're over in the Labour Movement."

The creak of the rocking chair stopped. Grace moved quickly to the door, the switched clicked, and in the sudden harsh flood of light, the faces in the room blinked and looked bewildered.

"When you've been in the Movement as long as we have," she said to Tom, "you'll know there's different ways of doing things at different times, and everybody isn't wrong that isn't doing them just the way you fancy! But this is a dull evening for you young folk! John, see if you can't get some dance music on the wireless, or something lively! Give me that coffee pot and I'll go and make some more coffee."

When the others had left, Mary called after Doris and Frank, "Go on, I'll catch you up," and hung back for a moment in the passage, her arms round her Aunt's neck.

"I haven't really talked to you and Uncle John! I'll come next time by myself when you aren't having all these tiresome people!"

"Come when you like, love. Your uncle gets talking politics and forgets it's dull for the young ones, but I know you don't mind."

"Of course I don't." Mary looked at the two standing together, the old man smiling apologetically, but undisturbed, his wife's reproachful tone barely masking affection and pride. Loving one another soundly, they had always had love to spare for her and for their friends. She was turning away, and then remembered.

"Oh, Uncle John, I met someone who wants you to talk to him about politics—Stephen Harding, in Ward's. He's interested and feeling his way. I thought you'd let him come here some evening?"

"He can come whenever he likes. He's a nice lad, but I didn't know he ever thought about anything of that sort. His father and I have been old friends and old enemies for many a year, ever since we were first on the Council together. Let me see, that would be . . ."

"Let Mary go now, dear," his wife cut in. "The others will be waiting for her."

"The Hardings were always a Liberal-minded family." Uncle John's mind was still focused on the past. "It was Mr. Lionel Harding's father, after that strike I was telling you about, who spoke up on the Council for the men, and said the hours were too long and the strike was justified. That brought the others round more than anything. They're a good family, they've done well by the town."

"There's Frank's horn, he's getting impatient. Good-bye, my darlings."

Mary flew out to the car, and climbed in, apologizing, for Frank had really borne a good deal that evening from his relations-in-law-elect. Settling down in the back seat behind the shoulders of the lovers, she felt happy, cheered and warmed as always by seeing Aunt Grace, and with an obscure satisfaction in Uncle John's remark that the Hardings had always been a Liberal-minded family. It seemed to matter so much just now what everybody thought about things.

Rosie, having finished her breakfast and put down a saucer of milk for the cat, suddenly saw what a great improvement it would be to her kitchen if she put a clean paper on the shelf under the pans. From some pocket in her mind emerged a vision of a shelf covered with clean paper whose edges were not plain, but cut in a tasteful pattern like battlements. Rosie was an artist under the compulsion of an idea. She pushed her breakfast things to one side of the table, and hauled the pans off the shelf, tumbling them on to the hearth-rug. The dingy paper under them was fastened by drawing-pins, but she could not be bothered to take them out. She tore the paper off in strips, leaving a fringe round the head of each pin. Snatching a roll of shelf paper from a drawer, she measured it roughly against the shelf, grabbed the scissors from her work basket, and began to cut the battlemented edge.

Beryl came in and saw her balanced with one knee on a chair in a welter of pans, torn paper and dirty crockery. One end of the clean shelf paper was in the cat's saucer of milk. The cat was springing and pouncing joyfully among the torn scraps. Beryl picked up the saucer and said mildly,

"What are you doing, Rosie?"

"I'm going to have me shelf nice under the pans!"

"Wouldn't it have been better to wash up the breakfast things and get the kitchen tidy first?"

Rosie could not explain that the vision of the shelf with

124

its decoration of clean, cut paper had seized her mind with so much urgency that she could not consider doing anything else first. She said, "I shan't be a minute!" and impetuously snipped off a battlement.

Beryl looked round. She herself had cooked their supper and washed up after it the night before, and had left the little kitchen spotlessly tidy. Since then Rosie had only made three cups of early morning tea and cooked breakfast for three people, but the kitchen looked as though it had been the scene of a dog fight or of a revolution. How, Beryl wondered, had the large calendar, a gift from their chemist, got under the table, and why were the mixing bowl for cakes and a vegetable tureen on the stove when breakfast had been fried eggs and bacon?

"How is it the kitchen has got so untidy, Rosie?" she said as severely as she could.

Rosie looked round. The kitchen wasn't what she would call untidy. It did not offend her eye in the least to see a few things in different places, any more than it worried her, when she went and picnicked in the park, to see the paper wrapping from her sandwiches blowing away across the grass. She knew that in come curious way these things did annoy people, and she made haste to reassure her mistress for the sake of peace and quiet.

"I'll soon hike all those back again."

Beryl picked up the calendar, looked for its nail, saw that the nail had come out of the wall, and propped it on the mantel piece.

"Did you have a nice evening?"

"Lousy!" said Rosie briefly.

"Oh dear! Why?"

"Well, it was that Olive would have us go out with 'er and 'er Tom to see some friends of theirs. So we hiked round to their house and then we didn't do nowt but just sat and talked! Ever such an old couple, they was. Nice, you know, but ever so old. 'E's a Councillor," added Rosie with a flicker of pride. "Councillor Allworthy, they call 'im. I'm sure I don't know what that means?"

"It means he's on the Town Council."

"I daresay. Summat o' that kind. 'E was talking about how he got sloshed by a copper when he was a lad."

"Good gracious! What was he doing?"

"Street fighting," said Rosie indifferently. "Mrs. Allworthy, she gave us some sandwiches; I don't know what was in them but they tasted right nasty. There was some cake, but of course I didn't eat much, any road."

"Why not?"

Rosie looked slightly shocked.

"Well, you don't like to eat much, do you, in other folks' houses? But when we came away I was that 'ungry I could have eaten a horse between two mattresses. So Fred and me bought some fish and chips and I had a right good tuck in. That's how I came to be a bit late," Rosie added candidly, forestalling a rebuke.

"I see. Well you must try to be more punctual, Rosie. It struck eleven before you came in."

"Aye, I'll think on next time," replied Rosie cheerfully.

Honour being now satisfied on both sides, Beryl ordered the meals, and went back to "do" the sitting-room.

Dusting with gentle care the family china which had been a wedding present to Robert from an old aunt, she thought, I believe I might like it if we were very poor and had no maid. It was not the management of Rosie that disturbed her. Rosie was a naughty girl, but company and a pleasure. It was a feeling as though her own days were empty. From the time when she left school, during her year in France, her grown-up years at home, her meeting with Robert, through her engagement, right up to her marriage her life had been a crescendo. The excitement and happiness had risen to a point. Now she was discovering that she had passed the point. Instead of going on and on, up and up, she seemed to be walking along a straight road, and almost along a road that began to slope down hill. She had been married to Robert for two years, and while she loved him dearly, she had a feeling that he was getting used to her. And so far there was no sign of a child, so that at times she felt herself a failure; she had a secret and morbid fear that Robert must mind much more than he admitted, and that his family must blame her. Perhaps some people thought she wouldn't have one. Jane Carr had almost hinted it the other day. If they only knew how she wanted one!

In the meantime she wanted something to do. Of course she had plenty in a way. There were always jobs she could find about the house, there was the household shopping, there were her clothes to look after. There were a lot of tennis-parties and tea-parties, she was friendly and popular. On any free afternoon she could go to Robert's old home and see his mother and father whom she loved, or ask Clare to go to a picture with her. There were plenty of pleasant things to fill her days. She thought as she shook up the cushions that it wasn't pleasant things she wanted. She wanted something to bite, some kind of work that she would have to do whether she felt like it or not, something that would be a nuisance and difficult and would make her tired, but remove this feeling of drifting gently along. It was churlish and ungrateful of her to be tired of her nice young friends at tea-parties and it was odd that after their pleasant gossip she should find herself glad to come back to Rosie's conversation, which was like something rough and tasty after a bit of sponge cake.

I must be very discontented, Beryl thought. She laughed, remembering an old nurse who would have told her that she had got out of bed that morning with a little black dog on her back. The sun was shining, and she played for a minute with the idea of going into town to look at the shops and have lunch. She could ask one of her friends to come too, she would enjoy it and forget all about her dissatisfactions.

But she thought, No, I won't, because I shall feel the same again to-morrow. She sat down on the sofa to think things out about herself. Why do I feel like this? Is it because I'm spoilt? I know I am! Haven't I got everything I want to make me happy? Anybody would say yes. And I am happy. No, I'm half happy. I think I feel that I'm not being used. But I'm Robert's wife, isn't that enough? No, it's funny, it isn't. I've got this nice house and lots of friends and enough clothes and money. But it isn't that I want to have things, she discovered with surprise. I want to *do* them. Rosie's night out is the night I like best in the week. I should be happier without Rosie! But Robert wouldn't like it and his people wouldn't; they'd all feel I was having a hard time, and Robert wouldn't iike people to know that I was doing all the housework, and anyhow, I don't want to do Rosie out of a job. I think she's happy here. But how funny that Robert should feel like that! How funny to like your wife to have things but not like her to do things! How odd that our sort of people have got to think such a lot of having and so little of doing!

The door flew open and Rosie burst in, her round face streaming with tears. Beryl jumped up.

"Oh, Rosie, what's the matter?"

"It's me sister!" sobbed Rosie. "Me brother's come. She's dying! It's Clarice—her that has Patreechia and Gloria! Me brother's come on his bicycle. They've taken 'er into hospital, and they're going to operate."

"What's the matter with her?"

"Appendicitis, me brother says."

"Oh, well, Rosie, she'll probably get better! Lots of people have that operation and get all right in a few weeks."

Rosie shook her head.

"She's been screaming and crying with pain all night, and they coom and took 'er off this morning. She'll not get better. Me brother's coom to fetch me so we can all go and say good-bye to 'er. Can I go? I've done me shelf and washed up; I was just going to straighten up a bit."

"Yes, of course you can go. I don't know whether they'll want you at the hospital, but you'll be able to look after the children. Is anyone with them, poor little things?"

"Me sister, Lily's there, and Rufus, that's Clarice's 'usband, you know, 'is brother Cliff and 'is wife coom and brought their little girl over, she's expecting another is 'is wife— Pauleen 'er name is, and me youngest sister will be there by now."

"Oh," said Beryl a little staggered. "Still, I daresay there'll be something you can do. You'd better put on your coat quickly and catch the tram. I'll look up the buses for you while you get ready. Did you make your brother a cup of tea?"

"'E's gone. 'E's going over to Kirklington to tell me auntie. Clarice was always me auntie's favourite. She was my favourite too," said Rosie, beginning to cry again. "She's that generous 'earted she'd give you the clothes off her back! It's always them ones that get taken!"

"But Rosie, she'll very likely get better! Now you hurry up and get your things on and I'll make you a cup of tea to drink before you go. You must be brave, you know, and help the others."

"I couldn't swallow!" Rosie said firmly and reproachfully. There were times when Mrs. Harding's social sense seemed to her to be strangely lacking.

Beryl saw her off at the back door, a sturdy childish figure in her tweed coat and beret with her round face swollen and stained with tears. "I'll telephone you," she promised, "and I'll come back to-night, choose how." Beryl patted her shoulder and slipped half a crown into her hand, "Perhaps there'll be some little thing she can have." Rosie gulped and said, "Thank you very much. I'll put it towards the flowers. Me brother was saying we'd get a much better wreath if we all join." She went off and Beryl returned to a kitchen still strewn with cut paper and with Rosie's discarded apron lying in the middle of the floor.

Unable to help a holiday feeling, Beryl tidied the kitchen thoroughly, turned out the cupboard, put clean paper on the shelves, and cleaned the electric stove. She decided to cook a special dinner for Robert, the things that he liked best. She thought that she would make a cake for her mother-in-law and Clare who were coming to tea with her to-morrow. She locked up the house and made an excursion to the shops for mushrooms and olives and cream. When she came back she scrambled herself an egg, taking it out of the pan while it was still slippery and soft as she liked it, and not the tight friz of permanent waves that Rosie never failed to produce. She ate it with brown bread and butter and milk in the kitchen and lay back luxuriously in Rosie's chair, smoking a cigarette and planning her labours for the afternoon.

When Robert came home rather late from the office he found her, flushed and busy, with a coloured check overall over her frock, stirring her pans on the stove. He exclaimed, "Hulloa! What's up? Where's Rosie?"

"Her sister's gone into hospital to have an operation for appendicitis, and she had to go. She went off in terrible distress."

"Poor Rosie!" Robert said kindly. "Has she gone to the hospital?"

"No, to Clarice's home."

"Oh, to see that the kids are all right, I suppose?"

"Well, there seemed to be a lot of people doing that, but she wanted to be on the spot, I think."

"If they brought her sister into the Infirmary, she'd be more on the spot here. You've had all the work to do two days running! What a shame!"

"I've enjoyed it. I've had a good day. I've got a lovely dinner for you!"

"You shouldn't have bothered, darling! We could have had scrambled eggs."

"I had them for lunch."

"Did you?" said Robert, sitting down on the table. "I had lunch at old Stephen's place. I went round to see him about something and he asked me to lunch in their staff room."

"Good lunch?"

"Yes, only I had to sit next to that old bounder Ward. By the way, he wants us to go to dinner one night next week. His wife is writing. I made a non-committal sort of mutter, and thought we'd have another engagement for the night when fixed."

"Robert, I think we ought to go. I think if none of us ever go it makes things difficult for Stephen."

"Do you? Well, I don't really mind. The food's always good. If you think we ought to go All into the Valley of Death with Stephen, we will. Especially as he seems down in the mouth nowadays. I don't know what's the matter with him."

"Is he worried about something?"

"I think he is. He talked an awful lot of rot to-day, I thought, after lunch. He seems to be turning Socialist. I expect it's his liver. Or of course he's still got Hilary staying in the house. That might give anybody a turn against the educated classes. For that matter," Robert added cheerfully, "I'm often glad I married you instead of Joy."

"Are you glad you married me instead of Sylvia?"

The question slipped out incredibly, catching both of them unawares. Not since he first told her about it had either of them mentioned Robert's two years engagement to Sylvia Johnson.

Robert looked at her, and replied seriously,

"Yes, I am. I should be a fool if I wasn't." He came over and kissed her and said more lightly, "Don't be a little goose, Berry Brown. Of course I am! We'd better have a glass of sherry before this grand dinner of yours. I'll bring it in here."

Of course, of course I am, he told himself, as he opened a fresh bottle of sherry. Beryl had been solace and infinite kindness after those bruised unhappy months; he loved her and she was the dearest possible person to love, the easiest possible person to live with. What had made her suddenly stir up the memory of those old wild feelings as if she put a finger into a forgotten wound? Did she think about Sylvia much? Was that why she sometimes looked sad? He would never have been as happy married to Sylvia, and it was only a queer perverse corner of his heart that had suddenly ached for a sting and splendour that was not there in ordinary life, not meant to be there, no, no, not meant to be. Well, ordinary life was good enough. But Beryl must not think things! He went into the kitchen with the bottle and two glasses, and for the rest of the evening while they feasted, and then while he helped her to wash up, he was less gay and casual, more tender and considerate. Beryl, who was feeling cheerful after her day's work, saw and thought, Poor Robert! But in the end I'll make it up to him. I can because I love him. And I shall feel I've wiped out Sylvia if I have a child.

Beryl was tired and Robert volunteered to sit up for Rosie who would, he said, come by the last bus if she came at all. Beryl thought it would be unkind to go to bed, and curled up on the sofa with a novel, while Robert, who had brought some papers home from the office, worked at a small table under the lamp, looking judicial and pre-occupied in his horn-rimmed spectacles, a real lawyer, and a clever one, people said. He was both sensible and clever, Beryl knew, under that half-serious manner. Sometimes in his fair and reasoned judgements, as well as in his small ways and movements, he was very like his father, though Stephen was really more like him. Poor Stephen! But why? He had a lovely wife and two jolly little boys and a job. Not at all a good job, but the great thing was to have one. At least, is it? The most necessary thing, to do something to earn money, but isn't what you do really more important, aren't we all wrong somewhere in this idea of living to earn your living, oughtn't these food and clothes and houses that you work for to be things you need and have and enjoy while you live for what you do? Isn't what you do the great thing? Beryl was growing sleepy. Her eyelids dropped, a warm drowsiness drugged her mind. She heard the back door open and she jumped up, shaking off her sleepiness, and hurried out to meet Rosie.

Rosie stood in the doorway, a great stuffed velvet rabbit and a large rose bowl of thick copper-tinted glass in her arms. Her face was very grubby, her beret, jauntily askew on tumbled curls, was adorned with a diamante brooch and a green quill which had not been there when she went out that morning. One cheek bulged with toffee. She shifted the rabbit in her arms, held out a sticky bag to Beryl and said indistinctly, "Have a bit?" She swallowed her lump of toffee, her broad cheeks expanded in a grin, and she said,

"Eh, we 'ave 'ad a bit o' fun!"

"Rosie!" exclaimed Beryl. "Your sister? Wasn't she ill?"

"Yes, she's going on nicely. She 'ad the operation this morning at ten o'clock, and Cliff's been in at lunch time and seen 'er. She was poorly, you know, but ever so comfortable and the nurse says she's doing fine and she'll be home again in no time and all the better for it. So when Cliff came 'ome and told us that, there was me and Gertie and Ada and Rufus and the two kiddies and me brother, Len and 'is Edna and 'er little girl and me auntie coom over from Kirklington, and the Feast was there, you know, that comes once a year, and me auntie says, 'Well,' she ses, 'Who's for the

Feast?' Always a one for a bit of fun, auntie is, so we all went."

Rosie held out the glass bowl. "I bought you this with some o' the money you gave me. It was only ninepence, but it's cut glass. It was rejooced, the man said."

"Thank you very much," murmured Beryl feebly, clasping the bowl.

"And I won this rabbit throwing at coconuts! I'm going to give him to the little boy that lives next door to Fred, 'e's a cripple, poor little soul! And we 'ad a good time on the roundabouts! But little Patreechia, poor little kiddy, oh, she was sick! She'd been crying all the morning, you see, because they'd taken her mother. And then Cliff's wife, 'er that's expecting you know, she coom over faint after she'd been on the swings, and we 'ad to lay her down on the grass and a gipsy brought 'er a glass of water. A proper gipsy she was with ear-rings and a little brown baby she was carrying. Oh, we 'ad some fun!"

"Good Gracious! I hope she was all right! Your brother-in-law's wife, I mean."

"Oh, she was all right. We all went to a stall and 'ad some 'ot pies and peas afterwards, and we bought some sugar sticks for Patreechia and Gloria and the other little kiddy to suck, you know, and we bought them ices."

"But I thought Patricia, oh well,—I'm glad your sister's going on all right, Rosie,—and"—I don't know that I quite meant you to have a day off, thought Beryl, but what can I say with the "rejooced" cut glass bowl in my arms. Besides, oh, I don't know—"Well, I'm glad you've enjoyed yourself. Now you'd better run up to bed."

Rosie lingered at the bottom of the stairs, conscience pricking her slightly. "I'm sorry you had to cook dinner again for Mr. Harding." Dinner, in Rosie's mind was always cooked for Mr. Harding. If he was out, she saw no occasion for dinner at all.

Beryl laughed.

"Oh, well, I enjoyed it." Remembering that discipline must be maintained, she added, "You must cook him a specially good one to-morrow."

Rosie leaned down over the banister and said, "I will that. It seemed a shame poor Clarice couldn't go too and 'er lying in bed poorly and all, but you might as well enjoy yourself, mightn't you? You've only got once to live!"

The month of August dispersed the various groups in the city to seaside and country and moor. Olive went with her brother, Herbert, and his wife and little girl to lodgings in Morecambe. There had been trouble about this with Tom Sutton, who wanted Olive to come camping with him. Rosie and Fred were going to a camp near Whitby, where they would lie in the heather and bathe and cook stews and strike up ardent friendships with other campers that would fade into thin air at the end of a week, like friendships made on board ship. Olive would not hear of it. Nobody would induce her to sleep in a tent and mess about with a Primus stove all day. Her heart was set on wearing all the pretty frocks that she had made and walking on the front at Morecambe. Tom was deeply disappointed and flung off in a temper to walk from Youth Hostel to Youth Hostel in the Lakes with Harold Pearson. He plodded wearily all the first day, growling and sulking, but fresh air and exercise and the happy freedom of the life did their work, and on the second day Harold had less to put up with. The two young men talked politics all day and scrambled eggs and joined in community singing in the evening. Sometimes Tom looked wistfully at the young women in shorts with their sunburnt faces and blown hair; if only Olive liked that sort of thing! But although he did not realize it, there was a certain relief from strain in being away from her, and his body was appeased by exercise.

Harold Pearson would have put up with much more than a day's bad temper from Tom. He was very fond of him, and nursed two secret ambitions, to get him away from his flimsy, petty-bourgeois girl, and to win him for the Communist Party. He was sure that in the end he should achieve both these ambitions, and he bided his time, firmly established in his own certainties, and potent because of that very security.

He was neither doubtful nor afraid. His pale, spectacled eyes had envisaged every possibility, battle, murder and sudden death, the triumph of hatred, the ruin of liberty, chaos, war, violence, starvation and dislocation, everything that might be necessary to bring the new social order to an agonized birth. He was a kind and unselfish companion. In the Youth Hostels at night, he often lent a hand with someone else's Primus stove. He made genuinely sympathetic inquiries in the morning for blisters or twisted ankles. When a kitten was brought in with a broken leg, it was he who put a splint along the tiny limb, handling it with delicate care. But he did not feel any discomfort at the thought of executions in Russia. If that was the only way that Stalin could secure the new order, then there was nothing else for it. At whatever cost in life or liberty the new world must be born.

Hardly aware of such intentions, the old world pursued its peaceful way. Robert went into camp with his Territorials for a fortnight while Beryl went down South to her mother. She gave a dinner party to all her relations-in-law before she went, "Showing off," as she explained to Robert, by cooking most of the dinner herself. The party should have been a success, for she and Robert were cheerful hosts and loved entertaining.

"Beryl is a dear little cheerful thing!" Alice said warmly on the way home. "Fancy her taking all that trouble for us."

"Yes," Lionel agreed, "Robert's lucky. I've always thought so."

There was silence in the car while both minds travelled the same way. Then Alice said,

"I wish Stephen was going to have his holiday before the end of September. I think he needs it."

"Well, I suppose he couldn't get off now with Ward just going away."

"No, I suppose not. But he does look tired. Anyhow, I shall have him at home next week while Joy goes to her people."

Alice was silent for a moment, thinking of the things that Stephen would like to eat, and determining to make a fuss of him and send him to bed early. She had never been a

135

fussy mother, but was inclined, if she worried about any of them, to worry about Stephen, although Clare, her companion and half her daily life, was dearer to her than either of her living sons.

Lionel said,

"We must be fair to Joy. She's straightforward and loyal and devoted to the boys."

"She's a very stupid girl," Alice said crossly.

"I don't think she can help resenting anything she doesn't understand."

"Why did she flare up like that when he said he'd spent an evening at the Allworthys'? Was it just snobbishness?"

"It struck me that they were both on edge about that. I think there must have been something more behind it. Perhaps she wanted him to do something with her. He can be obstinate and unreasonable, you know, Mother. I think they probably get on better when Hilary isn't there. He takes Joy back into her own home world again."

"When I heard that Hilary was coming home, I thought it might be nice if he married Clare."

"He'd bore her. He isn't her sort."

"He's the same sort as Joy, and Clare's very like Stephen."

Again there was a silence, at the end of which Alice said briskly,

"Anyhow, I'm glad Clare will be home before Stephen comes to us next week. I'm sure she misses the boys. It will be nice for her to see something of him again."

Alice's mind dwelt on her daughter, who had so terribly missed Neville that her youth had slipped by her, who in a few years would miss them and be left alone. But no, Hilary was no remedy. She sighed.

"Do you think it was true what Stephen was saying about this Abyssinian business? Do you think it is the turning point for the next hundred years? Joy looked as black as thunder when he said it. And then Hilary said that about nobody conquering Abyssinia yet, and the Wops never would. Hilary always sounds as if he were repeating a lesson! Stephen scowled so when he said it, I could have laughed, only I was sorry to see them all so touchy. Perhaps something has been happening at the office to upset Stephen. I know it's difficult for him getting on with Ward."

"Well, the Wards all go off to-morrow, so he'll have a rest from them."

"Where are they going?"

"A cruise, I believe."

"They would!"

"Don't be snobbish yourself, Mother! I daresay it's a good way of seeing foreign parts, for those that like everything cut and dried."

"Cut and buttered more likely! I suppose it's a cruise on a luxury liner!"

"You may as well have some fun for your money!"

"Yes, but they won't! A lot of fun those poor children will have putting on fancy dress and playing deck tennis with Pa and Ma watching them all the time! Well, anyhow it will be a holiday for Stephen!"

The cruise on the luxury liner was under discussion two miles away, where Marjorie and Leslie sat in the drawing-room at Grey Gables. They were not often alone together in the evening, but Mrs. Ward had a headache in anticipation of the journey and had gone to bed early. Ward was in the room that he used as an office, making some last-minute notes for his secretary.

"I expect I oughtn't to eat any more," remarked Marjorie, dipping into a box of chocolates. "I shall get fat. But I keep on trying to find a coffee and I can't. Have one, Les?"

"No thanks."

"Aren't you looking forward to it?"

"No."

"I think it may be quite fun. Mary says——"

Leslie kicked a footstool. Marjorie had been to morning coffee and a tradeshow with Mary the day before in defiance of her parents' orders. Her delight in Mary and her pleasure in her own spirit of independence had stimulated her, she was pleased with her new cruising clothes, and naturally excited at the prospect of a change and of fun. She was in the state which Leslie in his mind called "bouncing" and which irritated him the more because of his own depression. For he had funked the fence which Marjorie had taken. He had respected the prohibition on his friendship with Mark Forrester, and had refused an invitation to supper with him. He suffered from the loss of his friend, and more unconsciously from shame at his own betrayal. This made him angry with Marjorie and not inclined to listen sympathetically to her eager account of what Mary had said.

"I thought Dad told you to let her alone," he said, severe, because of his private wound. "Do you mean to say you went and had coffee with her after that?"

"I'm grown up," replied Marjorie, looking far from it. "I'm old enough to choose my own friends."

"You'll catch it."

"I shan't say anything about it."

"That's deceitful," Leslie replied, wishing that it had occurred to him.

"I know it is and I don't really want to be deceitful. But if they're going to watch everything we do and tell us not to do it, we shall just have to be deceitful at times, or never have any fun!"

"You won't get much chance on the cruise, anyhow."

"Oh, I shan't worry about that. I shall just enjoy seeing places and games and dancing, and I shall send picture postcards to Mary and perhaps bring her back a present, and as soon as we get home, I shall ask her to lunch in town."

"She may not want to come."

"She will! She likes me a bit! She's kind!"

"She works and she's intelligent and full of Socialist ideas. She won't have much time for rich, vulgar idle people like us."

"We aren't vulgar! How can you say it!"

"We are! We don't know how to spend our money. We have too much food and too many servants and everything in the house is beastly!"

"I suppose you think Mother and Dad are vulgar and beastly—and me?"

Leslie was brought up short by being crudely presented with one of the things he really did think. He was also rather frightened as he always was when anyone was angry. He temporized.

"I suppose Mother and Dad like the kind of things their generation did like. And you haven't had a chance yet to find out what you like or want."

"I'm a year older than you, anyhow! And I've got a lot more sense! Women always grow up earlier."

"That's a cliché."

"A what?"

"Don't you know what a cliché is? Your posh school didn't teach you much!"

Marjorie was dashed from her crest of happy excitement. Tears came into her eyes. She had always cried easily since she was a spoilt little girl.

"You needn't be so superior! I think you're horrid, sneering at us all! Mother and Dad give you everything you want, and you're just going to have a lovely holiday, and they've said you may do English at the University instead of something really useful, and they're going to make a study for you upstaris with a lot of new furniture, and you're going to have a car for your birthday. What *do* you want?"

What did Leslie want? He wanted to go to supper with Mark Forrester, he wanted to go to Oxford instead of to the local University, he wanted to talk to people who cared more for ideas than for money. He wanted to scrape the house clean and burn everything in it, he wanted people like Stephen's wife, Joy, not to despise him and his family, or he wanted to have a revolution and sweep people like Joy off the face of the earth. He wanted to go for a holiday by himself, he wanted to tell his father to go to hell, he wanted his father to love and admire him, he wanted to cry and be comforted. But Marjorie would never understand a tenth part of what he wanted, and if he cried she might try to comfort him, but her clumsy comfort would not assuage his confused misery. Besides, he often felt that she despised him. Once she had said that a lot of girls at school had such jolly brothers! The remark had pricked through his thin skin and

139

made a sore. Perhaps she would like him to be a great fat bounder like Billy Wilson who had come to supper last night, and told so many funny stories that Leslie did not think funny! Well, he wasn't going to be a jolly brother on this cruise anyway, thought Leslie with much foresight.

"Oh, I don't know," he said drearily. "I want lots of things, but I don't suppose I shall get them. You're eating too many chocolates! Come on, we'd better go to bed."

Ward's absence and the absence of Joy and the children gave Stephen a feeling of holiday. He came back to his old home with the relief of one returning to an earlier, easier life. Pressure was lifted in two places, and loafing about the garden with Clare or his father, he felt more able to think without the unacknowledged sense that for him thinking might be a disaster.

Once, as they were repairing a broken seat in the summer-house together, Stephen said to his father.

"Don't you think a change over is coming—ought to come—to a new system?"

"I think it has been coming for a long time."

"Only here and there in small things."

"More than anything else in people's feelings. When I was a boy, there was no general feeling that everyone ought to have a decent house to live in. Most people didn't think about houses except their own. And there wasn't the same concern about food for everyone. All this free milk in the schools is the result of a growing feeling that every child has a right to be fed, by the community if its own family can't feed it. All that sort of thing is a slow growth of Socialism."

"I went in the other evening and had a talk with John Allworthy."

"A good fellow, old John!"

"He was talking about his life and the early days that he remembered."

"We do, you know, Stephen, at our age!"

A smile of affection passed from father to son.

"He made me feel ashamed for people like us. It seemed to me that every piece of fairness and decency had been conceded by us, by Conservatives, prosperous people, our class, if you like, because the others pushed us into it by clamouring for it."

"I don't think that's altogether fair. You wouldn't say, for instance, that Mr. Baldwin only makes concessions when and because he's pushed into it?"

"No. I think he wants to be fair all round so far as the system will let him. But the trouble is that it won't let him. It's out-of-date. And most of you—us—don't want to be fair beyond a certain point and won't be fair beyond that point unless they're pushed."

"So you're going to push us?" Lionel said, smiling.

"I don't know. I don't want to, but I might feel I ought."

"What does Joy say about it?"

"Hates politics. Won't listen if she can help it, and can always only see one thing for decent people to say or do."

"And always does it. More than most of us can say, Stephen."

"Oh, I know." He had not meant to criticize his wife to his father. He added hastily, "Joy's a very feminine creature. She's interested in the people she loves and in individual lives."

It was Lionel's private opinion that Joy was not a very feminine creature, that she was an undeveloped schoolgirl of the kind who had taken refuge from maturity in being half a schoolboy. That, he thought, was part of the trouble. Stephen had been slow growing up, but Stephen, if he grew up, might grow out of her. It did not seem likely that Joy would ever grow up. And she was not interested in the people she loved, or in individual lives. She loved people without being interested in them, even Jack and Lin whom she loved dearly. She thought about their bodily welfare and about bringing them up in accordance with her code, making them plucky, honourable, good-tempered, sporting and modest. She had no curiosity about their reactions to her code or their minds and personalities. Probably a darn sight better for them, Lionel thought, than the way people brought up children nowadays, like gardeners taking up the plant every day or two to see if it was growing. Joy might try and prune the leaves to her own shape, but would not disturb the roots. She was adequate for Jack and Lin—but for Stephen?

They could not discuss Joy. Ward they could and did discuss freely.

"I never feel I know much about him as a person," Stephen said. "He's such a queer, grey, dry, secret being. And yet it's quite extraordinary the difference when he isn't there. I feel rather as if a weight was off the top of my head, and a lot of other people look as though they felt the same."

"What on earth does he do with himself on a cruise?"

"God knows! He told me he wasn't looking forward to it, but he won't let his family go without him. I shouldn't be surprised if he doesn't spend his time organizing expeditions and seeing that his children go in for competitions and arranging fancy dresses for them, poor little wretches!"

"I used to see something of him when we were both on the Council. I won't say we were friendly, but I think we had a friendly feeling. We always had a word or two. He was the ablest of us all, of course, and how the Labour people hated him! All the same, I used to think what a fine thing it was to see John Allworthy standing up and opposing him. He allowed John time off from the works for Council meetings and Committee work, but John went back and worked overtime for every hour he missed. He'd come and fight tooth and nail against Ward, then go back and work for him. That sort of thing's very English, Stephen, and very sound. It's the kind of thing I hope we shall never lose, whatever changes you make in your new world."

"Sometimes I suspect that Ward has a more human feeling for old John than for anyone else."

"Well, I suppose John is all there is left of his early life, and that counts when a man's getting on. Your mother and I and William and Isobel—we all played together as children, and there's a special feeling when we're alone together. You'll know it one day, you and Robert and Clare."

Stephen observed, "I'm just getting to know Clare again. I've hardly seen her since I was married."

"Clare is worth knowing." He sighed. He often thought and said to Alice that they had been selfish about Clare. They had drawn too close to her in their shared grief for Neville. They ought perhaps to have pushed her away from them, taught her to turn outwards into the world to fill the gap. Sensitive stuff took a deep print, and by letting her comfort them, they had stamped it deeper. It was hard to learn that affection could damage. His daughter was active, kind and cheerful, but he suspected that she was not happy. Perhaps she would talk to Stephen, her own generation, now that she had him without Joy, whom she did not care for.

On the Saturday of his visit Stephen went with Clare to the wedding of a collateral Marsden. The wedding was at a country church in the Vale of York. The bride and her bridesmaid sister were tall and fair, and although only comely, not beautiful like Joy, reminded him of her, as their parents and relations reminded him of Joy's people. Stephen looked with sympathetic interest at the young, ruddy Gilly Marsden, wondering if he realized the hundred small rubs and adjustments inevitable in any marriage, and particularly in a marriage between different worlds. He said this to Clare, who replied, "Surely not so very different, Stephen."

"More than it looks. I think the town mind, the industrial mind is very different from the country landowning mind."

"The country mind ought to be better," Clare mused, her eyes on the tranquillity of green field spreading beyond the looped stripes of the marquee and the gay frocks and black coats in the garden.

"Why?"

"Deeper. Moving to a natural rhythm. More in touch with nature?"

"I don't know. I think that so much of the life we have to live isn't moving to natural rhythm, that perhaps a mind that was wouldn't be able to adjust itself. We've got off the natural rhythm. Perhaps people who are off it too can keep in step better."

"Where would they be stepping to?"

"There, my dear, you've got me!"

"The only places where people always keep in step are totalitarian states."

"Don't you often feel now as though, whether you liked it or not, the rhythm was speeding up? Like something on wheels starting at the top of a hill and going slowly at first until it moves faster and faster and faster towards the bottom."

"And what's at the bottom?"

"Perhaps revolution or war, or the end of an era."

Clare murmured, "Revolution! Can you imagine it in England?"

"Not what you're imagining, a film picture of crowds rushing down a street and houses blazing, and the guillotine working. Isn't that what you were seeing?"

"Something like that. Barriers and furious faces and weapons and a mob loose."

"I don't imagine that. But I think,—I'm getting more certain every day,—that there's got to be a change over of direction, of the aim of most of our lives. After all, there've been revolutions of that kind before. Christianity was a revolution."

"Not a very complete one," Clare said sadly.

"No; if it had been, there wouldn't have been so much need for any others."

"Hulloa you two!" Robert's voice said behind them. "Couple of sober faces for a wedding!"

"Bob! I thought you couldn't get here!"

"Well, I thought I was going to play in a cricket match against the Vth, but they scratched—got a brass hat coming down to see them, or something, so I thought I'd slip over and see Gilly pushed off. Then I had to stop and see the R.S.M. about the sports, and my confounded subaltern wasn't there when I wanted him, and he'd taken my A.A. map, so I lost the way here, and that's why I've only just arrived, and I want a drink," Robert concluded. He was copper brown from the sun, bright-eyed and alert from a week's fresh air and exercise. He looked about him, nodding here, grinning there, all ready to enjoy himself. It seemed absurd to talk of revolutions!

"I'll see you later, shan't I?" Robert said, and plunged into the party.

"We shan't see him later," Clare observed, "unless we dig him out from half a dozen people. Don't you remember at children's parties when we were ready to go home, we always had to wait while they found Robert?"

"I often wish I was like him!" Stephen added ungrudgingly. "Somehow, he's a much more complete person."

"His capacity's less, so he's nearer to it. I think you're more like Neville, Stephen."

Aware both that she had paid him her highest compliment, and that Neville had not left much mark on his own life, he smiled at her, but was silent.

"It's hot in here. Shall we walk about outside a bit?"

Clare's soft dress, flowered with nasturtiums on a grey ground, flowed back from her body, the wind filled her chiffon sleeves with delicious coolness as they stepped from under the striped roof. What would it be like if it was my wedding? If all these people had come here for me? If Harry . . .? An ache of desolation filled her heart, and in the middle of it a certain relief because it was not her wedding, she would not have to make the supreme effort of loving and living with anyone, not even Harry, married and gone to Kenya five years ago. It was like old times to be at a party again with Robert and Stephen as though they were all still at home. She turned to say so and saw that Stephen was speaking to a girl, a very neat girl in a thin black and white frock, and a small white straw hat, turned up like a cup-shaped flower from her brown hair. Stephen's eyes beckoned, and Clare turned back. In that instant, when he smiled from her to the girl, she saw him look like Robert for the first time that afternoon.

"Here's my sister," Stephen said. "This is Miss Mary Welburn, she's doing the wedding for the *Y.G.* We can give her a lift back, Clare, can't we?"

Clare suddenly felt countrified in her flowery frock and big hat, she was a little dismayed by the exact poise of the up-turned white cup, and by the firm curve of the reddened lips, but the girl's eyes were frank and friendly.

"How do you do?"

Stephen said, laughing,

"We've been talking about revolutions."

"You generally are, aren't you?"

Oh, she's a friend of theirs, thought Clare. She liked to be able to place people. They were either friends, or people one met on committees or people who went to St. Jude's and helped at bazaars, or people who had been in the office or the works. If they were none of these things they were hardly people at all.

"I saw your uncle this morning," Stephen said.

"Did you? They're going away next week to stay with some friends near Derby."

"We had a long talk the other night!"

"Did it help at all?"

"I think it made things clearer in my own mind." Stephen turned to Clare. "You know Mr. Allworthy? He's Miss Welburn's uncle."

"Oh, yes, of course I know him." Clare tried not to show her surprise. So this girl was not a friend, but someone Stephen knew because of the works. Clare became at once a little less shy and more cordial. Cordiality with one's friends was a matter of mood and taste. With people in the parish, people attached to the works, it was an obligation. Clare had learnt that before she was ten by watching her father.

"Have you had anything to eat, Miss Welburn? Come and have some iced coffee with us?"

"Thanks awfully, but I think I ought to go round first and find out about everybody and get my notes for the paper."

"Well, we can take you back, can't we? Shall we look out for you after the bride has gone?"

"Oh, will you? Thank you very much."

Clare watched her as she moved off.

"Is she really old John's niece?"

"Oh, yes. She got a scholarship to the High School and another one from there to Oxford, and she's been on a London paper."

"That shows that you don't need so many revolutions, Stephen. There is a chance for those people to get on in the world!"

146

She saw that she had annoyed him. He said abruptly, "There's always a chance for exceptional people to get on in the world." He added, "I'm beginning to think that what you call 'those people' are worth a lot more than 'these people.'"

"That's sentimental! You can't size people up in blocks."

"I'm not so sure. What they have in common may be more than what's different; just now, especially."

Clare looked round the garden.

"What's the matter with these people on the whole? Taking them by and large, they're decent, honourable, plucky, affectionate and good-tempered."

Stephen answered, "They're blind!"

A friend came up to them, and they talked to other people for the rest of the afternoon.

On the drive home, Clare shared the back seat of the car with Mary. Stephen had picked up one of the ushers, who had come over in a friend's car but wanted to get back before the friend was ready to leave. They had put their top hats on the floor behind, and the backs of their heads before Clare and Mary were masculine and aloof as they jerked an occasional sentence at one another with spaces of silence in between. Clare and Mary talked. The girl was interesting, Clare thought, about her work on the paper. She told Clare that she wanted to write, had had one or two short stories published. She seemed to want to do a lot of things, and to feel as though she might be able to do them. Envy stirred in Clare for so firm a grip on life. Because Stephen's remark about "those people" had made a discomfort in her mind, she asked Mary to come and see her. Mary said that she would like to, but it was difficult to be sure when she would be free, might she ring up and ask if Clare could do with her? Faintly surprised that her invitation should be accepted quite so much as a matter of course, Clare agreed. When they had dropped Mary and the boy, Clare got into the front seat by Stephen.

"I like Miss Welburn," she said, feeling obscurely that she was making amends. "I hope she'll come and see me."

"Oh, I'm sure she will." Stephen patted Clare's knee

147

and said suddenly, "It's been nice going to a party again with you, Clare! Like old times. It's fun being at home this week."

Doris and Arthur were both out when Mary arrived at No. 4. Her mother, who was up that day, was asleep, dozing over a book in her chair by the small fire which she needed even in August. The evening sunlight, pouring through the window, made the fire a thin ghost of flame among the coals, but touched to a dazzling brightness the brass knob on the fender. These brass knobs were the first objects that Mary could remember; she could remember sitting on the hearth rug as a little girl and fitting their cold round smoothness into the hollow of her small palm. Arthur had complained the other day that the fender was ugly, and she had looked at it, feeling it impossible to see whether it was or not, it was so much part of the stuff of her life.

She stood on the hearthrug looking down at her mother. Relaxed by sleep, the face against the cushion looked worn, old and fragile, the skin strained over the bones, the once soft flesh dried and creased by innumerable lines. Her mother, like the brass knobs of the fender, had been for so many years a part of her life that she had been slow to see her. Her mother's life was a novel that she had skipped but never read. She had had glimpses of the little girl, going to school with her sister, Grace, both of them rather shabby and sometimes even hungry. She could see Grace protecting and encouraging the younger Emily and ordering her about, but coming quite often to a point when a stubborn and weeping Emily would not yield. It was perhaps harder to imagine the pretty, blue-eyed young woman taking the fancy of Harry Welburn who seemed so dashing, and worldly and gay, and who married her because he could not do without anything he wanted, and he dared not even suggest to her that she should have him on any other terms. Mary understood better now the years of their married life that she could remember, her father's bursts of gaiety and fits of

148

temper, the days when her mother went about with a face like a stone. She had been taught to think of her father as the family disgrace, but she felt some sympathy with him although her mother needed more compassion. It was not only that her husband had harassed and then deserted her. To have lived so long and done so valiantly, but never that Mary could remember to have enjoyed herself, never willingly to have given or received affection, there was her tragedy.

Emily opened her eyes and said querulously,

"Oh, there you are, Mary. I thought you'd be back sooner. Doris hasn't come in yet. I wish you'd tell Mrs. Potter she can go now."

Mrs. Potter, the "woman who came in" when they were all obliged to be out, was in the kitchen in her hat and coat waiting to be released. Left to herself, Mary began to prepare supper. Her family's idea of food often struck her as uninteresting. Sometimes she was too tired or too lazy to contest them, and left Doris to her final resort, going round to a shop and buying slices of cooked ham to be eaten with bread and butter and tea cakes and followed by buns. This evening, feeling energetic, Mary chopped up the ham, ready to make a ham omelette. What fun it had been with Jill in their room at Hampstead making omelettes for anyone who happened to come in! Nobody happened to come in here, except Frank, who was almost part of the family, and even his comings and goings were generally known and prepared for with extra scones and spice cake which he did not really like, being careful of his weight.

Doris came in as Mary was beating the eggs. She had been shopping at a Saturday afternoon sale with a friend from the office. She was flushed and triumphant, laden with small parcels. Her trousseau was a muddle. She bought too many lengths of pretty material of poor quality, she favoured undistinguished blues and pinks, but she looked happy and lovely as she tossed her prizes into the arm-chair, and pulled off her hat, ruffling up her fair curls.

"Oh, Mary! What are you doing? I meant to be back in time to get supper ready. I'm so hot! I've got ever such a lovely remnant of crêpe de Chine, shell pink, enough for two

149

cami-knickers." She took a glass out of the cupboard, crossed to the kitchen sink, filled it with water and drank greedily. She came back and perched on the table by Mary. "Tell me about the wedding. What was her dress like?"

Mary supplied details.

"How did you get back so soon?" Doris asked idly.

"The Hardings brought me,—Stephen and his sister."

"Oh!" Doris was impressed and pleased. "What is Miss Harding like?"

"Quite nice. Shy and a bit stiff and condescending without meaning to be, but kind and rather sad, I think. I'm going to tea with her one day, so perhaps I shall get to know more what she's really like."

"I danced with him once when I went with Uncle John to the Staff Dance. He was ever so nice."

"Yes, he is."

"And his wife's beautiful! What was she wearing?"

"She wasn't there."

"Are you tired, Mary. I can finish that."

"No, not a bit, thanks. You sit there and get cool and talk to me."

Doris leaned back in the kitchen rocking-chair with a sigh of satisfaction.

"Frank was talking about you last night, Mary. He admires you ever so much."

"That's nice of him. I admire him. He's so good-tempered and sensible and he's got such a beautiful body."

Doris stared and laughed.

"You do say funny things!"

"But don't you like the way he moves?"

"I think he's very handsome and I love his face and the way his hair grows. I don't think I've thought about his body." Doris suddenly flushed. "Mary. Do you think—all that part—will be awful?"

"No, of course it won't, darling!"

"I expect it isn't really so very important."

"I expect it's awfully important, and you'll enjoy it."

Doris's fair young face was suddenly like her mother's.

"I don't think you ought to say that, Mary!"

"But it will be so discouraging for Frank if you think of it as a painful duty!"

Doris primmed her lips.

"Frank has a nice mind."

"Do you mean I haven't?"

Doris, who had very nearly meant that, was shocked at the suggestion.

"Of course, I know you have!" She leaned forward, pulled Mary towards her and kissed her cheek. She went back to the earlier, safer subject.

"Frank thinks you're ever so clever and attractive." Doris added kindly, "You'll find somebody like him some day soon, Mary! Though he wouldn't be quite your sort, perhaps. You'd like somebody brainy." Her mind returned to a familiar track and she said eagerly.

"It's ever so lucky, isn't it, having the grounds of the Convalescent Home behind our house? We'll never get built up with a lot of ugly little houses, and when you look out of our bedroom window, it's like being in the country. Did I tell you, Mary, we settled on the light green for the bedspreads and curtains?" She added discontentedly, "I wish Arthur was a year or two older and not so shy. I would rather have been given away by my own brother than by Uncle John."

"Oh, Doris, he's always been so good to us! He's an uncle to be proud of!"

"I know you're very fond of him and of course I am too. But he is—he does look a funny old thing, and I don't think he'll get on with Frank's cricketing friends. One thing, I am glad we're having the wedding in St. Jude's. It's a lovely church but I do hope Canon Halliday won't be abroad then, and that Forrester have to take the service. He was preaching one evening when we went there to see the church, and he made Frank quite angry. Frank said he had bats in the belfry and was doing a lot of harm, stirring up bad feeling."

"You have to stir up feeling to get things done."

"Well, but I don't see it's his business to get things done, except," Doris added vaguely, "services and visiting and that. Frank says clergymen ought to mind their own business."

151

"I daresay they feel that the state of the world and the way people behave to one another is their business."

"Frank said that what Forrester was preaching was pure Socialism."

"Perhaps it was pure Christianity. They're much the same thing."

"Oh, Mary, what a wicked thing to say!" Doris suddenly and surprisingly burst into tears.

With Mary's arms round her and her face pressed against Mary's shoulder, Doris sobbed.

"I'm sorry to be so silly, it was so hot in the shops, my head aches and I seem to feel so excited all the time, nowadays, and it worries me when Frank doesn't like things, and I've always known you were so clever, but he thinks different from you, and I do want us all to be friends."

"Frank loves you, Doris, and so do I. That matters more than what we think. You've got too tired." Mary soothed and petted her, stroking the soft waves of hair that were like spun gold against her dark sleeve. In a minute Doris pulled herself together, and drew apart. She blew her nose and achieved a watery smile.

"I'm all right now. I'll go and get an aspirin and powder my nose." She kissed Mary again and said shakily, "There's Arthur coming. I don't want him to see I've been crying. I'll take all these up to our bedroom and show them to you afterwards."

Canon Halliday had always prided himself on his fatherly relationship with his curates. They had been made free of his house and treated as part of his family. To one of them, now vicar of a church in the South, he had married his elder daughter, Beatrice. He introduced them to his friends, and was fond of saying in company that he liked them to know people and to be asked to "nice houses," though he was less fond of saying this after his second daughter, Jane, remarked once, "Poor devils! It's so damned dull in nice houses!" Jane was seventeen, and passed the time with the curates, but stated often and emphatically that nothing would induce her to marry a clergyman.

She found it difficult to pass much time with Mark Forrester, but not nearly as difficult as the Canon found it to maintain a fatherly relationship with him. It was like taking a service with a congregation that did not know the responses. Canon Halliday had of course known before Mark arrived that he was an ardent Anglo Catholic. He did not mind that at all. He himself had Anglo Catholic leanings. It was rather convenient to have a curate who tried innovations, and to be able to say apologetically and tolerantly if his friends in the congregation objected, "Well, you know, he's young! You know what these young fellows are! He'll settle down. I don't like to be too hard on enthusiasm."

If Mark Forrester had kept his enthusiasm for extra Celebrations, and more Ceremonial, he would have found his Vicar the broad-minded, kindly elder of his own self-portrait. Unfortunately this was only part of his activities. He preached in season and out of season on matters which in Canon Halliday's opinion were no concern of the Church. He advocated something that the dismayed Canon greatly feared was Bolshevism, or anyhow would sound like it to the congregation. He scourged the rich and sentimentalized over the poor. He appeared on political platforms. The Canon lost a stone over him, and began to dread going to the club for lunch after a meeting, a little treat which he had always enjoyed, but which was entirely spoilt if some old acquaintance button-holed him and told him fiercely that his curate was no gentleman. What could he do? The young man was active, devout, indefatigable in his parish work, and effective. He started a Young People's Guild, and soon had a following of boys and girls from the new housing estate, although Heaven knew what ideas he was putting into their heads! He brought back lapsed communicants, and whipped up the largest Confirmation Class that St. Jude's had known for years. Worst of all, he filled the church on Sunday evenings. He had got himself noticed by the Press and people came to hear him for a stunt, all sorts of people who did not belong to the parish, and perhaps never went to church anywhere.

153

They came and stared and laughed and whispered to one another. It was all most distasteful.

Canon Halliday was sadly pondering the problem in his study one evening when Jane thrust her mop of sandy curls in at the door and said, "Are you awake, Dad? Savonarola wants to see you. Do have him in now, because I want to practise in the drawing-room."

The Canon had always preferred the naughty, idle Jane to her more sober sister. For an instant the burden of his difficult curate was lightened by her disrespectful words and mocking smile. While she stood in the doorway, her narrow, freckled face all one sparkle between the swinging curtains of bright hair, Mark Forrester was a foolish young man and not a tragedy. But Jane went out like a candle. The door slammed behind her, her light footsteps scurried across the hall, and in a minute or two, heavier footsteps came to the door. The Canon braced himself, feeling nervous and out of his own waters. Whatever his curate wanted to see him about, it was sure to be a difficult, possibly even a distressing half-hour.

He tried to smile genially at the unsmiling young face.

"Hulloa, Forrester! Good evening. Sit down. What did you want to see me about?" He added, "I'm going out to dinner. I'm afraid I shall have to leave you in about twenty minutes."

One of the disconcerting things about Mark Forrester was that he hardly ever answered a casual remark.

"You ought to try and learn some small talk," Jane had once said to him. "What do you do when you go visiting? Do you ring the bell and say, 'Good afternoon, do you believe in God?' You must frighten them off!"

It would have astonished Mark Forrester to learn that he frightened her father. He himself always felt oppressed and disconcerted in his Vicar's comfortable study. The college groups above the fireplace, the oar with a light blue blade fastened on the wall, the good, shabby furniture, the shelves full of used books, all were eloquent of an established world, and of the things in the established world most difficult to fight. It was not its extravagant luxuries and vulgarities, it was its ease and good taste and genuine culture that had such a hold on people! Almost anyone of any perceptions might be persuaded to topple over what Grey Gables stood for. Only the uncompromising would assail Lionel Harding's house and the Vicarage. Mark Forrester was uncompromising, but he had a worm of inferiority in his heart that made him more uncompromising in this study than on the common ground of vestry and parish room.

He thrust an evening paper across to the Vicar.

"Look!" he said. "Have you seen to-night's news?"

Canon Halliday almost groaned aloud. He always read the papers, of course; he read *The Times* and the *Yorkshire Guardian* every day. Sometimes he reviewed a religious or philosophical work for the *Guardian*. He had always kept abreast of the affairs of the day, but it seemed to him that since the arrival of Mark Forrester, there had been so much *more* news, and instead of lying quietly in the paper in a gentlemanly manner as news should, it got up and danced before his eyes in letters of fire. When he opened his paper in the morning, he often glanced nervously at the headlines, wondering what his curate would say on Sunday evening about the events of the week.

"No," he said, "I've been out visiting this afternoon." To his conscience, surprised at the remark, he said hastily that anyhow the Hardings were in his parish. It was pleasant to drop in there at tea time, and talk to Lionel, enjoy their hot scones, and be waited on by Clare whom he had baptized.

"Well, look at that!" Mark pushed the evening paper towards him.

The date was September 5th. Across the top of the paper was a large heading:

"ITALIANS WALK OUT OF LEAGUE COUNCIL."

"Ah, dear me! Dreadful! Dreadful!" Canon Halliday said heavily.

"What are we going to do about it?"

If Jane had been there she would have said, "Well, Mr. Forrester, you'd better ask them to come back!" But she was not there to support her father with her flippant common sense. Canon Halliday could think of no answer, and avoided one by reading further. One of the subheadings announced that the T.U.C. were solid in support of the League. There was an article on the Abyssinian warrior by a man from Wakefield who had been in Abyssinia three years before. His opinion was that the Abyssinian warrior was equal to five Italians. The papers blossomed every day with articles by people who had been in Abyssinia, sometimes saying that it would be impossible for the Italians to conquer it, sometimes saying that it would be impossible for the untrained Abyssinians to withstand the Italians.

Mark Forrester said vehemently, "The whole parish ought to be down on its knees in prayer and repentance."

"Come, I really don't think you can hold the parish responsible!"

Mark replied vehemently.

"We're all responsible. We were told the right way to live nineteen hundred years ago,—loving one another as brothers, having all things in common. We've all of us embraced Christianity just up to the point where it doesn't inconvenience our own greed and lust of power and possessions. We've had lesson after lesson and we've never learnt. Even the last war didn't teach us. So now we're at the beginning of the biggest war the world has ever known, a war that will spread slowly, dividing nations and cities and houses and families. . . ."

"My dear fellow," Canon Halliday said coldly, "don't let us get hysterical!"

Mark checked, stared at him dumbly. Canon Halliday pursued his advantage.

"I don't for one minute suppose that Mussolini will take on the whole League. How could he? Some compromise will be found. There are very able men at Geneva. Anthony Eden——"

Mark made a gesture of despair.

"He's a straw on the tide. Any individual man now is only a straw against the tide,—against the two great tides."

"In that case Mussolini is also a straw and his bombast must not disturb us unduly."

Mark, never read in debate, had no reply to that. Canon Halliday saw it, and said in a conciliatory tone,

"But you are perfectly right to suggest that we should take

some steps. We will have a special service of intercession after morning prayer on Sunday and a special intention at the early communion. Will you see about the service? Speak to Carter about the organ? And do try, my dear boy, to take things a little more calmly."

"I can't, Vicar! I feel there might still be a chance for us, for civilization, if people could be made to feel and accept their responsibility and turn to God. There's so little time to *make* them see, to *make* them accept it."

"Neither you nor I know how much time there is. Our times are in God's hands. If we don't have faith, how can we ask it of other people, laymen?"

Mark said abruptly,

"Faith isn't sitting still and hoping for the best. It should be an active, burning fire, setting fire to others."

The Canon pushed back his chair.

"I'm sorry, Mark, but unless there's anything else urgent, I shall have to ask you to go now. I shall be late." He added kindly, "You look tired. Have you got anything on this evening?"

"I'm going down again to Harebell Avenue to look in at old Mr. Trent. He's not expected to last the night, and I want to go into the club for an hour. That's all. I really want to do some reading."

When the curate had gone out, the Vicar sat for a minute or two playing with his pen.

"Unbalanced!" he said to himself, "unbalanced! Of course not quite,—but it's so difficult to get one that is nowadays. I made a mistake! I thought he seemed a nice fresh, eager lad; but dreadfully unbalanced!"

He laid down the pen. Suddenly he felt that he himself was getting old, was fat, scamped his visiting, hurried his private prayers. He knew that he avoided unpleasant facts, that he had long ago lost spiritual fervour, that a good dinner seemed more vitally real to him than a war in Abyssinia. Well, it would be a good dinner to-night, and over the Gardiners' excellent port in pleasant company of which he was not the least pleasant part, he would forget a raw, crude youth who preached at him in his own study, probably did not know port from claret, and overstrained a not very subtle brain by essaying all the problems of the universe.

Harebell Avenue was one of a block of streets in a new housing estate which, being called Harebell Terrace, Harebell Back Terrace, Harebell View, and Harebell Crescent, were known collectively as the Harebells. Perhaps the name enshrined the ghosts of lavender blue bells on fine stalks that had once blown on a disused mound of rough grass before the sods were taken up by the builder. The houses were of red brick, neatly roofed with ornamental tiles. Since the estate was three years old, nearly all of them were set in exquisitely tended gardens, miracles of skill and care that bloomed all through the changing seasons, from the first crocus to the last rusty chrysanthemum.

Mark Forrester took very little interest in the gardens. He hurried on his way to the dying John Trent, thinking about this housing estate, about the very little he had been able to do in it. He had barely scratched the surface. The neat red houses were full of people without faith, without ardour, without ideas. Religion was outside their lives. Politics meant for them leaflets blue or red with the unimposing photographs of potential M.P.'s. The leaflets were thrust in at their doors, and when they found them, they glanced at them and put them in the waste-paper basket, or gave them to the children to play with. If they could remember, they voted. When they had a baby, they brought it to be christened, for most of them were inbued by a desire to give their children everything that they could in Heaven or earth. Christening and voting were incidents that showed no vital feeling and were detached from the rest of their lives.

A voice said, "Good evening, Mr. Forrester," in Mark's abstracted ear. He stopped, looked, and recognized Herbert Walters, who was leaning on his front gate. Herbert was a clerk in an Insurance Office. He did not come to church himself as a rule, but his wife sometimes came, and his little daughter attended Sunday school.

"Oh, good evening," Mark said.

"A nice back-end we're having. We've just come home from Morecambe."

"Did you have a good holiday?"

"Yes, it was very enjoyable. You'll be going along to see old Mr. Trent, I daresay?"

"Yes."

"They seem to think he won't last the night, poor old gentleman."

Herbert was obviously settling down for a good conversation about Mr. Trent. Mark said abruptly, "Well, I must be getting on. Good night," and hurried off with long strides. Herbert Walters was one of those people who filled him with despair. It seemed to him that nothing would ever penetrate that careful respectability, that tepid kindliness. It would be impossible to rouse Herbert Walters to the claims of God or the needs of man.

Herbert finished his cigarette, looked proudly at his dahlias, exchanged a greeting with several passers-by, and then went back into the house. His wife, Mabel, was washing up after tea in the kitchen. Herbert twitched the cloth from the rack.

"Here, I'll dry these for you."

They worked busily side by side. Herbert was like both Fred and Olive, long, thin, pale with Olive's grey eyes, and Fred's smooth, light hair. Mabel was short, dark, rosy and plump, and had worked in a sweet shop before she was married.

"Where's Doreen?" Herbert asked.

"Gone to play with Ruth Myers. I told her to come in at half-past seven." Mabel, shaking the tea-leaves rigorously out of the tea-pot, began to laugh. "Eh, she is a caution! Do you know what she said to me at dinner-time?"

Herbert listened to the tale of Doreen's not very witty remarks with rapt admiration. Mark Forrester was wrong in thinking that all his emotions were tepid. Both he and Mabel worshipped Doreen with ardour and astonishment. No child could ever have been so pretty, so clever, so funny. No child before could ever have thought of such things to say, or said them in such inimitable ways. Her achievements at school were miracles, her cut knees and colds were disasters. She was the transmitter for a universe reborn. When she saw a daisy for the first time, or learned that the world was round, or wept for a dead bird, her parents shared the first lost sharpness of pleasure and interest and pain.

"I've just seen Mr. Forrester go past."

"He'll be going down to old Mr. Trent's, I suppose. The doctor was there again at six. Poor old man, it's to be hoped it will soon be over. Did Mr. Forrester stop and talk to you?"

"Just a word. He was in a hurry."

"He always speaks very short. Not what I should call friendly like. I shouldn't fancy him in the room if I was dying. But Mrs. Grey, over at the Terrace, can't say enough good of him for all he did for their lad when he was in trouble."

"Ah, well," said Herbert, "it takes all sorts to make a world. Is Olive coming up this evening?"

"No, she's going to the second house at the Empire."

"With Tom?"

"No, one of her friends; Maisie, I think it is. There, that's all. We'll go into the other room and see if there's anything on the wireless."

They had been in No. 9, Harebell Avenue for three years, but Herbert never sat down in the other room after tea without a glow of pride. He had been born and brought up in a house in a yard behind the Hardings' works, a house which because his mother was a good housewife was always neat and clean, but in which there was hardly room to move. The kitchen was also the sitting-room, Herbert, Olive and Fred shared as small children a bedroom upstairs, and later Olive went in with her mother, and Herbert and Fred shared it with their father, who snored heavily, and enforced silence at night and prompt early rising in the morning. There was no bathroom, and the lavatory was one of a row of privies in a yard round the corner. No. 9, Harebell Avenue, with its shining bathroom, its drawing-room suite of light wood trimmed with blue enamel, its glossy artificial silk curtains was not only a small Paradise, it was the hall-mark of success. It proved that Herbert Walters, son of Joe Walters who wore

160

overall suits and worked a riveting machine, had climbed above his father, had become a clerical worker in a white collar, part of that immense and varied army, the middle class. For Herbert the best moment of the day was this one when he and Mabel sat down in the other room, and he smoked a cigarette and looked at the evening paper, while Mabel sewed and knitted and talked to him or they turned on the wireless.

This evening Mabel picked up a little dress, threaded a needle and began to hem. As the needle moved in and out, her mind went back to something that had been worrying her all day. She said,

"You know, Herbert. I could see that your friend who came in the other night, Mr. Awning, was right taken with Olive."

"Was he?"

"Was he? Why anybody with eyes could have seen it! He was looking at her all the evening! And he was ever so keen to go on the same tram, and I'm sure I could have died of laughing when you would keep telling him that it was nearer for him to go the other way."

"But it saves him ten minutes!"

Mabel clicked her tongue.

"Yes, I dare say! And did you want anyone to save you ten minutes when you were taking me home?"

"It's no use Awning thinking about Olive. She's got Tom."

"I know she has."

There was a silence. Then in answer to some unspoken remark, Mabel said,

"Mind you, Tom's a decent, steady lad and earning a good wage."

"I wish he hadn't taken up with politics—with all these Reds! One of these days he'll be getting into trouble. Besides——" Herbert paused. He was not articulate and could not put into words his obscure feeling that Tom's politics threatened his hard-won elegance, menaced the shining bathroom, the drawing-room suite and the dahlias in the garden. Herbert knew without admitting it to himself that Tom despised him. He had seen a good deal of Tom, and had received those communications which are carried on all the time underneath surface relationships by currents of feeling. But it was part of Herbert's muddled and instinctive morality to try to be kind, as it was also the prompting of his safety-first instinct, which told him that he would be more secure in the little patch of civilization he had won out of the jungle, if he lifted his hand against no man and had no man's hand against him.

"Well," he said judicially, "Tom's young. When you've got on a bit and seen a bit of the world, you look at things differently. Now there's Mr. Dalton"—Mr. Dalton was the manager of Herbert's company—"as nice a gentleman as you could wish to see and ever so kind that time when Doreen was ill, sending me off home, and enquiring for her. And then there's people like the Hardings and the Marsdens, rich people that have done a lot of good for the town. You can't make everyone the same. It's only lads like Tom that think you can. I come from the working class just as he does, but I've got on a bit, and seen a bit more of the world, and I know well enough that the working class aren't fit to govern."

Mabel glanced at the ornamental clock.

"Oh, Herbert, it's a quarter to eight! I told Doreen to come in at half-past seven. I wish you'd go and seek her. I don't want to put this down."

Herbert went out to look for Doreen. He knew that he should probably find her at the end of Harebell Avenue in a small strip of wood which those who planned the housing estate had wisely left undestroyed, thus ensuring for twelve hundred people a daily glimpse in spring of delicate young beech and nodding bluebells, and in autumn of leaves which although rusty and curled by the smoke of the town, yet took on here and there a fire of red and a glow of yellow, and smelled heavy and sweet, and rustled under children's boots.

Doreen was jumping on and off a log with her friend, Ruth Myers. She saw her father coming and was glad it was not her mother. She could deal with both at a pinch, but Daddy was easier game. His authoritative "It's time you

162

came in, Doreen," impressed her not at all. She did not mean to come in, and he could not and would not make her, but she knew that his face must be saved.

"Oh, Daddy? Just a few more minutes! Please!" Doreen put her head on one side. She had been a very pretty baby, and though she was now thin, lanky, pale, and spoilt by irregularly growing second teeth, she still kept the manner of a consciously charming little girl.

"Your mother said half-past seven," Herbert temporized. Ruth Myers, who was round and plump with a square-cut fringe, struck in.

"My mother and Dad's gone to me auntie's and they won't be back 'til half-past eight. The house is locked and I can't get in."

"Can't I stay with Ruth till half-past eight?" Herbert looked at Ruth with some disfavour. Her mother and father were what Herbert called "rough." All the estate knew that they sat in the kitchen except when they had company. Mr. Myers was a tram driver, and rumour had it that Mrs. Myers had once worked in a fish and chip restaurant. If so, she had not lost the taste, for every time she came back from the town, she was seen to be hugging a greasy parcel. Herbert would much rather that Doreen had made friends with the little Barraclough girls at the corner of the Terrace. Their father was a clerk in the Gas Offices and Hilda and Violet were "nicely spoken" and went to a private dancing class.

"Well——" he hesitated.

"Oh, please, Daddy?"

"Are you warm enough without your coat?"

Doreen knew that she had won.

"I'm very hot! I'm boiling!"

"Well, you must come in at half-past eight whether Ruth's mother and Dad have come home or not."

"Ooh, yes! Yes, I will!"

"All right."

Mabel looked up as he came in.

"She didn't want to come, I suppose?"

"No, I said she might stay a bit longer."

"She's a little monkey! Well, the evenings are still so light, I daresay it seems hard to go to bed."

Herbert sat down and picked up the evening paper.

"Soon be no more cricket now. The papers will be a bit dull."

"Is there any news?"

"It says here the Italians have walked out of the League Council."

"What does that mean?"

"I suppose it means they won't discuss anything reasonable. There's one or two at our place properly worked up about it. They say we shall have a war with Italy in a month if we try sanctions."

"Whatever are they?"

"Sort of restrictions on food and oil and things that Italy wants, to prevent other countries selling them to her."

"It seems to me it's all a fuss about nothing! We don't want Abyssinia, do we? Well then, why not let that Mussolini have it to keep him quiet?"

"It's part of the League, you see. The League of Nations. And we've got to stand by the League. You heard Sir Samuel Hoare's speech on the wireless—Don't you remember?"

"There's been such a lot of them speaking on the wireless lately. I can't remember what they all said. I didn't know you liked speeches."

"I don't, not really, but I hear our fellows talking and it makes you think."

Mabel bit off a thread.

"You're a one! What does it make you think?"

Herbert did not answer. He stared at the opposite wall with unseeing eyes. He saw a series of vague and disconnected pictures; dark-skinned men in mountainous country wearing uniform that looked absurd on them and being taught to handle unfamiliar weapons: Anthony Eden in a black hat, other statesmen, British and foreign, who in newspaper photographs seemed to be eternally stepping from the doorways of imposing buildings: Mussolini, whom, in spite of many pictures, he persisted in seeing with the face of his old head master. What he felt was less clear than what he saw.

He felt bothered and irritated because things of the kind that did not interest him insisted on claiming his attention. He felt annoyed with the foreigner who was causing this disturbance; he felt a tightening of the bonds that bound him to his own country, a deepening of his national consciousness. As he listened to that speech which Mabel could not now remember, he had experienced a sensation of being all in it together behind Sir Samuel Hoare. Deeper than all these thoughts somewhere in his feelings and instincts he was touched by a cold edge of fear. The name of Abyssinia, so strange, so far, seemed, like Tom's politics, to hold a menace for the house of his life, laboriously built. He could not have said why this was so. He had never noticed the trouble between Japan and China in 1932. They were not in Europe, and for him anything that was not in Europe could hardly be said to exist. Besides, he had not heard people talking about it so much in the office. Even in his tram to-day the conductor had said to a passenger proffering a half-crown, "Where do you want a ticket for? Abyssinia?" Something was coming nearer. Herbert, although he still thought the papers would be dull when cricket was over, felt a twinge of uneasiness. The current sweeping over Europe had just touched him and given him a faint suspicion of electric shock, so that he could never again be quite so firmly settled inside his own life. He threw the paper down on the floor. "Let's see if we can get some music," he said. "We don't want any speeches this evening. Let's try for some variety, something cheerful."

To Lionel Harding those days of late September when Europe hung waiting on Geneva were like the last days before the War. Once again the ordinary man must wait and watch, impotent to avert disaster. This time the threat of war seemed both more and less surprising. Less because confidence and easy security had been shattered, more because in the last twenty years the English mind had come to think of war as a barbarous method of argument. In 1914 to the mass of the English people, war had been unexpected but not

165

unnatural. To the same solid mass in 1935 it was unnatural but they half expected it, knowing now that the worst could happen.

The feeling of living again through a part of his life recalled more vividly to Lionel the memory of Neville, never altogether out of his thoughts. For a day or two he had a curious feeling as though the boy were back with him an actual presence in the house. As he went up the wide, shallow stairs, he expected to hear the young voice in the hall below him. He looked up across a bonfire in the garden, half believing that he would see the eager face through the column of blue smoke. So strong was his sense of his dead son's presence that he looked more than once at Alice and Clare to see if they too were aware of it. Alice went on her way much as usual, concerned at the news, but more concerned in her household and committees, and in the company of her married sister, Esther, who was staying with William. Clare looked as though the summer had tired her. She was quieter than usual. Small, new lines were appearing round her mouth and eyes. Looking at her with the tenderness of stirred feelings, Lionel realized that she was no longer a girl. Her fresh youth had been thrown on the bonfire as surely as Neville's. Or perhaps they themselves had shut her off from life by too much love and care.

He felt this most acutely on the afternoon when Mary Welburn came to tea with her. Alice had gone with Esther to call on some old friends, but he was at home, and came into the drawing-room for a cup of tea. Moved by his continual curiosity and interest in other people, he wanted to see what old John Allworthy's niece was like. He saw a smallish girl, rather nice-looking, very much alive, and with the stamp of someone who had already had to struggle for what she wanted. She was not aggressive, but looked as if she could be determined. He felt humour in her and a shrewd judgement, but also delight in the varieties of life. She looked at him as he looked at her, to see what sort of person this was, ready to be interested and make friends.

They had been talking before he came in, but he fancied that they had not yet struck common ground. Clare was

166

nervous and with a shade of hostility in the nervousness, and he wondered why she had asked the girl. They began to talk about modern novels. He did not read very many himself, he had come to the time of life when it was pleasant to re-read and dip in old books. As he listened to the conversation, he detected in Clare a shrinking away from attitudes of mind which the younger girl accepted, if not as her own, as commonplaces of everyday life to which she was accustomed. He was inclined to accuse himself that somehow or other he had equipped his daughter badly for her contemporary world.

"Do you share your uncle's politics?" he asked Mary.

"Yes, more or less. He brought me up in them. I should like things to move a bit quicker than he would."

"Just as in thirty years time, your sons and daughters will want things to move quicker than you do?"

She smiled and he said, "The world changes very slowly, you know. But perhaps you don't think that's a fair argument?"

"Oh yes I do. I quite expect that my children will say I'm reactionary. I suppose I shall be. But I do think there's a speeding up all round, nowadays. Things change faster. They've got to, or else go back."

"Perhaps it would be better if they went back," Clare said.

"That's always a disaster, don't you think? Because they can't really. You can't go against a natural rhythm without doing harm."

Clare did not answer. Looking quickly at her, her father saw on her face an expression prim, closed and disapproving that reminded him of William. She was too young for that look!

"The great thing about the present revolution in England," he said, "is that it's going on so quietly that a lot of people will probably never notice it happening until it's over. Because there is a revolution going on. My complaint about your people, Miss Welburn, is that you never try to be fair."

She answered with a flash of resentment,

"How are we to know what fairness is? We've never been treated fairly. My great grandmother worked in a mill when

167

she was seven years old. My grandmother brought up eight children on thirty shillings a week. My mother and aunt were both clever girls and my aunt longed to learn and to teach, but they both had to leave school at thirteen and go to work to help to keep their families."

Clare looked down at her piece of cake, embarrassed. Lionel said gently,

"By your own people I meant your political party, which thinks itself the only one responsible for any progress. We've made a lot of reforms, you know. Aren't you going to allow us any virtues?"

Mary laughed at him.

"I think you'd give away and share anything you didn't want to keep!"

He countered,

"I think you'd grab anything you could get!"

"Some more tea, Miss Welburn?"

Clare wished that they would talk about something else, yet was touched by jealousy because they were leaving her out of the conversation. Mary put the tea-cup into her hand and smiled at her. For an instant Clare's liking for her revived, but it sank again as the girl turned eagerly to go on with the argument.

Lionel was smiling.

"Now that we've told each other what we really think, let's admit that there have been many years of unfairness on my side and that there is now unfairness on yours. Here are you and I, neither of us, I think, malicious people, nor meaning to be unfair. What are we going to do about it?"

"I should think it depends on how much we have to take and how much you are willing to give."

"But you mean to have it?"

"Yes, we mean to have it someday."

"At any price?"

"Some of us think so. People like my uncle don't, of course. They don't want anything done except by general consent."

"And you?"

"No, I don't either really, but," she laughed, "I'd like to give general consent a push!"

"You wouldn't kill me to get a piece of my land?"

"No, I wouldn't; I'd rather do without the land and hope your son would learn to share it with mine. But I'd keep on trying to make him see it that way!"

"Well, there's quite a hopeful prospect for you with one of my sons."

"With Stephen—yes, I know."

A little surprised at her casual and familiar reference, he said,

"You know him, do you?"

"He comes to see my uncle sometimes. He was there last night, when there were several of us there, talking."

"Do you know his wife?"

"Only by sight. I haven't met her yet."

When Mary had gone, he said to Clare,

"Stephen seems to be launching out in a new direction."

"He's different altogether, nowadays."

Her voice was dejected and he said kindly,

"You look tired. Did you enjoy your tea party."

"No. I don't think I like her much. She's so assured."

"She's probably had to be. The father ran off with someone else and left them, you know, when they were children. I remember old John telling me about it. I believe the poor mother had an awful struggle. This girl earned her education and now she's earning her living."

Clare said flatly,

"I've never earned anything, nor done anything. I expect she despises me. And I dare say she's right."

Tears came into her eyes and she turned away, but her father saw and put his arm round her.

"You've been everything to us, Clare"—but he thought as he said the comforting words—"How wrong we were to let you be!"

Joy came back from her own home with definite ideas about Mussolini and Abyssinia, of which the first was that Abyssinia was too near Egypt. Her father did not so much mind when Mussolini defied the League, but did not care to have him jostling the British Empire. There was also a feeling at Stackhouses that it was the business of the British Government to protect natives, and that it was impertinent for Italy, in fact for any other country, to want Colonies. So Joy and Stephen agreed on the immediate issue. They were glad to see one another again. In the warmth of reunion, they forgot that they had both been bad tempered lately, that Joy had been angry with Stephen for making queer friends and picking up odd ideas, and Stephen had resented Joy's absorption in Hilary, and had begun to think her stupid. The little boys were delighted to be home. They dragged all their toys out of the toy cupboard and threw themselves upon Stephen when he came from the office, and shouted and rampaged all over the house in their pyjamas, until caught and put into bed, where they fell asleep in two minutes. Stephen went in to look at them. Lin snuggled down in bed and only his ruffled fair hair and one side of his face were visible. His long golden eyelashes, Joy's eyelashes, quivered on the soft curve of his cheek as some tremor went through him and he stirred like a dreaming kitten. Jack lay high on the pillow as though he had just flung himself down. Against the white linen he was red and brown as an autumn berry. He still clutched in one square freckled hand a long necklace of chestnuts threaded on string.

"They're nice, aren't they?" Stephen said to Joy putting his arm round her. "Didn't your people think they'd grown a lot?"

"They were delighted with them. Dad borrowed a pony for them, so they got some riding. They ran round with him everywhere like two little dogs. Mum thinks Lin is exactly like Hilary. She said it was like having him back again at five years old. She's quite forgotten she so much wanted him to be a girl. I'm thankful he isn't! I shouldn't know what to do with a daughter."

"I should like one."

"Well, it's fair there should be one for you. If we have another, I hope it is. You'll have to bring her up!"

"Oh, she'll bring herself up with Jack and Lin."

"Yes," Joy agreed. "The most important thing for a girl is to have brothers."

She tucked Jack's arms under the bedclothes without waking him, and went off to wash before dinner.

They spent the evening exchanging news of family and friends, Joy's news rather than Stephen's. The dip into her old life had revived and refreshed her. Telling him about her family and about all the people in the village, she was eager as a little girl, and lovely in that unusual animation which only home and Hilary now seemed to rouse in her. She woke in him his old feeling for her as somebody beautiful, innocent and vulnerable, somebody whom he longed to cherish. In the days before they were married he had secretly written poems to her, comparing her to sunlight on the sea. Lately his vision of her as a female St. Michael with shining hair had been submerged in an irritated sense of her impenetrable mind, and obstinate temper. To-night his old vision was restored to him, until a chance word destroyed it. Joy said casually,

"Did you go to the Appleton's sherry-party yesterday?"

"Oh, no, I didn't. I rang up Clare to see if she wanted to go and she was going off walking for a day with Joanna and getting back late, so I didn't bother. I went round and spent the evening at John Allworthy's."

The eager little girl, the female St. Michael, disappeared. Joy said crossly,

"What on earth do you keep going there for?"

"Because I like them. Because I'm learning things from them."

"That's just it! What sort of things?"

"Things I ought to have been taught at school."

"They've probably got them all wrong. They're ignorant and prejudiced!"

"Not as ignorant and prejudiced as we are."

She stared at him unhappily, her face falling into sullen lines.

"What do you mean? You've had a much wider experience. What do they know that you don't?"

He gathered himself together for an effort that he felt to be hopeless.

"Joy, we never learnt how other people live. Don't you know how many people in England are having less food than they need?"

"It's because they buy the wrong things with their money. They spend it stupidly on tinned stuff and all sorts of rubbish." Joy spoke in the confident tone of a child who knows the answer to that one.

"Only sometimes. It's because they haven't enough money, and food's too dear. And yet there's enough food in the world to feed everyone. Can't you see that there's something badly wrong with the whole thing? When we leave it like that, because we're comfortable and all right, we're just as bad as Mussolini grabbing at Abyssinia! And if this flares up into war and the whole of civilization goes to ruin, it will be the fault of people like us, the greedy people, the exploiters, the ones who won't share. Can't you *see* Joy? If you put a plate of buns on the table and Jack bagged the lot before Lin could get one because Lin was smaller, wouldn't you say fast enough that Jack ought to share?"

"I can't see that's got anything to do with it. I think you're getting morbid, Stephen. I wish you wouldn't go and see these people." Joy stood up. "I'm tired," she said abruptly, "I think I'll go to bed. You put Chick out, will you?"

Perhaps I am getting morbid, he thought, standing on the doorstep in the September night, while Chick disappeared between the fruit trees. Perhaps we all are. He looked up at the quiet sky, and shining stars. He saw that sky filled with whirring machines, the birds of death flying nearer with outspread wings. The air was cool against his cheek, the night smelled of earth and leaves, the first faint tang of autumn. A fury of impotence possessed his heart. So good a world misused and in danger, so many people who wished no one any harm at the mercy of those who did, and all of them at the mercy of circumstances as uncontrollable as tides. Not altogether uncontrollable, perhaps. It would need a stupendous effort to roll back the tide. Reluctantly he felt himself drawn to share in that effort with half a heart and a whole tradition against it. It was as though he saw them lined up on the other side of a barrier, his father regretful, Robert

172

laughing at him, Joy hurt and indignant, Hilary astonished and uncomprehending. Between him and them a gulf was beginning to stretch. On the side of the gulf to which he was crossing were people still strange to him and, he knew, mistrustful of him. He saw the group with whom he had been talking round the fire last night, old John and Grace Allworthy, kindly, tolerant of his ignorance, a little amused at him as at an inquiring child, the young man Tom Sutton, ardent and suspicious, Mary Welburn,—she alone of the group did not seem alien, she was not suspicious of him, her mind met his and he had been aware every time he turned to her of release and understanding. He supposed that it was because she had been so much away from Aire and was more used to different kinds of people. Chick reappeared, a round white blob moving between the tree trunks. Stephen whistled him in, locked and bolted the door, and went upstairs to bed.

The reverberations of those fruitless talks at Geneva, and of the drums that beat in Addis Ababa reached even to Beryl's kitchen, where Rosie, reading the evening paper which she persisted in using for a tablecloth, put down her cup of tea and exclaimed,

"Eh! The cheeky monkey!"

"Who?" asked Beryl, who had come in to remind Rosie to start the joint in good time.

"This 'ere Micky-Mouse—Mussolini!" Rosie replied with her mouth full.

"I bought you a nice tablecloth, Rosie!" Beryl said in mild protest.

"I don't want to make that mucky while Saturday. I've asked me sister over to tea. That'll be all right, won't it?"

"Yes. But you should have asked me first."

"I meant to, but it slipped me mind." Rosie took a large bite out of a piece of toast, drank a mouthful of tea, and swallowed both together with relish. She said,

"If there's a war, Fred says him and me will get married

quick in a Quaker chapel, and then 'e won't have to go."

"Are you sure?"

"Oh, yes. Quakers don't have to fight."

"Is Fred a Quaker?"

"Oh, no, 'e's Chapel, but it's all the same to him."

Not at all sure that it would be all the same to a Military Tribunal, Beryl abandoned the argument.

"I shall have to send me sister the money to come with," Rosie remarked. "Me brother-in-law's on strike."

"Is he? Why?"

"Eh, I don't know. They're all out at the colliery."

Rosie dismissed the affair with a shrug of her shoulders. Sometimes her brothers and brother-in-law were on strike and sometimes they were working. She knew the difference in cash, but had very little idea of why either happened, and her brothers had not much more. They were a cheerful, ignorant, happy-go-lucky family, wholly unaware of the forces that controlled their destinies. By some strange law of nature, they believed everything that was told to them by people as ignorant and happy-go-lucky as themselves, and disbelieved with stubborn obstinacy any information from those who had more knowledge and experience. Rosie glanced again at the paper, and remarked with finality,

"Aye, 'e's a bad lot, that Musso! I never did like Eyetalians, but a boy that works in Fred's place, 'e ses it's all the Jews."

To that summary of the political situation she clung, in spite of the explanations with which Tom Sutton bewildered her and Fred, and attempted to stir Olive's interest. Tom suffered badly in these days from his inability to make anyone understand. Most of his fellows in the workroom realized that Mussolini was being a nuisance, but as to why or how or with what purpose, they knew nothing and cared less. They were interested in their homes and wives and children, in the prospects of their local football teams, and in what won the three-thirty. They were good-natured with Tom, but a trifle bored. Thwarted and depressed, he was obliged to find an outlet by helping Harold Pearson to address and distribute leaflets. Harold, like most of his party, had a passionate faith in the printed word. When anything happened, they got out a new leaflet with a bright red or yellow back and an arresting slogan. Harold Pearson and half a dozen other youths and girls folded these and stuck them in envelopes, pushed them into letter-boxes, placed them on chairs at meetings, or stood patiently outside cinemas in the rain, thrusting them into the hands of passers-by, who crumpled and dropped them without a glance. Tom grew impatient over the work, realizing that in spite of the snowstorm of leaflets, Olive and Fred and Rosie and Herbert and Mabel had no more grasp of the political and economic situation than they had acquired from the casual remark of an ignorant friend, or a headline in the daily Press. Harold plodded on with unwearied patience, too happy in his self-devotion to mind about immediate results. His temperament was religious and he asked no more of life than an object to live for and constant opportunities to serve it. It was happiness to him to hurry back from the offices of Ward's Works in which he was a respectful and reliable clerk, to bolt down his tea and refuse a second cup or another slice of tea cake, saying to his mother, "I can't stop. I'm a steward to-night and it's an important meeting."

In the afternoon of October 1st, Mary went to an Amateur Mannequin Parade got up by a Ladies' Committee to raise funds for a Children's Home. The dresses were provided by one of the big shops in the town, which lent its restaurant for the parade. Between the small tables at which their friends and relatives drank coffee, the prosperous young women of the town moved slowly up and down, displaying with the new evening frocks and coats, their pleasant faces and pretty hair, their uncontrolled limbs and ingenuous eyes. They looked their best when they stood still, Mary thought, hastily jotting down names and colours. Of them all, Joy Harding interested her most. She appeared once as a bride in a severe dress of white satin, long in the sleeves and high at the throat. She must have looked like that seven years ago when she

175

came up the church to a waiting Stephen. She was lovely even when she walked across the room and stood stiff with self-consciousness before the eyes of her friends. What was she like? Was she a warm, loving livable-with human being? Or was she a spoilt beauty, or an undeveloped girl, or as cool and unapproachable as she looked, standing there like a white statue? Whatever she was like, Stephen had loved her, had lived with her for seven years, and had given her two sons. The thought gave Mary so fierce a pang that she was startled, and wondered, Am I falling in love with him? I'd better not, it would be no good. She had been aware lately of something between them, a feeling as though she was on his wavelength and he on hers. In the hot room, with its dazzling lights and shining colours, its smell of coffee and cigarettes, she found herself trembling, filled with an astonishing sweetness and pain that there was no time to examine. She bit her lip, and broke the point of her pencil as she scribbled down, Mrs. Stephen Harding, white satin wedding dress, classical lines.

She had asked for a word or two with the London buyer of the firm who had come down with the models for the afternoon, and she stood at the entrance to the room waiting to catch her, while the women who had been sitting at the tables, and a little later the mannequins, back in their own clothes, laughing and talking, passed by her and went out. Well dressed and prosperous, with agreeable voices and incurious eyes, they looked as though nothing had ever greatly disturbed them. Their world no doubt had its personal irritations and distastes, but on the whole it seemed good to them. Probably they thought or heard their husbands say that the news in the papers was bad, but they felt no menace to their own security. Mary caught snatches of their talk as they passed her.

"Oh, my dear, I liked the way it was made but definitely not that colour on the blue."

"Anyhow, I'm too fat for it!"

"Didn't Joy look lovely?"

"Was that the tall fair girl, the bride? Oh, was that one of the young Hardings' wives?"

"You know, I couldn't make the two middle hooks stay fastened, so I didn't want to turn my back, and that was why I had to edge along sideways."

One or two, who had met Mary at other functions, smiled at her or nodded. A pair of friends, young mothers, stood by her for a minute or two, the clothes already forgotten in a discussion of a more urgent preoccupation.

"Are you taking Pat to Billy's party? I'm taking Susan. Did you find the blouses were the right size for Pat?"

"Do you know what Pat said?" They drifted away together, happily absorbed in Pat and Susan.

The buyer, small, crisp, dark, with heavy dark eye-brows above shrewd eyes, came across to Mary.

"You're the reporter? Well, come along now and I'll show you the dresses before they're packed up."

When Mary came out into the street, an early dusk had begun and a shower of rain was falling. She stood for an instant in the doorway, her cheeks flushed from the heated rooms, her eyes smarting with cigarette smoke, her mind conscious of some deep disturbance below, but busy on the surface with the lines of dresses, with brilliant colours and soft stuffs. She lifted her face to the falling rain. Even the town air felt deliciously fresh after the shop that had been warmed all day by central heating. Traffic swept past her in the narrow street, cars and vans jammed one behind the other, pressing forward like an army, stealing a yard here, a foot there, constantly checked by the check at the robots ahead. In this hour of dusk which seemed like a pause, a moment of unreality between the day and the night, any town was beautiful. Mary looked at her watch and saw that she had an hour and a half before the big meeting of the Society for the Prevention of Cruelty to Animals which she was due to attend. Although she had not had an honest meal since breakfast, she had had enough cups of coffee, savoury sandwiches and petit fours at the Mannequin Parade to reduce her to the unsatisfactory condition of being unable to eat any more at the moment, but knowing that she would be very hungry before the end of the evening. She decided to turn in at the nearest cinema and sit there for an hour or until she could manage to feel hungry enough to go and get something to eat.

The cinema was fairly full, but she found a seat near the back of the circle and dropped into it, glad to sit down somewhere where there was nothing that she need notice or remember and no one she need speak to. It was the musical interlude and the organ was playing, filling with a mournful, sugary sound the whole great building, too much decorated, too begilded, too warm. Still, it was a world in which you could vanish, in which you could lose yourself. Mary sat back and closed her smarting eyelids.

After dreaming for a minute, she opened her eyes to find that the Pathé Gazette had begun. On the screen before her unrolled a wild and desolate country, over which tanks were moving escorted by aeroplanes. The mechanical voice which accompanied the film elaborated, "Mussolini's Italian forces are now moving up to the Abyssinian frontier." More terrible than any picture of a marching army was that grim picture of the great machines moving through the air and across the barren ground to make war on human flesh. Mary sat upright, awake and tingling in every nerve. The tanks gave way to a stream of men in uniform, marching along a stony road over the shoulder of a mountain. The voice, like a chorus commenting on destiny, went on with its explanations. "The first Army Corps commanded by Marshall Badoglio *en route* for the Ethiopian frontier. They left——" The voice broke off suddenly, the marching men came forward out of the picture, the aeroplanes flying above them, the rocky, mountainous country unfolding on either side.

Another voice, speaking through a megaphone, interrupted on a more human note, "A message has just been sent round from the office of the *Yorkshire Guardian* to say that news has been received that the first division of the Italian Army has to-day crossed over the frontier into Abyssinia. The war has begun."

The picture on the screen changed to the Bay of Naples, and the mechanical voice of the commentator resumed,

"Italian troops embarking at Naples for the voyage to Ethiopia."

178

Before the eyes of the crowded cinema, young men in uniform laden with heavy packs jostled one another on the quay. Their faces were lively, eager, but one boy had his arms round the neck of an old woman. Another, a handsome dark lad, was turning away from a girl who carried a baby, and his face was distorted with weeping. They crossed the gangway on to the ship, and some indignant opponent of Mussolini on the ground floor of the cinema hissed them fiercely.

Mary sat with her hands locked together and tears running down her cheeks. These were not the enemy, these young men going to war. Hatred itself was the enemy, hatred, as always, by greed out of vanity, once more victorious, once more successfully loosed in Europe. It had all been in vain, the shattering lessons of the last war, the birth of the League of Nations, the growing desire for peace. Once again the sane, ordinary man who hated nobody and wanted to get on with his job was to be trapped by powerful forces, misled by his own generosity and idealism and broken on the wheel.

The Pathé Gazette had come to an end, and shots of the next week's film were being shown. The screen, blurred by tears, danced before Mary's eyes. She could not stay for any more. She stumbled out of her seat and up the steps, crossed the brightly lit foyer, indifferent to the curious glances of the attendants in fantastic livery, and found herself in the street.

The shower was over. The wet street shone like a black river, and on its brink the news-vendors displayed their placards and shouted out, "War begins in Abyssinia. Italian Army crosses the frontier." Mary bought an evening paper and walked along the pavement. At the corner of Highgate and Market Street she ran into Stephen Harding.

He said to her, "Hulloa! You've heard? They've gone into Abyssinia!"

She said, "I know. I've just heard it announced in the cinema."

They moved without thinking into the doorway of a jeweller's shop, a recess flanked on either side by lit windows, bright with cases of silver. In the light he saw her face pale and marked by tears. He had never before seen her distressed. One of those moments flared between them when life achieves an extraordinary simplification. It did not matter who they were or what they were, and saying what they felt was as easy as breathing. He said,

"Don't cry, Mary!"

"No, it was stupid. But I saw them all on the pictures starting off for the war. Young ones with wives and babies! Sometimes everything we do seems no good!"

"It's a bad world, but people like you make it better."

The words filled her with a stinging joy, although she thought that he hardly knew he had said them. He went on, almost as though speaking to himself,

"It seems to me this is the beginning. It won't be possible to be indifferent or neutral any longer. This has happened because we've all let things drift for so long. I've been thinking and reading and turning things over. I expect I shall have to come in on your side."

She thought of his wife and family, his work and friends, of what might happen, not now in these quiet prosperous times, when stresses were light and half hidden, but in the times to come.

"Aren't you glad?"

"Yes, of course I'm glad." Yes, oh yes, Stephen, I'm glad, but I am afraid for you, you'll be hurt by both sides, you'll be unhappy, your life will have to be broken up and made again. I'm afraid for myself, too, because of something beginning between us. But yes, I'm glad because you are too good for anything else, and because you will be nearer to me.

They stood for one moment staring at one another in the narrow passage between the lit windows. Footsteps hurried by them on the pavement, the newspaper placards flapped in the breeze. Above the noise of the traffic and of passing feet the hoarse voices of the newspaper sellers bawled out their tidings.

"Eyetalians cross the Abyssinian frontier. War begins."

PART II

"If there are two parties, a man ought to adhere to that which he disliketh least. For whilst he doth not list himself in one or the other party, he is looked upon as such a straggler that he is fallen upon by both."

Marquess of Halifax.

LATE ON A November afternoon, Leslie Ward drove his car out of the entrance to the University playing fields, which covered a great stretch of bare ground on to the northern outskirts of the city. He had been playing football, and, as usual, playing rather badly, but he was so happy nowadays that he did not mind. He only felt lively and alert from air and exercise, very hungry, and much elated at the prospect of his evening. As he curved from the narrow lane into the by-pass road, he trod on the accelerator and began to sing. He swooped into a hollow already filled with mist, climbed the opposite slope as though climbing out of a steam bath, and saw ahead of him the lights of the town. Until six weeks ago he had hated and loathed every stone of it and longed to live somewhere else. He had felt the city and especially Grey Gables, like heavy weights on his head. Now Grey Gables had receded into the background of his life, it was a hotel for bed and breakfast, and Aire had become the most interesting city in the world because it held his friends.

On the outskirts of the town, he stopped the car before a row of new, raw-looking shops, and bought a copy of a woman's magazine, and a tin of Edinburgh rock. Never before in his life had he felt so grateful to his father for giving him a generous allowance. He had never enjoyed spending it until this term, when he discovered the rapture and delight of being able to give small presents and treats to Angus and Grizel and the babies. At first he had proffered seats at the pictures and celluloid ducks with extraordinary diffidence. He was acutely self-conscious about money. He had revolted so fiercely against commercial values that he expected any-one whom he could respect to despise him for being rich. He soon realized with incredulous joy that Angus and Grizel did not despise him nor reject his offerings. He was their friend and they shared what they had with him, and accepted a share of his good things. Since they were really not con-cerned with money standards, the fact that Leslie's personal allowance was only fifty pounds less than the salary from the University on which Angus kept a wife and two children did not enter into their estimate of Leslie. Angus thought of him as a promising pupil, and they both thought of him as a dear boy, their great friend.

Leslie drew up his car at their gate. They lived in a solid, old-fashioned terrace house, which was too large for them, and too tall, and had basement kitchens, and was therefore cheap. It stood back from the road at the end of a narrow garden. There was room for the pram to stand on the strip of lawn in summer, and for a rug on which thin Bunny and fat Biddy could roll in minute bathing dresses. This evening the laurel bushes at the end of the grass were dank and heavy with mist, the stones of the path were wet and slippery, and the front of the house was dark. Leslie was not daunted. He sped up the path, lifted the old-fashioned knocker and rapped on the door. The bell, he saw, was still broken. He and Angus had meant to mend it on Tuesday, but had become absorbed in a discussion and had forgotten about it. There was no answer to his knock. He opened the door and walked in.

He switched on the hall light, and put his parcels down on the table, beside a bowl of autumn berries and late red leaves. He looked at their rusty colours and sighed with happiness, drawing a deep breath of the friendly air. From upstairs Grizel's voice said,

"Is that you, Leslie?"

"Yes. Good evening!"

"Good evening! Angus isn't in yet. He won't be long. I've just got Biddy in the bath. Oh, Leslie! Would you mind going in to the kitchen and saving Bunny's milk before it boils over? I was hoping Angus would be coming. My hands are all wet. Could you be a lamb and pour it into the mug and take it upstairs to him?"

"Rather!"

Leslie, walking on air, went into the kitchen. His heart was filled with happiness. He who had had no great friends at school, who had no great friends at home, now knew these enchanting people so well that he could walk into their house, and they shouted at him from upstairs to go and take the milk off in the kitchen. He turned on the kitchen light. The pan was on the electric ring, and the milk was just rising to the top in a foam of bubbles. Leslie retrieved it and poured it into the mug which stood on a tray beside two sponge fingers on a small plate. Leslie switched off the electric ring, put some coal on the fire, hung up a fallen tea-cloth on the rack, and carried the tray carefully upstairs.

Bunny, two and a half years old, slept in a room by himself, and was sitting up in bed in a brown dressing-gown bestrewn with white rabbits. He was a small copy of Angus, narrow pale face, grey eyes and shock of ruffled, light brown hair. He held out his arms to Leslie with a shout of "Juggins!" This was his name for Leslie because he had once heard his mother call him a juggins, when Leslie, having come to tea, had demurred about staying to supper. Bunny had thought this exquisitely funny. Leslie thrilled with joy every time he heard the friendly insult repeated. He had always believed himself to be a juggins, and to be called it in that way had taken the sting out of the belief. His secret diffidence and self-distrust had become a joke in this house, the password of a baby's affection. He smiled, said, "Yes, it's Juggins come with your supper," and sat down on the bed.

Leslie's own family would have been astonished to watch the tenderness and efficiency with which he restrained Bunny from the milk until it was cool enough, and then administered milk and biscuits, wiped the child's mouth and tucked him up in bed. In one brief term at the University, not yet finished, Leslie's education had advanced by leaps and bounds, and not only in English.

"Did you come in your car?" Bunny asked, lying down obediently.

"Yes, it's at the gate now."

"Will it be cold?"

"I don't think so. I've put the muff down and covered its nose with a rug."

"What will it have for supper?"

"It won't want any supper. It had a very good tea this afternoon, a lot of petrol and some oil and a long drink of water."

"Did it say, 'I've finished, please may I get down, thank you'?"

"No! It forgot! And the man at the garage who put in the petrol said, 'What have you forgotten?'"

"Did he?" The small voice in the dark was ecstatic, "And what did it do then?"

"It backfired—like that—*Bang!* because it was so surprised. And then it said, 'Please may I get down, thank you?' and I drove it out of the yard."

"Shall I go in your car again one day?"

"Of course you will. Any day."

"Which is 'anyday'?"

"The first day that Mummie says you may."

"To-morrow or for ever and ever?"

"We'll see. Soon, anyhow."

Grizel, who had come softly in during this conversation, thought, Leslie is a darling! She said, "I think that's Angus. Do run down and ask him to slip round for a loaf of brown bread before he takes his coat off. I've let us run short."

"I'll go!" Leslie said eagerly. "Angus will be tired."

"Well, I haven't got any money except a ten shilling note. I hoped Angus would have."

"I've got lots!" Six weeks ago he would have been covered with confusion at hearing himself make such a statement. Even now he felt a prick of discomfort, but Grizel only said, "Oh, good! then we can settle up afterwards. Will you buy to-day's—a brown cob, if you really don't mind going?"

Leslie grinned and nodded and flew downstairs as if he were a King's messenger entrusted with an important message. First the milk, and then the bread! He was busy, active, useful, a part of their household! His spirits were so high that while he was buying the bread in the shop, he burst into exuberant talk about the weather and the approach of Christmas. An elderly woman waiting her turn smiled at him with a generous pleasure in his youth and high spirits. He saw the look and felt it like an accolade; he, Leslie Ward, was young, gay, had friends, was someone whom elderly women in shops smiled upon and envied. He almost danced out into the street.

When he got back to Oak Lea, Angus had arrived, and was cooking sausages on the grill while Grizel made coffee. The two delicious smells combined in the warm kitchen. Angus looked up with his sweet, slow smile. Leslie did not know whether it was Grizel or Angus or the children that he loved most. He was in love with the whole house, with its warmth and friendliness and ease, with its casual ways and indifference to appearances.

"Let me do those, Angus!" he said, eager as a puppy to show good will.

"Do some toasted cheese," Grizel suggested. "It's a very scratch supper to-night, not a well-balanced meal. We shall all have indigestion, but never mind."

They ate their supper at the kitchen table, and sat afterwards, replete and content, smoking cigarettes in the warm firelight. They talked idly or were quiet.

"Good game, Leslie?"

"I played abominably. It was rather fun, though."

"What was your committee-meeting like, Angus?"

"Oh, long and dull and everybody very pompous. I went to sleep."

Grizel began to laugh. "I did a dreadful thing this morning. Do you know what I did?"

"What?"

"You know I promised I'd lend Naomi that new magazine that Clive brought, *Red Morning*, the very highbrow English-Russian one printed on a private press? I was rather pleased about it, because I could see that she thought more of me the other night for having a copy. For a minute she almost thought I was intelligent. And I put it in my basket and I just pushed *Woman at Home* in, too, because I thought I might want to buy some wool for the jumper in it, and I was too lazy to tear the page out. And I am quite sure I put the other one in as well, but it was a most extraordinary thing, when I got to their house, it had dropped out somehow, and there was nothing but a three months old copy of *Woman at Home*. I'm sure Naomi thought I'd never had *Red Morning*!"

Angus laughed. "Poor Naomi!"

"Have you come across them, Leslie?"

"Mr. Unwin spoke to me about joining the University Labour Club."

"Well, don't."

"I haven't yet. I used to think about politics a good bit my last year at school, but I haven't bothered lately. Why did you say, 'don't.' "

"Because it's a waste of time. You listen to illiterate speakers trotting out clichés by the score." [1]

"What are you, Angus? About politics, I mean?"

"God knows! I should think a Liberal if I'm anything. But I can't do with the really political mind. Whatever colour it is, it seems to me like a child's chemistry outfit. It makes a few bad smells and small explosions and that's all."

Leslie laughed. Politics were remote and he was ready to laugh at anything. He looked at his two companions, at Angus leaning back in his tilted chair and blowing smoke rings, at Grizel with her elbows on the table, her freckled chin cupped in her hands and the smooth curtains of brown hair swinging forward against her cheeks. A spontaneous cry broke from him.

"It's such fun! It's so lovely to be here with you two!"

Grizel smiled warmly at his happy face, but Angus recoiled a trifle from the naïve and unconcealed emotion.

"It won't be lovely in a minute," he said, "when we start washing up!" Then seeing a shade on the brightness of Leslie's face, he added, "The more you come, the more we like it, don't we, Grizel?"

Leslie was still in a glow from the evening when he drove home. He turned in at the gates of Grey Gables as the clock struck twelve. He garaged his car, locked the garage and came round to the front door, fumbling for his latch key. The door was unlocked, and as he pushed it open, Marjorie called to him in a low voice from the drawing-room.

"Les! Is that you? I've just come in. I left it open for you. There are some sandwiches in here. Come in."

Leslie locked the front door and went into the drawing-room. Marjorie was sitting on the floor by the fire, her coat thrown back, her dark chestnut curls ruffled above a face that had lost a good deal of its discontent.

"Good evening?" Leslie said amiably.

"Yes, rather. I saw Mary."

Leslie knew that for Marjorie nowadays that made a good evening. She, like he, was preoccupied with an entrancing friendship. He sympathized and yet was faintly irritated. He liked Mary, he was glad that Marjorie was enjoying herself and was so much better tempered, but there was a discomfort in his mind, a small irritable spot near this alliance of Marjorie with Mary. He hardly ever thought about Mark Forrester nowadays, and did not know that he felt a submerged twinge of shame because Marjorie had fought and won her battle and he had given in at the first gunshot. Marjorie had accepted Mary's invitations in flat disobedience, had wept, sulked and said that she would go nowhere and do nothing unless she might have Mary to the house. After an unnecessary expenditure of nervous energy and enough friction to justify a bankruptcy or a divorce, she won her point. Mary came sometimes, knowing that the Ward parents did not want her, but knowing, too, the fight that Marjorie had made for her. There was very little about Marjorie that Mary did not know by this time. The mere relief of pouring out unreserved confidence had sweetened Marjorie's temper, lifted the corners of her mouth and made her several shades prettier.

She pushed the sandwiches across to Leslie.

"I've had my share. You finish them. I'm going to begin helping at a Babies Welcome next week. Down in South Albeck. It's a very poor one, short of help."

"Will you like that?"

"I don't know. I can't just do nothing, can I?"

"What do Mum and Dad say about it?"

"Mum wanted me to help at the Oaktown one where the Bradley girls go and do jobs, but she doesn't really mind because helping with charities is all right. Nice girls do it. It gets them into things. I suppose Dad doesn't mind or he'd have told her to tell me not to."

189

Leslie noticed the new detachment in her tone. He said shyly,

"Marjorie! Do you talk to Mary about things at home, Mum and Dad and so on?"

"Yes, I talk to her about everything. Don't you to the Grants?"

"No, not about Mum and Dad. I—I don't think I could. I shouldn't feel it was decent!"

"I felt a bit like that at first,—but you know, Leslie, I don't believe I can manage to stand up to Dad unless I talk things over with somebody."

"But do you want to stand up to him? What do you want to stand up to him about? He's very good to you. He likes you much better than me. He's always giving you things."

"I know. He's very generous to us about money and anything we want. But he expects us to do exactly as he says about everything. I don't want to stand up to him now, except about being friends with Mary and they're getting used to that, but I want to be able to. I might have to any day. And I've got different ideas now about the kind of person I want to be. I don't just want to be rich and social and go to the right parties."

"What kind of person do you want to be."

Marjorie's ingenuous face flushed and softened. She said, "Like Mary! I couldn't, of course, but as near as I can. Oh, Leslie! She's only a few years older than me, but just think what she's done already! She's worked so hard and seen so much and done so much, she's so brave! And she's so much alive! Do you know, Leslie, I've never really cared much about poetry before, of course we did it at school, but I didn't like it much, but now I've found lots of bits that are just like Mary! I've got a book and written some out, perhaps I'll show you. There's one bit in a poem by G. K. Chesterton,

> 'Brave as a blast of trumpets for the fray,
> Pure as white lilies in a watery place,'

I think that's just like her! Do you see what I mean?"

Leslie did not. He thought that Mary was a nice person, quite easy to get on with, she did not make him feel shy, and she was intelligent, but as for trumpets and lilies, he did not associate them with her. She was not even what he called pretty, just nice looking. But he was touched by Marjorie's eager, flushed face and by her genuine feeling. He said warmly,

"I think she's very nice, awfully nice, Marjorie. I'm glad you've got somebody. It makes such a difference! We had such fun this evening! We cooked sausages and I made toasted cheese, and then we washed up, and afterwards we all sat round the kitchen fire and roasted chestnuts and Angus read poetry aloud. And Biddy woke up and cried, and Grizel brought her down for a bit, rolled up in a blanket." He stopped. He had no words to express the compound delights of that evening, the company, the firelight, the poetry, the Autumn bonfire taste of hot chestnuts, the sight of Biddy's downy head and exquisite baby cheek against Grizel's shoulder. He said, "Every time I go there I feel how *right* they are, how they know how to live. They're aristocrats, Marjorie. I don't mean in any snobbish sense, but really. They live richly, they have royal lives."

Marjorie smiled at him kindly. What nonsense he was talking! The Grants were nice people, rather shy and quiet when they came to dinner, and Angus used too long words when he did talk, and Grizel was not really pretty, though she had a pleasant face. Leslie was such a boy! But it was a good thing that he was happy! She had never bothered about Leslie very much as they grew up, but Mary, in discussing her home and family with her, always took it for granted that she must think a good deal about her brother and wanted him to be happy, so she was beginning to take him more closely into the pattern of her life.

She yawned and pulled her coat round her.

"We'd better go to bed, I suppose." She looked down at Leslie, who sprawled on the rug, contented, and tired, smoking a last cigarette.

"Look here, Leslie! We're grown up and beginning to want things outside our own family, different things, let's have a pact. I'll stand by you always, about your friends and your doings, if you'll stand by me?"

"All right, only I don't need it about the Grants. Mum and Dad like me to be friends with them. They're very well connected and all that tosh. Mum found out all about them. And you know she likes the babies. I don't think she and Dad want to go against us." He had thought much more kindly of his parents since a very successful Sunday tea-party at which his mother had made much of Bunny and Biddy, after which his father had dropped a dry, "I like your new friends, Leslie. I think their landlord is doing them over that kitchen range. Can't expect scholars to be up to these things. I'll have it looked into for them."

Marjorie, who had fought for her friend and talked things out more freely, saw further than Leslie.

"Yes, you're all right now, but you may want to do things and know people that Dad doesn't want, and so may I. And we must stick together, because we're the same generation."

"All right, of course we will. Good night, old Marjorie!"

"Good night, Leslie, dear." Marjorie bent down and kissed him, and suddenly he did what he had not done since he went away to school. He put his arms round her and they hugged one another heartily.

"It's fun being grown up, isn't it?"

"It's a relief!" Leslie admitted.

"Don't forget the lights, dear!"

"No. Right you are. Good night."

"Good night."

Alone for the moment in the bedroom, Mary twisted up her thick knot of brown hair, and pulled the soft waves forward on either side above her ears. It was one of the mornings when she looked plain, and the bridesmaid's dress lying across her bed would not improve matters. Odd clothes and odd colours became her, but this was a pretty dress without character. The soft blue velvet with its blue and mauve ribbons looked as though it could have no connection with her, or with the November morning, which was still muffled in fog. A red ball of sun hung above the housetops, but had not been strong enough to break through. In the main road at the end of Birchgrove Terrace the tram bells were ringing, and trams towered out of the fog like lighted ships, moving slowly. It was an unreal day, a day that reduced reality to people and objects within ten yards, and made everything beyond that radius an improbable world.

That was what it had felt like yesterday evening when she and Stephen were walking to the tram. She had gone round to Aunt Grace late with an urgent message about the wedding arrangements, and had found him there. There had been fog ever since tea-time, but it thickened while they were in the house, and when they left together, Aunt Grace in the lighted doorway was hidden from them by the time they opened the gate of the small front garden and stepped into the road. Side by side they walked down the pavement of Clement's Lane, cut off from everything else in the world but each other. Mary mentioned the wedding to-morrow, Stephen spoke once of some point that he had been discussing with the Allworthys that evening. Both conversations died unregretted. Their footsteps were the only sound in the street. Feeling rose and quivered between them, making a warmth and radiance in the cold world. Mary's tram, a different one from his, loomed up out of a bank of fog as soon as they reached the stop. He said, "Are you sure you'll be all right the other end?" She assured him that it was only a few yards from the tram to her door, and laughed a little, thinking how many late and lonely journeys she had made without escort. She saw his face for a moment, smiling and his hand waving to her, before her tram jolted her away and the fog swallowed him. She had lain awake for a long time after Doris had stopped turning over and was peacefully asleep, reliving the moment. This morning she had woken up with the glow of it in her veins although common sense moved her to wonder if, except in her own imagination, there had been a moment at all.

Doris came back from the bathroom, her old dressing-gown huddled round the new underclothes of soft satin and lace which she had made herself with so much care. She looked chilled and pale, her blue eyes piteous.

"Oh, Mary! I did hope it would clear! If only this fog would go and the sun come out I should feel different!"

"The fog's rather picturesque and it isn't really thick enough to stop anyone getting there. I expect it's quite clear outside the town."

"It makes everything look so dirty!" Doris sniffed miserably. "I believe I'm starting a cold!"

"You can't! Not on your wedding day. I'll get you a cup of hot tea and you can have an aspirin with it. I'll call out to Mrs. Renton and ask her to make one."

Doris picked up the comb and began to comb out the short strands of silky fair hair, letting them curl back again over her fingers. It was such pretty hair, and curled so easily and becomingly into place that she could not help feeling better. Iris at her wedding had to have the hairdresser directly after breakfast and then hardly dared move all morning for fear of disturbing his work, but Doris knew that at any time with a comb and five minutes she could make her hair look lovely. It would shine like gold through the veil, and her dress was beautiful. It was going to be quite an important wedding with all the Yorkshire team there and photographers from the paper and everything! And the house was ready and everything in it beautiful! She was a lucky girl, a very lucky girl, Doris told herself firmly. If only she did not feel so cold and discouraged, if only she could grasp that this really was her wedding-day! That all-important, all-exciting day seemed to be slipping past her, hidden in fog. She did not feel excited, or even very nervous, she just felt blank. She could not imagine going up the church nor the lunch at the hotel, nor changing into her going-away things, not even into the lovely fur coat that Frank was giving her for a wedding-present. Still less could she imagine going away with Frank in the car, and getting out of it at another hotel, going up to a bedroom which would be his and hers. She just felt at the moment as though she had no feelings, only small misgivings about various details.

Mary came back with two cups of tea.

"Here you are. You'll feel warmer when you've drunk it."

"I do wish Aunt Grace hadn't got that new red hat, Mary! I wish she would have had something quieter—a nice navy!"

Mary laughed, "Aunt Grace always must have a red hat for a party. It wouldn't be a party if she didn't."

"I hope Uncle John won't go on too long if he has to make a speech! When he gets remembering things——" Doris sighed. Mary was the only one of her relations whom she felt that she could trust in the company of Frank's friends, who seemed to her alarmingly sophisticated.

Mary tried to reassure her. Doris that morning was like her mother, a bottomless pit into which you could drop any amount of comfort and reassurance without effect. She cheered up a little when Mary twitched the sheets of tissue paper from the wedding-dress on the bed. The supple folds of satin, faintly tinged with pink, gleamed in the electric light.

"It's lovely, isn't it, Mary? And do you know, another present came last night from the first cricket club where Frank was groundsman for a bit? They sent a beautiful cake-dish—real nice china, it is. I am lucky, aren't I?"

Mary's heart cried out, you are, you are, but not because of wedding-dresses and cake-stands!

Doris slid the wedding-dress over her head. Her yellow curls came up through its folds like the heart of a water-lily.

"I can't imagine taking this off again when it's over! It will seem so funny when I'm Mrs. Varley and Frank and I go away together! It was ever so kind of Marjorie Ward to send me that lovely hand-bag!" Doris had the dress on and had looked at herself in the glass, her spirits were rising. "I'm glad she's coming to the wedding." She added naïvely, "It seems odd she should be a great friend of yours when Uncle John is just a workman in her father's works!"

"Yes! If we ever do have to be sorted into classes in England, especially in the West Riding of Yorkshire, it's going to be pretty difficult!"

Doris turned from the glass, smiling.

"Do I look nice, Mary?"

"Oh, my darling, you do! You look lovely! I daren't hug you very much for fear of crushing you!"

"I'm glad we've always been friends. We've never quarrelled

like some sisters do! I shall often see you! We shall always
be friends, shan't we?"

"Of course we shall."

"I wish I wasn't leaving you and Mother and Arthur!
I'm not going far away, anyhow!"

"No, of course you're not!"

"I believe that's Aunt Grace and Uncle John coming!
You'd better go down, Mary, and bring her up here, but come
back quickly and help me with the veil and wreath. The car
for you will be here in a minute! I do hope Mother will be
able to get into the chair all right the other end. Arthur's so
nervous about helping her, but Aunt Grace will be there."

Mary pulled the blue velvet cap to the right angle on
her brown hair, and ran downstairs.

Marjorie Ward, standing among the bride's friends, watched
the procession go up the church with no eyes for the bride.
Mary looks lovely! It's the way her cheek joins her neck and
her head is set on her shoulders behind! No it isn't, it's everything, it's her! I don't know how people can say the sister's
prettier. She is pretty, of course, but she's got such a silly
face compared to Mary! I'm so glad they asked me to the
wedding! To be at the wedding, Marjorie felt, stamped her
finally as one of Mary's great friends, a privilege which was
well worth the fuss that there had been at home because she
had refused a luncheon party to which she and her mother
had been invited for the same day. Marjorie was beginning to
feel a certain relish in opposition. So far, she had only had to
oppose her mother, and her father's opinions as delivered by
her. She had not directly withstood her father. Ward seldom
gave orders to his daughter. That department was his wife's,
and he only kept an eye on it to see that his wishes were being
carried out. It was unlucky that Marjorie, the bolder of the
two children, had the less formidable parent to contend with.

This is the church, Marjorie thought, where Leslie's curate
friend came from. Well, he's much happier with the Grants
and nobody minds about them at home, so perhaps it was a

good thing he dropped him. That was the evening Mary came to supper the first time! She glanced up the aisle to see if Leslie's Mr. Forrester, connected with so interesting an occasion, was anywhere about, but Doris's fears had not been realized, Canon Halliday was taking the service. His dignified figure and benevolent face were visible between the slender, white-veiled Doris, and Frank's straight shoulders. His voice, rich, sonorous, full of well-being, was exhorting them about their Christian life together. Shall I have a wedding, Marjorie wondered. Some day, perhaps. At the moment the prospect did not excite her. She thought, Mary will miss Doris terribly! She'll be alone in the house with her cross old mother and that young brother who never speaks. She resolved to make it her business to comfort Mary and take her sister's place to her. At the thought of being able to supply Mary's needs, an extraordinary tender pleasure flooded all her being. Aunt Grace, who stood like a sentry by her sister's wheeled chair, happened to turn her head, and saw the happy, glowing face. She thought, that lass of Ward's is a real bonnie lass and a good girl. I'm glad she's taken to Mary.

She turned her head again and from under the brim of the scarlet hat, which made a spot of colour in the foggy church, she inspected "the other side." Frank's parents, his father, rather like him, but shorter and broader, his mother in dark brown, portly and kind. A married sister with her husband who was something in business in Birmingham. The famous figures of the Yorkshire County team with their wives and families. Their presence had brought an enormous number of small boys, some with cameras, to join the regular spectators outside, the women with babies in perambulators who came to every interesting wedding and funeral. "The other side" looked prosperous and confident. By contrast Doris's party, her family, one or two friends out of the office, a neighbour or two and a few friends of her uncle's, looked shabbier and less solid.

Grace's eye moved to the bride, and to her own husband's thin, light figure and bald head beside her. My old man! What a wedding theirs had been, without a penny to spare for anything, with both families reluctant and uneasy that their chief bread-winner should take on other obligations! She recalled out of the past the image of John as she had first seen him at a performance of the "Messiah" in the Hasty Road Chapel down by Water Lane. She had been singing in the chorus, and loving it. She had a good, true voice and enjoyed using it in company. And after the performance they had all gone round to tea in the schoolroom, and there she had seen a thin, pale young man with ardent eyes and a sweet, crooked smile. He never came to chapel as a rule, he was an Agnostic he explained afterwards, but a great friend of his, one of his pals in the Movement, was singing the tenor solos and he had come loyally to support him. A few weeks later, it seemed to Grace and even to the Agnostic John that Providence had brought him. Two years they had kept company, and one year they had been engaged, and forty-five years they had been married, and I don't think I've had a cross word from him all that time, Grace reflected. He had continued to be an Agnostic, and she all her life had been to chapel, each going their own way and letting the other be. But Chapel or Agnostic, Grace had no doubts in her own mind as to which was the better of the two.

My old man is a saint if ever there was one! That's one of the things I've got against these young Communists, and Russia, too, the way they look at marriage! As if it could ever be the same, chopping and changing and doing whatever you like when you feel like it! We shall never take to those ways in England! But there isn't many as happy all their married lives as me and my old man have been! Tears came into her bright brown eyes, but she wiped them away as Emily leaned forward in her chair, whispering, "They're going into the vestry."

A few minutes later, Doris came down the aisle with her veil thrown back, similing, happy and lovely. Frank was a cheerful and unembarrassed bridegroom. He had too often walked out to bat before a ring of spectators to look sheepish when walking down a church at his wedding. A wave of sympathetic pleasure and goodwill followed the pair down the nave.

Mary as she came behind, feeling cold in her thin velvet,

aware of the acrid smell of her pink chrysanthemums penetrating the smell of fog, thought, all this would be so lovely
if I could have it with Stephen, but someone else has had it
with him. She smiled, as she passed, at Marjorie Ward, whose
face lit up in response with a smile so wide and beaming that
it stuck, and she could feel herself still grinning idiotically
after the bridal procession had reached the porch.

At the lunch in the hotel, at which everyone was very
hungry, cheerful and facetious, Mary found herself sitting
next to the best man, Frank's great friend, Huddleston, the
slow bowler who had got into the Yorkshire team in the same
summer. He was a dark, shy, silent young man, nearly as
good at rugby football as he was at cricket. He spent his time
in the winter giving football coaching at various boys' schools.
Frank in the winter travelled successfully and efficiently for
a firm of sports outfitters, and the two had a plan of setting
up a sports shop together when they should be too old for
first-class cricket. Huddleston and Mary had met several
times before and got on quite well. Her left hand neighbour
was Frank's brother-in-law from Birmingham of whom she
knew only that his name was Warburton, that he was in
business of some kind and said to be doing very well. He
seemed kindly, cheerful and energetic, and had a look in his
eye which suggested that he would in a few minutes begin
to tell her funny stories.

"They tell me you're on a newspaper, Miss Welburn," he
said.

"Yes, the *Yorkshire Guardian*."

"Well, now, I should think that must be an interesting job,
very interesting! When I lived in London I had a friend who
was a reporter on one of the evening papers. You wouldn't
believe some of the things he saw and heard about! I used to
enjoy a good talk with him, but since we came to Birmingham,
I haven't seen him."

"Have you been in Birmingham long?"

"Only eighteen months. I used to be in the London office,

199

you see, but I was moved down to the Birmingham branch."

"Do you like it better, or were you sorry to leave London?"

Mr. Warburton considered judicially.

"I hope you won't misunderstand me, Miss Welburn, if I say that if I have freedom in my love and in my soul I am free, it's all the same to me where I live. And Birmingham's a fine city. Now Frank's life, that's what I shouldn't like! Always moving about from one place to another, always in the train and on the go. I'm glad he's getting married and getting a house of his own, somewhere of his own to come back to, anyhow. And your sister looks a dear little girl and I'm sure she's as good as she's pretty, and they'll be very happy together."

"Do you mind travelling about so much?" Mary asked Huddleston, who replied, "No, I don't notice it now. I've got used to it."

"That's the really astonishing thing about life," agreed the loquacious Mr. Warburton. "The way you get used to things. Now take these two getting married here, Frank and your sister. I've no doubt they think at the moment that being married is the most wonderful thing in the world. I expect they're thrilled to death at the thought of spending years together, and terrified, simply terrified, I know I was! But in a year or two they'll have got used to it. It's got to be like that, you see, you've got to feel excited about a thing at the beginning to make you go in for it, and then before you know, you are in it, and it's part of your ordinary life. Now take this war in Abyssinia. When it began we were all in a flat spin about it and expecting to fight Italy at any moment, and now we just look in the morning paper to see how it's getting on, and don't eat gorgonzola—which is a loss to me, mind you. I was very fond of a nice bit of gorgonzola—but there it is, you see. We've got used to it."

Huddleston, who had to propose the health of the bride and bridegroom, was nervously scribbling on the back of his menu. Naturally a serious young man, he realized that the occasion demanded humour. While he was shaving that morning, he had thought of saying that Frank, who had caught so many people in the long-field, had himself been

200

caught at last. While he was driving in to pick up Frank, he had added to this, "caught by such fair hands," and had been pleased with the idea, but now a sudden cold doubt troubled him. Was it in quite good taste? Could he say something about old Frank and his bride going in to bat together and having a long innings and both retiring not out? This second inspiration seemed better, but the moment for the speech was approaching, and in the flurry of his nerves, he had not time to arrange his words. His knees felt weak and the wedding lunch that he had eaten was a solid lump in the middle of his body. He felt as if he were going in last to try and keep his end up while someone else made ten. He could not bat, he hated the very sight of a bat just as he loved the look of a clean, new red ball that would be so subtle and docile in his big hand, but he would rather go in to bat any day than make a speech! He saw somebody making a sign to him, and stumbled up. He glanced along the table, saw Doris's pretty fair face turned to him with the white veil floating back from her fair curls, saw Frank grinning at him, saw a scarlet hat, a couple of his fellow crickets looking amused, saw a confused vision of white tablecloth, carnations, champagne glasses, untidy napkins bunched by coffee cups. He took a deep breath and said in a voice that he himself had never heard before, "Ladies and Gentlemen."

Mary had been given the day off, but had to go in the evening to report the Charity Ball. She got high tea ready for her mother and Arthur. The house seemed empty and lonely without Doris. She felt irritable, tired and rather sick. Everything looked dingy from the day's fog, her mother was tired and in pain, Arthur yawned and drifted in and out, meaning to help her, but getting in her way. She thought that she still knew so little of Arthur. He was shy and quiet, he never talked about his friends or doings at school. He seemed to want to keep his two worlds separate. It was a feeling which she understood and respected, but she wished that she could really make friends with him. He hung about in the kitchen while she was cooking in a way that suggested he wanted company and consolation but that he did not really want hers. Probably he felt keenly the loss of Doris, the pretty, kind sister who had always lived at home with him. Mary reproached herself for selfishness, and resolved to give more time to him. After all, it was a dull home for a boy, an invalid mother, a sister out all day. It would not be surprising if he lived all his real life outside it.

When she carried a tray upstairs to her mother, she found her in tears. She put the tray down on the table, sat on the bed and slipped an arm round her shoulders.

"We shall often see her, Mother! It's such a little way, really, only fifteen minutes by bus from Station Square! And Frank's going to teach her to drive the car. And he'll be away so much, she'll always be coming in. It's really rather as if she'd married a sailor. We shall see much more of her than if he was in an ordinary kind of job."

Emily withdrew herself from Mary's arms and turned on her side. She said, "It's not that, but Doris was the only one of you that wanted me. You don't want to stay here, really, you're hankering to get back to London. And Arthur's a boy and only interested in school and his friends. I'm only a nuisance who has to be looked after. You've always cared more for Aunt Grace than for me, and I don't know what Arthur cares for, but you don't either of you need me, and there's nothing for me to go on living for."

There was so much truth in it that it was difficult to answer, and Mary felt as though she had not enough energy to answer it. She stood silent for a moment, stroking her mother's arm. Emily jerked it impatiently away. Mary began to talk soothingly and consolingly. But it was no use, Emily thought. Her children had wanted her while she could do things for them, but now that she could not, they did not need her. It was her tragedy that in her heart of hearts she had always thought of herself as doing her duty by them. In action she had never failed them, but feeling had always been locked up in her, and when the time for action was over, she had nothing more to give, and was shrewd enough to realize that her children were now doing their duty by her. She wanted more love and less virtue in their relationship to her, not realizing that it was born of her own locked love and austered virtue.

"You'd better go down, Mary," she said, moving against her pillows, "the tea will be getting cold."

Mary went down, wishing that she could have felt loving and not only pitiful. The front door opened as she came down the stairs and in the swirl of cold fog that filled the doorway she saw Aunt Grace wearing her second best red hat, and carrying a bundle under her arm. Mary ran down the stairs and threw her arms round her.

"I thought I'd come round and keep your mother company. I expect she's feeling a bit low this evening and I know you've got to go out. Your uncle's gone down to South Albeck to speak for Mr. Biggleswade at a meeting."

"You always come when we want you, Aunt Grace!"

"Well, I'll just pop upstairs and leave my hat in Emily's room and see how she's feeling, and then I can go and sit with her afterwards. I've brought my knitting. I daresay Arthur will like to go out." Aunt Grace leant down over the banisters, her dark eyes twinkling at Mary.

"Well, it was a grand wedding! I said to my old man, we've improved in weddings in the family since our time, champagne and waiters and all! And do you know what he said? He said, 'We shall never improve on our wedding.' It isn't often he says a thing like that without me jogging him, and not always then! I thought I could have died of laughing to-day at that young man's speech, poor lad, and he was a nice fellow, too. But we'll talk about that at tea, Mary. We've had ours early with your uncle going out, but I'll have another cup with you, if I may. There's a grand photograph of them in the evening paper, but I'm talking too much, I shall make you late!"

Aunt Grace ran nimbly upstairs leaving Mary in the passage below with renewed warmth in her heart.

Mary hugged her fur coat over her black evening frock, pulled on long leather boots, crammed as much of her hair as possible inside her beret, and set out into the fog. The taste of it was in her throat and the ends of her hair were wet and flat against her cheeks, before she had gone ten yards from the door, but it was not thick enough to hold up traffic or to prevent the whole town from setting out for the evening's engagements. The Municipal Elections were at hand. Lionel Harding was driving down to the Warbeck Ward to take the chair for the Conservative candidate. Although he had retired from the Council, he still went to a meeting or two in support of his old friends. John Allworthy was in a tram, bumping down the steep hill towards South Albeck. He was unopposed in his own ward, and was going to speak for the next door Labour candidate, Marcus Biggleswade. Tom Sutton was approaching the same meeting in another tram. Olive Walters was strolling up Highgate, arm in arm with a girl friend, towards the Tivoli, the big new picture house that was to her the height of beauty, and whose very cloakrooms had altered her standards of life and ideas of attainable bliss. Robert and Beryl were in their car on the way to the Territorial Prize Giving of C Company, prepared to sit on hard chairs in the Drill Hall and clap at frequent intervals as red-faced young men in uniform stamped up the floor, saluted with terrific vigour and precision, and marched back to their places bearing the cups and bowls of Regimental silver. Fred had gone up to visit Rosie and was sitting opposite to her by Beryl's kitchen fire, polishing the kettle for her while she embroidered a sideboard cloth for their future home. In a parish room filled with fog and the smell of radiators, Mark Forrester was conducting a discussion with the Youth Group on the place of the Church in modern life, while in the drawing-room at the Vicarage, Canon Halliday stood on the hearthrug with his hands clasped behind him, waiting for the gong to ring, and wondering uneasily what subversive ideas Forrester was putting into the heads of those boys and girls.

Stephen and Joy were driving in to the Charity Ball for which William Marsden had sent them the tickets that he felt obliged to buy but had no desire to use. Leslie was taking Angus in his car to a meeting of the English Association, at which a young poet was presently to explain that poetry, under pressure of circumstances, was coming back again into touch with common life. At least half his audience did not know that it had ever lost touch with it, or that common life had anything to do with poetry. They gazed with interest at the young, strained face of the celebrity, and heard his voice telling them of a crisis in the world of which they were hardly aware, and of a division of mind which they had remarked, if at all, in foreigners. Naomi Unwin, listening avidly, thought, Quite sound but rather pretty-pretty, rather on the literary side, the pill well coated with sugar for the audience. Angus thought, Nice gift with words, might be a poet someday if it wasn't for this eternal political propaganda, the squirrel cage mind! Claud Unwin, who did not know that he disliked seeing another man on the platform, thought, Sound in the main, but an affected ass! Leslie thought, He's quite nice but Angus would do it better! Grizel said when I took him back afterwards, I was to go in and we'd make tea and anchovy toast. What fun!

In the sitting room at No. 17, Harebell Terrace, Mabel and Herbert Walters sat by the fire, looking at a mottled exercise book full of her compositions which Doreen had brought home from school. Her writing and spelling, her amazing intelligence and erudition overcame them completely, and they could only gaze at one another, and smile and say, "Well!" In Grey Gables there was a feeling of relief because Ward was away in London. Mrs. Ward and Marjorie, each with a novel, sat at opposite ends of the hearthrug, friendly again after the dispute about the lunch-party and the wedding. Since Marjorie was full of the wedding, and weddings, even among the socially unacceptable, are interesting, Mrs. Ward found herself, in spite of her disapproval, hearing a good many of the details.

Guy Runnacre came into the offices of the *Yorkshire Guardian*, bringing a report of a big school prize-giving at which a Bishop had made a speech. He lounged into the news-room and glanced idly at the typed messages coming over the machine from the London office. There was a report that the Italians had gained ground in the South, but a rumour of heavy fighting in the North in which they had been held up. Guy Runnacre watched for a moment as the machine tapped out one neat letter after another on the white paper. He went into the sub-editor's room and handed over the Bishop's speech. It was news, for the *Guardian* had always stood by the Church, and the Bishop had a North Country See, and had spoken of the duty of preserving liberty and democracy in the modern world. The sub-editor put on the spikes an account of a lecture on art, cut several lines from a notice of a public dinner, and gave the Bishop half a column.

In the Town Hall, Mary was moving about among the guests, making a note of dresses, and looking out for those who would expect and were entitled to see their names in the paper next morning. She kept an eye on the dwindling stream of late arrivals, and presently saw the tall figure of Joy Harding, lovely in a dress of clear green, with Stephen coming behind her. They shook hands with the Lady Mayoress who was receiving the guests, spoke to one or two friends standing near the entrance, and then swung out together on to the floor, the yellow head and the dark head level. Stephen was speaking to his wife and smiling at her as they disappeared among the dancers.

A cold and numb misery succeeded to the furious beating of Mary's heart. This was that other life of Stephen's which she had sometimes forgotten, which had seemed unreal and unimportant when he was sitting by the Allworthys' fire, a little at sea, anxious to learn and looking to her for sympathy. This other life was not unreal. It was her own picture of it that had been unreal. She had made for herself a picture that pleased her of the intelligent and sensitive husband, and the narrow, unsympathetic wife with whom he lived in a dearth of understanding and tenderness. She saw a young man enjoying himself at a dance with his lovely wife. Her imagination swung over too far in the opposite direction, she punished herself by drawing with firm lines the picture of Stephen perfectly happy in his own world. Her mind fumbled vaguely with the idea of a story, some situation as it looked to a third person and as it was, but below the fumbling of her mind, her heart ached with loss and with a painful humiliation, because she had thought and felt absurdly. As the pair came round again among the dancers, she bent her head and scribbled in her small notebook that Mrs. Stephen Harding was wearing a dress of sea green crepe, cut on the new lines with a girdle of silver cord.

The meeting which John Allworthy was addressing in South Albeck was like other political meetings in that it was attended mainly by convinced supporters of the party holding it. There were not even very many idle people who had come in to see if there was any fun. There never was any fun at a Labour meeting in South Albeck. At a Conservative meeting, supporters of the Labour candidate sometimes asked questions, shouted insults, or even sang the Red Flag. Conservatives very seldom came and shouted insults at Labour speakers, or attempted to raise a performance of God Save the King, or Rule Britannia. This year the city was even more apathetic than usual about the Municipal Elections. It had just struggled through a General Election and helped to return the National Government to office for another five years. It was sick of public affairs. The one desire of most people was that the National Government should get on with the job of governing and leave them to get on with their own lives.

John Allworthy, an old hand, felt the temper of the meeting. Tired, listless, without much hope. It was, at the moment, the temper of the Labour Party. He spoke steadily and reassuringly, comforting them rather as a mother might comfort children tired with a long walk and still far from home. Tom Sutton fidgeted on his chair. The old man was losing his grip. There was nothing in that steady, go slow, all in good time business to give anyone heart, and while they were all steadying and going slow, the enemy stole a march on them. As soon as his time came to speak, Tom jumped to his feet, threw out an arm, cried "Comrades!" and began a rousing polemic.

Tom was a good speaker, ardent and vital, with a flow of plain, vigorous language, but this evening he could not get hold of his audience. They did not want to be roused to immediate action. They would vote and those of them who worked for the party would work, but they had just voted and worked for the General Election without success. Temporarily the stuffing was knocked out of them. They did not want new demands on their time and energies. They began to oppose to Tom's war-cry an invisible, steady barrier of resistance. We can't do any more just now, let us alone. Tom, always sensitive and doubly keyed-up when facing an audience, felt the resistance almost as though it were a palpable barrier, and being a fighter, hurled himself against it.

"Comrades," he cried, "we can't sit still! What's happening now in Abyssinia shows you! This is a world class war beginning! We've got to fight to the last ditch with any weapons, yes, I say with any weapons." John Allworthy's head turned towards him, but he did not notice it. He was unconsciously repeating things that Harold Pearson had often said to him. "If we can't move them by constitutional methods we can't wait while they ride rough-shod over us, we must use unconstitutional methods. Look at Russia. . . ."

The audience had perhaps been urged to look at Russia rather often, and were not without an innate and lingering distrust of foreign countries. After all, it was South Albeck that mattered. One or two of the younger ones kindled to Tom's glowing account of a perfect educational system, a world of culture, opportunity and leisure for all. Most of them simply did not believe in such things. Their view of life was that there was always a catch in it somewhere. They recoiled instinctively from haste, extremes or ruthlessness. They heard Tom to the end, but he knew that he was not getting that springing warmth of response which alone warms an orator to his climax. He felt as if he were pushing a large stone up hill. He sat down, wiping the sweat from his forehead. The audience endured a few votes of thanks, contributed pennies which they could ill afford to a collection for medical aid to the Abyssinian Army, and filed out into the fog.

The candidate was a small, pale-faced man who owned a

couple of fish and chip shops in South Albeck. He came up and shook hands with John.

"Always a pleasure to hear you, Mr. Allworthy!"

"Very glad to do anything, Mr. Biggleswade."

Mr. Biggleswade lowered his voice. "That young man, Sutton, now, is he a friend of yours?"

"Yes. I've known him since he was a baby."

"Ah, well, I don't want to say anything against him, and he's a fine speaker. Yes, a very nice flow, but a little injudicious, perhaps?"

"He's young, you know, Mr. Biggleswade. We want the young ones to keep us going."

"Ah," said Mr. Biggleswade. "But where are we going to? I don't like that talk of unconstitutional methods! We don't want any violence here. Russia's another story and what had to be there had to be, but it's a mistake to get up on a platform and say that kind of thing. It puts people off. But if he's a friend of yours, I daresay a word from you. . . .? I should be the last man to discourage enthusiasm," said Mr. Biggleswade, looking tired and harassed and particularly unenthusiastic, "but let's have steadiness, that's what I say. Let's have steadiness."

When Allworthy looked for Tom to have the suggested word with him, he found that he had already left. Tom was walking away from the hall feeling tired and deflated. South Albeck was the next district to Worbeck, where Olive lived. He had told her that he was going to speak in the Valley Road Hall, and a penny tram ride would have brought her to hear him. She had said at lunch-time that she might come. She had been sweet and friendly and had said, "Fancy seeing you up on the platform and hearing you make a speech!" Tom was always wanting her to come and hear him speak. He knew that he spoke well and often felt on top of the world when he was speaking, and Olive might think more of him if she heard him. He had carefully scanned row after row of the audience during the speeches that preceded his, but she was not there, and something of the impotent anger in his speech, which had rasped the nerves of the audience, had been due to his disappointment. He thought

209

that he would slip along to No. 10, Bankside Yard and see why she hadn't come. If she had gone with a friend to the pictures, he was prepared to be angry and injured.

But she had not done that, for she opened the door to him, and cried out, "Oh, come in, Tom!" in a voice much more freely welcoming than usual. Tom wiped his boots carefully on the mat and stepped into the kitchen, which was big and warm, lit by a ruddy fire. Olive's parents were sitting one on each side of the fireplace, her father smoking a pipe, her mother knitting a stocking. Both looked as though they had worked hard all day so that in the evening the mere pleasure of sitting down was enough for them. Both were so square, so solid, that it seemed incredible that the fragile Olive could be their daughter. No one, meeting Olive in the town, would have guessed that she came from No. 10, Bankside Yard, from a house with two bedrooms, and one kitchen-sitting-room, where every drop of water had to be boiled, where she shared a bed with her mother, and where the soot and smoke of neighbours' chimneys poured in at the window all day long. Olive's personal daintiness, her exquisitely ordered curls and polished nails, her fresh, fashionable clothes, were the result of much determination, and of a prolonged and valiant struggle. Her mother was a notable housewife. Her stone was always scoured to a bright yellow, the kitchen was always spotless, her pans and kettle shone. Olive attended to her own person with the same religious zeal that her mother bestowed on the house and with the same success.

"'Evening, Mr. Walters," Tom said, "'Evening Mrs. Walters. I thought perhaps you'd been to the pictures, Olive."

"We did go to the first house but it was that silly we came out, and I was coming down to your meeting, but when I got home there was Mum and Dad with a piece of news, and I was so excited I couldn't have sat still a minute." She smiled at him disarmingly, a dimple coming at the corner of her soft mouth. "Guess what's going to happen?"

He did not feel in the mood for guessing, but with his eyes on the dimple, he smiled and said,

"I dunno. Fred got a rise?"

"No. It's something for all of us!"

"You won a football pool, Mr. Walters?"

Mr. Walters grinned and shook his grizzled head. Olive, unable to contain herself any longer, cried out, "We're leaving this house! We've got to! It's been condemned!"

Her mother interposed:

"Don't you go saying it like that, Olive, making people think this house isn't what it ought to be with bugs and such! There's nothing wrong with this 'ouse. We could do with another bedroom, and the stairs is a bit steep, but it's always been a good oven, and it's a good solid house. What it is, Tom, they're pulling down the whole yard because of those filthy houses on the other side, and high time, too, and this side of the yard has to come down with it. It seems it's all part of a plan, to build a whole lot of new flats on this ground. There was a lady, a housing inspector I think they call her, come and explained it all to us, but I can't rightly remember all she said. But anyhow, we've to go, and they'll find us a new house on one of the estates. It's to have a bathroom and a sitting-room and a garden and I don't know what else. I ses to her, all very well, Miss, I ses, but who's going to clean this ere sitting-room and bathroom? I'm getting on and my legs is not what they were, and I've enough to do to follow these three rooms with the cooking an' all. But she says it will be so much cleaner out there and not these steep stairs. But I don't know, I'm sure."

"Oh, Mother," Olive cried, "I'll clean the sitting-room! I'll get up early every morning!"

Her mother turned on her an unresentful glance of complete disbelief.

"You might one morning, but well I know what would happen after that! You aren't in the house above an hour or two any day, except when you're asleep. You and Fred, I always say you're a pair of lodgers. But you can't go out to work and work at the house all day too, it stands to reason. Now you get the cups out and the tea-pot, the kettle's just on the boil, and I'm going to make Tom a nice cup of tea. He looks fair clemmed. Pull up that chair, Tom, and get warm."

"What do you think about it, Mr. Walters?" Tom asked.

Mr. Walters removed his pipe from his mouth, and brushed his walrus moustache with the back of his hand.

"He's not too pleased about it," his wife interpolated. "Ses 'e's too old now to change 'is ways."

"What I feel," Mr. Walters said heavily. "Why can't they let me alone? This 'ouse has been good enough for us all these years, hasn't it? Well, why isn't it now? What's this young woman want to come here for, talking about sitting-rooms and bathrooms? I didn't ask anyone for a sitting-room and a bathroom, did I? Then why 'ave I got to have one? A man's got a right to say what sort of 'ouse he wants to live in, and not have it pulled down about his ears! I'll tell you what it is, Tom, it's these 'ere Socialists of yours, a lot of busybodies nosey-parkering about, trying to make things different for people what don't want 'em different. I voted Labour last time because it seems right to stand by your own folk, but you won't catch me doing it again! Next thing is, if they go on improving the conditions a bit more, I shall find I've got to go and live in the Town 'All."

"Oh, Dad!" Olive cried, trembling with nervous impatience.

"Along with the Lord Mayor," said Mr. Walters, finishing his joke with determination.

Olive could have shaken him. Nobody, nobody knew how she hated this house, how it was her enemy in her long struggle for refinement, for elegance as she understood it. She hated the steep stairs up which she had to carry kettles of hot water every time she wanted to wash. She hated sharing a room with her mother, hated her mother's warm, heavy body in the bed with her. She hated the dirt, the sitting-room which was also a kitchen, the commonness of the neighbours. If what her father said was true, and Socialists had really got her out of this, she was prepared to believe that there was some sense in all Tom's goings-on. She did not often defend him, but now she said:

"Let Tom alone, Dad! Of course he's right if he wants people to have decent houses and not live like pigs!"

"Don't you talk about living like pigs!" her mother said sharply. "It's what I've never done and never will. I daresay this house would be a pigsty for all the cleaning you ever do in it, but luckily it hasn't got to wait for you!"

Tom, sipping his hot tea gratefully, sat and listened to them all with divided feelings. Of course he cared passionately for better houses for the people, and thought it right that the Walters should go to a better house in cleaner air, and have a bathroom and a sitting-room. He had been touched with extraordinary delight when Olive spoke up for him like that, and said a good word for the cause he believed in, even though he knew that she had very little idea of what she was talking about. On the face of it, it seemed that he ought to rejoice with her in this change, but he was troubled by misgivings. He could have given her a better house before now if she wanted one, but she had put him off and refused to be hurried. Now she was as pleased as a child about the move, and would be taken up with her parents' new house, and perhaps not willing to leave it while it was still a new toy. "And where do I come in?" thought Tom. He looked at her and ached in every inch of his body. She was wearing a grey skirt and a turquoise blue jumper, high at the neck, with a collar rolled over like a boy's sweater. The clinging wool showed the rounded lines of her young breasts. Her hair was dressed in a bunch of shining curls behind her delicate ears that looked whiter for the blue stones in them, new blue ear-rings bought for a shilling in the big multiple store at the corner of Highgate that was her Paradise. She had a way of putting her hand up and feeling that her ear-rings were safe, a way of just pinching her ear gently afterwards between finger and thumb that stayed in Tom's mind like a tune. Well, she was right happy and pleased about this new house, but it should have been his new house, his and hers. He was earning a good wage, there was nothing to stop them getting married.

Mr. Walters, who had been ruminating, turned to Tom for sympathy.

"It's all very well," he said, "but look at the time it will take me to get to my work from one of them estates and what it'll cost me in 'bus tickets! And what am I going to do in the evenings?"

"We'll have a nice wireless, Dad!" Olive cried.

"Nice wireless!" Mr. Walters said contemptuously, "I can't have a pint of mixed and pass the time of day with a nice wireless, can I?"

"You'll probably find much better pubs up there, Dad. Why, look at that grand one up by Herbert's, the Tracy Arms, don't they call it? Where old Mr. Trent that's dead now took you for a drink that Sunday morning? I'm sure that was ever so much nicer than the Three Bears!"

"That's all you know about it," Mr. Walters replied shortly. He did not attempt to argue or explain any more. A man had his dignity, his own life apart from his womenfolk. He did not expect his wife and daughter to understand that no great, red, staring public-house, more like a hotel than a pub, could be the same to him as the Three Bears, where they knew him, where they said "'Evening, Mr. Walters! The usual?'", where he had his own seat on the worn red-leather settee pushed back against the wall under the mirror with an advertisement for tobacco written across it. Women always thought that any pubs would do, that you just went there for the drink, not understanding that while you liked your glass of beer, you went there for company and familiarity and independence, to be a person in a life which was neither your work nor your home, so that your manhood could flower and expand freely, not restricted by discipline, nor altogether swamped in the affectionate domestic creature, the husband and father whom your family recognized. Mr. Walters did not say all that to himself, but he felt it. He puffed at his pipe in silence, foreseeing already his nostalgia for that worn leather seat so comfortable to his bottom, his isolation of the spirit in some improved public-house full of restless young people drinking cocktails.

"Whatever will Herbert and Mabel say about it!" Olive cried. "And Fred! It's time Fred was back!"

Fred came in just as she spoke, unwinding a long woollen scarf and throwing off his overcoat. His fair skin was flushed with the cold, and when he pulled off his cap, a cockatoo's crest of light brown hair rose up on his head as though glad to escape from restraint. Fred, like Olive, spent much time, thought and money on his clothes. He was a long, pale youth who by serving in a shop from the age of fourteen to twenty-two had acquired a permanently obliging manner. He was very neat and orderly, almost finicky, about all his personal belongings. It seemed odd that he should have chosen for his girl the sturdy, lively, untidy Rosie, but the background of his home was his mother's homely warmth, and a deep instinct below his refinements and small snobberies had made him look for the same qualities in a wife.

He nodded to Sutton, said "'Evening, Tom! Hulloa, everybody!" and came towards the fire.

"Fred!" Olive cried out, and burst into the tale of the new house. "They have to find us one, you see, if they pull this down, and it's to be in an estate with three bedrooms and a sitting-room and a bathroom! And there'll be a garden! And we'll never see this dirty old yard again as long as we live!"

Fred stood holding out his hands to the fire and taking it all in. Leave Bankside Yard! Well, of course he would have to leave it, anyhow, when he got married, but although he and Rosie had talked about houses, he had not really been able to imagine living anywhere else.

"Well!" he said, drawing a long breath.

"Aye, it is 'well'!" Mr. Walters said darkly.

"Aren't you pleased, Fred!" Olive screamed at him. "You'll have a bedroom to yourself and we'll have meals in the sitting-room!"

"I don't know so much about that," Mrs. Walters remarked, "I don't know as I'm going to spend my time carrying food about the house from one room to another and letting it get cold on the way. That's what I call finicky! But we'll see. I'm sure I hope you are pleased, Fred, for you young ones may as well be. Your Dad and me can't take to a change all of a sudden at our time of life."

Fred thought of having his own bedroom. Not having to undress in the dark because his father was already in bed and asleep. Not having to hang up his beautiful new suits, his sports coats and cycling jackets, his fine winter overcoat, on the pegs in the corner by his father's working clothes. Not sharing the big double bed with his father, hearing him snore, being roused by him punctually in the morning and made to get up and go downstairs and take his turn at the sink. Visions of incredible luxury swam before his dazzled eyes, perhaps a lavatory indoors and electric light. He drew a deep breath.

"Ah," he said. "Sounds like a bit of all right!"

"I must be getting along," Tom got up and reached for his cap. "How's Rosie, Fred?" he asked. He felt as though this business of the new house was going to draw the young Walters back into their own family life, away from Rosie and himself.

"Rosie's all right. Sent her love to you, Mum and Dad. She'll be coming along on Sunday."

"There's a Labour Meeting in your ward to-morrow evening, Mr. Walters, at the St. Margaret's schoolroom. Any hope of you getting along?"

"Nay, lad, I don't reckon much to meetings. There was a chap come here canvassing like the other evening. I ses to 'im, you let me alone and I'll let you alone. That's all I want," said Mr. Walters with rising passion. "To be let alone! And in this world nowadays it's the one thing you can't get."

With this stricture on modern life, he nodded to Tom and relapsed into sombre brooding over his pipe.

Tom stepped out of the door into Bankside Yard. The fog, surprisingly, had thinned, only stray wreaths of it clung round the houses, and the sky was visible, pricked by pale stars. The sky was like a ceiling, propped on the huddled uneven houses, jagged by the unsymmetrical chimney-pots. Of course the place ought to have come down years ago. The worn cobbles of the yard lay this evening in pools of water. He could smell the privies as he walked past them, and he knew that all the houses in the row called Bankside Yard Back were verminous. He was surprised to find himself feeling sentimental about the place. His heart had so often beat as he turned the corner by the fly-blown little shop, whose window was full of matches, tins of polish and sticks of liquorice. He had so often knocked at the door of No. 10 and seen Olive in the doorway framed by the warm firelight. He was jealous of the unknown new house for which she flushed and sparkled as she hardly ever did for him. It would be a house like Herbert's, full of irritating refinements and cold gentility, and Olive in such a house would be further off than ever from him and from the struggling army of workers. There was the difficulty! People lived in slums like rats in sewers, and you clamoured for better houses for them. They got their better houses with gardens and bathrooms, and at once they became different, more shut off from their neighbours. They were no longer an army living in a camp, they were separate families wanting to have their gardens and their curtains better than those next door. They grew frightened and polite and careful, grew like Mabel and Herbert, always saying to their child, "Sit up straight! Eat it nicely! Say 'thank you!' Pass the plate to Mr. Sutton first!"

There, thought Tom sadly, was the whole trouble. The things that the Labour Movement had fought for it had partly achieved, and what it had achieved had made Conservatives of them. They had fought for the right for working men to take part in the government and when they got there, they became the biggest Tories of the lot! They had fought for better houses, better pay, better conditions at work and had produced a race of petty-bourgeois who were far more interested in their private property than in any cause. And the result would be that one day they would all find themselves bombed among their gardens and wireless-sets or enslaved by a Fascist International which they hadn't even noticed.

In his mind, as so often on a platform, Tom flung himself against the incurable disposition of the English people,— against their laziness, their patience, their good humour, their individualism, their suspicion of all extremes, their distaste for violence, their unwillingness to think, their readiness to laugh. He saw that their real passion, if anything so steady and unconscious could be called a passion, was for respectability. It was exactly the same in the Labour members and Trade Union leaders proudly showing themselves anti-revolutionary, and in Mabel and Herbert buying afternoon tea napkins and talking about "the working classes." Nobody, nobody could stand the test of getting on! Even John All-worthy, old stalwart of the Movement, had betrayed the ardour of his youth, and was holding other people back. The whole trouble about England was that while Socialism was supposed to be a half-way house to Communism, English Socialism was simply a stage in the making of more Conservatives. Tom had a clear mind and had been trained to think politically. On this raw November night, with Olive glowing and thrilling, but not for him, the burden of a people who thought, if at all, with their nerves and feelings seemed more than he and a few like him could shift. He was tempted to give it all up and spend his money and his energies on getting on in the world, on having a nice house, a house better than Herbert's, better than the new one to which the Walters were moving, so that even Olive would be pleased and satisfied.

But of course he could not and would not give it up. He was too strongly bound to his own people, he had too often seen them suffer. He had seen too many unfairnesses, too many underfed children, harassed women, men without work. He saw all the issues, the inevitable struggle too clearly. He was aware of a deep sense of comradeship with those who like himself toiled to shift the great unheeding mass. That was the warmth and comfort of it, the sense of being shoulder to shoulder with like-minded men and women. Only to-night, his vision being cleared and sharpened, he knew that he would never be shoulder to shoulder with Olive, and he could have wept for his heart and body that betrayed him, making him feel that he could not do without her.

As he jumped off his tram and walked up the hill to the tram barriers in Highgate to catch the last tram towards his own lodgings, he passed a warehouse whose back entrance gave on to the wharves of the canal, and which had, besides the big door in front, a small door at the side opening on to the yard. He knew, for he had often been told, that by that small door more than fifty years ago the pioneers of the Labour Movement in the city had gone in after dark, had climbed to a disused loft above and squatted there by candle-light to build a new Jerusalem. There William Morris had come, escorted from the station by a young John Allworthy, pale and silent with admiration. There the great gas workers' strike had been planned, there the wet proofs of the first Aire Labour newspaper had been corrected. Tom was so used to passing the doorway that he did not give it a thought. No whisper of hope reached him from the stairs, no message from the young men who in their time had flung themselves into the battle, and had been defeated, but had won a yard or two of ground in their defeat, and had grown old and patient, life ebbing in them so that they could no longer go forward, but must sit down on the captured ground while younger men went past them into the fight. Nothing suggested to Tom that he too in his time would grow old and tired, would be afraid of losing what he had won, and would distrust the ardour of men still unborn. He had no conception of these natural tides in the life of man, he was young and strong and eager and sure that he should always feel as he felt now. Already in the lights and movement of the town his mood of discouragement was passing. He saw his last tram ahead of him just starting from the barriers, sprinted, caught it up, and swung himself on to the platform. Warmed by that successful effort, he climbed the stairs to the crowded, smoky upper story, dropped into a seat, lit a fag, and was jolted towards his home.

"In the end," Lionel Harding said, "the English tempera-ment may save us! I grant you changes are coming and ought to come, but I think perhaps we're capable of making them steadily and without rancour. You young fellows don't realize the changes that I've seen in my time. When I was a boy, South Albeck was full of children running about barefoot. You never see a barefooted child now. There's a levelling process going on, you know. I shall leave my children a quarter of what my father left me. The grandson of my father's old groom came to see me the other day. He's just down from Cambridge and off to America with a travelling research scholarship. He speaks English as well as my own sons, better probably. Classes are not solid blocks, there's a continual shifting to and fro from one to the other. The family is the strongest thing in English life and the greatest corrective to class consciousness! This young fellow was staying the week-end with his grandmother, the old groom's wife, who used to come in and help in the house, and he brought me a lot of messages from her and was fond of her and proud of her. There's always the family-grouping to prevent the class-grouping from becoming too rigid. Help yourself to port, Forrester, and pass it on."

"No, thank you. I don't drink."

An aggressive fellow, Lionel thought. Aloud he said:

"Conscience? Or don't you like it?"

"I don't think it's right to .indulge expensive tastes that most people can't afford. As a matter of fact, I don't really know how much I like it, I've never had much spare cash or any wealthy friends, so I haven't had much chance of trying."

"I hope you aren't considering me a wealthy friend? And I should have thought abstinence would have more value if you knew what you were abstaining from. But just as you like, of course. Help yourself, Unwin."

The young don filled up his glass.

"If I may say so, sir, I don't think those bromides about the English temperament go for much. To be slow in the uptake isn't a virtue nowadays, it's a crime, and a disaster, and I think you're attaching too much importance to superficial changes."

"Children were starving when I was young. No child starves nowadays. I'm on the Education Committee—they very kindly kept me on when I came off the Council—and I know how many free dinners are given at schools in this town every week. Do you call that a superficial change?"

"Yes. Entirely."

"Oh, you do, do you?" The young man, Lionel reflected,

had eaten his own dinner almost voraciously. "You know, if you found yourself starving, I doubt if you'd think it is superficial change."

"That's off the point, sir. So are free school dinners and other attempts to patch up an out-worn system. What we've got to do is to begin again from the objective realities. Here's the world—so much material in it—so many people. Certain problems of distribution and transport. What's the best way to arrange that a fair proportion of all the things get to all the people?"

"Only, of course like most simplifications, that's about one quarter of the truth—and a quarter of the truth is always a lie. What about all the other realities?"

"It's questionable whether there are any."

"Colonel Harding's right!" Forrester said emphatically, Very kind of him, thought Lionel with a faint smile. "Your dead philosophy is a lie. That's where all you dialectical materialists go wrong. Man shall not live by bread alone."

"I'm afraid I can't allow that a sentimental aphorism by a Narcissisitic Jewish philosopher proves anything."

The colour sprang in Mark Forrester's round face. The two young men eyed one another with hostility. The colour slowly faded in the curate's cheeks. He said with some dignity.

"I'm quite ready to argue with you. Cheap sneers are hardly fair argument."

"You men of God don't argue. You simply make assertions based on some mystical assumptions of your own."

"Your own assertions are equally mystical. How do you know that there is nothing more for any man than material reality? That's a dogma you can't prove."

"I can't, but I can prove that there is material reality, and I base my philosophy on what I can prove by touch and sight!"

You can't as a matter of fact, Lionel reflected, prove anything. There is no such thing as proof. You can only make another person aware of it. He listened to the two young men going at one another hammer and tongs. On matters of practical policy he disagreed with both of them, but he felt the division between them greater than the division between himself and Mark Forrester. The young don was as crude as though he had been reared on sour apples. What sort of a home and background, Lionel wondered. What an uncomfortable fellow to live with! But then his wife, with her nervously energetic manner and too bright eyes, did not look as though comfort entered much into her ideas of life.

He sat back in his chair and helped himself to half a glass more port. They did not want to include him in the discussion and since neither of them had any manners, they did not attempt to. Widely as they differed, they belonged to the same world and generation. In spite of their argument over the politics which had started the discussion, they were more angry with one another than they were with him. He was a Conservative, an elderly man. They expected nothing of him, but they were exasperated, furious with each other, each would have liked to hit the other on the head and bang him into submission to his own mind. And it was quite obvious that neither of them would submit. Lionel grew a little tired of them. He said, "Won't you have another glass of port, Unwin? Well, then, let's go into the drawing-room."

The Unwins parted from Mark Forrester on the doorstep of Mill Hall at 10.30. He was going out by the back gate which was nearer to his lodging. Naomi and Claud walked down the drive in the shadow of the trees. The night was frosty. The gravel was hard and rang under their feet. The branches of the trees made a tunnel, but through the cracks in the roof of the tunnel were visible wedges and scraps of sky, as oddly shaped as the pieces of a jig-saw puzzle, and brilliant with stars.

They walked in silence for fifty yards. Then Claud said, "The food was good."

Naomi was following her own train of thought and hardly listened to this succinct review of the evening.

"I think the Curate will join the Discussion Group."

"What's the use?"

222

"A lot of use. It reassures people to see a clergyman there."

"We don't want the sort of people that need reassuring."

Naomi sighed.

"Oh, Claud, those are just the people we do want! There aren't enough of the others! Besides, it's no use preaching to the converted! We want the gentlemanly waverers, like Stephen Harding, and the ignorant young, like that Ward boy, and the people brought up in old-fashioned Labour and just poking their noses outside it. We want to get them all there and used to ideas! We've got to get them past the stage when they say, 'Oh, of course not Communism!' as though they said, 'Oh, of course not small-pox!' We've got to give them the medicine without the label on the bottle!"

"If you think I'm going to spend my evenings giving economic truths in spoonfuls of jam to a lot of half-hearted sympathizers who'll jump back to their own side when the first gun goes off . . ."

"That's just exactly what you have got to do, so that they swallow the pills in the jam and absorb them into their systems without knowing it!" but Naomi sighed. There was no doubt that Claud was not the best man for the job. He might act Boreas, but he had never stooped to learn the art of persuasion. He was likely to make the shivering neophytes wrap their cloaks more tightly about them, and go home. It would perhaps be better to get someone else down to inaugurate the Group, some recognizably blameless member of the Labour Party, even a Liberal.

Claud said, "They won't be able to keep that house on surely, when the old man dies. How much do you suppose he'll leave them?"

"I don't know. How can I tell?" Naomi was always faintly disquieted by Claud's preoccupation with the incomes of his friends and acquaintances. She knew that he passionately wanted more money, and that he was ashamed of the want, and did not allow it to invade his consciousness. She herself did not really mind very much about it, they had enough to live on, and she did not think they ought to have more. If she wanted more it would be for one reason only. Secretly in her heart she wanted a child. Claud often said how foolish the Grants were to attempt two babies on their income. She knew that one of the reasons why he liked them and liked going to their house was because the Grants were much more straitened than they were, having four people to keep on the same salary. He enjoyed feeling superior and more sensible, and being able to afford an occasional concert ticket or holiday or theatre when they couldn't. He knew nothing of the queer, half-strangled feeling evoked in Naomi by the sight of the children's soft cheeks and rounded limbs and great, wondering eyes.

Harking back to their evening she said,

"It was like spending a few hours in another world! I felt sorry for that pathetic daughter."

"An obvious neurotic," remarked Claud. He was fond of classifying his acquaintances as different kinds of neurotics, but believed himself to be immune from all neurosis on the strength of having read Freud and Jung and their disciples, as though from the printed word he had taken in some immunization.

Naomi said in a low voice,

"I thought they were kind people." She had, in a way, enjoyed her evening. The Harding family were out of touch with the modern world, but there was a certain ease and geniality about them, they had welcomed her as though they were pleased to see her and wanted her to enjoy herself. She knew that they had said good-bye without much regret, and she had almost wished at one time that Claud would be less aggressive and uncompromising. She said half-apologetically, "They reminded me of the sort of people who used to ask us to children's parties when I was young."

"I daresay they're more in your line than mine." The bitterness in his voice meant that Claud unhappily could not forget that while Naomi's father had been a country doctor, poor but on friendly terms with the people in big country houses, his own had been an elementary school-master in a Lancashire town, whose social life was confined to the narrow circle of the chapel that he frequented. The sharp little red-headed boy had been so bored by that circle, so impatient of its flat pieties and indiscriminating kindliness that half the impatience and intolerance of his grown-up life was an attempt to avenge that boredom.

"When you come to think of that house and family, Stephen has done pretty well to get his eyes open at all."

"He'll shut them again when he's seen a bit more and doesn't like the look of it. I know his sort."

Naomi thought, you don't really. You don't know them as well as I do. You don't know anybody very well. You can do all kinds of things with figures, but you get hold of people like a clumsy workman getting hold of tools. At Cambridge, where they had met in a Labour Club, he had been so fierce, so independent and so lonely that she had been sorry for him, and pity had added a warmth of feeling to their pleasure in one another's minds, so that she had married him. Neither she nor he had been much in love, but she sometimes thought that they had been as near it as either of them could manage.

"His sort is half England, Claud! I don't mean that they've all been brought up the same way, all had the prosperous start that he had. But England's full of people with their eyes just opening, and they're the people who have the game in their hands and don't know it. We've *got* to swing them our way, and quickly too, but we've *got* to do it without frightening them too much at the beginning. When we get that group started, we've *got* to keep Stephen Harding in it."

"You seem to attach an extraordinary importance to him!"

"Oh, don't be a fool! He's a test case, that's all! We've got to get those people on our side and especially if they start, because if they come a little way and go back, they'll stiffen up against us. There's nobody so reactionary as someone who's gone a little way forward and got frightened. Here we are, thank goodness! I'm frozen! Have you got the key? I left some soup ready. We'll warm it up and drink it before we go to bed."

"Not one of our most successful evenings!" Alice remarked as the door closed behind their three guests. "I don't wonder poor Canon Halliday sighs over that young man! Look how he's crumpled the sofa cushions! It's most disconcerting

225

the way he drops a conversation that doesn't interest him!"

"More sincere than most of us, Mother! That's the trouble."

"People don't go out to dinner to be sincere! I thought that new sweet was delicious, didn't you? It's one Beryl gave me the recipe for. Anyhow, they enjoyed their food! That gaunt young man looks as though he burned every thing up, and the girl has hungry eyes. I should think they always have their meals at home in a hurry. What does she do? She kept talking about her work."

"Something political. I gather she works for half a dozen societies and is just starting a Left Discussion Group."

"At the University? Good gracious, I should think Sir George doesn't know about it! Her husband will get into trouble! I'm sure he's a bad influence!"

"Not at the University. For anyone who likes to come. She tells me Stephen is joining it."

"I don't know what's the matter with Stephen nowadays!"

"It's sporadic among his generation!"

"It's foolish! Ward will never put up with it!"

"I agree. I'm afraid Stephen's much more likely to get into trouble than Claud Unwin. After all, the young Marxist don isn't an unusual phenomenon, but you can't reconcile Karl Marx with a business like Ward's."

"Oh, dear! The silly boy! Can't you talk to him, Daddy?"

"I do. At least, I let him talk to me and I put our point of view. He's always very good-tempered and fair-minded, but it's like seeing somebody caught in a current and slowly swept away from you."

"I wish he'd never gone to Ward's! I can imagine feeling like a Bolshevik at Grey Gables! That is, if I can imagine feeling like a Bolshevik anywhere."

"I agree. I think he probably sees too much of our point of view at its worst."

"Well, there's one comfort, if he's going to a discussion group with the Unwins, he won't see the other point of view at its best! At least, I should think not. I don't know what it's best is, but not that very disagreeable young man, surely!"

"Oh, no. I'd rather have Forrester any day, or a decent, liberal, kindly old enemy like John Allworthy."

"What a nuisance it is when they get too big to be smacked! Clare, what do you think about it,—this business of Stephen?"

Clare had dropped into a big chair and was lying back with her eyes closed.

"Tired, old lady?"

"Yes, I am, rather." She was always tired nowadays at the end of the evening. She pulled her limp body out of the depths of the chair, and sat up, trying to give her parents her attention.

"I think it's Joy's fault."

Lionel looked at her, distressed by an edge in her voice that he had noticed lately when she spoke of Joy. He knew of course that she was fond of Robert's wife and did not like Stephen's, but she had always, until lately, been scrupulously fair to Joy. This tone, almost vicious, was new to her. He said,

"Oh, I don't think you can blame Joy. Why is it her fault?"

"She's stupid and rigid. She won't talk things over with him. She pushes him further than he would go by that sort of senseless opposition, and she makes it perfectly clear that her father and Hilary are the standard of what she admires, and that she doesn't consider that Stephen comes up to them. I think it was a pity Hilary came back, though you wouldn't think anyone with so little personality could make much difference."

"No, it's one of the surprises of this world how much difference the people without much personality can make to the people who have more. Though Hilary's personality, such as it is, is definite and unshakable. There's a certain power about people who never can and never could see any point of view but their own."

Alice, disregarding general reflections, said urgently, "Clare, you must talk to Stephen!"

Lionel was lighting a last pipe. His face bent down over the bowl, he said,

"You know I often wonder what Neville would have thought about all these things if he'd lived."

"He would never have gone against you! You know how

he copied you and adored you. Don't you remember him, that year of the election when that Liberal boot-maker was put up against you, don't you remember him walking round and round the ward with his blue ribbons on and hoping somebody would fight him?"

"Yes. But I remember when I was seeing him off at Victoria the last time he went back to France, he said, 'You know, Daddy, the people who come back won't ever be able to come back to the same world. It will have to be altered, a lot of barriers broken down and unfairnesses changed. Out there all those things seem so absurd.' That was ten days before he died. I've often thought of that while I've been trying to argue with Stephen."

If there was any imagined sanction from Neville, Alice thought, Lionel would not argue with Stephen at all, but would listen and sympathize. Perhaps she had better talk to him herself or get Robert to talk to him. Robert was sensible and level-headed, and the boys had always been good friends. Your brother was the obvious person to tell you not to be a silly ass, or what was family life for? She said with apparent irrelevance,

"I should think, wouldn't you, that both the Unwins were only children? Clare, you look absolutely tired out. I shall ask Doctor Long to come and have a look at you, I think, you must want a tonic. Come along up to bed."

Although very tired, Clare was reluctant to go to bed. She hated going to bed nowadays. She found it difficult to sleep, and when she did sleep, she dreamed, and grew unhappy in her dreams, and woke with the tears running down her cheeks. It was becoming very difficult not to cry in the day-time over nothing at all. The other night she had nearly cried at dinner because Robert teased her, a thing which had been as surprising to her as it would have been to him if it had happened. Not to cry when the boys teased had been a point of honour since she was six years old. This evening, she had gone in to speak to her mother while she was dressing for dinner, and Alice, picking up her favourite ornament, a chain of garnets which had belonged to her mother, had said, "I want you to have this after me, Clare, even if you decide to give some of my other things to Joy and Beryl." Clare had felt her throat swell, had murmured some answer and gone out of the room quickly to hide her springing tears. She had never been like this before, not even once a month when queer things happened to your temper. She must really pull herself together. She sat down on the low chair by her gas fire, and began to brush her hair, massaging it carefully, which she believed to be good for it. It was falling out, there were grey threads, and a whole grey wave over one temple which distressed her greatly.

She wondered why the evening should have been so depressing, why evenings were so often depressing nowadays when people came in, especially if they were people of her own age. With her parents' friends she was fairly happy, she was a young and kind assistant hostess of whom they were fond. They looked on her as a girl, and treated her with the half petting kindness of elderly people glad to be liked by the younger generation. It was her contemporaries who made her uneasy, as though they let in a cold wind upon her life. She recoiled from their ideas, but was not quite able to dismiss them. She imagined in these brisk and active young people a contempt which most of them probably did not feel.

But the worst of all, she thought, was her secret conviction that most of the things she did were not real, that her parties and societies and committee meetings, her work at Babies Welcomes and at the Girls' Home were not real life. She was beginning to realize that for her the only real life was the life of the affections. Her realities were her father and mother, the gap made in her life by Neville—and by Harry? Harry had seemed real enough in that summer before he went to Kenya. He had seemed for a short time to be the only reality, blotting out the rest, but if the test of reality was performance, he was not, he had faded out of her heart. During those weeks she had forgotten even the memory of Neville and thought only of Harry, but a year afterwards, Harry had been brushed away from the image of Neville as though he were a film of dust laid over a picture. For a short time she had dreamed of Harry, but Neville again came back to her in dreams. And yet he had died eighteen years ago. Other people would say that he could not be her reality, would call her morbid. She could not imagine what their guests of that evening would say of a life lived with such a centre, and yet her conviction persisted that she was nearer to a true reality than they were. It did not help her if she was, she was very miserable, unhappy at the dislocation between herself and the outside world, and tired by years of nostalgia. She began to cry, and since she was alone, she let the tears fall, making no effort to stop them.

She did not hear a tap at the door, nor hear it open. A soft exclamation behind her chair surprised her, she felt her mother's arms round her, and her head was drawn against her mother's breast. The silky surface of a dressing-gown against her cheek and the faint scent of violet powder were familiar as far back as she could remember, and brought memories of childish illnesses, and sudden, frightened wakenings in the dark.

"My poor little girl! What is it?"

"I don't know," Clare sobbed.

Alice asked no more for the moment, but stroked her dark hair.

"You aren't worrying about Stephen, are you?" Unless one is a mother one weeps so much more for one's own worries! Clare shook her head.

"I think we must see the doctor and get a tonic for you. Or do you think you want a holiday? Could Jenny go with you to Bournemouth for a week?"

Clare said surprisingly,

"I think I want to be psycho-analysed."

"Oh," Alice smiled. "Were you inspired by what that young man was saying about it this evening?"

"No, I wasn't." A watery smile broke through Clare's tears. "But I have heard sensible people talk about it. And I've read articles. I feel as though I wanted to get hold of myself somehow in my mind. I don't think tonics and holidays would help."

Really, Alice thought, with you picking up such a notion and Stephen turning Socialist, where are we?

"Well, if you like, darling. We could ask about it, anyhow."

"You wouldn't mind?"

"I wouldn't mind anything that makes you happy. Now I'm going to fetch you some hot milk and an aspirin, and you must go to sleep."

Clare stuck to her purpose, and, a week later, sat in the waiting-room of No. 40, Oxford Road, a street of square red houses behind the Infirmary. At one time they had been the fashionable houses of the town. Now they were mostly given up to doctors, nursing homes and dentists. This, thought Clare, was worse than going to a dentist, because it was a plunge into the unknown. You could at least imagine most of the things that a dentist might do to you. It was impossible to imagine what strange experience might be waiting for her in the room upstairs. Yet the waiting-room, with its green walls, polished table and bowl of flowers, was reassuringly ordinary. Even the *Tatlers* and *Spheres* followed established precedent, and were six weeks old.

Her heart beat and her knees trembled as she followed the overalled girl into the next room and found herself shaking hands with Doctor Bates. Her first impression was that he looked like a business acquaintance of her father's. He was broad, with a square, brownish face, grey eyes, and dark hair going grizzled on the temples. He did not smile very much, and she had the feeling of somebody whose personality was deliberately withdrawn from her. He put her into a chair which had its back turned to him. Sitting there with her eyes on a picture of a canal, a barge going along and a man leading a horse on the towing-path, she tried to say what was the matter with her and to answer the questions that came in a quiet voice from behind her. At first she was stiff and shy and could not find words, but presently she was weeping wildly, and pouring out a confused tale of not finding things real, Neville, her empty feeling, and a secret nervous terror of leaving home that she had kept to herself.

231

Sometimes she cried so much that she could not speak. When her sobs had abated, Doctor Bates said gently "Yes? Go on if you can." She was unconsciously surprised that he did not try to comfort her, or even sound very sorry for her. In a little while she stopped crying.

He asked her to start from a word—for instance "home" and say at once whatever came into her mind. She had heard that game played at a party, "thought chains" they had called it, and had noticed how very soon in the "thought chain" people had come to something that they did not want to say and stumbled, hesitated and obviously changed a word. She soon found herself in the same predicament. There were one or two things that she really could not say. She assured herself that they did not matter, and passed on, but the voice behind her said quietly, "The first thing that comes, please." She felt like crying again and saying, "I won't!" but a more sensible feeling restrained her and she forced the difficult words out of her mouth. Doctor Bates murmured "Yes. Quite. Go on!" He seemed undisturbed by her revelations, and it was borne in upon her that nothing in her mind could surprise him. Insensibly her limbs relaxed, she lay back in the chair and spoke more easily.

He stopped her after a time, and explained to her that if she was coming for treatment she would have to remember and write down her dreams. Dreams were the key to the unconscious life in which were the roots of the conscious life and of all her troubles. She could believe that, for she had for some time been aware of a hidden life which in her seemed to be detached from the outer covering. She asked him, "Do you think I need it? Do you think it will do me any good?"

He said, "Yes, I'm sure you need it. I'm quite sure it will do you good. You must feel, don't you, that your life is unsatisfactory, that you could be much more fully alive?"

"Will it take long?"

"It depends on how honest you are and how soon you can assimilate truths about yourself."

She said that she would do her best, and made an appointment to come again. Shaking hands with her at the door, he smiled and said, "The world isn't such a bad place as they make it out, you know. There's a lot to enjoy in it if you are really free." She went downstairs and into the street. She walked along behind the high walls of the Infirmary. She said to herself, half smiling, "Is that all?" She had expected something much more startling and dramatic, but the interview had been no more than faintly astringent. Relief from intangible fears, and the liberation of having talked out her troubles to somebody who, she felt, knew more about them than she did had revived her spirits, given her a sense of a new start, and made her quite extraordinarily hungry. She went into a café, ordered a cup of coffee and a ginger bun.

While waiting for them, she idly watched the people coming in and out. Their faces were preoccupied, a good many of them worried. They looked as though they were fussing about something, getting the right cake, getting home in time for lunch, remembering all the shopping they had come to do. Very few of them looked as though they were enjoying themselves, as though there were any pleasure in the mere fact of being alive, able to move and speak and buy cakes on a frosty November morning. Clare had a vision of people passing through life as through a railway station, squandering the moments they might have lived in because of some inner, compelling urgency that was making them always intent on some moment that was coming. We have got disorientated, she thought, pushed like a dislocated limb off this business of living! When her coffee came she was sharply aware of its aromatic smell, and of the rough, hot taste of the bun against her palate. She lit a cigarette and sat back, lazy and placid, looking at the bright and delicate colours of the Christmas crackers on the counter.

Preparations for Christmas began all over the town early in November with displays of Christmas cards, crackers and toys, with advertisements of the Pantomimes that startled the unready, who were still picking late roses in their gardens and had not realized that winter had begun. They observed the approach of Christmas with pleasure, impatience or boredom according to their nature and obligations.

Joy Harding welcomed with delight every string of tinsel in the tiny windows of the poorer shops, every catalogue that arrived from the big London stores. She had not been to her own home for Christmas for three years. She had not had a Christmas at home with Hilary since before her marriage. This Christmas at Stackhouses to which she and Stephen and the boys were going had become in her mind the end of her life. She did not think beyond it, she could envisage nothing happening after Christmas. She expected the holiday to put an end by magic to all troubles and difficulties. She said to herself, "When we go up there for Christmas everything will be all right, and Stephen will be like himself again."

In the meantime and without knowing it, she drew her preparations for Christmas round her like a covering. She was determined to take the exact presents they would like best to everyone, to her mother and father and Hilary, to the old servants who had been with them when she was a girl at home, to the gardener and his family, to the Vicarage children and the old woman who cleaned the church, to everyone she knew in the village. She emptied a small chest where she kept her shoes and filled it with parcels, letting the boys help her. She made a good many of the presents, and searched the shops carefully for those she could not make. She had not much money to spare and was never extravagant. She enjoyed her contrivances.

Stephen came home one evening early in December and found her by the fire in the sitting-room. She had a doll on her knee, and was tying a satin bonnet on its curls. She dressed dolls as they had been dressed when she was a little girl, in pink and blue satin frocks trimmed with narrow lace, and hats and bonnets to match.

Stephen came across to the fire and stood looking down at her bent golden head.

"Pretty!" he said. "Who is that for?"

"For Veronica, Mrs. Cartwright's little granddaughter,

you know. She's just been sent home from India; she's going to be at the Vicarage for two years. She'll be five. She's three months younger than Lin."

"How ever do you remember them all?"

"I remember everyone up there."

"I told you I was going out to-night, didn't I?"

"Yes. I've made supper early. It's only cold beef. I shall be glad to have a long evening. I want to do some cutting out on the dining-room table after the room's cleared."

She did not ask him where he was going. She was anxious to make his going out a convenient thing for both of them, something about which there need be no discussion. She wished that he would not say any more, but knew that he was going to. She went on hastily.

"Jack fell and cut his knee again this afternoon, took quite a bit out of it. He was very good. He turned round to me when I was bathing it and said, 'My blood is like a red, red rose. That's out of a song in the Song Book, Mummie.'"

Stephen smiled. "Did he?" The smile died. "I want to tell you, Joy. I'm going to a meeting of a new Left Discussion Group."

"I didn't ask you where you were going."

"No, I know you didn't, but I think it's fair to tell you."

"You know what I think, Stephen. I think it's wrong and foolish and stupid of you. I expect a lot of other people will go because you do, people who won't know as well as you do when they hear a lot of nonsense."

"Nobody will go because I do. Nobody knows I'm going. Besides, why should they?"

To Joy it was obvious that wherever her own kind of people led, other people followed. She tried another argument.

"You can't think your father is wrong, Stephen! You're so fond of him! He's a good Conservative!"

"He belongs to another generation that hasn't been able to grasp the quick-change history of the last few years. Besides, he isn't altogether against me."

Joy thought, Then he ought to be! You'd better talk to my father!

"I simply don't know how you can go against your own kind of people."

"I haven't gone against them yet. I haven't done anything. I'm only learning and seeing my way."

"You are going against them!"

"I think I shall have to!"

Joy said slowly,

"If you do, I shall never forgive you."

"I'm sorry you feel like that."

"It's wicked to stir up trouble in a peaceful country."

"Where everything is just as it ought to be, I suppose?"

"No, not quite, of course, but better than any other countries, and much better than it would be if your new friends got hold of it. Look what happened when there was a Labour Government."

"Oh, Joy! You don't even begin to understand!"

"I'm not interested in politics, but I know which kind of people are right and which are wrong! Daddy and Hilary . . ."

"If they and I disagree, you would be sure that they were right and I was wrong?"

"Yes," said honest Joy, the word slipping out of her. She was quite unaware how deeply she had hurt him. She explained. "Daddy's older and has had so much more experience. And of course Hilary has knocked about the world a lot."

"I see." He stood for a minute leaning his elbow on the mantelpiece and looking down at the fire.

"Well, I'd better wash. Next time I'm going to one of these meetings, I'll get something in town and not bother you to have supper earlier."

"Oh, it's no bother. To-night it's rather convenient."

He had gone out of the room. She began to put her bits of silk and satin together, sighing as she did so. It spoilt all the fun of looking forward to Christmas that Stephen should be so tiresome. Surely, surely, when he got up there, when he was in the country with Dad and Hilary to talk to, he would come to his senses. His own family were worried, she knew. His mother had said something about Stephen's new ideas, and about Ward not liking it, Stephen losing his job.

Joy was not going to worry about that, she did not consider that the hated Ward had any right to ask what Stephen did outside the office. The mere thought of his criticism made her feel a little more kindly to Stephen. She remembered that she had forgotten to put out the new jar of chutney which he liked with his cold beef, and went to the store cupboard to get it.

The room in which the Left Discussion Group had arranged to meet was on the top floor of a café, and was reached by four flights of stairs. Through glass-panelled doorways, the panting members as they climbed had glimpses of desolate rooms in which chairs were stacked one on top of each other round bare tables. In the room hired for the meeting, half a dozen tables were covered by dubious white cloths, and adorned by a couple of drooping chrysanthemums apiece in tall vases of electro-plate. The vases, narrow at the base and branching at the top, were of the pattern that holds least water and topples over most easily. On the table nearest the door, solid white coffee-cups stood in rows, marshalled behind plates of iced cakes in frilled paper cases. The general effect of a tea ordered for a parish outing was heightened by Harold Pearson, who stood at the door looking like a member of a Young Men's Bible Class, and handing out typewritten slips about the Group. To each slip he had carefully pinned a yellow leaflet giving particulars of a peace meeting, a blue leaflet giving particulars of a meeting to raise funds for Medical Aid in Abyssinia, a white leaflet heralding a series of lectures on Dialectical Materialism, and a scarlet leaflet bearing in bold black letters the arresting title, DO YOU SEE RED? Harold Pearson pressed these upon everyone who came in, and said with encouraging cordiality, "Do sit anywhere you like. Won't you go up to the front?" One of his friends had a makeshift bookstall just inside the door, stacked with copies of the *Daily Worker*, and of political literature from the Communist bookshop. Half a dozen youths stood ready to find chairs or pass leaflets. Word had gone forth that the party was to encourage this venture.

Marjorie Ward, who climbed the stairs in a compound mood of defiance, excitement and nervousness, was very much disappointed at the appearance of the meeting. She had imagined a dark attic, probably lit by a single candle, with black-browed revolutionaries in red shirts exchanging mysterious passwords at the door. She had been rather frightened of coming, wondering if they would refuse to let her in. She had put on her last winter's coat, and quite an old hat which she wore on wet days. This was a dreary place, the sort of place where every table had a bottle of tomato sauce and an ash-tray advertising something, but it seemed respectable. Marjorie hesitated in the doorway, wondering if she had come to the right room. Harold Pearson, of course, knew her by sight. He had seen her once or twice when the whole Ward family appeared at the works to receive royalty or to grace some public occasion. He was surprised and delighted to see her this evening.

"Would you like to go up to the front?" he said helpfully. "Or would you like one of those chairs at the back? I think you'd hear better at the front." Like all organizers of meetings he was anxious to fill the front seats, but had so far been thwarted by the invincible determination of any section of the British public to huddle together in modest retirement as near the door as possible.

"I—I don't know." Marjorie looked round the room for Mary. "I was really coming to meet a friend."

"Well, won't you sit down here until he comes." Harold flicked an eye at one of his aides-de-camp, who was instantly at his side.

"Find this lady a nice seat, Jack."

Jack took possession of Marjorie, said that it was a cold night, and advised her to sit near the radiators which had just been put on and would soon be warm. Marjorie sat down, a little disappointed by the general urbanity, but relieved of her worst alarms.

Grace Allworthy, who walked in a minute or two later, was not relieved but disgusted by the cordial welcome of the young men grouped round the doorway. She knew them all, as she knew everyone in the town who took any part in politics. Not a solid Labour man among them! Just these young whipper-snappers of I.L.P. boys and Communists, some of them not even with conscience enough to be members of their Trade Union! Silly lads that nobody would take any notice of in a Labour Division, so they had to go and make a noise and a stir somewhere else like children banging drums to attract attention to themselves! A jealous resentment surged up in her. If this discussion group was going to be run by young fools of Communists, she wasn't coming to it. She didn't see much need for a discussion group, anyway. All problems that mattered were well thrashed out at the divisional meetings of the Labour Party, and anyone that really cared for the cause and the movement could and would join that.

"I'll find myself a seat, thank you," she said, sniffing disdainfully. Holding her head high in her second best red hat, she marched up the room and plumped herself down in a chair next to Tom Sutton.

The first person whom Stephen saw as he came in was Marjorie Ward, her face round, rosy and solemn above the soft fur collar of her coat. He thought, Good Lord, she'll catch it if the old man finds out! It occurred to him that perhaps he was in the same boat. Neither for his daughter nor for his right-hand man would Ward consider this a suitable evening's occupation. How much he would mind, Stephen did not know. For Marjorie probably a good deal, and for himself? That was one of the many questions which had, perhaps, still to be answered.

Marjorie looked round, saw Stephen, and smiled with some relief. At that moment Joy would have been justified in saying, I told you so, for Marjorie thought, Oh, it's all right then! She would have been glad if Stephen had come to sit by her, but he nodded, smiled, and went further forward into a row divided from hers by several chairs.

With a jerk of his head, Harold Pearson promoted a colleague to his place at the door, moved across and sat down by Stephen to have a few words with him. Stephen was a genuine fish, the son of a well-known Conservative in the town, one of those middle-class sympathizers whose support had to be won, who must be wooed gently with comfort and reassurance. Harold knew his duty. He chatted pleasantly to Stephen about the weather and the news of the Abyssinian War. A soothing, unspoken message ran through his words, Look, we are all right, quite ordinary! There is nothing to be afraid of!

Mary knew that Stephen was there and where he was sitting before she came into the room, or else it seemed to her that she had known, memory and precipience running together in the first shock of delight. She slipped into a chair next to Marjorie, whose face lost its slightly anxious expression, and beamed with satisfaction.

"I'm so glad you've come! I felt shy without you. But I thought it would be different," Marjorie murmured.

"I think all meetings are pretty much alike, really."

"Everyone looks so quiet and ordinary!"

"What did you expect? Did you think they'd be dancing the carmagnole?"

"I suppose I did. Anyhow, I thought they'd all be more sort of rough and excited. Show me a Communist. Is there one here?"

"Several. That man moving chairs in front, and the fair-haired young man who's just gone back to the door with the leaflets."

"Good gracious! He seemed so respectful and obliging! He spoke to me when I came in. There's Stephen Harding just in front of us, do you see?"

"Yes. Does your father know you've come to this meeting?"

"No. I daresay he won't ask where I've been. He doesn't always." Marjorie pushed away from her the thought of what would happen if he did. She had learnt that the only way to enjoy any liberty was to leave such considerations until she got home and deal with them as the moment provided.

"Perhaps it would be better not to tell him that you saw Stephen here."

Marjorie looked startled.

"Oh! Yes, I see. Dad wouldn't like it, perhaps."

Her new-found security was shaken. Everyone might be perfectly quiet and ordinary, but all the same it wasn't the

240

kind of meeting her father would like her to attend. She said in an unhappy voice,

"The women and the little babies down at the South Albeck Welcome look so poor! A lot of the babies have to have free milk, and I found out that one family sold it again to buy some meat for Sunday. Besides, the mothers don't get anything. The babies get fatter, but the mothers don't." She fingered the clasp of her handbag, a lump of tortoise-shell that caught the light like peat water in the sun. She had seen and admired the bag yesterday in a shop window, and her mother had bought it for her, just for a little present. It had cost three guineas and she had been delighted with it. Perhaps she ought not to have it. But trade must go on, people would have been paid for making it. She sighed. The world was too perplexing for her. It seemed impossible to make everything fit in. She looked again at the door, and whispered to Mary,

"Oh, look, there's a clergyman coming in! Why, it's Leslie's Mr. Forrester. You know, he came to supper the first time you came. I haven't seen him since."

Naomi and Claud Unwin came in with the two speakers who were going to open the discussion. One was Mr. Averdick, the Labour member for a neighbouring constituency, a solid, quiet man who stopped as he went up the room to shake hands with Grace Allworthy. He was pleased to see her there and asked for her husband. They were sound people whom he knew well. His chief anxiety about this meeting was that he should not find himself appearing on a platform with a Communist, and he cast a doubtful eye on the other guest, a young woman with a delicate face, too lined for her age, and a mop of uncovered dark hair. She might very well be anything. He was somewhat relieved to see that there was no platform, only a table distinguished from the others by being at the top of the room and having two vases of drooping chrysanthemums instead of one. Standing up casually behind a table with a Communist was not quite the same thing, although if it should get about, his detractors would certainly make the table into a platform for purposes of argument.

He was also relieved to see that the chairman was Edward Lister, a man of blameless reputation, an ex-schoolmaster, a Liberal who had unsuccessfully contested several parliamentary elections, a Quaker, a Pacifist and a recognized supporter of the League of Nations. Lister had been persuaded by Naomi to take the chair on the understanding that the purpose of the discussion group was to work for peace and to preserve liberty. He was a good and kindly man who honestly cared for peace and liberty, and in their name sometimes sponsored causes and meetings whose ultimate aim was neither. He perceived only ideas and did not concern himself with their practical application. He opened the debate with a few remarks on the English heritage of free speech. Although determinedly international, he shared the widespread belief that free speech had been invented by English people and was enjoined by their laws. Nobody in the room was much stirred by what he was saying, but they all agreed with him, that is to say they were in favour of free speech up to a point, most of them feeling that Fascists ought not to have it, and Harold Pearson and his friends making a mental reservation about Trotskyists, who ought not to be allowed to speak at all. Mr. Averdick merely hoped that the speech would not be too free this evening.

The dark girl, Truda, leaned her head on her hand, and stared, seeing nothing of the faces before her. She had a German grandmother, and had gone to Germany as a governess to three young children, whose father was a doctor and an able writer on scientific subjects. He and his wife had been very kind to her, and she had loved them and had been devoted to the children, especially to the little girl, Hildegarde. It had been discovered that the doctor's mother was a Jew. He had been dragged from his bed, beaten with lead tubing under his wife's eyes, and carried off to a concentration camp. His wife was left without money to struggle on as best she might. In the winter the children were ill with measles, and Hildegarde, who had gone short of food and warmth, developed pneumonia and died. Truda came back to England and had a nervous breakdown. She had always been a quiet, reserved girl, but when she recovered, she was like something

242

hardened in great heat. She went everywhere working for the Communist Party and speaking against Fascism. She hardly saw the towns that she went to, nor the audiences to whom she spoke, having always before her eyes the beaten and broken body of her employer as he was dragged from the house, his wife's face, and the face of the little dead Hildegarde. She did not listen to the chairman nor to Mr. Averdick, who was making a sober, dull speech about the duty of every citizen to be interested in public affairs. She was waiting until her turn came to spring to her feet and bring home to these placid, safe people the horrors of cruelty which she had seen in that winter in Berlin.

All very well, Stephen thought, listening to her, but what about the other side? What about the people who could stand up there and tell stories of Russian nobles and bourgeois murdered and starved to death? He could feel that dark, thin girl, speaking with the sincerity forged out of bitter experience, was moving the audience whom the other two speakers had left untouched. But what was she moving them to? He saw the square brown hand of Tom Sutton crisp at his side. He saw the whole world moving in a deadly circle, hatred begetting hatred, cruelty breeding cruelty, violence spawning violent deeds and thoughts wherever it touched the lives of men. And humanity, decency, toleration, the kind and quiet virtues were King Canute to that terrible tide. Was there anything that could stem it? Any generosity wide enough to cover it, any love deep and strong enough to stand up against it? No longer religious, except that he occasionally went to church with Joy and the children, he found himself praying in his heart, Oh God, let me do nothing from hatred! It was so hard to see where hatred began! A little vanity, a little greed, small weeds that grew up by love and gentleness, and in no time at all were great plants choking them until they died at the roots. The worst of it was that hatred could grow out of the roots of love. Truda had loved Hildegarde and her parents and that love had made her a fighter and a hater. Of that kindly relationship with decent human beings this woman who lived only to be an enemy was born.

Truda sat down, exhausted and white-faced as though all

243

the strength had gone out of her. The audience stirred and rustled, released from tension. There was a moment's silence. The chairman looked rather helplessly round the room, and caught the eye of Harold Pearson which seemed to be goading him into action. He sounded inept and irrelevant as he said that the meeting had heard various arguments put forward in favour of starting a discussion group, a group of all progressive-minded people working together for peace and liberty. The matter was now open to discussion.

There was the usual pause. A dark-haired young man at the back leapt to his feet and said breathlessly,

"I am a member of the Independent Labour Party, and I say that we want a discussion group but we do not want anybody in it except the working class. We do not want the middle class coming in to try to be our leaders. They will only lead us to their own advantage, and abandon us in the struggle. There is a point when they will betray us. Let us get rid of them *now* . . ."

The Communists, displeased by his want of tact, tried to hush him down like parents hushing a child who is misbehaving at a party, but the young man was warmed and encouraged by the sound of his own voice, and went on,

"What do they want with us?" he cried, fixing a baleful eye on Stephen. "It stands to reason they cannot want our victory! There is no place for them in the new world. The workers are nothing to them. They have not been born in the working class . . ."

Stephen lost his temper. He jumped up and said, "Don't be such an infernal snob, sir," surprising himself, and making two-thirds of the meeting laugh. The young man stopped and stared with his mouth open, taken aback by the unexpected retort. Edward Lister, ploughing on for peace and liberty, said to him, "I think, sir, that surely all sorts and conditions of men should be free to express their opinion in a discussion group?" He rubbed his chin, perplexed. In the days when he had made his own revolt against his Tory, Anglican parents, he had believed with great simplicity that the working classes were democratic, and all his life it had surprised him if he found one of them who was not.

A tall, fair young man leapt up in the opposite corner of the room.

"I am in favour of a discussion circle, and I should like to propose to this meeting that we start next time by discussing the shameful departure of the U.S.S.R. from the true principles of pure revolution as maintained by Trotsky."

Harold Pearson rose to his feet.

"I should like to point out to the last speaker that Trotsky is the enemy of the one great contemporary experiment in Socialism, and that Stalin is the true revolutionary who has followed the course that alone makes that experiment possible!"

Every Communist in the room was now sitting upright, bristling like a tom-cat who has smelled another tom-cat on the wind.

The fair young man who was still standing up, said,

"Stalin is a traitor to pure revolutionary principles. Trotsky . . ."

Two or three Communists were on their feet at once.

"Stalin! . . ."

"Trostky! . . ."

"Stalin! . . ."

"Gentlemen! Please! Order!" Edward Lister rapped on the table. "This is not the boat race!" he said, trying to strike a human note, but striking one which failed to find an echo in the audience.

Grace Allworthy had been sitting with taut back, one hand tapping on her knee the familiar tattoo of her rising wrath. She jumped up.

"Mr. Chairman. I see no use in a discussion group at all if a lot of silly lads are going to get up and argue with one another like street corner boys! I'm not at all sure that there's any need for a discussion group, but if some people think they want one, let's have one, only let's discuss something sensible! Let's take the Labour Party Programme or some book that Mr. Unwin can choose for us, perhaps, and then we can think about it before next time, and come prepared to say something that isn't nonsense. It's all very well, but some of us are busy people and have too much to do to waste our time like this!"

She sat down, clasping her thin, strong hands together in her lap. You don't catch me here again! I only came to please Mary and see if there was any sense in it. Bad-tempered children playing a game, that's what they all are! It's always the same thing, a lot of young men in a hurry, knowing nothing at all and wanting to start something new, instead of going on with the work that's been doing all these years! Why ever it is, I don't know, that people must always be wanting to make a new start instead of going on with things!

Tom Sutton at her side shifted in his seat. Trotskyists are fair silly! Talk through their hats they do, always, but I reckon I'm not coming here again if this is going to be another Divisional Labour Meeting with Aunt Grace and Uncle John making a Sunday-school class of it! If we do discuss the Labour Party Programme, they'll hear something they won't like, thought Tom, forgetting that this was hardly a new experience to Aunt Grace and Uncle John after fifty years of politics.

An animated private discussion was now going on at the back of the room between the Trotskyist and two Communists. Naomi looked round and frowned impatiently. What curious law was it that made all the silliest people speak first in a discussion so that those who knew anything were discouraged before they could open their mouths? In another minute the meeting was going to die in Edward Lister's limp hands! She looked at him with such an intensity of will that her eyes drove him to action, and he rapped again on the table.

"Well, now. Will someone please propose a date for the next meeting and a subject for discussion?"

At the end of the meeting, Stephen stood by the bookstall, turning over the paper-backed volumes. The dark-haired young man from the Independent Labour Party came up to him and shook hands, saying, "Of course I didn't mean anything personal." Stephen accepted the overture cordially, and turned back to the bookstall. There was a pamphlet there advocating a United Front for England. He picked it

246

up and read one or two of the arguments. The arguments did not matter much. The point had been in the young man's outburst. Could people like him ever trust people like Stephen to go through with it? Were they, perhaps, right not to, considering the pull of tradition and upbringing? Stephen acknowledged himself afraid of stirring up faction and violence, restive at the mere thought of coercion or of any threat to the liberty of the individual. Did he really want a dictatorship of the working class? He did not. Did he think that Mr. Averdick, the Unwins, Tom Sutton, and the various disputants at the meeting were the sort of people whom he would trust to make important decisions? He did not. Then what was he doing with them? He believed and hoped that enough people like himself would be with them in time to make the change over to a new way of life by general consent. Suppose there were not enough? Would his new allies, when the pinch came, trust him to stand by them? Even more important, could he trust himself to stand by them? There might be a price that he could not pay for the new world, perhaps liberty. But liberty was comparative, each man was free only in certain directions. Liberty was the most important thing in the world, but one must be careful not to make a parrot cry of it, robbing it of meaning.

He was so deep in his thoughts that he did not see most of the people go out. A voice at his side said, "Good evening!" He looked up and saw Mark Forrester. As his eye fell on the clergyman's coat and collar, he realized why the table spread with small pamphlets seemed so familiar. Of course! It was like the tables at the bottom of churches with little books on the Christian faith and the Apostolic succession! It was really very much the same, for the little books of the Left like the little books of the Church tried to fit on to a disobedient universe the arbitrary pattern of a complete faith.

"I hear you are doing great things at St. Jude's," he said.

The young man shook his head.

"Very little. Not much more than we can hope to do here in a different way. It is possible to change a few men's minds, but I see no hope for the world unless we can change their hearts."

Mary was standing by the door with Tom Sutton and Naomi Unwin. She was going on with a conversation of which she herself knew little, and of which Naomi was obviously tired. If she let it end, she would have to walk out of the room without speaking to Stephen, and she could not face that blank drop into disappointment. She had already refused to go and have a cup of coffee with Marjorie, who had gone away disappointed. Now she was boring Naomi with disconnected remarks about a recently-published book on the Psychology of Dictators. She did not at this moment care two pins about the psychology of dictators, and was taking a mean advantage of the fact that Naomi felt it her duty to be interested.

Mark Forrester finished his conversation with Stephen and went out. Stephen came towards them, smiling at Mary. Her absurd happiness brimmed up so that she could not hold it.

"Claud has taken the speakers to the station," Naomi said. She pushed the dark hair back off her forehead and added, "Lord, I'm tired!" She looked this evening as though the burden of the modern world that she so unremittingly tried to sustain was too much for her.

"Let's all go and have a drink?" Stephen suggested. They trailed down the half-lit stairs, and out into the night of cold, gently falling rain that rayed the light of the street lamps and shop signs, and made a black gleaming river of the now half-empty street. Stephen said to Mary,

"We generally seem to meet in bad weather—either fog or rain!"

"Rather difficult not to if you meet people at all up here in the winter!" She was so happy that she could hardly contrive to answer him. They were walking along the pavement together, a few yards in front of Naomi and Tom. Naomi had seized upon Tom with the same avidity which Mrs. Allison would have shown in seizing upon a Duchess. She was now drawing him out with great perseverance, while Tom had retired into his shell, and was looking out of it suspiciously, wondering what she was driving at.

Stephen said again,

"Is it much good, do you think, this sort of thing?"

She wanted to say, Oh it is, indeed it is, look what is happening now! She subdued her dancing spirits and compelled herself to answer reasonably.

"I don't know. Not much at first, perhaps. But I suppose anything that brings people together and makes them think and discuss is useful. For the average, decent well-meaning person it is so much a matter of becoming conscious of the situation."

"Here we are." He pushed open the swing door and they all followed him.

They turned into a warm room where several people were already sitting at small tables with glasses and mugs before them. The walls of the room were red, and there was a glowing fire. After the chill gentility of the café and the wet night outside, the place was genial and welcoming. Tom Sutton looked more at home with them as he sat down in it, but Naomi, with her thin, eager face and restless eyes, seemed irrelevant in the middle of its ugly comfort. When sitting down, she always looked as though she were just going to get up. She sat forward on the edge of her chair, glancing eagerly about her. She was examining the people at the other tables. They were types, and this pub was a piece of social history. It was interesting and useful to know how other people spent their lives.

Stephen's mood of discouragement began to slip from him. He knew that he liked to be with Mary. Not only could he talk to her freely of his difficult new path in life, but some liberation that was not of the mind came to him from her. Everything became very clear and very simple, a matter for straightforward feeling.

"Your uncle didn't come to-night."

"No, he's gone to a committee meeting—the Housing Committee."

"Was he very much disappointed about the elections?"

"No, he didn't expect anything else!"

"He's a patient man!"

"He's had to be. Yes, he is patient anyhow by nature. Much more so than Aunt Grace, who sees red sometimes when things happen slowly. She's acquired patience by living with him, but he was born patient."

Their conversation was not really important. It was the light airs on the strings beneath which some deeper instruments played the tune. Once Mary thought suddenly and forlornly, It's no good! Then she yielded to the happiness of the moment, which seemed cut off from life like a dream.

A woman at the next table, stout, comfortable, with a broad, good-humoured face, smiled at her.

"You wouldn't think I'd just come from a church bazaar meeting, would you love? But I have. Talk, talk, talk, all the evening, a lot of us all magging together, and I said to myself, Marion Jennings,—that's my name, Mrs. Arthur Jennings, but he's been gone seven years, has Mr. Jennings, —I said to myself, You *shall* have a drink on the way home. Not that I come here often, mind you. It's just once in a way. I'm more broad-minded than some of them, you see. St. Oswald's, the church is; I daresay you'll know it. Mr. Jennings was sidesman there ten years. With the last Vicar that was, the Reverend Pratt. There was a good man, a real Christian! Not that I'm saying anything against the present Vicar. Live and let live is my motto. I'm not one to pick holes in people."

"I'm sure you're not!" Mary said, smiling.

"Well, it isn't Christian, is it?"

A young man sitting by the fire, who looked like a commercial traveller, had been listening with interest, and edged his way into the conversation at the first stop.

"It's a pity all Christians and all church-people don't think like you do, Ma'am! The world would be a different place if they did. Take Russia, now! There's a country in a terrible state and all because when there was a Church, it did nothing for the poor."

Tom Sutton had jerked up his head at the mention of Russia, and opened his mouth to speak, but Mrs. Jennings brushed him aside.

"I don't want to hear anything about Russia. We're none of us Bolsheviks here, I should hope! Besides, that wasn't the Church of England, now was it?"

"The state of Russia now is a great improvement on the state it was in before the Revolution," Naomi said, forestalling Tom, who had been going to say the same thing, and who looked only half pleased with her for taking the words out of his mouth.

"This is like a conversation out of *Alice in Wonderland*," Mary murmured to Stephen. He turned and nodded, and she caught his quick, sweet smile and thought, He is happy and amused, he likes all these funny people, he is here with me. Her happiness seemed more than she could hold.

"Well, I've not been to Russia," the traveller admitted. Fortunately he did not inquire whether Naomi had either. He was anxious to impart information. "But I'll tell you where I have been lately, and that's Germany. Now that's a fine country! Say what you like, it's wonderful what Hitler has done for that country! I was over there six years ago, and you would not believe the difference. I saw any number of new roads and new houses and new works and shops."

"See any concentration camps?" Tom Sutton asked roughly.

"No, I can't say as I did. Mind you," said the young man impartially, "I dare say there were some. But I was told the reports were greatly exaggerated."

"I'll be bound you were."

How odd it is, Stephen thought; here we are sitting, a casual company of people collected together by chance in a pub in the West Riding of Yorkshire, and we talk about Russia and Germany and are instantly divided, and yet we none of us really know very much about either. He said,

"Well, I haven't been to Russia at all, and it's some time since I've been to Germany, so let's have another drink all round and talk about something nearer home. Will you join us, sir?" he added, turning to the only other table near them now occupied, where a solid, elderly man with a bushy moustache was just finishing a pint, by no means his first, apparently, for when he spoke it was with the mellow deliberation of a man who had enjoyed his evening.

The traveller who had decided that Tom Sutton was his natural adversary, leaned towards him and said,

·I suppose you think all men are equal?"

"Reckon they all ought to have the same chance."

"It's nonsense talking like that," Mrs. Jennings said, comfortably. "Because they don't. Take the heathen, now, out there in Africa or wherever it might be, bowing down to wood and stone and knowing no better. It stands to reason they haven't had the same chance as you have, brought up in a good Christian country. Why, they haven't even heard of the Church! Well, of course, it may be a bit different now with the wireless, but then I don't suppose many of them understand English. But what I mean, if people don't start with the same chance about religion, why should you expect them to start with the same chance about other things that don't matter so much?"

Naomi shrugged impatient shoulders.

"Would you like to live under a dictatorship?" she asked the traveller.

"I don't see that it matters much. I'm an ordinary sort of fellow getting on with my job, and the men I met over there in Germany were ordinary sorts of fellows getting on with their jobs, and it didn't seem to make much odds that they were governed by Hitler and we have the British Constitution."

"Well done!" the elderly moustached man said approvingly. "Well done! Very good for this time of night."

Stephen laughed. The traveller, absorbed in making his point, smiled perfunctorily, and explained, "You don't really notice what you're being governed by when you're keen on your job and busy with ordinary life."

"Would you like to have to fight those other ordinary men you met in Germany?"

"I don't want to fight anyone," the young man replied sincerely.

"Well, some day you may have to, if you don't notice who you're being governed by, or who they're being governed by."

Stephen, who found Naomi a most exhausting woman, said, "Oh Lord, let's give politics a rest! We've been at them all evening."

The young traveller looked disconcerted. Naomi did not

believe in giving anything a rest. She shrugged her thin shoulders again. It was exasperating dealing with people like Stephen, who carried their easy, casual *laissez-faire* habits with them whatever party they joined! Left or right, reaction or revolution, their attitude was blow the whistle, keep the rules, stop for half-time, let's all go off to tea together when the game's over.

The elderly man with the large moustache had finished his last pint. He got up and paused on his way out by Stephen's chair.

"You're all right," he said impressively. "Qui' right. Politics—'s all talk! Religion—'s all smoke! S'behaving like human beings to one another—that's what matters!"

Outside on the wet pavement under the dark sky the party split up; Naomi and Tom went off to their separate trams. Stephen lingered a moment, saying good-bye to Mary.

"That old fellow had the last word, hadn't he? He was right, you know. Behaving like human beings to one another is all that matters."

He sounded relieved as though he had found a clue to the perplexing world. That's all he knows or wants really, Mary thought, to behave like a human being to other people and see they get treated as human beings. That's all he'll ever really grasp of politics. He seemed to her so simple, kind and boyish that her very heart was wrung. She wanted to cry, Keep out of it all, Stephen, keep out! You'll be used and exploited and hurt and find yourself twisted out of the very thing you care about, treating other people like human beings! It's different for me. I'm tougher. I've seen more of the worst sides of people. I don't expect much. I've made up my mind that behaving like a human being to people nowadays can't be done without politics; I've got to go through with it. But you keep out!

She felt almost as though she had said it aloud but she had not, for he was still smiling at her, it was only a second since he had spoken. That he should be happy and safe,

253

most of all that he should not be misled and forced into betraying himself, seemed to her at that moment more important than anything else in the world, but there was nothing that she could do to make sure of it. She said, "Well, Good night! See you at the next meeting, I expect!" and turned and walked away from him down the street.

On that same evening, Robert sat in the Drill Hall in Company Office swearing in a new recruit. The walls of Company Office were hung with regimental photographs, from a group of the heavily moustached volunteers at the time of the Boer War, to the officers of the battalion photographed in camp at Catterick last summer. The recruit, whose name was Clarence Baker, was a short, stocky young man with a ruddy complexion inclined to pimples, a snub nose, and a quiff of brown hair which sprang up on top of his head in spite of a liberal dose of oil. He was sweating, and breathed heavily through his nose, in awe of the officer, but even more in awe of the Company Sergeant-major, who stood by his side regarding him with the quelling eye of a man keeping a savage dog under control.

Robert stood up and handed Baker a Bible. Baker took hold of it gingerly, as though afraid his hands might dirty it. He had scrubbed them unsparingly before this ordeal, but they were the hands of a collier, ingrained with coal dust, the nails blackened and broken. Robert noticed that they were a good shape, sinewy and flexible. The recruit was physically a good specimen. He looked, as many of them did not, as though he had had enough to eat when young and had been sent to bed in good time. When not constricted in every limb by nervousness, he carried himself with a certain jauntiness.

Robert and the Company Sergeant-major stood up and took off their hats. The eyes of Clarence Baker grew rounder. He had no hat, but he ran a hand over the springing lock of hair that jumped up again under his fingers. Forgetting to be gingerly with it, he gripped the Bible for support.

"Now repeat the words after me," Robert said. "I swear by Almighty God that I will be faithful and bear allegiance to His Majesty King George V and his heirs and successors."

Clarence Baker, hoarse with alarm, mumbled the words in a broad Yorkshire accent.

"And that I will as in duty bound honestly and faithfully defend His Majesty, his heirs and successors in Person, Crown and Dignity——"

"Person, Crown and Dignity," Clarence Baker repeated, relaxing his hold on the Bible for a second to draw a hand across his wet forehead.

"Against all enemies according to the conditions of my service."

"Against all enemies according to the conditions of my service."

Being told to kiss the Book, Baker stooped his head awkwardly to meet it, and gave it a smacking kiss. The Company Sergeant-major at once took it away from him with the air of a man glad to recover regimental property. Robert shook the recruit's hand.

"Well, Baker, you're a soldier now. I wish you the best of luck!"

Robert and the C.S.M. put their hats on again. Baker muttered, "Thank you, sir," and looked as though a weight had been taken off his mind. The C.S.M. pushed the attestation forms across the table to Robert. As Robert signed them he thought, It's a funny thing, I've done this dozens of times, but it always gives me a thrill! Wonder if it gives him one? Clarence Baker to defend His Majesty in Person, Crown and Dignity. What does he make of that? Words linking up a young collier, who works underground and drinks his pint of beer and watches his football match or dog race, with history and tradition and the movements of empires? Probably he doesn't make anything of it. Just glad it's over. Looks a likely lad. His boots want mending.

Robert pushed the attestation forms across the table.

"All right, Sergeant-major. Anyone else to see me?"

"One or two more, sir."

While he waited, sorting the papers on the long table,

Robert thought about his subaltern, Jerry Garrod, who ought to have been there that evening but was not. A nice boy, Jerry, but there were too many occasions on which he ought to be there but was not. Spoiled at home and too well off, that was the trouble. Had romped through three years at Oxford driving about in a sports car, and entertaining his friends, and was now articled to the firm of solicitors in which Robert was a partner, and light-heartedly pursuing the study of law. A nice, friendly lad, but if he was going on in Robert's company, he must turn up at Prize-Givings and Sergeants' Dances, and having turned up, must keep sober at them. What he did at the monthly dinners of the Officers' Mess was his own look-out, and if he must make a bloody fool of himself, Robert's only concern was to see that he did not drive himself home afterwards. But I must have a word with him, he thought, about these Tuesday evenings. He must learn to do the thing properly.

"Private Hemingway to see you, sir."

"All right, Sergeant-major." Robert nodded dismissal. In theory the C.S.M. was present at all interviews, but in practice he often preferred to see the men alone. They spoke more freely, and in Robert's private opinion, Sergeant-major Gull, though reliable and efficient, was a bit fussy and apt to nag the men. And Hemingway was a good man, one of their best shots, who had won a divisional prize that year.

"Well, Hemingway?"

The man looked chilled through with the cold, Robert thought. His big hands, on which the knuckles stood up white, were raw and red, there was a bluish look on his face, and he had a sty on one eye that made him blink constantly. He was a quiet, steady fellow, a great fisherman, as Robert happened to know. He was on the committee of a local Anglers' Club, and spent a good deal of his spare time on it.

Hemingway swallowed nervously,—Robert saw the movement under the pale skin of his throat,—and said,

"Could you lend me a pound, sir, and stop it out of my bounty? I don't hardly like to ask, but I don't know where to turn. I've been on the Exchange three months, and my wife's been ill, and now we've got our little girl down with bronchitis, and we've got behindhand like. The rate's got to be paid this week. With one thing and another, we shan't have any food in the house from Thursday."

Hemingway made the statement simply and undramatically. He was ashamed because he had to try and borrow money. He was an engineer, and he had always been so careful to keep inside his wage, to put a bit by for chance. Only this autumn there had been so many chances. The loss of his job, his wife's illness, the little girl's illness, everything seemed to have come at once, and when it was one thing after another, you couldn't get your head up.

"Bad luck!" Robert said. He was thinking quickly. It was contrary to King's Regulations for an officer to lend money to his men. Robert, when younger, had done it more than once in defiance of King's Regulations, and knew that the officer seldom or never saw his money again. He had not been a Territorial officer for twelve years without learning to say no. But Hemingway was a good chap, one of their best men, and he looked as though he had not had a meal for a week.

The sweat sprang out on Hemingway's forehead. He moistened his dry lips with his tongue, and an involuntary cry broke from him.

"I shan't be able to pay my Burial Club, sir, this week."

Robert knew what that meant. Not to be able to keep up the insurance for your funeral meant to the Yorkshire workman not only the prospect of a pauper burying, but the loss of self-respect and solidity. Pride lay not only in looking after yourself and your wife and children when living, but in the knowledge that you could see yourself decently and almost handsomely underground when dead, as though even your corpse must maintain a sturdy independence until it became dust.

Robert took out his pocket-book.

"Here you are, Hemingway. I'll lend you a quid, and pay me back at your own time. I'm sorry you've had bad luck. I hope the child will soon be all right again. It's bad weather for bronchitis with all these fogs. You don't look very fit yourself. You've been worrying, I expect. You'd better cut along home."

His next applicant was Private Tolson, a loose-limbed, red-headed young man, who began as soon as he was inside the door. "I just wanted to know, sir, if you thought there was a chance of a start for me in your brother's place or anywhere?"

Robert considered Private Tolson dispassionately. A slack fellow, never kept his uniform properly. Odd how this so reasonable request for work was so often made by shysters, by people who would, he was convinced, be no good at any job for which he recommended them.

"Well?" he said. "What can you do?"

Private Tolson, a wordy person, began to expound his autobiography. From this two main themes emerged, the fact that he had never lost a job through any fault of his own, and that while actually an unskilled labourer with no training, he could do almost anything if given a chance. He seemed from his confused account of his career to have been given several chances, all of which, he gave Robert to understand, had been spoilt by the unjust disposition of his employers.

"I don't suppose I can do anything for you," Robert said, "but I'll make a note of your name in case I hear of anything."

"A chance, sir, that's all I ask," Private Tolson repeated fervently.

Robert thought that there were many better men wanting that same chance, but scribbled the name down on a pad, said, "I'll let you know if I hear of anything," and nodded dismissal.

At the next request, "Private Rogers to see you, sir," he groaned inwardly. Private Rogers had a passion for interviewing his Company Commander. During the past five years, he had visited Robert at frequent intervals to ask for promotion, and, when he did not get it, to ask why he had not been promoted, to suggest that he should be made one of the company cooks, to try and borrow money, to ask for a job, and to be reprimanded for not doing his drills. This

258

last interview alone was not of his own seeking. The attitude of Private Rogers to his Company Commander was that of a devout Christian turning to the Deity for help in every emergency.

"What is it, Rogers?" Robert refrained with difficulty from adding "now."

Rogers, a square, pale man with a drooping moustache, shifted his feet and cleared his throat.

"Well, sir, it's like this, I don't 'ardly like to ask you, but wasn't there some new law about divorce, you can get it straight away for nothing now, sir? You see my wife and I, we aren't getting on too well." Robert felt a vivid sympathy for Mrs. Rogers. "She's gone 'ome to 'er moother for a bit, and I thought we might as well split, and if you can get this 'ere divorce now for nothing, a chap at the works told me it was a new law, sir. I 'ope you don't mind me asking you, but I thought you'd be able to tell me."

"No, you can't get a divorce for nothing. There's no new law to make that happen."

Private Rogers looked incredulous, doubtful and dissatisfied, and murmured, "It was a chap at the works told me."

"Well, he told you wrong. A divorce has to be paid for."

"Well, what had I better do then, sir?"

"Try not to be a bloody fool," was on the tip of Robert's tongue, but he suppressed it. He had grown wary about giving advice on matrimonial problems, questions of separation allowances and illegitimate children, all of which various members of his company put up to him from time to time. It would not do to have anyone saying in court, "Well, the officer at the Drill Hall told me . . ."

"I'm afraid I can't interfere in a matter between you and your wife, Rogers. You can't get a divorce for nothing, and a sensible man thinks twice before getting it at all. That's all I can say to you. Think it over."

When the last of them had gone, Robert went into the ante-room of the Mess to get a drink. A bottle of whisky, a bottle of gin, and a dozen bottles of beer were kept in a cupboard for officers to help themselves. Standing drinks to one another was not allowed, a useful provision to prevent young fools of subalterns from standing one another half a dozen rounds and being unable to pay their mess bills at the end of the month. Robert took a bottle of beer out of the cupboard, entered it in the book, and glanced round. Horsfall, another Company Commander, was lying back in a big chair, smoking a pipe and drinking a whisky and soda. The Adjutant, Cartwright, was drifting about the room, because he had a feeling that he ought to be about, and that the Permanent Instructor might want to speak to him. He was continually amazed by the violent activity of the Territorial battalion to which he was attached, by people like Robert and Horsfall who worked all day at God knows what, and then came rushing into the Drill Hall at night full of tiresome energy. He could not quite grasp their lives outside the Drill Hall, he was still surprised at not being able to get them on the telephone when he rang them up at home at the gentlemanly hour of twelve o'clock in the morning. They made him feel hustled and tired, and he longed for the date six months ahead when his term of service with them would be up, and he could sink back into the peaceful arms of the first battalion.

Robert sat down in a chair by Horsfall.

"Seen the paper?" Horsfall asked.

"No. Any news?"

"A big Italian advance in the North."

"They're getting on a bit, aren't they?"

"Looks like it."

"Of course they haven't really come up against it yet. Neither the worst of the country, nor any big resistance."

"No. Extraordinarily clever fellow that Haile Selassie is. Everything he does, all his appeals to the League, so right and dignified. He makes them all look rather small."

"They say it's his son's French tutor who writes them all."

"Pity someone doesn't assassinate Mussolini.'

"Yes."

Both young men were silent, seeing in their minds again those pictures that now pervaded the morning paper, the advancing army with its tanks and bombers and guns, the mountainous country, the black men lying in ambush with their rifles. In the minds of both was shame and uneasiness because their own country, which did not want these things to happen, had been obliged to allow them. Horsfall knew what Robert meant when he said suddenly,

"It was those damned Labour fellows and that wave of sentimental pacifism all over the country.

"I know. Well, we shan't be caught that way again."

Robert was thinking about Stephen. He said,

"Look at our fellows here, Horsfall! How can anyone say they're fit to govern anything! Except for the theory of the thing, what's the sense of them having votes? Why, half of them don't know what the House of Commons is. They believe any yarn that any chap in the works tells them. One of my men to-night came to ask me if there wasn't a new law making divorce free. Someone had told him there was, and I told him there wasn't, but I bet he's gone away to think it over and decided I was wrong. People like that having votes are a potential danger. It only needs somebody to get hold of them, somebody like Oswald Mosley or a bit more convincing than that, perhaps, or some wild Red prophet, and where are we?"

"Yes. You know, I think there ought to be an intelligence test for voters, something like a test for a driving licence. When you're twenty-one, you ought to have to apply at the Town Hall to get an examination paper to fill in. Do you know what are the British Empire, the House of Lords, the House of Commons, Tariffs, the League of Nations, and so on."

The Adjutant, who had been fussing vaguely about the room, went out. Robert grinned after his retreating back.

"Think Cartwright would pass your test?"

"Oh, not a hope."

The two young men chuckled, enjoying their contempt. They expended much time and simple wit on the differences between themselves and the Regular Army. Like the divided parties of the Left, they obeyed that curious law which makes a man more interested in the clash with those nearest to him than in the larger clashes with the outside world.

Leslie was the first to return to Grey Gables that evening. He ran up the front door steps, whistling, about half-past ten, and let himself in with his key. To his surprise, he found his father waiting by the fire in the hall. Ward usually said good night to his family about nine o'clock, and went off to his study, where he worked alone or with his secretary for a couple of hours. To see him late at night sitting idle with *The Times* on his knee and the whisky and soda on the table by him was astonishing.

Leslie looked for a minute at that dry, grey figure in the big chair. A sense of his father's loneliness and isolation touched him for the first time. In the happy warmth of his own friendship, he realized that his father had no friends. He did not think that anybody, even his mother, was nearer his father. He himself had always been worlds away, admiring, wondering, fearing. He had never since he could remember been able to speak to his father naturally. He was nearer to it now in his new confidence than he had been for years. He called out, "Hulloa, sir! Good evening!"

Ward shifted *The Times* and looked at his son.

"Where have you been?"

"I drove Angus over to a meeting of the Helford Literary Society. He was reading them a paper, and it's rather a difficult place to get to by train or bus. We had a chop together first, and the society gave us some sandwiches and coffee afterwards, that made us rather late getting back."

"All the Grants well?"

"Bunny had a fall yesterday and cut his head; he had to have two stitches in, but he's all right to-day."

"You say they're going to be in Aire for Christmas?"

"Yes. They're too hard up to go away."

"Your mother thought of asking them here for Christmas Day and the week-end. Some sort of nursery could be arranged for the children in one of the spare rooms, and one of the maids could look after them and give Mrs. Grant a little rest."

"Oh, Dad!"

The sight of his son's happy, eager face pleased Alfred Ward, who expected to have his bounties received with enthusiasm. He nodded.

262

"Well, your mother will write a note to Mrs. Grant in the morning. You'd better get to bed. Don't go wasting too much time on all this literary stuff. It will never get you anywhere. I'm glad for you to have three years at the University, and I'm glad to see you enjoying them, but you couldn't have had them if I'd spent my time reading Shakespeare when I was a lad."

"I know." Leslie was abashed. It troubled him to think that his anyhow outwardly prosperous youth had been earned by his father's years of hardship.

Ward saw the boy's face fall, and was sorry in some obscure corner of his mind. He had been shy and stiff with the little boy, impatient and contemptuous of the nervous, sulky schoolboy. During these last few weeks he had felt a new stirring of pride and affection for the cheerful, normal young man who seemed to have superseded both. He did not altogether dislike the picture of his son dashing about in an expensive car, giving lifts to his tutors, and wasting his time on anything so utterly unremunerative as English Literature. It showed that Alfred Ward could afford to gratify his children's fancies.

"Well, never mind," he said, not unkindly. He almost smiled as he added, "You won't break me yet awhile."

"I'm—I'm awfully grateful!" Leslie stammered.

"You must help your mother to arrange a party for your friends and see about seats for the Pantomime. You'd better get to bed now. Leave the door unfastened. I'm waiting for Marjorie. Do you know where she is this evening?"

"No, sir."

"All right. Good night."

Marjorie came in a few minutes later. She was already feeling guilty and disturbed about her evening's occupation, and she was startled át the sight of her father sitting before the fire. His "Where have you been" struck an unhappy echo in her own mind. She hesitated and faltered,

"At a meeting."

"What sort of meeting? Where was it?"

"In a café. It was a meeting to discuss things—books." Hastily she told herself that the meeting had decided to

263

read and discuss later a book about the system of education in Soviet Russia. She added. "We're going to discusss a book about education."

"What for? You've had all the education you need, and you aren't rearing children yet!"

Marjorie murmured feebly that it would be interesting to hear other people's ideas.

Ward looked at her in silence. It was an extraordinary thing that he did not seem to have produced a sound, practical, sensible child! All this reading books and running after ideas and hearing people talk was sheer waste of time and didn't get them anywhere. What sort of people was Marjorie likely to come across at a meeting discussing books on education? Women teachers, probably, and a few young men with long hair and no money. His mind pursued one of its subterranean channels of thought, and his next remark seemed to Marjorie to be incredibly but reassuringly far away from her doings of that evening.

"You haven't seen much of the Wilsons lately."

"No," Marjorie agreed without much interest.

"Your mother is thinking of asking them to dinner on Christmas Day. And I thought you and Billy Wilson and Leslie and the eldest girl, the one who is away at school, might like to make up a party now and then and go dancing somewhere in the holidays. You can have tickets for any dance you fancy or money for whatever hotel you like to dine at. What's the girl's name. Violet, isn't it?"

"Violet's still at school," Marjorie murmured, raising the only objection she could think of.

"She's rising seventeen, isn't she? And I suppose she can dance? She's a sensible girl, or was when I last saw her, and not likely to turn up her nose at a few treats in her holidays. You'll want a couple of new dresses, I daresay. Well, if you've spent your allowance, you can have them for Christmas."

"Thank you, father," Marjorie said soberly.

He looked at her with impatience. He had always liked her better than Leslie, but he felt that she was pulling against him, that she wanted things that he could not give her by spending money on her. She was setting up standards that clashed with and criticized his. It all came of this girl on the paper, this niece of John Allworthy's. He decided that she was a bad influence and Marjorie must see less of her.

"Well, you'd better get to bed," he said shortly. "Good night."

Marjorie wished wildly that she had a different father or was a different person. She wished that she could come home and talk over all her doings and her problems to a parent who would be interested and uncritical, or that she had the pluck to say, I've been to a Left political discussion meeting. I feel unhappy about all the money you spend on me. I don't want to go dancing with Billy Wilson, who is like ourselves, only more cheerful and better tempered. I want to be a different kind of person, contributing more and taking less, and I want to be with people like that, like Mary. Of course she could not say a word of it. She must remain half defiant, half deceitful, wholly uncomfortable. She said,

"Good night, Father!" and went upstairs to bed.

The children had prayed as usual for snow at Christmas, but there was no snow on the stinging wind that whipped their faces as they scrambled out of the car at the door of Stackhouses, and flung themselves with shrieks of greeting on Tim, the red setter, and the wire-haired terrier, Ladybird. Joy's "Jack! Lin! Say 'how do you do' to Grannie and Grandpa first" was drowned in the noise. The grown-up people laughed at one another over the tumbling heap of boy and dog on the doorstep. Inside, the hall was warm and bright with the light of lamps and of the leaping fire. Glossy evergreens, the clean evergreens of the country, hung in thick wreaths above the mantelpiece and on the stair rail. Mrs. Norton shoo'd the dogs and the children inside, "We've left the stable door open for the car, Stephen." Hilary, who was carrying their bags into the hall, said, "I'll go round with you," and jumped in beside him.

The gravel sweep that circled the house towards the stables was a terrace cut in the side of a hill. The fields dropped steeply below it, and a stone thrown over the edge would fall on the first houses of the village, huddled with their backs against the rising ground as though for shelter. It was just getting dark, but the rounded shapes of the hills still stood out clearly against the sky. A light shone here and there among them, the window of some lonely farm. The air was pure and cold. There was great space and silence.

Stephen put the car in what had once been a horse box, lit a lamp supplied by Hilary, hung it on the bonnet, and hooded the bonnet with rugs. They walked back to the house together talking about the roads and the journey. In the hall, Joy, radiant between her mother and father, was warming her hands at the fire. She had thrown off her hat, and her hair shone and glinted as yellow as straw in a manger. The brass candlesticks on the mantelpiece were twisted with long chains of red berries. Joy touched them and said, "How pretty! What ages it must have taken to thread all those! Did you do them, Mummie?"

"No, Anne Armitage did them. She brought them all over yesterday, and some lovely Christmas roses that she had grown. She and her father are coming to dinner to-morrow."

"Have a glass of sherry, Stephen?" Hilary moved towards the table. Joy, not quick as a rule to notice people, looked at him quickly, feeling some shyness or excitement in him.

"They've generally gone South for Christmas before, you know, to the uncle, Johnnie Armitage, but he's been ill and had to winter abroad, so Anne and her father are at home alone and we thought they'd better come here. They're used to a large party. We've seen a lot of Anne lately. She's such a nice girl. She's wonderfully clever with the garden. She's brought me such lovely roses long after mine were all over. They're more sheltered than we are, you know, with Spurn Brow between them and the east winds."

Stephen, Hilary and Colonel Norton were standing by the table, laughing and talking. The boys had scampered off to the kitchen to say how do you do to Cook. Joy and her mother were alone together by the fire. Her mother was smiling a little as she spoke of Anne, she was telling Joy something about her, not that she was a nice girl and could

266

grow roses, something that she told with the curve of her lips and her eyes. Hilary! Joy's heart turned over with excitement, sympathy and a pang of loss.

Joy's father and mother were both tall and though now grey, had been fair. They had that likeness to one another which sometimes seems to grow upon a married couple who have lived together for many years in harmony. The Colonel was lame from a shrapnel wound in the leg at the battle of Loos. He had retired from the Army in 1913 but had raised and commanded a service battalion of his old regiment in 1914, and had fought in France for a year until invalided out with a D.S.O. Joy was like both her parents but more like her father. The young subaltern who saw his first active service on the Indian frontier in the eighties had been conspicuous by a head of the same shining yellow hair. They were a devoted and closely-knit family. The children had been taught as soon as they could walk to obey an order, to share sweets evenly, and to observe the rules of any game with scrupulous fairness. The opinion of the family was united on nearly all important matters, and as none of them liked abstract discussion, or even read a book unless they were ill in bed, nothing had ever disturbed this unity. Compared to them, the minds of the Marsdens and Hardings and their friends in Aire were flexible, their awareness of contemporary issues was almost modern. Stephen had never begun to feel like part of his wife's family. They were kind to him, but he knew that they would have preferred someone more of their own world for their daughter, they were faintly contemptuous of "trade," and disappointed that Stephen was a poor shot, and had never hunted. They saw that he was ignorant of country knowledge and suspected him of being clever. Loyal to Joy, they did not put their criticisms into words, they were at no time good at putting things into words. They gave Stephen presents on his birthday, Mrs. Norton remembered his favourite dinners, and they all did their best with him.

Electric light had not yet come to Stackhouses. From dusk

onwards, a row of candlesticks stood on the hall table, and an oil lamp on the window ledge half-way up the stairs made a circle of subdued gold. There was another oil lamp in the spare room and a wood fire burning on the hearth. Alone in the room, Stephen unpacked his bag while Joy had a bath. He was caught back by the smell of the house, smell of oil and wood fires, into the old enchantment. He had been so enraptured to find himself here on his first visit, had so trembled for the good-will of Joy's parents as he unpacked his bag in this very room! He had agonized all through dinner that evening because a lout of a young man who talked about hunting all the time was absorbing Joy's attention. When, after the dinner guests had left, Joy had remarked casually that Brian was putting on weight too much, something that seemed like an actual physical oppression had been lifted from Stephen's heart. That half-hour on that first evening when he had drawn round the fire with his hosts and shared the return to intimacy which follows the departure of strangers had seemed like a foretaste of happiness. There was nothing that he wanted more than to become part of the family whom he was to regard in a few years' time as his narrow and boring in-laws. The truth perhaps lay between his two visions of them. The aftermath of receding glamour had been unfair to people who were unmistakably good of their kind. Back again in their house at Christmas, warmed by their welcome and their sherry, Stephen felt nostalgia for his old view of them.

When they were in bed together that night, Joy said to Stephen,

"Mother says Anne is so nice. Just the right kind of person for Hilary. She thinks they'll be very happy together. They like all the same things."

There was an unconscious regret in her voice as though she had missed something and did not know what it was. Stephen felt that he ought to take her in his arms, but the evening among people who were so far off from his mind that he could not even disagree with them had closed him up and made him irritable.

Joy's voice went on in the dark,

"I've often wondered who Hilary would marry. He isn't the sort of person to fall in love easily. He's got very deep, strong, tenacious feelings. It would have been so dreadful if he'd married the wrong girl, someone who didn't fit in with him. It might have spoilt the whole of his life."

Stephen walked to church next morning between his two chattering little boys. A white frost had partly consoled them for the lack of snow. When they ran into the nursery that morning to open their stockings on the hearthrug by the fire, they found the nursery windows embossed with flowery patterns. The ruts and pools in the road were covered over with sheets of ice, shading from grey to white as though the ground were covered with gulls' wings. The little boys jumped on them, shouting as the ice crackled beneath their small, heavy boots. They fell behind the rest of the party, and Stephen took a hand of each and told them to run. All three arrived at the churchyard gate with glowing cheeks, their breath making three clouds of smoke before them on the frosty air. The churchyard rang with the noise of footsteps going to the church door. There were greetings and smiles and looks of friendly curiosity for Joy's two children. From the square grey tower the bells sent out rings of sound that widened and spread and sailed away into the pale sky. Joy, going into church with her mother, turned back and smiled at Stephen and the boys. She had a cap of green felt pulled sideways on her golden hair. Her cheeks were rosy and her eyes shone, she looked like a happy little girl. The indescribable smell of church met them as they followed her through the doorway, smell of childhood and tradition, of being good and Sunday morning. Lin pushed on, caught up his mother and insinuated himself between her and his uncle Hilary, but Jack hooked a woollen gloved hand into Stephen's arm and whispered, "Bags I sit next to you!"

Stephen knelt in the pew between Jack and his mother-in-law, joining in the responses.

"Endue thy Ministers with righteousness," the Vicar prayed, far up the church, in his old, precise voice.

The answer came in a murmur that rose and died like the sound of a wave.

"And make thy chosen people joyful."

"Give peace in our time, O Lord!"

Stephen thought, what a hope! and was abashed by the dignity of the response.

"Because there is none other that fighteth for us but only thou, oh God!"

The old man's voice rose and strengthened on the last prayer.

"Oh God, make clean our hearts within us."

The congregation, a few thinking of the words, some of their Christmas dinner, some of other matters, murmured together,

"And take not thy holy spirit from us."

Jack tugged at Stephen's arm and whispered,

"Is it Hark the Herald *now*, Daddy?"

"Not just yet."

During the Collect for Peace he looked along the pew at Colonel Norton and Hilary, two men trained for war and no doubt praying quite sincerely, aware of no incongruity, perhaps even aware in their nerves and blood though certainly not in their minds that to be undisturbed by incongruity was the only way to live in the modern world. But that was an old prayer and soldiers had prayed it before and meant it. Modern world was a cliché nine times out of ten! It was the whole life of humanity that was made up of incongruities, it was a shifting, changing stream of them through which you fumbled your way towards some half-formed vision of completeness. You wanted so much to apply a form and see a pattern, for it is the nature and desire of every man to be an artist, the artist is only the ordinary man a shade more articulate, a little luckier.

The congregation scrambled to their feet, straightening their backs and brushing the knees of their trousers.

"Is it Hark the Herald *now*, Daddy?" At Stephen's nod, Jack screwed up his face into a grin of ecstasy, leaned forward and signed to Lin, but Lin, who was sitting on a footstool, had occupied himself in unlacing his boot, and was now trying to lace it up again with a piece of string that he had found in his pocket. Always a child with great powers of concentration, he had forgotten all about "Hark the Herald," and was bent on trying to make the frayed end of string go through the holes. Joy looked down at him, smiled, and hauled him briskly to his feet. His mother might have done that to him, Stephen thought, making him behave with just that unresentful firmness. He thought of his own mother and father, of Christmas at home, with sudden longing.

Stephen's mother and father were sitting in St. Jude's Church, listening to a Christmas sermon by Mark Forrester. A sudden attack of flu, developing on Christmas Eve, had obliged Canon Halliday to go to bed. It was too late to get anyone else to preach on the morning of Christmas Day and he was reluctantly obliged to let his curate loose on one of the largest morning congregations of the year, and on what he could not help feeling was a most inappropriate occasion for a young man who specialized in gloomy warnings.

His temperature would probably have been higher than it was if he had been able to hear the use that Mark Forrester was making of his opportunity. Mark had had no time to prepare a sermon. He had made a few notes the night before when he got the Canon's message, but what he really wanted to say did not come to him until he stood in the pulpit, inappropriately framed in green branches of holly and flanked by two small Christmas-trees. He rested his hands on the rail and looked down at the congregation, who had just settled comfortably in their seats, glad of the respite from standing and kneeling, and prepared to put up with the sermon. His general impression of the rows of faces turned towards him was of an immovable complacency. They had come to church because it was Christmas Day, they were feeling benevolent, sentimental and cheerful. Soon they would go home to see what the post had brought, and to eat

271

their Christmas turkey, or in some houses, the cold lunch of pie and ham that was only a prelude to the evening's feast. They would listen to what he said to them with a mild interest, and perhaps criticize it afterwards, if they remembered enough about it. They would not let it disturb them. He burned with a desire to disturb them. He leaned forward over the rail, and his voice rang out in the big church.

"Peace on earth, goodwill towards men!

"Where shall we now find peace on earth? A European nation has in this last year embarked upon an unjust war against a Christian people, whom the nations were bound by their obligations to protect. They have not kept to that obligation. They have failed the solemn covenant of the League of Nations, and by that failure have delivered over our civilization to battle, murder and sudden death. Where shall we now find peace on earth? In Abyssinia, where the men who claimed the just protection of their brothers are being bombed and gassed? In Germany, where, day and night, preparations for war go on, and little children in the schools are taught to look forward to war and violence as man's estate? In the Far East, where Japan is gathering her forces to spring again on China? In our own country, where armament factories are busy again with the weapons of death? There is no peace on earth in our time, and the day is coming when that shall be brought home to us, here in this city, in our daily lives."

He paused for an instant. The faces upturned to his were not so much startled and shocked as disgusted. Their expression was that of children who have been given rice-pudding at a party. A few of them looked mildly amused. In the vicarage pew, Jean Halliday thought, "Poor Daddy!" and looked up at her father's substitute with wicked mirth in her green eyes. Robert Harding glanced at Beryl, saw her face grave and troubled under the brim of her hat, put his lips to her ear and whispered, "Here endeth the Pathé Gazette!"

Mark Forrester thumped suddenly on the rim of the pulpit.

"Why is there no peace on earth? Because there is no real goodwill towards men! Because greed and vanity still matter

272

more to men than doing to their neighbours as they would be done by. Because to most people—and especially to people in masses, to nations—love is a name and a dream, and greed and vanity are realities. There are nations called Christian, but their Christianity is only skin deep. It has never inhibited their pride, their lust for power and possession. You here in this church call yourselves Christian. Where is your own goodwill towards men? You will go home to your Christmas dinners. Does it trouble you that there are people in this town who will have no real Christmas dinner, or whose Christmas dinner, if they do have one, will have been given to them by charity? Does it trouble you that there are people living within a mile of you short of food, short of clothes, short of warmth, short of hope and comfort and security? Do you remember that there are in this country, not far from you, whole areas where men have no work, where their sticks of furniture are sold one by one for food and coal, until no more can be sold because the pawn-shops have no hope of selling them again? Do you know it? If you do not know it, go and look and see! If you do know it, down on your knees and pray God to forgive you for the selfishness of your own lives."

Something like a shiver of indignation went over the church. This was not what they had a right to expect on Christmas Day morning! Lionel said to himself sadly, God forgive us, I'm afraid he's right! Most of the congregation, aware of subscriptions to Christmas Dinner Funds, of presents sent to poor relations and unattractive friends, of hours spent on charitable committees, thought, The young man doesn't know what he's talking about! The dear old Vicar would be horrified to hear of his impertinence! A nice Christmas spirit! Robert, his eyes screwed up, his lips curving in a discreet smile, thought, Well, I'm damned, funniest Christmas sermon I ever heard! What's the matter with the poor fellow? Anybody would think it was Boxing Day already, and he'd had too much Christmas dinner the night before.

Mark's voice rang through the whole great building.

"Awake! Up! Shake yourselves out of your comfortable lives! Join God's Army, God's Red Army, before it is too late and fight in the one great battle against injustice and oppression and against the spirit that says, 'I'll keep what I've got and the rest is not my business.' That spirit is abroad and rampant and ruining the world. Why do the nations so furiously rage together and the heathen imagine a vain thing? Because love of God and love of man are defeated, have been trodden underfoot for centuries. It may be that this is the last challenge of the powers of darkness, one last chance to save civilization. The world is waiting for a new wave of generosity, or for a great wave of death. You will not be able for much longer to say, 'This is not my business.' Stir yourselves now and throw in your weight with God against the devil. You may be too late to save England, to save Europe or the world from great disaster, but at least you may save your own souls!"

He turned his back on the indignant congregation, and the quiet murmur of his voice in the accustomed words of the ascription sounded irrelevant and surprising. "And now to God the Father, God the Son, and God the Holy Ghost." . . . He came down the pulpit stairs and walked back to the altar, a square, clumsy figure in alb and amice, a prophet to his Youth Group, a friend to those who had needed help, to other members of the congregation, a Bolshevik agitator, a tactless ass, an interesting preacher or a young man who did not know his place, to himself, as the chasuble was slipped over his head again, the inadequate representative of God. Behind him in the nave of the church, women opened their bags and men felt in their pockets. The organist played the first lines of "Christians, Awake," and with a relieved sense of returning to the normal, choir and congregation together saluted the happy morning.

"Well!" Alice said as the Harding family left the church together, "I hope nobody tells Canon Halliday how his curate took his place until he's feeling better! He might have a relapse."

Robert remarked, "It reminded me of a story I once read in a Christmas number. A fellow went to the dentist's on Christmas Eve, and the dentist got him all fixed up in a chair and strapped him in because he was a big fellow who

274

might struggle, and then gave him gas and while he was under, the dentist had a heart attack and died. His housekeeper thought he'd gone home, so she just locked up the door, and locked the house, and went off, and when the patient came round, there he was locked in with a corpse and strapped down. That was called, 'A Christmas Story.' I should think it would have been Forrester's idea of good reading, wouldn't you?"

Beryl and Lionel Harding were walking together behind. Beryl said in a troubled voice,

"I've an awful feeling that he was right. That what he said was true!"

Robert turned and glanced back at her.

"Good Lord, Berry Brown, don't you join the mourners! It's bad enough having Stephen going about saying our number is up! Civilization isn't finished yet, by a long chalk nor this old country either. We're in a lot more thriving way than we were four or five years ago. Why, that silly fellow can't see facts when they're under his nose! Look at unemployment down, trade picking up, the country solid for rearmament whatever nonsense the Labour Party have to pretend in Parliament! And everybody knows that's all my eye like the way they vote against something at a Council Meeting here when they've agreed to it on a committee and know perfectly well it's going through anyhow."

He turned to wave and shout Merry Christmas to an acquaintance who was passing on the other side of the road.

Beryl said sadly to her father-in-law,

"That sermon did make me feel I wasn't a good Christian."

"I suppose that's what all sermons ought to make you feel."

"Not on Christmas Day morning," said Alice firmly. "On Christmas Day you ought to be made to feel that the great thing is to be a Christian at all! Let's wait for Clare a minute, shall we?" She stopped to speak to old Mrs. Crosland. "Well, I was disappointed that we couldn't have Stephen and Joy and the boys this Christmas, but I'm really rather glad he wasn't there. He might have started thinking after that sermon and gone on all day!"

"It's a good job you've got one son who never thinks, isn't it, Mother?"

Alice smiled. But Robert was no fool, he had a sturdy power of acceptance and adaptability that Clare and Stephen lacked.

"I know it's an accepted fact," Robert said, "that people like me, Conservatives, middle-class, public-school, play golf and all that, never think. For one thing, nobody in England ever really believes that you can think and look well and cheerful on it. You're only allowed to think if you look as though you'd got chronic dyspepsia, like that poisonous fellow, Unwin, or if you spoil everybody's Christmas morning, like Forrester, or if you begin to go broody, like Stephen. Well, they can have it for me. But you mark my words, every time they do their thinking and get into a mess, we have to come along and get them out of it. They've all swallowed more ideas than they can carry, and they've gone to their heads, and they ought not to be allowed on the road until they've sobered up a bit." He added with a chuckle, "Poor old Stephen! If he's doing any thinking up there this Christmas, I bet he's doing it alone!"

During the holiday a number of Christmas letters were written more or less willingly.

Angus, sitting in a big chair by the library fire at Grey Gables, wrote to Charles Allen, who had been his great friend at Oxford and was now a schoolmaster in Devon.

"DEAR CHARLES,

"The book for me and the box of sweets for the family arrived safely, and were welcomed with shouts of joy. Thank you very much! I hope you are having a good Christmas. Glad to hear you may be coming up North, all the trains stop here. We live the primitive life, overrun by babies, but we can give you a bed and a plate of porridge and even boil an egg for you.

"Just at the moment there is no question of boiled eggs,

we are living in luxury, spending our Christmas in the home of one of the captains of industry. I haven't come across the breed much, have you? His son, Leslie, is my pupil. Quite good, and writes pleasant verse of a young, sentimental kind. He has hated home and been miserable at school, but is just beginning to shake off his cares and enjoy life. We're very fond of him. He's desperately short of self-confidence. I should think he has been told early and often that he will never be as good a man as his father, and the family has been snubbed socially by the provincial nobs of the town. One doesn't just know anybody here, my dear Charles. If one belongs to the old Aire families, one knows the old Aire families! Age of family usually two or three generations, which perhaps accounts for them having to be careful! Snob? Yes, of course I am, we all are. But to return to Papa Ward. He's a grey, dry, shut-up person who lives inside himself like a spider in the middle of his web, but likes in a grey, dry, quiet way to manage the affairs of everyone outside. He wouldn't make a bad dictator, except that I don't see him bawling clap-trap into a microphone. The man behind the Dictator, perhaps? Or one of these here wicked financiers who really tell the Prime Minister what to do? On a small scale, of course, what he directs is the local Town Council, I imagine. He's most interesting to talk to if you can really get him going, but I've only managed it once or twice. I'm very sorry for him. Nobody likes him much, and his two children are growing up and pushing out in what he thinks are quite the wrong directions. So they ought, of course, but he's less elastic than most parents, and has fewer compensations. The girl is a bouncing, bonny lass, more guts than Leslie, but thicker quality. She'll be all right. A family called Wilson came to dinner on Christmas Day. There is a son called Billy, whom I think Papa Ward has marked down as a prospective suitor for Marjorie. The Wilsons have climbed up in the world too, and become captains of industry, but they get a lot more fun out of it than the Wards. Billy is a provincial young man about town, slaps you on the back as soon as look on you, and tells what he calls 'good ones.' Very nice to Biddy and Bunny. Will probably marry Marjorie after all, and settle down and have six dearly loved children and be the backbone of England.

"You ought to see this house! It wants gutting from roof to ceiling! I didn't know there were so many loathsome objects! How Leslie ever acquired the rudiments of taste I don't know, but he has. All the matches are in velvet boxes with gold tassels, *even in the bathroom* where they match the bath-salts. Probably in the kitchen, but I haven't penetrated. Mamma Ward is thin, genteel, straining for correctness, but when she forgets about all that, is simple and kind, and rather lost.

"I ought to be writing my *serious work*, but I've had too much lunch. I can't answer the part of your letter about politics. If you must join the Communist Party, you must. I hope you won't get sacked. If I had a school I wouldn't have Communists on the staff, nor, I hasten to add, Fascists either, nor 'ists' of any kind! I wouldn't entrust the young to anybody who had handed over his mind bound and gagged. You say 'One can't keep out of it nowadays or keep it out of anything.' I would remind you, my dear Charles, that the compulsive element is nearly always the element of the neurotic and obsessional. Will you forgive me if I say that the person least able to keep his mind off one thing is the lunatic? It's the fantasy that ties you, not reality, which may not satisfy you, but leaves you free. If I were a very learned psychologist, I think I would write a book about Europe at this moment, and about the ghastly damage done to the human race by ideas—or ideologies if you must use that god-awful word! Ideas spring out of the noblest part of the human mind, and almost always leads to inhuman behaviour. Cf. the Inquisition! It seems, on the whole, better for human nature to be a bit less noble and look what it's doing. See Yeats,

> "'We have fed the heart on fantasies,
> The heart's grown brutal from the fare,
> More substance in our enmities
> Than in our loves.'

"I seem to have written you an extension lecture, of your charity forgive me! Don't forget to come and see us. Grizel would send her love, but she is out with Mrs. Ward being driven rapidly through the country in a large Daimler. I hope she's enjoying it, bless her! Your godson disgraced himself yesterday by pulling the table-cloth off the tea-table 'scattering ruin and spreading ban.' I think he wanted to register a protest against the décor of this house. Nice to be at an age when you can do these things! I may have to be in town for a night before term begins. Any hope of meeting? Till then or for ever,

"Yours,
"ANGUS."

From Claud Unwin, 14 Towton Row, to Naomi Unwin, The White Cottage, Elmsted, Surrey:

"MY DEAR NAOMI,

"I was glad to hear from you that Wanda's child had arrived safely, and that she was well. Please give her my felicitations. One does rather wonder what sort of chance the child will have! Paul is brilliant, of course, but obviously a mass of complexes. It always seems to me there's a streak of perversion about him. How on earth are they going to manage to keep a child on their income? Or is Paul getting more now from the paper? I've sometimes thought his work liable to date, but I hope he's still in the swim.

"I went out to dinner unexpectedly on Boxing Day. I went for a walk in the morning and met Angus Grant and his wife and young Ward and a sister. The Grants were staying with the Wards, and Leslie asked me to go in to dinner that evening. We had a very good dinner, conversation puerile. Something undeveloped about Grant, I think. Old Ward is an admirable example of the kind of rich man who ought to be hanged from a lamp-post. Brutal, oppressive, greedy, stupid, except in the actual business of getting on in the world. He struck me as having paranoiac tendencies. The boy's an obvious case of œdipus complex. The house reeks of bourgeois comfort and Philistine bad taste. Grizel Grant sent her love to you and said she was so glad about your friend's baby. I've got Parrott's book on the Economics of

Modern Banking to review for the *Politician*. I always think Parrott is overrated—a memory rather than a mind!

"Remember me to Wanda and Paul,

"Always,
"CLAUD."

From Edward Bates, Psycho-analyst, Cloverfield, Mornside, Nr. Aire, to Dr. Thomas Crosby, 90 Thirlmine Street, Liverpool:

"DEAR TOM,

"Many thanks for the driving gloves. I feel like a Prince in them! I hope you all had a good Christmas. I've had a couple of days' golf. I'm a bit out of practice, but I enjoyed it. Do you get any nowadays?

"When are you and Christine coming for a week-end again? Angela says don't leave it as long as you did last time. We've put in a new rose-bed behind the house, where that dingy shrubbery was, do you remember? The children are flourishing, and Janet begins school next term. I shall take her in with me every morning. I'm up to my eyes in work, and I expect you are. Wish there were some more of us up here!

"Write and suggest your own week-end. Any time suits us. All the very best for the New Year to you and Christine and Robin. See you before long, I hope.

"Many thanks and love from us all,

"NED."

Mary, sitting in the reporters' room at the *Yorkshire Guardian* office on a slack afternoon, wrote to her great friend, Jill, in her Hampstead studio:

"DEAREST JILL,

"I'm sorry my letters have been so scrappy lately. I've been meaning to write you a decent letter, but I never seemed to have had time. Now I'm shamed into it by your lovely Christmas present. Thank you so much, my darling, it was kind of you. I wish I was back in the studio this afternoon, and we were just going to make a hearthrug supper, and Taddy and some more of them were coming in, and we were going to talk till midnight. The great difference up here is in the things people don't talk about. Conversation doesn't go where it likes, it keeps on the footpath. I long sometimes for an evening when it is allowed off the lead again, and can run all over the grass.

"We've had rather a difficult Christmas family party. First of all, Mother worried terribly about the preparations and I was so busy just before Christmas that I had to scramble them in when I could, and she was nervous for fear everything shouldn't get done. It did, but only after I'd got cross with her, and she'd worried herself nearly ill. The party didn't mix very well. You know all about Aunt Grace, and of course you met Uncle John that time when he came to supper at the studio. They were their usual dear selves, but Frank doesn't like them very much, and Doris is completely married now and thinks what he thinks. She's happy and looks well and lovely. She's nearly sure she's going to have a baby, so it's all as it should be. Arthur misses her a lot, I think. I've discovered that he has a secret, passionate desire to be a clergyman. Doesn't it seem a funny thing to want to be? Though it doesn't seem so funny up here, this is still a very religious part of the world. My father was more or less Church of England, though Mother and Aunt Grace are Wesleyans, but Arthur's been confirmed with his great friend at the Grammar School, and they both want to be ordained together. I've been finding out from a man on the paper about Theological Colleges.

"I haven't got your letter here, but I'll try and remember your questions and answer them. I do quite like the job. It doesn't keep you keyed up like the *Daily Tribune*, there isn't generally so much rush, and there isn't the same feeling of heartless efficiency. I spend at least half my time attending parties and performances and meetings in aid of something. It's simply incredible the amount of work done in this city for every kind of good cause! The better-off citizens of Aire, especially the older ones, have a colossal sense of duty, and seem to feel responsible for anyone or anything that needs help. Of course, partly, they like being important and managing things, but mostly they are filled with the desire to do

281

good. I think they like it better if they don't do anything just for fun. A bridge drive got up in aid of the Infirmary or of a Convalescent Home makes them feel much happier than a bridge drive got up because they want to play bridge. I'd forgotten how strongly Puritan the North is, and how costive and how shy of showing its feelings in any way. Everyone who comes to the theatre here says what hard work it is to move the audience, and yet very often you find out afterwards that they've really enjoyed the performance.

"You wanted to know about politics. Well, there's a solidly Conservative Labour Party with a younger tail kicking against the head, an active Communist Party, small, of course, but one of the larger ones as they go. The prosperous people are nearly all Conservative. Half of them used to be Liberal and still call themselves that, but of course are Tories now to all intents and purposes. The blocks are pretty definite up here. There aren't any of the Champagne Communists. There are a few Left Dons at the University, but on the whole, the Left are working or lower-middle-class people. Heaps and heaps of people aren't interested in politics at all and haven't noticed anything happening. The people who've noticed least are the ordinary workmen, mostly interested in racing and football, and the upper-middle-class, especially the women. The wife of the professional or business man up here seems almost insulated from contemporary life—of course with exceptions. Everyone got a bit worked up when Mussolini went into Abyssinia, but now they've got used to the war and don't connect it with themselves. They know Europe's behaving very oddly, but they don't expect much of foreigners, and I don't know that they're really afraid. Sometimes I think they're sensible. If we are living on the edge of a volcano, anyhow they're having the last bit of their lives in peace.

"That's all I can think of at the moment about the things you asked. Jill, I want to tell you something, because I shall burst if I don't. I've fallen in love, a lot, and quite stupidly and hopelessly, as far as I can see. He belongs to one of the old industrial families up here. He's married to a lovely, stupid girl and he's got two little boys. He's a sort of secretary

282

and staff manager to Alfred Ward, who owns the big ready-made clothing factory that Uncle John works in. He is a natural, friendly person tolerant of everybody's point of view, and likes all sorts of people, but he's been brought up inside a comfortable box, as his lot are, and it's taken him some time to get out of it. Now he's got interested in politics, partly through talking to Uncle John and Aunt Grace, and he's going to join the Labour Party. Going Left up here among his sort of people is quite surprising to them. His wife and family won't like it and Ward may not like it. Now they may just laugh at him and Ward may take no notice, but I often think when I'm going about up here, that although most people don't feel very violently yet, when the squeeze comes, the next slump or whatever it is, they'll divide like the Red Sea, and then he'll be away from all his own people and on the other side. I'm half glad because he's too good for anything else, and half sorry because he'll be torn in two. He has dark eyes and dark hair and square shoulders and a most kind mouth and a very quick, sweet smile. Oh, Jill—I think you'd better burn this letter. If I get too desperate I shall come up for a week-end and talk to you. I haven't tried to write any short stories for weeks. I just can't. Imaginary people and situations aren't interesting enough. I was allowed to do a signed review the other day of a life of George Eliot. I'll send it to you.

"Lots of love. I wish you were here!

"MARY."

Rosie, who had taken Fred to spend Christmas with her family while Robert and Beryl were at Mill Hall, wrote to her friend Kathleen:

"6, Church St., Hudholme.

"DEAR K.,

"I thought I would wait till Xmas was over be-fore I wrote to you as you know one cannot be bothered with triffles at such a festive time. I hope you have had a nice time with lots of pressents.

"Fred and I are re-turning home tonight and can assure you we have had a splendid time staying with my sister

283

Clarice, her husband doesn't alter much, still as daft as ever and had us in hystrics with laughing, I never want to see any more food for quite a while, that's how I feel now all blown up like a prized tea cake.

"Cliff and his wife came to dinner and the usual crowd and when they got going with the banjo and mouth organs you can guess what kind of a time we had and Cliff resited that very familiar piece of poity that he composed himself, you re-member the one about the old brown cow had layed a brick, it created quite a sensation with those who hadn't heard it before, then we had the usual drinks of port wine for the ladies and whisky and beer for the men. I wish you had been with us it would have been like old times. Clarice bought me a nice bed spread for my bottom drawer and I'm coming home with more than I went with, you know how generous she is, give you her soul, when I remarked about it Cliff wanted to know if I ment the sole of her shoe just like the ninny he is.

"I'm looking forward to seeing you so will now wish you a speedy goodnight, Fred is waiting for me and you know how these men hate to be kept waiting.

"Cheerio for now,

"Your loving chum,
"ROSIE."

From William Marsden, Greenoak Hall, to Sir Walter Dovedale, 89 Minden Gardens, Bayswater:

"MY DEAR WALTER,

"Thank you very much indeed for the Cambridge Diary. At our time of life, it is pleasant to be remembered and to be reminded of our youth. I should like to revisit the old place again some day with you, but you are still a busy man, and I find it increasingly difficult to uproot myself, even for a week-end. I was thinking the other day of our first holiday together in Vienna. Do you remember it? The younger members of my family go abroad a good deal for holidays, but not in the same way, nor to the same Europe. They travel with passports into foreign countries, and I find it difficult to make them believe that before the War there really was an international society, and an international life. They are under the impression that Internationalism was a novelty invented after the War by President Wilson, and recently destroyed by Mussolini. There has, of course, been none since the War. The nations have become not merely national but provincial in the worst sense, illiberal, pig-headed, assertive, self-enclosed, without magnanimity or care for æsthetic values. Day by day I see everything that makes life worth living destroyed in the world, as though I saw good wine being replaced everywhere by those harsh cocktails only fit for the uneducated palate of the very young. And how are the palates of the very young to be educated when that is all the world sets before them?

"I have a young nephew in the thirties who is waking up rather late in the day to a sense of other people in the world and of the desirability of progress. He should have become a Liberal, but for the young people nowadays to join the Liberal Party is, I am told, to walk at the tail of a pauper funeral. He is, therefore, with some solemnity, doing what he calls 'going Left,' to the great distress of his mother, my sister Alice, whom you will remember. He is a good, honest, generous fellow, a little absurd at the moment, and he will no doubt be disgusted very shortly by the illiberal and bad tempered disposition of his new associates. Whether he will then swing back towards Toryism or become one more bad tempered Socialist remains to be seen. I am growing old and tired perhaps and shall not remain to see it.

"Thank you again for the diary and for your good wishes, and for the pleasure of hearing from you.

"I remain,
"Yours ever,
"WILLIAM MARSDEN."

From Stephen Harding at Stackhouses, Callerdale, to Lionel Harding, Mill Hall, Aire:

"DEAREST DAD,

"Thank you very much indeed for the books and the tobacco. I shall be rich in both for a long time! I hope you've all had a good Christmas together. I thought about you a lot. We've had quite fun up here, Joy and the boys have enjoyed themselves no end. I'd rather have been with you, of course, but the Nortons are very kind. Hilary has just got engaged to a girl called Anne Armitage—nice but dull, very like him, I think. Joy is pleased about it.

"I've had quite a lot of time to myself this week-end, and I've been trying to get clear in my mind a good many things that I've been turning over lately. I want to tell you first of all the conclusion I've come to. You won't agree with me, but I think you'll allow for my point of view.

"I feel that I must take a hand in politics, and I'm going to join the Labour Party and work in my local division. I don't only feel that a social and economic change must be made to come, I feel that it is inevitably coming. All this terrific piling up of Fascism and Nationalism, this swing back to the barbarian, is the last struggle of the old world. I think that unless all of us who see this and want the change take a hand, we may be crushed by the weight of the dying, or the struggle may be so bitter that the things worth keeping, liberty, humanity, decency, toleration, art and culture, will go down in the ruin. I hope that in England the change-over will come without violence. I think that depends on how many of us are willing to accept it and help it on. Especially I feel that this is a time when moderate men ought not to keep out of things. If we do, we can't complain because the world is slipping away from moderation. It's so easy to talk about Liberty and Democracy and stand apart from either side doing nothing. I think we've got to preserve Liberty and Democracy by going into things and helping to save them out of the wreck. Anyhow, that's my personal feeling, so I must go by it.

"Don't think I'm not sorry to be in the opposite camp from you or that I'm criticizing you. My world is such a different one from yours. I don't admire any man more than I admire you. I think probably if you were my age you would feel as I do about it all.

"I know there are going to be difficulties. Joy hates it all, poor darling, and will mind very much when she knows I am definitely committing myself. I suppose there is just a possibility of losing my job. Strictly speaking, it isn't Ward's business, but I can never quite tell how he'll take things. I can't help it. For me this is the only decent thing to do. I wanted to explain to you before I do it. Believe me always,

> "Your loving son,
> "STEPHEN."

From Lionel Harding, Mill Hall, to Stephen Harding, Lane End, Barton, Nr. Aire:

"MY DEAR BOY,

"Thank you for your letter. I knew I should not catch you at Stackhouses, so send this to you at home.

"I respect your integrity and admire you for making, and being prepared to stick to, a decision which will cause you some discomfort if nothing worse. Of course, I don't agree with you. I agree with you that many things want changing. But, my dear boy, they are being changed, slowly and surely, and not by any one political party, but by the slow growth of social conscience and universal good-will. If you want to take a hand in politics, you could do as much in the Conservative Party, by whom at least two-thirds of the progressive legislation in the country is made. You could probably do more, because I can't help thinking that a fish swims best in its own waters. On the other side, you will be fighting against opposition all the time in your wife, your friends, your family, and, I think, in yourself. I should be afraid that the constant strain would cripple your effectiveness in action.

"I also think that it's most important to-day not to bring into England bad blood and hatred. The feeling about politics nowadays is nothing like as bitter as it was when I was young. My old friend and enemy, John Allworthy, will tell you that he suffered something like persecution in the early days of the Labour Party. We are a nation that grinds slowly. Any stimulating or speeding up of the revolution— and of course there's a revolution going on and has been for years—will make hatred and sharper divisions. That is the last thing we want when all Europe is rent with hatred and sharp divisions. You might make bad blood between yourself and your own people. There's a danger that you might make bad blood between yourself and your new allies, who will always half distrust you, whereas if you stayed in your own camp they would know you for a plain enemy, and might half trust you. You have thought about the position with Ward, I know. You can judge better than I how far he would let you go. I have always believed that a man's first duty was to look after his wife and children, but your conscience is your own. Only I beg you to think again before you take any definite step. You can't tell where that step may lead you.

"As for criticizing me or going on to the other side, my dear boy, never give that a thought! The generations must see things differently. I am getting on, behind the times. I have tried to do my best as I saw it, but I know that I have not done enough. As poor Forrester tells us in church, when eight million people in this country are underfed, none of us can feel proud of ourselves. I don't ask you to do nothing about it. I only ask you to think what you are doing and how you can do it with least damage and distress to yourself and others. Whatever you do and wherever you go, I am always,

> "Your very loving father,
> "LIONEL HARDING."

Stephen Harding, Lane End, Barton, Nr. Aire, to Lionel Harding, Mill Hall, Aire:

"MY DEAR DAD,
"I have thought carefully. I can't help it. I've got to do it.

> "Your loving son,
> "STEPHEN."

PART III

"We have fed the heart on fantasies,
  The heart's grown brutal from the fare,
  More substance in our enmities
  Than in our loves."

W. B. Yeats.

On the evening of January 20th, 1936, Grace Allworthy stood in the parish room of the Onslet Road Wesleyan Chapel behind a trestle-table heaped with old clothes. She was selling at a jumble sale to raise funds for the South Aire division of the Labour Party. It was still possible to do quite well out of a jumble sale in the poorest parts of the city, although the plentiful supply of cheap, ready-made clothes had reduced the demand for second-hand goods in any other quarter. And quite right too, Grace thought. No woman ought to be dressed in another woman's leavings. She watched the customers who pressed against the front of the stall. Most of them were elderly women with shapeless figures and worn, lined faces, but with unabated vitality. Their eyes were shrewd to assess the quality of the clothes; the movements of their work-worn hands were brisk. Love for them swelled in Grace's heart and brought hot tears to the back of her eyes. They asked so little of life for themselves and contributed so much. They kept humour and spirit unbroken.

One of them began to turn over a pile of old hats at the end of the table. The hats were marked sixpence each. She pushed the heap away from her and said to Grace,

"You 'aven't a red one, 'ave you, love? Or a green? I do like a bit o' colour! Seems to make you feel brighter like."

She was a thin slip of a woman with greying hair, cut short, and a sallow wedge of face in which two brown eyes sparkled undaunted.

"I'm afraid that's all we've got," Grace said, and then paused. Growing hot in the stuffy room she had taken off her own cherry red felt hat, and thrown it down on the bench beside her. She was seized by one of the sudden impulses for which John had laughed at her in her girlhood, and which she had never outgrown.

"Stop a bit, love!" she said. "There's one here, fallen down behind. A nice bright red! Try it on!"

"Is that one of the sixpennies?"

Grace nodded.

The woman perched the hat on her thin hair. Its colour was unkind to her yellowish skin, its gaiety incongruous above her worn cheeks and lined forehead, but she cocked her head jauntily and called out, "Mrs. Wade! Sitha, Mrs. Wade, how do I look?"

Mrs. Wade, a stout woman who was breathing heavily over a pile of coats, turned and said, "Eh, by gum, it suits you a treat, Mrs. Cookson! Your old man won't know you if you go home in a hat like that!"

"I'll take it!" Recklessly stuffing her beret into the pocket of her old coat, Mrs. Cookson tipped Grace's red hat a little further over one eyebrow, winked gaily at Mrs. Wade, and walked over to the pile of worn stair carpets, brass rods, pictures with cracked glass and oddments of china in the middle of the room.

Grace picked out the least battered from the pile of hats and dropped a sixpence into the bowl.

It was late when she went out to catch the tram. Her legs ached with standing and her back with stooping, but her spirits were high in the glow of successful activity. They had made nine pounds. Her pleasure in the result gave way to a mood of anger that these things should be necessary. Tom Sutton had jeered the other evening at a revolution built on jumble sales. Ah, but he was a daft lad, that was just the sort of thing that a revolution in England would be built on, small efforts and small sacrifices! It was better than having it built on dead and maimed bodies! He had said that their Labour Party Division was very like a parish. And Stephen Harding had said that everything in England that was any good was run on the lines of a parish, it was the natural rhythm of the people. Well, the Labour Party funds had been made up out of pennies, and pennies that could ill be spared. Grace, who had seen it grow from a handful of men to one of the most important movements in the world, knew well enough what sacrifices, what self-denial and loyalty and devotion had gone to build it. And then for Tom to jeer and young whipper-snappers like Harold Pearson that had

292

never suffered nor lost a penny for it! Grace shook with anger, with a desire to put Tom across her knee and smack him. An impatient jerk of her shoulders made the jumble-sale hat, which was too large for her, wobble on her head; and she relaxed, thinking, "My old man won't half laugh when I tell him about my hat!" She was not without a lively pleasure in herself as a character, a woman to whom people often said, "Eh, Mrs. Allworthy, you are a one!" It was part of her vivid delight in the whole adventure of life that she was aware of herself as "a one" adventuring in it.

She had been out since morning, first ticketing and pricing the things for the jumble sale, then selling them. She had been, as always, entirely absorbed in what she was doing, and had forgotten the outside world. She arrived home to find John in a big chair by the sitting-room fire, smoking a pipe and reading *Barnaby Rudge*. He was a great reader of Victorian novels. He had, as soon as he could afford it, bought complete sets of Thackeray, Dickens and George Eliot, and he generally kept one going as a relaxation from his political reading. The wireless at his elbow was silent, and Grace was surprised, for he generally kept it on and read serenely with variety, classical music or authoritative talks braying in his ear. He looked up at her over his spectacles.

"The King's dying. They're giving out bulletins from time to time as the news comes from Sandringham. They've just said 'The King's life is drawing peacefully to a close.' "

"It's been a short illness!"

"I reckon he's been a tired man for a long time."

Grace stood warming her hands at the fire. She felt stirred by sorrow and quickened by an unconscious pleasure in drama, in the life of the nation swinging into their private lives.

"I've left the kettle on for you, and I cut a few sandwiches. I left a cup ready but I didn't know whether you'd fancy some coffee or a cup of tea."

"Did they say when the next announcement will be?"

"No. It depends how soon the news comes."

"You'd like to sit up and hear it, wouldn't you? I'll make

some tea, and we'll both have a cup." Grace might trifle with coffee and cocoa or even chocolate for parties and on frivolous occasions, but for a crisis, domestic or national, tea was the only drink. She went into the kitchen.

John, smoking thoughtfully by the fire, remembered a time when he had felt bitterly opposed to royalty, and had even made impassioned speeches proposing the abolition of the Crown and the House of Lords. A smile crinkled the corner of his mouth. What a silly lad that young John Allworthy had been, speaking, he remembered, in the market on a Saturday evening near Christmas. He could remember the holly on the stalls and the fat swinging bodies of the turkeys. He had never tasted turkey in those days. He had been all for making things better then by pulling everything down; he had wanted to change the whole country next morning. He had grown old and patient since that time, and the more he heard of violent changes in other countries, the more he dreaded hurry and violence. There was a lot to be done, to the end of his life he would go on trying to do it, but he had come to have great respect and tenderness for the British Constitution, and for the slow pace of the British Nation.

Grace came back with tea and sandwiches. She put the tray down on the floor between their chairs. The fire glowed red. John was a rare hand with a fire. The room was warm and comfortable, the curtains drawn against the raw night. Grace lifted the fat brown tea-pot and the ribbon of tea, clear as cornelian, curved into the big breakfast cups, sending up its aromatic scent. Grace had made a plate of dripping toast, a particular weakness of hers. Holding out the plate to John, she said,

"Eh, old lad, I hope I die first!"

He answered thoughtfully, "I hope you do." He was remembering her agony of sorrow over their dead baby. Nothing that he had ever seen in his life had so wrung his heart. In all the years when he had suffered from his impotence to help his fellow creatures, he had never known such a pang as he had felt when neither he nor the doctors nor anyone else could save that small life for her. He had hardly been aware of his own loss till afterwards, so deeply had he

294

been moved by hers. He could not bear to think of her after his death, left alone to mourn for him without his comfort. Even the sight of her downcast face now distressed him. He sought in his mind for a more cheerful subject.

"We've settled that matter of the cutters' wages. The firm signed the agreement with us this morning. They've agreed to the halfpenny rise."

"They know well enough it ought to be a penny!"

"They've a lot of competition to face. I reckoned when we asked for a penny we might get a halfpenny. You've got to move a step at a time."

"Were the men satisfied?"

"Not all of them. Tom made trouble."

"I've no patience with Tom nowadays! What's come to the lad? Why, he used to follow you about like a dog!"

"I think that girl of his leads him a dance."

"Well, he'd better marry her or get shut of her! Why can't they get married? He's earning a good wage."

"She doesn't seem to be in any hurry. Doesn't want to give up earning, perhaps."

"She could go on."

"Tom's not the sort of man to let his wife go out to work!"

"You let me for many a year."

"I had to. I didn't like it."

"You old-fashioned old stick-in-the-mud! Call yourself a revolutionary! Why, you might be Hitler with your 'woman's place in the home.' Look at what women do in Russia!"

To have to admit, even to himself, that there were some questions on which he sided with Hitler rather than with Russia was unwelcome to John Allworthy. He only said, as he seemed to have said rather often lately, "There's things that are all right in Russia, and wouldn't do here." No one had ever known how much he had minded having to let his wife go out to work for the first ten years of her married life. He could never forget something which he hoped she did not know, that when she had had a hard time with the baby and the child was born delicate, the doctor had said to him, "She's not such a young woman, you know, and she's worked hard. She ought to have begun child-bearing ten years ago."

295

That was the price that they had paid for having their two families to support and help, for poverty and an unfair world.

The announcer's voice at John's elbow startled them both. "This—is London." Putting down their tea cups they heard the message. "Death came peacefully to the King at 11.55 to-night in the presence of Her Majesty the Queen, the Prince of Wales, the Duke of York, the Princess Royal, the Duke and Duchess of Kent."

Tears came into Grace's eyes, and she said, "He was a good man! I'm sorry for Queen Mary."

John Allworthy said, as so many like him were saying all over England,

"The new King will maybe do a lot for us. He knows us and he's always cared for the working man and the unemployed. There's thousands love him that didn't bother themselves about the old King. He'll stand our friend."

Grace stood up, stiff and tired. She yawned and switched off the wireless.

"I can hardly keep my eyes open. Let's go to bed. Rake out the fire, John. It's not safe to leave it like that. I'll wash up these few things with breakfast in the morning," she added with a revival of her earlier interest. "We made £9 at the jumble sale."

"That was good!" But he was not thinking about the jumble sale. He was thinking of the old King, his contemporary, lying dead at Sandringham, and of a new king, young enough to be his own son. He was thinking how odd it would be to belong to a generation older than the King, how queer it would be not to see that familiar, bearded face on stamps and pennies and at the end of a film. He was thinking how much less like a family England would feel, how some protection seemed to have been removed from it at a time when the outside world was threatening. He thought how he would never have expected to feel like this when he was a young lad pouring out his ardour and anger and impatience before the fat, swinging turkeys in the market. If he could only make the lads like Tom see that a man in his lifetime could do only a very small part of what he meant to do, and that probably it was all for the best, it was the great saving of humanity, since each man alone was ignorant and rash and a lot of what he meant to do, especially when young, would do more harm than good! Time and the real world and the natural pace of things sifted out the grain of wheat from the chaff in every young man's dreams. But you could not make them see it! Perhaps if you could make them see it, there would be no dreams, perhaps you needed the chaff for the grain of wheat. Or perhaps, as John sometimes thought, he was growing old and losing his power to make people see things. As he switched out the light, and followed his wife up the steep staircase, bending his knees a little stiffly, he said, as again thousands like him were saying, "It seems somehow like the end of an old world."

The old life at No. 10, Bankside Yard came to an end for the Walters family at dawn on a grey February morning, and the new life at No. 17, Alloa Crescent, Netherton, began in a gust of sleety wind, with feet trampling in at the door and straw blowing in after them, with bangs and bumps and shouts and a smell of new paint, with the voices of the Corporation removing men, who seemed to be in everybody's way, but whose departure left the Walters feeling as though they were abandoned in a foreign country. Mr. Walters expressed the view of the whole family when he answered the back door to a touting milkman, and in response to a civil inquiry as to what they thought of their new house, replied briefly, "Cold as Hell!" and slammed the door again.

The new estate of Netherton was a city built upon a hill. Two years ago, the hill had been green with grass or brown with ploughed earth. Corn had grown there, and on the banks of the narrow lane that meandered up the slope, children who had strayed so far from town found dog violets and cuckoo flowers and the red berried spikes of lords and ladies. Now the hill from base to summit was covered with row upon row of neat, improbable red houses. Each house had a small garden back and front. Each house had a bathroom and lavatory, electric light, and a gas cooker. Between

297

the asphalt pavements and the wide road stretched long strips of grass. The whole effect was clean, airy, spacious, and to Mr. and Mrs. Walters incredibly bleak and strange. Even Olive shivered when both front and back door were open, and the wind that tore through threatened to lift the house from its foundations and blow it away like a child's toy. Olive had half a day off from the works, Fred a whole da~ off from the shop. They both worked hard and willingly, delighted with the elegance of their new home, entranced by having realized one of the dreams of their lives, a bedroom apiece. Their greatest difficulty was the furniture. Fred had the big double bed which he had hitherto shared with his father, and which left very little space in his room for the washstand and chest of drawers out of his old room. A second-hand bed had been bought for Olive, and she herself had bought from a neighbour an old table, and a square mirror to stand on it. It was very unsatisfactory. The bed was an iron one with brass knobs, two which had been lost, leaving the ugly black shafts exposed. The frame of the mirror was of dark brown imitation mahogany, the table was of light wood, stained yellow. Olive looked at them disparagingly, thinking, If only I had a bedroom suite, like Mabel's, ever so dainty, with enamel handles and that light-coloured wood that looks like satin ! She had always thought that she could be perfectly happy if she had a bedroom of her own, but now that she had one, she realized at once that she would never be happy until she also had a bedroom suite.

It was just as unsatisfactory downstairs. The kitchen at Bankside Yard had been no more than a low, common kitchen which nothing could disguise as a parlour, but it had been a good-sized room which took the solid old-fashioned furniture bequeathed to the Walters by their parents, and left plenty of space between. In No. 17, Alloa Crescent, the furniture proved to be too large, too uncompromising, and utterly old-fashioned. In the eyes of Mrs. Walters, it looked too good for what she privately thought of as a gimcrack house. In the eyes of Olive, it disgraced a superior residence. Mr. Walters merely looked at it morosely and said, "'Ere, when do us get wer teas?"

"Oh, not yet, Dad, not yet!" Olive cried feverishly. "Let's get straight first! Look, Fred! Help me to pull that cupboard through into the sitting-room. It won't look so bad against the wall till we can get a cabinet, and there's no room for it here. We can't move!"

"Wait a bit, Miss," her mother cried. "All my spoons and forks are in that cupboard. You don't reckon I'm going to walk backwards and forwards from the kitchen to this 'ere parlour or whatever it is every time I lay the table or want a spoon to stir a bit of gravy? You leave that cupboard where it is."

"But we must have some furniture in the other room! It's nearly empty! It doesn't look as though we used it!"

"Nor we 'aven't used it yet," Mr. Walters said darkly. He did not like the other room. Anybody that had a good kitchen fire and didn't sit by it was in his opinion a fool.

"But we're going to use it! We must get a table and have tea there and sit there of an evening! We'll have the wireless in there. You can buy one on instalments, I found out from a girl at our place."

"You find out a lot of things at your place," her father said heavily. "Most of 'em things you'd be better without. You can go and have your tea there and sit there of an evening with the table and the wireless *and* the gold plate on the sideboard. I'm going to stop 'ere," and he sat down by the kitchen fire which had just got going and began to unlace his boots.

Olive burst into tears. Here was this lovely house and she would never, never make it what it ought to be, never get the kind of life in it that she wanted. She saw in a flash of vision that it was not only the furniture that was incongruous. Her parents were like the furniture, hard to move, without elegance, old. The tears ran down her delicately-painted cheeks, she put up a grimy hand to her eyes and made black finger-marks all round them.

"Oh!" she sobbed. "It's too bad! We've got a really nice house at last, a house fit for anyone to live in, and we could make it like Herbert's and Mabel's, and have it all ever so nice like I've always wanted, and you won't, just because it's a bit more trouble, and you don't want to give up your common ways!"

Mrs. Walters said sharply, "Them's what I call common ways, my girl, speaking like that to your father!"

But Mr. Walters, looking at the dirty-faced, weeping Olive, suddenly saw again a little girl who had fallen down in Bankside Yard and run to him for comfort, a little girl who had come in from playing in the street and whose face he had washed tenderly at the sink, being so careful with his big hands not to put soap in her eyes, or pull the rings of bright hair.

"Well, well," he said soothingly, "'appen we'll tek to t'new ways in time. You mun give us a chance!"

"Let's have our teas now," Fred suggested. "We can shift t'rest afterwards and Rosie'll give us a hand. She said she'd come up this evening."

Olive, still sniffling and gulping, frowned a little without letting Fred see her. She meant to have visitors to the house certainly, but Fred's Rosie, a servant, was one visitor she did not want in a hurry. In her heart of hearts she hoped that Fred and Rosie would part company. She had always kept the other girls at work from knowing what her brother's girl did. At Bankside Yard it had not mattered so much, and anyhow it would have been impossible to keep people from knowing, as Rosie ran in and out of all the other houses and chattered to the neighbours, telling them everything they did "up at Hardings" when they had a party, what sort of clothes her Mrs. Robert wore, and what kind of little mats they had on the table. Olive was determined if possible to keep Rose from chattering to the neighbours on the Netherton Estate. There were sure to be some nice people up there who would be even more scornful of a girl in service than her friends at work. Olive kept these thoughts to herself. Fred, usually docile in her hands, had a will of his own where Rosie was concerned, and she never dared to show open disapproval.

She flew upstairs to the bathroom and felt a keen thrill of pleasure in her new luxuries as she turned a tap and ran water into the shining, enamel basin. She darted back into her bedroom, rummaged in her handbag for her powder and rouge, and sat down on a packing case to make up her face. Even though the frame of the mirror did not match the wood of the dressing-table, it gave her a far better view than she had ever had in the dark bedroom at Bankside Yard. She felt cheered, rubbed in rouge with the tips of her fingers, and put on powder with the delicate, serious attention of an artist. She was always a long time over the business. When she came downstairs again, tea was laid and the family were sitting round the table in the kitchen. The table was large and there was very little room for their chairs and no room to pass behind them. Fred had to get up to let Olive come to her seat. Mrs. Walters said rather wearily,

"Reckon you're right, Olive. We'll have to shift some o' t'things into t'other room. You can't swing a cat in here, let alone bake. What this oven's going to be like I don't know. It doesn't look too good to me. Seems to me this 'ouse is like one o' them ready-made dresses you're so fond o' buying cheap, pretty enough when new, but no turnings at the seams, and t'colour runs in t'tub."

She saw Olive's brow wrinkle again with distress, and added, "Well, well, we'll see what we see. Sit down, love, and get your tea."

A front door bell was another novelty to which the Walters were unaccustomed. Its sharp ring startled them all as they were clearing the table. After a minute's surprise, Fred exclaimed, "That'll be Rosie," and went to the front door. He came back with Rosie and Tom Sutton behind him.

Mr. Walters was pleased to see Tom, another man who might give him the sympathy that he needed now that he was alone in a strange land, far from Bankside Yard and the Three Bears, marooned in an uncomfortable house with women and children, for Fred, and even Herbert, being his sons, did not count as men, but were "t'lads."

"Eh, Tom lad!" he said. "This is a do, this is!"

"I wish you good luck in the new house, Mr. Walters, and you too, Mrs. Walters!"

"What about me?" Olive might tease and neglect Tom, but did not like him to leave her out.

He turned and smiled at her.

"You too, Olive—but not for long! Reckon this house is only a lodging for you, until you're in your own."

Olive flushed and tightened her lips, but did not answer. Tom was always bothering, couldn't let her alone!

Rosie had brought a table-runner embroidered by herself in violent colours. She spread it out, admiring it with cheerful heartiness. "Only one and sixpence halfpenny it was without t'silks, and Mrs. Robert gave me the browns and yellows out of her box, so I'd nobbut the green and violet to buy. It's not so bad, is it?"

Olive, who knew that the colours were crude and that one should speak depreciatingly of one's own presents, and conceal their price, looked at it coldly, but Mrs. Walters put her arms round Rosie and gave her a smacking kiss.

"You should have kept it for your own bottom drawer, love."

"Oh, I've plenty. Me sister gave me ever such a lovely bedspread at Christmas, and two cushion covers, silk ones you know, with tassels at the corners—what they call artificial silk, like—real shiny!"

"Tell us a bit of news, Tom?" Mr. Walters said. He felt that he had heard all he wanted to hear about houses and furniture for the next ten years.

Tom was filling a pipe. He twisted a torn envelope, thrust it into the fire and lit the tobacco. He stood for a minute thinking hard, till the flame licked along the spill and nearly burnt his fingers. By some odd trick of the mind it was so that Olive often remembered him afterwards, puffing at his pipe, unconscious of them all, his blue eyes dark with thought and the strip of flaring paper in his hand.

"Well, there is a bit of news. You know they started a new system with conveyers in the cutting-room last November, Mr. Walters, so as to get more done in the time? We asked for a rise of a penny an hour on account of that and we got a halfpenny. And we're going to down tools on Monday week and come out on strike until we get the penny."

"A strike!" Olive exclaimed. There had been no strike at Ward's within her short memory, and she knew nothing at all of the strike as a weapon, of its rights and wrongs, or of strike procedure, but she smelled a threat to the even tenor of her life. She stared at Tom with wide, frightened eyes.

Mr. Walters looked puzzled.

"But a thowt the Union had fixed t'rate of wages? Didn't you tell me last month they'd agreed to t'halfpenny!"

"They have. They signed an agreement with the firm the day the old king died."

"Well, then?"

"We're not getting our rights, Mr. Walters. We ought to have the penny. The speeding up process is going to make a lot more money for them, and it means harder work and more strain for us. We've a right to better wages."

"Aye, lad, but you can't go against your Union!"

"We are the Union,—not a few old men that call themselves leaders and drag on us like a brake on a tram-car! They'll come in with us fast enough when they see we mean business. The strike won't last above a day or two. You'll get a nice little holiday at home, Olive, to straighten up the new house, and get to know the neighbours."

"Eh, well I don't know an' all!" Mr. Walters was puzzled. No politician, he was a regular member of his Union. He never went to meetings nor troubled himself to vote for delegates but he had always accepted the decisions of the Union as final and unquestionable. They fixed the wage at a certain sum and there it was. Employers presumably disagreed with them sometimes. Mr. Walters knew that the Union was there to disagree with employers, but the idea of disagreeing with it himself would not have occurred to him. He would as soon have thought of telling the wind not to blow or the skies not to rain. He looked at Tom with awe and doubt.

"Don't 'ee mek trouble for thysen, lad," he said dubiously. "I never heard owt come yet of a man going against his union."

"Things aren't the same nowadays, Mr. Walters," Tom said quite good-naturedly. "When you were a young man, t'unions put the workers first and fought for their interests. Now they put themselves first and God knows what they fight for, unless it's to be patted on the back by t'government and t'employers."

Olive, kneeling by the fire, was looking up at Tom with a puzzled frown. She exclaimed impatiently.

"Oh, you're always right! There's some of them that have been in the unions for years might know a little bit about it too, I suppose? What about Mr. Allworthy? What does he say to your strike and your penny an hour?"

Tom's face darkened. He bit hard on the stem of his pipe. After a minute he answered,

"Not what he'd have said once nor what he ought. He calls himself the Union Branch Secretary, but he's Ward's man. He signed for the halfpenny rise and put us all off with his everlasting talk of patience. I'm shut of him!"

"Oh, Tom! Why, you've always called him Uncle John and he was your oldest friend!"

"I'll have no friends, new or old, that betray our own people."

Olive got up from her knees with a pettish movement. She did not really care whether Tom remained friends with Allworthy, or how he behaved to Alfred Ward or to the Union, but her instinct warned her that he was going to make trouble for her. She was delighted to hear the front door bell ring again, for that must be Mabel and Herbert, her allies. She ran out to meet them, and brought them in with exaggerated cries of welcome and pretty, caressing gestures of affection to Doreen, who had come with them. It was not all affectation. Olive had always been really fond and proud of her little niece. As she knelt down again on the floor to unbutton Doreen's coat, the child threw her arms round her neck and hugged her, ruffling up her shining curls unrebuked. Olive returned the hug and said, "Are you glad to see your Auntie Olive, love!"

Seeing her for a moment natural and sweet, Tom's heart contracted painfully in his body. He felt that he was losing her. All that she cared for and all that he cared for must inevitably come between them. He felt himself alone in this room. No one there even understood the issues that he saw so clearly or valued the things that he was prepared to give

304

his life for. Mabel had brought a home-made cake and Herbert a bottle of port to christen the new house. They drank the port out of tumblers and tea cups, Olive murmuring apologetically to Mabel, "When I've had time to turn round, I'll get some real nice wine-glasses like yours," for in No. 17, Harebell Avenue, they drank port out of the glasses with cocks on, and Olive was ashamed of the thick tumbler she had handed to her sister-in-law. Nobody else minded at all. The kitchen was growing so hot and full that the feeling of bleak newness was wearing off, and it sounded if it did not look like the kitchen at Bankside Yard. Even Mrs. Walters began to feel more at home in it and less pessimistic about the oven. She realized, without expressing it to herself, that you changed your habitation, but that solid and unchangeable thing, the family, went with you. She heard Olive telling Mabel that they were going to get a sofa for the front room and a cabinet. She smiled, murmuring to herself, "Set her up!" She did not trouble to make any protest. She was tired out with the day's work, and still more with the strangeness of her surroundings. A very little port made her drowsy. Olive and Mabel were talking about curtains for the front windows, and forgot to consult her, but she could not be bothered to interrupt them. Time enough to-morrow to put Olive in her place!

She was still sleepy when they went upstairs to bed, and this cushioned her against the fresh jolts of novelty, washing in the bathroom basin instead of taking up a kettle, undressing by the blinding glare of electric light. It seemed perhaps most strange of all to have Joe in her bed again. They had not shared a room since the children were too big to sleep together. Joe took up far more room in the bed than Olive. The bedclothes were lifted up on to the mountain of his shoulders and allowed a draught of cold air to slip down the side on to his wife. When he rolled over, he took most of them with him, and she had to hang on to them and drag them back again, but at least he was familiar, comfort and company in a strange world. She huddled against the warmth of his broad back and fell fast asleep.

Olive was the last person awake in the house. In all the

intervals of her busy day she had looked forward to this half-hour when the others would be in bed and out of the way. She sat on the packing-case in her room, shivering with cold and excitement. She was going to have a bath, not the laborious bath by the kitchen fire prepared with an exhausting succession of kettles, but a real bath in the new, shiny bathroom. As soon as the doors had finally shut on her parents and Fred, she slipped across to the bathroom and switched on the light. The clean white bath was so lovely that it ravished her heart. She had bought a packet of bath salts specially for this occasion, and she recklessly poured the whole lot into the hot water. She undressed quickly, folding her flimsy underclothes in a small neat pile. Her young body, white, smooth, supple, was as lovely as a flower, but she was quite unaware of this, her ideas of beauty being entirely limited to fashionable clothes, a pretty face made up to what she considered smartness, and permanently waved hair.

With a sigh of rapture, she slipped into the steaming water. As it closed over her limbs, and the strong violet scent of the bath salts filled her nostrils, it was borne in upon her that she would be able to do this nearly every night, perhaps every night if she stayed up late and there was enough hot water. It seemed too good to be true. She slid lower down on to the floor of the bath, slippery as silk with the overdose of bath salts, and let the water cover her to her neck, a thing that she had never been able to do in the old tin bath at Bankside Yard. She thought confusedly how stupid people were that went talking against the modern world and saying old times were best. Why, things got better and better every day! The world was going on well enough if only people like Tom didn't get interfering with it, putting everybody's backs up and making trouble! Why look what a fine thing the Corporation or whatever it was had done, pulling down that dirty old Bankside Yard and giving them this beautiful house! That showed it was all nonsense people saying that nobody cared for working people; somebody must have cared! I'll get a big jar of bath salts, Olive thought, pink, and some pink cretonne curtains to match. She had never dreamed
306

of buying anything for the house in Bankside Yard, she had thought of that as her parents' house, but this seemed like her own. Her small face above the steaming water was relaxed and suffused with happiness.

"When they are put into better houses," Stephen's neighbour at dinner said to him, "it makes *no difference*! They simply turn them into slums again, and live just as they did before! I heard only the other day of a family that had all been accustomed to sleeping in one room, and do you know, when they were put into a nice new Corporation house with three bedrooms, they went on all sleeping together in one because they said it was warmer?"

"And I suppose," Stephen suggested, "that they put the coals in the bath?"

His tone left Mrs. Batley quite unruffled. Her husband owned a large printing works, he was on the Council, and both she and he played a considerable part in civic affairs. Cheerful, prosperous and expensive-looking, she was in great demand on committees, and as an opener of bazaars. She was not likely to suspect irony in a young man who, although he belonged to one of the oldest families in the town, was only Ward's secretary.

"I expect so," she said. "A lot of them do, of course. It's dreadful, isn't it? Really one despairs of making any difference to people of that sort! I can tell you a perfectly *true* story I heard the other day. A family had been removed during the slum clearance to a nice house with three bedrooms—there were five of them—and do you know what they did? *They started growing mushrooms in one of the bedrooms.* Of course the Corporation came and took them away. But wasn't it shocking?"

"Shocking!" Stephen agreed. "There's no liberty nowadays."

Leslie Ward across the table shot him a sympathetic glance, but Mrs. Batley, who needed only some kind of answer to punctuate her remarks, was perfectly satisfied and flowed on.

"Marjorie looks sweet to-night, doesn't she, in that new frock? I've been telling Mr. Ward he'll have to give a ball for her when she's twenty-one."

The Wards were giving a dinner party for Marjorie's twentieth birthday. It was not the party she had wanted, since Mary had not been asked, and she looked a little sulky at the beginning of dinner, sitting next to Billy Wilson in her new frock of apricot-coloured taffeta. The frock had a coat cut as severely as a mess jacket, with stiffened collar and cuffs. The spray of orchids on her shoulder had been sent by Billy and were pinned in place by a new diamond brooch, a present from her father. Her dark reddish hair, newly waved, was arranged at the back of her head in rows of fat curls. On the table in front of her lay a lovely evening bag of Chinese embroidery which her mother had given her that morning. Violet Wilson thought that Marjorie was very lucky and was having a marvellous birthday. Violet was not yet quite seventeen, but had been allowed to leave school at Christmas because she was bored with it, and her family thought that she had had all the education that was good for her. This was her first real dinner party, and she was enjoying it, although she was not at all hungry, for she had met a young friend in town that afternoon and had made an extremely good tea, beginning with muffins and proceeding by way of cream buns to banana sundaes. To Violet dinner was still a pretext for going out and wearing evening dress, but tea was business. She was like her brother, round-faced, fair, plump and pleasant. Unlike him she did not worry about being plump. Billy's weight was one of his very few problems. He had just sternly refused the most delicious-looking brown knobs of potato. He said to Marjorie,

"Sometimes I really almost think of going on the Hay diet. Good for the old figure, what?"

"If you saw the mothers and babies that I see down in South Albeck you'd think a meal like this was disgusting."

"I don't think I should, you know. I shouldn't think a first-class dinner like this was disgusting, not if I saw a whole Babies' Welcome. What you mean is we're disgusting to eat it."

308

"Well, I think we are."

Billy sighed. He was fond of Marjorie, who had always been a jolly kid and a friend of his, and had grown up a real good-looker. Unfortunately she also seemed to have grown up a prig and a high-brow or something of the sort. He blamed, quite unjustly, the extra year that she had stayed on at her expensive school, and felt glad that his own little sister had been removed before she took up ideas and forgot how to enjoy herself at a party.

"Well," he said, "what I say is, make the best of anything there is going, and don't grouse when there isn't any."

"But you wouldn't feel like that if you were one of the people who never get a good dinner?"

"I daresay not. I'd rumble around then until I found a way of getting one."

"It's so easy to talk!"

"That's just what I think, Marjorie. You don't do anybody any good by talking about the starving poor in the middle of a birthday party. If you feel as strongly about them as all that, you pop that diamond brooch to-morrow and buy tinned milk or Bovril and what-not for the mothers and babies. But let's have our fun to-night."

Overcome by his smashing common sense, yet feeling a flaw in it somewhere, annoyed at being laughed off her naïve but earnest attempts to put her point of view, Marjorie said between tight lips,

"Will you believe I mean it if I do!"

"Yes. Oh, rather!" Billy laughed. He was thinking that it was time he turned round and said something to his left-hand neighbour, Mrs. Stephen Harding. He admired her appearance very much, but found her difficult and alarming, too stiff for his easy taste. He cleared his throat nervously and asked her if she had been to the Pantomime. He was luckier than he expected, she had taken her little boys, and had enjoyed it as much as they had. Joy and Billy, both fundamentally simple people, found common ground in recalling it in detail. Joy thought, he's not a bad little man, considering! Billy, metaphorically slapping himself on the back, thought, keep it up, my boy-o, you're doing fine!

Mrs. Wilson, who sat on Ward's right, beamed on her husband at the far end of the table, on her two children half way down, and on the rest of the party. She and Gus Wilson had risen like Alfred Ward from dire poverty to great wealth. People liked them, their house was a pleasant place to go to, and none of the children was really spoilt. All this was probably due to the unspoilable sweetness and goodness of Martha Wilson's own nature. She had soft, untidy grey hair, a soft, broad pink face, and had, when her husband was Lord Mayor, looked homely and comfortable in her court dress, as though ready at any moment to have a nice cup of tea in it, or to lift a tired child on to her satin lap. She said in her slow, broad voice,

"I'm sorry to hear there may be trouble in your works, Mr. Ward. I've a little maid, you know, whose sister works in the canteen, and she told her they might all be coming out on strike."

Ward said dryly,

"If all the strikes that are talked about came off, there wouldn't be a works going more than a month in the length and breadth of the country."

"Oh, well then I hope it's only talk. Strikes are such dreadful things. They cause so much suffering and make such bad feeling. But I know you'll do your best to avoid one."

"I don't want my works closed down at our busiest season. But these rumours often get about and don't amount to anything."

"Well, I'm sure I'm very glad, for Nellie, that's my little maid, you know, was quite upset. There's been a lot of trouble in the family with the mother ill and the father out of work, and there's a little brother having special treatment at the Infirmary, so they were so glad when Mary, that's the other sister, got that good job at your place. And Nellie said something about she didn't know if Mary would even get strike pay. I didn't understand what she meant, I don't think she did, but it was something to do with the unions."

"I don't think you need worry at the moment on your maid's account."

310

"Well, I'm glad. I hate to hear of bad blood between master and men. There's too much quarrelling all over the world nowadays, isn't there, Mr. Ward? It seems so odd to me that people don't talk things over together more and try and do what's best for all! I don't believe there are many really wicked people. It's the good ones seem to get obstinate and lose their tempers and do nearly as much harm. But we mustn't talk about these things at a birthday party, must we, with all those young people here enjoying themselves."

She smiled kindly down the table at Leslie, the nearest young person. He smiled back because, like everyone else, he liked Mrs. Wilson, but he was not really enjoying himself. He was disappointed because the Grants had not been able to come to the party. Angus and Biddy were both in bed with flu, he had been told not to come for a week, and he missed the almost daily intercourse with his friends, and the feeling that he could run in at any time. He did not care for this party, it was too formal, too splendid, there was too much to eat, and nearly everyone at it was fat, civic and dull. He could not possibly have any intelligent conversation with the child, Violet, who was his partner. His social education had advanced far enough to make him despise pretension and formality, but not far enough to bring home to him any particular obligation to make other people enjoy themselves in their own way. Violet thought him nice-looking, but conceited and superior.

When the dessert was on the table and the port had gone round, Gus Wilson rose up from his chair next to Mrs. Ward. He was a stout, bald man with a fresh-coloured face. He combined great shrewdness and acumen in all business matters with an attractive simplicity outside business. He had been a popular and efficient Lord Mayor, he was a generous supporter of all good causes. He lifted his glass.

"Well, now, before we all go under the table as a result of our good friend's excellent wine, I think we shall all want to drink one toast. Why I should have taken it upon me to propose it I don't know, except that I can claim the privilege of old friendship. Mother and I have known Miss Marjorie Ward ever since she was a little thing in socks. Her father and I have done many a year's work together on the Council and in the Chamber of Commerce and other places, and our families, as you might say, have grown up side by side and been good friends, as I hope they always will be." His eye rested for a second with meaning on Marjorie's bent head, and on his son's face, turned towards him with an encouraging grin. "So here's many happy returns and long life and happiness to Miss Marjorie!"

"Marjorie!" "Miss Marjorie!" everyone said, scrambling to their feet.

Marjorie smiled and flushed and bent her head till her cheek touched the petals of the orchid on her shoulder. She felt pleased but foolish, and a little as though she were drowning in a sea of light and faces. Her eyes clung to the sun-warmed skin of a peach on her plate. Now they were all saying "Speech! Speech!" and laughing at her kindly. She shook her head, gave a schoolgirl giggle and said, "Oh, no, no, I couldn't!" Billy stooped over her bent curls.

"Allow me to reply for you? May I?" Marjorie nodded. Billy straightened himself, tuck a thumb in each armhole of his white waistcoat and began jauntily, "Ladies and Gentlemen." Leslie thought, oh my God, he's going to be *funny*! His worst forebodings were justified. Billy was what the rest of the dinner party thought very funny indeed. Only Leslie looked aloof, smiling no more than politeness demanded and enjoying the pleasure of superiority, while at the end of the table, Ward sat grey and silent, his face hardly moving. These people here to-night, the Wilsons and the Batleys, were his friends so far as he had any, but none of them were casual with him, none of them knew what went on in his mind, or had ever laughed at him.

As soon as the men had left the dining-room, he slipped away to his own room, leaving the responsibility for the rest of the evening to his wife and children, and to Stephen Harding, who would, it was tacitly understood, assume the position of a host, to supplement Leslie's efforts.

Ward sat down in the chair at his writing-table with a sigh. He had had as much of his daughter's birthday party as he could stand. He was by nature a solitary who could

312

not bear for too long the pressure of other people. He felt greatly relieved to be alone in his quiet room with his papers.

Glancing at his clock he saw that it was a quarter-past nine. Not too late to ring up the Allworthy's house and ask after old John, who was at home and in bed with a touch of flu. It was not often that Ward made such personal inquiries, but he was anxious to know when John would be back again. He had spoken firmly to Mrs. Wilson, but things were ticklish in the works just now. He pulled the telephone towards him and dialled a number.

Grace's voice was in his ear.

"Mr. Ward? Well, that is kind of you. He'll be pleased to hear you've rung up. He's much better to-day, he'll be up to-morrow, but he's got a nasty cough, he has to be careful, you know, since he had that bronchitis last year. He'll be back on Monday, I think. He's been worrying at being away now, he was saying there was a bit of trouble going on. Thank you very much. I'll tell him. Good night."

Ward replaced the receiver and turned his chair towards the fire. Awkward, very awkward, John away ill, when the men were trying to force the hand of the Union! It was a pity that he was not going to be about in the next few days. The men had been restless for some time, he had known that this was blowing up. They knew that times were good and that the spring was the busy season. They were spoilt! He thought of the restrooms and playing-fields, the health benefits and the delicious cheap meals in the canteen. It was a passing thought, and he did not waste much time in indignation. He understood the whole business as a war. You put in certain improvements to speed up the process and increase your profits. The Union asked for higher wages. You haggled with the Union, beating them down as far as possible. You were out to get as much profit as you could and the men were out to get as much for themselves as they could. No sentiment of justice or kindness came into it now that the men had their own organizations and advanced in close formation. It was pull devil, pull baker. The strike was their final weapon in that war, and if the men struck against the Union, they would more easily be broken. It was the worst time for a strike in this busy season with orders pouring in and competition keen, but it would probably not last long, and a strike, once broken, was the employer's best ally, taking the kick out of the men for a long time, and convincing them of the uselessness of making trouble. It might almost be worth it.

It was late when Ward got up, turned out his light and went downstairs to see if the front door was properly fastened. When he was at home he always looked at the locking up himself. On the stairs he met Marjorie, just coming up. Her arms were full of parcels half unwrapped, the presents that the guests had brought to her party. Most of the lights were out, but he could see the sparkle of the diamonds on her shoulder, and the bloom and shimmer of her rich taffeta skirts spreading around her. She had everything, he was sure, that a girl could want. He wanted to ask her if she had enjoyed her party, and she wanted to thank him for it, but they fumbled the moment somehow between them. She only said "I'm just going up now." And he said "Good night." She hesitated for an instant and then ran on upstairs.

In her own bedroom she tumbled her parcels on the writing-table. It was already covered with other presents given her at breakfast by her family, or sent her by post. There were so many that she had hardly had time to examine them. She stood for a minute fingering the envelope that held a cheque from her father, idly turning over a pile of fine silk stockings. Then she pushed them away from her and opened the drawer underneath the table. There was another present there, still wrapped in its brown paper. She turned back the wrapping and took out a book, a new cheap edition of *The Old Wives Tale* with "Marjorie with love and best wishes from Mary" written on the fly-leaf. It was Marjorie's nature to prefer cheques and silk stockings to books, but nothing that she had been given that day had roused the same delight as Mary's present. What were dinner parties, orchids, Billy Wilson compared to a person like Mary, so truly noble that Marjorie often said to herself that it was incredible and astonishing that such a person should ever have been born!

As she unpinned the diamond brooch from her shoulder, she remembered what Billy Wilson had said at dinner. Just for a minute then she had meant to do what he suggested, to shame and surprise him into taking her seriously. Now she was disconcerted to find that her resolution had cooled out of her. It was not that she would so much have minded giving up the diamonds. She was afraid of her father, she did not know how to set about selling or pawning anything, and she shrank from an action so extravagant and absurd. Such a thing could not belong to real life. Yet the underfed mothers and babies whom she saw at the Welcome belonged to real life. Marjorie struggled as she undressed with the clash of irreconcilable realities. Finally she put the diamonds away in their case, thought, I'll talk to Mary about it, put her precious book on the chair beside her bed, snuggled in between the sheets, and immediately fell asleep.

On Monday morning, Mary was in the reporters' room at the *Yorkshire Guardian*, glancing through her appointments for the week. Hudson looked in at the door, saw her alone by the table, and came in, beaming all over his pleasant face.

"I've had a bit of news this morning," he said. "My boy's got his scholarship."

"Oh, Mr. Hudson! I'm so glad! I do congratulate you! It's splendid. Isn't his mother delighted?"

"Yes, we're both up in the air. We said to him when he went in, Well, you've done your best and you can't do more. If you don't get anything, you won't hear a word from us. But he's got it! So now he'll have a public school education with the best of them. You know, Miss Welburn, my father wasn't able to give me any advantages. I went to the little grammar school in the town where we lived for two years, and then I had to leave at sixteen to get a job. Mind you, I got a kind of education in other ways, knocking about and coming up against different kinds of people and seeing things. There's nothing like journalism for seeing life. But

I've always said my son should have a better start than I had. It gives you a different position in after life. Of course this scholarship won't cover the whole thing, it will be a bit of a struggle to do it with the clothes and journeys and all that, but his mother and I are determined to do it for him whatever we have to go without. Well, I'm off to the station, but I thought I'd just like to tell you. I know you got to college yourself with a scholarship, so you'll know how we feel!"

"I'm awfully glad! I expect he'll do splendidly!"

"He's a good boy. I should like to show you the letter his head master wrote, sometime. But I must be off now."

Guy Runnacre strolled in a minute or two later and sat down in his favourite position on the edge of the table.

"Seen Hudson?"

"Yes! Isn't he happy, bless him!"

"Poor dupe of the snob system! His boy will go and pick up the code of a semi-monastic semi-militarist community, and learn to despise a father worth ten of him. He'll be even more unfitted for the modern world than he would have been if he'd rubbed along at home, absorbing Hudson's old-fashioned Liberal-Conservatism. And in a year or two he'll probably be bombed anyhow, so it don't make no odds."

" You went to a public school yourself, and whatever code you picked up, it doesn't seem to be semi-militarist. Why should he swallow it whole any more than you did?"

"Because it will be new to him. My going there was a matter of course, a boring but inevitable necessity. It just had to happen because it had happened to all my people. I was inoculated before I went, so to speak. This lad will go up like stout Cortez into an undiscovered world. I could say he'll be hanged with the old school tie only I don't like mixing metaphors, and we've heard so much about the bloody tie, I could be sick every time anyone mentions it."

"Your reactions are always a bit violent! Aren't you pleased, anyhow, about the Spanish elections?"

"I suppose so. Yes. Yes, I would be if I thought it would make any difference in the long run."

316

"I thought a Left victory might cheer you up!"

"The next thing after a Left victory anywhere is so often an unholy mess, and a dictator as the way out." He had lit a cigarette and was smoking quickly with restless movements of his brown stained fingers. He broke out fretfully,

"You're so lucky, Mary! You really do believe in humanity getting better, in Left movements doing good, in more justice on the way for more people. I can see that those are good things, but I don't really believe in them. You've got to be rather simple and, I think, very healthy, full of vitality, to believe in them as heartily as you do. All I see is that one lot of people have been in power and have made a mess of things and now another lot of people are trying to get into power, and after they've got there with a lot of bloodshed and destruction, they'll probably make a worse mess of things. Because we're all fools and man is born to trouble as the sparks fly upwards. Round we go in a circle. My family had the playing-fields-of-Eton-Sahib ideas for a century and I've grown out of them. Now young Hudson's going to start picking them up, and in another hundred years—no, less, the pace is quicker—he'll have a grandson who'll grow out of them. That is if bombs and gas let him have a grandson at all."

"Did you say all that to his father?"

"No, I didn't. I like Hudson. I have some human feelings."

He smoked in silence for a moment, swinging his long legs. He threw the stub of his cigarette into a waste-paper basket, and lit another.

"I think, really, I envy you and Hudson. You're both single-minded. You've both got such a lot of things you think worth while. I'd be quite glad to change places with either of you."

"Do you think you'd really prefer our simple faith to your Norman blood?"

Guy laughed, an unexpected, rather pleasant sound.

"I believe if you're left alive after the world's been reduced to a howling, stinking ruin, you'll start trying to build it up again. You'll collect some scraps, make a house, you'll rake together some old bits of stuff and make a dress, you'll find a way of snaring rabbits and cooking wild berries, you'll get hold of some sort of man and produce a child. With all the mess we've made of it, you'll think it worth while. I don't believe women are ever fundamentally disillusioned!"

"They've more sense! You've set the paper in that basket on fire! Do you mind doing something about it?"

Guy Runnacre emptied the basket on to the floor and trod out the charred and smoking fragments with his heel. He said,

"You're a sane person, which means keeping your balance like a skater, and looking where you're going and ignoring all logical conclusions. That's why English people are particularly sane. They live by equilibrium and ignore logical conclusions so firmly that they almost might not be there. But I've got a sort of uneasy feeling that this century is where logical conclusions are going to get back on them. What's going to happen at Ward's?"

"A lightning strike against the Union, I'm afraid."

"Afraid! You ought to be all for it!"

"My uncle's the Branch Secretary of the Union and it will be awful for him. But apart from that, I can't hold with people breaking their signed agreements."

"That's where your bourgeois mentality unfits you for the modern world. You'll have to adjust your mind to the idea that all pledges are breakable."

"I'd rather stay unadjusted. I do in a way sympathize with the Left Wingers in the Union. You do feel that the older ones think about going slow before they think about doing anything. Even my uncle."

"It's the usual circle. Make a trade union to protect the rights of the men against the masters, and about twenty years afterwards, you find the Union defending its own rights, whatever those are, against the men. Human nature's always the trouble!"

They were interrupted by the arrival of the musical critic, who had come in to verify some alteration in his programme for the week. He stood at his desk turning over his advance notices and muttering, "The Axbridge Musical *would* have Soldini for the Bach, she never could sing Bach and now she can't sing at all, she's so damned idle she won't even learn her stuff, and she looks like a cow that's just going to calve, but they've got her into their heads and they can't get her out again, and I have to sit through it once a year!"

Guy Runnacre went off to his own desk to write a letter. Mary sat on at the table thinking about the strike. The really important question about the whole thing was how it would affect Stephen. To this had all the years of her uncle's training, of her own sensible and intelligent observation, brought her. The world had narrowed down into the welfare of one young man, who except in her private heart was no more than a friendly acquaintance. On the face of it, this strike would be no affair of Stephen's. He was only responsible for the office staff and had nothing to do with the works. But a strike would stir up feeling in him, in Ward, in everyone connected with the place. How much did Ward know about Stephen's change of mind and how much would it matter? It was clear from Marjorie's talk that he would not put up with such things in his children, but men who were tyrants in their own homes were often reasonable outside. Ward was fair, even in his dry way kind to her uncle, but she suspected that Stephen had a lot to put up with. It was no job for him, it was not worth doing a job like that, even to keep a wife and family and any wife worth twopence would see it! Mary resented it for him, and yet was afraid that he might lose it. Perhaps her fears were absurd, intensified as every feeling about him was. But everything that happened nowadays was a catalyst thrown into a vat of badly assorted chemicals, and precipitating strange combinations.

Stephen's secretary, Miss Longley, brought him in some letters to sign at half-past twelve. As she laid them on the table in front of him and picked up the strip of blotting-paper to blot his signatures, she said brightly,

"The men are having a meeting on the recreation ground.

319

You can just see them from this window if you look, ever such a lot of them and some of the girls too! Someone was saying they may be going out on strike."

Privately she wondered whether, if there was a strike, the office would get a holiday. It seemed such a long time since Christmas, it would be a real treat to lie in bed a bit later for a morning or two! February was an awful month, nothing nice ever happened in it. It was just cold and grey and raw and the Christmas parties all over, and either you had flu yourself or you had to do extra work because other people had. Miss Longley found even the threat of a strike a pleasant relief from monotony.

"Miss Longley, I've told you a dozen times that 'all right' is two words. If you spell it 'alright' again, I shall sack you!"

Miss Longley, not unduly disturbed, laughed and said, "Oh, I'm ever so sorry, Mr. Harding!"

"Do you know if old John is back this morning?"

"I think he's here, Mr. Harding. I heard somebody say he had gone out to stop the meeting."

When Miss Longley had gone to her lunch, Stephen strolled to the window and looked out. He could see that there was a crowd on the far side of the recreation ground beyond the swimming-bath. The greater part of it was hidden from him by the walls of the bath. The groups of men and girls whom he could see stood still and attentive in the shrewd east wind, their faces turned one way as though they were listening to a speech.

His feelings about the strike were more divided than he would have expected. He had an idea of the extra profit which Ward hoped to make by the new processes, but the men had been granted an extra halfpenny, and it would be some time before the profit could be estimated exactly, or before it cleared off the cost of the machines. Stephen discovered in himself a critical sense that his new allies were rather grasping. To his imagination a strike was a desperate weapon against notable injustice or heavy oppression, not simply a move in a sordid struggle for more money. The struggle seemed as sordid to Stephen as such things do to

320

those who have never been in a position where a halfpenny an hour more or less can make any difference.

But wrong on both sides will happen, he thought, while the whole thing is so wrong, while there is this tug between the interests of the people who do the work, and the people who profit by what they do. It seemed to him so clear that he was amazed he had not seen it before. His mind went back to the General Strike, to that week when Robert and he had driven the mail vans. He remembered that first evening, driving the great red vans out of the yard into the street, the temporary staff cheering, the feeling of novelty, excitement and adventure, of rallying round the country. Sweeping down the great North Road with the red tail light of Robert's van fifty yards ahead of him, he had felt like a hero. Now it appeared to him that he had been a blind and rather stupid young man unconsciously resisting economic change and rallying round his own class.

He tried to remember, how and when did I begin to tumble to it that things were all wrong? In the slump we all realized much more sharply than ever before the fact of unemployment, but we felt that we were suffering too because our businesses were going down right and left, and our incomes were dwindling. I was in love, too, and trying to get married, and that took up nearly all my mind.

Anyhow, I hadn't begun to connect. I thought the unemployment was due to bad times. I didn't realize it was due to the protracted end of a dead system. I can't remember, now, exactly how I began to be uneasy. I read things, and uneasiness was in the air. I was like a lot of other people, I began to think because I was afraid. You don't get a lot of people thinking until they are short of something, either physically or mentally. What we are all short of to-day, those of us who have what we need physically, is security. It was the Italian Abyssinian business that woke me up in the end. That and talking to Mary.

He turned away from the window and went back to the table, thinking, Joy will never understand! I can't talk any more about that sort of thing to my own people! I hadn't realized how far away "our kind" live from reality. I don't mean personal and individual realities. You couldn't have anyone more genuine and more wise about personal things than my father. But "our kind" have lived so much shut up in their own comfortable box that they haven't connected. They don't see things as a whole or their world in relation to other people. And so they're dying. Because you only live through communication with external realities. It's odd how dead Ward always feels to me though he's a personality, and you feel such a tremendous difference when he isn't there. Sometimes I think he's a life killer, and that people always are whose own life has been killed in some way inside. What shall I teach Jack and Lin? How, with their mother set like iron against it all? What will be the end of all this? What do they need to learn for their world that's coming? He felt that he did not want to-day to go and lunch conversationally in the staff-room. He put on his coat, picked up his hat, and went downstairs into the street.

On an improvised platform behind the swimming-bath, Tom Sutton was speaking to a sea of upturned faces. A good many of the faces looked chilled and blue with cold, for it was a raw morning and an east wind was blowing steadily. John Allworthy, who stood just below the platform, coughed, and felt weak and hollow with the aftermath of 'flu, and with the bitter knowledge that the situation was slipping out of his grasp, had perhaps slipped altogether in that week when he had been ill at home. He had left men restive and returned to find them resolute. He had returned to find that in the works where he had been all-powerful a Central Factory Committee had sprung up with Tom Sutton as Chairman. Two of the men and one of the women on the committee were, he knew, Communist Party members. The others were people who had never played much part in their unions, and lacked, in his opinion, knowledge and experience. The whole lot of them were unbalanced and impatient, and had worked themselves up into a temper so that they were

322

incapable of long views or cool decisions. John distrusted them utterly. He shivered and folded his arms across his chest, trying to hug himself to a little warmth. He listened to what Tom was saying.

"Make no mistake, comrades! This is a war. If we allow the firm to exploit the cutters and fitters now for the sake of more profits, the same thing will happen in all other departments. To our employers we are not men but machines, machines for them to wring more money out of. But, comrades, we are not machines! We are men and women! If we are going to make more goods for them in the time, we've a right to be paid more money. . . ."

It was a simple, unassailable logic, sweeping away all considerations of patience or diplomacy. At the end of every one of Tom's periods came a round of applause, and his speech was often punctuated by deep, involuntary murmurs of agreement. John Allworthy was experienced in the temper of an audience. He knew that his own turn must come soon, and for once in his life he did not want to speak. He felt that these people whose rights he had upheld for so many years had become hostile to him. His chest was sore and his legs ached, he felt incapable of the physical effort of speaking to a large audience in the open air.

He realized that Tom had turned towards him and was saying something about him. He was speaking of their old friend Mr. Allworthy, the Branch Secretary of their Union and their representative who had organized the great strike in 1925, who had stood up for their rights all these years, and would stand up for them now. The face which he turned towards his old friend was not the sullen face which John had so often seen lately, it was eager, glowing, alive. Looking down from his trestle at the men and women before him, Tom was warmed by more than the orator's feeling for his audience. A warm love was released in him for his fellow men and women, so patient, so defenceless, so loyal to one another. He felt as though he could move mountains for them. He spoke to the audience of what John had done for them in the past, but he was really pleading with John not to desert them now. Let the workers stand together behind their

323

unions and the unions stand for the workers! He jumped down from the trestle among a storm of cheers. He put a hand on John's arm to help him up, and John felt the strong grip of the warm young fingers touching his sleeve.

"You'll stand by us, Uncle John?" Tom said. For months he had not spoken in that old, friendly tone. He could have said nothing that would have moved and touched John more deeply. In all his life he had never disliked any task so much as the one before him. He felt old and tired, he would have been glad to go home to bed, and let the younger men carry on, but he was an old war-horse, he had forced his inclination too often to give up now. As he climbed on to the trestle, a roar of cheering broke from the audience. They saw before them the hero of a hundred stout battles, their leader and their champion. After they had cheered for a minute, he lifted his hand.

"Listen, friends! I reckon you all know that when the new system was put into operation in the cutting rooms, I went to the firm for the Union and asked for a penny an hour rise in wages. We had a lot of discussion, and the matter was referred to our headquarters for advice, and we agreed to take a halfpenny. It was put forward on behalf of the firm that the new plant had been costly and that it would be some time before the new methods would show a profit. They were not willing to go beyond a halfpenny an hour, that was their outside limit, but they promised to look into the matter with us again in a year's time. We told you at a general meeting that we were making the best bargain we could for you, you agreed to it, and we signed an agreement on behalf of the Union.

"Now, friends, we've got to stick to that bargain. I don't pretend we've got all we wanted. There aren't many bargains where you do. We've got to stick to it because we've pledged the word of the Union, and if we don't keep to it, the Union's worth no more than a bit of waste cloth!" He paused for a minute, interrupted by a fit of coughing. The faces turned towards him showed surprise, indignation, but also some perplexity, as though half the audience had not yet grasped the drift of his speech. He mastered his cough and went on.

"If we don't stick to our word, we destroy the whole system of collective bargaining—the thing that we fought for—aye, and you younger ones don't know how we fought, in the early days of the unions! We've got our honour. . . ."

A man standing near the front cried out violently, "That's a class word!"

"It's a word for any class, Ben Outhwaite! We've signed an agreement and we'll stick to it. It's the end of all fair and peaceful dealings between men or classes, aye, or nations, when the signed word goes for nothing." His voice rang suddenly clearer. "I tell you all, if you go out on strike, you go against the Union. You'll get not a penny of strike pay. You'll have to come slinking back with your tails between your legs, and you'll tie our hands in what we do for you for the next ten years."

A confused sound of dissent and anger followed his speech. Before he could get down, Tom Sutton sprang up beside him on the platform. His blue eyes were blazing with wrath, he flung out an arm and shouted:

"To Hell with t'Union!"

There was a roar of applause. Tom waited for it to die, and then cried out,

"What do we want with a Union that sells us to t'masters? We don't want Union brass! We'll make our own terms with the firm at the end of a day or two and tighten our belts until we do. T'Union will come in with us fast enough when they see we mean business. Comrades! I'm a Union man, as you all know. I was a delegate to last year's Conference from this branch, but Union or no Union, I propose that we down tools and walk out of here at the end of t'dinner-hour."

Another young man had sprung up on to the platform, and was seconding Tom's resolution in vigorous language. The unsteady platform trembled under the three men's weight, but John was not going to get down. He must try at all costs for another hearing. At Tom's words such anger had sprung up in him as he had not felt for twenty years. It was not only Tom, who was like his own lad, turning against him. It was the Union man, the delegate, turning on the Union, and cursing it publicly. John, like many another Englishman, was personally modest and transferred his vanity and sensitiveness to the organization to which he belonged. What the School, the Regiment, the Civil Service, the professions were to others, the Union was to him. He was not only angry. He saw before him a crowd of ignorant people being hounded on to loss and disaster. There could be only one end to an unofficial strike.

The seconder finished speaking and there was another roar of applause. John had the feeling of being impotent in a nightmare. He caught Tom by the arm.

"Let me speak again!" It was bitter to him to have to ask.

Tom turned towards him, his blue eyes blazing. He shook off the hand from his sleeve and said,

"Reckon you've said enough on Ward's side!"

He turned again to the audience and shouted,

"Now, comrades! It has been proposed and seconded that we should down tools and walk out at the end of t'dinner-hour, and that the Central Committee should inform the firm we'll not come back until they are prepared to raise t'cutters a penny an hour. Those in favour?"

The open space became a sea of raised arms and waving hands.

"Those against?"

Allworthy raised his hand on the platform. A group of men on the left-hand side of the crowd raised their arms, a hand shot up here and there. One or two went up for a second, wavered uncertainly and then went down again as though ashamed. In one corner there was a scuffle as though a man had put up his hand and it had been pulled down by his neighbours.

"We don't need to take a count," Tom said triumphantly.

He began to issue instructions. The strikers would walk out quietly and go to the Halton Lane Park where there would be a meeting to appoint pickets and a finance committee, and to decide on procedure. There must be no disorder, shouting or disturbance. A deputation from the meeting could be sent to the firm with terms. In the last half-hour Tom seemed to have blossomed into an unhesitating leadership. He firmly quashed an attempt on the part of the crowd to sing the Red Flag, recommending that this should be kept for Halton Lane Park. The men began to disperse, going back to the works to collect their belongings. Tom jumped down off the platform, and was surrounded by a group of younger men, among whom was Harold Pearson. He was taking counsel and giving instructions. John heard him say, "We'll have to start at once organizing a collection. There'll be the expenses of printing to send round notices."

John Allworthy walked slowly back into the building. He remembered that he had promised Grace that he would get a hot dinner. He was not often hungry in the middle of the day, and sometimes only bought a sandwich in the canteen. Always a little short of food in his early years, he had learnt to do without much, and had never developed an appetite that satisfied his wife. He did not want to eat now, but he would not break a definite promise. He went into the canteen, and up to the hatch, and asked for a plate of hot pie and vegetables. He took it to a table and sat alone.

It was extraordinary and dreamlike to see the place so empty at this hour of the day. There were some girls laughing and giggling at a table in the corner, a few men who had not gone with the strikers and that was all. It was late, and those who had not been at the meeting had already had dinner and gone. Weary and dispirited, John laboriously swallowed the food, which he did not want. It made him feel a little warmer, but when he had eaten half of it he pushed the plate away from him.

One of the giggling group of girls left the others and came across to him. He recognized Tom's Olive, prettier than ever in a buttercup-yellow woollen sweater, belted round her slim waist. She said to him,

"Is there a strike, Mr. Allworthy?"

"Aye, lass," he said heavily. "They've just gone out this dinner-hour."

"Do we have to go home?"

"No! You'll stay here and work until the Union tells you to stop! This strike isn't right. It's against the Union."

She caught her scarlet lip between her small white teeth.

"Was it Tom made them go out?"

He nodded. He was too sick to speak of it. He did not know whether she was proud of Tom or angry with him, nor did he care.

"Oh!" she said. "I see." She walked back to the group of girls in the corner.

John left his meal unfinished and went down into the South Work Room. An extraordinary silence and emptiness smote him. The machines that carried the cloth to the cutters, the new machines that carried the cut sections to the big pressing irons were not working. Here and there at one of the long tables a man was in his place looking as though he did not quite know what to do. John recognized one or two of the older men who had not, he thought, been at the meeting. He went to his own place. His scissors were lying on the table beside a piece of cloth and the pattern of a coat sleeve. He could cut that sleeve and another, but after that, he would have to go and work the machine that cut off the exact length of cloth for a sleeve, he would have to set in motion the machine that brought it to his table, he would have to take the cut sleeve to the pressing table and iron it, and then see it taken to the table where it should be stitched into a coat, and the coat which corresponded to the sleeve by number would not have been cut. John himself would have to cut, fit, work the machines for sewing on buttons and making button-holes, press, take to the place where the linings were cut and fitted, and see the coat into the packing-room. He was an expert in all branches of ready-made tailoring, but the immense complications of the system were too much for him. He would not be able alone to make one coat this afternoon. He picked up his scissors and laid them down again. Then he began to walk about the room, covering such pieces of the machinery as he could, picking up bits from the floor with mechanical tidiness.

The meeting at Halton Lane Park sang the Red Flag, and after this concession to revolutionary fervour, became business-like, and elected sub-committees. Like bubbles rising to the top there emerged from the heterogeneous mass people who thought that they could do things and were anxious to do them. The disorderly movement showed a passion for order and self-government. Tom asked for nominees for the Finance Committee and for volunteers for pickets. Nominations were promptly made, mostly by Harold Pearson and his Communist friends, who knew pretty well the value and capacity of any man who had done any political work. They saw to it that they themselves were represented on every committee, but took care not to overweight them, knowing that the majority of their fellow workers did not like to think that anything was run by Communists, and being fairly sure that one member of the disciplined and uncompromising force would always be able to equal half a dozen of their vaguer brethren.

For the first time in his life, Tom Sutton was in full use of his natural capacities. Such times are the rarest and probably the happiest in the life of any ordinary man. He grew by inches, taking the whole impromptu machinery of the strike into his capable hands, and finding that the occasion produced a dozen administrators, able and willing to help him. A Little Bethel near to the works offered a room to be used for strike headquarters. The Local Labour Club agreed to lend a large room for general meetings. The Finance Committee briskly took a collection for strike expenses, and gathered together in a corner, discussing ways and means of raising money for a relief fund, if a relief fund should be needed. It seemed to them unlikely that it would. Everyone had received a week's pay on Saturday, and the next few days would be sure to see a settlement. Pickets were arranged for the coming forty-eight hours, and Harold Pearson had discovered a house close at hand which was willing to make hot tea for them from time to time. Tom gave out that there would be a general meeting next day at eleven o'clock in the Labour Club, and the strikers dispersed and went home quietly by bus or tram.

Some of them felt uneasy as soon as they got away from their fellows. They did not enjoy the prospect of going home and telling their wives that unless the strike was short-lived, there would be no money coming in at the end of the week. When they were all together in the Park, singing and cheering and voting, they had felt powerful and confident. Alone they lost confidence and became aware of misgivings about going against the Union. The younger men were the most cheerful, still feeling the glow of decisive action, and a conviction that youth was now taking the lead. For a good many of the girls the strike only meant a prospect of a day or two's holiday. After that it would no doubt all be over and things would go on as before.

When Stephen arrived at the office next morning, he found three chilled and bored pickets mounting guard over the big gate of the works' yard. A policeman, who looked warmer, but equally bored, was strolling up and down the opposite pavement. Stephen stopped and spoke to the pickets, who grinned at him amiably.

"A cold job!"

"Aye, sir, it is that!"

"Have you had many people trying to get in?"

"Not above a dozen, and two of them was girls that had been away ill and hadn't heard about it."

"Well, I hope you haven't got a long shift?"

"Four hours, sir. We came on at seven. We come off at eleven."

A thin, long-legged little girl emerged from a house at the end of the street, carrying three steaming mugs on a tin tray. The mugs were full of strong, hot tea, heavily sugared. The pickets warmed their hands gratefully and sipped and joked with the child. The policeman glanced enviously across the road, and then, as though disgusted at the domestic scene, turned up a side street and walked away.

Stephen went in at the office entrance and up to his own room. In the office everything seemed much as usual. He read through the pile of letters on the table, made one or two telephone inquiries to various departments, and dictated to Miss Langley, who was disappointed to find work going on in the same old way, and everything quite dull. In bed last night she had embroidered a fantasy in which Mr.

330

Harding was shut up in his room by strikers who threatened him and would not let him come out until he promised to use his influence with Mr. Ward, but she, his secretary, had stolen out through innumerable pickets,—who were shouting angrily and waving their arms, not drinking tea,—and had brought the police to the rescue. The fantasy had ended with a presentation of a diamond wrist watch from the firm, warm thanks from Mr. Harding, and Miss Langley's photograph in the papers. She was depressed by the difference between the dramatic, coloured world available in bed at night and the drab realities of next morning.

When she had gone out with the letters, Stephen found himself unoccupied. Ward was in consultation with his General Manager. Although there was no sign of anything unusual in the office, a feeling hung about the place as of a house in which there had been a death. Most of the office staff disapproved of the strike. They identified themselves with the firm, and spoke feelingly of the loss and difficulties that would follow at this busy season and with competition so keen. Between the office and works there was a great gulf fixed. Some of the clerks and travellers occasionally fraternized with men out of the works at football and cricket matches or whist-drives. The girls in the office, the typists and secretaries, were altogether remote from the girls in the workshops and never had any dealings with them. The consensus of opinion at the staff lunch was that strikes were always a mistake, and an unofficial strike, after an agreement had been signed by the Union, was unpardonable.

It would be useless, Stephen thought, to point out to them that the whole system was unpardonable. They would not be able to see that ready-made clothes should be produced because a great many people needed ready-made clothes, and not because one man wanted to run a profitable business. They would not be able to wrench their minds off the familiar track. The familiar track meant safety, and to play for safety was the ruling motive of their lives. There were so many things to be afraid of, losing their jobs, losing their health, losing the esteem of their neighbours and the appearances that they kept up so religiously. They had

331

climbed out of the working class into what seemed to them a higher platform, and hard as frightened people are, they would kick anybody down who approached and threatened that platform. It was no use suggesting a more equal division of luck to people whose whole self-respect lay in having acquired a little more luck than others. It was no use talking about a classless society to people whose parents had made it their life ambition to put them into a class a little higher than their own. Scrambling through the world, threatened on all sides, most men could not afford to be generous. Only an occasional rare spirit such as John Allworthy could begin to concern himself with other peoples' welfare before assuring his own. Tom Sutton whether mistaken or not, was taking risks and fighting for more than himself. That there should be people in insecure positions brave enough to do this showed that humanity had not quite been defeated by a constricting civilization. Or did it only show, as Robert had observed last night, that there were always fools in the world? Sensible men made the best lives that they could for themselves and those they loved under existing conditions. It was the fools and cranks and neurotics, Robert said, the men with an obsession, the men with a grievance who banged their heads against existing conditions, and hurt themselves. But sometimes it happened that out of their pain, out of their grievances and the distortions of their minds, conditions were altered.

There was not much to do in the office that afternoon. Stephen left half an hour before his usual time. As he drove along the street, he met the procession of strikers. They had spent the afternoon at a meeting in the Labour Club, and had decided to walk through the town before dispersing to go home. They hoped in this way to impress their protest and their demands on the minds of their fellow-citizens. They marched steadily in good order, four abreast, Tom and three other members of the strike committee in the front rank. A policeman walked along the pavement, keeping level with the leaders, and two more brought up the rear of the procession. All three looked large, rosy and well fed, compared to the marching ranks, most of whom had the small stature and sallow colouring of the indoor workman of the West Riding.

The procession came up Highgate, was kindly but firmly deflected by the police from Bank Street, the principal shopping street of the town, and finally turned down Upper Row, one of the new wide streets leading to the Town Hall. The swarm of small boys who had followed it from the Labour Club began to drop off. They had walked a long way, and it did not look as though anything interesting were going to happen. At the corner of the Upper Row, Mrs. Batley, who was shopping with a friend, looked round and said,

"Who are those men? The strikers from Ward's? How disgraceful! I wonder the police allow it!"

Naomi Unwin, who was coming back from the public library, saw the procession pass, and felt an immediate stir of sympathy with the men, and anger against the undisturbed police. She had been away, and had not read the accounts of the strike in the Monday evening or Tuesday morning papers. To her the details, the rights and wrongs of the case did not matter. Any strike was a move made by her own side in a war. She waved a hand to the advancing ranks and stood still to let them go past.

As she turned the corner by Harley's Store, she came upon Leslie Ward standing on the pavement, as though he had stopped there to watch the procession and had not moved since. Naomi did not know him well enough to remark that he looked like the old Leslie Ward of last summer, not like the cheerful undergraduate of the autumn term. His face looked drawn and strained and the muscles were twitching underneath it.

"Oh, Mrs. Unwin!" he said nervously. "Good afternoon! Did you see those men? They're out of my father's works, you know. They're on strike. They—they look very quiet, don't they? I mean they aren't making any disturbance. Just walking along quietly."

He babbled, hardly knowing what he was saying. The sight of those men, moving steadily with a collective purpose in that street full of detached groups and individual shoppers had disturbed him strangely. Those men were in revolt

333

against his father. To Leslie it was as though he had seen some secret feeling of his own embodied and walking down the street.

"I expect there's been some muddle," he said nervously. "Probably it will be settled to-morrow and they'll all go back. The Union . . . they'll talk it over, won't they?"

"This is a strike against the Union." Naomi had known the thing was brewing, and had read the makeshift banners and placards carried by the procession.

"Against the Union! Then—I ought to know about these things, but my father never talks business at home—— Is the Union on his side?"

"Yes, the Union is on your father's side."

"Oh! But—I thought—I thought the unions were only there to put the men's point of view."

"A good many of us used to think that!" Naomi said bitterly.

"It's so complicated!" Leslie murmured childishly.

Naomi looked at him with more attention. She and Claud had once talked of him as a possible convert, but had decided that he was ineradicably bourgeois, fit only for the escapist and immature company of the Grants. Claud had ruled him out. But then Claud ruled out so many people. It was worth while getting any recruit, and even a feeble recruit from the enemy's camp was a prize. Besides, the boy had a right to hear the other side. If there was anything decent in him, he must sooner or later revolt against the traditions of his upbringing.

"Shall we go in here and have a cup of tea?" Naomi suggested. "If you're interested, I could tell you something about this sort of strike, and about the whole question of unions and non-union strikes."

Leslie's first instinct in any perplexity or distress of mind was to look for somebody to relieve the strain for him. He knew that his beloved Grants only half-liked the Unwins, that pity, amusement and distaste were mixed with more friendly feelings, but the Unwins were in a way friends of theirs, they belonged to the fringes of his enchanted world. He was always eager to respond to any friendly advance.

"Oh, thank you!" he said shyly. "Yes, I . . . Yes, I'd love to

334

have a cup of tea. Er, I don't know what it's like in here, do you?"

"There's a café!" replied Naomi indifferently. "We can sit down somewhere and talk."

She pushed her way in through the swing doors, and Leslie followed her.

On Thursday evening, Angus sat at the kitchen table typing out a review of a new book, a biography and critical estimate of a great poet. At least, the publishers called it a critical estimate. Angus in his review had called it something else. The author appeared to him to lack all critical sense. She made emotional rushes at her subject which curdled his blood, and she varied these by deliberate retreats in which she denied the poet some undeniable virtue in order to prove to the world that she was not sentimental about him. She probably ought to be shot. Certainly the publishers ought to be shot, who had enshrined her luscious ardours and self-conscious withdrawals in such imposing and expensive form, and had printed such god-awful tosh about the book and the writer inside the jacket! Angus read through his typescript, wondering if he had been perfectly fair, or if he had allowed himself to dance on the woman's head too much because he felt tired and shaky after 'flu, and was worried about Bunny, and because he had just discovered that he would have to rewrite two chapters of his own book on account of some letters that had turned up in America, and he saw no hope of rewriting them this term. He flipped over the pages of the biography and his eye fell upon one of the passages where the author had let herself go. And after all, she had even misquoted. And one of the better-known sonnets, too! No, if anything he had let her down too gently. He folded his typescript, addressed and stamped it. Now there were his lecture notes for next morning. He leaned back in his chair rubbing his eyes, and pushing the long lock of fair hair off his aching forehead. The front door bell rang. Angus said "Damn!" and went to open the door.

Leslie was standing on the step. He said,

"Oh, I say, Angus, are you better? Are you busy? Can I come in?"

If he had been any other young man, Angus would have sent him away, but he was as glad to see Leslie as he could be at that moment to see anybody.

"You'll probably catch 'flu," he said. "But come in. Bunny's got it rather badly. He's had earache all day, and we're afraid of a mastoid. He's nearly 103 this evening."

"Oh I say! I am sorry!" For a minute his friend's trouble broke through Leslie's preoccupations. "Poor little Bunny! What bad luck! Is he feeling very miserable?"

"Yes, he's been crying all the evening, but I don't hear him now. I think he's gone off. Grizel's tired out. Come into the kitchen, Leslie, there isn't a fire anywhere else. We'll make some coffee, I daresay Grizel would like some. Perhaps she'll come down for a bit and let me go up."

Leslie followed Angus into the kitchen, but he did not as usual make any attempt to help him while he collected coffee, milk, percolator and cups. He stood looking down into the fire. Angus was tired and his nerves were sensitive. He became aware of something portentous in Leslie's manner. He was at once faintly irritated as he always was by any hint of the portentous. He said in a voice that he tried to keep from sounding impatient,

"Put a lump of coal on the fire, will you? I've let it get low."

Leslie put several lumps of coal on the fire with the manner of a man piling sods on his own grave. Angus, moving about the room, absorbed the boy's mood through the pores of his skin, and suddenly found himself wanting to shake him.

"Well," he said as pleasantly as he could, "what's the news?"

"I want to talk to you."

"Half a minute while I find the sugar." Angus began to whistle. He was protesting against some self-dramatization that he felt in Leslie. Whistling made him cough, and he broke off and came back to the fire.

"Well?" he said.

336

"I've come to the conclusion that my whole life is an offence against society."

"Good Lord! Have you been to a Four-Square Gospel Meeting?"

"No, but I've been looking into things, thinking about the whole construction of society."

"Do you mean you've been to supper with the Unwins?"

"Yes, I went in there yesterday evening, and I had tea with them to-day."

"I see. I know that can make the construction of society look a bit grim. I'd offer you a drink only I don't think we've got anything except the rest of the cooking brandy left over from Christmas. You'll have to wait for the coffee."

For the first time in his life, Leslie wished that Angus would be more serious. He did not want jokes or drinks. He wanted to relieve his mind of a flood of new ideas, of a burden of guilt and alarm and bewilderment.

"You know my father's men are all out on strike?"

"I didn't know. I'm sorry. Is he much worried?"

For a minute Leslie stopped short. A fragment of the conversation at supper yesterday recurred to his mind, Naomi Unwin mentioning the Grants, Claud saying, "I don't suppose Grant has heard about the strike yet. He doesn't trouble his head about anything much later than the nineteenth century." They had said very little about Angus. It was more by omissions, by a word and a look, that they had painted a picture of him turning his back on the urgent problems of the day, enclosed in his own small, selfish world. Leslie, easily impressionable, had seen that picture with unwilling eyes, and had rejected it. Now he saw it again.

"It isn't my father I'm thinking about," he said hastily. The picture of his father as the tyrant and oppressor had hardly been painted at all, but had been so vivid in the minds of the Unwins that Leslie had seen that too, and it had been coloured by deep feelings of his own of which he was unaware. He had shown them something of those feelings in his anxiety to dissociate himself altogether from the section of society that they condemned. Hysterically trying not to be the rich employer's son, he had ranged himself with them like a frightened animal taking cover. Angus's casual question upset him again by appealing to an instinct which he had firmly buried.

He began to pour out a medley of submerged feelings and half-digested ideas. His feelings, his old half-conscious revolt against his father, his new recent doubts about the way of life in which he had been brought up, were genuine, but sounded to Angus less genuine than they were because they were clothed in the second-hand language of Claud Unwin. Angus suffered from a disability not uncommon in educated people acutely sensitive to words. He found it difficult to believe in the sincerity of people who expressed themselves in clichés. Leslie was really crying out that he wanted to have a mind of his own apart from his father but did not know what mind to have, that he sympathized with those who could not help themselves, and felt a young man's generous rage at the injustices of a world with which he had not yet compromised. He did not know that he was crying it out in the pompous, bad-tempered and dogmatic voice of Claud Unwin. Angus listened, watching the coffee trickle from the percolator. Leslie probably had to get this some time like measles, but the red rash seemed to have come out suddenly and badly. Angus knew nothing of the latent germs caught from Mark Forrester, and put it down to the strike and the Unwins between them.

"And it seems to me," Leslie concluded, "that every decent person must care about those sort of things and think that way! It seems to me really nowadays that there's only one way of looking at things at all!"

Angus could not trouble himself to answer so ludicrous a statement. Leslie was being naïve and exclamatory and emotional, all things which Angus very much disliked. He had not even the energy to laugh at him. He poured out the coffee.

"I'll just take this cup up to Grizel, Leslie. I'll be down in a minute. Help yourself."

Leslie, alone in the kitchen, felt like a punctured tyre. He was, as he had been thinking all day, at one of the turning points of his life, and he had told his greatest friend all

338

about it, and his greatest friend simply went out of the room as though nothing had happened. Something else which Naomi had said came back to him, that the people who were unaware of politics to-day lost virtue because it meant that they had to be unaware of so much it was like depriving themselves of the use of their senses. He had been greatly impressed by the knowledge and conviction of Naomi and Claud. They had not only presented him with a new view of society, they had made him see his friend for the first time through alien eyes.

The door of Bunny's room was ajar. Angus gently pushed it open, and saw in the pale glow of a shaded night light, Grizel's figure by the bed. Her face was in shadow, but he saw the faint gleam of her fair, bobbed hair. Bunny was murmuring and whimpering and sounded half asleep. Angus stole across the room and put the cup of coffee into her hand. She turned up her face towards him and put her finger on her lips. He stooped and kissed her cheek, which felt cold, the hours she had sat in that room to-day, poor Grizel! He stood by her for a minute, his arm round her shoulders. Bunny stirred and moaned, a sad little cry of pain. Angus stole out of the room again, drawing the door softly to behind him.

When he came downstairs Leslie was standing in the middle of the kitchen with his coat on.

"I think I'd better go," he said. He spoke stiffly and looked sulky. It was an old look, but Angus had never seen it before. He wanted Leslie to go, but was aware of inadequacy. He made an effort.

"Oh, sit down and have another cup of coffee!"

"No thanks. It's getting late. I expect you want to go to bed."

"I've got some notes to look through first, but sit down again for five minutes. You've hardly got warm."

"Five minutes" flicked the old, absurd touchiness which Leslie had seemed to lose. He picked up his hat.

"I won't keep you any longer."

"Well, you must come round as soon as ever things are ordinary again."

339

"Thank you for the coffee. I hope Alistair will soon be better."

Angus wanted to cry out, "You absurd, touchy young ass!" but his instinct was to ignore a situation rather than to admit it. He accompanied Leslie to the front door.

"Don't swallow anything whole!" he said on the door-step. He smiled, but Leslie did not smile back. He still looked offended.

"Good night."

"I shall see you to-morrow. Oh, no I shan't. You go to your Anglo-Saxon, don't you? Well, see you soon. Good night."

Leslie stalked away down the garden path and slammed the gate. Confound him, Angus thought, he might have remembered Bunny. He didn't seem to care a bit! Angus locked up the front door and went back to the kitchen.

Half an hour later Grizel found him there by the dying fire, huddled up half asleep over his lecture notes, his long forelock nearly touching the paper.

"He's asleep, Angus. I think he'll be better in the morning. Come up to bed."

Angus lifted up a face sodden with drowsiness.

"Thank goodness!" He knelt by her on the hearth and put an arm round her. "You're frozen! Let's wake up the remains of the fire! Grizel, I think I've been rather a brute to Leslie."

"I shouldn't think so," Grizel said serenely.

"His father's works are on strike, and he's been taking counsel with the Unwins and come out in a red rash. And he wanted to tell me all about it and I just wouldn't listen. But suppressed measles are the worst. He was fed up and went off without a smile."

"The silly boy! He'll get over it."

"He's such a queer, sensitive creature I'm afraid I hurt his feelings. And he's nice, Grizel! I'm fond of him."

"I know you are. And he's very fond of you. The first minute we can, we'll fetch him round to supper and tell him not to be a goose and let him talk politics all night. Now come up to bed. You weren't really fit to go back to work to-day."

"I hope he isn't feeling very injured."

"Oh, Angus, nobody in their senses could for more than two minutes! You'll both have forgotten all about it in the morning."

"Yes, of course we shall, shan't we?" Neither to Grizel nor to Angus did it occur that you could really stay bad-tempered for long with your friends.

Clare awoke in the morning to the sense of an imminent duty. Hardly wide awake, she picked up the pencil and paper from the chair beside her bed, and struggled to recapture her dreams. It was like trying to catch trout that wriggled back through her fingers into the water. On some morning she could not remember them at all, only retaining a faint flavour in her mind like a taste in the mouth. This was a good morning. She had had a nightmare which remained vividly in her memory.

She had been walking along the pavement towards Dr. Bates' house, when she had seen a body of strikers marching down the street. They looked like the men whom she had seen two days ago in real life marching down Highgate, but in her dream one of them, who came first, was wearing fancy-dress, a highwayman's caped coat and cocked hat. She recognized the particular coat and hat, which had been a cherished property of their own acting box in schoolroom days. Neville had last worn the hat in a play in which Clare had been the heroine. Pleased with herself in powder and panniers, she had been travelling in a coach elaborately constructed of chairs and brown paper. She paused in her scribbling, smiling as she remembered that play. Robert had been the coachman, mounted precariously on the box, which had been made by propping up the music stool on a packing-case. She remembered Neville helping her out of the coach with one hand and pointing a pistol at Robert with the other, saying to her in loud and courtly tones, "Forgive me, Madam, for putting you to this inconvenience," and to Robert in an unrehearsed whisper, "Take care, you

341

fool! You're going to bring the whole thing down!" That was the play in which they had discovered half-way through that the storm-lantern, a necessary part of the plot, had been left upstairs in the attic. Stephen had been sent to fetch it, and the resourceful Neville had said to Robert, "We've got to keep the audience amused somehow! We'd better fight another duel till he comes. Draw the curtains, Clare! Come on, Bob! Insult me! Quick!"

Clare laughed as the vivid memories of those early days crowded into her mind. She recalled herself with an effort to her dream. She had turned and run and the strikers had run after her. She had the agonizing dream-sense of being pursued, of straining to run faster, and being unable to move her limbs. Just as she turned the corner of the street, she felt one of the men behind her touch her shoulder. She woke up with her heart jumping, relieved as she opened her eyes and saw the flowered window curtains of her own room swinging in the morning breeze.

She lay back on her pillows considering the dream. She knew enough now to be able to make a guess at its meaning. At first she had found psycho-analysis disturbing and difficult. She had not liked the things which it discovered to her in her own mind. She had always had without knowing it a picture of herself, of someone gentle, fastidious, honourable, kind, dutiful, modest, shy and retiring. She had now discovered that she had buried within her a creature whom to herself she called Mrs. Grubb. Mrs. Grubb, who appreared in dreams and fantasies in various disguises, was greedy for what she wanted, had shameless bodily desires, a strong inclination to self-display, a ruthless disregard of other peoples' interests, was in fact rather like a cat or any other animal, only what seemed charming and natural in animals was disconcerting in people. At first Clare had refused to believe in the existence of Mrs. Grubb. Then being sincere and not stupid, she had accepted her reluctantly as a fact, and suffered pangs of misery. It was now just beginning to dawn on her not only that everybody else had a Mrs. Grubb, but even that Mrs. Grubb was easier to manage when in sight than when locked in the cellar. Mrs. Grubb was in some ways a sensible creature, she had been cabined, cribbed, confined too much, and was obliged to mutter and grumble underground because she had no scope for her natural energies. Clare realized that there had been a considerable strain involved in keeping Mrs. Grubb battened down so tightly, and the relief from the strain was making her feel more free and vigorous. She no longer lay awake at night or was troubled by uncontrollable tears. Her hair had stopped coming out, her face had lost its drawn look, she found herself much more at ease with other people of her own age. Somehow, familiarity with Mrs. Grubb in herself had put her on easier terms with the outside world.

Doctor Bates reflected with interest that morning on the number of people who had used the strike as material for their dreams. A young man who had had a nervous breakdown and, besides other troubles, found himself completely unable to disagree with anyone, and particularly with his parents, had dreamed that he was marching through the town at the head of the strikers on his way to burn down his father's office. He rejected with horror the suggestion that his excessive meekness might be the reverse of a suppressed rebellion in his own mind.

"I'm devoted to my father, devoted," he kept on saying emphatically. "And I think strikers ought to be put down with a firm hand. I think the Government ought to interfere. I've always thought that sort of thing was much too leniently treated in England! They're much better about that sort of thing in the Fascist countries. They wouldn't allow it, and they're quite right. I've no sympathy with people on strike. I should put them in prison. That dream can't mean anything at all."

Doctor Bates allowed him to run down.

Then he suggested mildly,

"Don't you think that a child is bound to have rebellious feelings towards his parents sometimes? And if he was a very conscientious child, what is called 'very well brought

343

up,' he might suppress them and pretend to himself that he hadn't, and bury them in his mind, and they might stay embedded there and come up in his later life in dreams?"

"I never remember having any rebellious feelings," the young man said firmly.

"Still, don't you think it likely that any child would have?"

"I was always absolutely devoted to my parents."

"Yet in this dream you identified yourself with men who are in a state of rebellion against authority?"

"That must have been an accident."

"There are no accidents in dreams."

"Well, I'm sure it must have meant something else, because I've never sympathized with people on strike or socialists or subversive people of any kind."

The clock struck the hour. Doctor Bates pushed his chair back.

"I should like you to consider that possibility all the same, Mr. Ferriby, before you come to me next week."

"I really don't think it is a possibility," said Mr. Ferriby coldly. He picked up his hat and stick and glared angrily at Doctor Bates. "Good morning!"

Doctor Bates nodded "Good morning!" He was quite unmoved. They were so often angry with him when they left, but sometimes what he said sank in and they came back next time prepared to see reason. He glanced at his time-table. Miss Harding, and not here yet. Perhaps he would just have time to copy out that list of plants for the new border. Mr. Ferriby disappeared from his mind, he propped up his catalogue of herbaceous plants against his desk, and scribbled busily until the arrival of Miss Harding.

Miss Harding had been a slow case because like Mr. Ferriby she had been very well brought up. She inherited a sensitive conscience, which had been reinforced so early by religion and by the overpowering weight of nursery morals and manners that the natural animal in her had been nearly suffocated. He had been obliged to let her see it by

344

slow degrees, indeed her own resistance had kept her from any sudden shock. Patients complained and objected if they did not get on fast, and did not understand nature's own mechanism for a slow but certain cure. Even this dream after a month or two of treatment was filled with disguise and symbolism. He did not push her, but let her work it out for herself, and knew by her stumbles and hesitancy and the changes in her voice that she was quick enough to perceive that a body of strikers were nothing to her unconscious mind but men who were asserting themselves and might be violent, that fear might be a disguise for desire, that her real feeling for Neville had merged in a fantasy which filled the dissatisfaction of a mind that reflected an unsatisfied body. People did not like to think that their mental attitudes might be rooted in their attitudes to things of the body any more than they sometimes liked to be told that their high-sounding political theories and ideals had a basis in economics. Yet it was these unfortunate dissociations that caused all the trouble, divorcing ideas from reality, making politicians espouse impracticable theories, and private persons have nervous breakdowns. When the idea and the reality got too far apart, something had to crack.

Clare got up to go with a little sigh, feeling at once tired and invigorated.

"It's really rather like a detective novel!" she said, smiling. It was rather like a detective novel. Going back through the layers of memory into the past, you picked up, or rather you encouraged the patient to pick up a clue here, a clue there, until at last with infinite patience they reached the fossilized fantasy and said, "Is that all?" The emotion and event that had been charged with such intensity in the child's mind was so little to the grown-up person's intelligence, even while it still coloured his feelings.

His third patient, Mr. Harrison, had also woven the strike into his dreams. He was a serious, studious young man preparing to teach in elementary schools. In his last term

345

at the Training College, he had suddenly developed a tendency to kleptomania. He took books, money, small personal belongings out of the rooms and coat-pockets of his friends. He could not explain why, and was deeply distressed at his own anti-social behaviour. He was difficult to deal with because his mind was crammed with rationalizations and ready-made explanations of the Universe, which he hastened to interpose between himself and his shrinking, submerged feelings. He had dreamed that a body of strikers, waving sticks and shouting, were advancing on the Market to help themselves to everything in it, but that he with a companion, a policeman—he rather thought that in the dream he was a policeman himself—was shutting the gates to keep them out.

"It seems funny I should dream like that," he said loquaciously, "because of course actually my sympathies are with the strike. I think I've told you before, Doctor Bates, that I'm a Communist. Not a party member, you understand, because of course there's a lot of difficulty about that in the profession I'm taking up, but my political views. . . ."

Doctor Bates spent a good deal of this hour every week in disabusing Mr. Harrison of the belief that psycho-analysis was a Heaven-sent opportunity for talking about himself to an intelligent audience. Or rather, the self that he wanted him to talk about was the immature childish self whom Mr. Harrison firmly disowned, between whom and Doctor Bates he interposed like a screen a carefully constructed self, made on the best modern pattern, compact of every contemporary virtue. Doctor Bates recalled him to the point.

"Did you see any of these strikers, who they were and what they looked like? Just think a minute."

Mr. Harrison thought.

"One of them," he said in a tone of surprise, "was wearing my hat! It's a new hat I bought this week."

"Doesn't that suggest to you some identification of the men on strike with yourself?"

"That's what I was just saying," Mr. Harrison declared triumphantly. "All my sympathies are with the workers. I can't bear to see them herded about the town by the police.

The police have Fascist sympathies, you know. Their handling of Communist meetings is often most unfair and even brutal. Why, only the other day I read of an instance at a meeting in the East End of London. . . ."

"But in this dream you were a policeman."

"Well, I often say there's no account for everything that happens in a dream, is there?"

"Everything," said Doctor Bates, placidly.

"But when I read Freud about a year ago—you know, actually I've read most of his books and Jung too—I'm sure he said somewhere that there were things he came across in dreams that *he* couldn't interpret." Mr. Harrison flung this statement defiantly across the room, his face and manner saying clearly, "So you needn't think you can do any better."

Preserve me, Doctor Bates reflected, from patients who've read Freud and Jung!

"Doesn't it occur to you that since in the dream you were a policeman and also there is some reason to identify you with the strikers, you may have used these figures to dramatize a conflict in your own feelings?"

"I haven't any conflict of feeling about the strike. I've read a good deal about social and industrial questions and made up my mind some time ago."

"I mean a more personal conflict between the part of you that wants to take things that don't belong to it, and the moral part of you, the policeman in your mind, that disapproves of that and won't let you be conscious of it?"

At the personal application, the young man's argumentative, lecture-room manner dropped from him. He looked like a startled child, and like a stubborn, startled child, he said,

"I never *have* wanted to take things. I don't *know* why I did it. I did it without knowing."

There of course was the rub. The compulsion of the unacknowledged impulse, the painful and laborious shifts and disguises and suppressions by which the sensitive human mind continued to avoid acknowledging it. Doctor Bates persevered firmly, but gently. He knew that he was pressing on the nerve, and could feel Mr. Harrison's relief at the end of the hour, the relief of the man in the chair who hears the

347

dentist say, that's all for this morning. As he opened the door, Mr. Harrison recovered a certain jauntiness and said briskly.

"Actually I think it's a very good thing for a teacher to be psycho-analysed. I mean, one will understand so much more about the mentality of one's pupils. I'm really very glad to have had the experience."

It sounded sensible, but his powers of rationalizing and disguising his feelings were so great that it was probably an upside-down way of saying, I hate this and I'm damned if I'll come here any more. As he would come, as his face looked less harassed, and he had not lately been overcome by the desire to thieve, it did not much matter anyhow. Doctor Bates dismissed him with a cheerful,

"Tuesday afternoon, then? Good morning."

But it was not surprising, he thought, that strikes arose and bred hatred and bitterness and were difficult to settle! Not surprising that nations persuaded themselves that they went to war for an ideal, or that governments acting against the interests of two thirds of the population honestly believed that they were doing their best for the whole nation. It was not surprising that in a world of plenty large numbers of men, women and children went hungry. He dealt every day with people who had only to walk out of their home or put out their hand to enjoy a free, full and active life, but who did not walk out or put out their hand. He dealt with people who had persuaded themselves that they acted from certain motives and would have gone to the stake for them. In his inexperienced youth when he was a medical student at Edinburgh, he had been astonished that rich men could live happily with poor men before their eyes, and that politicians could sound so sincere in pursuing their own advantage. Now he realized that it was difficult to talk about sincerity. Nearly everyone was sincere according to the degree of his self-knowledge. Nearly everyone saw the world, politics, life and art in terms of his personal equation, of that part of his mind which he did not know. Only a few could bear to look at reality, the brief and unaccountable life of man. So they could not keep the flexible and easy pose of those adapting themselves to each reality as it came, but stiffened into attitudes, religious, political, æsthetic, social, and did their business a little clumsily, with constricted limbs. The surprising thing about it all, really, was that owing to the toughness and variety of human nature they did not make an even worse job of it. And learning, growing in conscious- ness of themselves they might yet make a better one, thought Doctor Bates hopefully, pulling his list of plants towards him.

The Conservative Ball was the great social event of the spring season. Politics, which can unite as well as divide, brought together the old industrial families, the Marsdens and Hardings and their friends, and the civic group, the Wards and Wilsons and Batleys, whose rise in the world had been more recent. Besides these there were, of course, a good many who had no political bias of any kind, but liked dancing, or wanted to be seen at the social events of the town.

Joy Harding had a new frock for the dance, and put it on with pleasant anticipations. Hilary and his Anne were going with them, and had arrived at tea-time with a basket full of clean snowdrops and ivy leaves from the country garden. They were looking forward to the party, and were as nearly excited as was possible for two placid people. To have them in the house meant for Joy comfort and reassur- ance which she needed, for Stephen had grown strange to her. Hilary's presence revived something of the old feeling with which as a little girl she had put on her Red Riding Hood cloak to drive with him to parties through the snow. She smiled at her own reflection in the glass. She was as little vain as any beautiful woman can be, she thought con- ceit of any kind rather bad form, but she was glad that she looked nice to go out with Hilary and his Anne. She could hear the bath water running across the passage. Stephen had arrived home late and was changing quickly. She knew

349

that he did not want to go, but that he would not disappoint her or his father. The Hardings had been to this ball in a party ever since Lionel was, just down from Oxford, a young subaltern in the Volunteers and neophyte in this business.

Another family party was setting off from Grey Gables. Marjorie too had a new frock, and in spite of the twinges of conscience which her unnecessary luxuries cost her nowadays, would have been prepared to enjoy herself, but for the fact that the nerves of the whole family were shaken by a revolution and its aftermath. Leslie that morning had refused to go to the dance. Leslie was now sitting on the front seat of the big car, complete in white tie, white waistcoat and button-hole, but angry, humiliated, miserable, ashamed. Like all unsuccessful revolutionaries, he was realizing that his position, both inward and outward, was much worse than it had been before the revolution. Alone in his bedroom he had wept secret, shameful tears. Waves of anger swept over him like physical pain. He could almost have hit his father.

His mother and father on the seat behind him were talking about the Grants. Bunny's illness, which had been crowded into a corner of Leslie's mind by other preoccupations, had roused far more concern in them. Mrs. Ward had driven round on the morning after Leslie's visit with chicken jelly, country eggs, and a teddy bear as large as Bunny. Ward had called in on the way back from work, and had made stiff dry inquiries, ending by an even stiffer and drier request that Angus would come to him for temporary assistance if the doctor should want to get in a specialist. Bunny, after another day of anxiety, had begun to get better, and Leslie knew nothing of the offer. He heard his father saying that he had sent round half a dozen bottles of good burgundy because Angus and Grizel both looked worse than the child. He felt that his friends were in the enemy's camp, protégés of his father. It did not occur to him that his parents had received from the Grants a simple friendliness and gratitude for kindness which they did not get from their own children. The Unwins were right, he thought, about the dividing lines nowadays. You could only be on one side of it or the other.

350

He and his father were on opposite sides, and perhaps the Unwins were with him and the Grants with his father.

It would have been a lovely night to go to a dance, Marjorie thought, if it had not all been so difficult about Leslie, and if only she had a really exciting partner instead of Billy Wilson! There had been a flurry of snow in the afternoon, lightly coating the house-tops. Now it was freezing, and the remnants of snow crackled under the wheels of the car. The air was as exhilarating as champagne. If only Billy Wilson did not get so hot when he danced, and if he did not make so many jokes and talk so much about what he allowed himself to eat and what he didn't! Who cared about his weight, anyhow, he wouldn't be nice-looking if he was thin, with those piggy eyes. Yet he was kind, and in some way that she did not understand, Marjorie found comfort in his easy philosophy and felt safe with him.

As the car turned into the Upper Row, the chauffeur slowed down. They had come upon the tail of a body of marching men.

"Good Lord! It's our men!" Leslie cried out nervously.

"Is it the strikers?" Marjorie leaned forward and peered over Tomlin's shoulder.

"Hadn't we better go another way round, Alfred?" Mrs. Ward's voice sounded anxious.

"No." Ward picked up the speaking tube. He said to Tomlin, "Go down the side. Drive past them." The car began to move along the side of the marching ranks. Leslie cowered in his seat with shame, fear and misery. It had seemed to him awful that the Ward family should be going to a dance to-night at all. Now to drive past these ranks of desperate men, to flaunt their big car and festive clothes, seemed to him an intolerable outrage on humanity. How could his father, how could he! It would serve him jolly well right if the strikers recognized them and stopped the car and dragged them out of it and stripped off the warm coats, the furs and jewels! Leslie shut his eyes, the sweat poured down under his armpits and he prayed that the car might go faster, faster, that the ordeal of driving past those rows of faces might be at an end.

351

They were about half-way down the column when the light from a brilliant shop window shone into the car and one of the men recognized Ward. He called out his name and it passed down the column. The men did not break step, but heads turned towards them and there were angry cries.

"Oh!" Mrs. Ward cried. "Tell him to turn up a side street!"

A man shook his fist at the window as the car slid past him. Marjorie gave a little scream.

"Be quiet, Marjorie," her father said.

Police Constable Hargreaves, who was marching at the side of the procession, dropped back a step or two and waited for the car to come up to him. P.C. Hargreaves had spent a good many hours in the last fortnight escorting processions of strikers about the town. He was sick of the sight of the bloody fools, wasting his time and their time. He stepped into the road and swung himself on to the running-board of the car.

"Oh!" Marjorie cried. "There's a man on the car!"

"It's a policeman, you fool!" Leslie almost sobbed. Nothing, nothing that could happen to him could ever be as bad as this! He felt as though something in him would crack if this agony and terror were not ended.

For a minute the line of marching men wavered, and looked like breaking. Ward had his hand on one of the loose cushions. He did not want to say to Marjorie and Leslie a minute too soon, "Put your heads down," but he must not risk saying it too late. He was afraid of broken glass. Tomlin's hand shook a little on the wheel, he said to himself furiously, "The buggers! You can't do nothing with the working class!" Police Constable Hargreaves put his whistle to his lips. Then a man came running down the side of the column. Ward knew Tom Sutton by sight, the others did not. They saw him spread out his arms as though to shield them. His back was towards them and with the windows of the car shut they could not hear his words. What he said to the strikers was, "Not yet lads! Aye, I know, but not yet!" The column, which had staggered for breaking, straightened again. P.C.

Hargreaves lowered his whistle. Tom fell into step beside the four men who were level with the car. He said something, Marjorie saw him throw back his head and open his mouth. The next minute the whole column were marching steadily and singing the Red Flag. Tomlin accelerated as much as he dared in the narrow space on the slippery road. The car drew abreast of the foremost ranks of the strikers, drew ahead and was in the middle of the road again. From behind it came a defiant shout, "Are we downhearted? No."

"The beasts! The beasts!" Marjorie cried.

Leslie, shaking in every limb, turned on her a white, twisted, furious face.

"Be quiet! Be quiet! We're the beasts ourselves!"

The string of cars, one pressing behind the other, crawled to the Town Hall entrance, their lights sweeping the dark stone walls and the sparkling snow that coated every projection. Robert and Beryl Harding ran up the steps together, both happily excited at the prospect of their evening. On a makeshift platform at the side of the steps, a man was speaking to a small crowd. Robert paused for a minute and looked down on him. Stray phrases came to his ear. "A class war! The exploiters and the exploited—a new economic system, a new social order. Class war! . . ."

"The poor devil looks frozen!" Robert said. "Not a good evening for making speeches out of doors! Why, hulloa, Tim! Hulloa, Jenny!" Greeting his friends and laughing with them, he passed in through the big doors.

The Town Hall was a solid, dignified Victorian building, good of its kind, and like most of its kind, better outside than in. The Committee had attempted to transfer the big concert hall into what they imagined to be a representation of Vauxhall Gardens in the eighteenth century. The effect, when you thought about it, was rather like a statue of Queen Victoria hung with paper flowers, but most people did not think about it too closely and were pleased by the festive look of the trellises and coloured lanterns. Boxes had been

353

made all round the hall and reserved for supper by various parties, who were too distinguished or too lazy to go and struggle in the supper-room in the crypt.

The Hardings had, as usual, decided not to afford a box this year, and had, as usual, taken one. Lionel Harding and Alice, William Marsden and Isobel were sitting in it looking on while the younger members of their party danced. The two women kept up a brisk fire of question and comment.

"Attractive little thing Jean Halliday is, absolutely sparkling with life!"

"I like Joy's new dress."

"Yes, she's looking lovely. That colour suits her."

"Who is Robert dancing with?"

"That's Anne Armitage, the girl who's engaged to Hilary."

"Clare looks much better."

"Yes, this queer new treatment is doing her good."

"There are a great many people here I don't know. I go out so little now, I don't know the new generation."

"And of course there's all the Ward-Wilson lot, those sort of people on the Council and all that. There's the Ward girl in turquoise dancing with the plump young man. I never did like dancing with men with hot hands, did you, Isobel? Do you remember Bertie?"

"Do you remember that Bachelors' Ball when Edward was late and our programmes were full because we thought he wasn't coming?"

"That was the year Janet and Giles had that fearful quarrel just before he broke off the engagement, do you remember? . . ."

They slid off happily into reminiscence. Lionel Harding got up.

"I think I'll just go round to Ward's box and one or two more and have a word with them. Like to come too?"

William shook his head.

"I feel no social obligations nowadays except to my friends. I don't know half those people by sight. You go by all means."

He watched with more affection than he ever showed his brother-in-law's progress from box to box. He had always felt older than Lionel. He had sometimes envied Lionel's easy touch with all sorts and conditions of men. He envied him now a certain elasticity that made him able at least to get on terms with the modern world. No one, not even Isobel, knew how much he himself disliked it. No sense of quality, no patience, the decay of the Liberal spirit, a world of skin-deep education and strident self-expression, of noise and hurry and mass-production. A world of people who had lost simplicity without gaining experience, who mistook sophistication for culture, and who ate, wore and used things made without taste or ardour. He was sorry for the young people, and sometimes thought that his dead sons had not missed much. His eye fell upon his nephew, Stephen, dancing with some young woman whom he did not know. A good boy with generous aspirations that seemed fated nowadays either to turn sour or to be ineffectual, the fate, he thought, of generous aspirations in an illiberal world.

The story was going round the ball-room that Ward's car had been stopped by strikers, that they had threatened to drag him out, that he and all his family had been turned out and made to walk to the Town Hall, that Mrs. Ward had fainted, that Ward had addressed the strikers from the running-board of the car, that all the windows had been smashed and the mounted police had dispersed the crowd. Robert heard two different versions of the story from two excited partners. Swinging the third, Jean Halliday, out on to the floor, he said, "Do you want to dance or do you want to tell me about the Ward affair? Because my last partner did both, and it wasn't a success."

"I only talk when I'm dancing with people who can't dance."

"Most rare woman! So if you open your mouth I shall know I've fallen below the standard."

Robert was well known to be the best dancer of all the younger generation in Aire. Jean at seventeen had already discovered that too many of the young men who came to dances either could not dance or did not really want to. She kept silence until the music stopped. Then she said,

"You'd better tell me about the Ward affair. You know them and I don't."

355

"You've had no loss."

"I think I have. I want to know all kinds of people. I do know a good many already. That's one of the advantages of living in a Vicarage. You see life."

"If you want to see the Ward life, I'll take you along and introduce you. Though whether your parents will think you're getting into undesirable company——"

"Don't be so silly! I've told you I'm going to get into every kind of company I can. But tell me first what happened?"

"I imagine that what really happened was that Ward in his expensive pantechnicon drove past a procession of strikers who are now living on short commons, and they looked as though they didn't like him."

"Is that all? I thought you'd heard a lot of much more exciting things."

"I have. But I'll bet ten bob that's what really happened."

"The strikers are wrong, of course. Why, their own Union is against them!"

"Oh yes, they're wrong. But I expect it was aggravating, toiling along hungry on a cold night and suddenly seeing the Ward family roll by."

"Do you suppose they know they're wrong?"

"Well, how many people ever do? About anything? We're all very good at making what we want to do into our duty. And somebody's done it for them, poor devils, and led them up the garden path. Here's the Ward encampment."

Robert was not altogether unwilling to satisfy his curiosity about the events of the evening.

The Ward encampment was unusually full, but Jean Halliday quickly disentangled the family from the casual visitors. Mr. Ward, grey and dry and thin, business-man-looking, didn't smile when he shook hands with you. Mrs. Ward, very complete all over, hair and clothes and manners and smile, looked as though she might be a bit hollow inside. A girl, Marjorie, pretty, lovely frock, looking excited, laughing rather a lot, and breaking in when other people were talking. Looked as though without noticing she had had one cocktail or glass of champagne more than she meant to.

356

I did that once or twice last year, when I began going to dances, thought the sapient Jean. There was a fat, cheery, common young man with Marjorie and a fat, cheery, common girl who smiled all the time and was eating steadily through a tray of cocktail biscuits and little savouries. Then Jean, who had been warmly welcomed by Mrs. Ward and Marjorie, was introduced to Marjorie's brother, and in the middle of the dance frocks and glass and laughter, was startled. He had, she thought, the most unhappy face of any young man she had ever seen. She said to him, "Don't you like dancing?" It was an inane remark, but she was so deeply disturbed by the trouble in his eyes. He answered as though the light question had taken a cork out of a bottle. "Not much, and I didn't want to come to this dance to-night. I hate spending all this money when the men out of my father's works are all out on strike." He shivered in the hot room, and the muscles twitched in his cheek as something almost like a cry broke out of him. "I think it's intolerable!"

Stephen was dancing dutifully with Anne Armitage. She was a bad dancer and did not much care for it. He loved it and was good, though not as good as Robert. He pushed her joyless and unrhythmical body round the room, and hoped that she was not as bored as she felt. Anne was not bored at all, her wildest moments of enjoyment were never hilarious, and she was pleased to be at a party with Hilary and Joy. She was a little shy with Stephen, and knew that Hilary did not much like him.

They went back to the box at the end of their dance, and sat down at one of the little tables with Joy and Hilary. Joy said to Stephen,

"Have you heard about your Wards?"

"No. What?"

"They drove past a procession of strikers on the way here, and the men shouted at them and nearly attacked them."

"Good Lord!"

"How dreadful!" Anne said.

357

"Can't have that sort of thing beginning here!" Hilary agreed.

"Of course you know, Hil, the Wards are quite impossible people." A faint sympathy with the strikers betrayed itself in Joy's tone.

"Oh, quite. But that doesn't justify a strike. It's all these Trade Unions, I suppose."

"No, even the Trade Unions are against it. In fact they've really behaved very well. It's some Communists in the works, one, specially, called Tom Sutton."

"Tom Sutton isn't a Communist," Stephen said. "He's a member of the Labour Party."

"Oh, well, it's all the same thing. He's behaving like a Communist. And he's simply made trouble for nothing."

"Not altogether for nothing." Stephen's mouth and chin were obstinate. "There is something to be said on their side!"

Joy flushed.

"I don't know how you can think they're right when their own Union thinks they're wrong! You're only saying it out of perversity!"

Neither Hilary nor Anne had heard Joy use that tone to Stephen before. Hilary blinked. Anne looked up with round, startled eyes.

"I didn't say they were right. In this particular case, I don't think they are. If they aren't satisfied with what the Union does for them, I think they should go to the meeting and vote different people into the management of the Union. But of course they know that the whole point of the present system is to make as much profit as possible on their labour. They know that two-thirds of the employers in this country want to get as much out of them as they can and would pay them less if they could—in fact always did, until the unions made it impossible. I don't say they're right this time, or only partly right. I do say it's a war, and you can't blame them."

The faces of Anne, Hilary and Joy were stiff with self-consciousness and displeasure. Two red spots of colour burned on Joy's cheeks. That Stephen should talk like this

358

to her or in his own family was bad enough. That Hilary and Anne should hear him, covered her with shame. She said, trying to speak lightly, "You do talk nonsense sometimes! Ward is a dreadful outsider, but I've seen enough to know that he's a most generous employer. The men and girls have every single thing in that place that they can want. They're simply ungrateful and spoilt and out on the make for themselves, grabbing and grabbing and wanting more, as they always do. Look what's done for them, free schools and clinics and things, and how it all comes out of us." Her voice shook with anger though she tried to steady it. "You know everything nowadays falls most heavily on the middle classes."

Stephen glanced round the ball-room. A new dance had just begun. The dancers in their black coats and vivid frocks swung by, a waiter crossed the front of their box, carrying a tray of drinks, topaz, amber, and chrysophrase in small glasses. Another went by with the gold-covered neck of a champagne bottle sticking out of a bucket.

"They seem to do fairly well on it, all the same!" Stephen said.

There was a pause. Hilary turned to Anne. "Let's dance again, shall we?" They fled from the table with obvious relief.

Robert came to the front of the box. He smiled at Joy, lifted his eyebrows and made a gesture of invitation towards the floor. Joy rose.

"I'm going to dance with Robert. Stephen, you know I don't agree with you. I never shall. I don't interfere with you, though I hate it! But I wish you wouldn't say those sort of things before Anne and Hilary. I feel disgraced! I can't bear them to know that I've married somebody who goes against everything we've been brought up to and our own kind of people!"

Stephen went out of the great hall into the corridor that ran round it. He wanted to get cool. He wanted to think that it was funny. He had opened a crack of window and

359

let a small draught of air into their warm, enclosed room, and they were absurd in their anxious haste to shut it again.

As he turned the corner of the passage he saw a girl in a stiff black dress with spreading skirts coming out of the hall by another door. It was Mary Welburn, and something in him clicked into place as though a dislocated limb had been put back. She stood still for a minute outside the door, reading something that she had written on her pad. She put the pad away in her bag, looked up and saw him. They had not met lately.

"Hulloa!" he said. "You've deserted the Discussion Group!"

"I don't get many free evenings round about Christmas, and since then we've had people away with 'flu, so I've been extra busy. What have you been doing?"

"Nothing very much. We're rather quiet at the office because of the strike. I haven't seen your uncle since it started."

"It's making him old! Have you looked out in front of the Town Hall?"

"No."

"There's a demonstration going on in the Square. Come and see. We can see out of this window, I think."

He followed her into a small room, an ante-room to the Mayor's Parlour. One or two Corporation officials had left their coats there, making use of their privilege to avoid the end-of-the-evening struggle in the cloak-room.

As they walked across to the window, they heard the music stop in the ball-room behind them. There was a brisk rattle of clapping. After a minute, the drums and saxophones began again, banging and wailing the emphatic tune.

The window looked sideways on to the Town Hall steps. The square below them was white with a thin covering of snow, black in the middle with a throng of men. Someone was speaking, standing above the crowd on the pedestal of a statue of the Duke of Wellington. They could not hear him through the glass, but saw his gestures, his arms flung out black as a crow's wing against the background of snow-covered roofs on the opposite side of the square.

"They've been singing," Mary said. "One or two people from the daily papers have been taking photographs and writing up paragraphs—sound of revelry within, strikes outside—you know the kind of thing. I haven't got to do that, thank goodness, the *Guardian* doesn't want it. They must be so cold standing there all this time with their feet in the snow, and they can't do any good. I wish they'd go home!"

She let the heavy curtain fall over the window. The music from the ball-room surged up and sank again.

"It's incredible," Stephen said. "That outside and this inside—after all these years!"

He spoke unconsciously, not thinking of his words. Something incredible was happening to him, something that he had never imagined would happen and yet had known all the time was coming.

"Mary!"

"Oh, yes!"

The moment swept over real life, submerging it in something which seemed much more real. He felt in the instant when he was moving towards her as though never in his life before had he been fully alive. Then all definite thought and feeling was merged in a confused ecstasy, their separate existence almost lost so that when they let go of one another and drew apart they might have been rescued from drowning, they gasped breathless and bewildered on the shores of their everyday world. Stephen said stupidly,

"Did you know?"

"Yes. Oh, a long time. Not about you. About me."

"What shall we do?"

"I don't know! We can't do anything now."

Real life was coming back to them. Mary heard footsteps and voices in the passage.

"I must go round to the paper. You'd better go back to your party!"

He tried to remember his party, who and what they were. He remembered Joy, moving off to dance with Robert, her cheeks white, her lips stiff with anger. He said, "Oh, God!" sat down on a Corporation chair of red velvet and buried his face in his hands.

"You must go, darling! They'll be looking for you. It isn't safe here!"

"We must meet!"

"Yes, of course, we must. To-morrow evening! No, oh, I can't. The evening after, Thursday. We'll go somewhere and talk."

"When—what time?"

She thought quickly and told him a place and time. Above the singing happiness in her heart she had an urgent sense of the need to be sensible for him, to give him time to collect himself. She said, "You can send me a postcard if you'd rather not come when you think about it."

He smiled and shook his head. There was a sound again of footsteps outside, and a girl's laugh. The dance was over and people would be coming out to get cool in the corridor.

"I'm going," Mary said. "You wait here a bit."

She slipped out into the passage and shut the door leaving him in the room behind her.

Robert and Beryl, instead of putting their car in the large and overcrowded park behind the Town Hall, had left it about five minutes' walk away in a small, open yard behind Robert's office. As they came out on to the steps, the Town Hall attendants were bawling through microphones the numbers of chauffeur-driven cars, while owner-drivers were going off to struggle and wait their turn to get out of the official park. Robert and Beryl congratulated themselves on their cleverness, made a way through the crowd, and walked together along a white pavement that crackled under their feet. The air felt brilliant. A few lazy flakes of snow fluttered indifferently to the ground. Robert was exhilarated by dancing and stepped out briskly, holding Beryl's arm and humming a tune.

"Good party!" he said appreciatively.

"Lovely!"

"I'm glad you had a dance with Dad. He does like it!"

362

"He dances awfully well. Much better than a lot of the younger ones."

"What's Hilary like?"

Beryl laughed. "Conscientious!"

"Anne isn't even that! She just dozed off and let me push! What was the matter with Joy?"

"Was anything the matter?"

"She was in a tearing rage once when I danced with her. I wondered what I'd done. Afterwards I thought she and Stephen must have had a row. I gathered from Brother Hilary that Stephen had been saying some very queer things, very queer indeed!"

"Good gracious! What about?"

"Politics. Of course it isn't very difficult to say anything that sounds queer to Hilary. All the same, I wish Stephen wouldn't make such an ass of himself."

"Sometimes I think he may be partly right."

"Don't you get morbid too!"

"Things aren't fair."

"No one ever said they were. But Stephen upsetting Joy and perhaps getting across with Ward isn't going to make them any fairer. What do you bet me the car won't start?"

Robert was right. He pushed the self-starter, flooded the carburettor and cranked with vigour, but the car remained obstinately dead. Hot and exhausted, with his dark hair ruffled up and a blister on his hand, Robert observed "Curse!" without much real ill-temper, and added, "We'll have to shove it down the hill to Station Square. If it won't go by that time, we can put it in the Midland Garage and get a taxi. Stay there and keep warm while I look for someone to help me. This first bit's uphill, she'll go all right after that."

Beryl was left alone in the car, huddled in the warmth and comfort of her fur coat. What a darling Robert was! Never really cross, always amused and with such a gift for enjoying himself that he made you see how seldom most people positively enjoyed themselves. The Harding family had that capacity, it was in their father and had been in Stephen, though he seemed to have lost it temporarily, and it was in Clare too, though something had quenched it, but from time to time it flashed out. It would be a lovely gift to hand on to a child, a child who would look like Robert, and be interested and curious and amused as he was, a sturdy little boy or a round little girl with rosy cheeks and bright eyes and ruffled dark hair.

Robert came back with two men who looked like workmen behind him.

"You steer," he said to Beryl, "and we'll shove. Put the brake on once we get over this bit, and I'll jump in, and then we'll let her rip down the hill. It's a mile, pretty nearly. It ought to get her going."

Beryl sat up and gripped the steering wheel. Robert and the two men put their weight against the back of the car. The ground was slippery, and their feet slid away under them as they panted and strained, getting hot even in the frosty air. The car began to move slowly before them out of the yard. Beryl slewed round the corner of the gateway, she felt a renewed effort behind the car. It climbed a yard or two up a slope, and then began to move easily at the beginning of the long hill that ran down to the Station Square. She put on the brakes.

"I'm afraid that was hard work," Robert said, breathlessly. He looked uneasily at the smaller of the two men who seemed distressed, and was bending nearly double. "I hope it wasn't too much for you." He put his hand in his pocket.

"Thank you, sir." As the taller man took Robert's shilling, he said, as though moved irresistibly to confidence,

"That's more than I've earned this week!"

"You out of a job?"

"On strike—Ward's."

Robert was like his father, in that he seldom wanted to break off a casual conversation, even at three o'clock on a frosty morning. Perhaps because of this, casual conversations and unexpected confidences often came his way. He said,

"Is it any good, really? Why don't you chuck it and go back?"

The taller man, Joe, had been saying the same thing to himself that evening, but he had no words in which to put

364

before Robert of the complicated mixture of loyalty to his fellows, fear of their condemnation, and inertia that restrained him. He was accustomed to acting in a body, in his union, in the workroom, and now with the strikers. He had made up his mind some days ago that he wanted to go back, but the difference between thinking that and going back on his own initiative was the difference between thinking it time to get up and jumping out of bed on a cold morning. He shuffled his feet on the frozen snow, and grinned.

His companion, David Sanderson, was one of the men who had been addressing the crowd of strikers that evening. He was a small, pale fellow, the child of a tuberculous mother, who looked as though he might have the seeds of the disease in him. During the strike he had discovered in himself for the first time a gift for fluent and fiery oratory. He was separated from his wife and lived with his daughter and son-in-law, who was out of work. They had all been on short commons for more than a week. He had been hanging round with Joe in the hope of picking up a sixpence by helping to start a car, but he bitterly resented the necessity, and had shoved and pushed behind Robert's car with a heart hot with resentment. They were standing near a lamp.

Robert looked at him again and recognized him.

"Why, you're the fellow who was making a speech by the steps as we went in?"

David Sanderson nodded.

"About the class war?"

Sanderson nodded again. There were a dozen angry and telling things that he could have said to this easy-mannered, laughing enemy standing there bare-headed with his dark coat open and the tails of his silk scarf swinging across his white waistcoat, but somehow he could not say them. It was one thing to make a speech and another to argue with a stranger in private life. He ran his tongue along his lips and stared with hostile eyes.

"Don't be an ass!" Robert said. "There isn't a class war,—not in England. But if there was, let me tell you this. You aren't the only class that would fight!" He put his hand in his pocket again. Sanderson took the coin automatically.

"Thanks very much," Robert said again. "She'll go all right now down the hill. Good night!"

He jumped into the car beside Beryl and released the brake. The car began to glide downhill. In a minute the two men left behind heard the engine start up.

The coin in Sanderson's hand, round and heavy, was a half-crown. He looked at it, then swore, and threw it violently down into the snow. Joe, who had pocketed his own shilling, glanced at him uneasily, thinking, a bob's a bob and we don't know where there's one coming from next week! He could see the coin lying where it had rolled, a small, dull spot on the white pavement. He went after it, stooped, and picked it up. Arf a crown too! Some folks had money to chuck about! And he had shoved the ruddy car as hard as David! He brought the coin back. "'Ere," he said, "No use leaving it for a kid to pick up and spend on rubbish."

Sanderson took the half-crown. He had known, even while he threw it down, that he could not afford his pride. He made a sound that might have been thanks, put the coin in his pocket, and shuffled off down the street.

Most people prophesied that the strike would last a week. On Saturday, when the week's money was finished, and there was no pay to draw, the men would begin to realize their folly and go back to work. Tom Sutton and his committee knew that the end of the first week was a dangerous time. On Monday morning, Tom went round early to see that the pickets were on duty and stood for a while chatting to them. A group of girls came and stood on the opposite pavement and giggled and stared, but made no attempt to force an entrance. One or two men arrived, and one had an argument with the picket, and shook his fist in their faces, saying fiercely, "I've three bairns and my wife's expecting. Do you want us all to clem? Let me in, you ruddy bastards, I've a right to work for them!"

The pickets argued and called him a blackleg, and in the end he went grumbling away down the street. There was

366

no real attempt to come back. The workers were solid, the strike held. Tom went round to the strike headquarters with a glow of pride and achievement in his heart.

It seemed as though the machinery of the strike had been running for more than a week. A small heap of papers and some newspaper cuttings lay on the table before Tom's chair as if he were a director arriving at his business. Harold Pearson and another young man were taking off copies of a notice from a jelly. A girl was banging a borrowed typewriter at a table in the corner. Above the fireplace were pinned up a notice of a big strike meeting to be held in front of the Town Hall on Wednesday, and telegrams of encouragement and congratulation from various branches of the Communist Party. Some enthusiast had also found and tacked up a photograph of Lenin, and a cartoon of Big Business from the *Daily Worker*. On the mantelpiece were stacked a pile of those pamphlets with which Harold Pearson made himself a home from home wherever he went.

Harold came across to the table, leaving the jelly and the purple ink to the vigorous attentions of his colleague. He sat down by Tom, and looked over his elbow at the correspondence.

"Were there many of them trying to get back to work?"

"Only one or two."

"It's a fine demonstration of solidarity."

"We shall need the relief fund this week. The collectors had better go out this afternoon."

"Ward's have another notice in the paper this morning promising work and protection to anyone who goes back."

"Let them. There's no traitors in our camp."

"Only the Union."

"Aye, only t'Union."

"It seems to me, Tom, you'd do well to go and see John Allworthy."

"I've seen him," Tom said shortly. "They've had a branch meeting and t'General Secretary came down. They've written us another letter telling us to go back to work before they can speak for us."

"I've been hearing that Councillor Allworthy gets £1,000 down from Ward on the day the strike breaks."

"Nay, that's never true!"

"He's doing well for them."

"He'd not touch their money! He's jealous and afraid o't' power in t'Union passing out of his own hands. He's like all the old folk, want to keep the younger men out of it."

"The men are saying he's bought!"

"I don't believe it! He's a stubborn old ox, is John All-worthy, but he's honest."

"Well, why not go and see him again and see what you can do? Very probably he wouldn't expect the strike to run into another week. If the Union comes in with us now, Ward's'll give way."

In one corner of his heart, Tom was perhaps not displeased that the Union were standing out. It gave him an opportunity to handle the strike which he would not otherwise have had, and he was able to indulge a pleasant feeling of superiority to John Allworthy, a back number, an old man, out of things! Riding high on a wave of energy and activity, he thought that they could do very well without the Union. Harold had expected that the Union officials, afraid of losing their leadership, would give way sooner. It was a matter of indifference to him who handled the strike officially. He was guiding Tom more than Tom knew, and if the Union came in with them, he hoped to be able to guide the Union. He did not care whether he himself got any credit or importance. He was willing to work day and night in the background.

He went with Tom that afternoon to the daily meeting in the Labour Club. The sub-committee met privately in the morning, and not much business was done at the big meeting. A few notices were read out, speeches were made, and comedians and singers among the men gave entertainments. The importance of the meetings was that they kept the strikers together. Courage that ebbs easily when alone revives in company, and men will stand fast in a body where they will run away as individuals.

Claud Unwin was addressing the meeting that afternoon on the Economics of the Modern World. He knew quite well that he might make things awkward for himself by doing this, but he had long ago decided that there were certain risks that had to be taken. He gave a concise and brilliant summary, using too many long words, but holding the attention of the audience by the clarity of his ideas and by his sincere, almost savage conviction. Naomi, who sat behind him on the platform, thought that she had hardly ever heard him speak better. He was at his best and happiest when addressing an audience. The rows of intent and listening faces appeased for a time the gnawing dissatisfaction in his heart.

While he spoke, the seething complexities of the modern world were present in some degree to everyone in the audience. As soon as he sat down, the meeting rapidly assumed the homely character of an entertainment at a church bazaar. Two men who might have been sidesmen thanked Mr. Unwin for his very interesting and thoughtful address. A serious tenor and a local comic singer entertained the company in turn. The tenor was very bad, and bawled out drawing-room ballads, putting in expression like Hell, and wallowing in his own pathos. The comedian was extremely good, racy and apt with topical allusions. The audience liked both of them, encored everything they sang, and roared with good-natured laughter when the comedian made jokes about strikes.

"I shall never understand these people!" Claud muttered. Naomi thought that he never would. In one of those moments when her vision went beyond his, she saw the great gulf that stretched between Claud and his kind and the men whom they wished to lead or follow. They would always find a few ardent disciples and sympathetic friends, but to the mass of what they called "the workers," she suspected that a Tory fox-hunting squire might be nearer, if only because he lived by his instincts and not by his mind.

The meeting dutifully sang the Red Flag. The sort of tune they would adopt, Naomi thought, a nation that meant business by its revolution produced the Marseillaise! Honour being thus satisfied, the meeting sang Tipperary, Swanee River, Daisy, Daisy, and Ilkla Moor Ba't'At, with very much more fervour. Tom read from the platform the letter

369

from the General Secretary of the Ready Made Clothiers Union informing the strikers that they must go back to work before the Union could undertake any negotiations on their behalf. There were shouts of anger, and a motion that the strike should go on was proposed and carried by a unanimous vote, but some, especially of the older men, looked uneasy, and women were murmuring together at the back of the hall. Tom went down from the platform and stood at the door, nodding to those who went out, stopping one here and there for a word. Their faces were resolute but anxious. There would be no money in the house this week except their savings, and some of them who had lately been thriftless or unlucky had no savings. Nearly all of them had weekly payments to keep up, payments to Burial Clubs and Insurance Societies and Clothing Clubs.

Tom knew all this and felt for them in every nerve of his being. His own father had been out of work more than once, he had spent all his life among people living just inside the safety margin. Even for the Unemployed there was the dole and public assistance, but for the men and women now leaving the hall, there would be nothing except help from a limited and uncertain relief fund to keep them from starvation.

The *Yorkshire Guardian* that morning had published a grave leader on the sufferings of those who took part in an unofficial strike, and the heavy responsibility of those who had inspired it and misled them to their own undoing. Tom did not see it as his responsibility. It seemed to him that it was the responsibility of the Union. The officials were causing all the anxiety by withholding strike pay, as they were hampering the workers by standing out against the will of the majority. It was not he but John Allworthy who was making housewives anxiously count the pennies that were left, and send the children off to school on chilly February mornings without the extra slice of bread and bacon fat that they asked for.

He knew that the Council were meeting that afternoon, and as soon as the last of the strikers had left the hall, he took a penny tram to Highgate, and walked across Upper Row to the new City Hall, hoping to catch John Allworthy as he came out. The Council was still sitting, and he slipped into the strangers' gallery, just above the bent heads and scribbling pads of the Press. After the meeting which he had just left, this one seemed sleepy, formal and dull. The Council seats, which had high backs and wooden ledges like the pews of a church, were built in a circle. Nearly half the circle was occupied by a solid block of Conservatives. The Labour opposition made another smaller block opposite to them. Between were two forlorn-looking Liberals, and a grey-haired woman who had stood as an independent candidate on the housing question, and was a thorn in the side of both parties, harrying them impartially till they withdrew together into corners, and laid aside their political differences in a common irritation.

A debate was going on as to whether in appointing the commissionaires and caretakers for municipal buildings, preference should or should not be given to ex-soldiers. The Conservatives were upholding this, making speeches about our debt to the men who had fought for us. Labour were opposing, making speeches about the danger of any kind of preference except that of preferring the best man for the job. Mr. Batley spoke for three or four minutes and John Allworthy replied. Both of them knew that the motion had already been discussed in Committee, and would in a few minutes be carried by a comfortable Conservative majority. Both of them knew that it was past tea-time and that there were two other minutes to vote on, but they also knew that principles must be maintained, and that the reporters had not been given much in the way of a debate that afternoon. Mr. Batley accused John of deliberate meanness to the men who had saved his life. John accused Mr. Batley of militarism, unfairness, class prejudice and the first steps towards Fascism. The reporters, bored and thirsty, picked up here and there a salient phrase, distorted it slightly and noted it down. They knew that it was perfunctory, but Tom, who had never been to a Council meeting before, took it all at its face value, grew angry with Batley and sided with John. Like a good many of his kind, he regarded ex-soldiers as a section of the enemy class and the Conservative party.

The debate petered out. The remaining minutes, those of the Gas Committee and the Parks Committee, were put through with almost indecent haste, nobody even pretending that they wanted to debate on them. The Council rose for tea. Tom hurried down the stairs from the Gallery. As he walked along the passage that led to the door of the hall, the Councillors came out, in a bunch, and crossed over to the tea-room. John Allworthy came alone, stooping a little, and looking frail and tired. Tom's heart softened towards him. He had just seen his old friend staunchly upholding the good cause and being beaten. He was going up to him, when Alderman Batley stepped forward, slapped Allworthy on the back, took him by the arm, and began to talk to him, turning towards him a good-natured, ruddy face beaming with smiles. He said something which made John laugh. Two other Conservative Councillors in front turned and grinned and joined in the conversation. Tom did not hear all that they were saying, but one man called out cheerfully, "You old devil, John!" Allworthy was swept through the swing doors of the tea-room in the middle of a laughing, jesting group of his opponents. Tom remained outside.

His heart swelled with fury. Allworthy was a snob and false, false as Hell. He curried favour with the other side and cared nothing for his own class. Through the glass panels in the swing doors, Tom could see him having tea in the middle of the Conservative party, laughing with Batley and Wood and Crow. John was a character, loved as such men are in England for his integrity, and because something quaint and homely in his speech and manner made people laugh. There was always a crowd round him in the tea-room, and it so happened to-day that the crowd was made up almost entirely of the other side. Tom turned away from the glass panels, sick at heart. Harold Pearson's suggestion of that morning recurred to him. In his sober mood, he would never have believed that John could take money from Ward. He knew what many people did not know, that John had regularly forfeited part of his wages to take time off for his Council work, and that he had always cared as little for money as any man could who had known what it was to be short of it. Tom's mood was not sober. He was strung up by excitement and anxiety, flicked on the raw by the sight of John hobnobbing with Conservatives inside a room from which he was excluded. Harold Pearson's suggestions always carried more weight with him than he knew. Besides, if John would not sell his own people for money he might sell them for favour, for the pleasure of being patted on the back by the rich and powerful. Wasn't that what all of them did, from Transport House downwards? Tom's anger grew, and overcame his natural shyness in official places. He walked up to a policeman who was standing near the door of the tea-room, and said, "Will you tell Councillor Allworthy someone wants to see him. Name of Sutton. He's inside."

Rather to his astonishment, the policeman went in with his message. A minute later John Allworthy came out through the swing doors. He saw the sullen young man glowering at him and sighed inwardly.

"Well, Tom?" he said.

"I've come to make another appeal to you, Mr. Allworthy, on behalf of the majority of the workers. We're not going in till we get our rights, but there's many a man will suffer this week, and his wife and kids, too, for want of strike pay. T'Unions used to stand for the workers, not to starve them. Ward's can't stand against us if you come in with us. Make it a Union strike! You can do it, and t'strike's over!"

John shook his head.

"I can't lad. This strike ought never to have happened. I signed an agreement about the wages on behalf of the Union and it was agreed to a general meeting. I can't go back on our word."

"It's the wish of the majority and the majority vote is what ought to count in a democracy!"

"The majority agreed to the rise of a halfpenny an hour with further investigation in twelve months. They've got to stand by their word."

"Reckon it wasn't their will! They were led into it!"

"And what are they now, Tom Sutton? Led into a mess they'll be crying to get out of before another week's up."

"So you'll stand by Ward?" Tom sneered.

"I'll stand by the Union's signed agreement. Look, Tom, if we don't keep to our side of a bargain, there'll be no bargaining, and that's what we've fought for and worked for, some of us, all our lives. If the Union gives in to an unofficial strike, it's the end of the Union."

"And a good job, too, if t'Union's on t'side of t'masters!"

"Don't talk like a fool! Is there anything we've got since Ward's was started, better pay, better quarters, a factory committee, shorter hours—is there any of those that the Union hasn't had a hand in?" Allworthy checked his rising temper and spoke more kindly, "You're young, Tom. You want everything to come at once. You haven't learnt patience. You don't know the long fight we've had. Go back and tell the men to go in. Ward's have said they'll take up the matter again with the Union as soon as the men go back." His tone deepened. "Tom! I'm an old man. I've seen unofficial strikes and maybe you haven't. I've seen a hundred families lose all their savings in three weeks and get nothing for it. In the end this business has got to be settled round a table."

The policeman had come out again, and stood near. One or two Councillors, having finished their tea, were lingering in the passage, half-listening to the dispute. Tom saw in Allworthy's face that he was beaten. He could have struck that unyielding mouth and chin.

"It's on your head, Mr. Allworthy!" he said, breathing hard.

"Nay, Tom. It's on yours."

A Conservative Councillor, listening to the dispute, said to his companion in a low voice,

"What seems so odd to me is that neither of them seem to think it's on Ward's!"

"I've said my say," Tom said. "I'll go back and tell t'men to-morrow that it's nowt to you what they suffer! You can stand by the firm as much as you like, but you'll not break t'strike! We'll break you before we've done, and we'll break t'Union!"

He turned and slouched off along the passage.

On Sunday evening, at the beginning of the third week of the strike, Mark Forrester preached a sermon in St. Jude's Church on the text "If these things be done in a green tree, what shall be done in a dry?" He warned his hearers that another slump was bound to come soon, and that this terrible dispute between the head of a firm and his employees was only a foretaste of what would happen then, unless they made haste to repent of their selfishness and apply their Christianity, if it was real, to the conditions of the modern world. He appeared to think that the strike was the fault of the congregation. The congregation, having been blamed for the Italian victories in Abyssinia, for rearmament, for the failure of the League of Nations, and for the Government's unwillingness to share out colonies and raw materials, might have been supposed equal to sustaining one more burden on their consciences, but the Ward strike, being near home, touched them much more sharply. Canon Halliday had a pile of indignant letters the day after from old members of his congregation and from strangers who had come to the evening service to hear Mark Forrester. He reflected miserably on the arrangements of the Church of England which make it impossible for a Vicar easily to dismiss his Curate. He might talk to the Bishop about it. He had no complaint to make of Mark Forrester as a parish priest, and he was not quite sure what line the Bishop would take. His own monthly letter in the Diocesan Gazette was apt to touch non-committally on international affairs and social questions. Besides, Canon Halliday did not want to prejudice him against Mark Forrester. Mixed with his laziness and dislike of drastic action was real kindliness and forbearance.

Lionel Harding, who had heard the sermon with a half smile for the young man's sweeping economics, walked home reflecting on the passion of the rising generation for simplifications. They made a clear and simple pattern and fitted it to so much that was neither clear nor simple, not even to experts. He had not been an engineer for years without knowing that there were times when the experts were wrong, but he thought that they were not wrong as often as the intelligent amateur supposed. His tradition and character inclined him to a respect for knowledge and training.

Herbert and Mabel Walters, who did not often go to church in the evening, were disappointed because Canon Halliday had not been preaching. They admired his fine presence and his sonorous voice.

"He's more like a chapel preacher, is Forrester," Herbert said disapprovingly.

Mabel agreed.

"Give me the old sort of parson! Canon Halliday would never talk about business in church."

They were on their way up to the Netherton Estate, to fetch Doreen. Olive had been to her midday dinner with them, and had taken her niece home for the afternoon. She was much less interested in the child than usual, and disposed to be intolerant of importunities. Once when Doreen pleaded, "Will you find me something to play with? You said you'd find me something to play with!" Olive replied sharply, "You must wait till I've set the tea! Don't be a nuisance!" The spoilt child stared at her in dismayed astonishment, then shrugged her shoulders and muttered, "You are horrid this afternoon!"

"Everything's horrid," Olive said petulantly. She banged the sugar basin down on the table, her eyes filling with her too ready tears.

All through the fortnight of the strike she had suffered the desperation of the thwarted. A dozen times a day she said to herself that it was too bad. Here she was in a real nice house with a chance to begin to have things nice. She meant to buy a cabinet for the sitting-room in instalments, she planned to get a small table and buy and work at once an afternoon tea-cloth; she had already bought some rosy cretonne for curtains for the bathroom and a shilling jar of pink bath-salts. Then came the strike and the sudden stoppage of her wages. She who loved going to the factory every day, and was perfectly willing to work, was obliged to stay at home and earn nothing for reasons which she dismissed in her own mind as "Tom's nonsense." It did not occur to her that she was among the lucky ones. Her father and her

376

brother were in good work, there was plenty of wholesome food at home, and she was not obliged to take her savings out of the Bank. She could have a shilling or two from her mother and from Fred to go on with, to pay for her tram fares and a picture, but she could not have anything for what Mr. Walters thought of as her fallals. Removing had cost something, prices were higher at the housing estate shops, and Mr. Walters and Fred had to spend more on getting to their work. It was no time to think about cabinets and afternoon tea-cloths until they saw where they were. Olive had to postpone the realization of her dreams. She missed very much the regular rhythm of her life at the factory, the company of the other girls, casual half-hours spent looking at the shops in town, and the luxurious habit of ordering from a varied menu a mid-day meal which she had not had to prepare. She even missed the soothing regularity of her button machine. She drifted about at home like an undergraduate sent down half way through the term, or a clubman cut off from his club during the summer cleaning.

She had been peevish with Doreen but she was very glad indeed to see Herbert and Mabel. She found a more active sympathy in them than in her parents, who were fatalistic, and had grown more so since the removal which had fallen upon them like an unsought visitation. There were always strikes and stoppages and people out of work and there always would be, they thought. There was nothing to be done but hold on until the strike or the stoppage was over. The urgency of new furniture and afternoon tea-cloths was nothing to them. Olive always did "tek on," about one thing or another. They were occupied in adjusting themselves to the new life, which both of them still found cold and alien.

Mabel was much more satisfactory.

"It's a shame, Olive, that it is! I've always said Tom would come to no good if he took up with these Communists and let them get hold of him."

"I don't know," Herbert meditated, "that you could blame Ward if he filled up the places with outside labour."

This dreadful possibility had never occurred to Olive.

"Herbert!" she shrieked.

"There's nothing to stop him as I can see." Herbert was always very careful not to say "Nowt" like his parents. "A chap at our place was saying the other day that would be the next thing."

"Then we might not go back at all!"

"Mind you, I don't say he will do that, but he might."

Olive was too appalled even for tears. Surely, surely, nothing so dreadful could happen! To be turned off at Ward's! To have no work, no money, to lose the company of her friends and the surroundings that she admired! Olive appreciated the Vitaglass and chromium and polished wood if Stephen did not. Ward's satisfied her æsthetic sense nearly as well as the Tivoli, although not quite, since its shining efficiency fell short of the delicate charm of the imitation eighteenth-century décor of the Tivoli cloakrooms. Losing her job at Ward's would also mean losing the Tivoli cloakrooms, losing her little jars of cream and powder compacts, her constant visits to the hair-dresser, all her personal elegancies as well as the elegancies of the new house. She could not be sure of getting another job at once. Mabel, who saw her blank horror, said kindly,

"Nay, Herbert, I don't think he'll do that. He's always been good to his people, has Ward. Don't you fret yourself, Olive, love. The strike will be over now in a day or two."

"Have you seen Tom?" Herbert asked.

Olive shook her head. She had not seen Tom since the beginning of the strike. He had sent a postcard to say that he was too busy to come. She was not sorry, for she was so angry with him that she did not want to see him. Sometimes she thought that she did not want to have anything more to do with him. Yet she would have shrunk from a break with him, he had become a habit, and in spite of the disparity between their minds and natures, his good looks pleased her fastidious eye, and that in her which fumbled blindly after quality was more at home with his austere and ardent spirit than with the facetious love-making of a more ordinary boy. Olive had, if not taste, at least the desire for it. She was bewildered and led astray by a network of artificial values, a mass of shoddy productions, and it was likely that Tom

378

would be the most genuine thing of his kind that she would ever want, even for a short time.

She was sorry when Mabel said that it was Doreen's bedtime and got up to go. The older couple were sorry too. The loneliness and chill of this bleak hilltop were relieved by having their own family round them. Mrs. Walters had arranged the kitchen to her liking and had found that the oven was not so bad and the constant supply of hot water was an astonishing convenience, but she was not yet acclimatized. Virtue had gone out of her. She did not rule this clean, new house with the same firm hand that had ruled Bankside Yard. She hesitated over small decisions and sometimes turned to Olive to make up her mind for her.

"You'll be coming again soon?" she said almost pleadingly to Mabel.

"Here's a penny for you, love," Mr. Walters bent stiffly and brushed Doreen's soft little cheek with his moustache.

"Say, 'Thank you very much, Grandpa.'"

"I was going to! Don't tell me! I always do!"

"That's a good girl!" The two grandparents, Mabel and Herbert and even the miserable Olive beamed proudly on this incomparable child, who, in her blue cloth coat and round hat of the same cloth, looked to the casual eye like any other thin, long-legged little girl, but to them was as much of a miracle as the first spring.

"I'll put you on the way to the 'bus," Olive said. She did not want to stay in the house with her gloomy forebodings for company.

When she came back, two of her friends, Maysie and Violet, had arrived, and were sitting with her parents by the kitchen fire. If only the sitting-room was ready and a nice fire burning there and the wireless on, and a silver box with cigarettes on the table! This dream had not yet taken shape, but her friends were politely admiring the new house, and Olive was able to assure them that it would look very different when they were really settled. She was glad, anyhow, that she was wearing her new green woollen dress, for Maysie and Violet, in spite of sleety weather, were both in their best fur-collared coats and little hats with eye veils.

379

They were scented, powdered and curled, their gloves and bags and scarves matched their clothes, they wore the latest jewellery from Haley's.

"What we come round for, Olive," Maysie said, "was to see what you were going to do about going back to work?"

"Is the strike over?" Olive cried eagerly.

"Nay, but some of us in t'gang have been putting our heads together and we're right fed up with the whole business. Seems to me no one's a penny the better for this strike and some of us are a lot worse. Maybe the firm's doing us over the halfpenny and maybe it isn't. T'Union agreed to it, any road. Some of us are beginning to think we were fools not to listen to Mr. Allworthy."

"We got to begin earning again," Violet said. There were dark shadows under her eyes as though she had lain awake at night. Maysie, like Olive, had a comfortable home kept up by her parents. Violet was the mainstay of her family. Her mother kept a small shop which made very little profit, and there were a young brother and sister at school. How Violet managed, in spite of the substantial help she gave them, to have the fur-collared coat and eye-veiled hat, the bag and gloves, powder and cream and permanent wave, and always to be abreast of the changing fashion among her friends was one of the lesser miracles of modern civilization.

"Did you read what Ward's put in t'paper last night, Olive?"

Olive never looked at the evening paper except occasionally at a pattern or a beauty hint on the woman's page. She shook her head.

Maysie opened her bag and handed her a newspaper-cutting from the front page of the paper. Olive read:

"The Management of Alfred Ward's are of the opinion that most of their work-people who are now on strike have been misled by a few extremists. It is to their interests that matters should be dealt with through the recognized channel of their Trade Union. Unofficial strikes cannot have any good results, and cause loss and suffering to all concerned.

"The Management believe that a large number of workers are anxious to get back to work. They wish to assure them that their loyalty to their employers will be greatly appreciated, and that arrangements will be made to ensure that they return unmolested."

"But we can't go back!" Olive cried. "It's picketed!"

"T'pickets can't touch us. They aren't allowed. My Dad says so. They can only argue with you."

"There's been enough arguing!" Violet said bitterly. She opened her bag with hands that suddenly trembled, and took out a small mirror and a powder-puff in a square of flowered chiffon. The sweet scent of her powder filled the room. She bent her face over the mirror, thinking, "That Tom Sutton!" Her personal daintiness and her obligations at home had prevented her from saving, and the fingers of fear and want were already gripping her heart.

"Are the men going back?"

"Not yet. Not till we show them the way. Like a lot of birds they are, frightened by a scarecrow! There's twenty of us going to meet at the end of the road t'morrow morning and go in past the pickets together, and I'd like to see them stop us," she added. "We said we'd go and see you and one or two more and ask them to join. But we all know it's a bit awkward for you, Olive, with your Tom leading the strike. Don't you come if you don't want to. He might play war with you. Likely we'll all be back in a week. My Dad says the first people who go back break a strike more than anything else. But you think on! You've been with Tom for two years now, I know, and you don't want to lose your lad over it."

"What time are you meeting?"

"Eight-twenty at the corner of Buckden Drive."

"I'll be there."

Maysie began to fasten her coat.

"Well, we'd better try and see Alice and Pauline before it gets too late."

"Have a cup of tea first, love," Mrs. Walters urged. "You get the tea-things out, Olive, and there's a bit of my fruit-cake left."

"Do have some tea," Olive urged, politely but insincerely. She knew that Fred and Rosie, who had been out to supper, would be coming in for a few minutes before Rosie went home, and she had managed so far to keep her most distinguished friends from meeting Rosie, even from knowing that her brother was engaged to a girl in service. She was much relieved when Maysie and Violet refused the tea and went off to recruit another of their friends.

"Are you going back, Olive?" her mother asked as the door closed behind them.

"Yes, I am."

"What'll Tom say?"

"I don't care what he says."

Mrs. Walters looked doubtful. She had never been in favour of the strike, and she did not want Olive about the house all day, complaining of this and wanting to alter that, and dissatisfied with the midday meal, picking at what was good enough for her mother, calling it "fatty food" and talking about the cutlets and tomato salads at Ward's. But she had a soft spot for Tom, always nice to her and a kind, steady, respectable lad who would be a good husband for Olive. Mrs. Walters did not think anybody's politics of much importance.

"Well, I'm going!" Olive cried, defiantly answering something that her mother had not said. She flung an appeal to her father.

"Don't you think I'm right, Dad."

Mr. Walters took his pipe out of his mouth and considered. "Aye, I dare say. I never knew no good come yet of going against t'Union."

The strike headquarters could not be used on Sundays, since the Little Bethelites required the whole building for their own mysterious rites. There was a big strike meeting on Sunday evening in the hall of the Labour Club, addressed by two prominent speakers on the Left who had come down from London for the purpose. The Ward Strike was now

382

national news as well as provincial. It had provoked a question in Parliament, a leader in *The Times*, and an article in the *New Statesman*. Mr. Worsley, the General Secretary of the Ready Made Clothiers' Union, had taken up his quarters in Aire, and sent letters and telegrams daily to Transport House. In two other towns, Leeds and Manchester, unofficial strikes had been started in sympathy by the workers in ready-made clothing factories. The Communist Party had got out a leaflet, and half a dozen local branches had sent contributions to the Relief Fund. Tom Sutton had been photographed and interviewed by several papers. Ward had refused to be interviewed, but his picture was already available, as he was a public figure in his own town, and an enterprising photographer from the *Daily Budget* got a close-up of him leaving the office in his car, and wrote underneath it, *"British Business Man Stands like a Rock against Surging Tide of Bolshevism."* The same paper indicated the amount of money that had been sent from Russia to finance the strike. One paper published a photograph of John Allworthy looking benign and gnomish, and said that tears had poured down his cheeks at the meeting which voted for striking against the Union. The *Yorkshire Guardian* maintained throughout an attitude more of sorrow than of anger, supported Ward temperately, praised the Union, pitied the workmen, said that unofficial strikes were un-English, and solemnly urged the extremists who had started one to realize their responsibilities, and give in before more strife and bitterness were provoked.

On this third Monday of the strike Tom awoke early, realizing his responsibilities, although not those enjoined upon him by the *Yorkshire Guardian*. There was to be a meeting of the Strike Committee at ten o'clock and a demonstration on Fordhouse Moor that afternoon. Tom could not help a feeling of disappointment about the demonstrations. Perhaps it was because there had been so many of them that they fell a little flat. The citizens of Aire were tired of seeing a crowd of men clustered round a speaker with microphones, and watched by a number of bored and indifferent policemen. Even the small boys had given up expecting anything exciting to happen.

Ward must give in this week, thought Tom, he must! He must surely be impressed by the solidarity and determination of the strikers. But of course he was sheltering behind the Union. They were all in it together, he and Allworthy and the General Secretary, all bourgeois who had climbed out of the rut and secured their own positions, and now they were sitting on the heads of their own people with their talk of collective bargains and official channels! The Union *must* support the strike! Tom thought as he dressed of a plan which Harold Pearson had suggested on Sunday evening. He had rejected it at the time, but it seemed worth trying. He remembered the men who had come to him for money out of the Relief Fund on Saturday morning. There had been so few of them and they had come so reluctantly, driven by sickness at home or some urgent need. He was vividly aware of the silent, stoical loyalty of those who had not come. And only John Allworthy and a few more of his kind, jacks-in-office, snobs, toadies of the rich, stood between those silent suffering men and their rights. They were traitors to the workers' cause and hanging was too good for them.

Tom lodged over a butcher's shop in one of the streets that began in Onslet and ended in South Worbeck. They were clean, homely, comfortable lodgings, and he was very friendly with his hosts, though he had never been able to persuade them to take any interest in politics. Mr. Akeroyd grumbled that times had changed, people didn't buy the good Sunday joints they used to buy, they bought four pennyworth of potted meat and went off for the day on tandem bicycles or on motor-cycles with the baby in the side-car on its mother's knee. This appeared to be his one reflection on social changes, but he and his wife were passionately devoted to the Royal Family, especially to the new King Edward, and to the little Princesses, whose pictures at different ages confronted Tom from every corner of the house. Mr. Akeroyd, when he voted at all, voted Conservative from a vague but ineradicable conviction that all Socialists were vegetarians. Tom might protest as he ate the succulent chops and savoury dishes of pork or tripe with his hosts in the back parlour, but Mr. Akeroyd had known a Labour man in his youth who said that meat was poison, and his political convictions had set early.

Tom snatched a hasty breakfast on that Monday morning, and set out early to catch a tram for the centre of the town. He would have to go into the strike headquarters before the meeting, read any letters or telegrams that had come, see the collectors who were working for the Relief Fund and consider any claims for relief. Before that he wanted to go along to Ward's and see that the pickets were on duty. Another Monday morning meant another turning point in the strike. Any men who tried to drift back would be likely to try it at the beginning of a new week.

The street outside the works was empty when Tom got there, except for the three men on picket duty lounging in the gateway. They told him that they had already been there for half an hour. A few men had been and argued with them, and then argued with one another for some time on the other side of the road, but they had gone away. One or two more had come to look and see if the pickets were still there, but had not come up to them. The strike still held. Tom's heart grew hot with pride and triumph. He lingered for a few minutes, talking to the pickets and glancing scornfully at the stolid policeman who was wasting his time on the other side of the street.

He did not know that the army that was to make the first breach in his barricade was advancing to his undoing, nor did he recognize it for what it was when he saw two girls, Maysie and Violet turn the corner into the street. Maysie, inflated by leadership, enjoying the excitement and cheerfully sure of herself, walked with a swagger and carried her blonde head high. Violet's cheeks were pale and her lips set tight. She was frightened but determined. The little brother and sister at home mattered more than any rights or any cause. Behind Maysie and Violet came a score of others, some self-conscious, a few giggling, one or two scared. There was an older woman with a worn, dark face, a widow who worked to keep her three small children. There was a young wife whose husband, two years unemployed, was looking after the six-months-old baby at home. There was

385

May, the canteen worker, the sister of Mrs. Wilson's Nellie. There were one or two young girls like Maysie and Olive, who had found themselves suddenly cut off from luxuries and thrust back from the working world into dull homes. There were girls whose families were already hard put to it without their weekly contribution. With their painted lips and burnished curls, their shining silk legs, and jaunty hats, the unconscious champions of order and tradition, of realism against ideas, advanced upon the pickets. The pickets drew together and made a not very convincing attempt to fill the doorway. The policeman crossed the road. Maysie, who minded no policeman, stepped boldly forward and cried,

"Get out o' t'light, you daft Daniels! We've 'ad enough of your flipping strike!"

She jerked one man in the ribs with her solid elbow, and he gave back hastily. Maysie, swinging her hips and cocking her head, stepped through the doorway into the yard, Violet, tense and quivering, at her heels. One of the men, puzzled and sheepish, put his arm across the doorway, meaning to check the procession and argue. Behind Violet came the pretty young mother of the six-months-old baby. She said to him, her face twisted with anger, "Some of us have bairns that mun eat!" She pushed his arm away and walked through.

The pickets, at a loss, looked at Tom for help. He stepped forward and caught a girl by the arm, exclaiming,

"Listen, Comrade!"

The girl giggled and plucked her arm away from him. She said pertly, "Miss Johnson to you, if you please." She and her companions laughed. Tom was beginning again, when suddenly he drew a breath and stepped back. The stream of girls went past him, and he made no more attempt to stop them. He felt as though the world had given a great jerk under his feet. He stood perfectly still, his fists clenched at his sides.

Olive was the last of the stream. She came alone, half timid, half defiant, her head up, her lips pressed together. In her joy and relief at going back to work she made an even more careful toilet than usual. She wore her best hat, an elf's cap of green felt with a stiffened eye veil. She was delicately made up, bright earrings swung from her pretty ears, her curls clustered below her cap in orderly rows. Perhaps she had felt that she needed all her armour. She saw Tom, checked, and came on again. The rouge stood out suddenly on her cheeks, but she walked steadily, looking straight before her. She could see, though she would not look at him, that Tom was smiling, a queer twisted smile that frightened her. She wondered if he would hit her, and shrank inwardly with physical fear. There was the policeman, but if Tom struck her quickly, the policeman, though he would run him in for it, might be too late to stop him. Olive had time to think of this. Her heart was racing so that she could hardly breathe, her stomach felt hollow, she was cold under her armpits. She came on, stepping daintily in her green suède shoes.

Tom did not hit her. He waited until she was abreast of him. He stared full into her eyes, and even in that moment, frightened for herself as she was, she saw the pain and torment behind his anger. Something in her heart that had almost loved him cried "Tom!" but her lips did not speak. His lips curled back in a curious shape that she noticed even then, showing his strong white teeth. He said "Black-leg!", raised his hand and let it fall at his side, and turned and walked away down the street.

John Allworthy was putting on his coat to go to a committee meeting of the local branch of the Union. Grace came to him with the muffler which she had been warming before the fire. She wound it round his neck and tucked the ends in over his chest.

"You'll mind and put it on when you come out of the Hall?"

John nodded absently. He was tired and felt discouraged. He had spent the afternoon with Ward arguing against his intention of getting in outside labour. He had told him that the Union would resist that to the limit of its capacity. He had felt while he spoke that he was like a man advancing upon a position with a skeleton army. The workers were not behind the Union. He had prevailed because Ward was anxious at all costs to keep on good terms with the Union, and to foster the division between the officials and the Strike Committee. He had agreed that he would not get in outside labour for another week. About a hundred of the girls were back, and half as many men. The strike was not broken yet, but to Ward's acute ear, the water was chittering below the ice. He said so to John, who did not answer, but silently agreed with him. He had not believed that the strike could hold out so long, and he was sick for the courage and solidarity wasted and misused. The Union Committee had agreed to receive a deputation from the Strike Committee this evening. "That'll be Tom!" John thought, and his heart hardened.

The Branch Committee met at eight o'clock in one of the smaller rooms opening off the Trades Hall. They were all men whom John Allworthy knew well, men with whom he had worked for years, whose value in the Labour Party and in the Union was as well known to him as the value of other county cricketers to Frank Varley. They met this evening with serious faces. "Hulloa, Harry! Hulloa, Dick! Hulloa, old lad!" had a sober ring, and smiles were less expansive than usual. They were leaders who suddenly found themselves defending the camp against their own army, and they felt the strain of the unnatural position.

The deputation was due to arrive at nine-thirty, when they should have finished the ordinary business of the meeting. None of them had any intention of yielding to it, nor any lively hopes of prevailing with it. Most of them were angry with a jealous anger. One man said to another, "It's that Communist cell in the South Work-room! Whenever there's Communists there's trouble! No real spirit of democracy!" He spoke with more indignation than he had used a few minutes before of a bad employer who was keeping his staff in unfit premises.

There was a noise of trampling feet in the Trades Hall. Harry Best, one of the committee members, looked at his watch.

"It sounds as if there was going to be a meeting in the hall! There can't be one at this time o' night, surely?"

"Must be a large deputation!"

"They ought to be here by now!" Allworthy looked at the gold watch which had been given to him on his sixtieth birthday by the office staff and works at Ward's. He smoothed down his rebellious wisp of hair with his platform gesture as though getting ready for action.

There were voices and footsteps just outside, then a loud knock on the door of the Committee Room.

"Come in!" John called, with a shadow of impatience in his tone.

The door opened to show Tom Sutton and Harold Pearson standing in the doorway.

"Will you come here a minute, Mr. Allworthy?" Tom's face had altered in this third week of the strike. It looked as though the skin had been drawn more tightly over the bones, the eyes seemed deeper set.

Allworthy got up and went to the door. The Trades Hall was full of men, whose eyes were turned towards him. When they saw him in the doorway, they broke into a strange sound, a wordless murmur of anger and reproach. Some of them shook their fists at him. He stood confronting them, his lips closed in a firm line, and the bitterness of hell in his heart. These were his own people for whom he had worked and struggled and endured all his life, and they had turned on him as their enemy.

"What's all this?" he said to Tom.

"There's your deputation," Tom sneered. "There's a hundred and fifty of us, and we don't let you out of this room until you agree to support the strike."

"That's illegal action!"

"Well, there's no one here to stop it. Some of us don't reckon so much to the letter o' the law as you do."

"You'll get nothing by threatening, Tom Sutton."

"We'll see how long you'll stand out!"

"You'll see fast enough!" John answered, his light eyes shining. There was a murmur of agreement from the other men in the room who had come up behind him.

389

John raised his voice to address the strikers.

"Listen to me, lads!" Tom pushed him back into the Committee Room, slammed the door and locked it on the ten men inside. There were twelve members of the Branch Committee, but two had been kept at home by illness.

Through the little group of indignant and ejaculating men, John Allworthy walked back to his seat at the table. Chief among his varied emotions was surprise. Did they think to frighten *him*? Him, John Allworthy, who at a Labour Party dinner in London had been called "The Lion of the North"? Who had stood for the workers when it was dangerous to stand for the workers, who had fought in the streets of Aire against the police protecting black-legs, who had opposed his indomitable courage again and again to all the forces of wealth and power? Did Tom Sutton and a handful of poor silly fools really think that because they shut him up in a room for a few hours, he would betray all that he had fought for, the right to collective bargaining which he and his friends had wrung from the masters, the Union which was his life-work? The idea was so absurd that he could almost laugh at it. He said to his companions:

"We may as well sit down again, till they tire on't."

The ten men sat down heavily in their seats round the table. One or two of them looked uneasy, but most were annoyed rather than alarmed. They had nearly all done a hard day's work, and wanted to get home. One man, Fred Gill, who had suffered in secret all his life from claustrophobia, had gone white about the lips as he heard the key turned in the door. He glanced furtively at the high window, and for a minute rising hysteria made his throat swell, but it had never occurred to him to mention his feelings and he mastered them now with an effort, thinking that the strikers would probably let him out if he really felt ill. John Allworthy glanced at him with the leader's instinct for the weak place that needed support.

"They'll tire a while before morning, eh, Fred?"

"They will that," Fred replied sturdily.

"If we'd a couple of packs o' cards, we might get up a whist drive."

390

Someone said dryly,

"Aye, and ask Tom Sutton to present the prizes."

In the Trades Hall outside the men began to sing. The Red Flag, a steady, concerted volume of sound, came through the locked door.

"Reckon they've learned that tune by this time," John's right-hand neighbour remarked.

"Tom Sutton's put in some good choir practice over this strike, if he's done nowt else!"

The tune came to an end. There was a thump on the door, and Tom's voice called out,

"Have you owt to say to us?"

"Plenty!" John called back. "But not what you want to hear."

After a few minutes, the men began to sing again. This time the tune was Ilkla Moor Ba't'At. One or two in the inner room smiled, insensibly relieved. Surely no crowd that meant anything more than a show of hostility could sing that cheerful, gloomy tune with so much vigour!

Fred Gill, strung up by nervous tension to a state of hyperæsthesia, thought, eh, well, I don't know an' all! The lads outside, and us in here, what's between us? Reckon what they want is what we've always wanted. Seems all we don't agree on is how to get it! They're in a hurry and we're maybe old and slow, but by gum, we ought to be pulling together instead of opposite ways! The absurdity of that locked door and of the dividing wall struck him sharply. He leaned forward and said to John,

"Won't you call out and ask one or two of 'em to have a word wi' us, Mr. Allworthy? Seems we might come to some kind o' sense sitting round a table."

"It's for them to come to us," John replied, folding his lips in a firm line.

Gill thought that they might want to, but were ashamed and afraid of feeling foolish. It seemed to him it might be worth while for the older men, who had seen and done so much more, to show the way, but he had never gone against John Allworthy, and he was ashamed of his own nervous tension that made him acutely anxious to end this miserable and ridiculous situation. He said no more, but began to tear strips from the sheet of blotting-paper before him, and roll them into tiny balls.

"What time is it?" Tom asked.
Harold Pearson looked at his watch.
"Close on two."
"Are the bastards going to keep us here all night?"
"They'll come out to us before long, surely!"
"A few of our lads have slipped away and gone home."
"We'd better start some singing again."

Fred Gill, who had dozed off uncomfortably, woke and moved his stiff limbs.
"What was that striking, Mr. Allworthy?"
"Three."
"We can't stop here all night!"
"I'd stop here a week before I'd give an inch to them."
Hysterical feeling surged up again in Fred.
"Nay, I can't stay shut up here till morning! I'll ask them to let me go home."
He was on his feet, swallowing nervously, his eyes still clouded by sleep. John Allworthy came round the table and took him by the arm.
"Nay, lad, if you go now they'll think we're weakening."
"That's right," agreed Sutcliffe, one of the oldest members there. He sighed and shifted his heavy body in his seat, trying not to think of the soft bed at home, and of the cup of hot cocoa that would have been waiting for him. They had put all the coal that had been left them on the fire, and it was now a smouldering heap of red embers.
"Walk up and down a bit!" Allworthy suggested to Fred. "It'll warm you."
He took him by the arm and began to walk him gently up and down the room. The movement, if it did not warm

him very much, relieved the tension of Fred's nerves, and now fully awake, he recovered his control.

"It's only an hour or two till the first trams run," John said soothingly.

In the hall outside the chilled and shivering men were grumbling.

"What was that striking, Bill?"

"Four."

"This is a daft business! T'trams'll be running in an hour."

"Aye. I'm barn 'ome."

Harold Pearson said to Tom, "It might be a good thing to organize some kind of demonstration? Frighten them a bit?"

In this cold and deadly hour of the morning Tom suddenly knew himself beaten. He knew perfectly well that no amount of demonstration would frighten John Allworthy. He also knew, because he did really know the men who followed him, that nobody in the hall wanted to make a demonstration. Their mood was too pessimistic and disillusioned. The most fatal thing of all had happened to the strike during this night, it had become ridiculous. Harold Pearson, who lived with ideas, could imagine a body of strikers rushing into the Committee Room, dragging out John Allworthy and the others and alarming them into submission. Tom knew that nobody wanted to do this or could do it. A patient and law-abiding race, they would grumble steadily for another hour, and would then jump on to the first trams and go home.

"It's no use," he said roughly to Harold, "we're done. We've made fools of ourselves. We'd better let them go as soon as t'trams are running."

Harold sighed. It was always the same thing, every effort failed because people would not go far enough! They went into these affairs without seeing the inevitable end, and when it appeared to them, they shirked it, and let the whole thing slip out of their hands. The English people, he thought bitterly, did not deserve a revolution!

At five o'clock most of the Union Committee were asleep, sprawling uncomfortably over the table. John Allworthy, still wide awake, sat upright in his chair at the head, his arms folded across his chest in an attempt to keep a little warmth in his body. He wondered what his wife was thinking, and hoped she had gone to bed and fallen asleep. He remembered that morning thirty, no nearly thirty-four years ago, in the great gas works strike, when, after the night of the resistance to the blackleg-labour, he had come home to her with his broken head in bandages, proud and undefeated. That night had been the first battle in the great fight that he had fought for Trade Unionism, perhaps this would be the last, since he was growing old. He was satisfied.

He had heard for some time subdued movement in the hall outside. Presently his alert ear caught the sound of a key softly turned in the lock. He got up, went to the door, and tried the handle. The door opened upon an empty hall, full of cold, stale air, and lit only by the light from the room behind him. He went back to the table. His movement, and the sound of the opening door, had roused men who were sleeping lightly in uncomfortable positions. They yawned, shivered, and blinked at him, their faces sodden with sleep.

"T'strike's over, lads," he said. "They've all gone and left us. We'd better get home."

The last pickets on duty at Alfred Ward's finished their last shift at five o'clock on Friday afternoon. Tom Sutton told them that the strike was over, the men and girls were going back on Monday morning. He spoke shortly, gave no details, and discouraged comment. He walked away from them, and went in at the doorway of the strike headquarters.

One of the pickets, Joe Hardisty, lived in Sutton's neighbourhood, and sometimes met him on a tram and had a talk with him. Hardisty was an intelligent man, who had understood and followed the course of the strike, and had foreseen its defeat. He said to himself with bitterness that he would resign from the Union. As soon as they could after

394

coming off duty he and his companions went and had a drink together. Hardisty had a wife who took in dress-making, and no children. He had been able to save, and had not run as short of money as the other two men on picket duty with him. They were frankly glad that the strike was over. One of them had applied to the relief fund, the other would have been obliged to at the beginning of next week. Hardisty paid for their drinks, lent one of them half a crown to buy a bit of meat for the Sunday dinner, and went off to his own tram, thoughtful and dejected.

He saw Tom Sutton waiting at the tram stop. Tom nodded, but Hardisty felt that he did not want to talk. He made no attempt to approach him. The two men climbed to the top of the tram, and sat down, Tom on the curving seat in front that faced the rest of the tram, Hardisty in a seat about three from the front. Tom was staring before him without saying anything. Taking it hard, Hardisty thought. 'E's a grand lad! He would have liked to do something to show his sympathy and admiration for his defeated leader, but he could think of nothing to do. He opened his evening paper.

The conductor, coming to take Hardisty's fare, grinned and touched the red rosette which the Central Strike Com-mittee and the pickets had all worn, and which was still in Hardisty's buttonhole.

"Been to a football match?" the conductor said, laughing.

Hardisty held out his penny without answering.

The conductor was a young man, ruddy, cheerful, with thick lips, a flat nose, and round, comical blue eyes. He had very few feelings so sensitive that he could not joke about them, and he did not suppose that anyone else had. He was amused at the defeated striker still wearing his red ribbon.

"Reckon you might as well take that off now!" he grinned.

A wave of bitterness swept over Hardisty. They had fought well and bravely, and they were beaten, not in fair fight, but starved into surrender, betrayed by those who should have been their leaders. It was all no good. The same thing would happen again. The weight on top of them was too great, the forces against them were too strong. He did not answer the young conductor. He took the red ribbon out of

395

his button-hole and let it fall on the dirty floor of the tram. T'lad was right, he might as well take it off now. It had never been any use wearing it. Feeling utterly disheartened and worn out, he leaned back in his seat, his body sagging with weariness.

He grew drowsy, and did not see Tom get up and come down the tram. He suddenly found him at his side, and looked up into a white, set face in which the eyes were so dark that they looked more black than blue. Tom stopped and picked up the bit of red ribbon from the floor. He threw it in Hardisty's astonished face.

Hardisty could say nothing, but only stared, the dusty red rosette poised absurdly where it had fallen on his chest. His hand to his own red ribbon, still in his button-hole, Tom walked off along the top floor of the tram and down the stairs.

In his own room, Ward said to his General Manager, "That's all, then?"

"Yes. We start normally on Monday. Are you going to fire Sutton?"

"Not now. We've promised general oblivion. I've had John Allworthy in here this afternoon."

"Trying to make the best of a bad job, I suppose?"

"Trying to do more for them than they deserve, and so I told him."

"A fine old fellow in his way."

Ward did not answer. He never attempted to put into words the secret feelings of affection, respect, pity and a queer, inconsequent envy which he felt for the man who had started work with him.

"Probably Sutton will resign from the Union," the General Manager reflected. "A good many of them will. The numbers always go down after a strike. They're desperately short-sighted, even about their own advantage. We shan't have any more trouble for some time."

"No. You can get on next week with the new system in the South Room."

Marjorie regarded the collapse of the strike as a triumph for her father. This primitive reaction enraged Leslie, who thus was obliged to be ashamed of every single member of his family.

"Don't you see," he said, "that they were *right*? They've simply been starved into submission. Like all the rest of us, they're the prey of an unjust system of economics?"

"I don't see that we're its prey, anyhow!"

"We are, we are! As much as the poorest family on the dole. We've got more of everything than we ought to have. We're forced into being rich and vulgar and greedy and complacent. We aren't living proper lives. Look at you! You ought to be working or looking after the house."

"Thank you! I hate housework! What ought you to be doing?"

"Earning my living! Not living on the fat of the land, and rolling about in an expensive car, and spending my time on the literary fantasies of a dead world that haven't any bearing on modern life."

"I thought you liked doing English!"

"I've no use now for anything but a living literature."

Marjorie, who had no particular use for any literature, living or dead, was quick on to the personal issue.

"Have you quarrelled with the Grants?"

"Certainly not. I haven't seen them lately."

"But surely you have to go to coachings with Angus?"

"I missed the last one. I'm thinking of changing over to Economics."

"Is that the ugly professor with red hair?"

"If you mean Claud Unwin, he's not a professor, he's a lecturer. He's an extremely brilliant fellow."

"And I suppose," said Marjorie with immense sarcasm, "that his hair is auburn?"

Leslie exploded. "You're childish and absurd! You simply don't know anything at all about life or the modern world! If you did, you'd be ashamed?"

"What of?"

"Of being your father's daughter."

"Leslie! You're disloyal and disgusting!"

"This isn't a time for the glorification of personal loyalties."

"No, it doesn't seem to be with you. You go about abusing your own family, and you've quarrelled with the Grants that were such great friends."

"I *have not* quarrelled with the Grants!"

"What have you done, then? You used to go there nearly every day."

"I've just grown out of them."

Marjorie went off into a shout of laughter which was spontaneous to begin with, but which she deliberately made longer and louder. Leslie's fingers curled into his palms. He had not wanted so much to hit her since he was twelve years old. The muscles of his face quivered and twitched, he swallowed, struggled for a sneer and said,

"You're the complete bourgeoisie, Marjorie!"

"Well, that's not a bad thing to be."

"It's the worst thing anyone can be!"

"Don't be so silly, Leslie! Of course it isn't. It's better than being a murderer or a thief, or a lunatic or an atheist, or one of the lower classes."

"Oh, Marjorie!" Leslie's groan rose to something like a wail. "Thank Heaven nobody but me heard you say that!"

"If you mean the Unwins, if you ask them here again, they probably will hear me say that. I didn't like Professor Unwin! He was very rude at dinner. The Grants are ladies and gentlemen, anyhow, I mean they are a lady and a gentleman, and the children are darlings."

"As if it mattered about ladies and gentlemen!"

Marjorie said with a flash of the shrewdness that was like her father,

"It only doesn't matter if you are one."

"Listen, Marjorie! It's the bourgeois mentality that is holding up progress and fostering reaction."

"I suppose you mean it's what stops strikes and makes business go on again."

"Oh, you're hopeless! You don't even try to understand."

"*You* don't understand, Leslie. You're just saying what the Unwins have told you."

Leslie changed his ground.

"What does your wonderful Mary think about the strike?"

"I haven't seen her since it began."

"Oh! Have you quarrelled with her?"

"No! She's been busy and I've been busy, that's all. You've no right to say such a thing!"

Marjorie was really angry now. It was true that she had supposed herself to be busy and Mary had really been busy but perhaps she had not tried quite as hard as usual to arrange a meeting. She had not been to the Left Discussion Club lately, and the strike had made her swing uneasily away from Mary's ideas. Because there was the smallest grain of truth in Leslie's gibe, she resented it furiously.

"I'm not like you! I don't chop and change my friends every minute!"

The discussion declined to the old level of vituperation.

"You think you're very superior, don't you?"

"I think you're silly and horrid."

It continued on these lines until at last Leslie said, "I wish to God I hadn't got to live in this hell-hole with you all!" and rushed out of the room and banged the door.

Marjorie shrugged her shoulders in a gesture of disdain. A minute later, her face puckered up and tears came into her eyes. She reflected that Leslie was her only brother and that he had said dreadful things to her. Her tears were not of the kind that flow for long in private. Since there was no one there to hear and agree how horrid Leslie was, she sniffed, gulped, dried her eyes and blew her nose and took two chocolates out of a box on the table for consolation. She looked at the clock and saw that she had only just time to change and get to South Worbeck. It was her afternoon on duty at the Babies Welcome. She said, "Oh bother," and flew upstairs, calling out to one of the maids on the way to tell Tomlin to bring the car round.

Leslie had been right in at least one of the things he said about Marjorie. She was profoundly bored and needed a job. She sometimes grumbled at having to refuse an invitation on Thursday afternoon for the Welcome, but she always refused it. She turned up punctually and did her work with an efficiency that would not have disgraced her father's office.

Even if she had missed a bridge drive or a tea-party, she felt more satisfied on Thursday evening than on any other evening in the week. She thought now that it was annoying to have to rush off there when she was so much upset, but by the time she arrived at the door of the St. Benedict's school-room, and greeted Nurse Hapgood, Doctor Collet, and the two other voluntary helpers, she had recovered herself; she looked a bright, pretty, healthy girl again instead of the sullen, lumpish child she sometimes looked at home when she had yawned in the drawing-room all afternoon and eaten too many chocolates. She knew herself to be the most regular and trusted of the voluntary workers. She liked the doctor, a crisp, dark young woman who spoke to her as to a colleague, and Nurse Hapgood, who was kind and friendly.

She also liked the work. Her job was to sit in the weighing-room and enter the babies' weights on a chart after Nurse Hapgood had put them on the scales. She could see every week how much each baby was gaining. She drew an upward line with satisfaction, and a downward line with regret, sharing the disappointment of the crestfallen mother, who would snatch back the naked, squirming infant from Nurse's arms, murmuring defensively that Donald or Doreen or Stanley had been a bit poorly this week, it was the cold weather. By this time Marjorie had her favourite babies. Gwennie Schofield, the beauty of the Welcome, a curly-haired blue-eyed two-year-old, like a baby angel in a Rey-nolds picture; Maurice Oldroyd, their particular pride, who had come to them at four months old weighing very little more than when he was born, and who now at seven months had touched average weight for the first time; the Barker twins, Donald and Dorothy, so much alike that when they were lying in their pram, even their mother needed the pink and blue bows to distinguish them; Eileen Lewis, a sharp little ten months old Jewess with great brown eyes. The babies were all freshly washed and brushed for the Welcome, dressed, most of them, in clean home-made woollies. It was their mothers who sometimes looked bedraggled, thin and worn as though more life than they could spare had gone out of them into the children.

As soon as the weighing was over, Marjorie went out into the big schoolroom to help to hand round tea and biscuits to the mothers, who sat in rows on the four benches, chatting sociably, often over the head of a screaming infant. A dozen of them were lined up in a row on the far side waiting their turn to go into the doctor's room. The tea-party had dispersed and the Welcome was over by the time the doctor had finished with the last of these. She came out, pulling off her white linen coat and lighting a cigarette. Seeing Marjorie, she called out,

"I haven't seen Maurice Oldroyd. Hasn't he been here to-day?"

"I don't think so. He didn't come into the weighing-room."

"I particularly told his mother not to miss a week! And she's been much more willing since he's been gaining! I really thought she was learning sense. I hope he's not got 'flu! It would be sickening if he had a setback just now. Perhaps Mrs. Oldroyd's ill herself." Doctor Collet looked at her wrist-watch. "I wish I had time to slip round and see, but I've got a patient coming at 5.30. I must get back."

"Shall I go?"

"Would you? I don't know how far it is, but she always carries him here, so I should think it's quite near. We've got the address on the cards, of course. Nurse will know where it is. I'd ask her to go, but I know she wants to leave early to-night, she's going to an anti-gas lecture. If you could go and then give me a ring after dinner I'd be awfully grateful. If there was anything wrong I could slip over to-morrow and see him."

Marjorie felt responsible and important and quite enough interested in little Maurice to be willing to miss her tea. She found the address on the card index, and discovered from Nurse that No. 9, Laburnam Yard was not far off.

"I've not been there," Nurse said. "It's not on my beat, but I once walked along the road with Mrs. Oldroyd, and I remember she turned down a back street and said her home was quite near. It's a poor part, all those yards are. You'll see some sights." She smiled kindly at Marjorie's ingenuous young face. But not a bad thing, she thought, that the rich man's daughter should see how the poor live.

Marjorie found Laburnam Yard without much difficulty. It was a dark place with an uneven floor of worn stones surrounded by unevenly-built houses. A couple of women were calling to one another from the doorsteps of their houses, and a group of children were playing in the mud in the middle of the yard. Marjorie advanced shyly, aware that they had all stopped what they were doing and were staring in surprise at the stranger in her fur coat. She asked one of the women timidly which was No. 9, and the woman, still staring hard at her, pointed to a doorway. Marjorie crossed the yard, knocked at a door and heard a voice call, "Come in."

The room was lit by firelight, and by a fan of light in an old-fashioned gas bracket high up on the wall. It had a queer, sweet, stuffy smell that revolted Marjorie's nostrils. It was full of people, two or three women, a man, two children besides Maurice in Mrs. Oldroyd's arms, and someone who apparently lay asleep on the table in the middle of the room. Marjorie looked, surprised, at the reclining figure, and felt a shock that seemed to stop all her pulses. Her knees shook, the surface of her body became icy cold all over, warmth and strength ebbing away from her. It was an old woman on the table with a cap over her hair and a white thing up to her chin, and surely she was—dead? Never in her life before had Marjorie seen a dead body. She had never fainted in her life, and did not recognize her own sensations, but for a minute the room darkened, the figures that crowded it receded to a distance. Instinctively she looked for somewhere to sit down.

Mrs. Oldroyd came towards her with Maurice in her arms, saying something about "my husband's mother." Mrs. Oldroyd, who looked very much more slatternly and down at heel than Marjorie had ever seen her, was at least familiar, part of the everyday world, and the small pale Maurice in her arms was alive. His blue eyes stared solemnly at Marjorie. She was wearing a bright buckle at the neck of her dress which caught his attention. He had the aged face of a delicate ɔaby, and it creased into a shadowy smile as he put out a hand in a vague gesture towards the bright thing against the dark cloth.

"Oh!" Marjorie stammered. "I'm sorry! I didn't know! I won't stop! I'm sorry. I—I only came to see if Maurice was all right."

She had got over the first shock but she was beside herself with embarrassment, that she had stumbled upon them at such a time. She had no idea that privacy is a luxury unknown to the poor.

"Sit you down, Miss," Mrs. Oldroyd said, wiping a chair with a bit of her skirt. She was pleased to see Marjorie, a distinguished stranger come to look at the corpse. It added a spice of extra dignity to the death of her husband's mother. She was also vaguely sorry for the girl, who stared at her with such startled eyes. She was, as Dr. Collet had often remarked, a woman without much sense. Her household, husband on the dole, mother-in-law, sister-in-law and four children, had been too much for her. She dragged through the days in a perpetual weary muddle, with life always on top of her, but she had been at close quarters with birth and death. Some dim maternal instinct in her pitied Marjorie's inexperience.

"Have a cup of tea, love!" one of the other women said, reaching for the black tea-pot on the hob.

"No, no thank you!" Marjorie could not have swallowed in that room. Her one desire was to get out of it and breathe fresh air, but there was enough of her father in her to make her stick to her purpose.

"Is Maurice going on all right?" she asked. "Have you had him weighed this week?"

Mrs. Oldroyd said comfortably that she hadn't, that he had fretted a good deal with her being upset like, but that he was all right. She was always either in despair about Maurice, or else convinced that the doctor and nurse at the Welcome were making a lot of fuss about nothing. At present, though she hugged his thin little body to her lank chest, she was in her casual mood about him, and Marjorie could get little satisfaction. She looked carefully at the baby, and thought that his face was thinner, his expression more elderly and patient. The other two children, a boy and a girl, were playing on the floor under the table with some marbles. They seemed quite happy, but Marjorie could not help saying.

"Must they be in here with—with their grandmother?" She had not brought herself to look again at the corpse on the table.

"We've nobbut the one other room," Mr. Oldroyd said, speaking for the first time, "and our Jimmy's lying badly."

Marjorie's senses reeled. Another child, one bedroom and the one sitting-room! No wonder Maurice was so delicate and Jimmy was ill! The wonder was that any of them were alive at all. She herself felt nauseated by the hot, stuffy atmosphere of the room. The queer, sickly smell was really due to the presence of vermin, but with a sudden horrified leap of her imagination, Marjorie wondered if it was the corpse. She had read about the smell of battlefields. In another minute she was going to be sick! She sprang up, saying incoherently, "I'll tell the doctor about Maurice. I mustn't stop."

The neighbour who had offered Marjorie tea rose to go out. As she passed the table she paused, looked down at the dead woman and said politely,

"She makes a lovely corpse."

Marjorie's curiosity was struggling with horror. It seemed rude to say "good afternoon" and go, without some tribute to the dead. She stood up and forced herself to a long look. It did not seem to her that it could be a real person, that yellowish waxen face with thin strands of yellowish grey hair parted below the linen, that jutting nose and chin, the folded hands in white cotton gloves—they were none of them real, but they were terrifying to her, as though someone had turned over the bright penny of usual life and shown her a grim image on the reverse side. She caught her breath and said childishly, "I expect she's happy!" It seemed to her to be a proper thing to say. She did not really feel that a living person had ever had any connection with that shell on the table, lying so still above the children squabbling over their marbles.

Mrs. Oldroyd said with mournful pride,

"She's insured for herself and two coaches. Always kept that up for 'er, we 'ave."

The words were Greek to Marjorie, who vaguely supposed that the funerals of the poor were provided by the Corporation, and was too confused to grasp anything new to her. The sturdy strain in her made her turn in the doorway and say to Mrs. Oldroyd with unexpected firmness, "You won't forget, will you, to bring Maurice to the Welcome next week?"

Marjorie had never had any particular feeling for Grey Gables. It was her home providing her with what she needed. She did not often think whether she liked it or the things in it. She had none of Leslie's recoil from bad taste and ostentation. This evening she appreciated its comfort and luxury in every nerve. The warm air, heated to an even temperature, closed round her like a welcome. The bright colours of the hot house plants in the hall pleased her eye. Goodness, how hungry she was! She ran up to her room and tore off all her clothes, feeling that she wanted to be rid of everything that had been into No. 9, Laburnam Yard. She turned on a steaming hot bath and put in an extra spoonful of bathsalts. Clean and rosy from the bath, with soft chiffon next to her skin, and the fluffy collar of her dressing-gown huddled to her ears, she sat down in front of her fire, and suddenly cried. Her tears flowed for longer than usual, and she was obliged to hurry into her evening frock and come down to dinner with a red nose and watery eyes. In answer to her mother's enquiring glance, she said defiantly, "I think I've got a bit of cold." She could not have described her experiences of that afternoon. Mrs. Ward murmured discontentedly, "I do hope you haven't caught anything. You know I wish you'd work at another Welcome and not down there in the slums. You might pick up anything from those sort of people!"

To distract attention from her own doings, Marjorie asked, "Where's Leslie?"

"Out to supper," her father said.

"With those new friends of his, the Unwins," her mother supplied.

Neither said any more but their unspoken condemnation was in the air.

Marjorie had been in no mood to defend Leslie, but suddenly her feelings swung towards him. The inequalities of the world had been sharply brought before her eyes. She felt that something ought to be done to make places like Laburnam Yard impossible. Leslie was bad-tempered and silly, but there was probably something to be said for his ideas. After all, some of them were Mary's. She thought that she would like to talk to Mary about what she had seen that afternoon. She went to the telephone, dialled the *Yorkshire Guardian* number, asked to be put through to Mary and stood waiting, the receiver pressed against her ear under her curls.

Her mother crossed the hall and called out to her,

"Who is ringing up, dear?"

"No one. I'm ringing up the *Guardian*. I want to speak to Mary."

"Oh! I shouldn't stand about all the evening at the telephone if you've got a cold."

Marjorie shrugged impatiently, irked not for the first time by constant, petty supervision of her affairs.

A voice informed her that Miss Welburn had gone out for supper, but would be back in half an hour.

"All right, thank you," Marjorie said. "I'll ring up in half an hour."

As she was going into the drawing-room, the front door bell rang. A minute or two later, the parlour maid showed in Billy Wilson, who rolled into the drawing-room—his walk always suggested a roll—rubbing his hands and calling out cheerfully, "Hulloa, hulloa—good evening, Mrs. Ward! Good evening, sir. I'm all on my own-i-o—Violet gone to a party, Mum and Dad out, so I came round to be cheered up."

Billy was the only person who ever dropped in casually at Grey Gables. He was quite impervious to the formal and unwelcoming atmosphere of the house. It appeared to his simple mind that he was always pleased to see his friends, and they were always pleased to see him. This single-minded conviction went a long way towards making itself true, especially with Ward, who, unable to meet anyone, was very nearly grateful to a guest who came three-quarters of the way to meet him and did not notice the other quarter.

"Well, sir!" Billy said, "strike all over and all your men back?"

"Yes. The works were running normally again to-day."

"Been an awkward time just in the busy season?"

"It means a big loss, of course."

"Still, you won't have any trouble now for a few years." Billy was both shrewd and sanguine. "Not an ill wind altogether, eh, from your point of view?"

"Not altogether perhaps."

"If I were you I should feel like presenting old What's-his-name, the old Union man, with a gold watch."

"Rumour says that I have—with more than a gold watch."

"No! What! Saying he's been bought, are they? Well, I do call that a shame! Decent old fellow, isn't he? Dad says he's one of the best of the Labour men—no bitterness. But we mustn't talk shop all the evening." Billy turned to Marjorie.

"Come and play a hundred up with me, Marjorie? If you're not tired?"

Marjorie followed him to the billiard-room. She was rather good at billiards but this evening she played badly. Billy, smoking a fat cigar on the hearthrug, watched her bending over her cue, the chestnut curls falling across her neck. She missed an easy cannon, and instead of saying "Oh, bother!" or "Look at that!" she drew back from the table and said indifferently, "Your turn!"

Billy took the cigar out of his mouth.

"What's up, Marjorie? Down on your luck?"

He was not Marjorie's idea of a counsellor, but he was of her own generation, he was kindly, and in his own way, sure of himself. Marjorie told him of her afternoon.

His instinctive reaction was the same as her mother's.

407

He wished she wouldn't go to those kind of places among that sort of people. He held his tongue about that, and offered sympathy.

"It must have been a bit of a shock. Poor old Marjorie! I don't wonder you look under the weather. Cheer up! You know," he added, "they wouldn't mind it as much as you think. They love funerals. They were probably enjoying themselves no end."

Marjorie did not immediately cheer up. She stood rubbing her fingers along the table. Presently she said with apparent irrelevance,

"I quarrelled with Leslie this afternoon."

Billy had his own ideas about Leslie.

"Oh well!" he said easily. "I mean, family life and all that!"

"It began about the strike. He thinks father was wrong and they were right."

"He doesn't know an awful lot about business."

"He thinks we oughtn't to be so rich."

"I bet he wouldn't really like to be poor!"

"He says people like us are doing a lot of harm—holding up progress. I told him he was silly and disloyal to Father. Then this afternoon . . ."

Marjorie's voice trailed off. She was not good at expressing herself. She felt that there was some connection between what Leslie had said to her and what she had seen in Laburnam Yard. Her old childish view of the scene of life as a series of unrelated incidents was beginning to slip from her. She was becoming aware that her own cushioned life in Grey Gables and Maurice, wasting because his mother had been undernourished before his birth, were in the same world, linked up, perhaps, in some way with the strike and her father and Leslie's irritating nonsense. Now that the first shock of her visit to the Oldroyd's house had passed, she was more profoundly disturbed by a dawning perception that things were not separate. Looking candidly at Billy, she said,

"I told Leslie he was silly, but I've got an awful feeling that perhaps everyone is responsible for everything."

It was not quite what she was trying to say, but Billy

knew what she meant, recognized unconsciously in the attempt to connect and relate the menace to the structure of his life, and with the true instinct of his kind, struck to separate.

"Now, look here, Marjorie. You've had a beastly afternoon, but you mustn't get morbid. Leslie's a kid. If he understood anything about business or real life he'd have the greatest admiration for his father. Where would he be without him? I mean, his father started from scratch like my dear old Dad and they both earned everything we've ever had. That's what a man works for, you know. To be able to do things for his family. Your father employs a lot of people who wouldn't have a job without him, and he treats them well. This strike was wrong. That fellow, Tom Sutton, wanted to dictate terms to the whole firm and that sort of thing won't do! Why, you can tell the strike was wrong! Their own Union was against them, and they back them up fast enough if they think they've got anything like a fair case! As for that house you went to this afternoon, that's another matter. There ought not to be families living in two rooms with a corpse on the table. I'm with you there. But there aren't as many as there used to be. Lots of people are doing their best to stop that sort of thing, and people like your father, who employ a lot of labour and pay good wages, are doing as much as anyone. So don't you be a little goose like Leslie," Billy concluded. "And let's start this game again because you've been playing in your sleep so far."

They started the game again, and Marjorie forgot her problems. It was only as she went up to bed that it occurred to her that she had also forgotten to ring up Mary. It did not matter, she could do it in the morning. Billy was sensible, Marjorie reflected, sensible and kind. It was a pity he was plump and had little, piggy eyes. But he was not a silly boy like Leslie, he knew things and understood life. Marjorie's last reflection before she tumbled sleepily into bed was that though the eyes were small and piggy, they looked at her as they thought her pretty. There was a satisfaction in that which soothed her after the day's agitations, and she was soon sound asleep.

Angus Grant had an uncle who in his youth had been attaché to the Embassy in Rome, and who still went back to Italy every year to revisit old friends. His contacts with his nephew were infrequent but amicable. He had not seen him since he was married, but he happened to be passing through Aire in March and spent a night with the Grants. He was amused and rather charmed by their casual and cordial hospitality, and took a great fancy to Grizel, whom he had only seen before as a composed little bride in white satin and lace which did not suit her. It struck him that his nephew and niece by marriage had their hands full, with their small income, their two great babies, and their big rambling house, and that they looked as though they needed a holiday. He wrote and invited them to come to Italy for a fortnight in the Easter vac. as his guests.

After a spring term which had seemed like a long dark tunnel, the Grants were transported with joy. They wrote to ask if Grizel's married sister could take the babies, and held their breath until the answer came. They dug out the old maps and guide books that they had taken on their honeymoon, reminded one another joyously of this and that, packed and planned gleefully. Once Grizel said, "Will it be rather beastly going to Italy now?" "Oh, not with Uncle Quentin," Angus replied confidently. "He's been writing some stuff about their point of view. He knows their high-up people. We may get a look at Mussolini. Anyhow, it will be interesting. How much Italian do you remember?" They began to practise, and dismissed international complications.

Two days before they started, Angus said suddenly in a distressed voice,

"I wish I could have seen Leslie."

"Ask him to supper to-night—or to-morrow. He doesn't mind scratch meals. Go and ring him up now from a box and see when he can come."

"I have asked him three times lately. He's refused every time."

"I expect he feels bad about changing over from English."

"It's a pity, but I want to go on being friends."

"Go and see him, Angus! He's probably shy and feeling

uncomfortable and doesn't like to come here. Go and take him by both ears and shake him and tell him not to be silly."

"He's always at the Unwins. I gather he's got the Red bug badly. He was such a nice boy, Grizel! I don't want to lose sight of him."

"Well, go up to the house and walk in and say, 'Hulloa, Leslie! Don't be an ass! Come and say good-bye to us.' "

"He probably wouldn't be there, or the Unwins would."

Grizel reflected that Angus would be very bad at any sort of emotional reconciliation. Except with her, he disliked any situation in which he could not laugh, and he was absurdly diffident about going to any house unless he had been asked. If anyone was going to gate-crash the Wards and recall the truant, it had better be her. After all, it would only be polite to call on Mrs. Ward. She set out the next afternoon, wheeling both babies in the pram since she had no one to leave them with. It was an afternoon of wind and flickering spring sunshine. The trees that bordered the drive at Grey Gables were brown and thick with unbroken buds, the crocus cups were open in the beds by the front door. Bunny, now quite well again, sang a wordless and tuneless song as they approached the house. Biddy complacently chewed the ear of a pink plush rabbit. Grizel laughed at the children, thought of the coming holiday, and felt hopeful and confident enough to drag Leslie back to Angus by the hair. Perhaps she would bring him back to supper. She rang the front door-bell, unloaded the pram, and was admitted to the long drawing-room, Biddy in her arms, Bunny trotting by her side.

Mrs. Ward and Marjorie were in, and were very glad to see her. They had spent a tedious afternoon together, expecting callers who did not come and yawning over magazines. Mrs. Ward rang for extra milk and sponge cakes, and fed Grizel with muffins and tea while Marjorie petted and played with the babies.

"Is Leslie in?" Grizel asked.

"No, my dear. I'm afraid he isn't. He was going to a lecture to-night at five and then round to the Unwins. He'll be sorry to have missed you."

"We've been very sorry to see so little of him lately."

Mrs. Ward looked embarrassed and murmured something about him being so busy. Marjorie, looking up from the hearthrug, said resentfully,

"*We* don't see much of him! He's always with those Unwins!"

"You know them, of course?" Mrs. Ward looked at Grizel.

"Oh, yes."

"Do you like them?" Marjorie blurted out.

The candid Grizel hesitated, never quite sure if she did really like them, displeased with them now because they had taken Angus's friend from him.

"Sometimes I like them. I'm always rather sorry for them."

"Sorry for them? Why?" Marjorie stared at Grizel with round eyes.

"Well . . ." To take themselves and everything else so solemnly, to tread so anxiously in the paths of minority culture, to mind being poor as much as Claud did, to live in a state of resentful fury about the social order, to have no Biddy and Bunny.

"Don't they get on with one another?" Marjorie asked, searching for an obvious cause.

"Oh, yes, oh, very well indeed."

It was, Grizel thought, so lucky that they had found each other, since Claud especially was not good at getting on with anyone else. She did not feel able to explain them to Marjorie. She said,

"They take everything very hard."

She collected her babies and made her good-byes, leaving affectionate messages for Leslie. Would he, perhaps, run in for a minute before they went? Mrs. Ward, embarrassed again, promised doubtfully to ask him.

"I know Father will want him to!" Marjorie said.

"Oh no! I mean only if he likes, if he has time!" Grizel cried, distressed. She did not want Ward to make them a duty. She guessed that Marjorie had already antagonized Leslie by urging their claims against the Unwins.

She walked home in a more sober mood, a little tired, pushing the two drowsy babies in the heavy pram. Her way led past the end of the road in which the Unwins lived, and she paused at the corner, wondering if she should run in for

412

a moment to say good-bye, and if she might find Leslie there. She did not like giving up her purpose. Biddy had got her strap twisted in the pram and her pillows screwed up under her. Grizel stooped over her, making her comfortable. As she looked up, Leslie turned the corner and came across the street.

He did not at first recognize the girl with the perambulator. It was Bunny who recognized him and called "Juggins," holding out a hand encased in one of those gloves where the fingers share a compartment. While she lifted her head and smiled at Leslie, Grizel had time to think "Clever!" of her little son, and to remember that Leslie had never seen those gloves before he came to their house and had thought them funny, exquisite and touching.

"Hulloa, Leslie!" she said. "I've just been to your home to try and see you. I am glad we've met! How are you after all this time?"

"Oh—oh, very well, thanks," Leslie jerked out. He looked at her and looked at the pram and looked at his feet. "How—how are you?"

"All right, thank you. We're going to Italy for a fortnight! With Angus's rich uncle! Isn't it lovely? But what have you been doing? Why haven't you been to see us? Angus has missed you."

She felt a shutter close down in his mind.

"I—I've been very busy," he said. "Is Angus well?"

"Yes—at least, very tired, he hasn't really got over his 'flu and the awful time we had with Bunny."

Leslie's glance wavered for a second to the child.

"I hope he's all right again," he said in polite and formal tones.

Grizel wanted to shake him. She could not keep reproach out of her voice as she said,

"Yes, he is, but you never came to see him when he was getting better! Your mother and Marjorie came several times, and he often asked where you were."

Something quivered in Leslie's face as though stiffness were breaking. He put out his ungloved hand with an awkward gesture and touched the soft little cheek.

413

"Where's your car?" Bunny asked.

The shutter closed down again.

"I don't use it much now," Leslie said, withdrawing his hand.

"Have you broken it?" Bunny inquired sympathetically.

Leslie did not answer. He said stiffly to Grizel,

"I mustn't keep you standing here. I'm going to supper at the Unwins."

"It's quite early. Couldn't you walk back with us first and just smoke a pipe with Angus and then run back here again? It isn't half-past five yet. Do, Leslie! He'd love to see you before we go away." She saw that he was going to refuse, and added impulsively, "He isn't annoyed, you know, at your changing over from English. He was talking about you last night and saying how much he'd like to see you. Come on, Leslie! You haven't quarrelled with us, have you? We've had such fun together, we were such friends!"

His face was working oddly and for a moment she thought that she had prevailed. He looked as though in a second he might burst into tears. Well, let him. What did it matter, people always made too much fuss about that sort of thing! Let him cry and then laugh at himself and come back with her and sit by the fire with Angus and boil the babies' milk and perhaps forget the Unwins and stay on to supper, and be friends again.

The quivering of his face stiffened into obstinacy.

"No, I don't think I can, thank you very much. I told the Unwins I'd be early. I'm going to a meeting with them afterwards."

Grizel felt angry. It was for Angus that she had pleaded with this silly, fickle boy, and Angus who had been refused. She lifted her head.

"Very well. I hope you'll enjoy your meeting. We shall see you next term probably. Good-bye."

"Good-bye."

He watched her walking off, her light figure in its shabby tweed coat, stooping a little over the handles of the pram. As the pram turned the corner, Bunny leaned out and waved to him. He had an impulse to run after them, to say, "I

414

was an ass, Grizel! I'm sorry!" to grab Bunny out of the pram and ride him pick-a-back all the way home, most of all, to go in and see Angus. He stood where he was and saw the pram and Grizel behind it vanish round the corner.

Five minutes later he was in the sitting-room of the Unwins' flat, a room filled with books, and modern drawings by their friends. There were always new magazines about with strange cubist squares of black and red on the cover, and foreign newspapers, sometimes printed on private presses. Above the mantelpiece was a board on which were pinned notices of meetings and cuttings from the *Daily Worker* and other papers. Leslie was always deeply impressed by the room. When he was in it, he felt himself really abreast of all contemporary movements.

Claud was writing at his desk in the corner. Naomi, sitting by the fire, was scribbling notes for a speech on a pad on her knee. She looked up to welcome him, smiled and said,

"Do find a seat. Clear those books off. I won't be a minute. I just want to add a note for the meeting at Manchester to-morrow. I've had a very interesting letter from a great friend in Spain, an Anarchist, and I want to make a point out of it. She's a most interesting girl. Her mother was a Roumanian Jew who went to New York as a child and grew up and went on the streets there. Then when she was very ill, some Spanish Catholics took her in and brought her over to Valencia, and this child——"

Her voice flowed on. Leslie was much less interested than he usually was in the biographies of the Unwins' international friends. He was not even enough on the alert to have to try not to be shocked at the profession adopted by the friend's mother. He spent a good deal of time at the Unwins' passionately trying not to be shocked, swallowing their accounts of the incestuous and lustful impulses of their friends, adjusting his mind to the wholesale destruction of the standards by which he had been brought up. You could say and do anything at the Unwins' so long as you were not bourgeois. Murder, violence, sadism, rape, homosexuality and insanity were tolerable and interesting compared to that sin against

415

the Unwins' Holy Ghost. Leslie often saw in their faces that he was trembling on the verge of it, and always felt that he could have avoided it so much better if he had understood exactly what it was. It was bourgeois to love your father and mother, fear God and honour the King. It was bourgeois to have roast beef for midday dinner on Sunday. It was rather bourgeois to be married unless you made it perfectly clear that you were prepared to stop at any moment. It was always extremely bourgeois to be shocked. The worst of it was that the values shifted about so. Leslie, who thought that he had grasped that repressions and inhibitions and œdipus complexes were always all right, had the other evening quoted Freud in his support in a political argument, and had been told repressively by Claud that Freud was bourgeois. And after that, where were you? He was obliged to hold his tongue and reconsider his standards for the rest of the evening.

This evening his mind was preoccupied. When they were all sitting round the table drinking Naomi's excellent soup from little china bowls, he said suddenly,

"I met Grizel Grant outside."

Not a glance but a flicker of intelligence passed between the Unwins. They thought that the Grants had been a bad influence on Leslie, retarding his development and confirming him in the values of a dying world.

"Oh. How are they?" Naomi asked casually. "I haven't seen them lately."

"They're going to Italy for a holiday."

"Italy! Now!" Claud's tone spoke volumes and conveyed to Leslie's sensitive ear that by going to Italy the Grants were making themselves accessories after the fact to the Abyssinian War.

"I—I suppose it is a bit awkward," he muttered.

His companions' silence was heavy with the opinion that it was indecent rather than awkward. From pure nervousness Leslie went on.

"They're going with Angus's rich uncle."

He was at once aware that it was probably bourgeois to go on a holiday with a rich uncle, even perhaps to have a

416

rich uncle. His pang of homesickness for the Grants faded. They did not belong to his new world.

Naomi said in a low voice,

"I think Grizel must need a holiday. I hope she'll enjoy it." The wish was genuine, the warm, natural feeling caught her unaware. She looked almost apologetically at Claud, but Claud was crumbling his roll and thinking, half consciously, I wish I had a rich uncle! I haven't been abroad for two years!

After supper they cleared the table and stacked the things by the sink, leaving them for the daily woman to wash up in the morning. They put on their coats and went out to the tram. Leslie had given up using his car, it was so expensive and convenient that it was obviously the hall-mark of a capitalist. He did not like to drive up in it to meetings attended by people very much poorer than himself, it eased his conscience to go in trams. Claud did not altogether welcome this particular manifestation of the new spirit, and had hinted to Leslie that the car might reasonably be used "in the workers' cause," but Leslie, while he agreed, failed to connect the workers' cause with driving the Unwins to meetings, and vaguely imagined his car carrying messages and even possibly ammunition during the next general strike or the revolution. There were times when Claud found him annoyingly unpractical.

The meeting, a Peace Meeting, was held in one of the large halls of the city, and was addressed by a Bishop, a Rabbi, two Members of Parliament, Conservative and Labour, a representative of a League of Youth, and Professor Allison. It was attended by a large audience, none of whom had the faintest desire for war, nor any idea, either at the beginning or end of the meeting, what to do to prevent it, unless possibly to support the Government's programme of rearmament. That did at least seem definite and intelligible. Claud Unwin might mutter to himself about the profits of armament makers and the inevitable results of a dead system of economics. The average man saw his next-door neighbour arming, and with a sigh reached for a gun. On the whole, the audience at the Peace Meeting went away dejected, feeling no nearer to peace and more vividly aware of possibilities of war.

Leslie came away feeling miserable. His encounter with Grizel had depressed him more than he knew at the time. It seemed to him that with Grizel and the pram there had walked out of his life human kindness, fun and friendliness, easy toleration and light-hearted laughter. He had left these things behind. He moved in a new, austere world where everything, art, letters, life itself, must serve one single purpose. Everything must be thrown overboard which would not help to bring the new order to birth. The Grants were quite clearly not bringing any new order to birth, working on the Romantic poets and going off to Italy with rich uncles. They must be thrown overboard too. It was Naomi and Claud who had opened Leslie's eyes and shown him the new world at grips with the old one. They had made visible to him a gulf between ordinary people of which he had not been aware. On one side of the gulf were his mother and father, Marjorie, the Wilsons, the Grants, most of his family's friends. On the other side were Naomi and Claud, and a few more like them. He had sprung over to the other side. He felt sad and superior, but to-night more sad than superior. He could not help remembering that at supper with the Grants there had been no pitfalls, no feeling of tension. It had not mattered what he said, he was not obliged to agree with them, and he could even have been bourgeois without shame. In the company of the Unwins he had to say and think and feel the right things; to rule out anything that was not to the purpose. Freedom, that was what he had left on the other side of the gulf. This evening he thought that he regretted it, not realizing that men are proved by their actions, and that he had handed over his spirit in chains.

On Saturday afternoon Mary was having tea with Doris in her new house. Frank was out, and the two sisters sat cosily together at a small table in front of the bright fire. Doris had been feeling ill that morning, but had slept on the

418

sofa all the afternoon, and woken up with pink cheeks and an appetite. She varied between moods of deep content and hours of querulous misery in which she complained endlessly to Frank of everything from her occasional nausea and headaches to the rattle of a window and the time that it took to boil the electric kettle. In these moods she was like her mother, and even fell back on a familiar phrase of her mother's. "It's no use!" she would say. "I can't get up for breakfast." Or "It's no use! The kettle just *won't* boil!" and the complaint would be followed by tears. On the whole, Frank bore with these moods patiently, believing that they would disappear when the baby was born. It seemed to him fair that he should put up with something. Doris discovered with surprise and even with faint disapproval that he was not embarrassed by the physical details of her pregnancy. He had great ideas about diet, fresh air and exercise. He took her out with him as often as he could persuade her to come, and tried to substitute tomatoes, salads and brown bread for the tea-cakes and puddings which Doris liked, in his opinion, too much. He was interested in health, which Doris had only thought about when she was ill, and he was anxious that his son should be a healthy child.

He was also, Doris discovered, very much interested in money. He gave her what seemed to her a lot, both for herself and for the housekeeping, but he did not like her to spend it unnecessarily. Doris had always been inclined to fritter, buying hats that did not go with anything, patterns that she would never use, and odd jugs and ornaments for no particular purpose. She loved sales, and bought things because they were cheap. Frank's idea was that things should be bought because they were wanted and should then be bought good. They fratched a little over this difference, but on the whole were very happy together.

Doris was enwrapped and enfolded in the new life. She had asked for her mother with some affection, but on hearing that she had had a good deal of pain, said easily that she would be better when the warm weather came. She asked how Arthur was getting on at school this term, and stopped listening in the middle of the answer. Once she said vaguely,

"Is there any news?" "The strike's over," Mary said, "they go back on Monday." "What strike?" Doris said. "Oh, you mean Ward's. I believe Frank said something about it last night when he was reading the paper. I've been to see my room in the Nursing Home, Mary. It's ever so nice, on the third floor, looking right over the town. I'm going to take his own cot in. There is one there, but I don't seem to fancy a strange cot for him that other babies have used, and it isn't a very pretty one. I want him to have his own, and I bought the blankets yesterday, sweet, they are, bound with pale-blue silk. We'll go upstairs after tea and see them."

That, Mary reflected, was probably how it should be. Doris was bending all her energies to her essential business. It was stupid of her to wish for her lost sister, who would have asked her what she was doing and would have listened with eager interest to all her small affairs. She gave herself up to conversation about the baby and his possessions, about Doris's health and feelings.

Frank, when he came in, greeted her cordially and seemed pleased to see her. She was surprised because when he had made due inquiries for his mother-in-law, he said with unusual friendliness, "How's Uncle John?" So far as Mary could remember, he had always before firmly called his wife's uncle Mr. Allworthy. She replied that Uncle John had been in bed with a chill, but was getting up again.

"That was the night in the Trades Hall, I suppose," Frank said sympathetically. "Very plucky performance! He's a game old bird, isn't he?"

"What did he do?" Doris roused to a faint interest. "I believe you did tell me."

"Yes, I did. He stood up to the lot of them and broke the strike. It was a very fine performance." Frank spoke in the tone that he might have used of someone who had knocked up a hundred on a sticky wicket. He added rather naïvely, "Everyone's talking about him."

Mary thought irritably that this was probably the first time that Frank's friends had heard of his connection with his wife's uncle. He was a shrewd young man who valued success and publicity. Well, after all, why shouldn't he?

Most of us do. It was odd how distasteful that sense of their value always was in other people.

"And that fellow, Sutton!" Frank said indignantly. "He was a friend of Uncle John's, wasn't he? Wasn't he the surly fellow who was at their house one evening when we went there? With a pretty girl he was engaged to? Yes, I thought he was. And Uncle John had got him his job at Ward's and always been awfully good to him, which makes it all the worse."

"Oh, Tom's all right, really!" Mary said.

Frank gave her a quick, disapproving glance.

"It depends on what you call all right. He's led a lot of ignorant people into trouble and caused serious losses to his employers all for nothing. Why, he even went against his Union!"

The Unions, Mary reflected, were the Conservatives' new pet, and going against them a crime which they spoke of as having been committed for the first time by Left-Wing Labour.

"You don't approve of him going against the Union, surely?" Frank said.

"Oh, don't you see?" Mary cried. "It's a war, and Tom knows it! I think he probably wasn't right this time. He tried to do something more than he could do. He led an attack against a strong position and the main body didn't back him up, and I agree, he broke a flag of truce to do it. It wasn't honourable. But modern war isn't honourable! And especially this war—on both sides. If you're fighting for your life, you aren't playing cricket by M.C.C. rules."

"People who don't keep the rules get shot out of the game."

"Yes, of course they do, as long as it is a game. But don't you see that this is getting more than a game? Because both sides are being pushed harder and getting angrier and more afraid. Why, look at Europe!"

"This isn't Europe," said Frank coldly.

Doris murmured, "I always thought you were so fond of Uncle John!"

"I am. He's a darling and I admire and love him. He's

421

got the old technique and Tom's got the new one, that's all."

"In other words, he respects a signed agreement and Sutton doesn't."

"Tom knows that he's up against people who won't stop at anything to keep the present system. You can't expect him to fight fair when they don't."

Frank got up and lit a cigarette as though he needed the movement to relieve his feelings. Standing with his back to the fire, he said,

"These things are all rather more complicated than they look from the outside, aren't they? You need a good deal of experience of business to understand them. Has Doris shown you the new things for the cot?"

He smiled at Mary. He was the master of the house deliberately turning the conversation to subjects more suited to the female intelligence, and for a second she hated him.

He did not come up with them to the nursery, but when they came down again, Mary ready in her hat and coat, he opened the front door for her.

"Well, come again whenever you can and cheer Doris up," he said pleasantly.

"Yes, I'd love to." Mary shook hands with him and smiled. They knew both that their relationship had become a shade less friendly that afternoon.

Doris and Frank stood in the doorway, watching Mary as she walked down the road.

"She is nice and slim!" Doris said enviously, sighing for her own growing unwieldiness, "I didn't understand what she meant about the strike. She can't have thought Tom was right really, can she?"

"Oh, she was talking through her hat. Come in, Dot, it's cold." Frank pulled her inside and shut the door. As he followed Doris into the sitting-room, he said,

"We've never asked Aunt Grace and Uncle John up here, have we, since the housewarming? Why don't you ask them to tea next week-end? I should like to hear just what happened that night in the Trades Hall, and I expect Aunt Grace would like to see the things you've got ready for the child."

422

Mary looked back as she shut the garden gate, and saw Doris and Frank standing together in the lighted doorway, both smiling, Doris with her hand through his elbow. A pang of envy shook her. How lovely for Doris, oh how lovely to see the visitor go off, and then to go inside the house and shut the door, shut herself into her own home with the man whom she loved, whose child she was carrying! How lucky she was, and how difficult it was not to envy her and be sorry for oneself. And yet she was really not enviable at all, for Frank was dull, ordinary and uninteresting. A whole half-century of married life with him would not be worth a few stolen hours with Stephen.

The bus swung down the hill towards the thickly clustering lights of the town. That was the worst of this thing that had come upon them, the hours were literally stolen, stolen from Joy to whom they belonged, from the things that other people expected both Mary and Stephen to do. They were worse than stolen, they were furtive. They had met twice since the ball and each time it was difficult to arrange, each time the meeting was so short that it left them quivering for more, as though, being very thirsty, they had taken only a sip of water. This evening they were meeting for half an hour before the Concert at which Mary was expected to report on the social side. Stephen often went to the concerts and usually alone, or to join Robert and Beryl there, since Joy did not like music.

They had arranged to meet at a cheap restaurant near the Town Hall which was quite off the beat of Stephen's friends, and not used, so far as Mary knew, by anyone on the paper. Stephen was waiting at the door when she arrived. At the sight of him a tumultuous joy wiped out all other feelings. There he was, and for half an hour they would be together. It was extraordinary how one half-hour could seem both longer and shorter than weeks or days and how one person, perhaps to most people quite an ordinary person, could absorb into himself all the light and colour in the universe, so that there was none left in other people or in a world which was drab when he was not there.

They climbed upstairs together to a room which at this

hour was still empty, although the tables were covered with white cloths, and laid with strong knives and forks and solid tumblers, preparation for a serious meal. They ordered chops, anxious only to get the waitress out of the room. She gave the order down a speaking tube, and their agitation grew as she hung about, moving the cruet stand and sauce bottles on one of the tables, and flicking at crumbs with her napkin. When at last she left the room, their relief was so great that they both laughed. They both thought, If only we could live like this always, being together, laughing at the same things, sharing everything, free to be ourselves, always loving. Stephen said, "Mary!" as though he were touching her name. Their eyes clung together and they stretched out their hands and caught hold of each other's across the table.

On the afternoon of Saturday, March 7th, William Marsden took the chair at a meeting of the Marsden Trust Committee. The Marsden Trust was a sum of money invested by his grandfather to provide loans for young men and women who wanted education or training that they could not afford. Old John Marsden had believed in education as the solution of all problems, had been an ardent supporter of lectures and libraries for working-men, and had been the first subscriber to the Aire Philharmonic Society and to the Society of Literature and Science which still provided a yearly programme of lectures in the Institute which he had helped to build. His portrait with keen eyes, long nose and a bush of hair on the chin and cheeks hung over the mantelpiece of the Committee Room in the Institute where the meeting was held.

William was tired, but never allowed himself to hurry. He considered in detail the cases before the Committee. A young man who had lost his father in his first year at Aire University wanted to borrow enough money to finish his three years. Another wanted a year at the School of Art. A girl wanted a loan for a Secretarial Course. William's inquiries were patient and searching, but did not encourage

424

verbosity. Under the influence of his dry manner, even Mrs. Allison began to speak briefly and to the point. The meeting ended at four. The Committee, glad to get off in time for tea, hurried away, and left William alone in the room with the secretary who was putting away some papers and with the portrait of his grandfather.

"Some very deserving cases indeed this afternoon," the secretary said in the pleased tone of a collector who has found good specimens.

"I never feel sure that this fund is doing what it was intended for. I should prefer to see it used more for education and less for training."

"Well, it's the same thing, isn't it!" the secretary said vaguely. He snapped down the lid of his despatch case, said "Good afternoon, Mr. Marsden," and bustled out.

William had ordered the car to fetch him from the Club at five. That would allow him time to have a cup of tea there before going home, as he did on a working-day. He valued more and more, nowadays, the interval of quiet between the day's activity, and his home life. It was not that either of them went against the grain with him. He would have been miserable if he had retired, as the doctor had recommended five years ago, and his sister Isobel was only a little less congenial to him than his garden; but he had always needed to withdraw into himself at times, even from the people he loved, and from things that interested him. The need increased as he grew older and more tired. In the sober dignity of the Club smoke-room, the very air was familiar; and at this hour on Saturday afternoon he was alone. It was not even necessary for him to ring for his tea. The waiter brought unasked the small pot of china tea and the two digestive biscuits which all the Club servants knew had been Mr. Marsden's order for tea for the last ten years.

Presently a page brought in the early edition of the evening paper, and laid it on the table at his elbow. William picked up the sheets and turned to the back page. He glanced at the staring headline, "GERMANY SENDS TROOPS INTO THE RHINELAND," and read the paragraphs below in heavy black print. He lowered the paper to his knee, and

425

picked up his tea-cup. His throat felt dry. His hand shook as he put the cup back in the saucer. What a world! First Italy and then Germany. He did not know which distressed him more, their barbarous self-assertion and repudiation of their pledged word, or the loud-tongued clamour of those who arraigned them as barbarian. He remembered a spring in Florence, and a walking holiday spent once in May in the Black Forest, when the floor of the forest was blue with dog violets and the wild cherry was in flower. He had not thought of Germany as the enemy who killed his two sons, but of their young men and his as caught together in a trap by the world's folly, and uselessly slain. Cut off by the war from German friends and connections, he had never picked up the old threads again, and the new Germany was abhorrent to him, but he disliked it as much for having swamped the old, as for its menace to Europe and liberty.

He finished his tea and went out to the car. His chauffeur, Naylor, had been in the Aire Rifles with his sons, and had crawled out under a brisk machine-gun fire to bring in young Bill Marsden, getting a bullet in the thigh himself as he tumbled over into the trench with the boy's body on his back already dead. As he opened the door of the car, he said,

"Seen the evening paper, sir? Looks like trouble again with Germany."

"It looks like trouble everywhere," William said.

Naylor thought that the old man looked tired, bluish about the lips. He spread the rug carefully over his knees.

"French been provoking them again I daresay," he said, disapprovingly. Ever since the War he had been convinced that the Germans were an innocent and quiet people, irritated beyond endurance by the French. He himself had found the French so extremely irritating. He was not, William thought, the only man to see European politics in terms of his personal equation. Besides, when you remembered the Treaty of Versailles there was a germ of truth in it. William had known it at the time for an illiberal treaty based upon fundamental ignorance. But what could you expect! He had never fully accepted Lloyd George as a Liberal, the fellow was a glorified Radical without tradition or political pride of

426

ancestry, a cheapjack crying his wares! He had killed the Liberal Party and the Liberal mind was dead or dying. Young men like Stephen who believed in humanity and progress had to call themselves Socialists, or Labour or Left or whatever the name was now. They were obliged to pursue humanity and progress by getting out of the state of life to which it had pleased God to call them, and they suffered an inevitable distortion.

When he arrived at Green Oaks, Lionel and Alice were there having tea with Isobel. Never expansive, he found it impossible to convey that he was even more glad to see them than usual. They had driven over to Stephen's to ask after one of the children who was ill. The little boy was better. It was a false alarm, Alice said, comfortably. Such a lot of children had had that kind of flu, running up to 103° or 104° one night, and then nearly normal the next morning. It was a great relief to poor Joy, though she was very sensible and always kept calm. There was something dutiful in Alice's tone when she praised Stephen's wife.

William carried off Lionel to smoke a pipe in his study. The prevailing fashion had obliged him to allow smoking in his drawing-room, and he concealed his distaste for the sight of his nieces with Virginian cigarettes sticking out between reddened lips, and even more for their messy saucers dabbled with ash. In vain he bought ash-trays and placed them on the arms of their chairs or on small tables near them. They said, "Oh, thank you, Uncle William!" and went on smearing the sides of their tea-cups. He had to endure, but, whenever he could, he removed his own guests to a room really meant for smoking. He himself had been limited to one cigar a day some years ago, and he invariably smoked it after dinner, but he supplied his brother-in-law, and sat down in the tall chair by the fire. He never lounged in an easy chair as Lionel was now doing.

"You've seen the news about Germany?"

"Yes. We saw a poster as we came through the town and stopped and bought a paper."

"In a way you can't blame them."

"No."

"What sort of world are we leaving our——" he had been going to say "our children" but checked himself, "the young to, William?"

William's dry voice answered,

"To the return of the Barbarian."

Lionel, always restless, got out of his chair and began to walk up and down the room, puffing at his cigar.

"Do you remember a novel called *When It Was Dark!* that made a great sensation in our day?"

"You know I never was a novel-reader."

"It was a melodramatic tale about some manuscript or inscription which was suddenly discovered and disproved the Resurrection of Christ. The news spread all over the world, and there was a downfall of faith and a general rush of calamity. I've forgotten the exact story, but the point was that a great restraining force was removed, and people did their worst, robbed, cheated and murdered. I think there was a collapse of credit and a threat of wars, and then the hero discovered that the inscription was a fake and the world righted itself, just in time."

"It sounds like a piece of melodramatic rubbish."

"In a way, but I think it was a prophecy, whether the author knew it or not. I think something like that has really happened. Most of the world to-day has lost its faith. It doesn't believe in anything. You don't believe in the Godhead and Resurrection of Christ and I do, but we both believe in God, William, and in a future life. The younger ones don't, and so as a generation they are 'of all men most miserable.' *When It Was Dark* has come true. They are walking in the darkness, and fear and chaos and hatred and death are unleashed. 'Wars and Rumours of Wars. Men's hearts failing them for fear.' I almost wonder if we are getting near the end of the world!"

A smile deepened the lines on William's thin face. Lionel had always seemed a boy to him, eager, romantic, impatient, hopeful. He leaned back, pressing the tips of his fingers together.

"If we are, I shan't see it, and if we aren't, I'm glad I shan't see the next chapter of this one. My day is over. I've seen the end of most of the things that I care for. I don't want to see what happens next."

Lionel, standing at the window, with his back to him, did not answer. He thought, William has no children or grandchildren alive, no stake in the game! Yet if he himself had not had Robert and Stephen and Clare and Jack and Lin, he thought that he would still want to see what happened next. He had not lost his taste for life, and his sanguine temper made it impossible for him to imagine a world that he would rather not see. He turned round towards William with an old pity in his heart. He had so often felt that William was not enjoying himself! His brother-in-law's honourable, reasonable and dignified progress through life had seemed to preclude the amusement and curiosity that had enlivened his own. He came back to the fireplace.

"How has Stephen taken the Ward strike?" William asked.

"I think he was disturbed and surprised at finding his new allies more at loggerheads with one another than with Ward. Stephen's very young. 'Going Left' apparently seemed to him a simple and whole-hearted matter."

"He thought he was getting on to a by-pass road, and finds himself at the junction of four cross roads with no sign-post?"

"Something like that. The odd part of Stephen's conversion is that it has made Robert interested in politics for the first time in his life."

"Robert, I presume, is not going Left?"

"Oh, no, Robert's a Tory bred in the bone. But reasonably progressive, William, not like you Liberal die-hards!" the two exchanged a smile for an old battle. "He's got a very pretty wit sometimes, and a lot of energy. I should like to see him standing for the Council some day. You ought to work for the Town you live in, I think. He made a speech at the Disraeli Club dinner the other night when Coppenger was ill and failed at the last minute, and everyone said he was very good and spoke exactly like my father, even to the trick of rubbing his chin. He's a regular Harding."

"Yes. I've always thought Stephen was the child of our family, Robert of yours, although they both look more like you."

Isobel put her head in at the door.

"I'm sorry, Lionel. Alice wants to go. She says you're going out to dinner!"

"Bless me, I'd forgotten. Don't come out, William."

William got up stiffly without answering. It was unthinkable unless he was in bed, that he should not see any guests to the door, even his nearest relations.

Outside a March wind was swinging the branches of the trees. There was still enough light for the thickening buds to be visible, and under the great beech, an early daffodil nodded above the ranks of green spears.

"Thank goodness, the days are lengthening!" Alice said happily. "Your bulbs will be lovely in a week or two, William! I pine for the summer! I always say that next year we'll go South for February, but somehow we never do! This year with strikes and flu and the news so bad, the spring seems worse than usual. Next year we really *will* go to Devonshire or the New Forest."

Lionel, with his foot on the self starter, said,

"We'll go when William goes."

"I shouldn't wait for that," William said.

"Go in, Isobel! Go in, William! The wind's freezing. Thank you for our tea."

"Thank you for coming." To his brother-in-law William added suddenly and unexpectedly, "Bless you!"

He stood on the doorstep watching as the car gathered speed down the drive and disappeared round the curve beneath the arching branches of the trees. Before going in, he walked along the terrace and stood at the corner, looking across the lawn and the field to the outskirts of the city on the rising ground beyond. The new red houses were still plainly visible, a light springing here and there among them. They were the sign of the progress that he had believed in and fought for. It seemed to him that the results of that struggle were mean, shoddy and ugly, that his belief in progress had betrayed him as much as his belief in humanity and civilization. He shivered and walked back to the house. Meeting Isobel in the hall he said, "I feel rather off colour. I don't think I want any dinner. May I have some soup sent into the study?" Isobel looked at him anxiously, but said nothing, knowing how much he disliked any fuss. He smiled at her, went into the study and shut the door.

At the funeral of William Marsden, Stephen sat in one of the front pews of the Unitarian Chapel and listened to the minister, who was delivering an address on the dead man's life and virtues. Beside Stephen, Joy sat upright, lovely but a little unfamiliar in the black clothes that she hardly ever wore. Beryl was next to her, and Robert, beyond Beryl, leaned forward, his elbow resting on the ledge of the pew before him, his chin propped on his hand. Poor old Uncle William, Robert was thinking, he was a good old sort, but I don't believe he ever had much fun. Still, it was a useful kind of life, and a good way to finish, just sitting down like that in his study and dying quietly without any fuss. He listened to the recital of his uncle's public and private virtues. His justice and unflagging devotion to duty as a magistrate on the bench; his energy and generosity on the Council of the Infirmary and other hospitals; his contributions to the Art Gallery and to the City Museum; his donation towards the new library of the growing University; the support which he had given every year to the Orchestra and Choral Societies of the city; his justice and generosity as an employer; his excellence in all private relationships, as husband, father, brother and son. The minister, an old man, wandered off into recollections of William's father, John Marsden, whom Robert did not remember. Yes, Robert thought, a good life, solid, useful and dignified. The value of something besides fun and earning your living was slowly growing upon him. Even while he smiled at the ugly building and at a certain pompous simplicity in the sermon, he felt that he should like, by the time he died, to have made some contribution to his world besides the work he was paid for. As William's body was laid in the earth, something of his spirit was reborn in Robert Harding.

Stephen thought, there goes the end of an old world.

Uncle William in his youth had rebelled against established order and tradition with what now could hardly be called a rebellion. Uncle William had worn a yellow ribbon to Lionel Harding's blue, and now in a world blue or red it seemed that William and Lionel had been colour-blind, and the yellow had only been another shade of blue. Or else the yellow had faded with age until its colour was no longer distinguishable. The progressive young man had become set and uncompromising in later life, while the conservative young man had become more liberal in his last span, his mind open to new ideas. Was it possible that each man in his life could only make a certain amount of progress, and those who made it early stopped progressing, made all at once that small step forward which is the limit of average human achievement, and then stood? There was John Allworthy, the ardent young radical, grown into a sober reactionary. Shall I, Stephen wondered, in twenty-five years be where I am now, a rebel, a progressive of the 1930s like something fossilized in time? And will Robert be accepting, at least with a partly open mind, the rebellious and progressive spirit of 1960? Is it like Joy's hats? She says that the most fashionable ones go most completely out of fashion. If it must be like that, it must. I have the feelings and the mind of my time, and I can't help following them. Perhaps we shan't be here in the 1960s, we or our civilization.

The service was over. The bearers lifted the coffin from the trestle. The heavy tramp of their feet sounded through the building. His Aunt Isobel, his mother and his father were moving out of the pew in front. Stephen stood up and prepared to follow them. Isobel Marsden passed the end of the pew, her face still and contained, as though her chief determination was to avoid the fuss that William had so much disliked. His father looked sad, Stephen thought, and almost old. William, whom he had often laughed at, had been dear to him, a part of his life from the days of nursery tea-parties. He was tender-hearted, living fully in his personal relationships, and the loss of their sons in the war, so seldom mentioned between them, had drawn him and William together. He moved down the aisle behind his wife and sister-in-law

432

without spirit enough for his usual glance of amused scorn at the ugly building.

Stephen, walking down the aisle beside Joy, saw one familiar face after another in the pews, and was suddenly reminded of their wedding. The clothes were a little darker, the expressions a little different, but that was all. His family and the Marsden family and all their friends were here, a solid block of prosperous, decent, kindly and rather simple men and women, among whom he felt so much an alien that he walked like a ghost. The Stephen whom they knew was the Stephen whom they expected to find, a younger Robert, not the real Stephen. Yet feeling their stability and security, he was conscious of regret for that old world. It was a world in which fear played a much smaller part, perhaps because they had grown up in less disturbing times, but probably also because death itself was less important to them; since they believed it to be a prelude and not the end. A world which had shed faith was conditioned by fear. Once again the life of man was the flight of a sparrow through a lighted chamber from darkness to darkness, and it was difficult to accept this with dignity and to move freely in a dwelling that had changed from a house set in limitless grounds to a narrow room.

They came out of the chapel into the brisk air and light sunshine of a March morning. Robert straightened his shoulders and murmured "Pity to be dead on a day like this! Poor old Uncle William! I suppose we can't cut the state lunch, can we, Beryl? Do you think Aunt Isobel would mind? It's a lovely day for golf. Oh, well, all right, perhaps we'd better go through with it. I hope we don't boil over on the way to the cemetery same as we did last week going to the races—our car is so temperamental about a slow march! See you later, Stephen! What about a game of bridge? Could you come over this evening?"

On Easter Monday morning, Beryl went into her kitchen to say good-bye to Rosie, who was going off for the day to her brother's wedding.

433

Rosie was standing in the middle of the kitchen, which was not as tidy as it should have been. She had been once that morning through the whirling process known as "straightening up a bit," but had afterwards cancelled this by searching in every drawer and cupboard for a bottle of nail varnish which Olive had given her at Christmas. The nail varnish, when found between the cakes and the mushroom ketchup, proved to be bright scarlet, and Rosie, overcome by sudden diffidence, decided that she would not put it on her nails, and impulsively drew a cat with it on the newspaper which she was using as a tablecloth, in spite of Beryl's protests. An odour of pear drops pervaded the untidy room, in the midst of which Rosie stood, looking very young, bonnie, and festive.

"Will I do?" she asked.

Beryl, who had already taken part in several consultations about the wedding toilette, surveyed her with serious interest. Rosie wore a new light tweed coat, bought fresh for the occasion. She had proposed to wear a knitted cap, but Beryl had lent her her last summer's hat, a fine, light straw with a drooping brim. Rosie had improved the hat by adding a large bunch of violets and a diamanté buckle. She had shining, artificial silk stockings and new shoes of imitation crocodile. Her hair had emerged from curling-pins that Beryl had pretended not to notice into rough, sunny curls.

"You look very nice. Haven't you any white gloves, Rosie?"

"Nay, I 'aven't. Ought I to have *them*?"

"I'll lend you a pair."

Beryl ran upstairs, and came down again with a pair of white gloves. When she came back into the kitchen, Rosie was drinking a cup of tea and munching a bit of cold apple-tart.

"I was that excited," she explained, "I couldn't eat any breakfast."

Crumbs of pastry clung to the front of her coat, and tea was dripping on it from the wet bottom of the tea-cup.

"Oh, Rosie," Beryl exclaimed, "that cup's dripping! Look what you're doing to your new coat! You are a child!"

434

"Care killed the cat!" Rosie replied cheerfully. "I forgot to put the towels in to soak, but they'll wait while to-morrow."

"I'll do them. You'd better get off. You'll miss your bus, and Fred will be wondering where you are."

"I'm off." Rosie banged the dripping cup down on the table. "We asked that Olive to coom wi' us, but she thinks my folk are common. Good riddance, I say. Me and Fred are going on our own, any road."

Fred, who was waiting at the bus stop, felt a glow of pride when he saw Rosie coming towards him, stepping daintily on her absurd high heels. How could Olive say the things she did about her? It was downright unkind! There was nothing wrong with being in service. Rosie was as good as Olive's silly, giggling friends and prettier than any of them. His heart warmed with tenderness as he looked at the happy, smiling face under the brim weighted with violets. It was a holiday, it was spring, they were together. The two of them sprang on to the bus and scrambled up to a front seat. As they sat down side by side, Fred, usually undemonstrative, squeezed Rosie's hand and murmured, "The next wedding we go to might be our own, eh, Rosie?" She snuggled against him and half closed her eyes, so that the advertisements on the big hoarding near the bus stop swam in a dazzle of sunlit colour. As the conductor came up, Fred pulled out a coin and said, "Two returns, Huldholme, please," in a lordly way. Not even giving me time to put me 'and in me pocket, Rosie thought with pride.

The mining village of Huldholme was about ten miles out of Aire. The drive there through colliery country was not beautiful, but neither Rosie nor Fred wanted more than the spring sunshine, the movement of the bus, and one another's company. They got down in high spirits. Huldholme was a straggling village of greyish-yellow stone, built on either side of the street, and extending for more than a mile from the Wesleyan Chapel at one end to the offices of the Huldholme Colliery Co. at the other. The church and the church schools were in the middle of the village, opposite to the co-operative stores. There were two pubs, the Green Man and the Queen's Arms. All the country around and behind the village was flat, broken by pit-shafts and slag-heaps, and grimed by smoke and coal-dust. Fred thought it seemed a dreary sort of place to live. Rosie, who had lived there until she was fourteen, was excited and pleased to come home. It had never occurred to her to think much about her surroundings.

Rosie led the way into the house where Clarice and her husband lived, Fred following a little shyly. He was rather at sea among Rosie's people. Her brawny collier brothers shouted and laughed so loud, swore with a frequency at which he was secretly distressed, drank quantities of beer that astonished him, and were apt to clap him hard on the back at their first meeting, and then take no more notice of him. He consoled himself by thinking them a rough lot, and by trying to look superior.

He was glad that Olive had not come when he saw the rich confusion in Clarice's front room. Clarice herself was pouring out cups of tea from a gigantic black tea-pot. The tea was nearly as black as the pot and looked as though it had been standing all night. A stout young woman, whom Fred vaguely remembered as Clarice's sister-in-law, was suckling a six-weeks-old baby in a chair by the fire. Her blouse, unbuttoned and pushed carelessly down, showed even more than the necessary flesh. She was shouting across the room to her husband, above the little brown head. Intent upon his own proper business, the baby nuzzled and drank with small sucking noises, as persistent as a kitten, and as little disturbed by his surroundings. Len, Rosie's other unmarried brother, was sitting in the window playing a mouth-organ. In the middle of the floor, Ada, the sister next to Rosie, was dressing the bridesmaids, Clarice's two little girls, Patricia and Gloria. One child, already clothed in pink satin, was sucking a lollipop on the end of a stick. The other little girl, still in dirty underclothes, was jumping up and down, resisting her aunt's attempts to thrust the pink frills over her head.

"Give over, now, Gloria!" Ada exclaimed, and slapped her. Gloria began to roar.

"Ah, you naughty girl, you!" her mother said, mechanically and dispassionately. The strains of the mouth-organ, yearning after a high note, competed with Gloria's screams. Nobody took any notice of either of them. Rufus, Clarice's husband, and his brother Cliff, the father of Gloria, were occupied in baiting the bridegroom, a sturdy, sheepish youth with a carefully oiled quiff of brown hair, who hovered uncomfortably by the fire. They were making primitive jokes about his marriage bed and the pleasures in store for him, which Fred tried not to hear. Rosie did not seem to mind them. She was embracing one relation after another, and as Pauline moved the baby from her breast, she caught him away from her and cuddled him in her arms, kissing his little, veined forehead and rapturously admiring his small, mottled hands and cold pink feet. Among the slatternly brood, she looked fresh and neat, and to Fred's eye elegant and lady-like, though already her hat was off, her curls were roughened, and her accent was broader. Still carrying the baby, she crossed to the window, snatched the mouth-organ from Len, and exclaimed:

" 'Ere, I'll give you a tune."

She began to play the Isle of Capri, and took a dancing step or two, the baby looking over her shoulder with surprised blue eyes.

The clock on the mantelpiece struck twelve. I thought, Fred reflected anxiously, that the wedding was at twelve. Nobody seemed to think that there was any hurry. Len snatched the mouth-organ back from Rosie, and began to play Abide with Me. Clarice went on telling Pauline the full details of her recent operation. The baby, restored to his mother, was sick, whimpered a little, and then settled off to sleep under her caressing hand. Ada thrust two little rose-bud wreaths on to the curled heads of Patricia and Gloria, hugged Gloria, now gulping dismally, and said, "There now, lovey! You do love your auntie, don't you?" Patricia laid the half-sucked lollipop down on the table-cloth and climbed on to a chair to look at herself in the glass. The men went on jesting by the fireplace. Fred stood shy and stiff, an alien, wishing that he had not come. Rosie saw his disconsolate face, moved towards him and whispered, "We shan't be

437

long now, lad. T'Parson's always late." She looked at him for a second regretfully, wishing that he could enjoy himself as she did. As she turned away to greet her Auntie Edie, who had just arrived, she thought, eh, he's a funny lad is Fred, but 'e's my lad. 'E's not what I'd call lively, but 'e's a good lad, and I'm that used to 'im, I couldn't do without him.

By seven o'clock that night, even the thought of enjoying himself had passed from Fred's mind. He stood at one end of the long room in the Green Man, nervously lighting yet another cigarette and wondering how soon he could get out of this. They had had a meal and copious drinks after the wedding, they had been shouting and talking and eating all the afternoon, and now they were having drinks again. Most of them had already had more than was good for them. The bridegroom was half drunk. The bride, with her curls all in disorder, and a spreading stain of port on her light blue satin dress, was leaning, half asleep, against his shoulder. Len was still playing his mouth-organ, but now without any attempt at a tune, producing squeaks and squeals and laughing uproariously. Pauline, who had laid her baby down in a chair, was trying to dance, a man's felt hat unsteadily perched on her head. The room was thick with smoke and smelt of beer and warm humanity and of the onions which had accompanied the roast pork. Except for Fred and perhaps Rosie, everyone was very happy. There had been enough to eat, there was enough to drink, the room was hot, full, noisy, they were all having a bit of fun.

Fred fingered the money in his pocket. Four rounds of drinks he had had to pay for at midday! He was not ungenerous, though he was careful of his money, and he would have thought one round reasonable—but four! So far as he could make out, none of these people had any money. There was a strike on, their pockets were empty, and he could not imagine how they were going to pay for the food and the hire of the room. He could not help feeling that he would like to leave before the question was raised. Mingled

438

with his disapproval of these people was a spice of envy. Never in his life had he let himself go as they did, never sprawled and shouted and put his arm round young women, and drunk himself carefree. All he had had to-day was one pint of beer and one glass of lemonade, and he didn't feel as though they had mixed well inside him.

He looked for Rosie, and saw her suddenly in a far corner of the room. She was backing away from two young men, brothers, Fred thought, of the bride. They were very much alike, red-headed, small, but with the muscular arms and shoulders of the miner. They were too drunk to speak straight or walk steadily, and they lurched towards Rosie, laughing and making grabs at her. She pushed them off good-temperedly but with decision. She hated beer and was quite sober, but she was excited, flushed with the heat of the room, and tired with the prolonged party, and with all the noise that she herself had been making. One of the young men took her by the shoulder and pulled her towards him. Something snapped in Fred. He took three strides across the room and pulled Rosie away from them.

" 'Ere!" he said. "This is my girl!"

"Get along with you!" Rosie added, giving the young miner a vigorous shove. He stumbled, reeled against a chair and brought it crashing to the ground. There was a roar of laughter. The young man, forgetting all about Rosie, stared stupidly at the fallen chair, and then staggered off towards the maid, who was coming in at the door with another tray of drinks.

"Fred!" Rosie exclaimed, "we'd better take the kiddies back to Clarice's! There isn't no one else to do it, and they're only allowed in 'ere while seven."

She was laughing a little, but she felt ashamed. She said apologetically, "Pauline, she 'asn't 'ad a bit of fun since the baby was born." She understood how Fred felt, and she felt rather like it herself, even while she sympathized with her own people. She had grown away from them into more orderly, civilized ways, and could not wholly get back.

She picked up the baby from the chair and collected Patricia and Gloria, Muriel, the baby's elder sister, a couple of small boys and a two-year-old girl, who had come with the bride's party. Giving the two-year-old to Fred, and carrying the baby herself, she marshalled the others and drove them before her out into the street. It was only a few yards to Clarice's house, and they were soon in the kitchen. Rosie laid the baby in a chair and began to blow the dying embers of the fire. After the hot room at the Green Man the kitchen felt chilly. All the children were tired out. They had been lavishly fed with pork and onions, given tastes of beer and port, alternately caressed and scolded by their relatives all the afternoon. Patricia's wreath was lost, and she had spilt gravy over her satin frills. Gloria had been sick, and was whimpering. The two small boys were squabbling over an impromptu whip, made of a stick and a piece of string. The baby woke up and began to scream. Rosie brushed him tenderly, rocking him in her arms, and murmuring, "Poor little soul, then," but he was hungry, and not to be put off with kind words. His small crumpled face grew scarlet, he screamed with the furious rage of one defrauded of his rights.

"He's hungry, poor lamb!" Rose exclaimed, and tried to give him a spoonful of milk, which he rejected indignantly. He tried to nuzzle at her breast, found her dress in his way, and screamed again with fury at this stupid woman who did not know what he wanted.

"You'll have to go and fetch Pauline, Fred."

Fred got up with a sigh. He did not in the least want to go back to the Green Man. He was not at all sure that Pauline would come, and there was no knowing what he might find himself paying for if he got into that room again. He hesitated, but was decided by a wail from Gloria, "I'm going to be sick again!" He fled from Clarice's kitchen to the adult horrors of the Green Man.

Rosie, having dealt with Gloria and given her a lump of sugar for consolation, sat on by the fire, still trying to pacify the howling baby, and occasionally calling out "Mind, love, don't touch that now!" to the other children, as they played about the room. Poor old Fred! It was a lousy day out for him, she knew that he was miserable. It was a good job that

Olive hadn't come. At the mere thought of the elegant Olive at the party at the Green Man, Rosie shuddered. Olive reckoned her not good enough for Fred anyhow, and since she had broken with her Tom she was cracked about the new house, always on at Fred to spend his money on it when he wanted to save for a house of his own. Poor Tom! Rosie thought. He was a good lad and a bonnie lad. When you had a lad that was steady and kind and in good work, whatever did it matter if he went in for politics, it was cheaper than betting or drink any day!

"There now, little soul of a lamb, there now!" The baby who had quietened for a moment, was off again, filling the room with cries of fury. Rosie hugged him to her more closely, thinking to herself, eh, I hope Fred and I have one of our own as soon as we can!

The door opened and Pauline rushed in, a man's coat thrown over her shoulders, a crumpled daffodil from the bride's bouquet stuck in her hair. Her movements were uncertain and her speech indistinct, but she grabbed the baby from Rosie, staggered into the chair, pushed down her blouse, and in a second the furious crying was stilled. Rosie saw Fred in the doorway looking even more fed-up, and did not quite know whether to laugh or cry herself. She jumped up and went towards him.

"Come on, lad! Let's get t'next bus and go home!"

They were both silent on the bus. In the shade of Beryl's somewhat battered hat, Rosie's face was paler than usual, with dark shadows of fatigue under her eyes. On their way to the bus, they had met a procession escorting the bride and bridegroom, both drunk, to their nuptial bed in a friend's house. Clarice had borrowed five shillings from Rosie because the men were out on strike. Pauline had borrowed half a crown. What their husbands and brothers had borrowed from Fred, Rosie did not dare to think. She stole a glance at his face. It looked pale and stern. She thought of his home, always so clean and comfortable, even at Bankside Yard. She thought of Olive, of the stifling elegance of the sitting-room in his brother Herbert's house, with the embroidered afternoon tea-cloth on the table and the cocktail glasses all in a row in the cabinet. She had as a rule a sturdy self-respect that kept her from being abashed by "other folk's ways," but this evening she was tired and upset, distressed by the conflict between her two worlds. She wondered if Fred wanted to get shut of her, if he could stand her common folk and their common ways.

Something of the same kind had been keeping Fred so silent. He imagined with horror a wedding of his own at which all Rosie's relations got drunk and spilt food and kissed one another. He could picture Olive's disdain, Mabel and Herbert hustling their precious Doreen out of the room, even the shocked faces of his sober, thrifty parents. He foresaw dismally that Rosie's relations would always be borrowing money off him. What with the bus fares and the rounds of drinks and the loan which he had been obliged to make to Cliff, this day out had cost him pretty near a week's wage. All gone like that in a few hours and nothing to show for it but a headache, and a flat feeling of disappointment.

They got off the bus and walked along the street to the tram stop. Fred always saw Rosie into her tram before going further down the street to the barrier from which his own started. Rosie took his arm, but did not try to talk. The pavement was full of boys and girls like themselves, home from Bank-holiday exhibitions, just out of the pictures or Variety Theatre. Some of them went into the fish and chip restaurants, but Fred was too tired and too dejected to suggest a fish and chip supper. Besides, they had spent enough money for one day.

As they drew near to the tram stop, Rosie sighed, pulled off her hat, and ran a hand through her thick hair, lifting it off her aching head. "The bus made me feel a bit queer," she said. Fred looked at her, and another image passed through his mind, not the rough and noisy revels of her family, but Rosie herself, sitting by the fire, with Pauline's baby hugged to her breast, and her face bent over it, warm and tender. Fred, like Olive and Herbert, valued respect-

442

ability and security, wanted to climb and get on in the world, but he knew, as he looked at Rosie's downcast face, that that was not all he wanted. A protecting love surged up in him as though to defend his girl from his own cold and carping spirit on the bus. He very seldom made demonstrations of affection in a public place, but among the jostling groups that were getting into a queue for the tram, he put his arm round her and squeezed her against him. "You're my girl!" he said. "And don't you forget what I said this morning! The next wedding we go to, maybe, will be our own."

PART IV

"The world is waiting for a new wave of generosity, or a new great wave of death."

D. H. LAWRENCE.

THE RUNNING FIGURE of Brierley came up behind the opposite wicket, finishing with the familiar crab-like jerk. His arm rose against the white screen, Frank saw the ball, made his half-conscious decision, opened his shoulders and felt the impact, firm, true, satisfactory in the middle of his bat. He moved forward a step or two, but he had driven comfortably clear of mid-off, young Oakley, sprinting in the long field, just failed to reach the ball and a rattle of clapping all round the ground saluted the boundary. Ninety-four, thought Frank. He always knew his own score. He grinned amiably at Fairford, who was batting at the other end, and stooped to pat an unevenness in the turf made by Carr, the fast bowler, when he had finished his run. If only they would put Carr on again! But they wouldn't. Frank had had far too much fun with him before lunch. A four and a six off Carr would be a neat way to get his century! There was a neatness altogether that pleased him about getting his century in the Yorkshire and Lancashire match on the day his son was born. It seemed to make the right start for the little beggar, would be something to tell him when he began to play cricket.

Brierley was coming up again behind the opposite wicket. He was taking a longer run and the crab-like jerk was accentuated. That usually meant his faster ball. It was very difficult to knock him off his length, but when he was being hit, he sometimes bowled his faster ball twice instead of once in an over. This ball, when it came, was not the one which Frank had expected. It was slow, soft and innocent-looking. He knew that if he left it alone, it would curl in with a sudden wicked twist and caress his off stump. Before it had time, he cut it, sending it, he thought, past cover point about a foot from the turf. He saw Bardsley at cover swoop and dive, heard a roar all round the ground, saw him throw the ball up into the air, and thought, "My God, what a catch!" for he was an artist who loved his art. He grinned ruefully,

447

nodded good-bye to Fairford at the other end, and walked towards the pavilion.

The spectators clapped and roared applause at him, delighted with him because he had made ninety-four in the most important match of the season, because it was already in the Midday Cricket Special that his son, "a future member of the County Team," had been born at five o'clock that morning. A squad of cameras, professional and private, clicked as he came in at the gate and ran up the steps, smiling and acknowledging the applause. Half a dozen small boys were waiting for him with autograph books and pencils, but he pushed past them and ran inside.

"Bad luck!" Huddleston said to him. "You ought to have got a century to-day!"

"Oh well!" Frank was disappointed, but not enough to spoil his general sense of well-being. "What a catch! I never thought he'd get near it!" He kicked off the pad he had been unstrapping and wiped his hot face. "Do get me a drink, Jack!" He added, "You'd better get your pads on. I bet Watson doesn't last an over!"

Outside the pavilion, John Allworthy sat basking in the sunshine while Grace at his side burst into ejaculations of pleasure and interest. "Well! He's a grand cricketer, is Frank! They do reckon a lot to him, don't they? It was a pity he didn't get his century, poor lad! But there! You can't have everything! It's a fine little boy, a real beauty!" She had called at the Nursing Home on the way to the ground, and had been allowed a glimpse of the baby. She had described him half a dozen times to John, who was touched by her raptures, but hoped that the old wound was healed, and that Doris's child was all pleasure to her and no pain. His mind went back to the morning after the birth of his own child in the Maternity Hospital. He had been worn out by twenty-four hours of agonizing suspense, and wrung by the sight of his wife so exhausted that she had hardly been able to whisper or move her hand, only to smile with her eyes. He had barely taken in the baby, a little creased yellow thing in a shawl. It was only when he had gone back to his empty house and made himself some tea before going to work that the first pride of his short-lived fatherhood had stirred in him, and he had looked forward to his son growing up by his side, sharing his hopes and ardours, carrying on the good work. He had imagined his son a young man helping and admiring and following him, such a boy as Tom Sutton had been. Ah, Tom! At the thought of Tom, the sunny day was spoilt for him. The mention of Tom's name was enough to spoil anything, to stiffen his muscles and send a tide of black poison through his veins. All his life he had hated injustice and oppression, all his life he had fought hard and well against the other side, but never before had he really hated another human being.

"Good afternoon, Mrs. Allworthy! Good afternoon, John."

Allworthy looked up and saw Lionel Harding standing by his chair, with a little boy very much like him hanging on his arm. Wonderfully young-looking, Mr. Harding keeps, he thought, smiling at his old friend and opponent.

"I've come to ask a favour. My grandson, Jack, is a great admirer of Frank Varley and wants very much to have his autograph. He doesn't like to approach the great man himself, but we wondered if you would ask for him? Later on, perhaps, if you are seeing him!"

"Here's my book!" Jack exclaimed, thrusting an autograph book and a well-chewed piece of pencil into John's hands.

"I'll do that, Mr. Harding, with pleasure. I'll take him up now, I can see Frank in the window. He'd like to have a word with Frank himself, maybe."

Jack gave a little jump of excitement.

Frank had no particular objection to giving his autograph so long as he was not stopped on his way back from the wicket in the middle of the cheering spectators. He looked down with more than usual interest at the excited small boy. Perhaps in a few years' time Wilfred John Francis, whose names were already decided, would be a sturdy urchin running up and down this stand.

"You come along inside with me, sonny," Frank said. "I'll get you half a dozen autographs."

Inside! Into that holy of holies where the Yorkshire team sat and talked and smoked, where you could see them quite close to, hear them speak! Jack's face flushed from brow to chin, he caught the hand which Frank held out to him and gripped it firmly in both his small, hot paws. He looked up trustfully with his great clear eyes at this hero who had made ninety-four, this god who walked with other gods. Frank laughed and took him into the professionals' room.

Allworthy went back and found Lionel Harding in his seat, talking to Grace.

"Don't you move, Mr. Harding!" he said. He sat down in an empty chair on Lionel's other side.

"I was just asking Mrs. Allworthy, do you remember the old stand that used to be here before this one was built? The steel work of this was one of our jobs, you know. I was proud and pleased to have Robert Harding & Son up here on one of the girders! That was in my father's life-time when I was a young man. Must be thirty-five years ago, wasn't it?"

"Ah, I daresay. I didn't come to cricket matches much in those days."

"Didn't you? I've been ever since I can remember."

He could not have been more than six, he thought, when he came with his father to his first county match. This sleepy, sunny afternoon, the great green circle, the smell of tobacco and mown grass took him back to some of his earliest memories, to cricket matches that now seemed like the fabulous battles of giants. There were no cricket pros in the old days like Frank Varley. The old ones were more like gamekeepers or foremen, rougher, simpler, speaking with broad Yorkshire voices. The whole thing used to be more like a regiment, officers in charge, men keeping their distance. This fellow Varley was the new type, more sophisticated, probably thinking himself a cut above his family, although he was evidently on good terms with his uncle by marriage. Lionel meditated not for the first time on the infinite gradations, shiftings and adjustments in the British middle-class. He said to Allworthy,

"I hear you're not going to be unopposed in November?"

He saw Grace tighten her lips and clasp her hands together in her lap, till the knuckles showed white through the freckled skin.

"Some time since you've had to fight an election, isn't it? We've always looked on that as your ward. Long John's preserve, Conservatives keep off the grass! But somebody told me yesterday that the Left Wingers were putting up a candidate against you. Is it true?"

"Aye, it's true enough. It's Tom Sutton."

Lionel pursed his lips for a whistle. So that was the sequel to the Ward strike and the reason why Mrs. Allworthy looked like a cat defending her kittens! There was no bitterness like the bitterness of friends turned enemies! Grace was tearing her score card into small pieces with deliberate fingers. He thought, She'd like to do that to Sutton! He was sorry that he had blundered into a sore subject. He had worked hard and conscientiously on the Council for years, but had never lost the feeling that Municipal Elections were more than half a game. He perceived that this one was no game to his companions. To change the subject he said,

"That's my son Stephen's eldest boy that you've so kindly taken to Varley."

Grace relaxed and lay back in her chair.

"He's a fine little lad! You know, Mr. Harding, we think a lot of Stephen!"

"He says that you've been very good to him."

"We've been very glad to do anything we could. We haven't done aught but talk to him a bit and let him talk." Allworthy paused and said rather shyly, "I daresay it's a bit of a trouble to you him going the way he has. It stands to reason you won't see it the same way as we do. But we admire him for it."

How much, Lionel wondered, had that admiration weighed with Stephen? How much did vanity weigh with the educated young men who went Left? Easier to be remarkable on that side than on your own? But Stephen was not vain as men and human nature went. Ashamed of a thought which had perhaps been unfair to him, Lionel said quickly,

"I don't expect my children to think the same as I do.

451

I can even believe that they may be right and I may be wrong. But I'm too old to change my own coat."

John Allworthy said with a simplicity that disarmed offence, "You know, I've often wondered how your sort of folk feel about things. Does it seem right to you that you should live in good houses and our people live in slums? Do you reckon it's all right to have your three good meals a day when some families haven't but one and not always that? Or do you just not think about it?"

Lionel considered, puffing at his pipe.

"When I was young, I don't think most of us thought about it at all. Social consciousness has developed enormously since the War. Now, well, some of us still don't think. Perhaps none of us think as much as we ought. There are people who really haven't enough imagination to grasp any lives outside their own. Some of us think and are distressed and don't do anything. Perhaps because it's difficult to see what we can do, perhaps because we are convinced that the necessary things are being done by slow degrees and that it's dangerous to force the pace. I think, too, that we're often selfish and lazy and nervous of changes and afraid that other people's gain might be our loss. It's difficult to apportion motives, they're generally so mixed. I don't know that I could be sure of my own."

"I've sometimes wondered how you felt about it all. You don't mind my asking?"

"Of course not! We're old friends. Besides it's reasonable enough to ask a man what he stands for. I think that I believe in slow and natural growth, and change coming by general consent. I've a feeling that private property and private ownership and private enterprise are more in line with the fundamental needs of human nature than any of your planned production and State control. My chief objection to socialism and communism is that I think they're against nature."

"I don't think they're against nature, Mr. Harding. I think they're against habit, that folk often mistake for nature, especially," he gave Lionel a quick, gleaming smile, "if the habit's comfortable for them."

452

Lionel laughed.

"I daresay you're right. I'll agree with you on the main issue anyhow. More fair play for more people."

"I've sometimes thought you were half a Socialist!"

"I've no doubt the young hot heads say you are half a Tory nowadays, John!"

Before they could say any more, Jack came flying back and flung himself upon his grandfather, crying out,

"Oh. Look! Look! I've got six of them! Six! And I've spoken to Sutcliffe and Leyland!" He proudly displayed the green page in his autograph book which bore the scrawled signatures of the Yorkshire team.

Tom Sutton resigned from the Union in the month after the strike, left Ward's, and got a job with a smaller firm of ready-made clothiers, a firm run on old-fashioned lines under the management of one man, George Clarkson, whose father and grandfather had owned the business before him. The buildings were old-fashioned, the conditions were much less comfortable and convenient. Clarkson had difficulty in keeping his place in the flood of competition, and could not afford rest-rooms or Vitaglass. He had a conscience and did treat his employees as well as he could afford, sometimes better. A good many of them were non-Union men whose fathers had worked under his father, and whose private lives and family affairs were known to him. The whole atmosphere was more leisurely and personal than at Ward's. The proportion of nervous breakdowns and other illnesses among the women and girls working on the machines was smaller. The garments made were as good in quality and workmanship as Ward's, but cost more to produce and looked a little less slick. Tom saw that in ten or fifteen years' time Clarkson would be driven out of business by the increased efficiency and mechanization of his rivals. Clarkson's machines and method were out of date and would become more so every year. He could not afford to bring them up to date and he did not really want to. He was the type of sturdy, individual

Conservative who says, what was good enough for my father is good enough for me. He hated Ward with a jealous hatred, and had been extremely pleased about the strike, so that he felt an odd sympathy with Tom and was glad to take him on at once when he applied for work. Tom despised him for an old-fashioned, short-sighted fool, was drawn to him unconsciously by their mutual antipathy for Ward, and also liked more than he knew the pugnacious humanity in him. Clarkson interviewed Tom on his arrival and said,

"I'm told you're a dangerous Bolshevik and I'm a fool to employ you. Now don't you go making any trouble here. I don't have strikes in my works. We're not a modern octopus and I can't afford to have you holding me up for three weeks as you did Ward." He chuckled, and a flash of sympathy passed between them. "You understand," he repeated, "if you're not satisfied, you clear out. If you make any trouble, I shall know about it, and clear you out. You look to me like a sensible fellow. See if you can't behave like one." He liked the look of Tom, and at the bottom of his heart was the feeling that any man of spirit might be excused for striking against Ward. The very smell of that great place was inhuman, and Ward was an inhuman creature to whom his employees were machines to be kept in good order. George Clarkson saw with disgust the whole trend of modern business towards the mechanical and impersonal. He thought that you couldn't altogether blame a workman, especially a vigorous young man, for jibbing when he found himself not a person but an infinitesimal part of a machine.

He would have been surprised to know that Tom's feeling against Ward was pale and formal compared to his feeling against John Allworthy. Ward was the acknowledged enemy who had fought like an enemy and won. Hatred of him was a straightforward emotion, almost an obligation. John Allworthy was the friend who had turned enemy, the hero fallen from his pedestal, the leader who had betrayed his own side. He and not Ward was the man who had thwarted Tom and caused his brief spurt of successful leadership to end in a bitter and humiliating failure. It was Allworthy of whom Tom thought at night when he lay tossing in bed

454

and could not sleep, Allworthy who haunted his mind by day. His feeling for Ward was no more than itself. His hatred of John was personal, had strong tangled roots in the dark places of his mind, where wounded vanity, innate jealousy, and a fury of impotence nourished the unhappy growth. He could not keep John out of his mind. He made Harold Pearson tell him every scrap of news about him. He scanned the evening paper for any record of a remark made by him at a Council Meeting. John was an aching tooth from which he could not keep his tongue.

He was in this mood when some of the younger Labour men in the Central Ward came to him with an astonishing request. Would he stand for the Council to oppose John Allworthy? His lodgings were just inside the boundaries of the ward, a triangular division which had its broad base north of the river, but ran a point down into South Worbeck. They were determined to put up somebody. To them, as to Tom, Allworthy was the villain of the Ward strike, the real enemy of the working class. They realized that it would be difficult to throw him out. He had represented the ward for fifteen years. He was an institution, a public character. He was also in their eyes a traitor and a stumbling-block. "Reckon we've had enough of these old men calling themselves Labour men and working against us with the Conservatives," one young man said to Tom. "Allworthy's against the workers. He's got to go. It's known he took bribes from Ward to stop the strike."

"He never did!" Tom said contemptuously. He was still not prepared to pass that story. As if Allworthy would have needed a bribe to make him fight for his own position and importance, for the leadership of the Union!

"There's plenty saying he did!"

An obscure pleasure soothed the ache in Tom's heart, though he said again and firmly that the rumour was absurd. He told the deputation that he would think about standing for the Council. He thought about it seriously for three days. The strike had whetted his desire for affairs, and now that he no longer had Olive to think of, he badly needed some activity besides his work. If Clarkson would let him take time off for Council work, he would put in overtime to make it up, and forfeit some of his wage, as John Allworthy had always done at Ward's. He had occasionally thought of standing for the Council some day, had once talked it over with John. He had imagined himself standing for another ward, working side by side with Uncle John, his mentor and friend. That dream was forgotten now. There surged up in him a wild desire to attack John on his own ground and beat him, to thrust him out and take his place.

His motives were not all personal. Like a good many others of his kind, he had watched with a growing concern the progress of struggle. He had read in May of the fall of Addis Ababa, had rejoiced in the same month in the victory of the French Front Populaire, had groaned over the outbreak of the Spanish civil war. Sometimes he wished that he could go to Spain and fight with the men whom he thought of as friends and brothers, though he could not speak their language. At least he would not be out of the fight here. If he put up for the Council, he would be moving forward shoulder to shoulder with the men of Catalonia, with the Frenchmen who had rolled back the Croix de Feu, with the Russian workers building their new state. He would be marching in step with that great army, so ill-armed, so ill-equipped, facing such heavy odds.

Before giving a final answer to the deputation, Tom told George Clarkson that he was going to stand for the Council, and that he would make up any time that he took off for meetings, or forfeit his wages.

"Counting your chickens before they're hatched, aren't you?" Clarkson said, grinning.

Tom had never been teased in his life. He flushed, looked sulky, and muttered,

"I reckoned I'd mention it to you first."

"Very good of you, I'm sure. Which ward are you going to contest?"

"Central."

"Central! I thought there was a Labour man there already! Isn't that old Allworthy? Why—oh, I *see*!" Clarkson's shrewd eyes twinkled. "Well, it's your affair what you

456

do outside my works. I've told you I won't have any politics inside them. You can stand for Parliament in your spare time for all I care. If you do get on to the Town Council, I wish you'd get something done about the traffic in Station Square. I was nearly run over three times this morning." He nodded, "All right. Cut along, now."

Tom went, ruffled by an unsatisfactory feeling that neither he nor the Town Council were much more than a joke to Mr. Clarkson. At his club that day at lunch, Clarkson said to his neighbour,

"You know I've got that fellow Sutton in my place who made all the trouble at Ward's? He came to me this morning and announced that he was going to stand for the Council. Said very kindly that he wouldn't let me suffer for it."

"What, Sutton, the Communist who ran the strike? Good Lord, I wonder you employ him!"

"I rather like the rascal. He wants his head smacking every other day, but he's a first-rate workman. He's putting up against old John Allworthy. Matter of personal spite, I think."

"What a shame! Old John behaved like a Trojan over the strike, apparently. We don't want men like Sutton on the Council!"

"Oh, he won't get in, and a licking will do him good. Not that I think it would matter if he did get on the Council." Clarkson's tone held all the comfortable indifference of security. No vision of a universal, advancing army troubled his dreams. When, a minute later, someone at his table observed, "This business in Spain is getting pretty serious. Are you for or against the Government?" he replied, "The Spaniards always were a blood-thirsty lot. I don't suppose there's much to choose between them. I can't think *why* we always have roast beef at this club on Monday! I suppose it's to revive happy memories of the week-end!"

Mary was having high tea with the Allworthys in their kitchen. Grace had been out all the afternoon, and the fire in the sitting-room had burnt low. She had spread the cloth on the kitchen table, and sat behind the squat, brown tea-pot, her eager face thrust forward in the firelight, the unruly dark hair ruffling back over her ears.

"Pass up your cup, Mary. We aren't making a visitor of you, having tea in here. We carry it into the sitting-room for Mrs. Frank Varley."

"This is the best place in the world to have high tea," Mary observed dreamily. She had been out all day at a race meeting, and was drugged by fresh air to a comfortable sleepiness.

"Whenever I'm away and think of home and the West Riding, I think about this room with a great red fire burning, and the blue tea-cups on the table, and warm loaves on the dresser, and a smell of new bread."

"Well, there's no smell of new bread this afternoon, for I haven't had time to bake. But there's a home-made oven cake, one that Mrs. Jackson gave me this morning. She said, 'Now, Mrs. Allworthy, I know you like a bit of my baking so I've just slipped round with it.' She's a grand little woman, is Mrs. Jackson. John! Pass up your cup, you've time for another."

Allworthy glanced at the clock.

"I ought to be off by seven."

His tone was unenthusiastic, and Mary, glancing at him, thought that he looked yellow and worn and had grown much older since the strike.

"You're tired, Uncle John!"

"I'm getting old. It's time I made way for the younger men!"

"Stuff and nonsense!" Grace cried vigorously. "You're worth any ten of them! Just you remember that! There isn't one of them to hold a candle to you!"

She bustled him into his coat and muffler, and saw him off from the door with more than her usual tenderness. She came back to the table and poured herself out another cup of tea. She sipped it slowly, beating her other hand on her knee as she did when agitated. Presently she broke out,

"He's too old, now, to fight an election after all these years! And it's not only the election. It's what they're saying about him! Do you know they've put it about that he took money from Ward to stop the strike? Him that never reckoned anything to money in all his life without he thought I was going short of something I wanted! Him that's done more for the workers, aye and risked more, than any man in this town! As much as any man in England!" Her keen face began to work, she gulped a mouthful of tea, and said furiously, "If ever I set eyes on Tom, I'll give him a piece of my mind, I'll make him sorry he was born! Like a son he was in this house and coming here night after night when his mother died and he was a lad and lonely. He's a black traitor!" She put down her cup of tea and burst into tears.

In Mary's arms, with her head against Mary's shoulder, she sobbed,

"It's hard to have these things said about you and your good name taken away at the end of a life like his!"

"Nobody could believe that nonsense! Nobody in their senses!"

"Half the people in the world aren't in their senses. Mary, they believe anything they're told loud enough! Oh, I'm not romantic! I come of working-people and I know what they're like. There's many a house in the ward where I've been canvassing this afternoon where I could see they believed it. I saw Tom's picture in one house on the mantelpiece, the picture that was in the paper while the strike was on."

"That'll only be a few houses! Uncle John will romp home!"

Grace, drying her eyes, said soberly,

"I don't know that he will, Mary. There's a lot of feeling about the strike. And there's new people come into the ward since the last election, and plenty of people that'll vote for Tom just because he's a change. If he turns my old man out, it'll break his heart and mine too."

"He shan't! We'll work and work, and we'll get that story denied!"

"You can get a story denied, but once it's there, it's there. Folk remember the story because it was interesting and they don't remember the denying because it's dull."

Mary knew that that was only too true. She stroked her aunt's hair, comforting and consoling her. She could not

459

remember that she had ever before seen her cry, or heard her ready to admit the possibility of defeat. In a minute or two Grace drew away from her, blew her nose, jerked back her hair, and said briskly,

"There, now, love, I mustn't make you late. Your tea's got cold. Let's boil up the kettle again and you and I will have a fresh brew."

Mary was due at eight at a Chamber Concert at the University, where she had instructions to get an interview with Madame Kantz, the solo violinist of the evening. As she swung herself on to a tram to go up the hill, she wondered, as she wondered every time she went to a concert or public function, whether Stephen would be there. So many of her evenings were like this. Her heart beat violently as she drew near the hall or house, she searched the crowded building feverishly until she saw him, or realized with a sickening drop of disappointment that he was not coming. Sometimes she knew that he would be there, and then it was almost worse for both of them, the meeting that must seem casual, the hurried word or two, the horrible feeling of deceit and secrecy. It had been better in the summer when there was not so much going on in the town. They had met once or twice for a walk and had gone out together in his car. The afternoon or evening out of doors, though there were so few of them, had been more bearable than the snatched, hurried moments and half-hours at the end of Labour or Left Discussion meetings, in the Town Hall foyer at concerts. If it was difficult for her, Mary thought, it must be ten times worse for him. She was at least free. He went back from their unsatisfactory meetings to be the husband of Joy, to the life in which his established character, husband, brother, father, son, was there like a shell waiting for him to fit into it again. She knew that he often felt that he was behaving like a cad, that he was only happy and at peace when he was with her, and paid for those brief hours by a continual conflict and heart searching. He was surprised at himself, he had been

460

brought up hardly realizing that these things happened, certainly not expecting them to happen to him. He was bewildered by the whole new vision of life which had lately been presented to him, torn by his own departure in other ways from the tradition in which he had been brought up. I am the only person who can be any use to him just now, Mary thought, and I probably ought to clear out and leave him. He had spoken of getting Joy to divorce him. He had not spoken of his children, his parents, his friends and his sense of honour and loyalty, but Mary knew that they were all in his mind. He needn't do that, she thought, I would give him everything he wants without. But she knew that he would not hear of that, anyhow at present. He was as much afraid of making her suffer as she was of hurting him. These things were more complicated than they had sounded in the glib talk of Mary's friends. In ordinary provincial life, among Stephen's kind of people, you could not change a wife or take a lover without shaking the very foundations of your own and other people's existence.

The concert had just begun when Mary arrived. She slid quietly into a seat near the door. Looking round the room, she saw at once that Stephen was not there. She felt bitterly disappointed, but nearly relieved. She was almost glad not to have to deal with the emotions roused by a tantalizing glimpse in a public place. She began mechanically to make notes of people in the audience who would expect to be noticed. They were not arranged in rows, the floor of the hall was dotted with small tables at which groups of from four to five collected. Across the room, Mary saw Marjorie and Leslie Ward sitting together at a table in the corner. Leslie was fidgeting restlessly, bending and twisting his programme, and smoothing it out again, scraping his chair backwards and forwards across the floor in spite of indignant glances from the next table. Marjorie was hugging her fur coat round her over her long black frock, and looked bored and cross. Mary, who knew that she did not like music, was surprised to see her there.

As soon as the interval began, both Marjorie and Leslie got up with a look of relief. Leslie hurried over to the far corner of the room to a table hidden from Mary by a group who were standing up. Marjorie came to her, and flumped down in the seat beside her.

"I didn't think you'd be here," Mary said.

"I didn't want to come. I don't like concerts. But I had to. It's such a nuisance, Mary! I've got to try and do more things with Leslie! And I don't really want to do the things he does, and he doesn't want me. But mother and father say I must, because he's always about now with such awful people. Do you know the Unwins?"

"Yes, I've met them several times. But they're not awful, are they?"

"No, they wouldn't matter so much, but he gets to know other people through them. He's got a new friend called Harold Pearson, a Communist. He was one of the people at that Discussion meeting we once went to, do you remember? And he's quite a common person and he's in father's works! Not even in the office, just a workman! It's terribly awkward! And then there are one or two students at the University, a dreadful Jewish girl with greasy hair, and two young men. But I don't see how I can prevent him going about with anyone he likes, do you, Mary? He rushed off now as soon as the music stopped to speak to the Unwins, he's sitting at their table. And he was so angry on the way here this evening he wouldn't speak to me; and he drove so badly I thought we should have a smash! It isn't my fault! I don't want to spy on him! I don't believe he'd be so silly if there wasn't such a fuss about everything he does."

"No, I'm sure he wouldn't. Can't you say so to your father, discuss it with him? You're Leslie's generation. You could make him see Leslie's point of view, perhaps, without making him angry?"

"But I haven't got the same point of view as Leslie. I think you're often a bit Socialist when you first grow up, but you grow out of it as you see more of real life."

Billy Wilson, thought Mary, smiling inwardly.

"I meant, couldn't you make your father understand how Leslie naturally wants to go about alone and choose his

462

own friends, and how awkward it is for you to have to hang on to him?"

Marjorie looked doubtful.

"I don't know. I don't think I could. I can't talk to Father. He wouldn't think anything I said could be sensible. And you know Leslie does go and do very silly things!"

Mary could well believe it. Through a gap in the moving figures she caught a glimpse of Leslie between the Unwins, gesticulating furiously.

"He looks ill, I think."

"He's got so silly about food! He won't eat luxuries, and he says all our food is luxuries! And he won't use his car. He was driving mine to-night because Father made him take me in it. And oh, Mary! Do you know what he's going to do? He's going to work for that dreadful man, Sutton, at the election for the Town Council! He's been to two meetings, and I believe he made a speech at one of them. It was probably very silly if he did. But you *know*, Sutton was the man who made the whole strike! Well, of course you know, because he's trying to push your uncle out at the election. And he's a most awful man! He's a Communist!"

"No, he's not a Communist, he's Labour Party. I've known him for years. He's not really awful. He could be a fine person."

"Well, if he isn't a Communist he's something almost the same. You *can't* like him, Mary! He's been against your uncle all the time! Don't you want your uncle to win?"

"Yes." She did, and it was no use saying to Marjorie that that was a personal feeling, and perhaps the times needed people like Tom more than people like her uncle. She could not explain how sorry she was that the two were enemies when they should have been friends working side by side.

"Of course it's dreadful for father Leslie helping Sutton. I don't know what he'll do! He'll forbid it, of course, but Leslie doesn't always obey him nowadays. He's still afraid of him but," Marjorie wrinkled her brows, "I don't know. He's queer. It's as though something inside him was sort of driving him so hard that he even had to disobey father." She sighed. "I'm so tired of all these bothers! I wish I had

463

a very jolly ordinary brother who liked dancing and playing games."

There seemed little hope that Leslie would ever fulfil that old wish.

"I expect it's all very hard for him too," Mary suggested.

"Yes, I suppose so. But he makes his own troubles. That's what Billy, Billy Wilson you know, said to him the other day. Leslie was terribly rude! He said Billy was a pig with its eyes shut! I was so ashamed! But Billy was ripping about it. He just laughed and said to me afterwards that the poor kid was loopy. Sometimes I think he is a bit. But all the same, I don't think he ought to help Father's enemy."

It was quite clear that Marjorie had as she said grown out of being a Socialist, and that family feeling and Billy Wison were predominant.

"I suppose I must go back to him." Marjorie got up. "Is it a terribly long second half? I thought that first thing was never going to stop!" She felt that Mary was a little bit too much inclined to sympathize with Leslie's sufferings, and not enough with her own. She was, of course, very fond of Mary, but not in the way she had been. The lines of Mary's cheek and chin no longer made something inside her tremble with ecstasy. Mary's presence could no longer redeem a dull evening. Mary was nice and it was nice to see her, but glory had departed.

Leslie was still standing by the Unwins' table. He was just going to leave them, when he stopped, turned back and began to talk to them rapidly and disconnectedly about a book which they had lent him. His sentences tumbled out in nervous jerks, and he put a hand on Claud's arm in a rare gesture of affection. He had just caught sight of Angus Grant sitting at a table behind with the Allisons. He suddenly felt that he could not stay in the Hall any longer. Cutting short his conversation, he said a hasty good-bye and moved quickly across to his own table.

"Let's go home now, Marjorie," he said abruptly. "I've had enough."

Marjorie had had enough in the first ten minutes, but felt it due to herself to make some protest.

464

"We can't go now, in the middle! It will look so funny! She's just going to play again!"

"Yes, we can. It doesn't matter! Come on."

"Are you feeling ill or anything?"

"I've got a headache. I can't stick it any longer."

If she had been a little less bored with the music, Marjorie would have resisted, but the temptation to escape from another hour of tedium was too much for her. She let Leslie hustle her out of the room and round to the car park. She said firmly,

"I'll drive if your head's bad! You can sit still and shut your eyes."

"No, I'll drive. Like a gentleman taking a lady out for the evening!"

"You needn't try to sound sarcastic about it, just because you can't behave like one!"

Leslie gave what he meant for a sardonic laugh. Whether sardonic or not the laugh was irritating. Marjorie exploded.

"I think you're the limit! You know I didn't want to come with you to-night! First I've got to come to this stupid concert whether I like it or not, and then you drag me away in the middle!"

"You were enjoying the music so much, weren't you?"

"As much as you were, anyway! You were fidgeting all the time, you must have driven those people crazy at the next table. I wasn't pretending to enjoy the music—like some of those people were," she added, "but I don't like behaving oddly, and going about with people who do."

"You'd better stick to your complacent, bourgeois friends, then, Billy Wilson and so on—for the little time they've got left!"

"What do you mean the little time they've got left? Billy doesn't look like the sort of man that dies young!" Marjorie's tone was faintly regretful. It was undeniable that a shade more of that sort of thing would have improved Billy Wilson.

"Of course I don't mean that! I mean before they all get swept away in the world revolution."

"Who by?"

"The workers."

"Leslie, you're childish! You aren't a worker and Billy is. Father was saying yesterday that he was a good business man and had a head on his shoulders! If you tried to sweep him away, you'd much more likely get swept away yourself!"

Leslie, who was opening the door of the car to get in, slammed it to with violence. Everything had suddenly become too much for him. His constant attempts to live up to the Unwins, Angus's face smiling under the ruffled forelock, his father's displeasure, his own scared defiance, the world revolution and family squabbles in car parks all pressed too hard on his unstable spirit.

"Drive yourself home," he shouted. "I'll walk! I wish to God I needn't ever come home at all! I wish I was dead!"

He threaded his way between the cars and disappeared among the University buildings.

In spite of their long years of association, Ward hardly ever spoke to John Allworthy of anything in their private lives. John was surprised when at the end of a conversation about some payments for extra piece-work, Ward said abruptly,

"How are things going in your ward?"

"Well, of course, we haven't really begun yet. Nomination day isn't while Saturday."

"I suppose you'll beat him?"

John raised his light eyes to the face of his employer and old friend. He smiled and shook his head doubtfully.

"He's got a chance, has he?"

"I'm told the betting's two to one on him in the public-houses."

Ward was drawing on his blotting-paper straight lines like prison bars. He said without looking up,

"I hear he had a meeting on Sunday and my son spoke for him. It was against my wishes. Not that he's likely to help him much. More likely make a fool of Sutton as well as of himself."

Allworthy looked at the bent head and moving hand with a feeling of compassion. He said gently,

"Mr. Leslie's only a lad. When you're young you're all for those that tell you they'll get things done quickly. He'll learn patience."

Ward laid down the pencil.

"Well!" He nodded dismissal and John went out.

Ward asked for a number and was presently speaking to the Secretary of the Conservative Association. The voice at the other end of the line received his proposition doubtfully.

"Well, I really don't know, Mr. Ward. We've never bothered our heads about the Central. Left it to old John, really. It's never seemed worth while wasting powder and shot on it. Of course, as you say, the split Labour vote makes a difference. If we'd thought about it sooner! But it's nomination day on Saturday and to-day's Wednesday. I don't know where we could get hold of a strong candidate. It must be someone living or paying rates in the division, as of course you know. And it's been a solid Labour ward for years. It would need a pretty good man to do anything, even with the split vote. Can you think of anyone?"

"If I can," Ward said, "I'll give you a ring in the morning."

He opened his desk and searched in a private drawer which he had not opened for some time. He had used it when he was on the Council for papers about Council business. It still held the minutes of meetings in his last session, notes for committee business, a few newspaper cuttings and a photograph of the Housing Committee taken outside the first completed house on one of the new estates. Tucked underneath these he found what he was looking for, a map on which he had marked in blue pencil the outlines of the different wards. He studied the Central Division for some time, the broad upper part of the triangle which took in a good many of the principal offices in the middle of the town, the tapering point that ran down below the river into South Worbeck. The map proved uninspiring. No name suggested itself to him. He put the map away in the drawer and rang for his car. He usually lunched in his own room or in the Staff Dining Room, but he had a meeting at the Station Hotel at two-thirty, and thought that he might as well lunch there first.

Leaning far back in the big car, he was driven through the streets without seeing them until, at the corner of Prospect Street, the car stopped in a line of traffic, waiting for the lights to change. The small check fretted Ward. He leaned forward impatiently and so caught sight of a man who ran down the steps from the doorway of a block of offices. It was Robert Harding, who seemed to have come from some interview that had amused him. He was smiling, he looked alert and cheerful. He was on his way to lunch at that club which would certainly have black-balled Ward if he had ever been put up for it. Ward spoke down the tube and opened the door of the car. He called out,

"Mr. Harding! I want a word with you. Will you come and have lunch with me?"

Robert was so much astonished that he accepted and got into the car.

"I have a proposition to make to you," Ward said. "I'll wait till we're having lunch, if you don't mind. We shall be getting out in a minute."

He relapsed into silence in his own corner. Robert, who thought this a queer do, and was amused and intrigued, suddenly perceived that his host was shy. He himself did not often suffer from that disability. He began a conversation about the weather and the war in Spain, and sustained it until they were both sitting at a table in a corner of the French restaurant and Ward had ordered lunch. It was a very elaborate lunch, far removed from the chop and pint of beer which Robert had been contemplating. It was the sort of lunch that Sales Managers gave to Borough Surveyors. He thought that Ward must want something, and waited with interest to hear what it was.

They had finished their oysters and were waiting for their trout before Ward said, "Do you take any interest in politics?"

"Oh, a bit, you know. You can hardly help it nowadays, can you? So many dictators about."

"Have you ever thought of standing for the Council?"

Robert smiled and shook his head.

"Your father did many years' work on it."

468

"Yes. Well, I suppose I might perhaps have a shot at it some day if I got the chance."

"I am authorized to offer you a chance now."

"Good Lord! I thought it was all settled for this year! Why, it's nomination day on Saturday, isn't it?"

"Yes. There's still time. It's the Conservatives of the Central Ward want you to stand for them, Mr. Harding. Your offices are in that ward, you know."

"The Central Ward? Isn't that old John Allworthy's? Oh, I don't want to try and push him out! Why, he and my father were knocking spots out of one another on the Council for years! My father's awfully fond of old John."

"It won't be you who will push him out. You've heard of Tom Sutton?"

"What, the Bolshie fellow who ran the strike in your works? Is he standing?"

"They say he's going to win."

"I see." Robert, being no fool about personal matters, did see. The conflict and bitterness of the strike was being carried into the Municipal election. Sutton, the ringleader, and John Allworthy, the Union man, fighting out the second round. Ward, of course, against Sutton, bringing in an outsider to beat him, which would be a good job if it could be done, for Sutton was the kind of fellow who did a lot of harm, getting all those poor, ignorant beggars into trouble, making them live on their savings for three weeks, and stirring up bad feeling.

"Do you really think Sutton's going to carry it?"

"John Allworthy told me so himself this morning."

"Poor old John!" Robert considered. "I shouldn't be much good, you know! I've no experience, and there isn't much time. Can't you find anybody better?"

"Your family is very well known and respected in the town, Mr. Harding. Your father was on the Council for years. You'll soon pick up the ropes. Your agent will put you in the way of things."

"Your agent" sounded rather good to Robert. He smiled at Ward.

"I must just think about it a minute."

Looking at the alert, sunburnt face, the eyes merry even in repose, the square shoulders, the lively turn of the head, Ward surprised himself by thinking, I wish this was my son. How was it that he, who had fought his way up in the world from the very bottom without help, should have fathered such a son as Leslie, a weak boy who picked up every sentimental idea as surely as he had picked up every childish ailment? Marjorie should have been the boy! Once when she was about fifteen she had wanted to come into the business, and both he and her mother had crushed the notion. Mrs. Ward thought it unladylike, and he wanted an idle, pretty daughter to run about and enjoy herself as one of the badges of his achievement. Now he half wished that he had encouraged her. He brought his mind back from his own family to his companion.

"I suppose I could make time for the meetings. That is, if I got in. But I probably shouldn't. It's always been a Labour Ward. Really, I suppose they just want someone to have a shot at it and take a few votes off Sutton?"

Twisting his lips to the unfamiliar language which seemed most likely to serve his purpose, Ward said,

"I think you might not get in this time, seeing you come in at the last minute. But it's a sporting chance."

Robert's brown eyes sparkled a little more brightly.

"All right!" he agreed. "I don't mind having a crack at it. It might be rather fun!"

To most of the inhabitants of Aire, the announcement of a Fascist march and demonstration in the city on the third Sunday of October was not vitally interesting. There was a general impression that Fascists were a bit funny, rather tiresome, and somehow foreign. Those who had read the newspaper accounts of the Olympia meeting, and the letters that followed it, did not even think Fascists funny. Things had happened at that meeting at which English people, who laughed at nearly everything, could not laugh.

Robert, glancing at his paper, said to Beryl, "Oh, those

damned Fascists are marching through on Sunday. If we're going over to tea at home, we'd better start in good time, or we shall get held up." Herbert Walters read the news out of the evening paper to Mabel, who said, "Well, who wants to see them, anyway? If it's a fine afternoon, Herbert, let's go up to the Park and have our teas at the café. It'll do Doreen good to get a breath of fresh air. She's looking a bit poorly since she had that cold." She added as an afterthought, "What are these Fascists?"

"Same as the Germans," Herbert said vaguely.

"Well, we don't want any Germans over here, nor Russians neither. What do they want to march for?"

"It's Oswald Mosley thinks he ought to govern the country. Like another Mussolini."

"One's enough! It's a lot of silliness, if you ask me, and idle lads that want to dress up. Reach me down my workbasket, Herbert. There's a button coming off your coat."

The Chief Constable of Aire gave orders to the police to divert the Fascist march from the Jewish quarters, ordered that the anti-Fascist march should proceed to the demonstration by another route, drafted a supply of extra police into South Worbeck, where the demonstration was to be held, and hoped against hope that everyone would be good, satisfying themselves with noise and speeches.

Harold Pearson, who was actively engaged in organizing the counter-demonstration, began to think that he could have got on very much better without the help of Leslie Ward. Leslie wept tears of rage because the Chief Constable did not forbid the Fascist march. He seemed to want Harold Pearson to arrange for barricades across the street to stop it. He would interrupt the details of the arrangements by breaking out into childish bursts of anger against Oswald Mosley, against Fascism. The discreet Harold spoke to Mrs. Unwin about him. He was in constant fear that Leslie, who now went about proclaiming himself a Communist, would do something outrageous and useless, and bring the party even further into public disfavour. They were being so careful, speaking so soberly, publishing the mildest manifestoes, trying in every possible way to soothe and appease the nerves of

471

the great solid mass of English people who still shied at the word Communist. You could raise an anti-Communist scare among them as easily as you could once have raised a scare of no Popery! Harold asked Mrs. Unwin to speak to Leslie Ward and persuade him to be reasonable.

He sighed as he walked away from the Left discussion meeting at which he had seen her. He did not want the Fascist march. He knew perfectly well what would happen. The Fascists would march to South Worbeck Moor, escorted by the police, and the anti-Fascists would march to another part of South Worbeck Moor, escorted by the police. Both parties would make speeches. Stones would be thrown at the Fascist speakers by a few unauthorized enthusiasts, or by some roughs and small boys who enjoyed throwing stones. The Fascists would retaliate by knocking about some members of the audience who had not thrown any. The police would make several arrests among the audience. Next day there would be articles in the papers about an assault on the Fascists made by Communists, and the British public, who did not naturally like Fascists at all, would swing a little towards them because they imagined that they had not been allowed free speech and a fair hearing. Harold felt all the anxiety of a general who is entering a town at the head of his army and wonders if he will be able to restrain his soldiers, and still more his camp followers, from looting.

"Me brother is coming over to see t'Greenshirts!" Rosie informed Beryl on Saturday evening.

"Greenshirts? Do you mean Blackshirts? Your brothers aren't Fascists, I hope, are they?"

"Well, they 'aven't not to say signed a pledge or owt like that. But there was a man come to Huldholme to speak in the schoolroom, about a place in America or Canada or such-like, Albert, it was called, and 'e ses if we only 'ad these Greenshirts or Blackshirts in the government we'd all be getting a bonus, like. As well as our wages, you know, at the end of every week."

"Did he say where the money was coming from?"

"Oh, it's in t'banks. Me sister's husband's brother, you know, 'e's a Labour man, and 'e ses t'banks is cause of all t'trouble. But if we all 'ad a bonus every week it would be a bit of all right!"

"You know, Rosie, I think your brothers have got mixed. It's the Greenshirts, not the Fascists, that talk about bonuses."

"Eh, well it's all t'same, any road! When I see any of 'em do owt but talk, I'll join 'em. A lot of daft Daniels! Me and Fred's going over to Long Tor to-morrow on the tandem with a coople we met at the tea place last week."

Frank Varley, coming home from a day's travelling round sports outfitters, went upstairs to the spare bedroom, which was now a nursery, with the evening paper folded under his arm. Doris was giving Wilfrid John Francis his bath. Flushed, with her fair hair ruffled, and a rubber apron over an old frock, she concentrated on the small, firm, white body. Without looking up she said, "Have you had a good day?"

He told her, but he did not think she listened to the answer. She was anxiously studying a patch of roughness on the child's shoulder.

"I do hope he isn't going to start eczema."

"I've told you you will eat too many sweet things! You want more fruit and vegetables."

Her lips shut in an obstinate line. She spread a warm towel on her lap and lifted her son out on to it. It outraged her primness that Frank should think about these things, and annoyed her that he should criticize and make suggestions, instead of petting and pitying her for her anxieties and exertions over the child.

Frank looked down at the baby's head. The fine hairs were ruffled up by the towel, the skin showed faintly pink through them from Doris's rubbing. He was proud of his son and delighted with him, but there were times when he grudged him the whole of Doris's attention. There seemed to be a union in the house of mother and child, enclosed together in a warm, secret, sensuous love which reached its apotheosis when the baby was feeding, his lips intent at her breast, her face drowsy and intent above him. At those times Doris and the baby were as one person. Frank felt an undefined jealousy, the more so as he had never achieved such union with her, she was a stiff and nervous lover.

He opened the paper and remarked that there was to be a Fascist march and demonstration in Aire on Sunday.

"How silly!" Doris said abstractedly. "I wanted to take Baby to tea at Mother's! Will the streets be blocked?"

"Oh, I shouldn't think so! They'll have gone through before we get there." He added, moved by an obscure desire to assert himself, "All this marching is silly, right enough, and we don't want a Fascist government. Well, of course, it's absurd, we never should have one in England, but there's a lot to be said for what Hitler has done in Germany for the nation! Why, look at the Olympic Games!"

Doris was putting on the baby's little flannel night-gown, warm from the fire. She said with complete indifference, "Yes, I dare say. Would you like to go down, dear, and see if she's begun laying the table? I shan't be long?" She liked to get him out of the room while she fed the baby. Not only did it seem to her more suitable, but Wilfrid John Francis was more her own if she was entirely alone with him.

Marjorie Ward said uneasily to Billy Wilson, "You know, I daren't say anything to Father, but I believe Leslie's going to join in a demonstration against the Fascists on Sunday. He's got his car out again and had it greased and filled up, and he's very solemn and important! I'm sure he's planning something."

Billy privately thought that that was just the sort of tom-fool thing Leslie would do.

"Can't you talk sense to him, Marjorie? Make him see that it plays into their hands to take any notice of them? I mean, these demonstrations are neither here nor there, anyway, but we don't want Leslie getting hit on the head by some tough in a black shirt. Can't he *see* that the whole thing's poppycock? Fascists will never cut any ice in England!"

Shears, the secretary of the Conservative Association, made the same comment on the Friday before the nomination day. He was lunching with Ward to discuss the prospects of the election.

"It was a stroke of genius, Mr. Ward, you thinking of young Harding. Of course he's had no experience, but with the name and his father's reputation he ought to stand a

474

good chance, and he's a good speaker, I'm told, and he seems to have an attractive personality. I'm sorry for John All-worthy! This tale about you bribing him—it's a dirty trick!"

Ward nodded.

"I shouldn't let your candidate hear about that if you can help it. It will mean some votes for him, and if he found that out, he might make difficulties."

Laycock, the agent, who was lunching with them nodded.

"We shan't encourage the rumour, of course. I daresay he'll never hear it. Young men of that stamp don't know half of what goes on under their own noses."

"What do you think of the chances?"

"Well, it's an outside chance. A ward that's been Labour for fifteen years doesn't go Conservative as easily as all that, but we've got a likely horse. With their own side pulling two ways, they may get fed up with trying to decide between them, and just not vote at all, and let our man in."

"I should stress the fact that Tom Sutton, during the three weeks of the strike, practically made himself a dictator. Once get the word fixed on to him, and he'll lose half the votes in the ward."

Laycock nodded.

"That's right. The English people won't put up with dictators."

"I'll have a word with the Press. The *Guardian* will back Harding, of course, without any pressure. I'll see to the others."

The Secretary and Agent, who knew that Ward was the largest advertiser in both evening papers, nodded. Laycock said,

"He ought to do well enough with you behind him, Mr. Ward."

Ward said deliberately,

"I'm going to see he wins this seat."

He pushed back his chair.

"If you'll excuse me, gentlemen, I have to catch the London train. Don't let me hurry you. Stay here and finish your cigars."

He called for the bill, paid it, nodded to them and went out.

Laycock and Shears immediately relaxed in their chairs.

"Have a brandy with your coffee, Mr. Laycock?"

"Well, thank you, Mr. Shears. I don't mind if I do."

"Wonderful fellow, old Ward! We shall pull off this election."

"Think so?"

"Sure. I've never known him to fail to pull off anything yet. You'd be surprised if you knew how many things in this town he was at the back of. There's a lot of personal feeling in this, of course. Naturally he doesn't want Sutton on the Council."

"It's true enough what he said. The fellow did almost make himself a dictator. That's our line."

"Scratch a Socialist and you find a dictator! Here's your very good health!"

"And yours! And luck to Robert Harding!"

"I see there's a Fascist march on Sunday."

"Busy day for the police! I'm hoping to get a round of golf on Sunday. I haven't played much lately. I've had my wife's people staying with me."

"Have you ever met a Fascist, Mr. Shears?"

"Not that I know of. Not a real one. I believe my nephew fancied himself one for a bit after he came back from Germany. Do you know any?"

"No. I don't think they flourish very much in these parts."

"We've more sense up here. It'll never take in England. Well, I must be getting along. Thank you for the brandy. Good day to you!"

"Good day, Mr. Laycock. Good luck for the election."

It seemed to Leslie that Sunday lunch would never come to an end. He ate a few vegetables, crumbled his bread and fidgeted in his chair. The mannerisms of his family got on his nerves, the way his father cut up everything on his plate before beginning to eat, Marjorie's habit of pushing back her hair behind her ears, his mother's trick of lifting her glass with her little finger sticking straight out. He dared not get up and go in the middle of the meal, he could sometimes defy his father on large issues but never on small ones. It was Ward's custom to sit on alone for a few minutes drinking a glass of port. Leslie, who did not like port, generally went out with his mother and sister. As he was getting up eagerly to go, Ward said,

"Stop a bit, Leslie. I want to speak to you."

Almost choking with impatience, Leslie sat down again.

Ward did not speak at once. He cracked a nut, filled his glass and pushed the decanter towards Leslie.

"Like a glass of port?"

"No, thank you, sir."

Ward raised his own glass and sipped slowly.

"I hear you're a Communist, nowadays!"

"Yes." Leslie, a little sustained by consciousness of heroism, stared at him with bright, nervous eyes.

"Ah." Ward sipped again, unmoved, his face inexpressive. "They tell me you're helping—or trying to help—Sutton with his election campaign?"

Leslie could not speak. He gulped and nodded.

Ward put down his glass.

"If you're going to be a Communist, you'd better do the thing properly. A poor Communist is a fool. A rich Communist is a fraud. I'd rather see my son a fool than a fraud. If you wish to go on with this nonsense, I shall stop your allowance. I shall no longer pay your fees at the University, and you will no longer live in this house. I shall not allow your mother or sister to help you with money."

"But—what shall I do?" Leslie cried, entirely dumbfounded.

"Work. Earn you own living."

Leslie stared at him. "But——"

"You've made speeches about the workers, I reckon. You'd better be one. Then you'll have a right to speak."

Afterwards Leslie longed to have said, "Very well, sir," in dignified acceptance. He did say, in a high, quavering voice,

"I—I haven't got a start at anything!"

"I'd no start at anything when I went to work at eleven years old. I'd no breakfast the first morning I went. There wasn't any food in the house. You're nineteen. I've given you what they call a good education. I'll give you ten bob for a send-off so that you can have breakfast the first week."

The cold brutality of the last sentence stung Leslie into a rare retort. He said,

"It's not my fault you brought me up differently!"

"That's true enough. I'm not blaming you for my folly. I'm talking about yours. You can take a week to decide."

"I can't change my opinions."

"I'm not asking you to change your opinions. You can think what you like. You'll stop calling yourself a Communist, keep away from political meetings and make no speeches, or you leave my house and the University and keep yourself. What are your opinions worth till you've earned your living? Why, a decent Labour man, a man like John Allworthy, would laugh at you! If you'd any real principles, you wouldn't touch my capitalist money. Well, you'd better think about it, and I'll speak to you again next Sunday. That's all."

He nodded dismissal. Humiliated, quivering with rage, on the verge of tears, Leslie rushed out of the room. He stood in the hall, hardly able to think or see. He clenched his fists until his finger-nails drove into his palms, and muttered childishly again and again, "You beast, you beast, you beast!" He was like somebody badly wounded and not yet able to feel the place or extent of the wound. He did not know how far his political theories had been a platform from which he could look down on his father. The blow went deep because the platform had been made unreal. In one sick, shamed moment he had known that he was not willing to give up his home, his comfort, most of all his security, for an idea. The idea had been all that he could pride himself on, and it was not real. He did not admit this, but he had felt it. He stood staring at the great bank of hot house flowers in the hall. He felt that he would never, never be happy again. In some way, the vivid, opulent beauty of the flowers accentuated his misery, they were the external world that linked his torment with reality. He was never to see a begonia again in his life without a sick feeling.

478

The clock striking two recalled him to immediate necessities. He had almost forgotten the anti-Fascist demonstration, but whatever he decided at the end of the week,—he was not going to admit to himself that the decision had already been made,—he supposed that he must go on with his duties that afternoon. He had arranged to pick up Harold Pearson, drive him to the starting point of the anti-Fascist demonstration and see it off, then go on ahead of it to South Worbeck Moor and wait for its arrival. After that, he was to be at hand with his car to take anyone anywhere that was necessary. Harold Pearson had not, like Claud Unwin, hinted that the car might be useful; he had said, "Can't you bring a car?" and when Leslie explained his conscientious objections about using it, had said that it would be all right for this afternoon, and whenever it was wanted for the party.

Leslie grabbed his hat and coat from the peg and ran round to the garage. He had turned the engine over that morning and the car started without any difficulty. To be in it and driving again soothed him a little, he had always been happy in his car, feeling himself master of something that ran smoothly and obeyed his touch.

He turned from the drive into the road, his resentful thoughts ticking over like the speedometer. Why should I be in his power just because he has money, why should things always be in the power of the people who have money? Oh, God, why can't I tell him to go to hell and walk out and find a job? I can. I will! I'll go to the Unwins, and they'll put me up. They couldn't keep me for long, they're hard up. Money again, always money that decides! It's because I've got none that I can't go. I am going! I shall be free of him! I shall be happy. I shall really be a worker and belong to the new world! What can I do? I cannot dig, to beg I am ashamed. That comes somewhere in the Bible. But I expect I could find a job. I'll ask Pearson. I could be in an office. I don't think I should mind the work, it's the awful sort of house I should have to live in and the beastly places where I should have meals, and never feeling safe, not knowing if I should keep my job. It's the same for all of them! I ought to be able to do it! But I mind things they don't! I haven't had the same start.

It's his fault! It wasn't fair! He brought me up to be a gentleman, and not to go to work young! He's always wanted us to spend money and have everything, what Mother, when she's sentimental, calls "Heaping kindnesses on us." But it was because that showed how well he'd got on. He likes Marjorie a bit, he's never loved me. And how he's got me in a trap! I'll get out! I'll walk out of the house and find a job! I can't! He knows I can't! He knows I'll give in. Oh, God! I won't! I'll starve, and let everyone know how it happened!

To arrive at the Park where the anti-Fascist demonstration was collecting, and to see Harold Pearson shoving it into place with his usual air of the churchwarden at a school treat, was like waking up to the morning after a long, bad dream. Harold Pearson came up to the car and said, "That's right, Comrade. We're a little late starting. We're just waiting for the Youth Peace Group. It seems they've made a mistake and gone to another part of the Park. I want to take Mrs. Fairhurst down with us, one of the speakers from the Women's Labour Movement. She's a very fine speaker, she always makes a very nice contribution. Just draw in to the side a little, will you! Do you know the Reverend Forrester? He's another of our speakers. And we've the Minister from Claverley Road. A very good representative gathering!"

Rosie's brothers, Len and Don, bicycled into Aire on that Sunday afternoon, looking hopefully for a procession of Greenshirts or Blackshirts who would, if adequately supported, add a bonus to their weekly wages. They had very little idea about the procession, except that they supposed it would be accompanied by at least one band. At the corner of a street, they came upon an orderly array of marching men and women, escorted as usual by one or two policemen. At the head of the procession, two men carried a large banner on which were inscribed the words, "For Democracy, Peace and Liberty."

There were other banners behind, with various inscriptions

of the same kind. A group of women carried a banner inscribed, "For Equal Citizenship." There was a banner which said, "To each According to His Need," although it flapped in the wind so much that it was rather difficult to read the words. There were various slogans which included the word Peace, and one large banner which was inscribed, "Peace and Plenty for All."

"That's them!" Len observed to Don. They waited for the straggling tail of the procession, and joined in. It was rather amusing for a time to ride at the pace of the marching men without falling off.

"Where's t'barn?" Len shouted to a man in the rear ranks, who fell back to tie his bootlace.

"To t'Moor. South Worbeck Moor."

The anti-Fascist march pursued its way along the prescribed streets through the dead and deserted Sunday afternoon town. A few girls and boys, waiting for trams, glanced at them indifferently. Here and there a family party, on its way to Grandma's or the Park, paused on the pavement, and observed, "Is't t'Blackshirts?" "Nay, it's t'oother lot," and went on without looking back. At one tram stop, Mabel and Herbert were waiting with Doreen. As the moving ranks of men went past them, Mabel clutched at Herbert's arm.

"Look, Herbert! There's Tom! There's Olive's Tom that used to be! Don't you see? There, walking in front of those men!"

Doreen jumped up and down.

"Wheer, mother? Wheer's Uncle Tom?"

"Where's Uncle Tom. Not 'wheer's'! There he is, just going past."

"What is he doing?"

"Walking in a procession."

"Why?"

"Well—you see, some other people that he doesn't like are marching in a procession too."

"Why are they?"

"You explain to her, Herbert," Mabel said hastily.

Herbert cleared his throat. His daughter's small, pale face was turned up to him, her eyes trustful, her mouth a little open to receive the worm of information.

"Well, it's like this, Doreen, some men called Fascists, Blackshirts, think if they keep on walking in processions they'll get what they want."

"What do they want?"

"Er—well, they want to make England like Germany. And Tom and some more people think if they walk in processions they'll be able to stop them."

"Don't they want to make England like Germany?"

"No, love, they want to make it like Russia," Mabel put in, with a sudden recollection of Tom's visits and conversations.

Doreen looked puzzled.

"Has it *got* to be like anywhere?"

"Certainly not," Herbert said firmly. "There's a lot more people don't want it like either of them, but they don't walk in processions, that's all. See, here's our tram."

Doreen's eyes followed the retreating figures of the anti-Fascists. She said eagerly,

"Daddy! If you tied your handkerchief on to your walking stick, we could have a procession when we get to the Park."

The procession crossed the river by the Victoria Bridge, and wound down into the industrial part of the city between the grim fronts of warehouses, or the high walls of yards, past rows of dingy terrace houses, past derelict spaces on which houses had recently been pulled down. Here was a church, its stone so blackened by soot that it was impossible to tell the original colour. Here an exquisite Queen Anne house of smoke-blackened red brick stood back from the road, once a gentleman's country house, now offices, or flats. Here a dismal-looking pub or a cinema with flaring posters offered pleasure to the neighbourhood.

Len and Don were getting bored. It was tiring to ride at a slow pace for such a long time. There was no band with the procession. Nothing seemed to happen. Glancing through an open gateway into a yard, Len saw some men moving about near a shed. They had sticks and were urging on a terrier. A rat hunt!

"Come on, Don!" Len cried. He wheeled and rode his bicycle into the yard, which was a long, narrow, open space with a gate at the far end.

The owners of the terrier were proud of her and had no objection to gate crashers. Len and Don spent an absorbing ten minutes. At the end of that time, there was a noise of trampling feet at the far end of the yard. One of the men opened the gate opposite to that by which Len and Don had come in. A procession was going past, men, some of them in black shirts, carrying banners.

" 'Ere's t'Blackshirts!" someone said.

Len looked up, surprised.

"What, more on 'em?" He nudged his brother. "Sitha, Don! 'Ere's some more o't' procession!"

Don, who was poking about with a stick under the wall of the shed, replied easily,

"Oh, t'hell with t'ruddy processions!" He cocked a bright eye appealingly at the owner of the terrier. "Let's put 'er in again!"

Stephen, walking with some of the Labour Party representatives behind a banner labelled, "For Peace and Democracy," thought, Is this any use? He was obliged to feel this about so many of the things that he did nowadays, and yet not to do them meant to join that great inert mass, whose apathy might allow the old world to suffocate the new that was stirring in its womb on the eve of birth. It was absurd and pointless to walk in a procession through an indifferent town on a fine Sunday afternoon. But it was those indifferent millions in Germany and Italy that had allowed reaction to win. It was better to be absurd and walk in processions, to fling one's tiny scrap of weight on the right side. To do nothing was to help the old world. In that twilight of the Gods, only the conscious could be born again. The inert and unconscious slid back when they could not stand still, adding their weight, without knowing it, to the terrible, dragging power of the frightened.

The man next to Stephen was an old soldier whose chest was covered with medals put on for the occasion.

"It's a long way to Tipperary!" he said cheerfully. "I'm getting a bit stiff in the joints from marching."

"I could do with a drink!" Stephen said.

His companion grinned in agreement.

Their feet rose and fell on the dry, dusty street. How odd to think of Joy now taking the children to Sunday tea at Mill Hall, Robert and Beryl going there, the family all sitting at the long dining-table, thinking, "Silly ass, Stephen!" or perhaps, "Poor Stephen, I hope he'll get over it," and some of them thinking, "Poor Joy!" and no wonder! Robert there, excited and amused about the election, so happy and sensible and well adjusted to life, anyhow to the life in which he had been brought up. Robert first interested in politics because he felt obliged to argue with Stephen. Robert, upright and simple, a piece ready to be moved by Ward upon the board because Stephen had given him the little push that sent him into action. For every man or woman who consciously takes action, one of the unconscious takes action or is taken by action. Every Redshirt makes a Blackshirt, every Blackshirt makes a Red. Stephen's feet, moving up and down on the setts within the tram rails, beat out the refrain that jingled in his mind. Every Redshirt makes a Black. Every Blackshirt makes a Red. Every Redshirt makes a Black—Black. . . . Black. . . . Black. . . .

It soothed Leslie more than he knew to be in the company of Harold Pearson, who was certain of what he wanted to do himself, and of what he wanted everyone else to do. As they drove down to South Worbeck Moor by a series of back streets, Leslie would have liked to consult him about his own urgent problem. He was prevented because they had two speakers, strangers to him, in the back seat, and because Harold Pearson extracted some sheets of paper scribbled with notes from his pocket, and was preoccupied with them. He had made out a complete time table for the whole afternoon, the only flaw being that he could not be certain that the Fascist demonstration would work out according to plan. Like a good general, he could only guess and hope to guess right.

Just as they were getting out of the car, Leslie, not unconscious of martyrdom, did manage to say to him,

"My father doesn't want me to help in Sutton's campaign. He says he'll turn me out of the house if I do."

Harold smiled as at a paternal joke, but said at once, "Well, you'll have to leave it be, then, won't you?"

"Do you think so?" Leslie asked, surprised.

Harold was not sorry to have a chance of disposing of Leslie's rather embarrassing assistance.

"Of course," he said. "You can't go against your father too much while you're living in his house, can you?"

There it was again, that infuriating insistence on the economic basis of the situation! All Leslie's sore and humiliated feelings returned in full force. He would have felt better if Harold would have counselled heroics and petted and admired him as a victim. Harold was much too full of affairs to do anything of the kind. He looked at the list in his hand and said briskly,

"Now will you go to the Upper Worbeck Labour Club and fetch two of the speakers that are waiting there? Comrade Godlove, you go along too in the car and show Comrade Ward the way. You know where the Club is, don't you? It's off Geldart Road."

Leslie thought indignantly that all that fellow Pearson wanted was to make use of him! He took an instant dislike to Comrade Godlove, a dark young Jew with intensely bright eyes, who bounded into the car as though it belonged to him, and said "Off we go!" quite unnecessarily as it started. Are these the sort of people, Leslie thought, that I'm giving up everything for? He was not at all sociable with Comrade Godlove on the way to the Labour Club.

Mary walked beside her Aunt Grace in the deputation from the Women's Labour Movement. Aunt Grace, for all

485

her sixty-seven years, stepped out briskly, like a light infantryman, her nose and chin pointing the way for the women who followed her, her scarlet hat their oriflamme. I should not care to be a Fascist, Mary thought, and run across Aunt Grace!

"Your mother's not alone this afternoon?"

"No. Doris and Frank are going to tea and taking the baby."

"I should like to have seen him! He's a grand little lad! But Frank doesn't like coming to our house much."

"He's a silly ass, then!"

"Nay, he's canny. He'll get on." Grace laughed without malice. "He can't abide me. His sort don't like women that have ideas and make speeches and get things done. They're frightened of being pushed off the top. There isn't all that much difference between Master Frank and Mosley's men or the Nazis. You can't be generous if you're frightened. Why, a good-humoured fellow like Frank would bite like a rat in a trap if he saw his privileges going!" She sighed and added wistfully, "But I'd like to have seen the baby. He's a grand little lad!"

Mary, who had seen him move off at the start, was thinking that Stephen was in this procession ahead of her. Her spirit went forward out of her body and walked beside him. This is how it ought to be always, he and I walking forward together into the new world. But he is tied to the old one! Tied to his work and his wife and his family and his habits and all his life so far! How can he ever get free? His own people will turn on him and hate him as they would never hate one of us, Tom Sutton, Harold Pearson. And our people, Tom Sutton, Harold Pearson, will never trust him as they would trust one of themselves, never think of him as one of themselves. She saw Stephen walking for ever in a no-man's-land between two armies, denationalized, alone. Alone because she could not be with him, doubly alone because of Joy who was with him, making the worst tug of all for him. Her heart ached fiercely, to love and comfort him in that world which she saw coming daily nearer, that world which, whatever happened, would be a crucifixion

486

for moderate and peace-loving men. What prevented them would not stand in the way of half her friends, and perhaps would prevent no one in another hundred years. How often people proferred that consolation and how irritating it was. "It will be all the same in a hundred years." It reduced Stephen, this procession, even a world conflict to a smallness against which Mary's spirit protested. Feeling a need to enclose herself in the solid present, she began to talk to Aunt Grace about the election.

South Worbeck Moor was a broad, trodden stretch of sooty grass, fenced in all round by a benevolent corporation with iron railings. It was fringed on three sides by streets of terrace houses in dirty red brick, on the fourth by a railway siding, over which trucks and wagons shunted all day long. The only thing to be said for it was that it was an open space. It let in some air between the houses, and made it possible for children to run on grass, and for boys and young men to play cricket and kick a football about. It was not a stimulating background for any kind of demonstration. Neither were the crowd who assembled to hear the Fascist speakers a stimulating audience. Some of them had come from curiosity, some with hostile intent to sing and shout, some because they lived near, and some because there was very little else to do on Sunday afternoon.

A young Blackshirt, standing on a cart, made a speech about England, prosperity for all, down with the Jews, the great danger of Bolshevism, the need for a firm hand, no sentiment, England for the English. He was a strapping youth whose eyes on a near view had the changeless, pathological smile of a recently converted Buckmanite, but in the distance, on top of the cart, he made an impression of health and vigour. He poured out his clichés in a resonant voice which the microphone amplified. He did not succeed in moving the indifferent part of his audience. He was just a young man making a speech. They had heard too many speeches from everybody in every party about prosperity for all. They did not believe in such a thing. Certainly they did not like Jews very much, but they did not want to take any particular trouble about them. And they knew in their bones that only foreigners talked about England.

The hostile part of the audience began to sing. They were divided in their aims and uncertain in their methods. They made a ragged noise, rather like the response to a Principal Boy's Appeal in the Pantomime. The speaker finished, and was replaced by another, an older man who looked as though he had been a soldier. He repeated with different emphasis what his predecessor had said. He had a habit of flinging out his arm at the end of a period and then raising it and shaking his clenched fist at an invisible enemy. Some wag in the crowd began to imitate the gesture. A wave of laughter, more destructive of the speaker's effect than any organized singing, swept over the audience. The Blackshirt was funny! Alone and aloof he stood above them, pouring out his fantastic nonsense, booming more loudly as he felt his own inability to sway them. He could see the faces upturned to him, grim or phlegmatic. He had once attended a Fascist demonstration in Rome. There the Duce need only cry out "Italia" and as the lovely word melted into the blue sky, cheer upon crashing cheer rolled in waves across the square and echoed back from the high walls. The sky above South Worbeck was an unexhilarating grey, and when he said "England!" the men who were presumably her sons looked as though they had never heard of her.

He struggled on until a stone flew past his cheek. A lump of sod dropped on the floor of the cart at his feet. Another stone just missed his ear. He felt encouraged, he was getting the response that he expected. This was a part of the business that he understood. He could see a swirl in the audience, his own young stalwarts in their black shirts moving forward into the crowd, a policeman's helmet above the bare heads and flat caps. Another stone flew and cut him on the cheek. He put up his hand to the stinging cut, and blood dripped through his fingers. There was a movement and a sound in the audience. As the first stone flew, the sympathies of the indifferent had swung towards the Blackshirt. They were

488

not at all interested in what he was saying, but they liked him because he was showing pluck, and some of them cheered him as he went on speaking, mopping up the blood from his cut cheek with a handkerchief that grew picturesquely scarlet.

Leslie very soon grew tired of the anti-Fascist demonstration, or, more accurately, he grew tired of acting as chauffeur to Harold Pearson. He had to fetch another speaker from a bus stop, and drive one who was obliged to leave early to the station. An elderly woman had a fit, and he was pressed into the service to drive her home with her daughter. He particularly resented this last demand, because it could in no way be construed as helping the anti-Fascist or any other cause. People who had fits should stay at home, Leslie thought. He was the more annoyed because the patient, in spite of his protests, had been put into the front seat next to him, had recovered with incredible rapidity, and was now enjoying the ride. "It's me kidneys you see, love," she explained to Leslie. She told him what the doctor had said and what the sister at the Infirmary had said, and what her brother's Ellen had said, who knew someone that was taken the same way, and who was quite obviously, in her view, a more reliable authority than doctor or sister. She gave Leslie the full benefit of a rich and varied medical experience. Was it not good manners to entertain with the most interesting conversation she knew the gentleman who was driving her home? Leslie sweated and almost wished that she would have another fit, only the one thing clear from her autobiography was that she did not die of them.

He put her down at her door in a narrow street of tall, dirty, red brick houses. Staggering a little, her odd-shaped toque on one side, she leaned on the arm of her thin, dried-up daughter, and said,

"Will you come in and tek a coop o' tea, love? T'kettle will be on t'boil. Eh well, thank you kindly! It's been a bit of change an' all, it has that! I don't know what t'neighbours will think to see me coming home in a car with a young man!"

Neither her pluck nor her genuine courtesy touched Leslie, who felt nothing but acute self-consciousness and a burning desire to escape from an intolerable situation. He made up his mind as he drove off not to hurry back to the quarter of the moor where Harold Pearson reigned supreme. He wanted to have a look at the Fascists. They were the bogey in his dark corner who haunted his dreams with threats of violence. He did not believe what the Unwins were always saying, that these particular Fascists, though ripe for damnation, did not matter, except in so far as they served as a smoke-screen for the polite Fascists of Westminster and Whitehall. These Fascists were mixed up with his fears of bombs and gas and war, and with all the long, terrified resentment of tyranny which had begun when he was a little boy in socks, very much afraid of his unapproachable father.

He came out of a side-street on to the road that bordered the moor, and saw a large crowd ahead of him. He drove slowly along. He could see a man raised up above the crowd, a tiny, gesticulating figure against the sky. Anger suddenly came up into his throat and choked him. There was the enemy!

He drove on faster. There was some confusion among the crowd, which to his timid and inexperienced eyes seemed more than it was. "God, they're fighting!" he thought. A policeman emerged, dragging with him a young workman whose coat was half off, and whose shirt had been torn open, leaving bare his strong, hairy chest. The young man's forelock was tossed over his eyes, he had his hand to his side, and a trickle of blood ran down his chin from the corner of his mouth. Somewhere inside the crowd a woman screamed. The sound made every nerve in Leslie's body quiver. He had stopped the car but started it again, moved by an impulse to do something. He felt that he ought to rush into the crowd and rescue the woman, who was probably being knocked about by Blackshirts, yet if he had meant to go, his body would not have obeyed him, so frightened was he of being knocked about himself. He did not know that he was

490

muttering under his breath, "you beasts, you beasts, you beasts!"

Most of the Blackshirt's audience were standing on the grass, and the road at the edge of it was fairly clear, except for a few people who had had enough and were straggling away from the meeting. As Leslie drove on, there was a swirl in the crowd on the edge of the road. A middle-aged man with a handkerchief round his neck ran out of it, a tall young Blackshirt after him. The Blackshirt had fair hair that crinkled above a forehead that was pink and patchy as though he always wore hats too tight for him. He caught up the older man and kicked him hard in the middle of his body. The man dropped down on the road, winded and gasping with distress.

Something snapped inside Leslie, something that had been growing thinner and fraying all his life, ready for this moment. He trod full down on the accelerator, and the long bonnet of his car shot forward. There was a shout somewhere near. Leslie saw the crinkled yellow hair and pink face of the Blackshirt above the nose of the car. Then he felt a shock that made the steering wheel shake in his hands. The Blackshirt disappeared. Leslie took his foot off the accelerator and without knowing that he did it, put on the brakes. There were shouts and people came running from the edge of the moor. Leslie looked back. The Blackshirt was lying on the dusty road, limp, sickening, horrible. Men were running to him and bending over him. One of them, a policeman, got up from him and came to the car.

"Is he dead?" Leslie asked.

"Lucky for you he ain't," the policeman replied grimly. He was taking out a notebook and pencil.

Leslie said, speaking very carefully,

"I ran him down. I did it on purpose. He was hurting a man. You understand? I was trying to do it." Then he cried suddenly, "Oh, go away!" and doubling up sideways on the seat of the car was sick as though he would vomit the very soul out of his body.

The Blackshirt whom Leslie had run down was in the Infirmary with two broken ribs, bad bruises and concussion. The *Guardian* gave a brief report of the incident and a short account of the Fascist meeting without any details of the speeches. Its line was not to encourage the Blackshirts to think themselves important. It did have a leader commenting on the events of that Sunday afternoon. The leader writer said that processions, uniforms and violence were all part of an unnatural growth in England. Most of the inhabitants of Aire had shown their good sense and dislike of extremes by staying away from both demonstrations. While expressing a grave and sorrowful disapproval of a young man, the son of a well-known and respected citizen, who had deliberately run down a political opponent, the leader remarked that still graver disapprobation was due to those who had influenced a boy at a generous and impressionable age. Free speech was one of the conditions of democracy, but in view of the deplorable results of inflammatory political propaganda on the young and unbalanced, it might be necessary to confine it within certain limits. Men who were in positions of responsibility should at least place some restrictions on themselves in dealing with those *in statu pupillari* who were not able to bring to theory the test of experience.

"I wonder he didn't say 'acid test,'" Guy Runnacre commented to Mary. "He generally trots out the whole pantechnicon. Have you seen what the other papers are saying about young Ward?"

"No. What?"

"The *Daily Tribune* has a large-type heading, 'COMMUNIST VIOLENCE IN AIRE.' It says that the City and University of Aire are hot-beds of Communism, that the wicked Reds stoned the poor Blackshirts, who were behaving like lambs, and that Leslie Ward was put up by the Communist Party—I wonder they didn't say by Russia—to go for one particular lamb. It's just their luck, the fellow's only been married six months and his wife's expecting a baby I need hardly tell you that the *Tribune* counted her tear when the news was broken to her, and took a photograph of her getting into a car to go to her husband's bedside. They'll

492

probably start a collection to-morrow for the baby's layette. I hope it's triplets!"

"The sickening part is that all that's true in a way. The Fascists didn't touch anyone until they were attacked. Leslie does call himself a Communist, and he did go for the man on purpose. Of course, it must have been a nerve storm. I should think he's been working up for it for a long time and probably went off his head for a moment. Still, there it is. In a way the *Tribune's* facts are true."

"Oh, yes, in a way! Like this liberty and democracy and free speech the *Guardian's* always talking about. God, what fools the British public are! They'll swallow any poison that isn't labelled! They'd put up with any dictator if he called himself a Prime Minister and said that he was all for democracy and had never sought office. You'll see, they'll lap up Fascism when it's disguised as National Health or Organization of the Unemployed, or whatever they like to call it."

"I don't believe the British public are as gullible as you think."

"You have a sanguine temper, my dear. Therefore, it's nice to be with you, but at this stage of the world's history you're generally wrong. I see we're sponsoring Robert Harding's election campaign with great ardour. We gave him a whole column for the speech he made on Saturday night."

"Was it good?"

"We might have written it ourselves. In fact I should think we probably did. It looks like a rehash of one of old Pullen's leaders. Spooner was at the meeting and told me that he did very well. First they yelled and hissed him and he grinned at them, and finally they got tired of it and let him finish his speech, and he made them laugh. He couldn't answer most of the questions, really, and he either let off a stock bit about democracy or better housing or something, or else he made a joke. Once he said 'I'm afraid I don't know anything at all about that. But I'll find out,' and they laughed at that more than anything."

Mary began to put her things together.

"What will happen to Leslie Ward?"

"I should think it depends on how far they want to make an example of him."

What will happen to Leslie Ward supplied a general topic for conversation at the evening party of the Literary and Scientific Society, which was held each year in the Art Gallery. The Literary and Scientific Society had been founded, mainly by the efforts of the Marsden family, in the year of the Crimean War. It provided its members with six lectures during the winter, three on literary subjects, three on scientific, and to encourage and reward the pursuit of learning, it gave a party at the beginning of each session. In the old days the ladies and gentlemen of Aire, even the boys fresh from school and the girls just coming out, attended both parties and lectures. Nowadays the lectures had been incorporated with another series held at the University, and the party, which preserved the tradition, drew a number of guests who had no intention of going to those or to any other lectures, although from long habit they or their parents still subscribed to them.

Robert and Beryl walked through the long rooms of the Art Gallery, greeted on all sides by inquiries and good wishes about the election. Robert smiled and answered gaily. Beryl tried to do the same. She was not quite happy about the election and did not know why. She had a headache and the rooms were hot, but her uneasiness was more than temporary. It was some weeks since she had last heard Robert and Stephen argue about politics, but whenever she did, she was aware that she agreed with Stephen. It was distressing to her to feel that she was not on Robert's side. She knew that what he called "Stephen's goings on" had ruffled his easy temper, and roused a certain obstinacy in him. She was glad that there had been no discussions lately. It so happened that the brothers had only met in public places.

Presently she saw Joy and Stephen, side by side but a little apart, walking down the Gallery. They both looked cross, and not at all disposed to enjoy themselves. They had, as a matter of fact, been arguing in the car on the way to the party.

"Now that Robert is standing for the Central Ward," Joy said, "you'll have to stop working for that man, Allworthy!"

494

Stephen had been revolving this question in his mind all day. He had begun canvassing for John not only on principle but out of gratitude and friendliness. He was sorry that the opponent was also on the Left. It seemed to him absurd for John Allworthy and Tom Sutton to stand against one another when there were seats where Conservative candidates were unopposed. The more he saw of the Left the more Stephen sickened at the divisions in it, the more hopeless he felt of its achieving a united front or doing anything without one. When he heard that Robert was contesting the seat, he had thought of going off and working in another ward, but Joy's peremptory tone irritated him.

"I don't know," he said, "I haven't decided."

"I shouldn't have thought there could be any question about it."

"You never do think there are two sides to any question."

"There are never two right ones. You can't possibly work against your own brother."

"I was working in the ward before he butted in. You might as well say he shouldn't come in against me."

"That's different. I don't suppose he ever knew you were canvassing in the ward for Labour. I hope he didn't."

"Ashamed of me, are you?"

"I'm often ashamed of the things you've done lately."

Stephen made an effort and bit back a savage retort. He hated this bickering into which they so often fell nowadays, but his nerves were strung up so that he could not always avoid it. He felt remorseful because he was unfaithful to Joy in spirit and intention if not in actual fact. He ought to treat her with special consideration, and instead he found himself continually relapsing into bad temper or childish argument. The whole situation was intolerable and somehow unreal. The strain of being both the person he had been brought up to be who was married to Joy, and the person he was fumbling his way towards who loved Mary was so great that sometimes he felt as though he were cracking. He did not know whether he was more glad or sorry that Mary would not be reporting this idiotic party, he knew that she was going up to London to-night to be there in the morning for a wedding, at which the bridegroom and his family came from Yorkshire. He walked along beside Joy thinking about Mary.

Stephen and Joy and Beryl and Robert came face to face in front of a modern picture of squares and lines, a recent acquisition to the Art Gallery. Robert grinned and jerked an elbow at the picture and said, "Look at that! I could do that any day with a couple of pots of paint, couldn't you?"

Stephen, who did not understand the picture himself, felt irritated by Robert's calm assumption that there was no sense in what they did not understand, felt and resented Robert's quick recoil from anything new and experimental. He said,

"Oh, I don't know. I expect there's something in it."

Robert raised his eyebrows and shook his head. Beryl interrupted,

"I ache with standing! Let's all go and sit down at one of the tables and have some coffee."

The Grants and the Unwins met among the shifting groups, but Angus, nodding a greeting, drew Grizel on. He did not want to talk to the Unwins about Leslie. Leslie had widened the breech between the Grants and the Unwins. It had always been there, but it had been possible to throw a bridge across it. Now it did not seem possible.

Grizel, who knew why Angus was unhappy, said,

"I've heard some people talking about Leslie Ward and saying that they think he'll get let off lightly. He's so young and obviously nervy." She added, "I wonder if the Unwins know it was their fault."

"It was partly mine."

"Oh, nonsense, Angus!"

"Yes, it was. I ought to have let him talk it all out to me before he got too deep in and lost his sense of proportion. I helped to do it."

"You certainly didn't! The Unwins did it. All you did was to keep out of it."

496

"I know—and there's the rub! I've always wanted to keep out of the whole god-awful racket, but you know, Grizel, the snag about people like us is that we keep out of things too much. With so many lunatics about, you can find you've done quite a lot of harm by keeping out of things."

Someone pointed out Dr. Bates, the psycho-analyst, to Claud Unwin.

"Will you introduce me?" Claud said with brightening eyes.

Dr. Bates was looking at a picture of Spanish dancers.

"One sees the suppression of the subconscious so clearly in that old-fashioned representational school," Claud said.

"I don't know anything about art," Dr. Bates replied placidly. "I like the colour in that picture. It reminds me of a holiday I once had in Spain."

"Aren't you an admirer of the French surrealists?"

"I don't think I've ever seen any of them, or if I have, I didn't know what they were. Are there any in this gallery?"

"There's one on loan. Over there. I'll show you."

Claud led Doctor Bates to the picture which Robert and Stephen had inspected. Dr. Bates considered it.

"No, I don't like that very much. It's beyond me. I don't see any sense in it. I like a good portrait or a landscape and I'm very fond of engravings."

There was a silence. Claud could not help feeling as though Dr. Bates did not know his part. Yet surely in this broad, calm, dispassionate man, there must be a spirit akin to his own, a spirit fed with all the newest thought. He tried again.

"It's been extraordinarily interesting from the psychological point of view to notice the various reactions to this affair of Leslie Ward's. The manifestations, for instance, of the unconscious sexual attitudes to violence. The way that sadistic tendencies have betrayed themselves. You would be surprised at the number of people who think he ought to be sent to prison."

"Well," observed Dr. Bates, "you can't have young men running people down with motor-cars."

Claud blinked for a moment in surprise, and then let the remark slip by him.

"Of course the whole thing is a political issue. One sees the immediate piling up of the forces of reaction, provoked by one act of defiance, just as one sees the conflict in the individual. I knew Leslie Ward very well, you know."

That, reflected Dr. Bates, may have been part of what was wrong with him.

"Of course the real trouble with him was the mother-fixation. He found it very difficult to grow out of his childhood. He was soaked in bourgeois tradition. By the way, Dr. Bates, I don't think you've ever been to our discussion group. It would be very interesting to have a paper from you on the neurosis of Fascism. All Fascists are neurotics, of course."

"Probably," agreed Dr. Bates, "and most Communists, too, I daresay."

"What?"

"Don't you agree?"

"Certainly not!"

"That is only a rough impression, of course. I haven't very much time for politics. I should venture a guess that Russia and Germany are both suffering from mass neurosis. Violence is always a sign of neurosis, you know." He smiled. "Perhaps you'd rather I didn't read a paper to your society, whatever it is?"

"Surely," Claud exclaimed, "you are on the Left?"

"Well, I should like to see a good many things changed, and a fairer deal all round. I think that a new economic system is coming; but I think that with Europe as it is, the important thing is to have the most competent and experienced people in charge, and I certainly think that although I don't always agree with them, and I wish they would show a little more spirit, I should at the present moment be inclined to vote again for the National Government."

Naomi was talking to Mark Forrester by the refreshment buffet.

"One longs to go to Spain," Naomi said, "where the issue is clear!"

"As I see it," Forrester replied earnestly, "the issue is clear here. God and the devil. Brotherly love and kindness against greed and self-interest and lust for power. Some people have too much of what we all need. Some people are in want. The issue seems to me so clear that I cannot understand why everybody does not see it!"

Claud came up to them, looking cross. He said to Naomi,

"I've just been talking to the local psycho-analyst. At least that's what he's supposed to be."

"Oh!" Naomi's eyes seemed to come forward out of her face with eagerness. Had she been missing something? "Where is he? Is he interesting?"

"Not at all," Claud said coldly. "It's my belief he isn't really Freudian!"

Mrs. Allison said to Canon Halliday,

"Where is the French picture—the one they borrowed? I saw a note about it in the *Guardian*."

"I believe it is this one."

They contemplated it for a minute in silence. Canon Halliday had no feelings about it at all. Mrs. Allison felt resentful. It was new, unintelligible and therefore a threat, in some obscure way, to her prestige and security. Almost wholly ignorant of a changing world, she smelt a threat in anything new and unintelligible as homing birds smell the Northern Spring.

"It is interesting!" Canon Halliday said guardedly.

"In my opinion," replied Mrs. Allison firmly, "it is pure affectation."

"Let me get you some more coffee, Beryl?"

"Yes, please." She did not want any more coffee, but she would be quite glad to get Stephen away from the table for a minute, he and Robert were looking so cross, and Joy so white and stiff. All about Leslie Ward who did not matter to any of them, except perhaps a little to Stephen, who had had a connection with the family for a long time. Now, of course, Robert and Mr. Ward were working together over this election, and she and Robert were going to dinner there on Thursday. A year ago she had been obliged to persuade Robert to go occasionally to make things easier for Stephen, and now Stephen was not asked much, but Robert was. How oddly things turned out.

Joy was saying in her final way,

"I always knew that boy was no good. Nobody would ever think he'd been to a decent school."

"You know, Joy, I blame the people who filled him up with all that nonsense. It's always the same. Somebody does a little Communist propaganda and feels noble and enjoys it, and then a lot of fools go and try it out and get into trouble."

"That's what I tell Stephen. Other people will do things because he does, and won't know where to stop. I'm coming to drive a car for you at the election, Robert, if you'll have me. Oh, and Hilary sent you his very best wishes. He said 'Tell him I know he'll scoop the pool.' "

"That's awfully nice of him."

Beryl felt a trifle left out of the concordat on the other side of the table. Robert, she knew, had been annoyed with her because she had echoed Stephen's hope that Leslie would get off lightly. Robert really hoped it too for Ward's sake, and had already remarked to her that the boy must have lost his head for a moment, but to Stephen he said that it was as well to stop that sort of thing at once with a firm hand. Watching Robert and Stephen to-night had been like watching two people give one another little pushes in opposite directions, until each of them had got somewhere that he did not expect. Her head ached so much that she felt despondent, and wondered where they would get to in the end.

Stephen came back with the coffee. Beryl as she smiled her thanks at him, thought that he looked ill and strained, his face had grown thinner, he was not happy. He broke out, "I've never in my life heard so much rot talked in one evening as I've heard at this party! You'd think Leslie Ward was a world revolution instead of an unbalanced boy seeing a bit further than some people, and driven half crazy by circumstances!"

Robert looked up quickly.

"The circumstances being a comfortable home, a good education, lashings of money, and a reasonable chance of doing anything he wants to do. What do you mean, anyway, by 'seeing a bit further than most people'?"

"I mean he's unstable and neurotic and he's behaved like an idiot, but he has looked outside the comfortable box he's been brought up in, and got a glimpse of what the world's like and what's coming."

"Oh! What is coming?"

"The end of people like us, sheltered, secluded, living on other people's work with our eyes shut."

"Stephen!" Joy said sharply. "Don't be absurd!"

"It will be a bit of a job," Robert said, "to make an end of us."

"Of course it will. No end of a job."

"But you're going to do it, are you? What about yourself? Are you going to be made an end of too? Or are you going to save your skin by ratting to the other side?"

"Robert!" Beryl said quickly. "That's not fair."

She got a sudden flash of his dark eyes.

"You keep out of it, Beryl. You don't understand these things."

"Stephen doesn't want to make an end of anyone. He means there won't be such a favoured class any more. And," Beryl added bravely, "I really think there oughtn't to be."

"There are differences!" Joy cried. "There always have been and there always will be! It's natural."

Stephen and Robert were both red to the roots of their hair and looked extraordinarily alike.

"I'd better tell you that I've been canvassing for John Allworthy in your ward, and I'm not going to stop!"

"Don't stop! Unless you'd like to begin canvassing for Tom Sutton."

"I'd rather——"

"You'd rather him than me, eh! Well, they won't get in, either of them. They've cut their own silly throats by standing against one another, as your side always do and always will!"

Beryl stood up.

"Robert, I've got an awful headache and I feel ill. I should like to go home."

The other three looked at her for a minute as though at the end of an act of a play they were adjusting themselves to an interval. It's so lucky that I really feel ill, Beryl thought confusedly, as she held on to the back of her chair, while the room swam round her.

Seeing her dead white face, they were all ashamed of themselves. Robert jumped up and put his arm round her.

"Poor little Berry Brown! You do look all in! Could you take her to get her things, Joy, while I get the car?"

"I'll get your car," Stephen offered. "You stay and look after her. Where is it?"

He went out into the cool night. He thought, Oh Lord, what are we coming to, quarrelling like a couple of children at a party! What is the matter with us all, with everyone! Of course I can't work against Robert, really. And of course he doesn't want Leslie to get it in the neck any more than I do! What did take hold of us? When these things take hold of everybody good and hard, what is going to happen to the world?

He brought the car round as Joy and Robert brought Beryl down the steps. They tucked her in with rugs, and Robert thrust his head out of the window.

"Stephen! Thanks for bringing the car!"

"I hope she'll be all right. Sorry I lost my temper!"

"Same here! Couple of mugs, aren't we? Good night, old boy!"

"Good night!"

Marjorie sat alone and disconsolate in the drawing-room at Grey Gables. She had cried a good deal in the last few days, so much so that she felt to-day as though she had lost the capacity for crying, even though there was nothing else to do. Her father, more unapproachable than ever, had gone as usual to the office. Her mother was lying down upstairs with a headache. Leslie was in a nursing home, and had particularly asked that none of his family should come and see him. The mere idea of seeing them aroused such hysterical distress in him that the doctor advised them not to attempt it, so Marjorie and her mother could do nothing but ring up and send fruit and flowers and books. Leslie had been brought before the Police Court and committed for trial at the next Assizes at the beginning of December. He was allowed out on bail on condition that he was under medical supervision. The papers had been full of him. He might be sent to prison. They were all, the whole family, utterly and hopelessly disgraced, they could never go anywhere in public again, and no one decent would ever know them.

Now that the first shock of distress was over, Marjorie felt, and was ashamed of feeling, that the worst part was things not being ordinary. Her mother had said to her, "Of course you can't go to the Welcome this afternoon. Ring up the secretary. She will understand." Marjorie had rung up the secretary, who had understood with prompt and painful tact, and had said, "Of course not," and had promised at once to get another helper as substitute. But Marjorie would really have liked to go to the Babies Welcome. She would have been glad to go to the dullest civic lunch or the most boring stiff tea-party, to anything, anything that would have made her feel as though life was going on in a normal way and she was part of it again. It had been different at the beginning of the week when she had wept, felt sick, stayed awake at night till almost two, agonized over Leslie and tried to comfort her mother. She had slept soundly all last night, she was not feeling at all sick, and her mother's maid was much better than she was at putting eau-de-Cologne on her forehead and making cups of tea. Marjorie suddenly thought that she would like to go into town, see a picture and have tea at a café. She was shocked at herself for such a thought! Of course she would not really like it with all her family in such distress. If only she had someone to talk to! She did not talk intimately about her family affairs to any of her acquaintances except Mary and she had not seen much of Mary lately and did not want to see her now. Mary was all mixed up with the kind of people and ideas that had brought Leslie to disaster. Her father had been proved most terribly right about Leslie's friends, and he had never liked her being friends with Mary. Older people were sometimes right after all! You did not believe them when they warned you of dangers and tried to interfere with you, but look what happened!

Tea was brought in. Her spirits revived a little, it was at least something to do, and there was a new chocolate cake. Marjorie was beginning on the hot scones, when she heard the front door bell ring, and in a minute, a man's voice in the hall. The drawing-room door opened and Billy Wilson was shown in.

Marjorie had never been so glad to see him. The trouble about Billy Wilson, as she had often secretly acknowledged, was that he was so ordinary. That very quality now endeared him. From his smartly brushed hair and small, shrewd eyes to his neat spats, he belonged to a competent and prosperous everyday life, remote from disgrace and disaster.

"Hulloa—'ulloa—'ulloa!" Billy Wilson said cheerily. "All on your own-i-o? What luck!"

He established himself comfortably in an arm-chair. She gave him some tea, and he explained that he must not touch scones or cakes, then murmured, "Well, just this once as it's an occasion, I mean, I haven't seen you lately," took a large slice of chocolate cake, and salved his conscience by saying, "I'll give the pudding a miss to-night. That ought to work out about even." As a rule Marjorie was bored by the constant guerilla warfare between Billy's figure and Billy's appetite, but to-day she was glad to be with someone preoccupied with usual things.

"Well? How's Leslie?" Billy inquired.

At once Leslie became something more like an ordinary invalid instead of a secret shame. Marjorie gave the report from the Nursing Home.

"He'll be all right after this, you see!" Billy said confidently. "This will have given him a rare old fright and made him learn sense. People have got to learn it one way or another when they first grow up. He's had his dose, all at once, and now he'll go ahead."

"You don't—you don't think they'll put him in prison?"

"Well, of course, can't have people running down other people with their cars, you know! But he's very young and he's obviously been in a queer state for some time, and I expect they'll let him down lightly."

Marjorie had not yet dared to discuss the dreaded possibility with her parents. She said in a shaking voice,

"If they do put him in prison it will be the end of all our lives."

"Oh, no, it won't! I daresay it feels like that now, but it won't be. You can take it from your Uncle William, only one thing's the end of your life, and that's dying!"

Marjorie bent her head over the tea-pot, ashamed of the tears in her eyes. Billy looked at the bent head, at the fat chestnut curls bunched on her round neck.

"Look here!" he said. "Let's go and dine somewhere."

"To-night? Oh, I can't!"

"Why not?"

"Well——"

"Your mum's in bed, your governor will go off to his study and work. You can't do anything for Leslie. What's the use of moping here? You go up after tea and put your best frock on and I'll go home and change and be back here in half a shake. We'll go and have a spot of dinner and dance afterwards."

"Wouldn't it look very queer? People would think . . .?"

"Nothing like keeping your end up! Besides, we won't go here, we'll run over to the Grand. If there's anybody there we know, they'll only think, There's that lucky fellow Billy Wilson dancing with the beautiful Miss Ward!"

Marjorie felt a rush of affection for Billy who was cheerful in a gloomy world, who wanted her when in her own eyes she had become undesirable. She began to smile. She had a new blue velvet frock upstairs which she had not even

505

worn. It would be lovely to get out of the house. She hesitated.

"Will Father——?"

"Bless you he won't mind! More sense! If you like I'll ask him."

It was another of Billy's virtues that he was not afraid of her father.

"Well, thank you awfully. I'd love to come," Marjorie said.

Edward Crossley, the young man in Doctor Bates's room, could not keep still. He sat humped on the edge of the chair with all his muscles tight instead of lying back at his ease. He kept on fidgeting with his tie, putting up a hand to his cheek or smoothing his hair. There were deep purple shadows under his eyes. His trouble was that he could not sleep. When he did sleep, he dreamed horribly of a coming war. The details of his dreams were extraordinarily clear, he was usually in bed at home when someone woke him or he heard the first noise of aeroplanes. He saw bombs fall and houses blaze up, heard dreadful cries, ran out to meet an advancing cloud of gas and woke struggling in an agony of suffocation. The dreams had become so frequent that he dreaded the night, and the fear of them never left him in the day-time. He could not eat, lost weight, and was unable to do his work. He was in his uncle's firm, learning to be an account-ant. He had been sent away by his doctor for three months' holiday which had done him no good. His doctor was of the old-fashioned school, deeply distrustful of psycho-analysis. How could you cure a man, he said, by talking to him? But Edward's father had a friend whose daughter had been cured of a nervous trouble by it, and he was anxious that his son should give it a chance.

Edward was sulky because Doctor Bates had suggested, what neither doctor nor specialist had been heartless enough to suggest, that he should try and go back to work again. Edward was more than sulky, he was outraged. For a year he had been the object of most tender consideration to his

506

family and friends. The whole household had concentrated on doing anything that might make Edward sleep that night, and on inquiring the next morning whether he had slept. After such delicate sympathy, Doctor Bates seemed like a cold wind.

"You see," Edward explained. "What sleep I do get is generally in the morning."

"If you don't get it in the morning," Doctor Bates suggested, "you'll perhaps be more likely to go to sleep at night. Especially if you are tired after a day's work."

Edward did not answer. This was not at all the sort of thing he had a right to expect. Why didn't Doctor Bates begin talking to him about his complexes? Why, Good Lord, this was rather the kind of thing his father had said before he gave it up in despair! He didn't come to a psycho-analyst just to hear him talking like his father! He said sulkily,

"I really don't feel fit to work."

"But you soon will," Doctor Bates replied with cheerful firmness.

A pity, he thought, that Edward's father was comfortably off. The neurotic who was obliged to earn his own living was never able to cling so firmly to his neurosis.

"You see," he explained, "there must be some childish fantasy, some desire in the bottom of your mind which is being gratified by these dreams of yours. When we get that out and you accept it in your consciousness, you won't have the dreams any more."

"If you had my dreams," Edward said bitterly, "you wouldn't think they could gratify anything! Besides they aren't fantasy and nonsense. Look at the situation!"

He proceeded to give Doctor Bates an admirable summary of the position in Europe. He was an intelligent young man who had got a good class in history at Oxford, and who read the papers.

"So there it is," he concluded. "The upward surge of humanity piling up the forces of reaction against itself as it rises, so that there is bound to be a clash that will split the world in two. It seems as though we are moving towards a war that will destroy the whole of civilization."

507

He looked with bright, terrified eyes at Doctor Bates, half hoping for reassurance, half expecting to be snubbed. Doctor Bates answered kindly but with no note of easy reassurance.

"Things look bad certainly, but no one can tell what is coming. It's not so easy to destroy the whole of civilization so long as any civilized people are left alive. No doctor can get rid of reasonable fears for you. I can, I hope, cure you of these obsessional terrors that are making you ill and preventing you from playing a man's part in the world, which after all, Mr. Crossley, you would surely wish to do, whatever happens?"

Some spark of pride, some fibre of genuine courage in the young man vibrated suddenly. He answered in a more normal tone than he had yet used,

"Yes, I should. I'm not much good to anyone at present."

"You soon will be, especially if you want to be."

Doctor Bates began to explain to him about remembering and writing down his dreams.

Miss Harding, who came next, was here for the last time. Miss Harding was quite well again, had returned to active life, was going to look for a job, or perhaps go abroad for a bit, looked alert and interested and much prettier, no longer a limp, sad, fading girl, but a lively young woman. As she said good-bye and thanked Doctor Bates, she remarked,

"It makes such a difference being at home with everything in your own mind."

"It's very funny," she added, "I always thought, from things I read and from bits in the papers and from the things people say, that either you were full of repressions or you were one of those people who do exactly what they feel like at any moment. What it really amounts to is that when you know what you really feel like, you can deal with it better, anyhow."

"It's a common delusion that the escape from repression means anarchy. Whereas of course it should mean the full and balanced life of conscious control and harmony. The unrepressed person is by no means a person who follows every impulse. Anarchy is not freedom, it's repression worn the other way round."

"It would be interesting to work that out in bigger things—national affairs and politics. I suppose we've had a lot of repression—repression of one half of the world by the other half to start with?"

"Yes. I think so. And of all civilized countries by the demands of civilization."

"And now it looks as though the other side of the medal was coming round and we might all be plunged into anarchy," Clare laughed. "What seems to be wanted is somebody to psycho-analyse Europe."

"I think that Religion served the purpose in the civilized world that repression served in the individual. Now on the whole it's breaking down. You get the release of everything that it helped to repress, a time of anarchy when war and brutality are exalted, and the pledged word means nothing. The best hope that I can see for the world is the growth of real consciousness, that unless we are all destroyed by the blind warning impulses, we may struggle through somehow to the beginning of an adult mind, a state of self-knowledge and self-control."

"Don't you believe in any kind of religion at all?"

"I believe in the probability of some kind of creating mind or spirit, but I don't expect to know any more and I can't make any assertions about it. As for civilization, when I see the people who come here day by day with their personalities cramped and warped, and their lives maimed and impoverished, I'm quite sure that a lot of it wants destroying, although I don't want to see it destroyed by bombs and gas. Well, you'll be all right now, Miss Harding. Good luck to you! Good afternoon."

Rosie was waiting in the bus station for a bus to take her up to the Netherton Estate, when she saw Tom Sutton walk in and take his place at the stand for another bus. He was preoccupied and did not see her. She thought that he looked thinner and older. She had always liked him, pitying him for what Olive made him suffer. She had not seen him since Olive broke with him during the strike, but she had seen several pieces in the paper about him, his picture and something to do with an election or such-like. She walked across and stood in front of him.

"Tom!"

He started and looked at her. His face broke into its rare, sweet smile.

"Rosie! I didn't see you. How are you?"

"I'm all right. I'm just off up to Netherton for the evening."

"Not married yet?"

Rosie shook her head.

"Looks like we shan't be married in ten years. Poor Fred, 'e can't do owt for 'is own 'ouse! 'E's always 'aving to pay for things for theirs. I was that fed oop the other day I'd 'ave got shut of 'im, only I don't want t'trouble of courting another lad all over again. Besides, 'e's the only lad I ever 'ad. 'E's not much to look at and 'e's slow, is Fred. Takes me an evening sometimes to persuade 'im to give me a bit of a cuddle. But I'm used to 'im and I don't seem to fancy any oother lad, not t'same."

"Fred wants to get married, surely?"

"Oh, 'e does but . . ."

She stopped, a natural delicacy checking her.

"Olive?" Tom asked in a low voice.

Rosie nodded and then broke out,

"Ah, that's right, it's Olive. Always on at 'im, she is, to help her get this and that for t'house and they must have a suite because Mrs. Hardcastle at No. 10 has got one, and all them fiddling little spoons and glasses and such-like— daft, I call it! She reckons I'm not good enough for Fred, you know, because I'm in service."

Tom caught hold of her wrists and shook them.

"Now, see here, Rosie. Don't you believe that nonsense! You're good enough for any man. Fred's in luck. Don't you let Olive come between you, nor any house either, new or

510

old. You take and marry Fred and make a home for him."
He added again in a tone more envious than he knew,
"Fred's lucky!"

Looking at her kind mouth and smiling eyes, at her face
still chubby with her barely outgrown childhood, he wondered
why he did not find a girl like this and forget Olive. He could
easily find a score of girls who would be decent and kind
and not too genteel to love him at a street corner or on the
grassy slopes of the Park in summer. He did not seem to
want them nor have time for them, yet he was conscious of
loneliness and yearning. It was a shame if Olive's snobberies
and bourgeois vanities were going to spoil sport for Rosie
and Fred! A stick like Fred was in luck to get a girl like
Rosie, a good, hard working, honest piece of natural flesh
and blood with a warm heart and a lively tongue.

"You stand up for yourself, Rosie," he said. "Here's your
bus." He added, as he walked across with her, "Your Mr.
Robert Harding's putting up against me in t'election."

"He's a nice sort of gentleman, is Mr. Harding."

"Ah, I daresay," Tom said bitterly. It was so easy to be
a nice sort of gentleman if you were brought up with every
chance, every kind of happiness and comfort, with parents
that had never felt insecurity so that you did not know in
your bones the fear of being without work, food or shelter.

Rosie looked down at him from the step of the bus. His
face touched her, although she didn't know why. She put out
a cold red hand and said,

"You must come and see us when we're wed. You and
me were always good friends."

As she was carried off in the bus, she looked back and saw
him standing under the light, she said to herself, "Reckon
Olive won't do better! But Tom's well out of it!"

Olive had been thinking about Rosie as she got off an
earlier bus at Netherton that evening. If only Fred could
find another, a nicer girl, not in service, not speaking with
Rosie's broad accent nor with Rosie's rough ways! Rosie

went about town without a hat. When she made tea for the family, she forgot to put out saucers, seeing no need for them. She had a whole horde of uncouth relations who sometimes came over to Aire for a day out, and by evening often got drunk and argued with tram conductors, and went singing and shouting along the pavement. Olive had always told Fred what to like and what not to like. It was infuriating to find him, for the first time, with a mind of his own that she could not share. Since she herself had broken with Tom, she had two ambitions, to make Fred break with Rosie, and to beautify the new house and raise the Walters' standard of living to new heights of elegance.

As she got off the bus, a woman who had been sitting just behind her, smiled and said,

"Good evening!"

"Good evening, Mrs. Ashworth!" Olive smiled prettily.

"Rather cold to-night, isn't it?"

"Yes. But seasonable."

"Oh, yes, very seasonable. We shall have it colder before long, I expect. The wind does catch you up here."

"Yes, it is rather a cold neighbourhood."

"But it's healthy."

"Oh, I'm sure it's very healthy."

"Good night, Miss Walters."

"Good night, Mrs. Ashworth."

Olive was delighted by this conversation. Mrs. Ashworth, who lived at the corner house in Waterloo Road, was one of the neighbours to whose acquaintance she aspired, for Mrs. Ashworth belonged to the aristocracy of Netherton. The Ashworths had taken their own house and come there of their own accord before the Corporation decided to clear a belt of slums and put the inhabitants in the Netherton Estate. All the original householders in Netherton were furious and signed a petition asking that their good class estate should not be used for slum clearance. A harassed Corporation, having nowhere else to put the slum dwellers, and assailed on all sides by clamours from societies and individuals who had suddenly begun to concern themselves about housing, disregarded the petition and hoped that everyone would shake down together in time. So far their hopes were not justified. The estate seethed with rivalries, jealousies, snobberies and heart burnings. Social barriers were many and impassable. Almost everyone was cramped by the fear of knowing undesirable people, except for half a dozen Irish families from the lower end of Bankside Yard. They had been removed, deloused, counselled and inspected, but as soon as they got over the shock of finding themselves in clean, cold houses, they proceeded to re-establish the only conditions of life in which they could flourish. They screwed up all the windows against the cold air of the hill-top and stuffed the joints of the frames with rags, they made the houses dirty, frowsy and untidy as soon as possible. They bred more vermin and threw their rubbish out into the front gardens, from which it blew across the fence and distributed itself on all the gardens in the row. They were much more free and happy than most of the other people on the estate because they were willing to know anybody who would know them. They provided casual visitors with confirmation of their faith that it was a waste of time putting the working class into good houses, and they were an endless source of discussion to the original inhabitants who felt that they justified their petition.

To Olive they were a nightmare. It was not even as though they were strangers. They knew her, and greeted her when-ever they saw her as a fellow exile from Bankside Yard. There was Mrs. Murphy only two streets away. Once at the Yard, Mrs. Murphy had come in and sat up every night with Mrs. Walters during a bout of pneumonia. Every evening for a week, after she had put her own family to bed, she had appeared like salvation to a scared, twelve-year-old Olive who did not know what to do, and thought her mother was dying. It was true that ever since then Mrs. Murphy had borrowed things from them and either had not given them back at all, or had given them back filthy. Olive had hoped that when they moved, the Murphys would be a long way off, and there would be an end of this habit, but three hundred yards was not far, and Mrs. Murphy still came round, her hair in pins and her stockings in holes, to borrow the baking-tin or a frying-pan. What with such acquaintances, and what with Fred walking out with a girl in service, Olive felt that she was a good deal handicapped in her attempts to know the right people.

She concentrated on the house with all the intensity of her stubborn little nature. She had some opposition to contend with, but both her father and mother had grown older and less sure of themselves since the removal from Bankside Yard. They were like peonies whose roots had bled in transplanting. In Bankside Yard Mrs. Walters would have settled everything about the house without hesitation. At Netherton she murmured and grumbled but allowed Olive to override her. Neither she nor Mr. Walters would sit in the sitting-room if they could avoid it, but they let Olive have her way with it, and were even a little proud of its chaste splendour. Mr. Walters went in to the Three Bears every Saturday evening, but otherwise sat at home in the kitchen with his pipe and the evening paper. The great new red Trust House on the estate with its car park and tennis-courts was not in his opinion a pub at all, and he only ventured into it occasionally with great discomfort. Goaded by Olive, he tried his hand at gardening, but though he kept the square of grass cut, and put in the plants which she bought from Woolworths, he was too old to find a garden a new and entrancing adventure as so many people on the estate were finding theirs. He smoked, ruminated, did more or less what Olive told him, and at the Three Bears on Saturday night came out with surprisingly sardonic comments on modern ways and the changes going on in the world.

When Rosie arrived at No. 17, she found the whole family in conclave in the kitchen. Herbert and Mabel were there too. She had the feeling that she had broken in on a discussion which they would not continue in her presence. "Seems like I'm a stranger!" she said to herself. She looked quickly at Fred and met his shy, welcoming smile. Oh, Fred was her lad and no one should take him from her! She remembered what Tom had said, and greeted Olive with a casual, impudent nod. Mrs. Walters filled the kettle and began to put out tea-cups. Rosie jumped up to help her, and being in a mood to show what she could do, put out a saucer and a teaspoon for every cup and a separate spoon for the sugar. She knew how to have things nice as well as that Olive when she liked, and better, for she had lived two years with Mrs Harding, that was a real lady and had things that Olive had never seen, little crystal glass dishes for sweets on the dinner-table and mats like lace collars and tiny glasses no bigger than thimbles to have sticky little drinks out of with the coffee. It was all a lot of silliness and not worth a good cup of tea, but Rosie could do it if she liked, and Mrs. Harding said she set the table as well as she did herself, and she wished that Olive could hear her.

"Sit yer down, love," Mrs. Walters said to Rosie, "there next to Fred." She gave Rosie a specially good cup of tea, waiting till the water was nearly down to the tea-leaves so that it came out black and strong as treacle, and putting in several heaped spoonfuls of moist sugar.

"We've been talking about the pàrlour furniture," she said. "Our Olive wants a suite. But I says there's three chairs in there now and nobbut Olive and Mabel and 'Erbert ever sits on 'em, so where's t'sense of wasting brass?"

"None of those chairs match," Olive said sulkily.

"Well, lass, if tha's done a good day's work a chair feels none the worse to your bottom for not being spit o't' next. How much is this suite?"

"I've seen one for twelve pounds ten."

"And who's got twelve pounds ten to throw away?"

Olive had not wanted to explain the position before Rosie, but there was no help for it.

"We could buy it in instalments. That was what you did, Mabel, wasn't it? Me and Dad and Fred each paying so much a week."

Mr. Walters said, "Maybe Fred doesn't want to. He's got his own house to save for!"

"Oh, but not for a long time!" Olive said.

The words, coming on top of her thoughts and her conversation with Tom, stung Rosie like a challenge. She stopped stirring her tea and leaned forward.

"Me and Fred thought of getting married next summer, didn't we, Fred?"

Fred was a little startled. Certainly they had talked vaguely about a wedding in the summer, but he did not know that anything definite had been said about next summer. His heart began to thump. He wanted Rosie and his own house, but he was always a little afraid of Olive's tears and tempers.

"Aye, we did that," he said.

"You'll never get a house by then," Olive said coolly.

"Reckon we'll find somewhere if we make up our minds to it."

"You could coom 'ere for a bit while you look round," Mrs. Walters said comfortably. "There's room enough in this 'ouse, and there's a double bed now in Fred's bedroom. Aye, you can coom 'ere for a bit if you want, we'll be right glad to 'ave you."

The house would be warmer and more homely, she felt, with Rosie in it.

Olive was dismayed. Rosie and Fred in the house like lodgers, Rosie running in and out of the Murphys', leaning on the gate in her overall, asking her dreadful relations here! She said in a hurry,

"I'm sure they'd rather have a house of their own."

"Well, lass, you've just said they might not be able to get one!"

Rosie put down her cup and saucer with a thump so that the slop of tea in the saucer splashed over on to the table-cloth. Facing Olive squarely, she said,

"Seems you don't want us to get married!"

Olive's weapons were not much good against a frontal attack. She flushed and her mouth dropped open.

"Maybe you think I'm not good enough for Fred? I know you look down on me because I'm in service. Well, what if I am? I've got one mistress, and a good one, and you've got a lot o' masters. When I'm wed there's nothing I can't do for Fred. I can cook and clean and bake and mend——"
the words coming from the red-cheeked Rosie with her broad face and curly hair sounded like the refrain of a folk-song,

but the Walters family knew no folk-songs and only stared at her aghast. "I've worked in a house instead of a mill and I know my job. There's nothing I can't do for him. Since we've been walking out, I've saved five shillings every week. When we go out together, I pay my share. I'm not one to put all t'money in my own bank and let t'lad put 'is 'and in 'is pocket all t'time, without it's summat special and 'e's treating me." Rosie stopped for breath. Olive was frightened and had drawn a contemptuous expression over her face with difficulty. Rosie saw the sneer and not the alarm. "Don't you talk!" she cried. "You'd a good lad—too good for you 'e was, and you played Hamlet with him many a time instead of giving him a bit of love and kindness, and then let him go for some nonsense or other! Reckon you didn't want to leave earning and make a home for him. But me and Fred's going to get wed. You can mek up your mind to that, and we aren't going to buy no parlour suites for any other 'ouse till we've got our own!"

Olive burst into tears. Herbert looked at Mabel, said, "Come, come!" in an uneasy voice, pulled out a packet of cigarettes and began to light one, occupying himself with it as ostentatiously as possible. Mr. Walters removed his pipe from his mouth, put out a large hand and stroked his daughter's hair. Mabel patted her shaking shoulders, but Fred, looking and speaking like a man, said,

"That'll do, Olive. Maybe Rosie said more than she meant, but you don't treat her right. You're always on at me to spend my money on things we don't need, when I've to save up for my own house. You and your friends are always on about girls in service. Rosie's my girl and good enough for me, and we'll be married next summer."

"That's right!" Mrs. Walters said comfortably. "There's nowt like a wedding for a bit o' fun," she added. "Rosie's a good girl." She was thinking how often she felt better when Rosie came running in, her broad face all smiles, and how it was always Rosie who came to help her with a bit of washing up or ironing when her back was tired.

Rosie jumped up and went to Olive.

"Nay, don't tek on, Olive! I'm sorry I spoke sharp!"

517

She printed a smacking kiss on Olive's cool, painted cheek, and added jubilantly, "Eh, look, you'll be a bridesmaid! You and me sister Ada for the grown-up ones, and Patreechia and Gloria, that's Clarice's two kiddies, for the children. In blue satin, with pink flowers!"

Olive's spirit was broken. Fred would not contribute to the suite for the sitting-room, he was going to marry his common girl, and the only consolation for her was the prospect of walking up the aisle of a church among a gang of Rosie's dreadful relations, dressed in blue satin with pink flowers. It was hopeless, Olive thought, hopeless, trying to get on and raise a family like hers in the world. What would Mrs. Ashworth have thought if she had been here this evening and heard Rosie's outburst? There was only one consolation left. Olive murmured that she had a headache and slipped away upstairs. Safe, locked into her palace of delight, Olive threw off her flimsy garments, flung a handful of pink salts into the water, and plunged into the scent and steam, soothing her spirit with the one part of the new life that never failed her.

For the third time in the year 1936, the City of Aire found itself prominent in national news as well as provincial. An enterprising reporter from a daily paper came down to try and interview Ward about Leslie's assault on the Blackshirt. He was a good-tempered and persistent young man well worth his salary. Being put out on the mat by Ward, and having failed in his attempt to extract from the Vice Chancellor a pronouncement on Communist influences in the University, he cast about for easier prey, and stumbled on the fact that Tom Sutton, the leader in the great Ward strike, was opposing John Allworthy, the Trade Union representative who had resisted him, in the Municipal Elections. Here was a story, and a new one which the other papers, preoccupied with Leslie, had not noticed. The pages of his organ blossomed next morning with large headlines.

"SEQUEL TO WARD STRIKE."
"LEFT WING CHAMPION AGAINST THE UNIONS."
"FRIENDS BECOME ENEMIES"

The whole story was there. Tom's early friendship with John who was described as having been "father and mother to him" after the death of his parents: a recapitulation of the strike, with an account of how Tom went down on his knees to John to beg him to bring in the Union and John turned away in tears: photographs of John and Tom. The paragraph about John began, "Employed, it is stated, as a shop steward in the factory of Alfred Ward, whose son, Leslie, has so lately figured as the victim of Bolshevik propaganda in the tragedy of Lower Worbeck Moor, a tired, thin, elderly man..."

Next day, the reporter discovered Robert. Fresh headlines appeared in his paper.

"GALLANT LAST MINUTE ATTEMPT."

"Young son of old Tory family contests the Central Ward against Labour and Left Wing."

Then in inverted commas,

"Only wants to serve his fellow-citizens."

"Oh, God!" remarked Robert with horror. "I *couldn't* have said anything as bad as that!"

He read the rest of the interview with growing alarm. He was described as dark-haired and debonair.

" 'The hair's all right and I suppose the other's for alliteration,' Mr. Harding said," ran the paragraph, " 'I have never thought of going into politics. I am quite happy in my spare time with my wife, my dog, my garden and a game of golf.' " I *told* him I hated gardening! I wish the damn fellow had to cart all those stones for the crazy paving! Besides, he's left out the cat! Let's see what else I said. "Mr. Harding said, 'I had no idea of standing for the City Council, but when they asked me to stand because the Left Vote was split, I thought I might as well try and win a seat for the Conservatives. What do I think about foreign affairs? I think we should keep out of any bloc, Fascist or Communist, and stand firm for liberty and democracy.' " Yes, that bit's all right, Robert said, recognizing it. " 'In this city, I am anxious to see better housing, more playing-fields for the schools and more money spent on the social services.' " Well that might have been worse! He asked me what I thought

519

about Leslie Ward's affair, and I wouldn't say anything. There isn't anything to say except that the poor boy must have been crackers, and I wasn't going to say that. Ward's been very decent to me over this election.

Beryl said nothing. She felt tired and listless this morning. She had felt a long way off from Robert during the last few days in which he had been excited and amused with this new game of the election. He had forgotten that she had wished he was on the other side. He had not taken it seriously, had thought it only a mood. He was not in the least jealous or rancorous, he had been irritated at the moment because she was supporting Stephen, and had forgotten all about it half an hour afterwards.

After breakfast he kissed her affectionately, told her that she looked a bit washed out, went off and, she was sure, forgot her before he had gone ten yards. His mind was full of speeches and meetings, he made a joke of his new import-ance, but he was enjoying it. At the end of a week he was tackling his meetings quite differently. He had answers and ready retorts to the questions, he spoke with confidence. His agent was delighted with him. The *Guardian* backed him solidly, expanding his speeches to the length of a column and photographing him in genial attitudes. After the young reporter's interview, he became, to his own great astonish-ment, the hero of the Conservative Daily Press. People in cathedral towns, in South Country sea-side resorts and Midland villages, were confronted at breakfast with Robert smiling under the brim of a Foreign Office hat. They realized dimly a picture of a smoky Northern town full of chimneys and warehouses, and saw Robert maintaining tradition, and established order against a rabble of quarrelling socialists.

Tom Sutton had not at first thought of Robert as danger-ous. He knew that he himself was winning supporters every day from John Allworthy. The story of the strike was still fresh. A good many people believed in the rumour of bribes from Ward. The younger men of the Labour Party were tired of John's talk of steadiness and moderation, and per-haps detected some fear in it as well as weariness. "Reckon he's like Transport House, more afraid of what his own side'll do than of what t'other side'll do," Tom said in one of his speeches. Men felt without knowing it that John's prestige, waxing through fifty years of political life, had begun to wane. It was said he had taken money from Ward to hold up the strike. If that was true, there was no knowing what money he had taken on the Council. After all, he and Ward had been lads going out to work together, it was not unlikely that they should do a deal together. And this Tom Sutton spoke well and vigorously, and looked as though he might get things done. Besides, he was a change.

John, with fifty years' experience of electioneering behind him, felt the swinging tide, and realized that he had to make a fight for it. He summoned all his energies, and discovered for the first time in his life that there were no more to summon. He was sixty-nine and had called on his reserves too often. He felt that he could no longer put warmth into a cold audience nor life into a wooden one. When, now, he went up on to a platform, he knew that there were men and women in front of him who believed that he had been paid to betray them, and the knowledge sucked his spirit down into his boots. He never failed to deal with a meeting adequately, but he was like an old singer whose technique remained perfect but whose voice had failed.

Grace, on the other hand, burned with a fiery intensity, the desperate energy of one fighting with her back to the wall. She was out canvassing most of the day. She would rush home at the end of the afternoon, light the fire and cook and make tea so that John found everything ready when he got back from work. In the evening she went with him to his meeting or to some other meeting which he could not fit in. She spoke in her old racy, incisive style, dealing shrewd blows at any hecklers in the audience. She might have been a woman of forty instead of sixty-six. John watched her with amazement. He had never seen her throw herself into public affairs with such concentration since the winter after their child died, when for months she had been just like this, taut and tireless. He had understood what drove her then. Now she was driven by love and hate, protecting love for him and hatred of Tom. It seemed to him that she did not suffer as he

521

did from his hatred. Hers was a healthy emotion, that drove her into action. His was a heavy pain that hampered performance.

He did not realize the full strength of her feeling until one evening two or three days after nomination day, when they came home from a meeting. The evening paper was lying on the mat. Grace picked it up and glanced at it in the kitchen while she was waiting for the kettle to boil. There was a picture of Robert addressing a midday meeting in the yard of a works. Grace showed it to John.

"He's like his father," John remarked. "Many's the time his father and I have been on opposite sides, and never any ill feeling."

"I believe you're half sorry he won't get in."

"I'm none so sure he won't."

"He won't, but better him than Tom Sutton!" Grace said with passion.

A sudden realization smote John. Was this the end of the ardour and effort of their lives, their long devotion to the cause? Grace who had fought and sacrificed freely fifty years for Labour wanted a Conservative to beat one of their own people! He knew that the same wish was somewhere in his heart. He did not believe that he would carry the seat. To lose it to the young son of his old friendly enemy would be a far less bitter pang than to lose it to the friend he had come to hate. He was ashamed of the wish.

"Nay, lass. The Party comes first." He added, surprising himself by doing so, "Maybe I ought to stand down for Tom Sutton if there's any doubt about the seat."

Grace set the kettle down with a thump.

"You do that, John Allworthy, and I walk out of this house and leave you! Tom's not fit to be on the Council. A man that reckons nothing to the signed word of the Union! How could anyone trust him! This lad of Harding's will be an honest fellow, anyhow, like his father before him! But you'll beat the pair of them! Never let me hear you speak again of standing down! You that they called the Lion of the North? Do you want me to call you a rabbit?"

She saw the dejected droop of his shoulders as he turned away, and her tone changed.

"There, old lad! You're tired! Drink up your cocoa and we'll go to bed. But don't talk to me of giving up, for you and I have never done it yet and reckon we're too old to learn new tricks."

Tom, who happened to have a free evening, slipped into the back of the hall where Robert was having a meeting. The hall was hot and full of smoke. Near the door where Tom had found a place, a score of young men and lads were standing, a roughish-looking lot come in, Tom thought, to make trouble. He knew that his supporters, who had concentrated on shouting and singing at John's meetings, were now giving a good deal of their attention to Robert. He did not want to be recognized and turned his head away from the group who shuffled and spat and grinned within a few yards of him.

Robert, his chairman and one or two supporters, Ward among them, filed on to the platform from a side door, and took their seats. Robert, who was nervous, did not look up. He sat easily, his face alert and cheerful. His glance travelled round the hall. A tough lot! Looks like a gang of rowdies there by the door come to make trouble. Rather fun if Gilly brings his crowd, but I don't know if he'll have had time to raise 'em. Nice of him! I hope to God I've thought of everything they're likely to ask me! What's old Backhouse saying? Worthy son of his father touch. Dear old Dad, I wish I was! He's pleased about this election. Grand fun if I pull it off and pretty good fun anyhow. I hope old John doesn't mind. Queer faces do look in an audience! Especially these faces, they look hungry and pathetic. Probably aren't either. Waiting to howl me down. But decent enough people really, I expect. Most people are decent if you can get at them. Old Backhouse is having his money's worth! I hope he isn't going to make my speech for me like Thornton did the other evening! Jolly awkward! Oh, he's finished. Now for it.

For an instant Robert's knees quaked and the room swam before his eyes in darkness. He stood up smiling, looking easy.

"Ladies and Gentlemen. . . ."

The men and boys at the back of the room began to sing the Red Flag. They made a ragged and tuneless noise which Robert, by now experienced, was able to recognize. He waited until the first verse had straggled to an end. Then he raised his voice,

"If you *want* the Red Flag, Ladies and Gentlemen, for Heaven's sake let's sing it properly! It's not much of a tune at the best of times, but it's not as bad as that! Now then! All together, please."

Robert raised his fountain pen as if it were a conductor's baton.

The audience were taken by surprise. Those who had started the Red Flag to annoy Robert did not want to sing it to oblige him. Those who supported Robert did not want to sing the Red Flag, and anyhow did not know it. The tune, even more uncertain than before, rose and wavered for two lines.

"There's a gentleman at the back not singing!" Robert said, pointing his pen at the gang by the door. The Red Flag collapsed in a gale of laughter.

"Well, then, Ladies and Gentlemen, if you will allow me to make my speech . . ."

The door near Tom opened, and half a dozen young men came in. Tom looked at them curiously. He did not know Gilly Marsden by sight nor Ronnie Harding nor Tim Creswell, nor any of the others, but he saw that these young men did not come from south of the river. They were too prosperous-looking, too well dressed, too confident. They were the Harding lot. Friends come down to hear their man make a speech, probably. Tom looked at them with hostility. Their unconscious air of ease and well-being, of being comfortably on top of a comfortable world, rasped his spirit.

He turned his attention to Robert's speech. It was an echo of leaders in the *Guardian*, delivered with simplicity and sincerity. Tom watched his adversary across the packed, smoky hall. He was filled unexpectedly with a curious half-scornful pity. The young man on the platform knew nothing! He did not know how half the people in his own city lived and felt and thought. He saw Spain as a lot of bad-tempered fellows fighting one another, Germany as a threat that made rearmament necessary, Russia as a suspicious and incomprehensible phenomenon. He liked the League of Nations, but saw that it wouldn't do at the moment. He did not understand what his own party aimed at, it was doubtful if he had ever heard or read the aims of the other side, although he smelt them and wrinkled his nose whenever they appeared. He was obeying his instincts, running true to form. For a minute, Tom saw him as he was, not a deliberate and oppressive tyrant, but a decent, kindly and innocent young man brought up in an enclosed world, and working unconsciously to preserve the enclosure.

Ah, but he was dangerous! Tom's eye travelled to Ward sitting beside him. He was dangerous because men like Ward could use him for their ends! He was dangerous because when he felt the walls of the enclosure going, he would fight even without knowing why he fought! Tom's reflections were interrupted. The gang of youths near him began to shout. Robert went on speaking, but their noise made it impossible to hear him. The chairman got up, called for order and alluded to the Englishman's right of free speech and a fair hearing. Robert began to speak again. He spoke faster but showed no other signs of disturbance. He had been howled down at two meetings that week, and at each meeting had finished his speech, although only the front rows of the audience had heard it.

Gilly Marsden was standing just behind Tom's chair. Tom heard him whisper,

"Now then. Come on!"

He stepped forward and took the most vociferous of the interrupters by the collar of his coat.

"Out you go!" he said. He propelled the astonished youth vigorously through the door. Robert's young cousin, Ronnie Harding, hustled another of them out. The men who had been shouting and singing were utterly taken aback and dumbfounded. They had always considered that it was their privilege to get rough at meetings, not the privilege of the other side. A weedy youth, struggling in Gilly's grip, said furiously, " 'Ere you! What are you doing? I've a right to speak, 'aven't I?" "So's the candidate," replied Gilly. "Hop it! Open the door, Tim. This gentleman wants to finish his speech outside."

The whole of Tom's body tingled with the desire to join in. He was not a weedy lout who could shout but could not show fight. He was a tough and vigorous man, a match for any well-fed gentleman. He had had boxing lessons. He longed to land his fist on the point of Gilly's chin, to blacken the laughing eye of the young man called Tim. He restrained himself with an effort. A candidate must not be found brawling at the back of the hall at another candidate's meeting. He, like the sulky youths who were being hustled out of the door, had the feeling that the Conservatives had stolen the part of his own people. In a flash of perception he thought, They're a lazy lot, but if we teach them to fight, they'll fight fast enough. He waited until Robert had finished his speech and the scuffle at the back of the hall had subsided, then slipped out of his seat and left the meeting.

Lionel Harding felt in Robert's brief campaign a renewal of his own youth. There were differences which he noticed when he spoke for his son at one or two meetings, and sat behind him on the platform at others. He himself had fought his first campaign against a Liberal. A Labour man on the Council in those days was unheard of, as unheard of as a woman. He had been very like Robert, amused, excited, "having a shot at it," quite as unconscious of the hours of laborious work for which he was letting himself in. He had always done the work thoroughly and conscientiously, and so would Robert. Robert would be responsible, good-tempered and impossible to bribe, although there was much less of that sort of thing nowadays in any party. The handling of municipal affairs had certainly grown more honest, just as political feeling had grown milder. This young Sutton had never had as much to put up with as old John. There was a lot of talk about politics, but little real enmity. In England

and in the City of Aire any affair of paramount importance immediately became a non-party matter. The mass of England was non-party in all but name. The English people caught the prevailing germs from the Continent in their mildest form, inoculated, perhaps, against severe attacks by humour and laziness. In France a revolution, the guillotine at work all day, the prisons crammed, an aristocracy wiped out. In England a few Luddite riots. Blake, Shelley and Wordsworth. Was it possible that to-day the new state in Russia and the Nazi persecutions in Germany would only infect England with a rash of Left and Right book clubs?

Lionel was pleased by the congratulations of his friends. Elder men at the club spoke warmly of Robert. Good of him to give up his time, the right sort of young man to manage the affairs of the city. Not enough like him on the Council, too many of those new men, these Batleys and Wilsons and Wards. Robert was popular with his seniors as well as with the men of his own age.

One evening, Lionel was down in South Worbeck and had a fancy to turn in to one of Tom's meetings. The room was full, the audience on the whole sympathetic, except for a solid block of men in the middle of the hall who rose to ask questions. They were Allworthy supporters, old, steady Labour men who attacked Tom at once for disloyalty to the Trade Unions.

"Are you now, Mr. Sutton, a member of your Union?"

"Nay," Tom replied, "nor of the Conservative Party neither."

He did not get much of a laugh. A good many of those in the hall grumbled about their unions, but they belonged to them.

"Is it true that you appeared on a platform last week with a member of the Communist Party?"

"Aye. It's true," Tom answered sturdily. "I'm for the union of all progressive parties."

Lionel smiled. Strange bugbear of official Labour, that appearing on the platform with a Communist! He himself had appeared on so many platforms with so many different people, and had never attached this mystical significance to it. "Thou shalt not appear on a platform with a Communist!" seemed to be the first Labour commandment. From the point of view of his own side, it was no doubt a good thing, but at the moment, he was interested in the point of view of the other. The young man on the platform was urging a united front and urging it well and boldly. He had a hard row to hoe, for the Left was as fissiparous as Dissent!

"Look what they did in France!" Tom cried. "Look at the fight they're putting up in Spain! Don't you see our only chance is to stand together shoulder to shoulder, all of us that are against war, against exploitation, against the present unfair system?"

The fellow looks and sounds sincere, Lionel reflected, probably is, but there he is fighting John Allworthy tooth and nail, and if Robert pulls it off, he'll have lost a seat for Labour by splitting the vote. Well, sincerity in a man was like fog in a town, a queer thing of pockets and patches! To be very sincere meant not only good will but a degree of consciousness, a power of relating one thing to another which most people lacked. Willingly or no, you played hide and seek with the things in your mind, often losing sight of them for your convenience. Interesting, the things that Clare had picked up from this new treatment of hers! Not quite so new, perhaps, as she and the enthusiasts thought them, but it was new to be able to handle them so much and to use them towards wholeness. Was there such a thing as a sincere Socialist, anyhow, with an income of more than £3 a week? Was it natural to want to share as much as you wanted to win, to mind as much about humanity as about your own wife and children, your own ambitions and vanities? In fact, nature or original sin was what the Reformers had to reckon with, in themselves and other people. If there was a sincere Socialist anywhere, it was probably old John. Drawing towards his own generation, Lionel felt that if would be hard if either of those youngsters should beat him.

A young reporter from one of the evening papers sat at the back of the hall during Tom's meeting. He was a shrewd young man who understood his business. He knew that his paper did not want a long and accurate account of Sutton's speech. It wanted some item from the speech or from the questions and answers afterwards which would make news, and if possible, news of a kind unfavourable to Tom Sutton. His paper was backing Robert heavily and Ward had already increased his advertisements. The young reporter lounged uncomfortably on the form, which was hard to his tired body. He had been at various meetings all the afternoon.

There was nothing in the speech. The usual stuff. The young reporter yawned wearily. Perhaps he would be able to get a paragraph out of the questions. "Sutton accused of sharing platform with Communist," but they had had that in already, he believed. That business of going against the Union had been squeezed dry, there was nothing more to be made of that. Those Labour fellows of Allworthy's always came to Sutton's meetings and asked the same questions. Very solid, that old-fashioned Labour lot. Allworthy might pull it off yet. How boring it all was, the endless repetition of the same phrases, the same catch-words, all the promises that no one would keep! Come to think of it, it was extraordinary that the people of a great city, 400,000 of them, should sit still and let a question like whether they had houses or not be bandied about between Conservatives and Labour! The amount of complication and quarrelling and graft and foolishness that got between two simple things, one man wanting a house and another man able to build it for him and wanting work! The young reporter felt superior. Not so would he have ordered the universe.

He sat up with a faint revival of interest. A new questioner had arisen in another part of the hall, a small, elderly man with a face at once pugnacious and timid behind a large brown moustache. He owned two cottages at the end of a street in Lower Worbeck on the fringe of a condemned area. He said with a nervous defiance,

"I should like to ask the candidate if he thinks it right that property should be pulled down for these new 'ousing schemes and no compensation paid to the owners?"

Tom looked at him across the heads through the veil of

529

tobacco smoke, seeing not a frightened man trying to defend his bit of security in a difficult world, but one of those obstructive creatures who held up the well-being of many, and whose individual wrongs became a test for Conservatives. He answered with some asperity,

"I don't know about compensation. A bad house isn't worth much, and if the owner gets the site value, he gets as much as its worth. I'll tell you one thing. I don't hold with dictators, but if I were a dictator, I would pull down every rotten house in this ward in three weeks."

The young reporter had got what he wanted. He scribbled on his pad, snapped the elastic over it, and went out.

Ward opened his evening paper next day in his car on the way home from the office. He glanced at the long report of Robert's meeting, with a photograph of Robert speaking to a couple of small boys outside the hall. Robert had actually been saying to the small boys, "Leave my car alone, you little devils! If you've scratched the paint, I'll skin you alive!' The caption underneath the photograph ran "Candidate has friendly chat with young supporters." There was a brief an unexhilarating account of John Allworthy's meeting. Tom had been given rather more space, and one question and answer were reported in black type.

"I should like to ask the candidate if he thinks it right that property should be pulled down for these new housing schemes and no compensation paid to the owners?" The candidate replied: "I don't care about compensation. If I were a dictator, I would pull down every rotten house in this ward in three weeks."

Ward, folding the paper deliberately, thought, "Got him!" For the first time since the Sunday of the Fascist demonstration, something like satisfaction filled his heart.

Exactly a week before the election, the citizens of Aire going out to their business in the morning, saw on every hoarding and advertisement space a new poster, larger than any of the others. It said in big blue letters on a white gouund:

"Sutton says, 'IF I WERE DICTATOR . . .' VOTE FOR HARDING, DEMOCRACY AND LIBERTY. DOWN WITH DICTATORS!"

Some of them laughed heartily and said, "What, that Bolshie fellow, Sutton, wants to be a dictator, does he? Some hopes!" They would not have dreamed of voting for Sutton, anyhow, and thought no more about it.

The electors in the Central Ward were more seriously troubled. The papers were laying great stress on Tom's remark about compensation. Sutton says, "I don't care about compensation." It was not, the evening paper said, as though he was attacking the rich owners of large property. It was often the poor man, the widow, the single woman who owned one or two houses in South Worbeck and lived on the rent. Were their rights not to be respected? Was there to be no reward for thrift, no security for those who had invested the hard-earned savings of a life-time in house property?

Those of the electors in the Central Ward who had either savings or property considered this seriously and decided that Tom was a menace. Besides, he had said that he wanted to be a dictator. The word produced the inevitable reaction. Who was he, anyhow? Dictator indeed! We don't want no dictators in this country! Who asked him to be a dictator, anyway!

Tom wrote to all the local papers explaining what he had really said. His letter was printed, and given a prominent place in the *Guardian*, but most of his electors did not read the *Guardian*, and seldom read the correspondence in any paper. Besides, they could not see much difference. He had said, "If I were dictator." Very well, then. He was only trying to now explain it away afterwards. It did not matter that he had really said, "I don't hold with dictators, but . . ." The word dictator was fastened round his neck.

Lionel Harding also wrote to the papers, saying that he had been at the meeting, and corroborating Tom's statement. He had telephoned to Robert before doing this, and Robert had agreed quite cheerfully, but had been much less distressed by the posters than his father. He said, "Oh, yes, of course, Dad! I don't want anything he said misrepresented. As a matter of fact, first I heard of it was when I saw one of the posters on my way to the office this morning. You write anything you like. Quite O.K. by me. Only I don't think it makes much odds what he said exactly, because if a fellow's talking about being a dictator, he obviously wants to be one, whatever words he uses. But you go ahead. I don't want to take any unfair advantage of him."

Tom Sutton read Lionel Harding's corroboration with surprise and suspicion. He thought, "What's he up to?" John Allworthy laid down the paper after reading it and said to Grace, "Mr. Harding's always a gentleman. What's more, there's nobody knows the difference like the Labour Party." He had not been able to help rejoicing at the posters. Even if they had twisted Tom's words a bit, the substance was true enough. He had made himself a dictator during those three weeks of the strike. If you were not willing to learn patience and work in with other people, you were bound to want to be a dictator or to want someone else to be a dictator. It was all a matter of time. Tom was like a child, saying, "I want it *now.*" When you learned that you couldn't have it *now*, and yet learned to carry on wanting it and trying to get it, that was where you grew up and became a man. Tom's a long road to go yet, John thought, not with sympathy, but with scorn and satisfaction.

A good many of the electors in the Central Ward who had always voted Labour from instinct and class feeling more than from any political conviction, were bewildered. Here was John Allworthy, who had apparently been bribed by his employer to stop a strike, and Sutton who had said that he wanted to be a dictator and would pull all their houses down in three weeks, whether they liked it or not. It was difficult to make out which was the better man. On the whole it would be less trouble not to vote at all. The more lazy minded decided to leave it till the day and see how they felt about it. Some of the more energetic decided as a matter of curiosity to go along to one of young Harding's meetings.

532

The election opened on a colourless November morning with the air raw, the sky low and heavy above the house-tops, and the streets coated with a film of greasy mud, dangerous for cars. The supporters of the various candidates sat shivering and bored in their respective committee rooms, ticking off an occasional voter on their list. The citizens of Aire, going to business or to shop, saw a car pass with a large poster on the back proclaiming in blue letters, "VOTE FOR HARDING," and thought, Oh, of course, it's the municipal elections to-day, isn't it! One or two who had been following events more closely, reflected, I wonder what will happen in the Central Ward.

At this stage in the proceedings, all three candidates ardently wanted to win, and each had a private conviction that he would. John's conviction was the least firm, but in the last few days he had recovered something like his old energy and confidence. He had spoken the night before to a packed meeting in the Central Schools with fire and pride, had warmed up his audience, and felt cheered himself by their warmth. He was not dead yet, he nor the movement that impatient young man arraigned so lightly!

Tom Sutton was in his South Worbeck Committee Room at nine o' clock. He felt restless and impatient because there was nothing he could do. The smooth fair head of Harold Pearson, soberly bent above the lists, annoyed him.

"Maybe I'd better be getting round to some o't'other committee rooms?" he suggested.

"You could have a run round at midday," Harold Pearson agreed. "But there won't be much happening while six. Our folk can't vote till they've got home from work and had their tea." He sighed. "We've only the two cars, I wish we'd one or two more! Mrs. Unwin said she'd try and borrow one and come for a couple of hours this evening. It makes a lot of difference between six and eight."

"Aye," Tom said bitterly. "It's t'same all through. Cars, ships, aeroplanes! Same in Abyssinia, same in Spain! That's how they beat us! They've got the armaments every time!"

Later in the morning he took a tram and went up to his committee room on the north side of the river. This was

533

Robert's stronghold, a part of the city in which he felt himself an alien. His own committee room with its yellow placards looked small and deserted. John Allworthy, on the other side of the road, had one or two red-ribboned cars standing at the door, and showed a few more signs of activity, but both were eclipsed by Robert's, who was using his own offices for committee rooms. The office building was gaily decorated with posters and blue and white streamers. Sympathizing friends ran in and out all the morning to see what was doing and ask if they should lend a hand. Prospect Street was choked with the cars of Robert's supporters. There were the big Bentleys and Daimlers of the Wards and Wilsons and Batleys and the less opulent Armstrongs and Austins of the Marsden and Harding cousins and their friends. Territorial subalterns, young men who played golf and cricket with Robert, brought their ten-pound second-hand cars, and rattled gaily about the town. Robert's dancing partners and the young wives of his friends, turned up in their neat Morrises and baby Austins. There was not nearly enough for them all to do. They besought the flustered men behind the table in the committee room for jobs, and were sent off in search of voters who had died, voters who had removed to another ward, voters who had not yet got their names put on the roll, and voters who said, "I can't come now. Later on, maybe, when I've cleaned myself, when *he* comes home." Gilly Marsden, who was hard at work all the morning, brought up three voters, one of whom turned out not to have a vote. It was an inadequate return for so lavish an expenditure of petrol, time and energy, but Gilly felt that he was contributing enormously to Robert's success by dashing up and down Prospect Street as fast as the greasy surface would let him. It was a day off, and rather fun, and everybody said that from five to eight at night things would really get busy. In the meantime, there was a steady trickle of Conservative voters. Gilly and a bunch of young friends went and snatched a hasty but adequate lunch at the Quick Lunch Bar in the station hotel. They could perfectly well have been spared to sit down at a table for an hour and a half, but their sense of fitness would never have allowed this, and

534

they said to one another, "Just snatching a bite, must get back on the job. I wonder how we're doing? I do hope poor old Robert's getting some lunch!" The candidate had become for the time being a romantic figure, something between Royalty and a convalescent, entitled to special consideration.

All this activity at the Conservative committee rooms depressed Tom's spirits. He stood in his own doorway, watching their big cars roll by, their blue ribbons, which had grown damp in a shower of rain, flapping gaily in a drying breeze. He saw the stream of prosperous, confident people going in and out of Robert's office. He did not know how many of them were voters. It was not so much the thought of the number of votes that troubled him. It was the security and solidity of Robert's world. These well-dressed young women and casual young men looked so much on top of life. He could tell by the way they called out to one another that this election was half a game to them. They were playing it without knowing why they played. If it ever became more than a game in England they would play harder, sticking more closely together. Just as now they turned out with all their cars to beat the men who had none, so under pressure they would use those arms and machines that they were now piling up, against the men who were making them. These people running up the steps of Robert's committee rooms, calling out, "I believe I'm out of petrol!" "Where the deuce is Mafeking Street? Oh, Tim! I think I left my cigarette-case in your car!", this cheerful picnic party would, when pushed, become a solid and unrelenting army, strong in its unity and in the possession of money and weapons. Tom, watching them from the windows of his committee room, felt impotent, bitter and dejected. What had he to oppose to them but the strength of unarmed men and a justice that they did not recognize?

Allworthy's committee rooms were on the opposite of the road, about twenty yards further down than Robert's. As Tom stood idly looking out of the window, he saw a car driven up, red ribbons fluttering on the bonnet. John Allworthy got out, rather stiffly, Grace jumping briskly after

535

him. They shook hands with one or two people who were standing in the doorway, and went inside.

"Reckon he and Harding would be on same side o't'road!" Tom thought. He had just had a glimpse of the Conservative strength, and he was sharply aware of his own side's weakness. It was hampered by too many people like John Allworthy, Conservative in all but name, and doing more harm in the Labour Party than they would do if they were on the other side. Anger swelled in his heart. It wasn't the car and blue ribbons and that young fool Harding that were going to prevent him getting this seat. It was an old man that ought by rights to have stood aside long ago in the Trade Union and on the Council, an old man holding on to office for its own sake, and jealous of those coming up after him.

I was wrong, Tom thought bitterly. They'll never need to use their bombs and planes to crush the revolution. It'll have been crushed long before it gets to that by t'Labour leaders.

He could not hang about any longer doing nothing, especially in this part of the town where he felt like an intruder, and where his confidence was ebbing rapidly before the overwhelming superiority of the other side. He spoke a word or two to the men in the committee room, and then set out to walk to the bottom of Highgate, get a bite of food in a café and go back across the river, to his own part of the world.

John Allworthy watched the activity around Robert's committee rooms with a smile. He had far more idea than Tom of its actual value in votes. His experience of every election was that Conservatives looked like winning in the morning. Leisured women, particularly, had time to vote then, whereas working women could not leave their houses. The owner of a business or shop could slip out for a minute or two, and record his vote. Men and women working in factories and in shops or offices had to wait for the end of the day's work. As for the cars, John had seen a fleet of

Conservative cars at every election yet, and for all that, had sometimes seen their candidates beaten. He did not think that the cars made so very much difference. People who meant to vote got to the poll somehow. How often had he seen the town alive all day with blue-ribboned cars, and the tide turned between six and eight by Labour walking up to vote in the rain?

Grace was bending over the shoulder of the man at the table, looking at the names ticked off on the list. Presently she straightened herself and came to the window. She and John saw Tom Sutton step out from the doorway of his committee rooms. He stood on the pavement for a moment looking down the road towards the Conservative head-quarters, then across at theirs.

"He looks like a hungry Tom-cat!" Grace said. For an instant she felt how absurd it all was, Tom, the boy who had always been about their house, Tom who had worked with John many a time over these elections, going off with him to speak for somebody in another ward. Many an evening they had all three had tea together first in her kitchen and right glad she had been, for after his mother died, she was never sure that Tom got proper meals. She had always felt happier about him when she had given him plenty of apple pie and cheese and home-made bread. And now there he was, an enemy. She was strung up, and tears burned under her eyelids. For a minute she felt that she was getting old, and John was getting old, and life and the Labour Movement were not what they had been. The young man whom they were fighting to-day had come nearer than anyone else in their lives to replacing their dead child.

She looked at John and was startled by his grim face. She knew that his feeling about Tom was a painful obstruction in his mind like a growth in the body. Her own heart hardened against Tom for having caused that feeling. She touched her husband's arm. "Come on, old lad. Let's get a bit of dinner somewhere, and then go to the other side of the river."

Rain began to fall steadily towards evening. The workers in the committee rooms told their candidates that it was the quietest election they ever remembered and looked like being the smallest poll, especially with the weather turning bad. To the three men who had been working hard night after night, the election day itself seemed an anti-climax. Even the experienced John felt it, for he had never stood before with the same tension of personal feeling. Robert and Tom, about three o'clock in the afternoon, both yearned for their ordinary day's work. It seemed to both of them that nothing was happening at all. They went from committee room to committee room, shaking hands with a great many helpers who were hanging about and glancing at lists scored with blue pencil, from which they could only come to the conclusion that all the people who had cheered them at meetings had decided not to vote.

Robert was touring the division in Ward's big car, accompanied by Beryl, his agent, Laycock, and Ward. About five o'clock they went into the Station Hotel and had tea. When they came out into the dark, dripping night, Laycock said, "Better go south of the river now. There won't be much more doing up here. The next two hours down there will make all the difference."

There was certainly a renewal of activity at the South Worbeck Committee Room, which was a parlour opening off a tobacconist's shop. Beryl was given a chair by the fire. Through one door she could, see people coming in and out of the shop. When the other opened she had a glimpse of the kitchen, where the tobacconist's wife was doing some ironing at the table. The warm smell of freshly-ironed clothes came through the door. It's a nice little house, Beryl thought. I could be very happy living in it. It doesn't matter where you live. A warm content enveloped her although she felt a little sick and tired. My baby is nearly certain! It was extraordinary how, since the doctor had told her that yesterday, everything in life had become simpler. It no longer mattered that in her heart she disagreed with Robert and agreed with Stephen. She no longer felt that she needed to be useful. She could let everything go and wait tranquilly for nature to make use of her. Things sorted themselves out when your personal life was all right. It must be something like that with Stephen.

Robert came across and stood by her.

"Tired, Berry Brown? Like to go on home?"

"No. I'm quite all right. It's very comfortable here. I shall be asleep in a minute."

"They've phoned up for some more cars to come down. Voters are fairly rolling in now. Wrong side mostly, I think. I'm just going across to the polling station to see what's doing."

The polling station had come to life. A steady stream of voters were arriving, the men behind the tables ticking them off, and even the policemen on duty looked more interested. Robert went outside again and stood on the steps. One of his cars dashed up with damp blue ribbons flying, and disgorged an old woman, a young woman with a baby in her arms and two small children, who were bidden to "Get back in t'car, love, and stay with t'gentleman while we come back." Gilly, who was driving the car, grinned at Robert and said, "Well, so long as I haven't got to hold the baby! I've got the technique now. I don't waste time when I get to a house asking who has votes. I bring the whole family and let them sort themselves here."

Another blue-ribboned car drew up behind, and the voice of Tim Creswell called out,

"Here, Gilly? Lend us a hand!"

Tim and Gilly between them half hauled, half carried up the steps an extraordinarily stout old man who walked with a crutch, and who panted and wheezed and groaned alarmingly in response to their cheerful encouragement. Gilly, coming back to Robert, remarked,

"I've almost got to that stage now where I'd yank a voter out of his coffin."

"Awfully good you are, Gilly! All of you!"

"Oh, rot! It's rather fun. Here comes my lot. I hope the baby hasn't voted! Hi! Ronnie! Can you give Tim a hand when he comes out, he's got a stretcher case in there."

Robert turned sharply to run down the steps, and almost collided with a young man in a mackintosh and felt hat who was running up them. In the light from the door, Robert recognized his opponent, Tom Sutton. He held out his hand.

"Hulloa! Good evening! Beastly day we're having for it, aren't we?" He saw that the face under the sodden brim was unsmiling. Tom did not know how to reply to that cheerful greeting. He had been watching the blue-ribboned cars roll up. The capitalists, the exploiters, the rich, overfed bourgeoisie had invaded even his own part of the world, and here was their champion speaking to him as though the whole thing were a game. An enemy was an enemy and class war was class war. He stared back at Robert with hostile eyes.

Surly fellow, Robert thought, annoyed because Tom did not know the rules of the game, and was not trying to play by them. He persevered, but his tone was less friendly.

"Think this rain will keep a lot of people from voting?"

"Not your people," Tom said. He glanced at Tim and Ronnie, who were helping the lame old man down the steps. He added with bitterness, "I can't get my cripples here. I haven't got cars."

Robert flushed. It was as though he had been accused of starting in the race before the pistol went.

"I'm sorry," he said shortly. "Take one of mine. I shall be glad to lend it to you."

He glanced round. At the foot of the steps, a girl in a leather coat stood by the door of a neat four-seater Standard. Beryl had come out of the committee room and was talking to her. Robert ran down.

"Peggy!"

"Yes?" Peggy, who was young and blue eyed and thought Robert very nice-looking, sprang eagerly to attention.

"Do me a great favour?"

"Of course!"

"Will you take my poster off your car and bring up a few disabled voters for Mr. Sutton? He's short of a car at the moment."

Peggy, astonished, glanced past Robert to the dumb-founded young man standing behind him on the steps. So that was the Communist! She had vaguely expected him to be wearing a cloth cap and a red neckerchief, not a blue

540

suit and mackintosh and felt hat hardly distinguishable from Robert's in the rain and dark. How cross he looked! How generous Robert was! She did not want to bring up people to vote against him, but she was overwhelmed by his noble gesture and would not fail him.

"All right, Robert. If you like."

She got his quick, dancing smile.

"Thanks awfully." He turned to Tom Sutton and said rather stiffly, "Here you are. Miss Thicknesse will drive for you."

Tom began to say, "I don't want your car." He would have said much more if he had been alone with Robert, but he was tongue-tied in the presence of Beryl and Peggy. Before he could collect himself, Harold Pearson appeared out of the darkness and said to Peggy,

"Thank you very much, Miss. I've got a list here I'll just give you if you don't mind waiting a minute. I'll give you one of our posters. Perhaps you'll come inside and look at the street map?" A car was a car to Harold Pearson.

Tom made an angry, despairing gesture with his hand, and flung away from them. Beryl and Robert were left standing at the foot of the steps. Beryl said, "Oh, Robert! I wish you hadn't done that!"

"Why? It isn't fair, really! And I didn't like the fellow suggesting I was going to win on cars!"

Beryl said in a low voice,

"I expect he would rather have lost the seat."

"He's going to do that anyhow," Robert replied cheerfully. "You're getting wet out here, Berry Brown. Come back inside."

A larger crowd than usual assembled outside the Town Hall on the morning after the election to see the results announced on the board. The figures for the Central Ward were not out at noon, and a good many workers from Alfred Ward's came along to find out what had happened. There had been much betting and speculation in the works and opinion was divided between John and Tom. It was mostly the men who came, but a few girls and women drifted along with them. Among them was Olive, who could not help feeling curious and interested. It was odd to think that she might perhaps have been the wife of a City Councillor!

It was about a quarter past twelve when the figures for the Central Ward were run up on the board.

Harding	Con.	1,246
Allworthy	Lab.	1,065
Sutton	Ind. Lab.	807

The *Yorkshire Guardian* celebrated the Municipal Elections with a leader which picked out the Central Ward results for special notice. Here, it said, was an epitome of the feeling in the country as a whole, a miniature of national history in provincial. The casting of the votes proved clearly that the British people, whatever their political bias, had a profound distrust of extremists. They had not forgotten the history of the strike, the loss and suffering caused to ignorant men and their wives and children by the unjustifiable action of agitators who did not respect the principle of collective bargaining. They were not to be led astray by the rash promises of those who advocated immediate millenniums obtainable by unconstitutional methods. They had shown once again their steadiness and good sense and their appreciation of the peace and prosperity enjoyed under the National Government at a time when so many nations were torn by faction and violence.

The *Guardian* touched on John Allworthy's long and honourable career in Municipal politics, reminded its readers of the part that he had played during the strike, and referred magnanimously to his connection with the early days of the Labour Movement and the beginnings of Trade Unionism. It commented on the value in civic life of the old Aire families, mentioned the tradition of public service established by the father and grandfather of Robert Harding, and extended a warm welcome to him on the City Council.

542

"Well?" George Clarkson said to Tom Sutton. "Had enough of politics?"

Tom did not answer. His scissors snipped on steadily through the fine cloth of a gent's striped suiting. Clarkson looked at his bent dark head with a not unkindly amusement.

"Anyhow," he remarked, "you've won us a seat."

All the rest of that week Tom worked hard, withdrawing himself at dinner-time and in the evenings from the company of his fellow men. He refused to go with Harold Pearson on Saturday afternoon to a private show of Russian films organized by the Left Book Club Circle with which the Discussion Group had now merged. Harold pleaded that they were films everyone ought to see, and that he needed someone to help him to put leaflets about a Spain meeting on all the chairs. Tom shook his head. He wanted to go for a walk alone.

After dinner he took a tram to its terminus, left the main road by a side path, and climbed up to the hills that looked down upon the city. The November afternoon was clear and still. There was frost in the air, and in these high places white rime still covered the coarse tufts of grass. Against it the sheep looked nearly the same colour as the walls of unmortared stone. Tom's own breath made a little cloud before him. His cheeks glowed and in spite of the heaviness of his spirit, his body quickened with its own joy, moving freely and vigorously after the cramping weeks of town life and indoor work.

His mind had been numbed for the last few days since the election, but up here in the space and silence, the frozen currents of feeling began to melt and flow. Great bitterness rose in him. Twice that year he had tasted defeat and humiliation at the hands of John Allworthy. It was true that Ward, if anyone, had profited by the strike, and that Robert Harding had won the seat, but Allworthy had helped them both to their victories. Their figures were obscured to Tom's mind by that figure always before him, that old man's face with its thin cheeks and firmly cut mouth and chin, its light eyes and the wisp of hair on the bald forehead. Well, anyhow, Tom thought, he didn't get in! He's out after all these years. I've done that on him.

It was a hollow, empty victory, for it was true enough what Clarkson had said. He and John between them had given away a seat. It was the same about everything. The young pushed on and the old men betrayed them, the rank and file were solid, and the leaders handed them over bound and gagged to the other side. A purpose, half acknowledged in Tom's mind all through the week, came to the surface. He thought, I'm shut of it all, the divisions and muddles here, having to hang back all the time for the timid ones and being held up by snobs gone middle-class. I'll go to Spain.

As soon as he said this to himself, he realized that it had been in his mind for weeks. The thought of those men, his brothers and comrades, making their great fight had never been far from him. There, so he supposed, the issues were clear. There, he imagined, were no old men's councils, no talk of constitutions and tiresome legal formalities. If he went there, it would be to fight an open enemy on the other side. No more of this endless, sickening business of proposing motions and having them ruled out on a point of order by nervous elders who were afraid that they might be carried. There it would be a matter of digging a trench and firing a gun. To Tom, a vigorous and healthy young man, living a sedentary life in a city, the thought of adventuring with his body was alluring. He had never been far away from Aire, and it would be worth a lot to see the world. Monday, he thought, I'll give in my notice and find out where you enlist. I've had enough of Yorkshire. I'm off to Spain.

He felt more peaceful after the decision, as though already the strike and the election and John Allworthy, his double defeat and humiliation had slipped into the past. He walked along the ridge of hills until he came to a farm with a board that said "Teas" by the door. The people at the farm did not often have customers in winter, but they gave him some tea, and buttered home-made tea cake and jam by a roaring kitchen fire that made him sleepy after the cold air.

When he came out, it was dark. He did not go back on to the crest of the ridge, but took the narrow cart road from the farm that wound lower down across the shoulder of the hill. It was freezing keenly now, and the ground rang under his

544

feet. He lit a pipe and walked along, enjoying the taste of the tobacco, feeling placid and quiet, enclosed in the dark night and far off from the world.

He had walked about four miles from the farm when the road curved round the hill and the whole valley suddenly opened before him, a floor of velvety darkness spread with lights, a great cluster of lights that was the city, strings of lights like evenly spread golden beads that marked the main road, sprinkled lights of villages and groups of houses, sparse lights of lonely farms on the hill-sides. The valley might have been the sky turned upside down and filled with new constellations that had changed their silver for gold. The sight was familiar to Tom, this was a favourite Saturday afternoon walk of his, and he had often come round this corner before in the dark, although never without pausing to admire.

This evening he paused for longer than usual. He was still at some height above the valley, and the cold wind from the hill-tops blew in his face and ruffled his hair. He could hear the noise of water on his right. A little stream, not yet frozen, was trickling down a bed of stones. He suddenly became conscious of an extraordinary affection for this queer country of his, these long valleys full of work and smoke and noise enclosed by the round, silent hills, this corner of the world in which you could climb so quickly from streets and millyards to heather, and from the noise of trams to the sound of wind and water.

Spain! He thought, What's Spain to me? I belong here! Spain was a good deal to him, another front in the war, an encouragement and perhaps, if it were needed, an example, but he saw now that he could not go there. Here, where he had grown up among his own people, here, where he knew their needs and their nature, here was his work. He had not done much so far. He had put up two fights against heavy odds and had been beaten. He had even damaged his own side by fighting, although he thought that was not his fault, but the fault of the others who had failed him. Reluctantly he acknowledged that the enemy were solid and the workers were not. It would need an almost unattainable amount of work and sense and unselfishness to make

545

a Left United Front. The Conservatives were a united front without making one.

But in the end, he thought, we can't be beaten. We can be checked and slowed down and scattered, but we should come together again, and go on. We might, I reckon, be imprisoned, punished, starved out, some of us even killed. But we can't be beaten, because we are the future. You can hold back change but you can't stop it. Seems you can kill yourself by holding on to the past, and half kill the present and make the future look like a dead hat, but you can't quite kill the thing that's growing any more than you can stop the spring. We're the winners. We've a lot to do and a lot to fear, but we haven't the worst fear of all, the fear in the heart of those that are finished. Whatever they do to us before they die, they can't make an end of us. We're the new world.

The sensation of Leslie Ward's trial at the December assizes and of his sentence to six months' imprisonment was almost blotted out for his fellow citizens by the major sensation of the Abdication. During that week in which like two-thirds of provincial England, they gasped with surprise, felt shocked and disappointed, regretful but firm, applauded Mr. Baldwin, said good-bye to an imaginary figure very dear to them, and accustomed their minds to a new King, the punishment of one inconsiderable young man, who had played the fool in a car, faded out of notice. Marjorie could not help feeling that it was very lucky, although she was ashamed to say so. Billy Wilson did say so. No one, he said, would remember what had happened to Leslie, and when he came out, he could go abroad for a bit, and send everyone a lot of picture postcards, and then come home as though nothing had been wrong. In a world where such extraordinary things happened every day, a spot of jug after a motor smash was neither here nor there, said Billy Wilson. Anything that might still be here or there in Leslie's mind was beyond the scope of his practical nature.

The Unwins were less resigned. They saw Leslie as the victim of political tyranny, and got up a petition to the Home Secretary, which was signed by a good many people for reasons of political bias, sentiment, and compassion for Leslie's youth. A number of other people said or wrote to the *Guardian* that Leslie's sentence was too light, an example should have been made of him. He ought, one old Colonel suggested, to have been flogged in public. An enterprising Daily began to get up a collection for the Blackshirt and his wife and coming child, but dropped it in favour of a series of intimate articles about Mrs. Simpson's style in dress and favourite dishes. Christmas was coming near, and both Leslie and the Abdication became happenings of yesterday, buried under shopping, preparations, family meetings and obligations, attempts to make money go further than it would, and all the suspension of ordinary life which makes Christmas so enchanting before it arrives and so demoralizing afterwards.

Nobody knew what Ward thought about his son's sentence. He was quieter than ever at home, and spent more time in his own room, so that his wife and daughter saw very little of him. Marjorie was preoccupied with Billy, Mrs. Ward absorbed in her own shaken nerves. Marjorie was amazed at the magnificence of her father's Christmas presents, a new car, a fur coat, a pair of diamond ear-rings. She supposed that he was sorry for her distress about Leslie, and knew that he was pleased at her all but avowed engagement to Billy. She did not realize that he was trying to make one of his children do him credit in the only way he understood.

Once, as she was making out her list for Christmas cards, she said to her mother,

"We haven't asked Stephen and Joy to dinner for ages. I don't believe I've seen them since the summer."

"I did mention them to your father when we had our last dinner party. He didn't want them. I think he's annoyed with Stephen. He said something about him preferring other company."

"Well we always knew Joy was stuck up and superior and bored."

547

"I don't think it's that. I think Stephen's been getting mixed up with some kind of politics, with Labour people and people like the Allworthy's."

"Oh, yes," Marjorie said and then stopped. She had almost forgotten that she herself had once begun to mix up with those people. "I shouldn't think Joy will like that!" she said with some satisfaction.

Joy would have been glad two years ago if Ward had stopped asking them to his house, but now she was troubled. She said to herself that they had all got to know him better over the election. She felt that although he was an outsider, vulgar and ostentatious, he was on the right side, on the same side as herself and Hilary and Anne and her father and mother, Robert and the Harding parents. About Clare she was not sure. Clare was beginning to have what Joy called "queer ideas." She had bought some new clothes and had her hair waved, so that she looked pretty but different, and she was going to Germany to teach English in a school for a term as a substitute and to see what was happening. It was altogether unlike Clare to be so adventurous, and Joy, who preferred people to be consistent, was surprised and faintly distrustful. Of course it was a good thing that this treatment had made her so much better, but it had altered her in other ways. She seemed now to laugh at a lot of things and question others, and they were not things that Joy thought ought to be laughed at or questioned. Sometimes she talked as though she agreed with Stephen, sometimes she cheerfully disagreed with him. Joy no longer felt sure what she would say or do next. Really she sometimes thought that Robert was the only reliable Harding.

She thought about Robert and Clare and Ward and Christmas and the children because she did not want to think about Stephen. She did not want to admit to herself that nowadays she was nearly always angry with him and sometimes almost hated him. He had become not only a Socialist, but difficult, moody, queer. Their quarrels sprang

548

up out of nothing and made them both miserable. She had asked him if he was ill, and had suggested that he should see a doctor, but he said that he was perfectly all right, and though he did not look it, she could not make him say any more. He often apologized after quarrelling with her, and sometimes when he did not know that she was watching him, she saw him looking so miserable and hopeless that she would have liked to comfort him as if he had been one of the children, only something made her feel shut up and unable to begin. She did not know what was the matter with them both. She groped in a fog of perplexity, and tried to forget it and to concentrate on the children and on preparations for Christmas.

When he had any attention to spare from Mary, Joy and himself, Stephen sometimes thought uneasily about Ward. They had never been on intimate terms, there was no change in Ward's always dry and reserved manner, but Stephen knew that a barrier had come down between them. He thought that Leslie's disaster had hardened something in Ward to a point of fanaticism. The tension of his already strained nerves was increased by the feeling that Ward was an enemy. If only he could walk out and leave the whole place! If only he could throw up his part in a system which he believed to be wrong. If he could take his family to live in a cottage and work at some job about which he had no qualms, even a chicken farm or a market garden to feed people! That was absurd, of course, how could he take Joy to live in a cottage, or deny his sons and hers the kind of education that he had had himself and that she would insist on for them? What could you do in this time of transition, if you were not free? You must live under the old system till the new was born, and do what you could to help on the new in the intervals of earning your living. You were forced into insincerity by circumstances. With Mary he could be free! If he could make enough money at some other job to provide for Joy and the children, if Joy would divorce him—

and she was too fair not to—he and Mary could live in the light of the new world and shake off the old, they could be poor and careless and untrammelled by what is expected of people brought up in prosperity. Brought up! The thought of his mother and father, his home and family tugged at his heart. He pushed them away, for they stood beside Joy, dragging him back from Mary, they were on the side of the established way of life, the ordered way of behaviour, and he wanted to break free from these in living as he was painfully breaking free in politics, he wanted Mary, Mary, Mary, more than anything else in the world.

Grace Allworthy had spent the December afternoon at a committee meeting making arrangements for the Labour Party Annual Dance. She came briskly home through the lighted streets, smelling Christmas in the fog. She stopped at a shop and bought some peppermint humbugs, the kind that she had always bought for Mary when she was a little girl. She was expecting Mary to spend the evening with her. John was going straight on from work to a Union meeting. She and Mary would scramble eggs and make tea and sit by the kitchen fire and be cosy together and have a good talk.

Mary had a latchkey to their house, a present which John had given her on her sixteenth birthday so that if she was coming to supper with them and they were out in the afternoon, she could walk straight in from school and get on with her homework. A good deal of her work for her scholarship had been done in the undisturbed peace of their house. Grace expected to find her there this evening, perhaps laying the table or making toast, but she saw no light in the kitchen window. Perhaps she had been kept late on the paper. She fitted her latch-key in the lock but found that the door was not latched. She opened it and went in. The kitchen fire, which had burnt low, still glowed red, and someone stirred on the hearthrug before the fire, someone who was crouching there with her face buried in the shabby cushions of the old rocking-chair.

"Mary?" Grace said.

There was a sound, hardly a word, and the chair creaked under a movement. Grace had put out her hand to the light, but she let it fall. She came towards the fireplace and sat down in the rocking chair. Her hand found the ruffled brown head and drew it towards her knee.

"There, there, my lamb, don't cry! Is it Stephen?"

"How did you know?"

Mary lifted her face, her voice was startled.

"I saw months ago when you both used to come here, and he thought he came to ask John about politics." Grace smiled sadly in the dark. Her hand stroked the rumpled waves of hair and touched the hot wet cheek. She sat quietly waiting.

"I can't, you know, Aunt Grace." Mary's voice, thick with tears, stumbled on in the dark. "I thought I could, but I can't. He wants to let her divorce him and marry me. I've told him I can't. I would if it was only me. I don't mind anything. And I don't care about her. I suppose I ought but I don't. It's because I know he only half wants it. He doesn't know that, he thinks he wants it altogether. But I know him, he'd never have any peace of mind again, he would feel he'd injured Joy and the children and his father, all his family. It isn't only that, he'd be going against his nature. I know it's nothing much to some kinds of people, to lots of my own friends. They'd laugh at me. But it's so much to someone like him that it's only worth doing if it's everything in the world to him. And—I want to feel it is but I don't. I wish it was."

Grace sat silent, only the touch of her hand telling her love and pity. She thought to herself, He's a nice enough lad but there isn't enough of him for Mary. Poor little lass!

"It's so difficult for people like him. The tug that's going on all over the world is going on inside them. And his wife doesn't understand. She never will. He's so unhappy. I could. . . . He's so gentle and honourable and kind, he touches other people's minds so gently. . . . He needs people to do it to him. . . . I can't bear it . . . but I can't do anything else."

"No, love, you can't," Grace said gently but decidedly. She thought, but did not say. It wouldn't be respectable!

There was a silence. She heard a long sigh and felt the girl at her knee gather herself together. Mary moved away from her caressing hand and spoke in an attempt at an ordinary voice.

"I've nearly let the fire go out. I'll put some coal on, shall I? It's quite early. We needn't put the lights on just yet."

"Oh, not for a long time." If it would comfort her, Grace was perfectly willing to sit all night in the dark.

Mary knelt on the hearthrug shivering and holding out her hands to the reviving fire. She said in a dreary tone,

"I can't stay here. It's too difficult for both of us. We can't help meeting at things. We so often have to go to the same ones. It makes it too hard for him. But what can I do? There's Mother and Arthur. In a year, when Arthur goes to Kelham, Mother will be quite alone. Doris only comes occasionally as a visitor, she's got the baby and her own house. I have to be out a lot, but I'm there, somebody to look after them."

"Your mother and Arthur could come to us, until Arthur goes, and then we'll look after your mother."

"You wouldn't want to! You're so busy, you've so much to do! You couldn't do all your work on committees and have an invalid in the house!"

"It's time I gave up some of my work, Mary. Not that I feel old yet, or that there isn't a lot of good work left in me, but it's fair to let the young ones take their turn, and it's not good for them or for the movement to have the older ones always on top of them. Besides, now your uncle's off the Council, he's more at home, and I like to be with him. We've both worked hard all our lives. We've a right to a little peace at the end. But what about your work?"

"I don't really want to stay on the *Guardian*. I don't know whether I could get back on to the *Tribune*, but I could do free-lance again for a bit while I was finding something There's nobody else with Jill. She wants me back."

Mary's tone was dull. She could not feel at the moment that it mattered very much where she went or what she did

She would be all right. At the moment she was empty of feeling.

Grace put an arm round her shoulders.

"Now you go upstairs and wash your face, and I'll make some tea and when you come down we'll talk about it and see what we can arrange."

When Mary had gone upstairs, Grace did not immediately get up to put out the tea things. She rocked herself gently backwards and forwards in the chair, the one piece of their furniture which had come from her mother's house and which she remembered since she was a little girl. She had always thought that if Mary wanted to get married or go away, they would have to take Emily. She sighed. She and John had been looking forward to more quiet time together, time to read books and talk and remember. There had been so much to remember in their full lives. She did not want Emily. She was fond of her sister and sorry for her, but she was always at odds with the querulous spirit that resigned itself instead of fighting, with Emily's satisfaction in denying joy and hugging sorrow. She did not want Emily but she would have to have her. She and John had talked it over in bed at night after Doris's wedding and he had said before she did, that if ever it was necessary they must set Mary free.

For she's all the child we've got, thought Grace, we've no child of our own. Her mind went back to the frail little five months' old son, whom they had buried on a bleak March morning. She had thought as she saw the earth dropped on the coffin that there was nothing left, there was an end of life, hope, happiness, of everything in her that had made it worth while to live. That was how Mary was feeling now. It was no use telling her that it would pass, that life itself, the flow and movement of it, triumphed over everything. The dead baby was still a pang in her heart, but they had had many a happy year since then, she and John, with good friends, and Mary growing up almost their child, and Tom like a son to them. For the first time since the strike she thought more kindly of Tom. She saw the stupidity of the whole thing, she and John and Tom who had loved one another and wanted the same things fighting one another to get them. Perhaps some day they might meet again and be able to make friends. As you got old, you saw how foolish most quarrels were, and how easily they could have been avoided.

Grace's mind went back to herself and John. They'd saved a bit of money and planned to have a bit of fun on his summer holidays, perhaps to go abroad, for that Trade Union expedition to Russia had been their one expedition to foreign parts, and at sixty-seven, she was eager to see the world. They'd talked of going to the theatre sometimes, and taking week-ends in the Dales. Now they would have Emily always in the house who could not be left, who would need more and more nursing, care and attention.

"Ah, well," Grace thought. "I've been a working woman all my life and I reckon I'll be a working woman to the end."

She got up, switched on the light, and began to put out the tea things.

The train slid past the platform. Aunt Grace stepped back, smiling and waving so vigorously that her new red hat, flat and round as a pancake, tipped over one ear. As the train come out from under the dark arch of the station into the cold light of the January morning, and began to gather speed round the curve, Mary saw the waving hand and the red hat, a warm spot of colour against the drab background. She drew in her head and sat down in her corner.

A light fog covered the West Riding. The valleys were filled with it, the lines of the hills were blotted out or dimly visible. By the side of the railway line, chimneys, houses, warehouses appeared suddenly and disappeared, dim shapes crowding upon the train and receding from it.

Mary was alone in her carriage. She sat with her book and paper unopened on her knee, staring out of the window at the half-hidden world. It was about eighteen months since she had so reluctantly come back home, and she was

554

even more reluctant to go. She was running away from what she most wanted, and what was worse, from what Stephen most wanted, and perhaps she was wrong, absurd, obeying an unconscious Puritanism inherited from her mother. She did not know, she had argued it out with herself so often that she was incapable of arguing any more. She only knew that she could not do anything else.

She was leaving him behind her to struggle alone in a difficult world, a world on the surface serene and peaceful, but disturbed by hidden fires, those same fires that were breaking out into flames all over Europe. In England, in this time of waiting and comparative prosperity, the fires burnt low. What would happen when the stress came, whether it came first by war from without, or privation from within? What would happen in the life of a provincial town, or of the nation, when these rival loyalties and conflicting claims were no longer the preoccupation of a few, and a matter of indifference to many, but when they could not be ignored by anyone, when they were life and death in ordinary lives? How much damage must be done to liberty and humanity in the inevitable transition from unconscious to conscious use of the world's resources, its painful struggle to an adult mind? It seemed to Mary that if there was a chance for anyone to make the transition without too much loss or disaster, there might be a chance for England, if she were left alone, to do it. The only real hope was the growth of consciousness in people who valued justice and kindness. The English people were lazy, casual, slow to use their intelligence, but they were by nature just and kind.

The train slowed up to the platform in Sheffield station. A family party got in to Mary's carriage and filled the other seats. She leaned back in her corner and opened her paper as the train ran out of the station, heading through the green and mist covered Midlands for the South, leaving the industrial North behind.

MAGNOLIA STREET

Louis Golding
New Foreword by Rabbi Lionel Blue

Set in the fictional city of Doomington, a classic novel of Jewish immigrant life inspired by working-class Manchester.

"A most heartwarming book and a lovely read" – Rabbi Blue

ISBN 0 575 03842 X

FIVE SILVER DAUGHTERS

Louis Golding

Continuing the saga of Doomington, Louis Golding follows the lives of five women caught up in the whirl of events in pre-war Europe.

"A great novel ... beautiful, powerful and important" – *Daily Mirror*

ISBN 0 575 04063 7

MISTRESS OF CHARLECOTE
The Memoirs of
Mary Elizabeth Lucy (1803-1889)
Edited by Alice Fairfax-Lucy

A unique picture of fashionable Victorian society and country life drawn from the unusually vivid recollections of a high-spirited and intelligent woman.
   "A real Victorian find" – *Sunday Times*

ISBN 0 575 03693 1

JANE AUSTEN
Elizabeth Jenkins

A highly enjoyable biography, regarded by many as the finest.
   "A book I shall never lend to anybody – I should so dread its loss" – Molly Keane *Sunday Times*

ISBN 0 575 03877 2

NICHOLAS AND ALEXANDRA
Robert K. Massie

The internationally bestselling biography of Russia's last Tsar and his family, whose violent deaths still provoke speculation and debate.

"An exquisite story of love and compassion" – *The Times*

ISBN 0 575 03589 7

THE FILE ON THE TSAR
Anthony Summers and Tom Mangold

The definitive investigation into the fate of the Romanovs, in particular the Grand Duchess Anastasia, by two of Britain's most respected investigative journalists.

"A superb, real-life unputdownable mystery" – Len Deighton

ISBN 0 575 04128 5

❂ GOLLANCZ PAPERBACKS ❂

THE BALLAD AND THE PLOUGH
A Folk-History of the Scottish Farmtouns
David Kerr Cameron

Threaded through with their famous bothy ballads, a warm-hearted history of the great Scottish farmtouns and the men and women who worked them.
  "A vivid portrait of old Scotland" – *Observer*

ISBN 0 575 04076 9

YOU'RE A BRICK, ANGELA!
The Girls' Story 1839-1985
Mary Cadogan and Patricia Craig

This witty, enlightening, thoroughly researched and hugely entertaining look at girls' stories ranges from Victorian moral tales, via the schoolgirl yarns of Angela Brazil, to the novels of the eighties.
  "Such brilliance, energy and expertise. It's all super!" – Arthur Marshall

ISBN 0 575 03825 X